LEEFDALE

BY THE SAME AUTHOR

Magnificent Britain

A Single To Filey

Julia's Room

Learning Lines?

LEEFDALE

Michael Murray

Copyright © 2018 Michael Murray

All rights reserved

This is a work of fiction. All names, characters, places, organisations and incidents are either products of the author's imagination or are used fictitiously. No reference to any real person is intended or should be inferred.

ABOUT THE AUTHOR

Michael Murray was born in Stepney, East London and educated at Sir John Cass's Foundation School in the City of London. At the age of nineteen Michael successfully auditioned for a place at the Royal Academy of Dramatic Art and also for an ILEA Major County Award which enabled him to take his place at the Academy. After graduating from RADA, he trained as a teacher of Drama and English at the University of Birmingham. He has a Diploma in Education from the University of London and an MA in Educational Studies from the University of Hull. After many years acting and teaching, Michael now writes full time. In addition to Leefdale, he has written the novel Magnificent Britain, the novella Julia's Room and the best-selling detective novel A Single To Filey. Michael is also the author of Learning Lines? A Practical Guide for Drama Students and Aspiring Actors.

For Catherine

How shall we find the concord of this discord?

Theseus, Duke of Athens

A Midsummer Night's Dream V.1

William Shakespeare

Table of Contents

CHAPTER ONE	3
CHAPTER TWO	18
CHAPTER THREE	26
CHAPTER FOUR	39
CHAPTER FIVE	46
CHAPTER SIX	60
CHAPTER SEVEN	67
CHAPTER EIGHT	86
CHAPTER NINE	92
CHAPTER TEN	112
CHAPTER ELEVEN	120
CHAPTER TWELVE	129
CHAPTER THIRTEEN	135
CHAPTER FOURTEEN	160
CHAPTER FIFTEEN	166
CHAPTER SIXTEEN	169
CHAPTER SEVENTEEN	179
CHAPTER EIGHTEEN	183
CHAPTER NINETEEN	193
CHAPTER TWENTY	197
CHAPTER TWENTY ONE	213
CHAPTER TWENTY TWO	221
CHAPTER TWENTY THREE	232
CHAPTER TWENTY FOUR	241
CHAPTER TWENTY FIVE	250
CHAPTER TWENTY SIX	255
CHAPTER TWENTY SEVEN	266
CHAPTER TWENTY EIGHT	280

CHAPTER TWENTY NINE	289
CHAPTER THIRTY	318
CHAPTER THIRTY ONE	335
CHAPTER THIRTY TWO	346
CHAPTER THIRTY THREE	362
CHAPTER THIRTY FOUR	372
CHAPTER THIRTY FIVE	379
CHAPTER THIRTY SIX	390
CHAPTER THIRTY SEVEN	406
CHAPTER THIRTY EIGHT	421
CHAPTER THIRTY NINE	435
CHAPTER FORTY	447
CHAPTER FORTY ONE	471
CHAPTER FORTY TWO	480
CHAPTER FORTY THREE	491
CHAPTER FORTY FOUR	511
CHAPTER FORTY FIVE	533
CHAPTER FORTY SIX	540
CHAPTER FORTY SEVEN	550
CHAPTER FORTY EIGHT	560
CHAPTER FORTY NINE	569
CHAPTER FIFTY	589
CHAPTER FIFTY ONE	613
CHAPTER FIFTY TWO	629
CHAPTER FIFTY THREE	639
CHAPTER FIFTY FOUR	651
CHAPTER FIFTY FIVE	664
CHAPTER FIFTY SIX	680
CHAPTER FIFTY SEVEN	691

PART ONE
Tuesday 10th April 2001
to
Monday 16th July 2001

CHAPTER ONE

Whenever Major Howard Roberts was depressed, which was quite often, he would go up to his study and stand at the window looking out. His gaze would take in his extensive front garden and the road beyond it, and finally fix on the house opposite which directly faced his own. This was The Old Rectory. At times of great remorse, of which he'd known many, Major Roberts would stare intently at this Georgian residence until its sublime symmetry, its soothing expanse of Virginia Creeper and the perfection of its front lawn had emptied his mind of all destructive thoughts and self-recriminations. Only then, comforted by The Old Rectory's soothing presence, could he obtain some temporary relief from his despair.

Today, Howard was once again at his study window, staring out. Yet, he was far from depressed and for once the exquisite building opposite wasn't being used to exorcise his demons. He was in an unusually buoyant mood because on his word processor lay the fruits of his morning's labours: the gardening column for April's edition of The Leeflet. The column had taken him more than three hours to complete and had involved several re-writes. Now, after a sustained period of intense concentration he was taking a well-earned break.

The Leeflet was a monthly newsletter produced for the four hundred or so inhabitants of Leefdale, the exquisite East Yorkshire village in which Howard lived and was chairman of the parish council. He'd established The Leeflet shortly after he'd been elected chairman and its purpose was to disseminate information and improve communications between the parish council and the villagers. However, some unkind people who frequented Leefdale's only pub, The Woldsman, had been heard to remark that The Leeflet was the means by which "that bloody Major" could tell everybody in Leefdale what to do and what to think.

These days, Howard's pleasure in his contemplation of The Old Rectory was greatly enhanced by the knowledge that his own labours were helping to maintain its splendid appearance. When Bruce and Ruby Corbridge had put the house on the market before leaving for Capri, they'd entrusted him with the maintenance of its gardens until a purchaser could be found. This had been a shrewd move on their part for no-one was more suited to the task than Howard. The Corbridges knew that as chairman of Leefdale's Magnificent Britain Sub-Committee he had a vested interest in ensuring that the gardens of The Old Rectory remained consistently at their best. The rectory was the most prestigious house in Leefdale, and, as everyone agreed, was the main reason the village had won the gold medal in the Magnificent Britain Gardening Competition for four consecutive years. Thus, with Howard's assistance, two birds could be killed with one stone: the village's next gold medal would almost certainly be assured and the Corbridges, despite their absence abroad, could look forward to having their gardens maintained to the highest standard whilst they sought the best market price for their property.

As Howard stood relishing the substantial dwelling opposite, enjoying the mellowing effect of the spring sunshine playing on its ancient bricks, only the estate agent's vulgar For Sale sign intruded on his rare happiness and prevented it from being total. The ugly wooden object had violated the rectory's front lawn for several weeks now, reminding Howard of life's latent uncertainties. He stared at the sign with a familiar sense of regret. Bruce and Ruby Corbridge had been perfect neighbours whose consuming passion, like his own, had been for gardening. Too bad they'd decided to sell up. It was unlikely that the new owners would be anything like as congenial. But whoever they were, it was absolutely essential they were committed to maintaining the perfection of the rectory's gardens.

As always, the thought of the rectory's new owners filled him with dread. The house was large enough for a good-sized family but he so hoped there wouldn't be a lot of teenagers, with all their noise, disturbing his peace and quiet. His greatest wish was that the purchasers should be a retired couple: people of prominence with a great interest in horticulture. People who would be an asset to the village and participate enthusiastically in the Magnificent Britain Gardening Competition. People, in short, like him.

He suddenly frowned as, with some concern, he noted that several blades of grass in the rectory's front lawn were getting slightly overlong and required immediate attention. Few people would even have noticed; but Howard wasn't only a lawn expert, he was also a perfectionist. He glanced at his watch. Yes, there was still time to give it a quick mow before he and Isobel drove to York.

Howard went downstairs to the shed in the rear garden where he kept his old gardening clothes. It took him but a few minutes to change into them. He hastened back into the house and was collecting a set of keys from a drawer in the kitchen table when his wife entered from the front sitting room, where she'd been working at her cross-stitch.

'What are you doing?' she demanded.
'The lawn needs a quick cut.'
'You did it yesterday.'
'Not ours, the rectory.'
'The rectory.' She pursed her lips. 'It can wait until tomorrow, surely.'
'No, it can't.'
'But we have to set off at twelve-thirty.'

Isobel had been looking forward to the matinee of "The Picture of Dorian Grey" for weeks. She'd a horror of arriving at the theatre after the performance had started and of there being a "fuss".

'Don't worry. There's plenty of time.'

'If we're late I'll never forgive you!' she screamed, stomping out of the kitchen.

****

Parker and Lund, the estate agents responsible for erecting the For Sale sign which was the source of so much of Howard's angst, had a branch in the main street of Luffield, a reassuringly old-fashioned market town some ten miles to the south of Leefdale. The Luffield branch was staffed by three estate agents: Sharon, Tracey and Karen. The desks of these three young women were permanently turned to face the double fronted windows of the estate agency's premises, and so, when seated, they always had a direct view of Luffield's main street.

At about the same time that Major Roberts had taken it into his head to mow the rectory's lawn, estate agent Sharon Makepiece was entering into her computer details of the small mid-terrace cottage she'd valued in Luffield the previous evening. (Two bedrooms - one reception - dining-kitchen - bathroom - separate w/c - small garden to rear). A photograph of this modest dwelling would shortly appear in the "New on the Market" section of Parker and Lund's window, accompanied by the information that the property would suit first-time buyers.

No matter how busily absorbed they might be, Sharon, Tracey and Karen were always alert to those punters who stopped and took an interest in the properties advertised in the estate agency's windows. Like fish nosing up to the sides of an aquarium they came: staring at the photographs of the available dwellings with a touching, fish-like vulnerability; for whether they were serious buyers or merely indulging in a spot of wishful thinking, this was where their dreams interfaced with the means of making them come true.

Sharon was aware of the motorcyclist before he'd even approached the window. She saw him pull up at the kerb, watched him remove his crash helmet and took pleasure in the leisurely swing of his long legs as he dismounted from his machine.

He came up to the window and began to scrutinise the advertised properties. Sharon watched him intently. His position indicated that he was interested in their most expensive houses. But he was wearing black motorcycle leathers. No-one in motorcycle leathers had ever asked for the details of a property valued at £500,000 plus.

All three women were now staring at him.

'He looks fit,' said Karen, the youngest.

'It's David Beckham,' said Tracey.

They all laughed.

There was certainly a strong resemblance to the footballer. He had the same fine, leonine features and he was tall, six feet two at least.

'Hang on,' said Karen, 'he's coming in!'

He strode into the shop, stopped, and contemplated each of the three estate agents in turn. He hesitated, unsure which one to approach, and then moved towards Sharon. She had an impression of black, knee high boots, tight fitting motorcycle leathers and a blonde fringe lolling over brilliant blue eyes. She could hear the other girls mentally sighing.

Her hand pulled at the hem of her skirt. It was a reflex action she was hardly aware of, but it didn't escape the notice of the motorcyclist who was sensitive to such nuances.

'Can I help you?'

'The Old Rectory, Leefdale. I'd like the details, please.'

His southern voice was slightly posh and its deep notes continued to resonate long after he'd finished speaking.

Sharon moved away from her desk and quickly crossed to the wall where the A4 sheets of property details were filed. Dylan observed her unexpected height, admired the length of her black-tighted legs and the tangle of dark brown hair tumbling to her shoulders.

She picked up three sheets of stapled A4 and brought them over to him, her knees lifting high, each step a kick to his heart.

She watched as he scanned the property details quickly.

'The Old Rectory's empty at the moment. The owners have moved out,' she said.

His eyes locked with hers.

'Would you like to see it?' she said, blinking.

THE LEEFLET
The Newsletter of The Leefdale Parish Council
April 2001
Pages 3-4
In the Garden with "The Major"

I was chatting to one of our new neighbours the other day, when he said, "Come on, Major. You've gardened in this chalky soil around here long enough to know a thing or two. Tell me, which shrubs do best in it?"

I made one or two suggestions and then we moved on to other topics. But his question set me thinking. Over the past twelve months we've welcomed several new residents to our little community here in Leefdale. (And standards of horticulture have certainly not declined as a consequence, let me say that at once!) But if we are to surpass ourselves yet again and win the Magnificent Britain Gardening Competition for an unprecedented fifth year running, then it is essential that all newcomers should be made aware of the plants that really thrive in our chalk soil; particularly those which are at their best in late July when the Magnificent Britain contest is judged.

Roses are an obvious example. Of course, people say that roses do not like alkaline soils, especially chalk. But I say not so! I have found that if the ground is properly prepared with plenty of humous and the plants are carefully nurtured, there are many roses that will grow well in chalk. If anyone is in doubt, take a look at my own front garden.

By contrast, Buddleia Davidii requires no attention at all, save some hard autumnal pruning, and is happiest in well drained soils, which, of course, makes it ideal for chalk. An added bonus of the buddleia is its attractiveness to butterflies. Indeed, colloquially speaking, it is known as the butterfly bush.

Another shrub which is irresistible to insects is Lavatera Olbia. It will grow up to five feet high in a single season and displays its deep pink flowers month after month. Lavatera is found in abundance in the gardens of our lovely village and bees love it.

Hypericum Hidcote (St John's Wort) also adapts well to our soil and from July to October never fails to delight us with its large, golden flowers. Try too Abelia Grandiflora which eventually reaches six feet high and also flowers in July.

Other suggestions for plants that succeed well on chalk: Spiraea Anthony Waterer and Cistus Silver Pink. Finally, don't forget lavender, one of our most popular shrubs -- my own favourite -- is Lavandula Hidcote.

Of course, there are some plants, just like some people, who never thrive when planted here and never become established. It is often stoutly maintained that one such species is the hydrangea. Certainly, it is very hard to grow certain hydrangeas on chalk and high pH soils but with nurturing and perseverance it can be done. (A moral there, I think!)

Well, happy planting everyone. Next month I shall be suggesting suitable climbing plants.

The Major.

(Howard Roberts)

Howard was on the ride-on mower cutting remarkably straight stripes in The Old Rectory's front lawn. He looked up, his eye arrested by a movement opposite in the drive of his own house, Rooks Nest. Isobel was passing through the front gate and was carrying a large mug of something that he assumed must be tea. She crossed Church Lane, which separated the two houses, and strode towards him across the rectory's lawn. Howard continued on until he'd completed the stripe then cut the mower's engine. He stayed sitting on the machine watching her approach, all the while noting the pinched, anxious look she'd acquired of late.

She handed him the mug. He was pleased to see that it did, in fact, contain tea.

'Thanks.'

Isobel nodded at the ground. 'Finished?'

'Not quite. I need to dig out those borders.'

'What on earth for?'

'Because I want to!'

'Oh, for heaven's sake!'

'It won't take a moment.'

'Can't you leave the bloody place alone for a minute?'

'It can't be neglected. Particularly with the competition coming up.'

'Oh yes. The competition!'

He raked a hand through his greying, sandy coloured hair. 'What's wrong now?'

'Nothing. Absolutely nothing!' She started to go then turned back. 'If you're not ready in half an hour I'm leaving without you. This is so unfair. You know how I hate to be late. You're such a selfish bastard!'

He watched her retreating back and felt a profound despair. Recently it seemed every small difference of opinion between them was inflated by her into a major incident. Every conversation became an engagement with the enemy. For heaven's sake, where had her kindness gone? She'd once had such immense capacity for kindness. It was kindness, more than anything, he needed now.

He switched on the mower and began cutting the next stripe.

****

Sharon had no appointments that morning so it was convenient for her to take the motorcyclist, whose name she'd now learnt was Dylan Bourne, to view The Old Rectory.

They left Parker and Lund's office together and stood next to Dylan's motorcycle. It had a distinctive red petrol tank and no passenger seat. Even

Sharon, who knew nothing about motorbikes, could see that it was something special.

'That's an unusual bike,' she said.

'Yes. It's an Ariel Red Hunter.'

'It looks old.'

'It was built in 1939.'

'Really?'

'Yes.'

Her shrewd hazel eyes seemed to be inviting an explanation.

'I've a passion for collecting antique bikes. I've inherited it from my father.'

'You inherited the bike from your dad?'

He held her eyes in a long, penetrating look. 'No, not the bike, my passion.'

Sharon blushed.

Dylan eased himself astride the Ariel. 'Sorry I can't offer you a lift to Leefdale but as you can see it's only built for one.'

'That's all right. I hate motor bikes anyway.'

'Why?'

'I don't know. I always have.'

His gaze became slightly solicitous. 'You know, sometimes, if you draw a picture of the thing you're afraid of it can make it less terrifying.'

Oh God, she thought. How disappointing. He's one of those.

Dylan wondered how old she was. Twenty seven? Twenty eight?

'Leefdale's about ten miles away,' said Sharon, slightly unnerved by his stare. 'Directions to the property are in the details. Or you can follow me, but I must warn you, I don't do more than fifty.'

'That's OK.'

'All right, let's go.'

Dylan hesitated. The Ariel Red Hunter suddenly seemed a poor consolation for the loss of Sharon's presence.

'Hang on,' he said, smoothly sliding off the bike. 'On second thoughts I'll go with you.'

Now why's he done that? Sharon wondered.

'You can fill me in on the property as we go along,' he said, removing his crash helmet.

****

'Presumably you're not a first-time buyer,' said Sharon.

Dylan stole a discreet glance at her knees as she changed up to fifth. They had left Luffield well behind now and the road was running between the green slopes of a secluded valley dotted with sheep.

'No. I'm not a first-time buyer.'

'We have our own mortgage advisor back at the office. Would you like a word with her afterwards?'

'It's not necessary, I'll be paying cash.'

'I see.'

Dylan had the impression that Sharon was looking at him approvingly; and so she was: she was working out her commission. The new dining room suite was becoming a feasibility.

Her eyes returned to the road. 'So there's no chain?' she said, mentally listing all the other £500,000 plus properties on Parker and Lund's books she could recommend should The Old Rectory fail to interest him.

'Chain? No.'

'Have you just sold a property?'

'No, I'm renting at the moment.'

She slowed for a cattle grid. Strange. He hadn't sold anything and didn't need a mortgage so where had he got £500,000? 'I see. Are you looking for a second home or are you intending to re-locate?'

'At the moment I live in London but I thought the country might be a pleasanter place to work. I'm an artist.'

An artist! Sharon, whose brain had been made dizzy with speculations about the source of his income, was re-assured. So that's why he'd suggested she should draw pictures of motorbikes!

'Well, you're in luck. We have lots of excellent rural properties.'

'So I saw. But I'm hoping The Old Rectory will be OK.'

'It's certainly a beautiful house.'

The next question was obvious. But Sharon had never been deterred by the obvious.

'You said you're an artist. Are you famous?'

Dylan laughed and looked thoughtful. 'If I were, you wouldn't have to ask.'

She affected a faux cringe. 'Sorry, I'm completely ignorant about Art. I've heard of Van Gogh and Picasso, of course. What I mean is, are you well known in the art world?'

'I have a certain reputation.'

'What sort of things do you paint?'

'All sorts.'

'Oh. Do you do modern art?'

'That description's as good as any.'

'Do you throw paint around and that sort of thing? Chuck a load of junk together and call it something?'

'Neither, I hope. Ever heard of a painter called Mondrian?'

'No.'

'Some of my work is a bit like his.'

'Oh.'

PARKER AND LUND

THE OLD RECTORY, CHURCH LANE, LEEFDALE, EAST YORKSHIRE

A magnificent Grade II listed property built in 1780, lovingly restored, full of character and charm, yet offering all the benefits associated with modern day living and set in the lovely village of Leefdale, in the heart of the Yorkshire Wolds. The coastal towns of Sandleton and Scarborough are less than twenty miles distant. The cities of York and Hull are easily commutable.

The property offers an oil central heating system and accommodation comprising entrance hall, drawing room, dining room, study, sitting room, shower room, dining-kitchen, utility room, cellar, conservatory, seven bedrooms and a bathroom/wc.

The property has extensive gardens to the front and rear occupying an area of approximately one and a half acres.

OFFERS IN THE REGION OF £500,000

DIRECTIONS

From Luffield follow the Malton road for approximately eight miles then turn left onto the single track, passing place road towards Oxenholme for approximately two miles. On your left you will see a sign for Leefdale. Follow the road for another half a mile and you will come to the village. As you enter Leefdale, take the first right into Church Lane. The Old Rectory is set back from the road on the left.

EXTERNALLY

The property offers a wide road frontage to Church Lane, enjoying a slightly elevated location close to the village church. The property is fronted by a north facing garden area of approximately half an acre which is extensively lawned, hedged with privet and contains a number of mature shrubs and trees. There is a front boundary wall together with a gated drive access. Contained within this front garden area is the brick and tile garaging 27' 3" x 14' 6" with optional remote controlled electric garage door, two exposed roof trusses and with power supply connected. In addition, there is convenient parking in the gravelled courtyard area adjacent to the main front door.

To the rear of the property is a south facing garden area of approximately one acre, extensively laid to lawn. The rear boundary is hedged with privet and there are a number of mature shrubs and trees including flowering cherries, plum trees, apple trees, ash, silver birch and willows. The superb gardens which have been lovingly tended by the present owners have helped Leefdale secure first prize for four consecutive years in the Magnificent Britain Gardening Competition.

ACCOMMODATION

All measurements are approximate.

ENTRANCE HALL

Staircase to the first floor accommodation with under stairs storage cupboard. Parquet flooring, radiator and doors leading into:

DRAWING ROOM

23' 4" x 21' 6" max

Open fire period fireplace with basket grate set within a Palladian style marble fire surround, parquet flooring, wooden panelling, moulded ceiling with centre ceiling rose and cornice frieze, two radiators, windows to the front elevation.

DINING ROOM

23' 4" x 21' 6" max

Open fire period fireplace with basket grate set within a Palladian style marble fire surround, fitted shelving to recess, dado rail, moulded ceiling with centre ceiling rose and cornice frieze, two radiators, windows to the front elevation.

SITTING ROOM

21' 6" x 15' max

Open fire set within an Adam style wooden fire surround, wooden panelling, moulded ceiling with centre ceiling rose and cornice frieze, two radiators. Window to side elevation.

STUDY

16' 6" x 15' max

Open fire set within an Adam style wooden fire surround, moulded ceiling with centre ceiling rose and cornice frieze, single radiator. Window to side elevation. Built in bookcases.

DINING-KITCHEN

39' 6" x 15' 3"

This spacious kitchen is partially tiled and fitted with a range of solid wood wall and base units incorporating drawers, wine rack and preparation surfaces. Inset sink unit, tiled splash backs, integrated dishwasher. Aga with tiled surround, tiled flooring and window to the rear elevation. Doors giving access to the shower room, utility room and conservatory.

SHOWER ROOM

Comprising shower cubicle, housing Mira power shower, pedestal wash basin, bidet,

w/c, extractor fan, radiator, tiled flooring and window to the side elevation.

UTILITY ROOM

The partially tiled utility is fitted with a range of solid wood wall and base units incorporating drawers and work surfaces and plumbed for an automatic washing machine. Belfast sink, tiled flooring and window to the rear elevation. Grandee central heating boiler. A trap door is set into the floor giving access to the cellar.

CELLAR 21' 6" x 12' 7"

Tiled throughout and fitted with a range of built-in storage units.

CONSERVATORY

20' 2" x 15' 5"

Radiator, tiled flooring and double doors giving access to the rear garden.

LANDING

Split level landing with staircase to the second floor, airing cupboard containing cylinder immersion heater, radiator, windows to the front and rear elevation and doors off passage leading into

MASTER BEDROOM

20' 6" x 20' max

Built in wardrobe, built in cupboard providing storage, radiator, windows to the front elevation.

Dylan's eyes glazed over at the prospect of reading the description of the six remaining bedrooms. He folded the property details, placed them on his lap and turned his attention to Sharon's lovely presence beside him. Much more diverting.

****

'Well, here we are,' said Sharon.

As they drove into Leefdale, Dylan was struck by the village's all-pervading atmosphere of peace. He knew instinctively that the inhabitants respected tradition and continuity, yet despite having a strong attachment to the past they were not entirely resistant to change. This was evident from the eclectic pageant of charming dwellings that lined Leefdale's main street: Elizabethan timber frame buildings stood cheek by jowl with imperiously symmetrical Georgian houses; converted seventeenth century barns were neighbours to respectable Victorian villas. Yet the occasional presence of modern cottages built in the vernacular style suggested that, even here, in this most conservative of communities, some modest degree of innovation was accepted.

Although he was cautioning himself to be detached and objective, Dylan couldn't help but be seduced. Leefdale was so picturesque: the quintessential image of an English village in bloom that is carried nostalgically in the heart of every English exile. It seemed that the front garden of each house, no matter how small, burgeoned with leafy shrubs and masses of flowers in all the glorious colours of April; climbing plants colonised all available walls, their advancing green tendrils complementing perfectly the bricks, chalk and other materials to which they clung; the roadside verges trembled with white, gold and purple crocuses, petals agape and open to the sun like the hungry mouths of young fledglings; and there were yellow daffodils and creamy narcissi too, nodding in the gentle breeze. Spring had startled itself out of the earth and dressed in its many hues was delighting in its own existence, promising hope and renewal. The artist in Dylan was deeply moved.

'It's lovely,' he said.

'You should see it in summer.'

In some of the front gardens keen gardeners were already at work, scrupulously maintaining that high standard of horticultural perfection which seemed to characterise most of the village. What Dylan couldn't know, of course, was that some villagers thought there was something rather sinister about the way their neighbours pursued this pleasant outdoor pastime with such competitive industry, uncompromising will and obsessive perfectionism.

'Beautiful, isn't it?' said Sharon, sounding almost proprietorial.

'Superb!'

'It's won the prize for best kept village four years running.'

'Best kept village in Yorkshire?'

'No. In the whole country!'

'So that's why they're all so hard at it. I thought we'd blundered into a recording of Gardening Club.'

✧✧✧✧

Despite his wife's objections, indeed, precisely because of them, Major Roberts was now on his hands and knees vigorously weeding The Old Rectory's borders, flinging the weeds angrily into the wheelbarrow at his side.

The tyres of Sharon's Passat crunching over the white gravel of the Corbridge's extensive drive halted Howard in his labours. Somewhat shakily, he got to his feet and stared at the vehicle with a look of pleasurable recognition.

The car stopped close to the house and Sharon and Dylan got out. Sharon gave Howard a smile and a quick wave. She then joined Dylan who was taking in the rectory's impressive Georgian frontage. Howard watched as she gave Dylan information about the exterior. At one stage she became quite animated and pointed out the date above the spider's web fanlight: 1780.

Sharon touched Dylan lightly on the arm. She said something to him and then, with a gesture, indicated Howard. Together, they set off across the lawn towards him.

With a good deal of displeasure, Howard assumed that the young man accompanying Sharon had come to view the house. This was not good news. Hopefully he would find it unsuitable. Howard had always regarded young men who wore tight black leather as profoundly suspicious; but he was courtesy itself when he wished them both good morning.

'Hello, Howard,' said Sharon. She turned to Dylan. 'This is Major Howard Roberts.'

'Dylan Bourne!' Dylan offered his hand to the Major and was surprised by the limpness of the hand that gripped his in return. 'You're a soldier?'

'Retired,' said Howard. He quickly changed the drift. 'Here for a look round?'

'Yes.'

'Well you won't do better than this. It's a magnificent property. Finest in the village!'

'Are you the gardener?'

Sharon laughed loudly. Just long enough for Howard to convert his affrontedness into jovial good humour.

'Good heavens, no! I'm just keeping everything neat and trim. I promised Bruce, that's the owner, I'd look after the gardens for him until the place was sold.'

'I see,' said Dylan. 'Sorry.'

'The Major's chairman of the Magnificent Britain Sub-Committee,' said Sharon.

Dylan looked bewildered. 'Magnificent Britain?'

'The best village contest.'

'Ah, yes,' said Dylan. 'I hear Leefdale's won first prize four times.'

'That's right,' said Howard. 'All down to this place, of course.'

'You shouldn't overlook everyone else's modest contribution,' said Sharon.

Dylan thought she sounded a little miffed.

'I don't,' said Howard. Realising he'd been tactless, his hand lightly touched her arm. 'And I would never overlook your contribution, my dear. But you've got to admit that the gardens of this house are the jewel in the crown.'

Dylan turned and surveyed the lawn. 'It's certainly very well kept. Certainly... um... very tidy.'

'That's because the Major's a fantastic gardener,' gushed Sharon.

'Not at all,' said Howard. 'It was Bruce who transformed the place. Spent a lot of money on it.' He fixed Dylan with a searching glance. 'You keen on gardening?'

Dylan grinned. 'No, my flat in London doesn't even have a window box.'

The Major looked concerned. 'You'd be taking on a lot here. There's an even bigger rear garden.'

Dylan shrugged, non-committedly.

'From London, are you?'

Dylan nodded.

There was a long pause. Howard, who believed strongly in first impressions, was finding Dylan intensely irritating. The Major had an aversion to blonde, slack jawed young men who, in his experience, invariably turned out to be mummy's boys. And what kind of a name was Dylan for Christ's sake? Welsh background, was it? Named after the poet? Fortunately, he didn't seem to have a wife or family in tow: and he looked in his very early thirties, so hopefully wasn't old enough to have teenage children.

Howard nodded towards The Old Rectory. 'It's a very big house you know. Got seven bedrooms.'

Sensing that he was being probed, Dylan became guarded. He saw no need to divulge any more than was necessary. 'I know. I like a lot of space.'

Now that's ominous, Howard thought.

'Mr Bourne's an artist,' Sharon explained, and immediately shot Dylan an apologetic look. 'Sorry, I hope that wasn't confidential.'

'Not at all,' said Dylan, wondering if he'd given too much away.

Howard said, 'An artist? Really? I like Constable and Joshua Reynolds. And, of course, military art. I've got a couple of good prints of "The Death of Nelson" and "The Death of General Wolfe". Do you do that sort of thing?'

'No. I paint abstracts.'

'Ah.'

Major Roberts seemed at a loss. He pointed towards Rooks Nest. 'That's my house over there. Finest rose garden in the village, even if I'm the only one who thinks so.'

Sharon touched him on the arm. 'Now you know everyone agrees with you. Stop fishing.'

The Major grinned back at her urbanely.

'Well, time's getting on,' said Sharon. She looked to Dylan. 'I'd better show you around.'

'And I must get back to my weeds.'

'See you later, Howard.'

Dylan gave Howard a nod, and then he and Sharon walked off towards the house.

The Major stared long at their retreating backs, his greying moustache accentuating his disappointed moué. 'Oh dear! I don't think you'll do! I don't think you'll do at all!'

CHAPTER TWO

'You'll have to wait here until I've switched off the security device,' said Sharon. She unlocked the front door of the rectory and pushed it open. At once the alarming sound of a siren reverberated around the hall. Sharon darted inside. A few moments later the din stopped and she called out, 'It's all right. You can come in now.'

Dylan entered and found himself standing in a spacious hallway.

'Sorry about that,' said Sharon. 'Once the alarm goes off you only have fifteen seconds to stop it before it alerts the Luffield police.'

'How do you de-activate it?'

She regarded him suspiciously. 'With a number code. That's why I had to ask you to stay outside. Mr Corbridge is paranoid about anyone finding out what it is.'

'Understandably.'

Sharon indicated the interior with a turn of her head. 'Well, this is the hall. The staircase is original by the way.'

Dylan approached the staircase for a closer inspection. It rose up the wall to his left and was thickly carpeted. He noted the mahogany handrail which terminated at the bottom in a spiral of balusters.

'No sign of woodworm yet,' he said, lightly.

Sharon frowned. 'I should hope not. The property's received extensive anti-woodworm treatment. Certificates are available, if you require them.'

Hmm. No sense of humour, thought Dylan. He observed the five white doors which led off the hall and the numerous examples of eighteenth century portraiture which adorned its walls. He admired the high ceiling and its elaborate plasterwork. He noted the oak parquet floor showing in the spaces between the opulent oriental rugs. He was amused by the eighteenth century carriage clock and the tastefully positioned spinet. All this, and they'd only got as far as the hall. Someone had obviously gone to great lengths to create a definite period "look". He felt as though he'd stepped into a play by Sheridan.

'Very Georgian, don't you think?' said Sharon.

Dylan could do little else but agree.

'Mr Corbridge was so thrilled to own an eighteenth century house. He was determined to recreate the Georgian style.'

'Oh. Which one?'

'Which one?'

'There are examples here of early, middle and late.'

'Really?'

Sharon wondered if he was a bull shitter. Bruce Corbridge had assured her that the house had been authentically restored.

'Shall we go on?' she said.

She opened a door to her left and showed Dylan into the first reception room, which she referred to as the drawing room. It was at the front of the house and overlooked the lawn. The room struck Dylan as ideal for his purposes: it was high ceilinged, spacious and brilliantly lit by the natural light pouring in through two huge sash windows that seemed to rise almost from floor to ceiling. But the furnishings! They were so oppressively vulgar: heavy, red, silk wall coverings finished with a gold fillet; sumptuous, red curtains held back by gilt acanthus leaf embrasses and topped by a pagoda style pelmet; obtrusive, coarse mouldings on the cornice and fireplace; ugly, squat bronzes adorning the mantelshelf; even the chandelier chain disguised with red silk and fringing. The furniture was mainly eighteenth century repro with a couple of genuine antiques, and, incongruously, two enormous, contemporary sofas that were so padded and comfortable they were obviously the property of affluent couch potatoes. There were far too many pictures in hideously elaborate frames, and the original wooden floor was all but obscured by modern oriental rugs.

'All the furniture is going to be removed and shipped out to Capri in a few days,' said Sharon, who'd observed Dylan's disapproval. 'Mr Corbridge and his wife are retiring there.'

Thank God the furniture's not included in the sale, Dylan thought. He was beginning to suspect that the whole house had been designed to create some loose, contemporary notion of a holistic Georgian "style", which had resulted in a travesty of anything Georgian or stylish. It was a bourgeois shrine to self-indulgence, ostentation and the comfort of excess.

'Is Mr Corbridge an American?' Dylan asked.

'No. He's Australian. A film producer.'

'Of course!' exclaimed Dylan. 'It's a film set!'

'Mr Corbridge and his wife are both very nice,' said Sharon. Her tone had become chilly. 'Is there anything that you do like about the room?'

'Oh yes. The light. It's magnificent. It would make a wonderful studio.' He regarded her for a moment. 'You didn't say you lived in Leefdale.'

'I didn't think it was relevant.'

'Well, it could be a recommendation. If you're personally happy here.' Something in her expression made him feel reckless. 'Are you happy here?'

She seemed surprised. 'Of course.'

'Do you live alone?'

'No.' Sharon moved towards the door. 'I'll show you the other reception rooms. But I warn you, they're all in the same style.'

'That's all right,' said Dylan. 'I can't say that I admire Mr Corbridge's furniture or his fittings but his taste in houses is perfect.'

Sharon moved through the doorway and back into the hall.

'All the carpets are included in the sale but not the curtains or rugs.'

'Has anybody ever painted you?' Dylan asked, following her.

She stopped, surprised. 'No. Why?'

'Because I think you'd make a wonderful subject.'

She took an involuntary step away from him. 'Oh, come on!'

'What?'

She turned back, wary, sceptical. 'Not that corny old pitch!'

'I'm serious. I'd like to paint you.'

'You said you only do abstracts.'

Dylan started to feel foolish. 'I started off doing conventional portraits. Seeing you has given me the urge to do one again.'

You've got the urge all right but it's got nothing to do with painting, Sharon thought. She said, 'Well, I'm terribly flattered, of course. Let me see, how does the next bit go? I ask you if I'd have to pose nude. That's right, isn't it? And you say, "Only if you want to" and then I say "but I'd be embarrassed" and you say, "Don't worry, I won't get aroused by your naked body, as far as I'm concerned it'll just be an object." That's about it, isn't it?'

Dylan smiled. 'I thought you said you didn't know any artists?'

'I don't. But I've met plenty of piss artists!' She opened another door leading off the hall. 'This is the dining room!'

She entered the room and Dylan followed closely behind her. He immediately saw that she was right: the Corbridges' execrable taste was as much in evidence in this room as the previous one.

Sharon stopped and turned to face him. She'd obviously made up her mind about something. 'Look,' she said, 'why don't you wander round the rest of the house by yourself? You can take your time and have a think about it.'

The strength of her hostility disconcerted him. 'It's all right. I'm quite happy to have you show me around.'

Sharon was adamant. 'No. I'd rather you went round on your own.'

'What I said about wanting to paint you. It's disturbed you, hasn't it?'

'Frankly, yes. We're on our own here and I've had some very unpleasant experiences with male clients.'

'I assure you I've no intention of coming on to you.'

Sharon went silent. She stared at Dylan grimly. 'Take as long as you want. I'll wait for you down here.'

****

She left him in the dining room, crossed the hall and moved purposely back into the drawing room. Fighting her desire for a cigarette, she sank into one of the overstuffed modern sofas. Her confrontation with Dylan had left her shaken, and now that the adrenalin which had emboldened her to be so recklessly assertive was beginning to recede, she was having misgivings about the wisdom of her behaviour. She'd called him a piss artist to his face! What a stupid thing to have done. Supposing he complained about her? He'd indicated that he was strongly attracted to the house. What if her rudeness had affected his decision to purchase? Her attitude would have lost the firm a cash sale and with it would have gone the new dining room suite. The thought made her almost laugh out loud. Shit! Was she really so abject she was willing to be sexually harassed and humiliated just to protect her commission?

Hang on, though, wasn't she overstating it a bit? He'd only offered to paint her. Many women would have taken it as a compliment. And it was she who'd suggested he might want to paint her nude. Now why had she done that? He'd never even mentioned it. Yes, but hadn't he followed her into the dining room just a little too closely? Hadn't he invaded her personal space? Wasn't that why she'd put him in his place? And rightly so!

Immediately she was recalling the many bad experiences she'd had viewing properties with single males. The short, fat one who'd patted her bum as they'd climbed the stairs at Killingholme Grange; the racehorse trainer who'd tried to grope her in the bedroom at The Ridings; the ugly businessman who'd stood in the kitchen of Oxenholme Farm and promised to purchase the property on condition she had sex with him. (Just joking love; just joking). After all those experiences how could she have allowed herself to enter the dining room in front of him? Why hadn't she said "after you" and let him go on in front of her? But then what exactly was it he'd actually done? Nothing! He hadn't laid a finger on her. But that was the point: they were so clever, they never did anything that couldn't be explained away as an accident; and it was the apprehension of what might happen that made the situation so threatening: the way they invaded your space and accidentally brushed their shoulder against your nipple; the way their knuckle came into contact with your thigh, again accidentally, as they bent to inspect something; the unblinking stare as they looked deeper and deeper into you, and then...

She got up suddenly and wandered over to the window. Christ! She was really getting paranoid. Was being with Greg and all the secrecy and everything finally getting to her after all these years?

But such thoughts were instantly forgotten by what she saw through the window. Outside, on the front lawn, a little drama was being enacted. Howard had now been joined by his wife, and they were obviously involved in some kind of row. Isobel was gesticulating angrily and jabbing her finger at the Major, who was on his knees by the border digging out weeds. She bent down, brought her mouth close to Howard's ear and shouted into it. Howard sprang up bawling savagely. Isobel screamed, kicked out at the wheelbarrow and then, sobbing, fled across the lawn in the direction of Rooks Nest. Sharon turned away: she'd no wish to witness Isobel's distress.

Up above, through a first floor bedroom window, Dylan too was observing the unpleasant scene taking place on the front lawn. It was obvious that Major Roberts and the woman - who was almost certainly his wife - had marital issues. He hadn't much liked the Major but he couldn't help feeling a certain sympathy for him. He knew from experience how draining it was to live with someone who was neurotic. For a moment or two he watched Isobel's tense back retreating down the drive. He then returned to the centre of the room and flung himself onto the vulgarly draped four poster bed.

Stupid of him to have suggested painting her. But how was he to know she'd react like that? He reflected on various ways in which the situation might be retrieved, and concluded that to follow up on any of them would result only in making matters worse. Still, it was interesting that she'd introduced the notion of posing for him in the nude, although he'd done absolutely nothing to encourage it. Was her professed abhorrence of the idea of being painted nude, real? Or was it being used to mask a fantasy which she secretly cherished?

He tried to think of something else, but Sharon's image continued to insinuate itself into his mind. Surely it was inconceivable that a woman like that could ever be his type? Had meeting her suddenly released within him a long suppressed fetish for short skirted business suits, dark tights and high heeled shoes? Ludicrous thought. So ludicrous he felt himself smile. Normally he regarded women who power dressed like that as a joke: unthinking subscribers to notions of male stereotypes. Clones of Margaret Thatcher. So why was he finding her so adorable? Why couldn't he stop thinking about the way her chestnut brown hair framed the perfect symmetry of her face: its locks and tresses so attractively curling and twisting down to flick the shoulders of her jacket with every turn of her lovely head? Why couldn't he stop seeing her big hazel eyes, that combination of tawny brown and flecks of olive green always so difficult to represent in oils? Why was he obsessing like a frustrated teenager over her voluptuous mouth and her delightful snub nose? Recalling her perfect bow lips and the enticing way they parted ever so slightly when she was thinking? Christ, he could even remember the tiny crater just above her left eyebrow, presumably some relic of a childhood chickenpox attack. And he could still see the almost imperceptible scar on her right cheek, close to her ear.

What was happening to him? OK. So he hadn't had sex with anyone since Zoe. But surely this infatuation with an obviously hard-nosed Tory estate agent was uncharacteristically excessive? Of course, it was the curse of the artist to absorb and retain a more intense impression than other people. Which was probably why he was falling such an easy victim to nature's timeless confidence trick: his preoccupation with the gorgeous Sharon was just an atavistic call for him to reproduce.

Perhaps the quickest way to exorcise her disturbing effect on him would be to sketch her. He took out a pen from his inside pocket and turned the property details for The Old Rectory over, so that the blank side was uppermost. From memory, he began drawing a full length portrait of estate agent Sharon Makepiece, starting with her black business suit.

****

'But we know Mrs Brand won't go any lower... I agree... but if Morrison won't budge, I think we should look for another purchaser...'

Dylan was descending the last flight of stairs. Realising that Sharon was in the hall speaking on her mobile, he halted halfway down and waited. She was partially turned away from him, standing with her weight thrown back on one leg. The other leg was slowly pivoting back and forth on the ball of her foot. Christ! He'd never imagined a woman in a business suit could be so sexy. But it wasn't just the suit or the way she was standing: it was the combination of beauty and assured competence that was so compelling. Her voice was attractively low, yet full of warm ripples and little cadences like a clear, fast running stream. Her accent was Yorkshire but softly rural, like others he'd heard in the Wolds. As she issued instructions confidently into the phone she exuded certainty of purpose. For him, who'd never truly been certain of anything, this was a potent aphrodisiac.

She changed weight from one leg to the other, and, in turning, became aware of Dylan standing on the stairs.

Now that was a detail he'd forgotten. The single string of creamy pearls enhancing her graceful neck and complementing the silky smoothness of her white top.

'Just a minute Tracey...' Sharon took the phone away from her ear and called up to Dylan, 'Have you seen all you need?'

'More than enough.'

She returned to the phone. 'I've got to go. I'll be with you in half an hour.'

Dylan continued down the stairs. Sharon was standing by the front door waiting for him.

'The house is perfect. Just what we're looking for,' he said, as he approached her. 'I've decided to make an offer.'

'Good.'

'I haven't fixed on a figure yet. I'll call you about that tomorrow.'
'Fine.'

Sharon went over to set the alarm. Almost immediately she stopped and turned back to him. 'Oh, you haven't seen the rear garden.'

'That's OK. I saw it from the window upstairs. It's the size of a small park. Mr Corbridge must have employed an army of gardeners.'

'No. Amazingly he and his wife did it all themselves.'

They stood around awkwardly.

'Well, I'm ready to go if you are,' said Dylan. 'Are you confident that I'm safe enough to travel in your car without molesting you or shall you call me up a cab?'

Sharon smiled. 'Don't be silly!'

'I'm serious,' he said. 'I don't want to cause you any unnecessary stress.'

'It's all right. I over-reacted, I'm sorry.'

****

She couldn't believe it, she was actually telling him about the little shit who'd touched her up at Killingholme Grange. And the racehorse owner. She'd never told anyone about that.

He wasn't saying anything, just listening. She hoped he wasn't too shocked. His understanding blue eyes and concerned expression were ineffably extracting her intimate secrets. She told herself to be careful.

Finally, he said, 'It's obviously affected you. Perhaps you should get some counselling.'

'I don't believe in all that stuff.'

They were passing through Leefdale's main street on their way back to Luffield. On impulse, as they reached the village pond, she indicated right and turned into a side road. The car travelled a short distance and then she parked opposite a terrace of three whitewashed Victorian cottages.

'The middle cottage is mine,' said Sharon. 'I thought you might like to see it.'

They stared at it together.

'Honeysuckle Cottage,' said Dylan. 'Lovely name.'

'Yes. But as you can see, no honeysuckle.'

'Even so, it's charming. Have you lived there long?'

'All my life.'

She seemed compelled to keep staring at it. He could tell that just the sight of it gave her pleasure.

'It was my parents' house. They're dead now.'

'I'm sorry. They must have died quite young.'

'Yes. They were in their late forties. They were killed in a car crash while they were touring Scotland.'

'That's awful. How old were you?'

'Seventeen. I thought my world had ended.'

They both stared at the cottage in silence.

Dylan said, 'What does your partner do?'

She turned to him, slowly. 'I don't have a partner.'

'I'm sorry. I got the impression you did.'

'No. I said I didn't live alone.'

She gazed back at her house. 'I love it here,' she said.

She started the car, executed a three-point turn and returned to the main road leading out of the village.

Now why did she show me that? Dylan wondered.

****

Sharon and Dylan parted outside Parker and Lund's. He took her hand and shook it slowly, holding on to it just beyond the point when it should have been released, so that the formality was protracted into something more intimate. 'Well, goodbye. Thanks for showing me around.'

'I can hardly claim to have done that!' she said, quickly extricating her hand from his. 'Look, if you'd like someone else to view the rectory I'd be glad to show it to them.'

'How do you mean?'

'Your wife or partner?'

'No. Not necessary. I don't have one of those.'

'Oh!' She looked confused.

'What?'

'Well, earlier, you said "we".'

He laughed. 'I was thinking of my friends. They're very interested in my next house purchase.'

'I see.' She gave him her closing-the-transaction smile. 'OK. I look forward to receiving your offer.'

'Right,' he said. 'What about my other offer?'

She stared at him blankly.

'To paint you. Fully clothed, of course.'

She smiled, shook her head and took a step or two back.

Laughing, Dylan pulled on his black leather gloves and mounted the Ariel Red Hunter. He started it up, gave her a wave, and accelerated off.

CHAPTER THREE

Sharon moved hurriedly around the bedroom, tidying it up. She quickly made the bed, placed several days-worth of used clothing in the laundry basket and stuffed three pairs of shoes in the bottom of the fitted wardrobe. Ideally, she'd have liked a shower before he came round but there was no time. She had Louise's tea to cook.

She went over to the dressing table mirror, thinking again about the letter which Louise had pressed into her hand when she'd collected her from the after-school club. She ran a comb through her hair and dabbed perfume behind her ears. Then she picked up the letter from the dressing table and re-read it for the fourth time.

Leefdale Primary School,
Blackberry Lane,
Leefdale,
East Yorkshire.
10th April 2001.
Dear Ms. Makepiece,
This afternoon Louise was involved in an unpleasant incident with Jade Maynard. They were sharing a computer during the Information Technology session and became involved in a quarrel. In the course of it, Louise hit Jade several times and pulled her hair.

I have spoken to both girls about the incident. Jade maintains that Louise was making fun of her acting ability. As you know we are at present rehearsing the school production of "Oliver". Worryingly, Louise refused to give me any explanation at all for her conduct.

Of late, I have become increasingly concerned about Louise's deteriorating standards of behaviour. She continues to be anti-social and aggressive. Please would you come in to school at your earliest opportunity to discuss the situation with me.

Yours sincerely,

Sally Henshall.
Head Teacher.

Sharon replaced the letter on the dressing table, wondering how she was going to re-organise her work commitments in order to make time to visit Mrs Henshall before the Easter holiday. She set off to consult her diary and then stopped. The phone next to her bed was ringing.

It was Ruby Corbridge, wife of the owner of The Old Rectory, calling from Capri. She'd received Sharon's message that a potential buyer had viewed the house.

'Yes. I showed him round this afternoon.'
'Oh, did he like it?'
'I think so.'
'What's he do?'
'He's an artist. His name's Dylan Bourne.'
'Never heard of him. Has he got any money?'
'Well, he must be doing all right. He's going to call me back tomorrow with an offer... a cash offer.'
'Cash? That's good.'
'I don't know though.'
'What do you mean, you don't know?'
'I don't know... there's something about him that keeps nagging at me... something doesn't feel quite right.'
'Is he married?'
'He said not, but I think there's someone in the background.'
'Young? Old?'
'Early thirties, I'd say.'
'Tall?'
'Yes.'
'Dark?'
'No, blonde.'
'Good looking?'
'Very good looking.'
'Maybe that's it.'
'What?'
'The thing that keeps nagging at you.'
Sharon giggled. 'Ruby, you're always trying to find me a man!'
'Come on. Don't tell me you didn't find him a bit attractive.'
'Well, all right, a bit.' Sharon smiled. 'But he wears too much leather.'
'Leather?'
'Yes. He rides a motorcycle.'
'A motorcycle, and he wants the rectory?'
'Yes. Oh, and he wants to paint me.'

'Paint you?' There was a sharp intake of breath from Ruby. 'Now something about him is starting to nag at me.'

The bedroom door opened and Louise came in. She went straight over to Sharon who was now lying back with her head on the pillows, taking the call. Louise jumped on the bed and snuggled up to her mother. Sharon stroked Louise's hair.

'What did he say about the big flaw?'

The vicarage was affected by rising damp in certain places, particularly the cellar. Ruby's great fear was that this would affect the sale.

'Nothing. It never came up.'

'Well, don't bring it up unless he does.'

'I won't. Stop worrying. I told you before, if anyone makes a big deal out of it we just go down a couple of grand.'

'Call me tomorrow and let me know what he's offered.'

'OK.'

Ruby sighed heavily. 'Now, I won't sleep all night!'

When Sharon had finished the call she put her arms around Louise and gave her a hug.

Louise said, 'So? What's the letter about?'

'Come on, Lou, you know very well what it's about!'

Louise lifted her head off Sharon's breast. 'You mean Jade?'

'Yes. Why did you hit her?'

Louise scowled. 'She was being horrible to me again.'

Sharon waited.

'She was winding me up. She asked me if my dad was coming to see me in "Oliver".'

'The little bitch! Is she starting all that again?'

'I told you she's jealous because I'm playing Nancy. She wanted that part.'

'And that's when you hit her?'

'No. Not right away. It was when she said, "Oh, of course, you haven't got a dad have you? I forgot".'

'Christ! I'm glad you hit her.'

'So I said, "Of course I've got a dad. Everybody's got a dad. As a matter of fact, your dad is my dad".'

Sharon pushed Louise off and sat bolt upright. She stared at her daughter incredulously. 'You didn't?'

Louise nodded.

Sharon got off the bed and paced over to the window. She turned away from the window and walked up and down the room.

'How could you, after you promised us!'

Sharon made a sudden lunge at Louise. She grabbed her by the shoulders and shook her. 'I ought to kill you! Kill you! Do you know what you've done?' She shook her more violently. 'You stupid little girl!'

'Of course, I didn't tell her!' screamed Louise. She pushed her mother away and leapt off the bed. 'But that's what I wanted to say. It's what I always want to say. But I never can. So I hit her instead.'

Sharon sank back onto the bed. 'Thank God!'

Louise started to sob.

Later, when Louise had stopped crying and was being comforted in her mother's arms, she said, 'Why can't we just go away? Why can't we just go away?'

Yes, why not? Sharon thought. Why not just go away? Inevitably she thought again of all the reasons not to, and surprised herself by dismissing them. 'Is that what you really want, Lou?'

'Yes. If we could move somewhere else, away from here, I'd be happy. I wouldn't have to keep pretending about dad and everything. Can we go mum? Can we?'

'All right,' said Sharon.

Louise squealed and hugged her mother tightly. 'Oh mum! You promise?'

'Yes. If it makes you happy.'

'But you really, really promise?'

'I just told you.'

'Oh fantastic. When will you tell dad?'

'I think he's coming round tonight. I'll tell him then.'

Louise hugged her again. 'Thanks, mum. Where will we go? Luffield?'

'One thing at a time, Lou.'

****

Later, Sharon sat in her armchair in front of the fire sipping Australian Cabernet Sauvignon. On the sofa sat Greg Maynard, Louise's father. He was a burly, dark haired man aged forty and was wearing a suit and tie. Next to him sat Louise, reading aloud from her school reading book. Occasionally, Greg made appropriate comments about Louise's efforts.

Louise completed the last page and closed the book.

'Well done,' said Greg. 'You're really improving.' He gave Louise a cuddle and kissed her on the cheek. Looking across at Sharon, he said, 'Don't you think she's improving?'

Sharon's lips tightened fractionally. 'At reading she is!'

'What do you mean?'

'Didn't Pam say anything?'

'No.'

Pam was Greg's wife. Jade's mother.

Sharon looked incredulous. 'You've been home, haven't you?'

'Yes.'

'And she said nothing?'

'What about?'

Sharon turned to Louise, who'd become deeply engrossed in her book. 'You'd better tell him what happened today.'

'Not now, I'm reading.'

Sharon started up from the sofa and stood over Louise, with her arms folded. 'Tell him now!'

Louise's attention remained on her book. Almost casually, she said, 'I hit Jade.'

Greg brought his face closer to Louise. 'Oh? Why?'

'She was saying horrible things about me again.'

'It was the usual thing,' said Sharon. 'About her not having a father.'

Greg stroked Louise's hair. 'We agreed you were going to ignore all that.'

'I tried, but she went on and on.'

'That's because she knows it upsets you. When you hit her she knew she'd won. You shouldn't have done it.'

'Why shouldn't she?' said Sharon, flaring.

Greg looked away. He hadn't the stomach for this old argument again. 'I can't understand why Pam never said anything.'

'Jade's obviously not told her. She must be ashamed of it.'

'How did you find out about it?'

'A note from Mrs Henshall.'

'Then Pam must have had one too. I'll ask her.'

'Don't be stupid, she'll want to know how you found out.'

'I'll say you told me, of course. She knows I'm dropping in here before the meeting.'

Sharon sighed. 'That's the trouble with this situation. You always have to think one step ahead.' She found herself craving for a cigarette. 'Anyway,' she went on, 'it gets worse. Louise nearly told Jade who her real father was.'

Greg stiffened and sat up very straight. 'Did you?'

Louise scrambled off the sofa. 'I'm going, if you're going to be horrible.'

'I'm not going to be horrible,' said Greg, standing up. 'I just want to remind you of the promise you made to me and mummy.' He placed his hands on her shoulders. 'I know it's difficult but you know how much it'll hurt us if the truth gets out.'

Louise shoved her father's hand away. 'Don't give me that. You don't care about me or mummy. You're only worried about yourself and what people will say when they find out you've got two families.'

'Louise!' warned Sharon.

'Well it's true! Have you any idea what it's like hiding who I am day after day? Never being able to be normal like everyone else?'

Louise rushed from the room. Shortly afterwards they heard the front door slam. Sharon got up and went over to the window. She remained there watching Louise stomping off down the street. When Louise was out of sight, Sharon returned to her arm chair and sat down.

'She worries me,' said Greg.

Sharon knew that Greg was not speaking out of fatherly concern but because he regarded Louise as the weak vertex in their fragile triangle of deceit. 'Don't worry, she'll never say anything.'

'Shouldn't you go after her?'

'It's all right. She's got a rehearsal.'

Greg began to complain about how difficult and unmanageable Jade had become recently. He explained that her behaviour had deteriorated at home and confessed he was at a loss to know how to deal with it.

'I suppose it's her age,' he said, finally.

'Are you sure she hasn't discovered something?'

'About us?'

'Yes.'

He smiled. 'No. It's nothing like that.'

Sharon was unconvinced. 'Maybe Pam found out something and passed it on to Jade.'

Greg's smile was intended to be reassuring but it merely made him look smug. 'Pam knows nothing.'

'Then why does Jade keep taunting Louise about not having a father?'

'They're kids. You know what kids are like. Evil little sods, sometimes.'

'People aren't blind. They see you coming in here. They put two and two together.'

'Come on. No-one would think it odd that I drop in from time to time.'

Sharon accepted that this was probably true. He'd gone to great lengths to create the impression that all his visits to Honeysuckle Cottage were connected with his chairmanship of Community Watch and the Leefdale Primary School Governing Body. With his encouragement she'd become secretary of the Community Watch and a school governor. He'd correctly reasoned that this would provide a sufficient smokescreen behind which he could legitimately pay her regular visits on the pretext of discussing their joint civic responsibilities. Tonight he had a meeting of the parish council, and she knew he'd have told Pam he'd be dropping in to Sharon's first to update his Community Watch report. That's why he was dressed formally in his best suit, the navy blue one, wearing a crisp white shirt with the blue silk tie she'd given him for Christmas. She always thought blue suited him best.

It occurred to her that she too was dressed more or less formally, still wearing the clothes she'd worn that day for work. What a shame Louise rarely saw her father and mother together dressed casually. The girl had never seen Greg in his pyjamas because he'd never stayed overnight; no amount of Community Watch business could have justified that! And then there were all the other experiences Louise had missed because of their bizarre domestic arrangements. She'd never eaten breakfast with her father and probably never would. Nor had she ever seen him in a swimming costume or a beach shirt, for they'd never been on holiday together. On Christmas Day she'd never exchanged presents with him under the Christmas tree. She'd never gone to a cinema or a bowling alley with him. And, of course, he'd never once discussed Louise's progress with a teacher at a parents' evening. All of that was the privilege of his legitimate family. No wonder the poor kid was fed up. Sharon could feel the promise she'd given Louise asserting itself at the forefront of her mind. She steeled herself to tell him that the situation was untenable and would have to end. That she'd decided to move away from Leefdale.

At that moment an ice cream van passed by in the street outside. Its tinny chimes flooded into the room through an open window creating a nauseating atmosphere of synthetic happiness. How she loathed the sound.

'Fancy an ice cream?' Greg asked, smiling.

She reacted with a scoff. The question didn't merit a response. She knew that being seen joining the queue for cornets was the last thing he wanted.

A silence fell over them. A certain tension had entered the room. They were both acutely aware that they had the cottage entirely to themselves. Sharon knew how embarrassed Greg was about making love when Louise was in the house, even when the girl was asleep. She wondered if he was thinking about risking a quickie. Now was the perfect opportunity.

The knowledge that they had the place to themselves and could have uninhibited sex would normally have excited her. But even though she'd known Greg for over ten years and he was the father of her child, tonight she felt unusually inhibited in his presence, as though he were a total stranger. Reminded of her promise to Louise, she again willed herself to tell him that they couldn't go on, that it was all over. But she stopped short. The enormity of the step frightened her.

'I took someone to view The Old Rectory today,' she said.

She described Dylan Bourne and the reasons for his interest in the property. Once started she didn't want to stop. She was surprised at the unexpected delight she took in uttering his name aloud, and of her pleasure at the thought of him.

Greg expressed perfunctory interest but she could tell from his tone that his mind was preoccupied. As she spoke she caught him eying her intently. She had a fair idea what he was thinking. It was already seven-thirty and his meeting was at eight. Louise was at a rehearsal. This was his rare chance for a shag. Should he take it?

She'd guessed his intention correctly but had no inkling of the trepidation with which he was approaching the opportunity. He was feeling uncharacteristically awkward and unsure. She looked so unattainable in her office clothes: white blouse, short black skirt, black tights; shoes off, feet curled under her as she sat on the arm chair. He was conscious of how young she was; how composed; how full of latent energy she seemed, and, more than ever, of the ten year age gap between them.

His instinct was to go over and kiss her, but he was afraid she might rebuff him. She seemed so cool and self-contained; so impregnable. When she was in this mood his recollection of their passionate and uninhibited fucking seemed like some remote sexual fantasy he'd indulged in when he'd been lying in bed beside his plump, motherly wife. He stared at Sharon again and mentally removed her clothes. Her naked image filled his mind. He savoured the memory of her heavy, swinging breasts, her black triangle of pubic hair and the full, rounded loops of her buttocks. Then he thought of the many, many times he'd breached that iron self-control of hers, and with just the touch of his hand or tongue inflamed in her such intense physical cravings she'd overcome all inhibitions and dissolved with him in an all-consuming, self-extinguishing, wildly abandoned lust. Such thoughts reassured and encouraged him. He felt his flesh stir and begin to thicken.

She saw him staring at her with that intense, preoccupied watchfulness that could only mean one thing. The thought of it sent a quiver of anticipation through her. Suddenly, tiny iron wings seemed to be beating under her breastbone; she felt her breathing quicken and was aware of that delicious spreading ache. Now she too, like him, was thinking only of one thing. She knew she should resist it but was incapable. Her determination to keep her promise to Louise receded as her will weakened and leached out of her. She felt powerless and heavy with acquiescence; thrilled at the futility of resistance; comforted by resignation. She was becoming inert and yet purposeful, like an egg. She wanted him. And with this admission came momentary despair. It was this need to fuck him which made life so difficult: prevented her from taking control or changing anything. The ecstasy of naked contact and penetration obliterated all rationality and logic. It reduced everything else to irrelevance. When they were locked together male and female she wanted it like that for all eternity and nothing ever to change. It had been weeks since she'd had him, and the thought of gorging greedily on such pleasure created a momentum within her which she knew would never be satisfied until her flesh was exhausting itself on his.

He watched her change position in her chair, uncurling her legs and swinging them out until they were planted firmly in front of her. He saw her knees move slightly apart.

He stood up and went across the room towards her. His bulk loomed over her. He stretched out an arm towards her.

She felt the touch of his large practical hand on her cheek. She closed her eyes and pressed her cheekbone hard against his steady palm.

He levered up her face to look at him.

'We haven't got much time.'

She stood up. In one smooth movement he bent towards her until his face completely filled her vision. It was his familiar face but with something added: the imperative of lust. Immediately she felt the press of his lips on hers; the warmth and intimacy of his breath; the overpowering musk of his after shave. Her lips parted at the insistence of his tongue and it was instantly inside her mouth, melding with hers, arching, coiling, exploring. The source of all awareness, all sensation seemed to be focussed entirely in this tiny point of connection between her tongue and his, so there was no sense of separateness only this blind and all-consuming commingling and exchange of sensation They kissed and kissed and kissed, their tongues arching and twisting them away into a swoon where there was only the blind ecstasy of hands feeling for all the secret forbidden places and a haste of unbuttoning and unzipping as they tore and pulled and tore and pulled until the last flimsy obstacles to their overwhelming desire were removed.

She grabbed him by the hand and began tugging him across the room towards the stairs.

He resisted and pulled her to him. 'No, here. Let's do it here.'

'The curtains. I must close the curtains!'

****

'Are you going to stay there all night?' Greg asked.

She was lying on the carpet, naked, watching him as he hastily dressed. She'd been lying in this position ever since he'd extricated himself from her. Her blouse was scrunched up between her legs absorbing the last residue of fluids. She wanted only to stay like this for a while, staggering her return from that far, far shore on to which she'd been transported by the crashing waves of her orgasm. Why was he talking to her? She wanted only to be quiet and still and facilitate her soul's reunion with the material body from which it had partially and rapturously separated; a body that was still registering faint yet unpredictable aftershocks of indescribable pleasure. They were only an echo of their former intensity but she'd no wish for these exquisite little tremors and shivers to cease. She couldn't bear the last vestiges of ecstasy to vanish, restoring her again to the plane of the ordinary. Yet how difficult it was to sustain the thrill of that orgasm: to maintain her tenuous hold on those ineffable sensations. She wanted those feelings to last forever. She wanted to lie still and quiet and think only of the sex; she wanted to postpone all thoughts of that broken promise to Louise. She wanted to forget that, yet again, sex had made her her own gaoler.

She watched Greg putting on his underpants. Those same underpants that Pam had probably washed and ironed. Don't go there, Sharon, she told herself. Better to recall the way he'd stared at her bare breasts in rapt admiration: how he'd spread his fingers wide and stroked both of them, lightly at first, so she could feel nothing but the tantalising brush of his hands over her soft, bare skin. And then his tongue going and making quick, urgent licks and kisses all over her breasts and in the cleft between them before taking each nipple between his teeth, gently bringing his teeth together over it and then the nipple going deeper into his mouth, his tongue flicking and agitating it into hardness. The memory made her nipples swell and grow hard again. She felt a faint renewal of the blind, moist welling up from the depths of her.

She smiled at him and said, 'I'll get up in a minute. Just coming down to earth.'

He looked conceited. 'It was that good, eh?'

'No, it was terrible,' she said, and laughed. He laughed too, but afterwards the look he gave her was uncertain.

****

He was pulling on his trousers and telling her about the items that were on the agenda for the parish council meeting. But she wasn't listening: she was recalling him urgently peeling her knickers and tights down her long legs, easing them off over her feet and flinging them behind him into the corner of the room, where they now lay in a twisted tangle like the sordid cast of some strange creature that rejuvenated itself by shedding its skin.

He sat on the arm of the chair to put on his socks. She thought of his probing tongue and of the way his hands had feverishly fondled every part of her: grasping and clutching at her naked flesh as though he was desperate to plunge his fingers beyond it, deeper and deeper into the bones and tissue beneath. What was it about sex, lust, that reduced us to this frenzy? Made us behave like creatures obsessed? Caused men and women to forget their families? Made people break their sincerest promises? Yet now he was calmly putting on his socks as though nothing had ever happened.

She watched him force his feet into his shoes, and as he laced them with his big, spatulate fingers she recalled the pleasure of his hand travelling up her inside leg, tantalisingly stroking its way towards the waiting junction of her desire; and she recalled with pleasure his fingers settling there and heard again an echo of her long, long sigh; and now there was the image of his head going down and she remembered the shock of his hard stubble against the softness of her inner thighs, the touch of his lips on her bare flesh, and once again, even though it was all gone and past now, she still felt that blind, irresistible moist welling up from the depths of her.

Now his shirt was going on and she was remembering him lying her down and the sudden and unfamiliar roughness of the carpet pile against her bare buttocks, and how his tongue had sought the back of her throat, seeking, seeking the deepest recesses of her. And then that weird sense of detachment; and the feeling, no, the certainty, that mum and dad who'd sat in this room so many times were somehow floating in the space between floor and ceiling; revolving around her; watching as she was greedily kissed and sucked by this strange man. The man they'd never met. The father of the grandchild they'd never seen. And the thought of her daughter brought guilt as she remembered the promise she'd made and broken.

He was putting on his tie now and as his fingers twined and knotted the different sized ends of silk, every movement seemed to be carrying him further and further away from her, expunging the exquisite intimacy they'd just shared.

'I need a pee.'

She watched him hurry across the room and go up the stairs to the bathroom that was directly above. She lay back and listened to him urinate straight and forcefully into the pan and the sound of it was like a cascading torrent.

She lay back with her hands clasped behind her neck. She spread her legs and felt the carpet's pile against the soft skin of her buttocks. That was how her legs had been when he was between them. Then, in response to some subliminal signal, they'd rolled over as one, exchanging positions so he was on his back and she was astride him, heaving a huge sigh of fulfilment as her own weight drove the thickness and hardness of him deeper and deeper in, so that she was enclosing all of him and there was only this wonderful feeling of him swelling and swelling inside her as she arched herself back and forth, rocking his thighs so that the contact intensified all the way through her, each movement forcing from her a short, sharp cry of unbearable pleasure.

She could tell that he'd finished in the bathroom now and was moving about upstairs. How could she leave him? How could she give him up? Louise's demands seemed so unreasonable. She'd forced a promise from her without giving her time to consider all the implications.

Greg came down the stairs. He was carrying a garment. He came into the room and threw the item of clothing at her. It was her dressing gown.

'We can't open the curtains until you've got something on,' he said.

'It's all right. Leave them as they are.'

'No, I'm not leaving here with the curtains drawn. How would that look?'

Slowly, languorously, she got to her feet and covered her nakedness. 'I wish we could do it all over again,' she said.

But his mind was elsewhere. He nodded absently and put on his jacket.

Prompted by her powerfully erotic thoughts she went over and kissed him passionately. But he responded with only the husk of his former desire: almost chastely. She could see he was surprised, even repelled by the fervour of her renewed lust. She was shocked by the occluded separateness of him now: his diffidence; his distance. How could this be when just minutes ago they'd been so rudely intimate?

'I said, I wish we could do it all over again.'

'So do I.'

She didn't believe him. He was a dog that had mated with a bitch in the street and was anxious to re-join the pack. He was dressed now in his civic armour and ready to resume his politicking and his petty jousting. What was she, compared to the lure of all that? What was his wife compared to the lure of it?

She went across to the window and drew the curtains back. The summer evening radiance instantly illuminated the room. Turning back to him, she thought, I should tell him now: tell him what I promised Louise. But the old inertia immediately enveloped her. After what had just happened she knew she'd never have the inclination to give everything up. It wasn't much but it was her life and she hadn't the courage or the will to walk out on it. Perhaps she never would. Besides, after sex like that it was hardly appropriate. "Thanks for the brilliant fuck. By the way, we'll be leaving next week". How would that go down? Louise was asking too much. Why had she given her that promise? What had possessed her to do it? Yet she knew very well why she'd given it. Because she was sick at heart with the situation; because she wanted out and Louise had provided her with the perfect reason.

As the immensity of her betrayal became clear she excoriated herself for her weakness. For the sake of a few minutes of sordid squelching she'd sacrificed her opportunity for freedom; thrown away her prospect of a new life and real emotional fulfilment; her chance to become an adult. At once she felt intense resentment towards him for inveigling her into the sex; furious anger with herself for allowing lust to enslave her yet again.

'Thank God for Louise's extra rehearsals,' she said.

'Yes. Brilliant,' he said, and laughed. 'I'm looking forward to the next one.'

'That's on Thursday.'

'Bugger. Can't do Thursday.'

'When then?'

He paused, savouring the duplicity. Devising excuses for meeting her; the thrill of discovery; the deceit; how he loved it. It brought an element of the clandestine into his life and was the biggest aphrodisiac of all; it gave him almost as much pleasure as the sex itself. What a cocksman it made him feel. 'She'll be rehearsing same time next Tuesday, won't she?'

'Yes.'

'Good. I'll tell Pam I need to pop round to see if you've got a copy of the minutes.'

'Which minutes?'

'The governors.'

'But that was weeks ago.'

'I'll say I've lost them.'

She wrapped her arms around his waist pulling him to her tightly. 'I don't want you to go.'

He kissed her lightly on the forehead and extricated himself. 'I have to. They'll be starting.'

He set off for the door and turned. 'Next Tuesday then. And don't forget. Tell Louise to take no notice of Jade. Whatever Jade says, she's to take no notice.'

She let him out, closed the door and went and sat down. What the hell was she going to tell Louise?

CHAPTER FOUR

After parting from Sharon outside her office in Luffield, Dylan Bourne set off for his immediate destination which was York. In this ancient, walled city the Station Hotel had served as his base for the past six days. It was from here that he'd ventured forth every morning to motorcycle all over North and East Yorkshire searching for potential properties; and every evening he'd returned, having left behind him several happy estate agents, each one under the impression that they'd definitely be receiving a cash offer from him for one of their overpriced pieces of real estate. Unfortunately, he'd never possessed the authority to make such a promise: the decision to purchase a property required the agreement of his colleagues. But Dylan was one of those people who wanted others to be happier than reality usually permits them to be.

He arrived at the hotel mid-afternoon and headed straight for the lounge where he settled in to a comfortable arm chair and ordered a cream tea. Whilst waiting for it to arrive he again studied the property details for The Old Rectory and indulged himself in a pleasant recollection of Sharon Makepiece's memorable eyes and her other undeniable attributes. Later, after scones, strawberry jam and clotted cream washed down with two cups of Earl Grey, he went up to his room where he showered, changed his clothes, packed his few belongings and checked out. He then drove the Ariel Red Hunter back to London via the A1 and M11, at times approaching speeds slightly in excess of seventy miles an hour, and arrived at the outskirts of the capital just after nightfall.

His destination was a luxury riverside development in Narrow Street, Limehouse. This was the home of Charles Reynolds, who, after his elevation to the peerage by New Labour, was now known as Lord Reynolds of Sandleton-on-Sea. The popular East Yorkshire fishing resort had been chosen by Charles as the territorial designation for his title because in 1951 he'd been born there into a family of hotel keepers. His all-consuming ambition in youth, however, was not to be an hotelier but a painter. In order to realize his dream he'd deeply antagonised his parents. On his eighteenth birthday, they'd been shocked when their gift of a fourteen bedroomed hotel had been ungratefully rejected in favour of a place at The Slade. Sadly, in the years following graduation, Charles discovered that a combination of rejection and lack of material comforts was vitiating what little single-mindedness of purpose he possessed for the creation of Art. Five years and dozens of unsold pictures later, he humbly returned to Sandleton to claim his birthright, and then rapidly achieved the material success his parents had always wished for him. His first fortune had been made from property; his second from buying and selling Old Masters. These early, seminal experiences gave him an ineluctable faith in the transformative power of Art, and the unshakable conviction that in a civilised country no-one should ever be denied access to decent accommodation. Which is why, in 1995, he'd broken with decades of family tradition and joined the Labour Party. It was also at this time that he'd established The Sandleton Trust, a not-for-profit organisation dedicated to using art and art therapy to transform the lives of young people who'd been excluded from mainstream education because of their anti-social behaviour.

Charles opened the door of his penthouse apartment and greeted Dylan warmly. He then ushered him into the main reception area where a man and two women were sitting drinking white wine. Their names were Eric, Toni and Zoe. Eric was in his late twenties: his caramel skin tone, springy black hair and light blue eyes indicated a lineage rich in racial diversity. He was smartly but casually dressed in a white open necked shirt, brown leather jacket and beige chinos. His long hair would have suggested non-conformity if it hadn't been so stylishly cut. Toni was several years older than Eric. She wore a navy blue cardigan over a pink blouse and her grey skirt was knee length. Blue tights and navy blue high heeled shoes completed her outfit which was vaguely redolent of school uniform. Her fair hair was cut short and her rimless spectacles gave her a slightly severe look which vanished on better acquaintance when you saw that her face was actually radiating kindness and integrity. By contrast, Zoe was dressed fashionably but sportily in white trainers, white joggers with a drawstring waist and a pastel blue T shirt. She wore only one piece of jewellery, a necklace in blue coral. These colours perfectly complemented her long titian hair and cobalt blue eyes that glinted with unusual lights. Her hair and skin had the wholesome glow of those who spend as much time as they can in the open air. Her face was striking and had a perfect balance of features but was prevented from being conventionally beautiful by a slight twist of pugnacity about the mouth. She'd studied drama at university and had acted professionally for a while. Like many actresses her face was unusually expressive: so sensitive an instrument for conveying mood and emotion that she appeared to feel things much more keenly than others; and often did. Charles was dressed formally in the businessman's standard uniform of light grey suit, blue shirt and red silk tie. He was a man in his late forties, of medium height and with closely cropped greying hair. Only his stylish Italian spectacle frames prevented him from appearing completely stuffy and boring, and indicated the possibility of a slightly more intriguing hinterland. In this smart company, Dylan, who was wearing his unwashed grey T shirt and faded blue jeans, looked somewhat under-dressed. Yet, despite his recent long journey, he appeared to be the only one who was completely at his ease.

Eric waved a greeting and smiled. Toni said, 'Hello.' Zoe nodded coolly. Then Toni and Eric started to bombard him with questions.

'Hang on!' said Dylan. 'I'm dying to go to the loo.'

When he returned he found bowls of chilli con carne and salad had appeared. Charles offered wine. Dylan declined and asked for mineral water. They started to eat and the questions began again, polite banal questions: how had he enjoyed York? What had he done in the evenings? What had the traffic been like on the motorway? Dylan's responses were perfunctory because he was not only tired but disorientated. Outside the penthouse, dark, warm night had fallen. The Thames was winding luminously between canyons of post-modernist apartment buildings, its flat surface iridescent with the reflected light from thousands of domestic light bulbs. Downstream the aircraft warning light on the roof of Canary Wharf was pulsing with mesmeric regularity. But the built environment was competing for attention with much more compelling images in Dylan's mind: the Yorkshire landscape and Sharon Makepiece. He was surprised to find himself yearning for both.

'So, what have you got for us?' asked Charles. The meal was over; coffee served; the real business of the meeting had begun.

Dylan opened his canvas duffle bag and took out the details of properties he'd identified as suitable for the establishment of the first social inclusion unit in Yorkshire. He placed them on the coffee table. 'As I told Charles on the phone, there were an enormous number of properties in the target area which met our criteria and fell within budget. I've managed to reduce them to a shortlist of six.'

The estate agents' descriptions were passed around and scrutinised while Dylan gave his personal impressions of the six properties he'd identified as potential purchases. He was then subjected to rigorous questioning about them and the advantages and disadvantages of each property were discussed in full. Disagreements were aired; positions taken up; opinions began to harden like cement.

Although he thought Cold Dale Farm probably came nearest to meeting their needs, Dylan didn't attempt to promote the purchase of any particular property. He simply described the merits of each and was happy to answer questions and provide further information whenever it was appropriate. Otherwise, he was content to rest his aching limbs and relax as best he could on Charles's uncomfortable minimalist furniture. He'd have given anything to have gone straight home to bed but he knew that wasn't an option. Charles was flying out the following day to Washington. He was part of a delegation of members of the Upper House who were touring the United States researching the work of social inclusion units. He wouldn't return for three weeks. A decision on the property had to be made that night.

Charles removed his glasses and fixed Dylan with an unnervingly myopic blue stare. 'Well, Dylan. We seem to have reached an impasse. You've had the opportunity to view all of these properties. Which one do you think is the most suitable?'

Dylan smiled and was astonished to hear himself say, 'The one that's made the least impact on you all: Leefdale rectory.'

Zoe picked up Parker and Lund's property details and scanned them to remind herself why she'd previously objected to the rectory. Suddenly, on the back she saw something she'd missed before: Dylan's sketch of Sharon Makepiece. Zoe held it up for Dylan to see. 'Who's this?'

The shock of seeing Sharon's image in such incongruous surroundings made Dylan start. 'It's the estate agent who showed me round.'

'I hope it's not the reason you prefer The Old Rectory?'

Everyone laughed.

Zoe returned her attention to the property details. 'Yes, I can see why you like it. In some ways it's just what we want.'

Dylan leaned forward in anticipation of her qualification. 'But?'

'It's right in the centre of a village!'

'What's wrong with that?'

Zoe sat back and folded her arms. 'Don't you see it as a potential source of conflict?'

'No. Why should it be?'

'Come on! This place Leefdale is an up market village full of smug little Englanders who think they're the bees' knees because for years they've won some poxy gardening contest. They're hardly going to be delighted when we fill their exquisite rectory with inner city yobbos.'

Eric grinned and affected shock. 'They're not yobbos!'

Zoe sighed patiently. 'Of course, they're not. We all agree on that. But that's how they'd be seen by the inhabitants of Leefdale.'

Toni wrinkled her eyebrows satirically. 'That's very defeatist of you. Why should these Leefdale people be insulated from reality?'

'Ordinarily I'd agree. But by basing ourselves in the rectory I think we'd be giving ourselves and the kids unnecessary grief.'

'So, to avoid that we have to hide them away. Is that what you're saying?' said Charles.

'No, I'm not!'

'Yes, you are,' said Dylan. 'That's why you prefer Cold Dale Farm. It's isolated and off the beaten track. The perfect place to hide them away!'

Zoe sighed and treated him to one of her "I've been unjustly misunderstood" looks. 'I don't want to hide them away. It's just that I don't want them put under any unnecessary pressure. They've all had crap experiences one way or another. The time they spend with us should be a period of relative tranquillity.'

'Tranquillity yes. Isolation no!' said Dylan. 'Of course we want to provide them with a secure environment. But security isn't just about feeling safe. It's about having the confidence to go out and deal with the world as it is.'

'I quite agree,' said Charles, who had to be at Heathrow at 7.30am. 'If they don't get involved with a community how are they going to have any sense of social inclusion?'

'I'm sorry. Did I get something wrong here?' said Eric. 'I thought the idea was that through art we were putting them on the path to being healed.'

'Sure,' said Dylan, 'that's part of what we're trying to do...'

'A big part, I hope!' said Eric. He threw Zoe a look.

'Yes. A very big part,' said Dylan. 'But not the only part. There's also a social dimension to the work we do. Look, the people I met in Leefdale seemed very reasonable. I don't think they'll give us a problem. Anyway, I'm sure we can pre-empt any antagonism by involving the clients in the Magnificent Britain Competition.'

'Now, that's an excellent idea,' said Charles.

'I think it's crap,' said Zoe 'Why should we let these Leefdale people dictate our agenda?'

'Because we want the clients to feel included,' said Dylan.

'I'm sorry,' said Zoe, 'I still think Cold Dale Farm is much more suitable.'

Eric shook his head. 'It's very small.'

'Nonsense. It's got tons of land,' said Zoe.

'It has. But the house itself is tiny. We don't need lots of land but we do need a good-sized house. And Leefdale's rectory is huge.'

Zoe gave him a sharp look. 'You weren't interested in the rectory until Dylan suggested it.'

Eric looked slightly sheepish.

'But Eric's right,' Dylan said. 'I've seen the accommodation at Cold Dale Farm. There's not much space for art and drama studios.'

'But with all that land surely we could build an arts block?' Zoe persisted.

Dylan shook his head. 'Not unless we can talk the price right down.'

Eric laughed. 'Would they come down a hundred thousand?'

'That's what they'd have to do,' said Charles. 'Otherwise, it's way beyond our price limit. After all, I have to ensure that the Trust gets value for money. I'm sorry Zoe, but at that price I don't think we'd be able to afford purpose-built studios. We need to just move in.'

Zoe grimaced. 'It's such a shame. The kids would love a big open space like that. They'd experience a real sense of freedom. And we could build a huge sculpture park.'

Dylan and Charles exchanged a knowing look. The creation of a sculpture park was Zoe's obsession. Unfortunately, none of the units she'd worked in had ever possessed sufficient land to make her dream a reality.

'Leefdale rectory's back garden is big enough for one,' Dylan told Zoe, helpfully.

But Zoe was adamant. 'There's not as much as land there as at Cold Dale Farm.'

Persistence was in Zoe's genes. It had brought her great grandparents out of Poland at the height of the Pogroms when all their neighbours were telling them it was a mistake to leave. Their foresight had saved themselves and their descendants from Auschwitz, and ultimately enabled Zoe to be born. Zoe's Catholic great grandparents had fled Northern Ireland for America in the 1890s but had pledged to return, and, indeed, had done so when the Irish Free State had been established. Zoe had told Dylan all this when they'd been lovers. He reflected on it now.

'Cold Dale Farm's too isolated,' said Toni, who was impatient for a decision.

'I agree,' said Dylan, again surprising himself. Hadn't he always said he preferred isolation?

'All right,' said Zoe. 'You're obviously not having Cold Dale Farm. But I do think that before we make a decision on any of these properties we should all be given the opportunity to go and view them.'

'I don't think we can do that, Zoe,' said Charles.

'Why not?'

'You know very well why. We promised all the interested parties we'd be up and running by the summer. By the time we've viewed all the properties separately the one we finally decide on might have been sold to someone else. We need to make a decision now.'

'But how can we make a decision if we haven't seen the properties?'

'We agreed to delegate the task to Dylan,' said Toni. Behind her glasses her light grey eyes regarded Zoe scornfully. 'I was perfectly OK with that. He is, after all, our team leader and he seems to have gone into everything very thoroughly. We must trust his judgement.'

Zoe was a drama therapist and an expert in assertion techniques. Reasonably but firmly she said, 'I don't mistrust Dylan's judgement, but as we're the ones who'll be working there I do think we're entitled to see what the conditions are like for ourselves.'

'You could have come up to Yorkshire with me,' said Dylan. 'I invited all of you.'

Zoe's expression became slightly tense. 'I explained in the clearest terms why I couldn't possibly do that.'

Dylan said, 'That's right. You did.'

But had it really been so impossible for her to renege on her speaking engagement at the drama therapists' conference? He doubted it. Actually, in the circumstances he couldn't understand why Zoe was going to be working with them at all. It was several months since he'd engineered the ending of their affair. His handling of the break-up had been clumsy and callous and it had come as a devastating shock to Zoe who, until then, had been completely unaware of his disenchantment with their relationship. In the months afterwards, although they'd continued as colleagues they'd barely spoken; and when Dylan was promoted team leader and assigned to establish the new East Yorkshire Inclusion Unit, he'd assumed they would never work together again. He was therefore staggered when Zoe applied for a place in his new team. What kind of a person after a break-up applies to work alongside their ex? It was so unusual he'd wondered if she'd done it deliberately to provoke him. At Charles' insistence (and against his own better judgement) he'd agreed to appoint her. Of course, Charles may have taken a different view if he'd known that she and Dylan had once been lovers and of the acrimony with which they'd parted; but it wasn't even suspected, by him or anyone else within the confines of their professional world. Yet why was Zoe kicking up such a fuss about the properties now, at this late stage? Could it be she was having second thoughts about working with him and was trying to wriggle out of her commitment to the new unit? He hoped so.

Zoe turned to Eric. 'Don't you think we should go and see for ourselves what these places are like?'

'Hey, I'm cool,' said Eric. 'I was happy to leave it to Dylan.' He wiggled his finger archly at Zoe in a faux reprimand. 'So you can leave me out of this.'

Zoe grinned and tapped him lightly on the thigh.

Zoe and Eric? Dylan thought. Zoe and Eric? Surely not?

'Look, I'm going to the states tomorrow, remember?' said Charles. 'I'm sorry but we've got to make a decision tonight.'

Their discussions continued until well after midnight. Eventually, Lord Sandleton, an experienced chairman and committee man, persuaded everyone to reduce the properties to a short list of two, which was then put to the vote. The Old Rectory at Leefdale received Dylan and Toni's votes. Predictably Zoe voted for Cold Dale Farm. Dylan found it significant that Eric did too. Lord Sandleton exercised his casting vote in favour of The Old Rectory. It was decided to make an offer of £495,000 for the property.

Dylan, Eric, Toni and Zoe left the apartment together. In the street, all four lingered briefly around Dylan's motorcycle. Toni offered Zoe a lift home.

'No thanks,' said Zoe. 'Eric's giving me one.' She said goodbye, turned to go and then turned back to Dylan. 'Well, you got what you wanted, as ever. I just hope it turns out all right. I've got a really bad feeling about it.'

CHAPTER FIVE

Louise had been both thrilled and apprehensive when Mrs Henshall had announced that, in order for the adult musicians to rehearse with the children in the school orchestra, there were to be extra rehearsals of "Oliver" in the village hall on Tuesday and Thursday nights. Louise had known that the grown-ups would be joining them for rehearsals at some point but hadn't expected it to be quite so soon; and she'd desperately wanted her performance as Nancy to be perfect before exposing it to critical eyes. Now, she was wondering why she'd been so worried. She was having a wonderful time! The addition of the adults and their instruments had transformed the thin and scraping noises usually made by the school's ten and eleven year old musicians into a wondrously full and sonorous sound. It seemed to ascend from the floor of the village hall, buoying her up and up on a musical thermal while the lyrics poured effortlessly out of her. It was truly magical, and she knew she'd never sung "As Long As He Needs Me" better. And then, when it had finished the whole orchestra had started applauding. All the kids in the cast and the choir had applauded too; even Jade, who'd looked really jealous. Then Mrs Henshall had called a short break. While they were all queuing up in the back room to get their coffees and orange squash some of the grown-ups had said really nice things about her acting and singing. Even old Mrs Phillips and Mr Rawson who'd come along to make the drinks had told her she had the best voice they'd ever heard. They said it was better than Kathy Kirby and Helen Shapiro put together, whoever they were. Still, it made Jade look even more sick. So that was all right.

Now she was watching Mrs Henshall rehearse the scene in which the Artful Dodger attempts to steal Mr Brownlow's handkerchief and Oliver Twist gets caught and arrested for it. Eddie Arkwright, who was playing the Dodger, and Tim Bainton, who was Mr Brownlow, were both terrible actors, and she felt frustrated because Mrs Henshall didn't stop them often enough to improve what they were doing. Mr Evans, the drama teacher at the youth theatre in Sandleton wouldn't have let them get away with so much: he'd have been much harder on them. But she didn't mind. Even though she wasn't acting in the scene it was nice to sit and watch the rehearsal. Somehow it made her feel she belonged. It was great to feel part of this amazing thing they were all making. It made her feel normal, as though it was what she'd been born for and there was nothing else more important in the world.

But she couldn't really concentrate much on what the other actors were doing because her mind kept twisting and turning like a swallow in flight. She kept thinking about all the work she'd just done in rehearsal; going over the bits she'd got right and delighting in her execution of the moves and the business, worrying about her timing and the things she'd failed to bring off successfully; for like all artists, young or old, she was a perfectionist and her curse was that she could never be satisfied. And yet, into all these stimulating thoughts an even more delicious one kept intruding: the thought that at last everything was going to change. Mum was going to tell dad they'd be leaving and going far away, never to return. And then they'd be free of Leefdale and all the lies and the pretending. The dreadful burden of secrecy would be lifted from her forever. This rare certainty made her feel gloriously happy and she was sure that everything was at last going to be wonderful.

How she loved the thought of change and the excitement of the new! That's why she wanted to be an actor. You didn't stay in one place: you toured with the play or musical and if you were a movie actor you filmed all over the world. She knew it was true because of the play on the radio. It was set in the olden days, in the Tudor period. All the other kids thought it was weird to like listening to plays on the radio. She didn't care. It was lovely listening to the radio because you could make up your own pictures. There was nothing nicer than being alone in your own room, lying on the bed and listening to the different voices of characters that seemed to come from outer space. They changed in tone ever so slightly every time they spoke so that you knew exactly what they were thinking and feeling. The play on the radio had seemed as real to her as anything that had ever happened. A band of travelling players were going from place to place and every night they'd perform at another village or remote farm. It was lovely listening to the sound of the actors' voices and the noise made by the wheels of the carts and the horses' hooves as they travelled along from place to place. But the best noise, and the one she remembered most, was the sound of the footsteps crisply crunching over the ground when the actors arrived at a new place and made their way to the barn or the yard of the inn where they were going to do their show. Just listening to those footsteps made her feel wonderful things were going to happen. And all the time there was the strange Tudor music being played on instruments that sounded like recorders and drums but weren't really proper recorders and drums at all, and were slightly off key and muffled. Travelling players! That's what those actors were called and that's what she wanted to be. Her whole life would be like that, now mum had promised to tell dad they were leaving. They wouldn't go right away, of course. She'd do her part in "Oliver" first. But then, at the end of the term they'd be off. She'd leave Leefdale and never come back. She had to get away from Leefdale. Not just because of the secrecy and having to hide who you really were, and having to be careful all the time not to let on that Jade's dad was your dad too and he secretly came round to see you and mum. She had to get away because only then would life change. She could feel the new life beckoning, tugging her off to endless possibilities. She was so glad mum was going to tell dad they were leaving. At last life was going to change for the better and she was going to be happy forever and the bullying would stop.

****

As soon as Greg left the cottage Sharon went upstairs for a shower. Afterwards, she returned to the sitting room dressed in a loose top, jeans and trainers and sat pondering what to tell Louise. She knew the child would be bitterly disappointed. Best not to mention then that she hadn't even told Greg they'd be leaving. But what to say? What excuse could she give for breaking her promise?

Sharon glanced down at the carpet and was immediately reminded of what she and Greg had been doing there earlier. It was the sex which had made it impossible to keep her promise to Louise. It had reminded her that imperfect as the present arrangement was, she didn't want to give it up. She was happy with the way things were. She'd never expected Greg to leave Pam, but if she told him she was leaving Leefdale he'd assume that's what she was trying to get him to do. The last thing she wanted was to set up home with Greg and endure all the mess of his divorce; see Pam deprived of her kids at weekends and holidays. All that blame and guilt, who needed it? It wasn't as if she actually loved him. Or rather, she didn't think she loved him anymore. Love had been replaced by habit. But habit had its advantages. Right now she didn't want any radical changes that would drastically alter the balance of forces in her life. The present situation was quite convenient. Besides, she had no intention of leaving Honeysuckle Cottage. To move out would be to acknowledge that her mother and father were actually dead, and even now, at the age of thirty, she wasn't able to do that.

Sharon looked around the room that contained so many of her mother and father's possessions. While she remained in these familiar and secure surroundings, mum and dad would always be alive and she'd feel close to them, as she'd always done. She was sure any number of people would tell her it was stupid to cling so obsessively and irrationally to the past. But that was easy to say when you weren't obsessive and irrational, wasn't it?

Invariably, such uncomfortable reflections on her circumstances precipitated the opening of a bottle. She stood up, went into the kitchen and returned with a big glass of Australian Merlot. She resumed her seat and took a long sip. That was better! Of course, she knew how desperately unhappy

Louise was, particularly with all the taunting from Jade and others about her absent father. It was a horrible situation for the child to be in: living a life of deceit. She was determined to do everything she could to make Louise happy. Everything, that was, except leave Leefdale.

Despite the consolation of the wine, Sharon found she was still vexed. "Never make a promise you can't keep". That's what her father had always said. So why had she made that rash promise to Louise, knowing she'd never go through with it? She struggled to comprehend the thought process that had led her to make such a crazy decision, but could only recall the wonderful feeling of relief when she'd made it. There was no use denying it, a big part of her longed to be free of a situation that was becoming more and more abnormal. She wanted to leave Leefdale just as much as her daughter. That's why she'd promised Louise she would tell Greg they were leaving. At the time it had seemed the easiest promise in the world to make. But, almost immediately, all the usual doubts had returned along with that inner voice urging her not to tell him.

But why not tell him? It was ludicrous for a woman of her age to be so unwilling to let go. To be paralysed by her fear of change. After all, it was hardly an ideal or desirable situation to cling on to, was it? To be living just down the road from your secret lover, whilst stopping your child revealing to his family that she was his daughter? Surely, if only for Louise's sake, she should leave? But that would mean conquering her fear of the unknown and she wasn't up to it. She knew it was unhealthy and preventing her growth as a human being but there was nothing she could do about it. She was comfortable with the person she was. If she left Leefdale that person would no longer exist, and she was terrified of losing that person.

More practically, if she moved away there would be no more popping in by Greg on some gubernatorial or Community Watch pretext. Their relationship would be difficult to sustain. The sex even more impossible to organise. It might even result in discovery. And then what? He'd be forced to choose. She didn't want to be the one responsible for breaking up his marriage and destroying his family.

How could she possibly explain to Louise all the complex reasons for breaking her promise to her? No, it looked like she'd just have to lie. Perhaps she could say she'd started telling dad they were intending to move, but he'd got so upset and distressed at the thought of it she'd backed off and promised they wouldn't. She'd no wish to disappoint Louise and upset her, but she couldn't allow her life to be dominated by the needs of an eleven year old.

After an inner struggle, Sharon succumbed to a second glass of wine; and then, much later, a third. At nine fifty-five the darkness outside her window reminded her that the "Oliver" rehearsal finished at ten and Mrs Henshall had specifically asked that all the children involved be collected from the village hall by a parent or another responsible adult.

Leisurely Sharon went upstairs and slipped on her fleece. She then returned to the sitting room and picked up her car keys from their usual place in the empty fruit bowl. Immediately, remembering the three very large glasses of wine she'd consumed, she threw the keys down again.

'Fuck!'

She went over to her handbag and rummaged around in it for her mobile. She accessed the number of Louise's mobile and pressed "Call". There was a short delay and then Louise's phone signalled its presence somewhere in the house. Sharon darted up the stairs and into Louise's bedroom. The unmistakable ring tone was emanating from a wardrobe. Sharon flung it open. Louise's waterproof was still hanging in its place on the rail. The disturbing noise was coming from one of the pockets. Sharon ended the call and the sound stopped.

Carrying Louise's waterproof, Sharon ran downstairs to the sitting room. Without the car she was going to be very late. Louise would be the last child to be collected. She visualised Mrs Henshall's disapproving expression. What kind of a mother would she seem to her? Panicking now, she let herself out of the front door and set off down Leefdale's almost pitch black main street.

The half mile between Honeysuckle Cottage and the village hall had never seemed longer, and she suddenly broke into a curiously inelegant half-running, half-loping trot. As she hurried on past the curtained and lighted windows lining the street, she imagined that behind them the parents who'd already collected their kids from the village hall were self-righteously condemning that appalling Sharon Makepiece who'd sent her poor daughter to the rehearsal without a coat or a mobile phone and hadn't even bothered to come for her when it was over.

She continued on into the darkness, cursing the refusal of the parish council to erect street lights. Greg and the Major had done their best but in the end had been defeated by the conservatism and intransigence of the other councillors.

Fortunately, ahead of her were the brightly lit windows of The Woldsman. She shivered slightly as she drew near the pub. It was still only April and although the days were warmer, the nights were very chill. Without her coat the poor kid would be freezing. She hoped Louise was waiting outside the village hall, as she'd promised, and not taken it into her head to set off alone. Sharon forced herself on, stealing a quick glance into The Woldsman as she passed, to see if Greg or any of the other parish councillors were in there. But there were only the regular faces around the bar. The meeting obviously hadn't ended yet.

She hurried on, consoled by the thought that as she was so late there ought to be no risk of meeting Pam who'd probably collected Jade already. She felt awkward enough in Pam's presence at the best of times. It made her cringe to imagine them standing outside the village hall chatting mumsily about the advantages of different secondary schools knowing that just a couple of hours ago she'd been shagging the woman's husband senseless.

Sharon had only gone a few yards beyond the pub when a car appeared in the distance, its headlights flooding the black and unlit street with artificial daylight. The vehicle drew nearer. Oh no! It was one of those owned by Greg and Pam. The driver tooted and pulled up. Sharon peered in. Pam was driving and next to her in the front passenger seat was Jade. Louise was in the back, sitting next to Pam's younger children. Pam pressed a button and the car's nearside window slid down. Sharon bent towards the opening.

'We thought you'd got lost so we gave her a lift,' Pam trilled in that infuriatingly calm and complacent way of hers that suggested nothing ever mattered or was any trouble. 'She looked so cold and forlorn waiting on her own, poor thing.'

'Thanks. I didn't realize it was so late. And then the car wouldn't start.'

'Hop in.'

That's all I need, thought Sharon. She cursed herself for drinking those extra glasses. 'Thanks, but there's no room.'

'We can squeeze you in.' Pam turned to the children in the back. 'Gwen. Ian. Shove up and make room for Louise's mum. Come on, chopity chop.'

Mindful of the alcohol on her breath, Sharon pursed her lips, opened the rear passenger door and slid in next to Louise.

Pam said, 'Do you want me to send Greg round to have a look at the car?'

'No, it's all right, thanks. I've got the AA.'

'Did he manage to catch you?'

Sharon was never sure how much Pam knew or suspected. That's why she always examined everything she said for nuances, subtle insinuations.

'Yes. He got his minutes.'

Louise's highly sensitive nose immediately detected that her mother had been drinking. So that's why she hadn't been there to collect her! The child experienced an inexplicable feeling of apprehension.

'He's hardly in the house five minutes before he's off to some meeting or other,' said Pam. 'I told him you don't have to be on the parish council and the Magnificent Britain Sub-Committee. You don't have to be chair of school governors and the Community Watch. Give something up. Let someone else do it.' Pam continued to complain about her husband's civic commitments at some length. Sharon wondered if Pam was implicitly criticising her for monopolising his time. She often wondered what interpretation Pam put on Greg's visits to Honeysuckle Cottage, and if in private she harangued him about them.

'He thinks more about his parish council commitments than he does about his own job,' said Pam.

How can mum bear it? Louise wondered. Why doesn't she tell her he comes round to see us whenever he can and I call him dad and he listens to my reading? Why doesn't she tell her Jade and Gwen are my half-sisters? And Ian's my half-brother? Why does it have to be like this? I can't stand it. Thank God we're leaving. We'll never have to speak to them again.

'Did you have a good rehearsal?' Sharon asked Louise.

'All right.'

'She's been thrilling everyone with her singing and dancing,' said Pam. 'And she acts brilliantly too.' Then, noticing her own daughter's altered expression, she added quickly, 'Jade was good as well.'

'I'm only one of Fagin's gang,' said Jade.

'You do it well, though,' said Pam.

Jade regarded her mother from beneath resentful brows. 'How do you know? You weren't there.'

'I came in at the end.'

'It was better with the grown-ups playing,' said Louise.

'It's a difficult score,' said Pam. 'It needs experienced players.'

An image appeared in Sharon's mind of Pam's husband and herself naked on the carpet.

'What on earth are we going to do about these two girls?' asked Pam, driving off.

Sharon said, 'Yes, I got a letter from Mrs Henshall, too.'

'It's very worrying. I mean they used to be such good friends.'

'Yes.'

'I've asked Jade what it's all about but she won't tell me.'

'No, Louise won't say either.'

Louise pulled a face and mouthed at Sharon, 'I did. I did.'

'Shh.'

'I did!'

Fortunately, apart from Sharon, no-one heard Louise. The car was a noisy diesel and in need of servicing.

'It's so strange,' Pam went on. 'I've told them they've got to make up and be friends again and stop all this silly nonsense.'

'It's Louise's fault,' said Ian, seizing the opportunity to make trouble. 'She's always picking on Jade.'

'I'm not,' Louise protested. 'Jade's always the one that starts it.'

'I don't.'

'Yes, you do. You're always saying I've got no dad.'

Pam's equable composure vanished. She was plainly shocked and embarrassed. 'Do you Jade? Do you say that?'

'No!'

'I should hope not!'

'I don't. I don't.'

'Then why's she saying you do?'

Jade said nothing. Sharon felt inexplicably sorry for her. Yet she wanted to tell her to stop lying and tell the truth.

'Louise has got a dad just like you,' said Pam. 'He's not at home that's all.'

Fortunately, they had now pulled up outside Honeysuckle Cottage.

Sharon could see the conversation was taking a dangerous direction. She quickly opened the car door. 'Well, we'll have to see what Mrs Henshall says about it.'

'Yes, she'll sort it out,' said Pam. 'Six of one and half a dozen of the other, I expect.'

****

They'd only just entered the cottage when Louise burst out, 'Well? What did he say?'

Sharon didn't reply immediately. She was moving around the room switching on the lamps. When she'd finished she went back to the light switch by the front door, turned the overhead light off and started taking off her fleece.

'Come on, mum. What did he say?'

Louise gazed at her mother beseechingly. Her whole being was animated. Her hazel eyes radiated optimism. Her expression overflowed with the prospect of good news. She looked supremely happy and sure of herself, confident of the anticipated happiness her mother was about to deliver. This visible evidence of her daughter's blind, innocent trust hurt Sharon more than anything. More than her own weakness; more than her cowardly and cruel betrayal.

'I didn't tell him,' she said.

For Louise this had never been a possibility. For several seconds there was complete silence.

'What do you mean?'

'I didn't tell him we were leaving.'

The significance of what her mother had said began to spread across Louise's features. 'You didn't tell him?'

Sharon flung her fleece on to the sofa. Casually, she said, 'No. There wasn't time.'

Louise's face was a rictus of incredulity. 'But you promised!'

'I know. But there wasn't time. He had to get to his meeting.'

Sharon set off for the kitchen. Louise immediately followed her. She had a strong suspicion she was being lied to. 'You had loads of time. His meeting wasn't until eight o'clock.'

Sharon began filling the electric kettle. 'He had to be there early to talk to Major Roberts.'

'What about?'

Sharon returned the kettle to its stand and switched it on. 'I don't know.'

Louise was now sure her mother was lying. 'You could have told him. It would only have taken a minute. "We're leaving Leefdale and we're not coming back". See! You could have told him. You only needed a couple of seconds.'

'Don't be silly, Lou. I couldn't just say it like that.'

'Why not? I just showed you. It's easy.'

'That's because you're a child. You don't understand. It's hard to tell people things like that. It takes more than a few seconds. For Christ's sake, he's not a stranger. He's your father. Now, what do you want for your supper?'

Louise was standing stiff and sullen. 'You're changing the subject.'

'No, I'm not. I'm asking you what you want for supper.'

The child's voice swooped in sudden insight. 'You were never going to tell him, were you?'

'Of course I was.'

'No, you weren't.'

'It wasn't the right time, Lou.'

'But you promised!'

'I know. I'm sorry. There wasn't time. Really, there wasn't.' Sharon felt the need to offer Louise some hope. 'But when there's time, I'll tell him.'

'You're a liar!' screamed Louise. She looked around wildly. On one of the kitchen surfaces was a round biscuit tin. She picked it up and hurled it at Sharon.

Sharon was so astonished she had no time to react. The tin caught her on the shoulder and ricocheted. When it hit the floor the lid flew off and several biscuits spilled out.

'I hate you!' cried Louise.

She ran past Sharon and up the stairs to her room.

****

Sharon's first instinct was to drag Louise downstairs and force her to pick up the biscuits. But she knew from experience that giving the girl ultimatums only made her more stubborn. She decided she'd leave the tin and the biscuits on the floor and see how long Louise left them there.

Sharon winced as she moved her right arm to see if it hurt. She pulled down her top to expose her shoulder. It wasn't bruised but if the tin had caught her on the face it could have given her a nasty injury. She wouldn't allow Louise to forget that in a hurry.

Sharon poured herself a glass of Australian red, went into the living room and sank into an armchair. She would wait and see if Louise came down and apologised. How hateful the girl was when she was in one of her moods. Although this was the first time she'd actually been violent at home. That was worrying. Such an ungrateful little cow. Always thinking of herself. Yes, her situation was horrible but why did she have to keep going on and on about it? She was no fool though. She'd seen through the lie. And lying to her had only made things worse. Why couldn't she just have accepted there hadn't been time to tell him, and left it at that? Yes, it was difficult for her: it was difficult for all of them. But it wasn't as though she'd just been told. It never seemed to bother her before. Must be the part she was playing. Playing Nancy had turned her into a drama queen.

The more Sharon considered Louise's reaction the more resentful she became. At least Louise had a mum she saw every day, and a dad who popped in a couple of times a week. How many kids could say that? Or adults, for that matter? Sharon would have given anything to see her parents again: hug them, kiss them, ask their advice; which was why she considered Louise a very selfish, ungrateful little girl. If they moved away she'd hardly ever see her father at all. Was that what she wanted? And where would they find a house as nice as Honeysuckle Cottage? The state of the market was such that even if she got her price she'd need another hundred grand to find anything comparable. And the last thing she wanted was to live on some horrid little estate in Luffield or Sandleton.

Sharon knocked back the remaining wine in her glass and went for a refill. Forty minutes later, when Louise had still not made an appearance, Sharon decided she could wait no longer. She went upstairs to Louise's room. Unusually the door was closed. Evidence that Louise was still in a strop.

Sharon knocked and when she received no answer, opened the door and entered. Louise was playing with a game on her computer. She didn't look up.

Sharon said, 'Don't you want to know if that tin hurt me?'

Louise said nothing. Her eyes remained riveted on the computer screen.

'No, of course you don't. Well, I was lucky. It could have taken my eye out. Don't ever do that to me again.'

Sharon waited for a reaction. None came. All of Louise's attention was directed at the game.

'I've left the tin and the biscuits where they are. They can stay there until you pick them up.'

Again, there was no reply from Louise.

'I suppose it's a waste of time expecting an apology.'

Sharon continued in this vein for several minutes but failed to elicit the slightest response. Eventually she admitted defeat. 'For God's sake!' She turned and moved to the door.

'Wait, mum!' cried Louise.

Sharon stopped and turned back. Louise had lifted her face from the computer. The puffiness around the girl's eyes and the streaks on her cheeks showed she'd been crying. She got up and came towards her mother. 'Your arm. Does it hurt?'

'Quite a bit,' lied Sharon.

Louise launched into a profuse and tearful apology.

'Oh, Louise!' Sharon placed her arms on Louise's shoulders and pulled her into a hug.

'I was sure you'd tell him you see,' Louise let out, between sobs. 'I was so sure we'd be getting away from here.'

'I know you were.' Sharon was stroking the girl's heaving shoulders: solacing away her sorrow.

'I can't stand it anymore.'

'I know. I know how hard it is for you.'

'It was horrible being in that car with them. It's always like that when I'm with Jade. Knowing and not being able to tell them.'

'I know.'

'But it didn't matter because I thought we were leaving. And then you said we weren't.' She sobbed again.

'I'm sorry.'

'That's why I threw the tin. I didn't want to hurt you.'

'It's all right, Lou. But you must try to control your temper. It'll get you into trouble.'

Louise stopped crying and looked her mother full in the eyes. 'I never thought you'd break your promise. You always say never make a promise you can't keep. That's why I believed you.'

'That's right, you shouldn't. And now you can see why. Because when you break a promise it makes people very unhappy. I'm sorry. I shouldn't have done it.'

'So tomorrow you'll tell him we're leaving?'

Sharon realized she could evade the truth no longer. 'No. I can't do that. I can't leave Leefdale.'

Louise stared at her, dumbly.

'I'm too frightened.'

'Frightened?'

'Yes. I'm frightened to leave here and start again somewhere else in a strange place with people I don't know. I've lived here all my life. I don't want to leave.'

'So we're going to have to stay here forever?'

'Not forever. But at least for the time being.'

'I knew it!' Louise cried, bitterly. She shrank from her mother's embrace and took several steps back.

'You're asking too much of me, Louise! I don't want to leave here. I love your dad and I love living here and I don't want to leave. I know it's hard for you and it's not what you want to hear, but that's the way it is.'

'But I thought you did want to leave?'

'Well, in a way I do. But not yet. It's very complicated. You're too young to understand. I can't give up my whole life. Think what it would mean. We'd lose our lovely cottage and we wouldn't see dad.'

'At least I wouldn't have to see Jade anymore.'

'Don't be ridiculous. Think how hurt dad would be. He loves us. It would kill him if he couldn't see us.'

Louise's expression became suspicious. 'I bet you did tell dad we were going and he talked you out of it.'

'No, honestly, I didn't. I never said a word to him about it. I couldn't.'

Louise looked confused. 'You said you didn't tell him because there wasn't time.'

Sharon cursed herself for the slip. 'That's right. I lied.' Gently, she added, 'Only because I didn't want to disappoint you. If I'd realised how important it was to you, I'd never have made the promise. It was wrong of me to raise your hopes like that. I'm sorry.'

Louise lowered her eyes and said nothing. Her face was completely impassive. She was obviously very affected by what her mother had said but it was impossible to guess what she was thinking. She was so sensitive; felt everything so deeply. Suddenly she said, 'You're lying about the car too, aren't you? There's nothing wrong with it, is there? You didn't drive because you were drunk.'

'I wasn't drunk. I had a couple of glasses of wine. It would have been irresponsible to drive.'

'If you hadn't drunk the wine you could have collected me and we wouldn't have had to come back in Pam's car.'

'Yes. I'm sorry about that.'

'It's awful when we're with them. It always feels wrong.'

Sharon didn't quite know what to say. The situation had never been foregrounded in this way before. Their bizarre existence as an adjunct to Greg's legitimate family was something that was never articulated, never alluded to overtly, even though it had been an accepted fact of their lives for years. It was a secret so shocking it could only be normalised by never being mentioned. For years, Sharon and Greg had managed to prevent Louise from ever openly talking about it, until tonight.

Louise said, 'So we're never, ever going? We're staying here forever?'

'Well, I don't know about forever. Who knows? Certainly for the foreseeable future.' Sharon suddenly saw a way of reconciling Louise to the situation. 'Look, I know Jade's being horrible, but all that will change soon. You only have to put up with it for a couple of months and then it'll be the summer holidays, and after that you'll go to secondary school. Things will be a lot better then.'

'No, they won't. Jade's going to Luffield too. We'll be in the same classes.'

'There are other schools, you know. I thought we might try and get you into one in Sandleton.'

'Sandleton?'

Encouraged, Sharon went on, 'There's the Girls' High School. Or the comprehensive. You could drive in with me to Luffield, take the train, and come home on the bus.'

Louise's face fell. 'I'd still have to come back here.'

'But you wouldn't see so much of Jade.'

'You don't get it do you? I hate it here. I don't understand how you can put up with it.'

'What do you mean?'

'Seeing dad only now and then.'

'It's better than nothing. At least we see him. I'd love to see my dad again. And my mum. But they're dead, so I can't. You don't know how lucky you are. I'm sure your friend Roger would love to see his dad.'

It occurred to Sharon that she'd drunk rather too much wine. Normally, she would never have used the death of Roger's father as some sort of emotional blackmail. Or spoken so frankly about her own feelings of bereavement. But the extraordinary thing that Louise said next, put all thoughts of this out of Sharon's mind.

'Roger's the lucky one. His dad's dead. It might be better if my dad was dead.'

'Louise! How can you say such a thing? How could you?'

'I don't care if I never see him again.'

'You know you don't mean that.'

'I do, I do! Why can't we be like normal people? Wouldn't you like to see him every day? Have him living with us all the time?'

'You know that's not possible.'

'Why not? Why can't he leave them and come and live with us?'

'Don't be silly. Think what people would say.'

'If we moved away he could come and live with us. It wouldn't matter then.'

Sharon was alarmed by Louise's attitude. She obviously thought that was what her mother wanted. One day she'd make it clear to her that it had never been her intention to set up home with Greg. But not yet. Louise was too young, and she didn't know how to put it to her. Her feelings were so conflicted about the situation: pitching and tossing all the time.

Sharon said, 'I know you want dad all to yourself but you've always known we have to share him.'

Louise shook her head vigorously. 'I don't care about sharing him. I just want people to know he's my dad too. I'm sick of hiding it all the time.'

Sharon placed her hand on Louise's shoulder. 'That's never going to happen, Louise. You'd better get used to it, otherwise you'll only give yourself grief.'

Louise nodded gravely. 'It was horrible in Pam's car. I can't stop thinking about it.'

'Yes.'

'Don't you feel funny when you're talking to Pam? I do. There's this great, big terrible secret there all the time. That's how it is when I talk to Jade and Gwen and Ian. It makes me feel horrible. Doesn't it make you feel horrible? That's why I want to move away.'

Sharon couldn't bear to look into her daughter's eyes: they were so full of unhappiness and reproach. But she said nothing. The conversation was leading her further and further on to that disturbing terrain she'd always managed to avoid. 'I'm going to get your supper,' she said. 'Hot milk and chocolate biscuits OK?'

'All right.'

Sharon left the room and went downstairs feeling a lot happier. Her mood was completely altered and she was sure it wasn't just the effect of the wine. She felt that on the whole she'd handled it rather well. Telling the truth had been the right thing to do. It had enabled her to say what she really felt, and put all thoughts of leaving out of Louise's head. She was sure that once Louise started going to school in Sandleton she'd feel much more positive about things.

CHAPTER SIX

'Have there been any changes in the circumstances at home?'

Sharon considered the head teacher's question carefully and suppressed her initial response which was to say, "No, of course not. That's the problem: the home circumstances are as bizarre as they've ever been".

They were in Mrs Henshall's office and had been discussing Louise for over twenty minutes. Sharon had already been shown her daughter's behaviour report: this was a little note book that Louise was required to present to her teacher at the end of each session for a signed comment on her behaviour. Louise had been placed "on report" three weeks after the term had begun. The intention behind the system was dual: the child's behaviour could be monitored on a daily basis and hopefully being "on report" would incentivise them to incrementally inch their way back to a reasonable standard of conduct. In Louise's case it clearly hadn't worked. The majority of the comments in her behaviour report were negative. It was a depressing account of Louise's inappropriate attitudes, and included descriptions of her non-cooperation, swearing and isolated acts of sporadic, low level violence. As punishment for these serious infringements of school discipline she'd forfeited many playtimes and other privileges.

The head teacher had sought to elicit from Sharon reasons for the unexpected decline in Louise's behaviour. She'd already asked the more obvious questions: had Louise been behaving badly at home? Had she become involved in undesirable friendships outside school, perhaps involving children older than herself? Had she started menstruating? To all of these questions Sharon had answered "no".

And now Mrs Henshall was asking if the home circumstances had changed; a question which Sharon regarded as an implicit criticism of her own lifestyle. Why didn't the woman come right out and ask if she'd installed a toy boy in the house? Or if she was shagging a different guy every night? Why be so coy about it? Mrs Henshall's perceived prurience and moral superiority only increased Sharon's sympathy for Louise, and she had a sudden and overwhelming urge to smash the edifice of bland respectability that the school represented and expose its hypocritical foundations. How satisfying it would be to outrage this confident, poised, professional woman by revealing the real reasons for Louise's bad behaviour. You want me to shock you? OK. How's this? I've been fucking your chair of Governors for nearly twelve years now and Louise is his daughter! The liberating effects of even thinking this in front of Mrs Henshall made her feel lightheaded and reckless. But she drew back from such a potentially catastrophic indiscretion. There was too much at stake. If she revealed what was causing her daughter such acute distress it would quickly become staffroom gossip and then the conflagration of disgust would engulf the village. Every household would be discussing Greg Maynard and his two families and wondering how the whole sordid scandal had been kept secret for so long.

'Do you mean have I moved a new boyfriend in with us? Something like that?'

'Yes.' Mrs Henshall looked embarrassed. 'Have you?'

Sharon smiled. 'No. No new additions in that department. Look, I really can't understand why Louise's behaving as she is. Perhaps it's something to do with the school. As you know, she was perfectly all right until this term. I think she's being bullied.'

Mrs Henshall immediately went on the defensive and automatically produced her standard response to such accusations: there was no evidence of anyone being bullied in the school; the children had been told that all bullying incidents had to be reported immediately; teachers had been trained to react sympathetically to alleged victims; the school had an anti-bullying policy which had been commended at the last Ofsted inspection.

Normally, Sharon would have accepted Mrs Henshall's assurances. But today she was feeling vindictive. She'd suddenly understood precisely what it must feel like to be her daughter, entering this place day after day, crushed by the burden of subterfuge and deception that her parents had imposed on her. Living a lie, unable to reveal who she really was. This act of empathy made Sharon feel guilty and resentful on Louise's behalf. Why did Louise have to bear the brunt of it? Why should Jade and the rest of her family escape the burden of secrecy and duplicity so easily?

Sharon said, 'Well, for all that, I think Jade Maynard is bullying Louise. She's jealous of her and says horrible things about her.'

'What sort of things?'

'About her not having a father. That's why Louise hit Jade and pulled her hair.'

'I see. Has Jade teased Louise in this way before?'

'I'd hardly call it teasing!'

Mrs Henshall instantly reminded herself that she was interviewing a touchy parent who was quite naturally protective about her child. More care with her vocabulary choices was required.

'Perhaps "teasing" is the wrong word. But has Jade made such comments to her before?'

'Yes. Several times.'

'You say Jade's jealous. Why?'

'She was desperate to play Nancy in "Oliver". Ever since Louise got the part Jade's been making her life hell.'

Mrs Henshall's brown eyes radiated concern. 'Louise has never complained about Jade to me. Whenever I ask her why she behaves as she does she simply becomes silent and withdrawn.'

'That's because she's embarrassed. Possibly even frightened.'

Mrs Henshall could understand why Louise might be embarrassed to talk about her absent father, but she considered it unlikely that she'd be intimidated by Jade Maynard as she towered a good six inches over her. However, Mrs Henshall's prudence and tact told her that it might not be politic to mention this. She said, 'Well, it's good that she's at last providing an explanation for her behaviour. I'll speak to both girls and get to the bottom of all this.'

Sharon became alarmed. Had she said too much? Given the chance, would Louise, in her vulnerable and volatile state, bring down the whole fiction they'd elaborately erected? She felt too weary to protest. 'Good,' she said.

But Mrs Henshall was far from mollified. 'I'm still very concerned about Louise's general behaviour. Whatever the causes, there's no justification for swearing at teachers or behaving aggressively. Until recently, I always felt confident that I, at least, could control her. Now, she's stopped obeying me and is even speaking to me in a most inappropriate manner. I'm afraid that if her bad behaviour continues I'll have to exclude her for a short period. Which means she'll lose her role in the school production. That would be a tragedy: we've only just started rehearsals but I can already see she's going to be brilliant.'

'I'll tell her that,' said Sharon. 'It should bring her to her senses.'

Throughout their discussion Mrs Henshall had been writing notes. She'd acquired this strategy on a course some years ago. The course tutor had explained that taking notes formalised interviews with difficult parents, it made them speak more slowly - less emotionally - and gave them an opportunity to calm down. It reduced their aggression, prevented the interview from escalating into a confrontation, and conveyed the impression that the head teacher was authoritative and in control: that something would be done. Mrs Henshall also found it a useful means of terminating an interview. She always followed the same procedure, which she now repeated with Sharon. She stopped writing and gave Sharon a professional smile. 'Good. Now, is there anything we haven't covered? Or are there any other issues you wish to raise with me?'

'No, I don't think so.'

Mrs Henshall placed her pen decisively down on the desk. She tore the page of writing from her A4 pad, folded it and put it in an empty wire basket marked "For Action". She stood and the backs of her legs made contact with the light swivel chair she'd been sitting on, sending it gliding smoothly backwards on its castors. Taking her cue, Sharon stood too.

'Well, Goodbye. And once again, thank you for coming so promptly.'

'That's all right. It had to be sorted out.'

And so they moved towards the door, in the course of which an obvious question occurred to Mrs Henshall.

'Are you in contact with Louise's father?'

Sharon was completely thrown. There was a very long pause. Finally, she said 'No.'

'But you know where he is if you wish to contact him?'

There was no choice but to continue the lie. 'No. No, he's disappeared. I haven't seen him for years.'

'Has Louise ever met him?'

Tentatively, Sharon said, 'No. Why?'

'I just thought that if Louise could meet him it might help with her behaviour.'

'I've no idea where he is,' said Sharon.

'So presumably he doesn't provide you with any financial support for Louise?'

'No.'

'You know there are ways of tracing errant fathers.'

Sharon opened the door of the office and turned back to Mrs Henshall. 'He's out of my life. I've no wish to contact him again. OK?'

Mrs Henshall registered the aggressive tone and remembered that she was no longer taking notes. 'Of course,' she said. 'I quite understand.'

THE LEEFLET
The Newsletter of The Leefdale Parish Council
May 2001
Page 6

Letters to the Editor

The Burrow,
Leefdale.
7th May 2001

Dear Sir,

I was most disappointed to read last month's "In the Garden with the Major". I got the distinct impression that Major Roberts was patronising those of us who have only recently moved to Leefdale.

I myself moved here just six months ago from Northampton. Others have come from the South and Scotland. We are all experienced gardeners and are very well aware that the local soil is a chalk one and need no advice about which plants thrive best in it.

Actually, I was very surprised that a number of common shrubs which do well on chalk were not included in the Major's list of recommendations. I am thinking particularly of Ceanothus Gloire de Versailles which provides rich blue flowers from midsummer to autumn. Another is Philadelphus Microphyllus Littleleaf Mock Orange which bears highly scented white flowers in early and mid-summer. Neither should one disregard Potentilla Fruticosa Red Ace which has dark green foliage and rose-like, vermillion-red flowers from spring to autumn.

I would also remind the Major that many plants which tolerate chalk are not always at their best in July when the Magnificent Britain Competition takes place. We all want to see the village win for the fifth year running but we mustn't forget that our gardens need to be at their best throughout the year, not just in July, and plant accordingly.

Yours sincerely,
Lucy Birkinshaw.

THE LEEFLET
The Newsletter of The Leefdale Parish Council
May 2001
Pages 3-4
In the Garden with "The Major"

Wonderful news! Yesterday I received a telephone call from Lady Brearley. She was delighted to inform me that Leefdale had yet again reached the final stages of selection in the Magnificent Britain Competition. (Village with less than 500 inhabitants category). Congratulations to all the hardworking gardeners in our village who have contributed to our success. The other villages which have reached the shortlist are:

Molesbury (Gloucestershire)
Kirkbuchan (Clackmannanshire)
Weasle (Kent)
Llarabeg (Gwynedd)
Larch-on-Ouse (Suffolk)
Fiddle (Lincolnshire)

The other good news is that Leefdale will be the last village to be adjudicated. Judging will take place on Friday the 20th of July. Make sure you put the date in your diaries.

Being judged last gives us the advantage of a little extra time in which to make a special effort to ensure the village is at its best when the judges come round. Incidentally, Lady Brearley tells me that she will be among them yet again this year. As many of you know, Lady Brearley's late husband, Sir Maurice, inaugurated the Magnificent Britain Competition over fifty years ago.

I hate to be a wet blanket at a time of such jubilation but, disappointingly, it has come to the notice of the Magnificent Britain Sub-Committee that there is still a small but significant number of gardens in the village which are not, shall I say, quite up to the mark, and might affect our chances of securing that record fifth consecutive gold medal. If, for some reason, you are unable to give the necessary care and attention to your garden don't forget that there are lots of volunteers in the village who are most happy to help you keep your garden up to scratch. Just call Greg Maynard on 756798 and he'll arrange it.

Now, as promised, here are my suggestions for climbing plants that do particularly well in chalky soils. I'll begin with some of the limited garden climbers which are able to cling to a wall or fence without the assistance of trellis or wires. Varieties of the common ivy, Hedera Helix, and the Persian ivy, H. Colchica Dentala Variegata are natural clingers. So too is the climbing hydrangea, Hydrangea Petiolaris, which blooms in July and produces creamy white flowerheads. My own favourites amongst the clingers are the Virginia Creeper Parthenocissus Quinquefolia and the Boston Ivy P. Tricuspidata

Veitchii. Train these two over a wall or strongly built fence each autumn and they will reward you with intense shades of scarlet, crimson and purple.

Climbers which are not self-clinging are often referred to as "scramblers" or "smotherers" and for a very good reason: they colonise every available space and smother every plant in their way! So, don't plant them anywhere near plants you regard as precious. There are numerous examples of scramblers. If you have a fence or wall which receive a good deal of sun the honeysuckles are an excellent choice. One which thrives particularly well in our chalky soil is Lonicera Periclymenum Serotina. Train it onto a support or up a large shrub. It has deciduous, oval leaves and from midsummer bears very fragrant, rich red-purple flowers.

Now, I suppose that clematis is probably everybody's favourite scrambler. C. Macropetala has violet-blue flowers which appear in late spring, and C. Nelly Moser produces large, mauve-pink flowers in early summer. Another clematis worth mentioning is C. Orientalis which is also known as the "orange peel" clematis because of its striking, yellowy-orange sepals. These clematis do particularly well on chalk but remember, clematis are water lovers. Plant them in shady areas and keep the roots moist with a heavy layer of organic mulch.

Finally, I would like to draw your attention to a letter which appears in this edition from Lucy Birkinshaw. Lucy accuses me of patronising newcomers. May I say that it was certainly not my intention to patronise anyone, Lucy, and if I have done so inadvertently I sincerely apologise. I was simply responding to a request for advice from one of our newest residents who had never gardened on chalk before. Furthermore, my list of recommended shrubs for chalky soils was never intended to be exhaustive. Any suggestions which enhance the horticultural splendour of our little community are always welcome. However, I will not apologise for encouraging our gardeners to choose plants that will flower in late July when the Magnificent Britain Competition is judged. Surely it makes sense to have as many plants as possible in bloom at that time.

I would remind everyone that I am a virtual newcomer myself, having moved here in the early nineteen nineties. On my arrival I was most grateful for the advice given to me by the village's experienced gardeners. Sadly, many of them have now passed on. They are greatly missed.

Happy gardening!
The Major.
(Howard Roberts.)

CHAPTER SEVEN

Dylan was in the art therapy room unpacking tubs of paint and other art materials when Zoe arrived. Through the windows he watched, with renewed apprehension, her white transit van appear in the rectory's drive and park up behind his. For days he'd been anticipating her arrival from London with considerable trepidation.

Zoe swung her bare legs out of the van and stood in the gravelled drive and yawned. As she stretched her arms out wide and flexed her athletic body, Dylan noted that she'd abandoned her usual joggers for a short, white summer dress that seemed as insubstantial as a cobweb. It provided the perfect contrast with her shoulder length, auburn hair which was so ablaze with colour he felt he was seeing its glorious russet and coppery tones for the first time. As he contemplated this lovely vision, Dylan was forced to acknowledge that any red-blooded man would have thought him crazy to have given her up. Easy to say, of course, if you were unaware of the more unattractive and alarming aspects of her strident personality; and recently, even by her standards, her behaviour had been pretty irrational, if not bizarre. Why would any woman deliberately seek to work with him again after such a bruising split? Was she engaging in some subtle form of stalking? Was she trying to make him feel guilty about the way he'd dumped her? Or was she in denial: refusing to believe that the relationship was over and hoping that their close proximity in a different location might stimulate it into renewal? And what were the implications of all this for their professional relations?

Zoe ended her sequence of sinuous stretching movements and went back to the van. Its offside door was still open and, bending from the waist, she leaned inside and reached out to retrieve her handbag from the front passenger seat. In doing so she unknowingly treated Dylan to a view of her shapely bum, igniting in him an unexpected flicker of dormant lust. He'd been afraid it would be like this. Already her actual presence was exerting its powerful physical attraction and nullifying his rational objections to her. As much as he consciously wanted to reject her, he couldn't deny that she was an incredibly sexy woman. No-one else would be arriving at the rectory until Wednesday.

The thought of being alone with someone so physically attractive and so unpredictable was unsettling. It was going to be an uncomfortable couple of days.

Dylan sidled reluctantly into the hall. He opened the front door and advanced onto the portico, adopting a suitably welcoming attitude. Zoe waved and walked swiftly up the drive towards him. The difficult problem of how he should physically greet her was now quickly resolved. She came straight up to him, smiled broadly and gave him a fierce hug.

'Lovely to see you,' she said. 'You've no idea how much I've been looking forward to it.'

And also dreading it. On the drive up to East Yorkshire her thoughts had constantly returned to the vicious row which had preceded his ending of their relationship and the many harsh things he'd said. For example, that she was consistently negative, which, was obviously absurd. But the other charges he'd flung at her: that she was too outspoken, didn't accept anyone else's right to a point of view and had no capacity for social restraint; well, these couldn't be so easily ignored, and she'd taken them greatly to heart.

Dylan accepted Zoe's embrace with rather less enthusiasm on his side. He quickly extricated himself. 'Welcome to The Old Rectory,' he said.

They stared into each other's eyes. Struggling with the ineffable, they grasped for the words that would allow them to transcend the impediments of the past.

'I hope you're pleased to see me,' Zoe said.

'Of course.' He touched her arm lightly, enquired about her journey, and while she told him all about it he led her down the hall and into the kitchen.

Zoe looked around her approvingly. 'What a fantastic place. This is certainly a lot different to Dulwich.' Before Dylan had been appointed Leefdale team leader, he and Zoe had worked closely together at the Dulwich inclusion unit.

'What a beautiful kitchen,' continued Zoe, determined to be positive. 'And the view!' Eagerly she moved into the conservatory. Dylan followed her and wondered how much of her enthusiasm was manufactured. They both stood and stared at the garden.

'Impressive, isn't it?' said Dylan.

'Much, much bigger than I expected.'

'Apparently it's the garden that helped Leefdale win Magnificent Britain four years running.'

Bully for them, thought Zoe. She opened the side door of the conservatory and eagerly went out across the patio and down the steps that led onto the extensive lawn. Dylan followed her. The grass was quite high and spattered with blotches of yellow and white where colonies of buttercups and daisies were announcing themselves. There were many more colours too, nestling shyly amongst the grass stems where other opportunistic but delightful little weeds had taken root, their seed broadcast by the great celestial gardener. The sight would have greatly displeased Major Roberts who'd been on holiday in Portugal for the past two weeks, for which reason the rectory's lawn had escaped his frequent attention. Despite that, (indeed, some might have said because of it) the grass had never looked lusher or healthier; as did the whole garden, which although slightly overgrown, wasn't at all unkempt. The flowers, the herbaceous borders and the trees were just entering that period when every leaf is glaucous or vibrant green and all plants seem to be immanent with their summer bloom. As Dylan ambled with Zoe along the gravel path that skirted the grass and ran in parallel with the privet boundary, he took delight in naming the trees, some of which appeared stranded on small islands amidst the lawn. To Zoe's astonishment, Dylan picked out and identified Plum and Apple trees, flowering Cherries, Ash, Silver Birch, Beech, Laburnum, Walnut, and many more.

'How do you know all their names?'

'You forget, I was brought up in the country. Several people in the commune were into plants and birds and things. They taught me.'

'Ooh. Look.'

They'd reached the rear of the garden. Close by the boundary hedge and partly obscured by shrubs stood the objects of Zoe's heightened interest: two white statues. They were some feet apart, each statue turned slightly towards the other as though vaguely acknowledging its companion's presence.

'Who are they meant to be?' asked Zoe.

Dylan pointed to the statue on the left, a half robed male figure holding a musical instrument. 'That's Apollo, a Greek god,' he said.

'Why's he holding the harp?'

'It's not a harp, it's a lyre. He's holding it because he's the god of music and poetry.' Dylan indicated the other statue, a woman wearing a long flowing robe and cradling a sheaf of wheat in her arms. 'And that's Demeter. Goddess of fertility and the harvest.'

How typical it was of Dylan to try to impress her with his knowledge. Such a big head. 'Well done,' she said. 'You seem to know a lot about them.'

'I don't. I read what was on the base of the statues. I expect the Corbridges bought them at some garden centre.'

Zoe's eyes sparkled. 'They're an omen.'

'An omen?'

'For my sculpture park.'

Dylan just stopped himself from groaning aloud. For some time now, in furtherance of her interest in the integration of art and drama therapy, Zoe's ambition had been to obtain a piece of land on which her clients could create what she termed "three dimensional personal constructs". These were not strictly sculptures but artefacts or installations with which the youngsters could interact and involve themselves in various psychodrama enactments. Dylan had already spent over a week in The Old Rectory and, although the house and its gardens legally belonged to Charles and The Sandleton Trust, he'd become almost proprietorial about it. Zoe's promotion of her sculpture park project was no surprise but it induced in him certain misgivings, and he couldn't help feeling she was trespassing on both his land and his subject territory. He instantly dismissed these reactions as irrational. Nevertheless, they niggled. When they'd worked together at the Dulwich unit, due to the lack of available land there'd never been any chance of Zoe's plans for a sculpture park materializing. Then, he'd been prepared to humour her, but now there was the possibility of her plan achieving fruition he was feeling less sanguine about the prospect.

Something amidst the grass at his feet caught his attention. He bent from the waist to peer at it.

'What are you looking at?'

'A blackbird's egg.' He pointed to it. 'See?'

Zoe bent to look too. 'It's broken.'

'And sucked out.'

She looked around. 'There's no sign of a nest.'

'Probably carried here by a predator.'

'What a shame.'

'Let's go back in,' he said.

They returned to the kitchen. Dylan put the kettle on while Zoe made a quick visit to the downstairs loo. When she emerged she was keen to be shown the rest of the house at once, but Dylan persuaded her to sit with him at the kitchen table and recover from the journey with a cup of tea.

As they waited for the kettle to boil there was plenty for them to talk about. Much had happened since it had been agreed to purchase The Old Rectory and convert it into an inclusion unit. The Corbridges had accepted the amount offered for their property without demur, and after contracts had been exchanged their furniture, carpets and curtains had been shipped out to Capri. Completion had taken place in the second week of June, and in the days since then Dylan had been staying at a hotel in Luffield and overseeing the transformation of the house. Specialised equipment had been delivered from London. Carpets, beds, televisions and much else had been purchased from suppliers in the local area. Formal contacts had been established with social services and GPs. All that now remained was for the rectory to be given its final preparations and it would be ready for the clients. They would be arriving on Wednesday in the mini-bus with Eric and Toni. The eight clients were teenagers from as far afield as London, Leicester, Manchester and Bradford. Much of this was already known to Zoe. Over the past weeks, and especially since Dylan had taken possession of the property, he'd been in consultation with her about these matters and much else besides. Their discussions had forged the basis of a good working relationship and had gone some way to repairing their damaged personal relations. Nevertheless, Dylan felt a curious need to impress her with all that he'd achieved. He attributed this to his role insecurity.

'So,' said Dylan, passing Zoe a mug of Earl Grey. 'How do you like the Yorkshire Wolds?'

She was determined to be positive. 'They're beautiful. The kind of place you imagine when you're a kid and your teacher asks you to draw a picture of the countryside.'

'There's loads of great walks to take the clients on.'

Zoe frowned. If only he wouldn't call them "clients". She said, 'The kids will love that.'

'The light's great for painting too.'

'Yes. Lovely big skies. I can see what you mean.'

There was a pause. Zoe sipped her tea.

Dylan said, 'What do you think of the village?'

'Very pretty. I've never seen so many flowers.'

She was about to go on and say she still thought Leefdale was much too posh and the kids would find it very intimidating but she quickly stopped herself. It would only provoke Dylan and reinforce his view that she was consistently negative about everything. She said, 'Although I'm not sure it's worth abandoning my flat in Blackheath for weeks on end, and giving up my social life and the best theatre in the world.'

'So why did you?'

There was an awkward pause. Ah yes, why had she? Should she tell him the real reason? That irrationally, she still loved him and couldn't bear to be separated from him geographically as well as emotionally? Oh yes, she'd love to see his response to that. She took a sip of tea before she spoke. 'You know why I wanted it. The challenge of starting up a unit from scratch.'

'That's what you said at your interview. But is that all?'

'Well, Charles can be very persuasive.'

Dylan certainly knew that. Charles had told him he'd be mad to reject the services of their best drama therapist.

Choosing his words carefully, Dylan said, 'I was very surprised that you applied at all.'

'Oh?'

Was she being deliberately obtuse? 'I mean because of our former relationship and the unpleasant way it ended.'

The look in her eyes was reasonable almost to the point of being patronising. 'I don't see that as relevant. We're professionals. We should be able to work together despite our personal feelings.'

'I agree.' Disingenuously, he went on, 'But I was surprised Eric applied too. After all, he has a wife and family in London. I gather he's leaving them behind. That's going to be tough on them. Perhaps he's having marital problems and that's the reason he applied.'

Zoe shrugged, dismissively. 'How would I know? You'll have to ask him.'

Deftly changing the subject, she told Dylan she'd been delighted to discover that not only was there a theatre in York but also one at Scarborough and Sandleton as well.

'So, it's not quite the backwater you thought it was?'

'I never thought it was a backwater.' She took another sip from her mug. 'There's also a karate class in Luffield. I've always wanted to find out more about karate.'

'Good,' said Dylan. 'Then at least you won't be bored.'

'Oh, I don't know about that.'

Knowing her fondness for sushi he told her that sushi bars in Leefdale were thin on the ground but there was a good Chinese in Luffield and the fish and chips in Sandleton and Filey were great. Their discussion continued on and included the preparations still to be made for the arrival of the clients; the problems Dylan had experienced obtaining the right equipment for the unit and the excellent opportunities the area provided for another of Zoe's interests, running. As they spoke it occurred to Zoe that they weren't really talking at all but simply using discourse to help them adjust to their new and uncomfortable situation. The topics they were selecting for discussion were very much on the periphery of their real concerns; in fact, were being deliberately chosen because they were safer alternatives to what was really on their minds. She listened with half an ear to his description of the new equipment he'd purchased, whilst wondering if he just occasionally regretted dumping her; if he'd shagged anyone since, and if the thought that she might be sleeping with someone else ever bothered him. Dylan, meanwhile, was considering whether he ought to apologise for the graceless manner in which he'd told her it was over. He was also speculating whether he would end up in bed with her; and wondering if he actually wanted to.

He finished his tea and stood up. 'I'll show you around,' he said.

****

Dylan led Zoe towards the ground floor rooms at the front of the house. What a relief it was for him to exchange the awkwardness of personal relations for the certainties of his professional role.

Opening a door off the hall, he said, 'This used to be the dining room. I thought it might make a good drama studio.'

Zoe followed him into the room and her experienced eye was immediately making a professional audit of its potential as a drama space. Her first thought was that it was better than she'd expected. The tall, double windows provided lots of light. The original floorboards, ornate decorative plasterwork and the chandelier made the room less austere than a purpose-built studio; but, ideally, she'd have preferred a much larger space. She suspected that once the rostra were brought in and set up, the working area would become hugely diminished. However, mindful of her determination to be positive, instead of complaining, she said, 'It's fine. You'll make sure I get some art materials, too, won't you?'

Dylan had been watching Zoe take it all in, nervously awaiting her verdict. Her request made him start. In the early, heady days of their affair they'd often discussed the overlapping connection between art and drama therapy. He recalled a particularly stimulating and trenchant discussion they'd had about it one Sunday afternoon lying in bed after sex. On that occasion he'd been defensive because he regarded art therapy as his territory. The recollection was evoking a rarer, happier time for him. Was she recalling it too? If so, was it similarly affecting her? He studied her expression but it was inscrutable.

He said, 'Just ask for anything you want.'

Somewhat imperiously, she said, 'The usual things please: a small supply of paper, paint, crayons, pastels. Perhaps some collage materials.'

'No problem. You can use the stuff in my room any time. Just take what you need.'

She was sure he'd automatically interpret her response as ungrateful, but she was determined not to let that stop her. 'Thanks, but it's important for me to have the materials to hand so they can be used spontaneously. If the kids had to go next door to get them the mood would be broken and the moment lost. So, if you don't mind, I'd like my own supply in here.'

Dylan conceded defeat. Zoe continued to speak approvingly about certain aspects of the room and then they left and drifted across the hall into the art therapy room.

As they entered, Dylan said, 'This was originally the Corbridges' drawing room so I thought it might be the ideal place for doing some... well, er... drawing.'

She affected a wince and groaned. 'Your puns get worse.'

'Actually, I read recently that punsters are more flexible thinkers.'

She laughed. 'More flexible somethings.'

She went beyond him into the room, looking all round without a word. Her silence discomfited him.

He said, 'I know it's slightly bigger than your room but I chose it because it gets most light. And I need a lot more space for equipment than you do.' This came out as defensive and weak and not at all like a team leader, so he added, 'I'm sorry but it's non-negotiable.'

Zoe stared at him satirically, raising one eyebrow. Really, playing the hard man didn't suit him at all. If he was going to do that he'd need her advice on role-play.

She took in the desks, storage units, easels and art materials that were all crammed anarchically together in the centre of the room. Knowing how obsessively tidy she was, Dylan guessed what she was thinking. He made an apologetic gesture. 'There's still a lot to do in here.'

Zoe nodded. 'What a beautiful parquet floor. It would be a pity to drip paint all over it.'

'You're right. I'd better find something to cover it up.'

'You're so impractical.'

Dylan said nothing. Her remark had carried with it a suggestion of their former intimacy. It was just the kind of familiarity he was anxious to avoid. Totally inappropriate!

Zoe feigned interest as he explained to her, at some length, his reasons for choosing the especially long desks and other items of furniture. She was trying very hard to keep her mouth shut. The room Dylan had grabbed for himself was, in her opinion, much more suitable for drama therapy and the one she herself would have chosen, if she'd been consulted!

'Did this belong to the Corbridges?' asked Zoe, pointing towards a battered leather Chesterfield.

'No. I picked it up in a junk shop. Luffield's full of them. It's the only growth industry. I got quite a lot of stuff for the chill-out room too. Come and see.'

They left the art therapy room, moved back down the hall and entered what had been the Corbridges' back sitting room.

Zoe clapped her hands together. 'Oh great. Table tennis!'

The table tennis table was in the middle of the room. Arranged around it were more old sofas and chairs that Dylan had bought from junk shops. A television set was in one corner. The chill-out room was aptly named: everything had a casual, informal look about it, suggesting that this was the sort of place you didn't have to worry about spilling anything; it was somewhere you could be yourself and relax.

Zoe looked around approvingly. 'The kids will love this.'

She picked up a bat and used it to repeatedly bounce a table tennis ball on the surface of the table. 'Fancy a game?'

'Later perhaps,' said Dylan. 'Come and see Toni's room.'

Zoe followed Dylan across the hall and found herself standing in a much smaller room lined with bookcases.

'This used to be the study,' said Dylan.

It was now a fully equipped classroom with desks and a whiteboard. Most of Mr Corbridge's bookshelves looked incongruously empty and had just a couple of piles of exercise books and textbooks on them.

'You've been busy,' said Zoe.

'Not me. That was Toni. She came here last week with all this stuff. Spent the day setting it up and then drove straight back.'

Zoe slowly circled the room, inspecting it.

'Oh, I mustn't forget,' said Dylan, 'she doesn't want it called a classroom. It's to be known as the "encouragement room".'

'What? So, in the other rooms we don't encourage them?'

Dylan laughed.

'Or am I being too negative?'

The good humour froze on Dylan's features, but he refused to rise to the bait. 'Shall we go upstairs?'

As they climbed up to the first floor, Zoe silently rebuked herself for provoking him. What was the point?

They arrived at the first floor landing. Dylan pointed to a door on his left. 'I thought you might like this for your bedroom. It's got a lovely view of the rear garden.' He indicated another room across the landing, the door of which was partly open, providing glimpses of a wash basin and a w/c. 'It's very handy for the bathroom too.'

'Where are the kids sleeping?' she asked.

'They're all on this floor, at the front.'

Zoe gestured towards the door of her intended bedroom. 'So, you've put me in there to keep them in order? Thanks.'

'That wasn't the reason but if you're unhappy about it we can swap. I'm on the floor above, next to Eric. You can have that one if you like.'

Was it her imagination or did he mention Eric's name with a leer? 'Let's have a look at it first,' she said, and set off across the landing. She opened the door of her allocated bedroom and Dylan followed her inside.

It had been some time since they'd both been together in a room with a bed in it. They pretended to ignore its unavoidable and curiously reproachful presence.

Zoe's eyes took in the room and focussed on the cast-iron fireplace. 'Oh, look. How lovely. I can have a fire in the winter.'

'I haven't tested the chimneys yet.'

'Well you can do that, can't you?' She glanced all around again and then upwards. 'I like the size. It's so big and roomy. Look at the height of that ceiling.'

Dylan recalled Zoe's cramped flat and felt encouraged. It seemed she liked the room.

Zoe went over to the fitted wardrobe and opened it. She spoke approvingly of the substantial storage space and then went across to the dressing table and opened the top drawer.

'This is just like the dressing table I have at home,' she said, turning to him, delighted.

He hadn't been aware of this but she was undoubtedly right: it certainly was like the one she had in her bedroom at Blackheath. Had his choice been subconscious?

She closed the drawer and turned the full force of her redheaded charm on him. 'Did you choose it?'

'Yes,' he said, almost defensively, although he didn't see why he should be on the defensive. 'I bought it in Luffield. I suppose it is a bit like the one you have.'

She gave him a knowing smile. 'More than a bit.' She moved over to the window. Dylan followed but kept his distance. The window overlooked the garden at the back of the house. Beyond it lay a field of oilseed rape limned to a golden sheen by the afternoon sunlight, and after that, going on and up, was the green hillside grazed by a small flock of contented sheep. The idyllic view was marred only by the presence of a large, agricultural building located to the left of the garden on neighbouring land: a brutal construction of metal and brick.

'You see what I mean about the view?' said Dylan.

Zoe was clearly enthralled. 'You get a much better idea of the size of the garden from up here. So much bigger than I expected. It would make a wonderful sculpture park. I know you didn't want to talk about it down there but I'm really serious about creating one.'

'I know you are.'

'Eric's in favour of it,' said Zoe. 'He thinks it's a great idea.'

Was that a dig? She knew he'd always been lukewarm about her sculpture park project. 'I've certainly no objection to it being discussed,' he said.

'Good. Because I'm really going to push for it.'

They'd now run out of things to comment on other than the unmade bed and neither of them could ignore it any longer. Zoe went over to it. 'This looks comfortable.' She placed both hands flat on the bare mattress and pressed down on it with all her weight. 'Nice and firm.'

'Yes, it was a good buy. All the beds I bought for us are the same.'

She stood up and turned to him mischievously. 'It's a long time since you were in my bedroom.'

She didn't wait for his response but threw herself backwards on to the bed and bounced up and down on the mattress. 'It's fine. Want to try it out?'

She continued bouncing lightly on the bed. Her short, thin summer dress was riding up her legs. He could see tanned knees and several inches of bare, smooth thighs.

'No thanks.'

She stopped bouncing and lay back on the mattress. Her hair splayed around her, a swirl of deep, pre-Raphaelite titian that always reminded him of Rossetti's paintings of Siddall. She smiled and made a noise of appreciation deep in her throat. 'Mm. This is really comfortable.'

Now Dylan experienced more than just a flicker of lust. He turned away and went over to the window.

'I hadn't expected a single bed,' she said.

He turned to look at her. She was still lying flat on her back. He said, 'Why not?'

'I don't know. I just expected a double. Like the one in my flat.'

There was a long pause. 'Look, maybe this is a good moment to get a few things clear,' he said, and stopped, halted by her searching stare. What extraordinary eyes she had: a light shade of turquoise blue with a shimmer of green, like a robin's egg. Full of depth but simultaneously brittle, shell-like, impenetrable, like the egg. This was going to be harder than he'd imagined. 'I mean, I'm hoping that despite what's happened we can still be mature and professional.'

'Of course,' she said.

'I want us to be good colleagues.'

'We always have been, haven't we?'

'Yes. But that's all.' He cleared his throat twice. 'I mean, I want you to know I'm not hoping to re-start anything.'

He couldn't have been clearer. Once again, she felt the force of his rejection. That terrible eviscerating pain around her heart. Only this time it was worse because she'd travelled hundreds of miles in the hope that her terrible feelings of worthlessness would go if he took her back and renewed their relationship. That's why she'd applied to work with him, because only resuming their relationship would stop these awful feelings of worthlessness and restore her to life again. This pain was unlike any pain she'd ever experienced; unlike period pain; or the appendicitis she'd had at nine. It was so bad because it was the worst imaginable pain you could have without actually feeling anything. It was like a pain in the soul. As though the soul was being pulled out of your body and only he could help you put it back. But all he could do was say he wasn't hoping to re-start anything! It was unbearable. She'd been crazy to come all this way to be knocked back again.

She sprang off the bed and stood up, tall. 'Did I say I wanted to re-start anything?'

'No.'

'I was only joking. I mean about trying out the bed.'

'Sorry. I thought...'

'I've no designs on you or your body.'

'No, I never thought...'

'I was kidding. The only relationship I expect from you is a professional one.'

He looked relieved. 'Good. That's what I want, too. But surely we can also be friends?'

Friends? God, why did that hurt so much?

She said, 'I've always thought we were friends.'

'We are, of course we are.' He was embarrassed now. 'So, friends and colleagues it is then.'

'Yes.' She turned to go.

'There's just one more thing.'

He paused. She turned back and looked at him expectantly.

He knew he was going to sound like a prudish prig but it couldn't be helped. 'We're all in an unusual situation here. Unlike the other units we can't get back to our homes on our days off. Obviously, we can't entertain people in our bedrooms, so if we want a private life it will have to be off site.'

'Entertain? What's that a euphemism for?'

'You know what I mean. We can't invite people into our bedrooms.'

'Christ, you're not suggesting I can't invite Eric or Toni or you into my room for a chat are you?'

'I wasn't saying that at all. I was talking about inviting outsiders into our rooms. When the clients are here.'

'Oh, come on! You don't have to remind me of that! I do know what's appropriate behaviour you know.'

She turned and marched her churning feelings out of the room on to the landing. Impulsively, she set off for the rooms at the front of the house. She then bethought herself and came back and darted into the bathroom. Dylan had now arrived on the landing. He stood outside the bathroom and through the open doorway watched her inspect the bath and turn on the extractor fan. She seemed extremely displeased for some reason.

Then, suddenly she turned to him and said, 'Have you got any cleaning stuff?'

The question was unexpected. 'Cleaning stuff?'

'You know, mops, cloths, disinfectant.'

'Oh, yes. Why?'

'Whoever lived here before didn't have a very good aim. Every toilet smells of pee.'

'I see.'

'Unless it's you.'

He looked affronted and then laughed. He was about to remind her of something but seeing that her expression remained severe, he stopped himself. It was an intimate and funny experience they'd once shared but it was too personal now. It belonged to their previous relationship. He said, 'Not me. Definitely not guilty. But I believe Mr Corbridge was quite old. Perhaps he had a prostate problem.'

'Well, after you've shown me around we'll get started. This place needs a good going over before the kids arrive.'

'OK.'

'Have you got a scrubbing brush?'

'No.'

'Thought not,' she said. 'Good thing I brought one.'

The first floor rooms at the front of the house had been designated as bedrooms for the clients. Zoe now set off towards these with Dylan following. The clients' bedrooms were the largest in the house and each one was furnished with two double bunk beds, wardrobes and chests of drawers. One bedroom was for girls and the other for boys. As she and Dylan stood in the girls' bedroom, Zoe knew why she'd always been opposed to The Old Rectory. It didn't have enough rooms. Many of the kids they worked with lacked privacy. They lived in overcrowded accommodation or terrible housing conditions. In her view it was essential they each had their own bedroom during their stay. She was desperate to mention this but bit her tongue. After all, what was the point? The Great Team Leader had obviously made up his mind.

'I hadn't expected they'd be sleeping four to a room,' said Zoe.

'They're very big rooms.'

'Yes, but at Dulwich they each have their own room.'

'There isn't the space for that here. Anyway, I always felt that isolated them. Don't you think it isolates them? Shouldn't we be encouraging them to be sociable? So many of them have such poor social health. Shouldn't we be facilitating them to function in groups?'

She shrugged non-committedly. 'Yes, of course. But they also need their own personal space. And what happens if one of them is sick? They'll need their own room then.'

Dylan considered this. 'If it were only a minor thing, they'd be perfectly all right. But if it was something more serious I'd be happy to give up my room.'

'Oh. Where would you sleep?'

'If it was just for a couple of nights I'd crash in Eric's room.'

She was about to make a flippant remark about her own door always being open but decided that in his present mood it probably wouldn't be appreciated.

They climbed the stairs to the next floor. When they reached the second storey landing, Dylan said, 'They're all bedrooms up here too.' He pointed to the door of one of the front bedrooms. 'By the way, I've chosen that one for my studio.'

Charles had given Dylan permission to use one of the rectory's rooms partly for his own art work. This had created some resentment.

Zoe didn't respond. Her face remained impassive.

Dylan regarded her tensely. 'I hope that's all right?'

No, it wasn't all right. He should give up his studio and share a bedroom with Eric. She and Toni should also share a bedroom. The encouragement room could be used as a bedroom and Toni could teach in the conservatory. Dylan's office could be located there too. The conservatory was huge, so there'd be plenty of room. Each kid could then have a bedroom of their own. If Dylan opposed these changes on the grounds that each member of staff needed their own room too, for privacy, she'd remind him that was exactly why she'd always thought the place was too small. But she knew that would only get them off to a really bad start. She looked around her silently, determined to keep her objections to herself. But it came hard; very, very hard. She said, 'I suppose it's all right. It was agreed, wasn't it?'

Dylan entered his proposed office-cum-studio with Zoe trailing after him. She wasn't surprised to find it almost as disorganised as his art therapy room: at its centre was a jumble of filing cabinets, easels and half unpacked boxes.

The only evidence of organisation was provided by Dylan's canvasses, some of which were neatly stacked against one wall. 'This room needs a little more work done on it too,' she observed, dryly. 'Have you brought all your paintings?'

'Yes.'

'Not just the abstracts?'

'No.'

There was a long pause. Zoe's feelings had been turbulent ever since Dylan had spelled out to her the purely professional nature of their relations.

'So, we've each got a bedroom?' she said.

'Yes. We've all got some degree of privacy.'

'And you've got two rooms? A bedroom and a studio?'

'Yes. The studio is actually my office but Charles said I could use part of it for painting. He knows how important that is to me.' Dylan couldn't read her expression but it certainly didn't seem approving. 'You think that's unfair, don't you?'

She certainly did think it was unfair. She didn't object to him having a studio to himself but surely he didn't need a bedroom as well? However, she was resolved not to be difficult and so merely said, 'No. Not if it's what's been agreed.'

As though he'd read her thoughts, he said, 'You know I couldn't sleep in the studio. The smell of the oils would keep me awake.' Her expression still seemed resentful, and so he said, 'Nothing's set in stone, you know. As soon as Eric and Toni arrive we can review the allocation of the rooms. But I was on my own and decisions had to be made.'

She gave him a sympathetic glance. 'Yes, it can't have been easy. You know very well I couldn't get up here to help you. I wanted to come but they couldn't find anyone to replace me.' This was true. Zoe had been required to continue working at the Dulwich unit until a suitable replacement had been found. 'But Eric and Toni could have come,' she continued. 'They certainly could have done a lot more to help.'

'Well, Toni did come for a day. As for Eric, I suppose he had Rachel and the children to think of.' Realising that in the circumstances his remark about Eric's family might be construed by her as insensitive, he quickly added, 'Besides, I'm the team leader. It's my responsibility.'

'Yes.'

She looked away, preoccupied.

He said, 'Look. I'd appreciate it if you didn't mention to anyone in the village our reasons for buying this place, yet. You know, if we happened to be in the village pub.'

'Why?'

'I want to tell Sharon Makepiece personally why we bought it. I don't want her finding out from someone else.'

Zoe looked perplexed. 'Who's Sharon Makepiece?'

'The estate agent. The one who sold us this place.'

Ah, the estate agent! Zoe recalled the biro drawing Dylan had made of her on the back of the property details. A hard looking power dresser with scissor legs and fuck-me heels. 'It's none of her business, is it?'

'Well, not strictly. But I feel guilty about it. She thought I was buying this place as my own home. I want to apologise for deceiving her and explain why we had to be so devious.'

'You're too nice. It's estate agents who make us behave deviously. She should be apologising to you. By the way, I've changed my mind. I don't want the bedroom you've chosen for me. I'd rather sleep up here.'

****

'You've brought everything but the kitchen sink,' said Dylan.

Zoe wrinkled her eyebrows and grinned. 'No, I'm sure there's a kitchen sink in there somewhere.'

They were standing at the rear of Zoe's transit van. The back doors were open and they were contemplating all the things Zoe had transported from London. These included drama resources, suitcases, pots and pans, bedding, cleaning equipment and much more besides.

'Some of the stuff belongs to Eric and Toni,' Zoe continued. 'Their cars don't hold much.'

Dylan suggested they unload the drama equipment first.

Zoe pulled a face. 'No. That's not very practical. We need to clean all the rooms before we arrange things. Otherwise it'll make double the work.'

Dylan had to concede she was right. They unloaded the vacuum cleaner, mops, buckets, dusters and cleaning materials and carried them into the kitchen. He stood peering at them looking at a loss. 'OK. Shall we get started?' he said, unsurely.

'Don't you think it would be a good idea to have a plan first?' said Zoe. 'So we both know what we're doing and what our responsibilities are?'

He shrugged. 'OK. Let's make a plan.'

Dylan fetched pens and paper, then he and Zoe sat at the kitchen table discussing what would be necessary to ensure that the rectory was ready for the arrival of Eric, Toni and the eight clients. When the plan was finalised, Zoe stood up and said, 'I can't clean toilet bowls in this dress. I need to change. This might be a good point to decide which bedroom I'm having.'

'Well, you've made it clear you don't like the one on the first floor. So which one do you want?'

'I hope you don't mind but I'd like the one on the top floor next to your studio.'

Dylan looked at her suspiciously.

'That won't disturb you will it?'

Dylan considered. The thought that he might be working in the studio at night with Zoe sleeping in the next room, did disturb him. Was there a subconscious reason for her decision? He wondered why she hadn't chosen one of the rooms at the back so she could contemplate the prospect of her beloved sculpture park.

'No problem at all,' he said.

It occurred to him they were now getting on rather well. It was amazing what a little sensitivity and consideration on both sides could achieve. A bit of give and take, that's all it took.

Zoe treated him to her loveliest smile. 'Good. I'll go and get changed.'

She went out to the transit van to get one of her cases. Dylan heard her lugging it up the stairs to her chosen room. When she returned to the kitchen a few minutes later she was wearing a pair of old jeans and a T shirt.

'Right,' she said, 'If you dust and hoover all the workrooms and bedrooms, I'll make a start on cleaning the lavatories and bathrooms.'

Dylan's expression was unenthusiastic. 'Is there a need to hoover all the rooms? I mean, some look quite clean to me.'

Zoe regarded him scornfully. 'Haven't you seen the dust? There's a fine film of dust on everything.'

Dylan resented the fact that she was taking charge. Surely he was the one who should be making the decisions? However, in the interests of harmony he let it pass. He carried the vacuum cleaner into the drama studio and began to hoover the bare floorboards. After their conversation in the bedroom he'd hoped for some indication that Zoe's attitude had changed, but no, she was still bossy and overbearing, even when it came to allocating the house cleaning tasks. She seemed to have forgotten that he was the team leader. Or was it she didn't recognise his right to the role? It had always been like this. She'd always intruded on his emotional and intellectual territory without the slightest regard for his feelings. She was perfectly aware that he was the art therapist and she was the drama therapist, but refused to observe the discrete boundaries of their professional domains. Certainly there was some overlap and reciprocity between them, but she'd always wanted to take over the art therapy side as well as her own. Her so called sculptures were an example. And now she was laying down the law about housework! It really was too much.

Dylan's suppressed anger found its outlet in the cleaning chores, and he set about them with a will. When he'd finished hoovering and dusting the drama studio he had to admit that it looked a whole lot cleaner. As he carried the hoover across the hall to the art therapy room he heard Zoe cleaning the downstairs lavatory. He stopped to listen. The knowledge that there was someone else in the house apart from himself, and they were both engaged in a joint activity, gave him a comforting, secure feeling.

It took Zoe almost an hour to complete her unpleasant task of cleaning and disinfecting the lavatories. Next, she turned her attention to the kitchen. She spent nearly an hour in there too: cleaning surfaces and cupboards, and methodically storing away pots and pans, crockery and cutlery in places where they would be most accessible. She set up the microwave and found out how to start the Aga. As she worked, she reflected that it was a good thing she'd arrived when she had. Dylan was an excellent art therapist but he was a dreamer with no practical organising ability whatsoever. In fact, it had been a great surprise to her when Charles had appointed him as team leader. But then, Dylan was the only senior art therapist working for The Sandleton Trust who'd been prepared to up sticks, leave London, and relocate hundreds of miles away to establish the North's first inclusion unit. Thinking about this, a question occurred to her which she'd asked herself many times before: why had he decided to do that? Not to get hundreds of miles away from her, surely?

Just after four, Dylan appeared in the kitchen. After congratulating her on the progress and improvements she'd made, he said, 'I've finished my jobs now. Do you need any help in here?'

'No thanks, but I'm just about to do the kids' bedrooms. You can give me a hand with them.'

Together they carried duvets, sheets and pillows up to the clients' bedrooms and deposited them on the lower bunks.

As they stood in the boys' bedroom, Zoe said, 'You make up the bunks in here and I'll do the girls' room.'

Dylan experienced a surge of irritation. Bossiness was another aspect of Zoe's personality which had contributed to their break-up. He was the team leader and here she was again dictating what his tasks were! It was childish, he knew, but the need to assert himself forced him to say, 'Hang on. They should make their own beds surely? We want to encourage them to be self-sufficient, don't we?'

Zoe assumed an expression of faux reasonableness which was deeply patronising. 'Not very welcoming, though, is it? To come miles and miles and be asked to make your own bed? We're not admitting them into youth custody, are we? We want them to feel cared for.'

Dylan knew she was right, of course. It was just her bloody manner. 'OK. I take your point,' he said.

Zoe went into the girls' bedroom and set to work. As she manoeuvred the double bunk beds away from the wall she reprimanded herself for being so bossy. It wasn't a nice characteristic and it only made him petulant.

Zoe was a fast worker and she'd soon made up all the bunk beds in the girls' bedroom. Afterwards, she went next door to the boys' room to see how Dylan was getting on. She wasn't surprised to find that, as yet, only one top bunk had sheets, a duvet and a pillow on it. She said, 'It'll speed things up if I do the bottom bunks while you do the other top one.'

'Thanks.' Sheet in hand he climbed up to the top bunk and started struggling to place it on the single mattress.

She laughed. 'No wonder it takes you so long. You need to pull the bunks away from the wall first. It makes it easier for tucking the sheets in.'

Dylan sighed and came down off the bunk. They moved both sets of bunks away from the wall and worked on, silently.

Although he resented Zoe's manner, Dylan grudgingly admitted that when it came to housework he was quite inadequate and was very glad of her assistance. As they worked he was aware that their shared physical activity was inducing a sense of camaraderie which seemed to be soothing away their previous awkwardness. Really, things weren't working out too badly. Obviously, it had been right to insist that as far as their personal relations were concerned there could be no returning to the status quo. Fortunately, she seemed to be in complete agreement with him about that. Yet despite feeling overall that he'd clearly defined the terms of their new relationship, he still had the impression that in some obscure, indefinable way he'd lost out somehow.

When they'd finished in the bedrooms, Dylan helped Zoe unload the drama resources from the transit. They carried rostra, masks, puppets, video equipment and lots of other stuff into the drama studio, which, to Zoe, seemed to be diminishing in size with every new item deposited there. Encouraged by their new-found comradeship and sense of purpose, Dylan offered to help Zoe organise the room. He was disappointed when she told him she wanted to spend some time in there on her own considering the layout before making a final decision about where everything should go. The truth was she was very annoyed at the total lack of space, which had only become obvious now that all the drama resources had been moved in. But as she and Dylan seemed to be working so well together she was reluctant to spoil things. She was paying a high price for the harmony that Dylan was taking for granted. It went against the grain for her to suppress her fundamental need for honesty and assertiveness, the creed she promoted through drama therapy. Her inclination was to tell him that the space available in The Old Rectory was inadequate, the building totally unsuitable and the drama studio should be in the room he'd selfishly appropriated for his art therapy.

As Zoe no longer required his assistance, Dylan returned to the art therapy room and resumed arranging the furniture and equipment. Yet he couldn't give these tasks his complete concentration. Her presence in the next room was affecting him more than he'd expected.

At around five, Dylan heard Zoe go upstairs. Ten minutes later she was back. She'd changed out of her jeans and T shirt and was now wearing a blue sports bra, hip hugging black lycra shorts and white trainers. The outfit clung to her like a second skin and left very little to the imagination. It was very disturbing. His retinas seemed overwhelmed by all her body's dips and contours, her acres of toned, bare flesh. He was no fool. He understood exactly the nature of the message she was sending him. 'See? You could have had all this. Look what you gave up.'

'I'm going for a run,' she said. 'I'll be about an hour.'
'Fine,' he said. 'I've got a map if you need one.'
'Why would I need a map?'
'In case you get lost.'
She laughed and shook her head. 'I won't get lost.'
She set off for the door.
He said, 'The Woldsman does bar meals. How about eating there tonight?'
She kept going but gave him a backward glance and a smile. 'OK.'

He went over to the window and watched her leave the house and set off running down the drive: her breasts bouncing slightly; her hair streaming out behind her like the tail of a comet. He noted that after passing through the gate she turned right into Church Lane. She was probably going to run the length of the village. Just as well to know where she was headed in case he had to go in search of her. He returned to his work but his heart wasn't in it. His mind was filled with images of her. He wondered if he'd got it all wrong. Perhaps there was nothing between her and Eric after all? He was surprised to find himself hoping so.

CHAPTER EIGHT

Like many remote villages in the Yorkshire Wolds, Leefdale was a linear settlement which had developed along both sides of a single road. Prior to her arrival at The Old Rectory, Zoe had driven backwards and forwards through the village many times while she prepared herself for her crucial reunion with Dylan: postponing it as long as possible, even though she yearned for it. Now, as she emerged from the rectory's drive and turned into Church Lane she already had a good idea of Leefdale's topography. Her intention was to run from one end of the village to the other and then find some path or track that would lead her out into the surrounding countryside.

The first building of any significance Zoe passed was St Wilfred's Church. Yet, although the cold, grey stones of this exquisite example of Norman Perpendicular were transfigured by a luminous patina of late afternoon sunlight, she barely noticed it. She was still recovering from the shock of her face-to-face encounter with Dylan. During the previous weeks when she'd spoken to him over the phone, their conversations had been solely about the unit. Consequently, they'd been short and business-like and had exhibited no trace of the former intimacy which had once existed between them. Disappointingly, it appeared that Dylan had no intention of abandoning this dispassionate, formal tone. In fact, he seemed determined that it was to be the manner in which all their relations should be conducted. Naturally, she'd assumed her first meeting with him in Leefdale wouldn't be easy and had prepared herself for some initial awkwardness and embarrassment: but she hadn't expected to be received with such coldness and reserve, nor a body language which communicated that Dylan wished she were a million miles away.

She came to the end of Church Lane and was confronted by its junction with Leefdale's main street. She didn't pause but turned right and continued running towards the centre of the village.

Back in February it had seemed an excellent idea for her to apply for a job at the Leefdale unit. After Dylan's callous and unexpected termination of their relationship her consequent feelings of rejection, failure and worthlessness had been unbearable. For weeks after the split she'd moved through the world like a ghost in her own life: full of the despair and grief of someone who'd suffered a bereavement. Fortunately, her positive nature and her own professional discipline saved her. She became her own counsellor and advised herself that she could draw a line under the experience, move on and try to forget about it, or she could use it to achieve emotional and psychological growth. The latter meant challenging Dylan's false characterisation of her behaviour, which he'd cowardly blamed for the failure of their relationship and had used to justify ending it. Serendipitously (or so she'd thought) around this time a vacancy for a drama therapist at the new Leefdale unit had occurred, and after some deliberation she'd decided to apply.

Anyone aware that she and Dylan had once been lovers might have considered her decision rather strange, if not downright peculiar. Fortunately, no-one knew of their affair. At her insistence she and Dylan had concealed it from all their colleagues, so no-one they worked with knew they'd even split up. She was aware it was unconventional and "not done" to pursue a former lover in such a way: but as well as a desire to right a perceived wrong, she also believed that the terrible damage done to her ego would only be repaired by getting him back. And if that meant following him to Leefdale, well, that's what she'd do. Now she wasn't so sure it had been such a great idea. And yet, the extraordinary relief she was already deriving from being in his company again was sufficient to make her feel that her original decision had been the right one.

With a surge of pleasure, she recalled the moments they'd spent together a short time earlier, chatting and working as they'd prepared the rooms for the kids. This recollection convinced her it was absurd to assume Dylan no longer wanted her. For the past few hours they'd been speaking to each other as civilized, rational people, and getting on incredibly well. So different to the last occasion they'd been alone together, when his stark announcement that their relationship was over had precipitated that terrible row. Today, it was as though none of that had happened. It allowed her to hope that she and Dylan would soon be restored to their previous state of emotional and physical intimacy. She was mindful that she'd less than two days in which to persuade him to admit that his original assessment of her personality was completely wrong and get their relations back on to a more intimate footing. There'd be no chance of that when Toni, Eric and the kids arrived. And then, when they'd become lovers again and he was feeling secure of her love and affection, if she so wished, she'd be able to dump him as abruptly and unceremoniously as he'd dumped her. But at least, then, it would be her decision. And if that caused him only a fraction of the annihilation of self that his cruel behaviour had caused her, then so what?

If Zoe had been accused of consciously formulating this ignoble plan she'd have been appalled and replied that vengeful acts of retribution were unworthy of an educated, rational woman and not the way to achieve good social health.

But she'd probably have added that anyone knowing of the circumstances might surely have understood her yearning for a little revenge.

The truth was that the balance of forces in her secure, predictable life with Dylan had been violently sundered, creating in her a blind, irrational desire to restore the settled life she'd once known. And it was this that had made her apply for the job at Leefdale. There was no specific plan in her mind, just a vague hope that if she followed her instinct it must ultimately lead to some kind of resolution and closure. Hopefully, by her actions, she'd convince him that he'd been completely wrong about her and prove it was his perception that was at fault and not her character. Hopefully too, she'd then be freed from her dreadful feelings of utter worthlessness. How all this would come about, she hadn't a clue. For life, in the course of being lived, is always a series of plunges into the unknown, and only in retrospect do these extemporisations acquire anything like the prescience of objective, rational design.

An old man working in his front garden called out 'Good Afternoon' to her as she ran past him. Without stopping she waved and ran on. Having spent most of her life in big cities this authentic human contact, made apparently without any ulterior motive, cheered her. If someone had done that in London she'd have been immediately suspicious and wondered what they were after. But here, in Leefdale, it seemed to be as natural for complete strangers to wish each other good afternoon as for sheep to bleat and for cows to low. Yet, this simple and pleasant encounter didn't stop her mind roiling with the perceived slights and resentments occasioned by her first meeting with Dylan for many weeks.

For example, the tenor of so much of their conversation: forced; awkward; unnatural; as though they'd been talking around things, not about them. Understandable, after all that had happened, but so cold and horrible, as though they were strangers. And then there was his attitude to her proposed sculpture park. When they'd been a couple he'd always been so supportive of her ideas: had genuinely encouraged her interest in the cross fertilisation of art and drama therapy. Had he been deceiving her all the time? Or worse, simply humouring her? And how awful it was to have to muzzle her natural spontaneity and forthrightness for fear of being accused of being too outspoken. What could be worse than being so constrained in someone's presence that you were unable to express yourself naturally and spontaneously? "Don't block, unlock!" Wasn't that her daily mantra? "Don't suppress your reactions!" Wasn't that what she was always telling her psychodrama students? And wasn't it the goal of every oppressor to shut you up? She was so angry with herself. Why hadn't she told him the rectory simply wasn't big enough and pointed out how the sleeping arrangements could be altered so that at least each teenager had a room of their own? And when he'd asked her why she'd really applied for the job at Leefdale, why hadn't she told him the truth? Anyway, she'd made sure his oppression hadn't extended to depriving her of her own supply of art materials. She was pleased with her assertiveness about that. She was definitely going to have her own personal stock of them. She'd fought him on that and won. And in time, too, he'd find out that Leefdale was too posh and the kids would find it terribly intimidating, just as she'd predicted. How outrageously cruel of him to tell her there was no question of re-kindling their relationship and expecting her to be just a friend and a colleague after the passion they'd shared? How dare he lecture her on how to behave professionally, as though she'd be dragging men in off the street and up to her bedroom? That had really upset her. So insensitive; so patronising. And then he'd made all those snide allusions to Eric. Why had he mentioned Eric's wife and children and hinted at his marital problems? And followed it with that insinuating look? Did he know something or just suspect?

She ran on, rehearsing many of her other grievances, both real and imagined. So vexed by her turbulent thoughts and intense reflections, she was oblivious to the looks she was receiving from passing motorists, whose attention was being violently wrenched from the road ahead by the riveting sight of her lightly clad body in vigorous motion.

Although not so high in the sky now, the sun was still a fierce force on her head and she was working up a sweat, but the thought of Eric sent a cold shiver of regret through her. It should never have happened. And it wouldn't have happened if she hadn't been at such a low ebb after the break-up. In a sense, it was all Dylan's fault. If he hadn't broken with her she wouldn't have gone on that course where she'd met Eric; or gone with him for the inevitable drink and accepted his offer of a lift home. It had been a consolation shag, that's all. (And not a very good one, at that). A marker indicating the end of her and Dylan, nothing more. She hadn't expected it to have such significance for Eric, and was appalled when it quickly became clear that his marriage was in trouble and he'd seen her as his deliverance. The need to get away from him had partly motivated her to apply for the job at Leefdale. What a shock it had been to discover he'd applied for a job there too. She'd begged him to reconsider: pleaded with him not to destroy his marriage or deprive his children of their emotional security. But his obsession with her had made him deaf to reason. So, she'd had to be blunt and cruel; told him she couldn't possibly love him; didn't want him around; didn't even fancy him. (Not quite true). But nothing dissuaded him, and he'd remained adamant about applying for the job at Leefdale. And, of course, he'd got it. So now they were all on some sort of emotional merry-go-round to Leefdale, with her pursuing Dylan and Eric pursuing her.

Her great fear was that Dylan might assume she and Eric had conspired to get jobs together because they were having an affair. Surely, Dylan couldn't suspect such a thing? How could he believe that their relationship had meant so little that she could cheerfully accept it had ended and then move straight on from him to Eric? How insulting was that?

And what was his interest in that estate agent all about? He'd already mentioned her twice that afternoon; and he'd drawn her too, on the back of the property details for The Old Rectory. Now he wanted to take her out to dinner. He said it was to apologise for deceiving her over the house sale. Surely he was deluding himself? Didn't he realise that when it came to women his ulterior motives were always completely transparent?

She'd been running now for several minutes and was fast approaching the end of the village. To her left she spied a track signposted "Bridle Path". It appeared to lead up and out of the village and go on and on, running between fields and climbing right to the top of the valley. Without hesitation she took this path, and before long was soon jogging alongside a field of ripening wheat. The chalky soil of the Yorkshire Wolds provides perfect drainage because it doesn't retain moisture for long. That summer there'd been no rain for weeks, and as the earth was bone dry the wheat was even drier, bleached a pale green by the merciless sun. She was sure that if she touched one of the plants it would crumble to pieces in her hands, so she avoided them and ran on past the unnaturally dry and static crop of wheat, through the windless, still air, every step sending up little clouds of dry dust each time her trainers came into contact with the sun-scorched, friable earth.

She ran on with the arid smell of the parched wheat in her nostrils, and as the path moved more steeply upward and the incline increased she felt the land's resistance more keenly in each calf and she began to pant ever so slightly. Now that she was forced to focus her mind on the hill before her and concentrate entirely on the task at hand, she'd no time for the thoughts that had vexed her previously. All her energy, will and determination was fixated on maintaining her pace, despite the increasing steepness and the tugging gravity of the land that made every step heavier than the one before, and seemed intent on demonstrating to her how unfit she was. Yet she was glad of the compulsion because it was driving out all her troubling thoughts and reminding her that, in the end, this is all we are, this determination to keep going.

The field of wheat had ended now and given way to a field of oil seed rape. A new smell entered her nostrils, and the pungent musk of the tall, yellow plants almost made her choke but she kept on because, although it was extremely arduous to run, it was pleasant not to have to think about anything except reducing the distance to the ridge, still over a hundred feet above her. She could feel the burn now, the delightful pain in every cell that intense exertion gave her, and she knew she had to keep going because she was very near to that moment when after many minutes of running her mind would wipe clear, empty itself of all thought and there would be only the sensation of soaring and gliding over the land.

At last she made the top of the ridge. She snatched a quick look over the other side of the hill and saw green pasture spotted with sheep sloping steeply down into another valley; but she didn't allow herself the luxury of stopping.

She turned and jogged left along the ridge, moving parallel with the village which she could see lying far below her like a child's model. All around were hillsides chequered green and yellow and occasionally blue: fields of oil seed rape, wheat, linseed and borage; crop and pasture undulating away, rectangles of green and yellow and blue going on and on, creating an earthly paradise; but she took little notice because she had concentration only for the running. No longer out of breath, and relieved of the exertion of the steep climb, she shot forward as though from a slingshot and increased her speed along the level path which ran atop the ridge. Now, finally, after all those many minutes of running came the altered state she sought. Her mind went suddenly clear, wiped clean, emptied of all thought, and there was only the sensation of being just an empty space moving through more infinite space, and the feeling of flying on land.

On and on Zen-like she ran, emptied of all thought, all emotion. There was only the perfect peace of her body moving effortlessly in complete harmony and oneness with everything, so that it was hard for her to know whether she was in the world or the world was in her: for there was no distinction between anything, not the slightest membrane separating the world outside from the world within, and thankfully, at last, there was no longer the clamour of a mind full of competing thoughts: there was only emptiness and silence, a big sky, vast views over the idyllic land, and an Olympian detachment.

CHAPTER NINE

Zoe was delighted with The Woldsman. She was charmed by its low ceiling and exposed, roughhewn beams. She was drawn to the many horse shoes and horse brasses adorning the bar. While Dylan ordered the drinks she moved up and down the pub, gazing at the ancient farm tools such as scythes and sickles that were mounted on its walls and the many photos of Leefdale's villagers and farmworkers taken in Victorian and Edwardian times.

The regulars seated at the bar were equally enchanted by Zoe, but as they were all men and she'd now changed back into her short, white dress this wasn't entirely unexpected. Even so, she found their lengthy stares and the way their eyes penetrated her with a mixture of suspicion and lustful speculation quite discomfiting. So, when she and Dylan had obtained their drinks and menus she steered him towards a table at the far end of the room, as far away as possible from the bar and the men lolling around it.

They sat down and took long sips from their pints of ale.

'Great pub,' said Dylan, looking around.

'Yes. Is this where you intend to bring your estate agent?'

Dylan laughed and turned his attention to his menu. He saw no reason to mention that a few days ago he'd rung Sharon Makepiece at Parker and Lund and, after expressing his concerns to her about the rectory's damp cellar, had suggested that they might go to The Woldsman for a drink sometime. Her response had been less than enthusiastic.

Zoe consulted her menu too, and shortly announced that she would settle for the vegetable lasagne. She could have killed for the steak and ale pie, but her diet dictated that she chose the healthy option. She was therefore quite put out when Dylan told her he was going to have the pie. Knowing that he was aware of her obsession with healthy diets and her struggle to adhere to them she wondered if he'd deliberately ordered it to provoke her.

After they'd made their decisions about food, there was a long pause as they both considered the range of neutral, or at least uncontentious, topics for conversation available to them. Unfortunately, most of these had been exhausted during their walk to The Woldsman.

Undaunted, Zoe began telling Dylan yet again how much she'd enjoyed her run through Leefdale and the surrounding countryside, and how attractive the village was.

'I was sure you'd fall in love with the place the moment you saw it,' he said.

'Yes, it's lovely.'

Even so, she felt intensely irritated that she couldn't say what she really thought about the village and The Old Rectory. But what was the point of spoiling the evening by antagonising him?

They went on to discuss mutual colleagues and clients they'd both worked with at the Dulwich inclusion unit. Gradually the beer and the conversation combined to produce a slight thaw in their relations. At this point, a waitress appeared and took their order. Just as she was about to go, Zoe surprised Dylan by saying to her, 'You have a beer garden here, don't you?'

'Yes.'

'Can we eat there?'

'Aye. I can bring your meal out, love.' She pointed to a door at the side of the room. 'The garden's through there.'

When the waitress had gone, Dylan regarded Zoe quizzically. 'You should have said.'

Her eyes held him in a brief caress. 'Well, it's a shame to be indoors on such a lovely evening.'

She pushed back her chair and stood up. 'Come on.'

Stimulated by her sudden movement the eyes of the men flickered in her direction. They appraised her salaciously as she bent forward to pick up her pint glass. As she went towards the door to the garden they watched her, riveted by the movements inside her flimsy white dress. Not once did she glance at these men who were now sprawling proprietorially around the bar. She didn't even look back to see if Dylan was following her: she just pulled the door open and went outside.

A few minutes later they were seated in a beautiful rectangular garden. It was enclosed on two sides by the exterior walls of the pub, and on the other sides by high, yew hedges. This gave the place a secluded, sequestered character. Pink, yellow and white climbing roses clung to the pub's ancient chalk walls like organic filigree, artfully wrought by gardeners long dead; whilst areas of more modern brickwork were partly obscured by hanging baskets: mauve, red and white blooms pouring over their sides like currents of rich colour arrested in mid-flow. All these flowers were illumined by the expiring radiance of the setting sun, which, high above, was also mottling the underbellies of the fluffy, white clouds with an intense yet delicate melding of carmine and orange. Gradually, as the light faded, these colours diffused and softened into a subtle salmon pink which dappled the beer garden in a soothing Turneresque sheen. This imparted a faintly bibulous glow to the other two couples who were sharing the space with Dylan and Zoe, but who were seated some distance away.

What a good idea of Zoe's to come out here, thought Dylan. He immediately told her so and she smiled back at him happily. There was no point in telling him the real reason she'd wanted to move.

He said, 'I'd love to paint that sunset.'

'Yes, it's beautiful.' She looked at him earnestly. 'But how would you depict it as an abstract?'

'I wouldn't. I'd just paint it.'

'I thought you'd given up all that representational stuff.'

If they'd still been in a relationship he might have felt inclined to reveal to her how his thinking about Art had developed recently, and then gone on to explain that he didn't see it now as just a choice between the abstract and the representational. He might have told her that his move to Leefdale and his re-connection with the rural was inspiring him to integrate more natural forms and recognizable features of reality into his work: yet underpin them with abstract concepts and techniques to make his canvasses resonate the intense fluxions that underpinned the stable surfaces of life. That his aim in Art now was to combine both the abstract and the representational in order to suggest the interconnectedness and universal nature of everything. To produce a new understanding of reality.

'Oh no,' he said, 'I haven't given up on the representational entirely.'

'So that's why you drew that sketch of Sharon Makepiece?' Zoe asked, caustically.

He said, 'That was just a doodle I did while I was killing time.'

Zoe recalled Dylan saying that if people were afraid of something they should draw it. Was he afraid of Sharon Makepiece? Was that why he'd drawn her? But why could he possibly be afraid of her? Unless he was frightened of the power of her sexual attraction? Could that be it?

She said, 'So you're going to paint pretty sunsets from now on?'

He said nothing, just smiled back at her enigmatically. She could tell he didn't want to say anything more about it, and wondered if perhaps he'd arrived at some sort of artistic crisis. She said, 'They're doing "The Seagull" at York next month. I think I'll go and see it. Like to come with me?'

Dylan was immediately on his guard. When they'd been lovers they'd often visited the theatre together. He'd no wish to agree to anything which could be construed by her in any way as an implicit return to their former closeness. Fortunately, he had a good reason for declining her offer. 'Sorry, I can't. At least three of us need to be with the clients constantly. Only one of us at a time can have their day off.'

Disappointment appeared in Zoe's eyes. 'Oh. I see.'

'I'll be constructing a leave rota,' said Dylan. 'Let me know which days off you want.'

He returned to talking about people they'd worked with in the Dulwich unit. Anything to avoid reminders of their former intimacy, which obstinately kept intruding. They discussed the latest news of these former colleagues until the waitress arrived with their food. Dylan decided he'd like another drink. Zoe said she'd have one too, and so he ordered another couple of pints.

As they ate, Dylan described some of his plans for the inclusion unit. Soon they were discussing the clients' individual case histories, even their medical records. Zoe was extremely well briefed and it pleased Dylan that their discourse was reasonable, impersonal and objective: above all professional. He was also gratified to find that Zoe appeared to be in accord with him over everything.

Zoe, however, wasn't finding the conversation so agreeable. She felt it was all one way and dictatorial. Dylan seemed to have adopted a male chauvinist leadership model that was paternalistic and autocratic, and imposed policy decisions upon co-workers without consultation. This was a great shock because when they'd worked together at Dulwich the ethos had been completely collegiate, and she'd assumed he would have continued that approach. Another thing that rankled was his constant description of the kids as "clients". This had always been a source of contention between them. She forced herself to bite her tongue whenever he used this term for the kids; but when he told her that only two "clients" should be allowed to accompany a staff member on weekly shopping trips for groceries, she could take it no longer.

'Still calling the kids "clients" I see,' she said.

'Yes.'

'I've never understood why.'

'I know.'

'Why can't you just call them kids, like we all do?'

'Because, as I've explained before, it creates distance. It produces a psychological and emotional space between us. It enables me to remain objective about them.'

'But they're human beings. You can't help becoming personally involved with them at some level. If you don't empathize with them and understand their needs how can you help them?'

'Calling them clients doesn't stop me understanding their needs.'

Zoe was clearly exasperated. 'Christ, I'm only asking you to call them kids.' She tried to refute his argument with a counter example. 'You call them by their first names, don't you?'

'Yes.'

'And they call you by your first name?'

'Yes.'

'So why can't you call them kids?'

He sighed. 'Because they're not kids. They're adolescents. But above all else they're our clients. If I called them anything other than clients it would affect my ability to judge what's in their best interests. It might affect the course of therapy I'd recommend for them.'

'Just calling them kids won't do that, surely?'

'It might.' His expression softened a little. He was tired of the direction the conversation was taking and wanted to end it amicably. 'But just for you, I'll call them kids.'

'That wouldn't do any good.'

'Why?'

'Because you'd still think of them as clients.'

Dylan laughed. 'Because that's what they are. Words matter.'

'Not if they're the wrong words. Surely that's the whole point. These kids come from a range of de-humanising circumstances. Some have been appallingly abused by their own parents. The last thing they need is to be treated coldly and clinically by people like us. They're human beings, not just machines that need putting right.'

Dylan was recalling how frustrating it was to discuss anything with Zoe. She never accepted that anyone else's argument might be valid and always had to have the last word. He wished she hadn't followed him to Leefdale. If only she'd never applied to the unit. If only she'd left him in peace!

And yet, even as these thoughts occurred to him, the sight of her face and hair in the fading, mellow light gave him a powerful recollection of the touch and feel of her and reminded him of the time when he'd had certain entitlements over her gorgeous body. If he hadn't broken up with her he'd have been free now to reach out and take hold of all that loveliness. Perhaps he didn't want her to leave Leefdale at all. Perhaps he just wanted to stop being reminded of the great physical relationship they'd once enjoyed.

They argued about the merits of using "kids" or "clients" until the subject was exhausted, and then Dylan returned to discussing his plans for the unit. At one point the conversation lagged, and apropos of nothing, Zoe said, 'It must be great riding the bike round all these country lanes.'

'It is.'

'I'm glad you brought the Ariel up here. I'd love to take it out sometime.' She shot him a doubtful look. 'Would you mind?'

'No. Not at all.'

'Does your insurance still cover me?'

'Yes. It hasn't expired yet. You're still the other named driver.' He wondered how many other ties that bind there were.

'Good.' She paused, unsurely, and then plunged in. 'Do you remember when you used to bring it over and we'd take turns to ride it on the Heath?'

'Of course.'

They reminisced about the lanes that criss-crossed Blackheath and the road that cut through Greenwich Park. They recalled their days and nights in The Princess of Wales and the nearby pond where kids sailed their model yachts.

Although he found them enjoyable, these reminiscences made Dylan uncomfortable. It seemed to be wrong, sharing recollections in this way. He was wary of crossing such borders to the past because there was always the danger they'd both be seduced back into deeply intimate and sensitive territory. The nascent professional relationship that was slowly being wrought out of the wreckage of their old intimacy had to be protected from rose coloured memories of their former warmth and physical affection. There could be no airbrushing away of their previous conflicts and resentments. It was essential that neither of them took an idealised and unrealistic view of their past, and allowed it to subvert their new platonic and professional relationship with falsely idyllic reminders of its very opposite. He hoped that Zoe was as committed as he was to resisting these seductive intrusions, attractive and tempting as they might be. Now she was here in the flesh and he was experiencing the compelling power of her presence once more, he was afraid they might get pissed. Then, through sentimentality and loneliness they'd make the mistake of becoming involved with each other again, which he was sure would bring only more pain for both of them.

Despite his misgivings, their delightful reminiscences continued with many jokes and shared laughter as the food and beer melted away what remained of their awkwardness and reserve. Zoe began to feel encouraged. It seemed that their former intimacy was being restored. It gave her hope that she and Dylan must surely get it back together before the others arrived. She said, 'I've been thinking. All four of us deceived your estate agent, so why should you be the only one who takes her for a meal? We should all come, shouldn't we?'

She had a teasing, provocative look.

Dylan thought quickly. 'That's impossible. I've told you, we can't all be absent from the unit at the same time. The clients can't be left unsupervised.'

Zoe nodded. 'Ah, the clients. I'd forgotten them.'

'Besides,' Dylan went on, 'I'm the one who lied to her face. None of you did. That's why I should apologise to her personally. I feel terrible about the way I misled her. I gave her the impression I was buying the rectory for my own home.'

Dylan's obvious concern for Sharon's feelings angered Zoe. He hadn't shown the slightest bit of concern for her own feelings when he'd so cruelly dumped her. He obviously fancied the estate agent like mad. Zoe thought this was very strange. She'd only his drawing to go on, but Sharon didn't seem at all his usual type. Unless he'd suddenly developed a taste for power-dressed businesswomen.

'You're far too considerate,' said Zoe. 'I shouldn't worry about her feelings. Estate agents only care about making sales and getting commission. She got what she wanted, so why should any of us apologise?'

Zoe's remark annoyed Dylan. It was obvious to him she was determined to thwart his plan to take Sharon out to dinner. Surely she wasn't jealous? She had Eric now, didn't she? And even if she were jealous, she'd no right to interfere with his sincere desire to explain to Sharon why he'd been forced to deceive her over the purchase of the rectory.

Zoe added, 'I'm sure if you spoke to Eric and Toni they'd both agree with me.'

So far, that evening they hadn't spoken of either Eric or Toni. Professionally, Dylan knew neither of them very well. Toni had never worked for The Sandleton Trust before. Prior to being appointed to the Leefdale inclusion unit she'd been a special needs teacher in a comprehensive in north London. Dylan knew Eric a little better, as he'd been an art therapist with the Acton inclusion unit, and they'd occasionally run into each other on various professional courses. It occurred to him, not without a slight tinge of regret, that Zoe was the one who probably knew Eric better than any of them! Dylan decided it was time to insinuate Toni and Eric's names into the conversation. He dropped them in casually, observing to Zoe that as they'd worked with neither of them before, a certain period of accommodation or adjustment might be necessary.

Zoe said, 'I still don't understand why Toni came up and sorted out the encouragement room but didn't stay overnight.' Her expression became playful. 'She wasn't afraid of being left alone with you, was she?'

Dylan laughed. 'No. Her school would only allow her one day off.'

Zoe took a drink of beer. 'I'm not sure she and I are going to get on.'

'You don't like her?'

'I don't have a very good feeling about her. She seems quite uptight. Almost anal. And rather judgemental.'

Dylan smiled inwardly. Uptight. Anal. Judgemental. The severest adjectives in Zoe's critiquing vocabulary. He said, 'Eric seems to be a very competent therapist.' He stared at her directly. 'What do you think?'

Zoe wondered why he was looking at her so knowingly. Was he insinuating something? 'How should I know?' she said. 'He seems quite competent.'

'You know, I've been thinking,' said Dylan. 'We'll be living cheek by jowl with Eric and Toni. They don't know about us, and given at times there may be emotional tension, perhaps even personal conflict between us, don't you think we should tell them that we were once lovers?'

Dylan stared almost facetiously into Zoe's eyes. He was gratified to see them agitated by surprise and amazement. After a long pause, she said, calmly, 'I don't think that's necessary. Besides, we agreed we'd never tell anyone about us.'

'But we'll all be living in the same house. It won't be long before they start suspecting.'

'Why should they? Unless we give them good reason. Anyway, I don't accept your premise. I don't see why emotional friction between us should be inevitable.' She smiled grimly, and added, 'Not if we remain professional.'

He said, 'There's also the question of fairness.'

She looked at him with sudden suspicion. 'What on earth do you mean?'

'Well, is it fair to keep the people who work with us forever in the dark about our relationship?'

'It didn't seem to bother you when we worked at Dulwich.'

Dylan acknowledged that this was true. After their split they had continued working together for several months without anyone knowing they'd once been lovers.

Dylan's proposal had made Zoe angry and fearful. The last thing she wanted was for Eric to discover she'd been having a year long relationship with Dylan. And it would be an absolute catastrophe if Dylan found out about her quick thing with Eric. He'd never believe it was just a consolation shag. It would only convince him she'd encouraged Eric to dump his wife and kids and join her at Leefdale. It really was too much. If only she could shake Eric off like one of those irritating leaves that get stuck to your shoe.

For his part, Dylan couldn't understand why Zoe insisted on keeping their affair a total secret. Especially now that it was over. It was contradictory in someone who made honesty and forthrightness their credo for living, as well as the basis of their drama therapy (or at least, asserted they did). And yet, she'd refused to allow their relationship to be revealed to anyone, even their colleagues. She'd said she was afraid of the threats that other people presented to it, and was sure that once their relationship was public knowledge it would be destroyed. Just as her mother and father's marriage, also a union of artists, had been destroyed by others and the stresses and strains of daily life. But Dylan's experience as an art therapist had taught him that people always gave plausible reasons for their behaviour and frank and simple explanations should be distrusted most.

She said, 'I don't want anyone hearing about us OK? It's none of their business.'

Her jaw was set and her eyes were emitting dangerous lights. Dylan recognised the all too familiar signs, and in deference to her unnerving volatility his good sense warned him to back off. But for some reason he couldn't help picking at the scab.

'I still think that in certain circumstances, say when we're under stress, we might not always behave civilly towards each other. In those situations, Toni and Eric might wonder what the hell was going on. If they knew we'd once had a relationship they'd understand and not be so concerned.'

You really are a cold fish, aren't you? thought Zoe, as though seeing him clearly for the first time.

'Besides,' he continued, 'what does it matter now you're with Eric?'

Zoe stared at him incredulously. My God! He knew! When he'd warned her about entertaining people in her room she'd assumed, amongst other things, he'd been intimating there was no way he and she could ever have sex while they were working in the unit. But all the time he'd really been talking about her and Eric! So that's why he'd been dropping all those heavy hints. But how did he know? Eric had sworn he'd never tell anyone. Maybe Dylan was just fishing. She decided she had no choice but to bluff it out. She gave him a derisory smile and said, 'Eric? You must be joking. What makes you say that?'

Yes, he wondered, what had made him say that? He'd no evidence to speak of except for the way she and Eric had related to each other in Charles' flat all those weeks ago. 'Oh, just a certain familiarity I noticed. Body language. Warm vocal tones when you spoke to each other.' He gestured lamely, 'Vibes, I suppose.'

She tossed her head back contemptuously. 'That just shows how utterly unreliable appearances can be. Eric and I have been on lots of courses together. That's why we're quite relaxed around each other. There's absolutely nothing between us.'

Something told Dylan she was lying. After all, she'd never wanted anyone to know about their own relationship, so why would she want anyone to find out about her and Eric? And if she wasn't lying, why had she and Eric applied to work at the unit? Dylan had assumed the only reason Eric had wanted to join the unit was because he'd left his wife for Zoe, and she'd already got a job there. But if there wasn't anything between Zoe and Eric, then why had she applied for the job? Dylan began to fear that the only reason Zoe was there was because he was there. Had she really given up her stimulating metropolitan life and come all that way just to be close to him? The thought made him feel curiously pleased and yet at the same time immensely vulnerable. It made her much more dangerous. They were going to spend two whole nights alone together, and she was already awakening old longings. A few minutes ago she'd made him laugh, and he'd realized how lonely he'd been for so long.

He said, 'I'm sorry. I've obviously made a mistake.'

'You certainly have.'

Zoe loathed herself for lying to him. She was basically honest and hated any kind of deception. It always made her feel sordid, dirty. 'Tell me something truthfully,' she said.

He looked at her warily. 'All right.'

'Have you ever regretted breaking up with me?'

He took a long sip of beer. 'Yes, several times. But I've always persuaded myself it was for the best.'

'Why?'

The sun had almost vanished over the horizon now: its last visible rays tinting the dark sky a barely perceptible red. The lengthening shadows had merged into deep dusk. A slight breeze had sprung up. Dylan and Zoe were the only people left in the garden.

'We're no good for each other, you and I,' said Dylan. 'You're too volatile and hot headed for me. I can't cope with your unpredictability. I need someone more...' He paused. Dare he say "stable"? No, best not. But, how to put it to her without causing offence? How to explain that her unpredictability and hot headedness made him deeply insecure and he couldn't stand insecurity? That her Jesus Christ complex and mission to save the world were deeply wearing? Or that she wasn't sufficiently grounded to be his partner? His father had always maintained that the best partner for an artist was an uncomplicated, practical woman with common sense, who would stop the artist going off the rails, keep his nose to the grindstone and put a lock on his wallet. "You know why we need other people, Dylan?" his father would say. "To supply the qualities we know we're deficient in ourselves." How could he tell her that?

Zoe was still waiting for him to complete his sentence. 'More what?' she asked.

'More ordinary,' he said.

If he'd been able to read her expression better in the failing light he'd have seen her astonishment. 'But I am ordinary,' she said.

'No, you're not. The last thing you are is ordinary.'

She was suddenly angry. 'I'm trying to be. I really am. You've no idea how hard I'm trying. I just want us to get back to the place we were once in. When you ended our relationship it did terrible things to me. It was so sudden and unexpected. So final. It came out of nowhere. I was completely devastated. It destroyed my self-esteem.'

There was a long pause. She hadn't meant to be so forthright about how she felt. But it was her nature. She couldn't do otherwise.

Dylan said nothing. They both sat in the descending dark for several minutes until they could no longer see each other's faces clearly. The only light was from a small upper window in the inn.

Finally, he said, 'It's late. We'd better get back.'

****

Dylan had never walked through Leefdale's main street late at night. He was surprised at how dark it was without street lights, although he didn't comment on this to Zoe. Neither had said a word since leaving The Woldsman. They'd walked in silence, preoccupied with their own thoughts, stumbling occasionally on the uneven pavements in the pitch black, the only light coming from the curtained windows of a few houses.

Zoe was already castigating herself for expressing so forthrightly the emotional damage their break-up had caused her. Why had she been so recriminatory? It was exactly the kind of note she'd wanted to avoid. She'd sounded vindictive and pathetic, completely unlike her usual confident, assertive self. It had probably reinforced his impression that she was some kind of neurotic harpy. What a shame, when the evening had been going so well and they'd recaptured some of their past familiarity. She stole a sideways glance at Dylan but it was too dark to be able to tell what he was thinking. She hoped she hadn't gone too far and frightened him off. Was it still possible to claw back some of the ground she'd lost by her outburst?

She needn't have worried. Her sincere expression of emotional anguish had profoundly affected him. He felt disgusted with himself for treating her so callously. Breaking with her had been the right thing to do, but he acknowledged that it should have been done more sensitively, with greater regard for her feelings. After all, he'd loved her once; or, at least, had thought he had.

'I can't see a thing,' said Zoe.

It really was very dark.

'Hang on.' He stopped and took out his mobile. He switched it on and searched the menu until he located the torch facility, then activated it. At once a thin beam of light issued from the phone in his hand, piercing the impenetrable gloom ahead and making their passage along the street a little easier.

They continued on in silence, until Zoe said, 'I'm sorry I spoke out like that. About the break-up, I mean. Confirms all your prejudices about me, I suppose. But I really hadn't intended to go there at all.'

When Dylan replied, there was a gentle, contrite tone in his voice. 'What you said was entirely justified. I was a shit to spring it on you like that, without warning.'

He meant it. The way he'd broken the news that their relationship was over had been crass and boorish. He couldn't have been more insensitive if he'd informed her by email. He was supposed to be a sentient and understanding man, yet hadn't appreciated the effect it would have on her feelings. But he knew why he'd been so brusque and abrasive: he was a coward about ending affairs. A coward about many things, really. He hated having to say or do anything unpleasant, so when it had become necessary to tell her they were finished he'd been uncomfortable and desperate to get the business over and done with as soon as possible. That had obviously affected his manner. The kindest, gentlest people can be monsters when forced to act against their better natures, he told himself.

'Thank you,' she said. 'I appreciate you saying that.'

Why was he thinking like this? Was it the beer making him sentimental? He'd resolved never to get entangled with Zoe again, and to keep their relations firmly in the professional domain. He was still determined to do that, but Zoe's presence and close proximity was making it very difficult. It was reminding him of what they'd formerly meant to each other. And that was the problem. She really wasn't such a bad girl, was she? They'd shared some incredibly happy moments together. He was glad she'd cleared up the matter of Eric. It was excellent news that she and Eric weren't an item after all. For some reason, imagining them in bed together and Eric running his hands all over her naked body had been torture. Not that any man was her keeper. She had the right to go with anyone she wished. Even so, it would have been intolerable for him if Zoe and Eric had conducted a full blown affair right under his nose.

He said, 'I'm sorry I made the mistake of thinking you were with Eric.'

'Well, yes. It was a bit of a shock.'

Dylan had a sudden and uncomfortable thought. If Eric's marriage was bust, naturally he'd be looking around. Might he try and start some sort of relationship with Zoe? There'd be nothing to stop him. Particularly if he wasn't aware that his team leader and the drama therapist had once been lovers. It occurred to Dylan that if he didn't give Zoe any encouragement, despite all she'd said, she might turn to Eric for consolation. Or anybody. How would he cope with that? If there was really nothing going on between Zoe and Eric, there was no reason why he and Zoe couldn't get back together. The thought of spending the night with her was becoming more attractive by the minute. But he'd have to move quickly, before the others arrived. At once, he rebuked himself for this dangerous, reckless thought. Hadn't he broken up with her because it was apparent they were completely incompatible? Was he going to row back on that because a few beers and some shared reminiscences had opened the possibility of a casual jump? Yet, it had to be admitted, he was in a strange mood. He hadn't been with a woman for months. In fact, the last one in his bed had been Zoe. And Art couldn't compensate entirely.

'You said something about Eric's marriage,' said Zoe. 'Is it going through a bad time?'

'Yes. Apparently.'

'And you thought I was the cause of it?'

For a moment he was tempted to deny it. Instead, he said. 'Yes. I did. Stupid of me. Sorry.'

Lying to him was making Zoe feel squalid, and she knew that sustaining the lie would only make her feel worse. But there was no way she could risk telling him about her brief affair with Eric, because she wasn't sure how he'd react. She said, 'I'm astonished that you could think I'd go straight from you to Eric. You know how much you meant to me. I couldn't imagine going with anyone else. Even now, after all this time, I couldn't.'

He said nothing and they took several more steps in silence. Her words were making him feel emotional. She quite obviously still loved him and it was clear that the break-up had hurt her terribly. Until now, her pain had been an abstraction for him, but her presence was forcing him to confront it: introject it, experience it as she was experiencing it. How disturbing to think that his actions were the cause of such distress in another human being. It was making him feel ashamed, and he wasn't even sure now that he'd been right to end their relationship. Perhaps with a little understanding and conciliation on his part, things between them might have improved. He'd forgotten how happy he'd been with her at times. And how wonderful she'd been in bed.

She felt his hand take hold of hers. The unexpected sensation made her wonder if he was simply supporting her. She'd stumbled badly once or twice in the dark. Perhaps he thought she needed a steadying hand? Or was it an expression of something deeper? If so, she wondered if now might be the time to tell him the real reason she'd applied for the job at Leefdale. But then again, it might not.

'Is it professional to hold hands?' she said.

He laughed. 'Trapeze artistes do it all the time.'

'Yes. But from necessity.'

'We're more than just colleagues,' he said. 'You know that.'

She said nothing. He told her that the way he'd announced their break-up was unforgivably callous. That he was ashamed of himself. That he could have handled it better. 'The way I behaved was awful. I wasn't thinking of your feelings at all.'

'Yes, but there's no easy way of doing something like that, is there?'

'Even so, it was wrong. I'm sorry.'

She wondered if it was just a perfunctory apology or a serious attempt at reconciliation. It excited her to think that when they got back to the rectory they'd be entirely alone. She said, 'I don't know why I told you how hurt I'd been. I've no idea what came over me. I honestly had no intention of bringing these things up again.'

'Well, I'm glad you did.'

Hand in hand they turned into Church Lane.

After a while, she said, 'You've no idea what it's like to be a woman.'

'That's a reasonable assumption,' he said, slickly.

Why did he have to be such a clever dick? 'No, what I mean is, you've no idea what it's like to be the prey all the time.'

'I don't regard you as prey.'

'Not you. I was thinking of those guys in the pub. The way they kept leering at me all night.'

'Which guys?'

'The ones taking up all the space around the bar. They kept staring at me.'

'So that's why you wanted to move into the beer garden?'

'Yes. I got sick of them undressing me in their heads.'

'You can't arrest people for what's in their heads.'

'No? I'd like to sometimes.'

'Anyway, being stared at is an occupational hazard if you're a beautiful woman.'

His hand squeezed hers more tightly and he thought, why would it be so wrong? After all, Zoe was probably willing. Sure, it was potentially dangerous. They'd be resurrecting a relationship that hadn't worked out. Well, not for him, anyway. But had it really been so bad? Was it any worse than the sexual and emotional limbo he'd been existing in for the past couple of months? All his instincts told him to hold out for Sharon. But Sharon was just a fantasy; Zoe was real, living flesh. Sharon had positively discouraged him. She'd certainly been lukewarm about his offer of a drink in The Woldsman. But Zoe was no fantasy. He recalled her familiar body. How uninhibited she was when naked. The noises she made. Zoe was the available option. Sharon was a fantasy. Unattainable.

Zoe said, 'So, you still think I'm beautiful, eh?'

'I always have.'

It hadn't stopped him splitting up with her though, had it? But she decided to let that go.

They'd arrived at the entrance to the rectory's drive. Dylan released her hand in order to open the gate.

They entered the drive, skirted round the two parked transit vans and went up to the front door. Dylan produced the key from his jeans pocket and was about to insert it into the lock when he froze.

'Sod it!'

He remained fixed in the same position for several seconds, thinking.

'What is it?'

He turned to her, and even in the dim light of his phone-torch she could see he was panic stricken. 'I can't remember the alarm code.'

'That doesn't stop you opening the door though, does it?'

'Yes, it does. I told you, as soon as it's opened you only have fifteen seconds to turn off the alarm. Otherwise it'll alert the cops.' He sighed, made a frustrated gesture and screwed up his eyes as he attempted to recall the elusive sequence of numbers.

'So, we can't go inside until you remember it?'

'No.'

She giggled. 'We'll have to sleep in our vans. That'll be fun.'

'It's serious.' He was irritated by her flippancy. 'I've completely forgotten it.'

'You must have written it down somewhere.'

'Yes. It's in my diary. But that's in my room.'

'Not much good there, is it?'

Zoe scrabbled in her handbag and produced a piece of paper. 'I wrote it down too, but even better, I've got it with me.' She was holding it high in the air, just out of his reach: tantalising him with it.

Remembering that he'd given her the code earlier, he almost collapsed with relief. Thank God she'd written it down! He snatched the piece of paper from her, and was about to put the key in the lock when she said, 'You go ahead. There's a few more things I need to get from the van.'

Dylan let himself into the house, switched the hall lights on and quickly deactivated the alarm. He was about to set off for the kitchen when it occurred to him that Zoe might need the phone torch.

He went back outside and found her standing at the rear of her van; the doors were open and she was peering into the black recesses of its unlit interior.

'Just what I need,' she said, taking the torch from him. 'Can't see a bloody thing. Must get the interior light fixed: needs a new bulb.'

'What are you looking for?'

'My duvet. Sheets and stuff. I forgot to make my bed.'

She shone the torch into the van. Dylan stared at the bewildering array of boxes, cases and containers.

'I'm surprised you can find anything.' He placed his hand lightly on her arm. 'Leave it for tonight. There's loads of spare bedding in the airing cupboard. All you need.'

'No thanks, I prefer my own.'

Simultaneously, they both became aware of several much stronger beams of light emanating from a source directly behind them. They were illuminating the van's interior much more brightly than the feeble light from Dylan's phone.

Together they spun round. Three men were standing inside the gate directing their torches straight up the drive and staring.

Dylan and Zoe stared back.

The three men advanced up the drive towards them, crunching over the gravel.

Zoe said, 'Who's this?'

'Our neighbours perhaps?' Dylan suggested.

The men came up and stopped. They didn't say anything but their suspicion and hostility were evident.

'Good evening,' said Dylan.

'Good evening,' said the tallest of the men. 'Would you mind telling us what you're doing here?'

'Who wants to know?' said Zoe.

'We do,' said one of the other men.

'Well, who are you?'

'Community Watch.'

Zoe laughed. 'Community what?'

'Just answer our question,' said the first man.

'Why should we?'

'We're the new owners,' said Dylan. He knew Zoe had a fiery temper and was anxious to avoid a scene. 'We're just moving some stuff in.'

The younger, taller man said, 'And you can prove that, can you?'

'This is fascist!' cried Zoe. 'Get that light out of my eyes!'

'Well,' said the man, lowering his torch, 'you say you're moving stuff in, but from where we stand you could be moving stuff out.'

Zoe scoffed. 'What? Stealing from our own house?'

'I'm Dylan Bourne and this is Zoe Fitzgerald,' said Dylan. 'Sharon Makepiece of Parker and Lund can vouch for us. She sold us the property.'

'We don't have to convince them, Dylan. They've no right to interrogate us. They're not police officers.'

'It's all right, Zoe,' said Dylan, curtly.

The taller man's demeanour suddenly changed. He held out his hand to Dylan, who took it and shook it firmly. 'Welcome to Leefdale, Mr Bourne,' said the man. 'I'm Greg Maynard. Sorry for the intrusion. We were patrolling the road and saw a light. The house is usually in darkness. It's been uninhabited for ages so we thought we'd have a look. We were only concerned for the property.'

'That's all right,' said Dylan. 'I've actually been moving stuff in for the past week but at night I've been staying at The Lamb in Luffield. That's probably why you thought it was still uninhabited. It's reassuring that people are keeping a look out.'

Greg Maynard introduced the two men with him. They were both elderly. They too welcomed Dylan and Zoe to Leefdale and made appreciative comments about The Old Rectory and its previous owners.

'We've had a lot of burglaries in the village and there's only two policemen to look after a hundred square miles,' said one of the older men, whose name apparently was Rawson. 'That's why we do these patrols.'

'Once you've settled in perhaps you'll join us,' said Maynard.

'You must be joking,' said Zoe.

'It's better than sitting on your arse and doing nothing.'

Zoe stiffened and took a sudden step towards him. 'Get off our property!'

Dylan moved closer to Zoe to be in a position to take a firm grip of her hand if necessary. He didn't want the situation to get out of control.

Zoe continued to square up to Maynard. She was only an inch shorter than him. He was clearly surprised and intimidated. There was a long, tense pause.

'Well, we'll bid you goodnight,' said Maynard.

'Goodnight,' said Dylan.

Wordlessly, the three members of Community Watch turned and walked back up the drive. Zoe followed closely behind and clanged the gate shut after them.

When she re-joined Dylan, even in the meagre light of his fading torch, he could see that she was in a foul mood.

'Thanks very much for all your support,' she said.

'You seemed to be doing all right without me.'

'Someone had to stand up to the fascist bastards!'

Quietly, he said, 'Fascists, that's a bit extreme, isn't it?'

'You don't think they were behaving like fascists? Throwing their weight about like that?'

'All I saw were some men doing their job.'

'It's not their job. Community Watch people are volunteers. I suppose you think I was being completely unreasonable?'

'Yes, I do. They were perfectly entitled to be suspicious. It's late at night. It's dark. They saw two unfamiliar vans parked in the drive. The door of the house was wide open. I haven't been staying at the rectory at night. This was the first time they saw the lights on. We could easily have been burglars carrying stuff out to the vans.'

'But you've been filling the house with furniture for days,' Zoe protested. 'They must have known the house was occupied.'

He knew that logic was on her side, but her strident tone made him obdurate. 'Not necessarily. As I hadn't been here at night they'd naturally assume the house was uninhabited and no-one had moved in.'

'In a small place like this where everybody gossips to everybody else? Come on use your imagination.'

Dylan folded his arms wearily. 'All right. Tell me why they were fascists.'

'They enjoyed throwing their weight around too much. They were getting off on intimidating us. There's a certain kind of man who enjoys doing that, intimidating people. Especially women. These Community Watch squads are full of officious bastards like that. People who'd love to be in the police and security services, so they can push people around. Really they're just excuses to engage in vigilantism.'

'Rather paranoid, don't you think?'

She glared at him. 'That's right. Don't listen to my justifications. Just categorise me as a case study. Poor Zoe, the alcoholic father; the workaholic mother. She was powerless as a child you know, so she compensates for it by having unrealistic expectations of others; by being over-assertive and paranoid.'

'That's not my analysis and you know it. But I do find it interesting that a drama therapist can fail to see her own psychological flaws.'

'Flaws?' she scoffed. 'My emotional intelligence, you mean? My highly developed affective domain? Well, at least my default position isn't the line of least resistance. You're so frightened of confrontation you're unable to function in your own interest. You can be too reasonable for your own good, you know. Seeing the other person's point of view is all very well as long as they don't interpret it as weakness. And fascists always do.'

'I'm going to make some coffee,' he said. 'Would you like some?'

'That's right. Go and find a displacement activity to hide behind. Anything to avoid taking a stand. That's what your Art's really all about, isn't it? Retreat from reality?'

He smiled broadly. He didn't want her to see how offended he was. 'Art isn't a retreat from reality, it's the means of addressing it. Surely, as a former actress you know that?'

Without waiting for her reply, he left her and went into the house.

Zoe watched him go, furious at his pusillanimity. She vented her anger on the contents of her van: indiscriminately and violently slamming bags and boxes around as she ransacked the vehicle's interior for the black bin liners containing her duvet, bed linen and other, more personal, items. It was intolerable that instead of lending her his support and standing up to those three thugs he'd tried to stop her defending her civil liberties. And then he'd had the gall to criticise her actions, suggesting she was the one who'd acted unreasonably. Not the fascists!

Realising she was achieving nothing despite all her efforts, she stopped and took a rest. This wasn't how the evening should have ended. Not after they'd started to get on so well again. Why, they'd even held hands! She should have gone straight into the house with him. They'd probably be in each other's arms now: perhaps, even in bed. Why had those fascists come along and ruined everything?

What angered her most was that, knowing how much Dylan deplored her outspokenness, she'd spent all day restraining herself from speaking out. But having an extremely low tolerance of injustice, it was counter-intuitive for her to keep her mouth firmly shut when creeps like those in the Community Watch were oppressing and walking all over her. And at that crucial moment, when physical and moral strength was most needed, Dylan had turned out to be a chocolate teapot. His greatest flaw, in her view, was his willingness to avoid confrontation and find compromises that pleased nobody. He didn't seem to appreciate that she came from a discipline of drama therapy where openness, honesty and spontaneity were encouraged and seen as the goal. He seemed unable to appreciate that for women, assertiveness was a highly desirable social behaviour. Whenever she displayed it in his presence, he patronisingly characterised her as strident and aggressive. Paranoid, even. Obviously, it had been a terrible mistake for her to follow him to Leefdale. There was an old saying, wasn't there? Something like, "You can't put your feet in the same river water twice". Yet, knowing all this, why did she still love him? Well, want him, anyway? Why did her existence seem so incomplete without him? Why?

While Zoe engaged in these reflections, Dylan was in the kitchen making coffee and congratulating himself on a narrow escape. Zoe's attitude to the Community Watch had convinced him he'd been absolutely right to break off with her. What the hell had he been thinking of, holding her hand and entertaining the idea that they might have sex? Even resume their former relationship? Was he some kind of masochist? He recalled other examples of her bizarrely outspoken behaviour; her lack of restraint; her absence of concern for the feelings of anyone other than herself; and her obsessive need to forcefully and bluntly advance her perverse and eccentric point of view. The countless times it had happened: at dinner parties, on courses, at meetings. Good thing no-one had known they were a couple. The social embarrassment of being involved with someone who spoke her mind candidly at all times without any regard for the consequences, was deeply stressful and upsetting. In fact, since they'd been estranged he'd never felt more at ease with himself. The thought that he might have given up his peace of mind for the pleasure of a quick shag appalled him. In the beer garden she'd said she was trying very hard to be conventional. Well it certainly didn't look like it. Her absurd clash with the Community Watch had deeply disturbed and unnerved him. It confirmed that his original conclusions about her had been correct. He was well out of it.

He spooned out the instant and poured hot water into the cups. Her jibe about the coffee being a displacement activity had been particularly galling. So, what was she saying? That Art was a displacement activity for those who were afraid to confront the realities of life? That he was some sort of coward? Utter bollocks. He'd spent his entire career as an art therapist advising his clients how to address the realities of their lives.

He heard her slam the rear doors of the transit van. He heard her footsteps coming in and going upstairs heavy footed as though she were carrying something. He heard her go all the way up to the second floor and slam the door of her bedroom.

He looked at the coffee cups, unsure what to do. Should he leave her coffee downstairs or take it up to her? He was afraid that if he took it up to her it would increase the chances that they'd have a screaming row or end up in bed.

He went down the hall to see if she'd closed the front door, and found it slightly ajar. Perhaps she still needed to get things out of the van. He felt he ought to check with her before he closed and bolted the door and set the alarm. For God's sake, he told himself, stop vacillating and make a decision. He went over to the big front door, closed it and shot the bolts home. Then, collecting her coffee from the kitchen, he climbed the stairs to her bedroom and knocked on the door, gently.

'Come in.'

He pushed the door open but didn't enter. She was leaning over the bed in the act of forcing her duvet into its cover.

She stopped and looked up. There was a pause. She seemed amused. 'You can come in, you know. I won't attack you.'

He took a step into the room. 'I came to tell you I'm about to bolt the front door and set the alarm. In case you needed anything more from the van.'

'Thanks, but I've got everything.'

He placed her mug of coffee on the dressing table and considered offering her a hand with the duvet but was worried where it might lead.

'I'm dead tired,' he said. 'I'm off to bed.'

'So am I,' she said. 'Goodnight.'

So that was it. He felt relieved but, simultaneously, disappointed. 'Goodnight.'

****

So that wanker was the famous Dylan Bourne, thought Greg Maynard, as he and his fellow Community Watch volunteers continued on their beat through Leefdale.

When Greg had challenged Dylan and Zoe in the rectory's drive, demanding to know what they were doing there, he was being completely disingenuous. He'd known very well that the rectory's new owner had taken possession of the property because Sharon had already told him that completion had taken place and the keys had been handed over. Naturally, Greg had kept this fact from the two Community Watch colleagues. He'd no wish to fuel speculation about the closeness of his relationship with Sharon Makepiece, which he constantly worried was the subject of salacious rumour.

Greg was one of those men who enjoyed being officious and using the petty power afforded him by his Community Watch role to throw his weight about, feel important and abuse his position. Particularly when Sharon, whom he regarded as his property, had expressed (rather too often for his liking) her appreciation of a certain good looking, Dylan Bourne. Greg also enjoyed humiliating attractive young women. Therefore, all in all, he'd had rather a good evening. Zoe's highly developed powers of observation and interpretation had not misled her.

CHAPTER TEN

The next morning Dylan and Zoe breakfasted on toast and cereal, and with admirable civility and professionalism discussed their assigned tasks for the day ahead, studiously avoiding the events of the previous night.

After breakfast, Zoe took herself off to Luffield to do the shopping in preparation for Wednesday's arrivals. Dylan remained behind and continued with the laborious task of unloading all the packing cases and boxes which still seemed to be flowing through every room in the house. During the course of the day he spent considerable amounts of time on his mobile speaking to Lord Sandleton, as well as Eric and Toni, reassuring them that all would be ready for Wednesday.

Zoe returned to the rectory just after three. After storing away the provisions she'd bought, she went out to her van and finished unloading her possessions. She then retired to the drama studio to continue with its preparations.

Just before six, Dylan cooked a quick dish of pasta, mushrooms and pesto which he and Zoe ate at the kitchen table. Afterwards, Zoe suggested a game of table tennis. She was two games in the lead when the doorbell rang. Dylan went to answer it. A middle-aged man of medium height stood on the doorstep. He possessed a proud, upright bearing, thinning sandy coloured hair, and a neatly trimmed moustache.

'Good evening,' said the man. 'I'm Howard Roberts. I live across the way at Rooks Nest. We met when you originally came to view the house.'

'Of course,' said Dylan. 'The Major.'

'Just thought I'd say welcome.'

'Thank you,' said Dylan. 'Come in.'

Howard hesitated. He was extremely curious to find out more about his new neighbours but was wondering how genuine the invitation was. 'Are you sure?'

Dylan's heart sank. 'Absolutely.'

'All right. Thank you.'

As he followed Dylan down the hall, Howard said, 'Actually, I would have come over sooner but we've been on holiday. I'll only stay a moment. You must have your hands full.'

In the chill-out room Zoe was bouncing a table tennis ball with her bat.

'This is Major Roberts,' said Dylan.

Major Roberts affected a wince. 'Howard, please.'

'Hello, Howard. I'm Zoe.'

Dylan noticed a mischievous gleam in Zoe's eye.

Howard strove very hard to hide his shock at the transformation of the Corbridge's back sitting room. The elegant Georgian furniture had been replaced by second-hand sofas from a junk shop. As well as the table tennis there was a table football game. It looked like some inner-city youth club. Howard now suspected the worst: that their children were teenagers. But why was there no sign of them?

'Howard lives across the road at Rooks Nest,' said Dylan. 'He's called to welcome us.'

'That's nice,' said Zoe. 'The thing is will the welcome last?'

Howard thought this an extraordinary thing to say. He turned to Dylan and, smiling urbanely, said, 'I sincerely hope so. Why shouldn't it?'

Zoe smiled archly. 'Well, you never know.'

'Someone as pretty as you will always be welcome here,' said Howard, warmly. She was indeed strikingly attractive. He'd already noted with appreciation her stunning figure, her auburn hair and riveting blue eyes. No, blue wasn't entirely their colour, there was a flash of something else. Green? Gold? Anyway, they were mesmerising. A real cracker.

Dylan knew the Major's remark wouldn't be appreciated by Zoe, who was a committed feminist. He prepared to intervene but before he could do so she'd retorted scornfully, 'So if I was ugly you wouldn't welcome me?'

Howard looked taken aback. 'Of course, I would.' He immediately categorised her as "politically correct". 'Do you play a lot of table tennis?' he said.

'Quite a bit,' said Zoe. 'Do you?'

'I used to. In the army. Not now.'

'In between killing people?'

There was a long, uncomfortable pause, during which Howard strove to relax his expression which had instinctively hardened. He knew very well when he was being deliberately provoked by those who were anti-military. However, he'd been given extensive training in the appropriate response. He smiled graciously, reached into his trouser pocket and produced a key. 'Here, you'd better have this. It's the spare for the garden shed.' He handed it to Dylan. 'You did say you weren't a gardener so I expect you'll have to buy a lot of equipment. Bruce took all of his with him, of course, but I'm happy to lend you anything you need.' He hesitated, and then continued, 'Actually, I hope you won't think it impertinent but I was wondering if you wanted me to continue doing the gardens. Mowing the lawn, weeding, keeping them tidy, that sort of thing. I'd be more than glad to.'

'We were looking forward to doing that ourselves,' Zoe said, quickly. 'We've got a lot of exciting ideas for the gardens.'

'Of course. I understand,' said Howard.

'But thank you very much for offering,' said Dylan.

'Not at all,' said Howard. 'Just the two of you are there?'

Zoe seized her opportunity for creating more mischief. 'Oh no,' she said, 'Toni and Eric will be joining us soon with the kids.'

Dylan shot Zoe a warning look. He knew exactly what she was up to. She knew very well he didn't want their real reason for purchasing the rectory revealed until he'd told Sharon personally.

'Yes. There are several of us,' Dylan said.

'Really?' Howard was perplexed. He was well aware that young people now had rather complicated domestic arrangements. He'd assumed that Zoe and Dylan were a couple. Was Tony an ex-husband perhaps? And who was Eric? He wondered if these children shared three fathers. Or if Zoe had re-married and inherited a number of step children, as his own sister had done. Casually, he said, 'How old are the children?'

'Teenagers,' said Zoe.

'Ah,' said Howard, his worst fears justified. And then, knowing it would be almost certain to provoke her, with old-fashioned gallantry, he said, 'You don't look old enough to have children of that age.'

Zoe laughed. 'Oh, they're not mine.'

Howard nodded. He was determined she shouldn't enjoy his perplexity.

'No,' said Dylan. He stared hard at her. 'Zoe's not much more than a child herself.'

Zoe smiled charmingly and resumed batting the table tennis ball up and down. 'So Major, which country are you going to invade next?'

Howard affected an urbane laugh. 'None, I hope. I'm retired.'

'You must have fought in some though.'

'I've seen service all over the world.' Again, he felt the urge to provoke her. 'My last tour was in Northern Ireland.'

'Britain's last colony?'

'Some have called it that.' Why did these people never give up? He smiled at Dylan. 'Well, you've obviously got a lot to do so I'll leave you to it. But if I can be of assistance in any way do let me know.'

He said his goodbyes and Dylan showed him out. When he returned to the chill-out room he found Zoe setting up the balls on the pool table.

'Fancy a game?' she said.

'Why did you do that?'

'What?'

'You were winding the poor bloke up.'

'Well,' she said, chalking her cue, 'he's such a nosey old sod. And what a chauvinist!'

'I thought you were going to tell him everything.'

'I wouldn't do that. Not until you've told your sexy estate agent.'

He instantly became defensive. 'I feel Sharon should be the first to get an explanation, that's all. I'd hate her to find out second-hand.'

Zoe looked at him brightly. 'She might think a lot less of you, eh?' She picked up a cue and bent low over the table, sighting up on the cue ball. 'No, I was just having a bit of fun that's all. Giving him something to get his imagination going.' She suddenly stood up, laughing. 'I'll bet it's running riot!'

Despite himself, Dylan found he was laughing too.

THE LEEFLET
The Newsletter of The Leefdale Parish Council
June 2001
Page 6

Letters to the Editor

The Burrow,
Leefdale.
3rd June 2001

Dear Sir,
Once again, I must protest at the content of your column "In the Garden with The Major".

Major Roberts implies that I'm ungrateful and unable to accept advice. This is simply not true. I'm prepared to accept advice about horticulture from anybody. It's the Major's autocratic, patronising attitude I object to.

I'm as delighted as anyone that Leefdale has reached the Finals of Magnificent Britain. But doesn't it occur to Major Roberts that others might not share his enthusiasm for the contest? Some people prefer their gardens as they are, even though they might not measure up to his standards of tidiness. I think his offer (or is it a threat?) to send volunteers round to tidy up the gardens of those he thinks are letting the village down, is an outrageous idea. It's an invasion of privacy as well as an abuse of people's individual human rights. My garden, as it happens, is immaculate, but that's my choice. It might not be everybody's, Major!

Yours sincerely,
Lucy Birkinshaw.

Editor's note.
Major Roberts' reply to Lucy's letter can be found in his column on page 4. This correspondence is now closed.

THE LEEFLET
The Newsletter of The Leefdale Parish Council
June 2001
Pages 3-4
In the Garden with "The Major"

I know that all our thoughts at this time are with the family and friends of Walter Marsden, who has died, aged eighty six. Walter was a resident of Leefdale all his life, and his death is a huge loss to our small community. He served tirelessly as a parish councillor for over forty years and his death creates a vacancy on the parish council that will be extremely hard to fill. His knowledge of horticulture and gardening lore also made him an invaluable member of the Magnificent Britain Sub-Committee. He was the committee's longest serving member, having served since 1946, the year in which the Magnificent Britain Gardening Competition was inaugurated. It is no exaggeration to say that Walter had one of the finest gardens in Leefdale and his annual display of sweet peas was without equal.

Walter's passing means that a vacancy has now arisen for a parish councillor and also for a member of the Magnificent Britain Sub-Committee. Community spirited individuals who wish to put themselves forward for co-option to these positions should apply to Mrs Phillips, the parish council clerk. If there is more than one candidate for the position of parish councillor a by-election will be called.

There are fewer than six weeks to go now until the judging of the Magnificent Britain Competition. I know that there are always severe demands on working people's time, but can I make a plea for more hanging baskets? I notice that there are still some dwellings around the village that have spaces on their walls, where, with a bit of effort, an extra hanging basket or two could be mounted. In past years Leefdale has always had a profusion of hanging baskets. They are the simplest and easiest way to provide a splash of colour, cut a dash and create the impression that every inch of the village is in bloom.

For those who have never created a hanging basket nothing could be simpler. They come in many materials and designs and can be obtained from most garden centres. The Magnificent Britain Sub-Committee has produced an excellent leaflet which provides step by step guidance for preparing and planting up a basket. It also recommends the most appropriate plants that will bloom in June, July or August. If you would like a copy of this leaflet please contact Greg Maynard on 756798. If you require assistance with hanging your basket, members of the Sub-Committee will be delighted to help.

If you haven't the time to prepare and plant up hanging baskets yourself, remember they can be purchased pre-planted from a garden centre, and then all you have to do is attach them to the exterior of your home. When they are in bloom not only will their beauty enhance your property but it will increase the village's chances of winning the Magnificent Britain Competition. There are a huge number of plants suitable for hanging baskets, depending on the season. Ideally, a basket intended for hanging during the summer months should boast a variety of species. I recommend a mixture of fuchsias, yuccas and geraniums, as their warm and vibrant colours are so redolent of the summertime. However, if you wish to restrict your hanging basket to a single colour I personally don't think you can beat lobelias or trailing petunias. Of course, an additional advantage of hanging baskets is that you can fill them with soil other than that found locally, and this greatly increases the number of different plants you can show. Remember, in order for Leefdale to win we need to provide the judges with evidence that a huge variety of plant species are on display in our village.

I do hope that no-one will take offence at my plea for more hanging baskets or think it paternalistic of me to recommend plants for them. I wouldn't wish, for one moment, to be thought patronising; a charge which is yet again levelled at me, I'm sorry to say, by Lucy Birkinshaw, in a further letter reproduced in this edition of The Leeflet. Once again, I categorically deny the objectionable accusation. I cannot understand how the proffering of my well-intentioned, expert guidance could possibly be described as "patronising". And no, Lucy, in my last column I certainly did not imply that you are ungrateful and unable to accept advice.

Furthermore, I also stand accused by Miss Birkinshaw of infringing the privacy of individuals and depriving them of their human rights. Why? Simply because in my last column I announced that if some villagers, either through pressure of work or incapacity, were unable to enter fully into the spirit of the Magnificent Britain Competition, there were plenty of keen gardeners in the village willing to give up some of their precious time to help improve those people's gardens, so that they look their best on adjudication day. What could be more neighbourly or community spirited than that? Such selfless volunteers should not be denigrated but applauded, Lucy. Surely we all want Leefdale's gardens to be at their best on Friday the 20th when the judges come round? If Leefdale is to win the Magnificent Britain Competition for the fifth consecutive year we must all pull our weight. I'm sure that most reasonable people who are unable to get their gardens in good order for the competition by themselves, would welcome the offer of extra assistance from fellow gardeners. I am also certain that they would regard the suggestion that such an offer of help constituted an abuse of their human rights as ludicrous!

Of course, there will always be a minority whose gardens are in a sorry state, yet have no wish to improve them. Such people are perfectly entitled to refuse the help so generously offered. That is entirely their choice! Who could possibly complain about people exercising their free choice in our democratic country? I take great exception to Lucy's suggestion that by offering support to people who are struggling to maintain their gardens in peak condition, I am somehow behaving autocratically, and engaging in an attempt to coerce them into taking part in the Magnificent Britain Competition against their will. How preposterous! It was in defence of the right of every British subject to exercise freedom of choice that we defended our country against the Germans in two world wars. I am the last person to deny the inhabitants of Leefdale their right to turn down assistance if they do not wish it. As an army officer it has been my duty on numerous occasions to defend and preserve the rights of the citizens of these islands, and I have never shirked my duty. It saddens me to say so, but I find Lucy's accusations deeply offensive.

Happy Gardening!

The Major

(Howard Roberts)

CHAPTER ELEVEN

By Wednesday afternoon most of the rectory's rooms were ready and the essential preparations for the arrival of Eric, Toni and the clients had been made. At around five o'clock, Toni phoned to confirm that all the clients had been collected: the mini-bus was just leaving Leeds on the A64 and they expected to arrive at Leefdale sometime around 6.30pm.

At six o'clock, Zoe began preparing the evening meal. Dylan left her to it and went up to his studio-cum-office on the top floor. When he got there, he stood around helplessly contemplating his desk on which there were metal baskets full of unanswered correspondence, and a brand new computer, so technically daunting just switching it on reduced him to blinding panic. His gaze shifted away from the desk to his personal possessions: the boxes of unpacked paintings; the stack of white, virginal canvasses awaiting the marks of his genius; the tubes, pots, brushes and all the other paraphernalia he'd accumulated during a lifetime in Art. He wondered if it had really been such a good idea to combine his studio and his office. It had seemed such a great solution at the time. He'd assumed that one activity would provide a welcome diversion from the other; so, when he grew tired of administration he could find relief in his canvasses, and vice versa. Yet the reality wasn't like that at all: the demands of admin were all consuming, leaving him virtually no time for his art. When there was a rare opportunity to paint, he was so exhausted he was hardly able to lift a brush and the thought of it was anathema to him, intensifying his frustration and plunging him into despair.

He stared at the computer as though at an oracle: yet again, its cyber authority was sternly reminding him that neglect of his admin duties for Art would under no circumstances be tolerated. It was also forcing him to confront the decisive question he'd long been avoiding. With all his art therapy responsibilities and the insatiable demands of admin, had taking on the role of team leader really been such a clever move? And if so, when was he going to be able to paint?

He went over to one of the large boxes and removed its lid. He reached inside and brought out his favourite Mondrian print: "Rhythm of Black Lines".

He placed it on one of the easels, then pulled up a chair and sat contemplating it in silent appreciation.

It was at times like this that his father's opinion seemed particularly pertinent. "If you want to paint, just paint. If it makes you hard up, borrow from other people. Let them look after you. If you can't afford a home, doss on a friend's couch or find a squat. It's everyone's duty to give you support. And they'll be glad to, because you're special. Whatever happens, never get sucked into the nine to five. It's death for an artist." And, of course, Bernard hadn't. He'd joined a commune. They kept their own animals; grew things; made things. The proceeds were shared collectively. For a time, anyway. Many, like his father, had just painted all day and sold their work to the galleries in the local seaside towns. Bernard always sold the most. That's when his first disputes with the collective over money had started to surface.

Dylan glanced disconsolately over at his desk. He knew exactly what his father would say if he could see him now. That's why he hadn't bothered to tell him of his promotion. Congratulations would have been the last thing on Bernard's mind. "If you're forced to work because you've got nothing to eat, make sure it's a simple job with no responsibility, like street cleaning, picking strawberries or washing dishes. If you're a writer or painter or musician, never get a job that carries responsibility: get a simple job that frees you in the evenings to write or compose or paint."

Well, that might have been OK for Bernard but Dylan had never intended to waste his intelligence or his education. He couldn't understand how anyone who was clever and industrious could be satisfied with working in low grade occupations that gave you a pittance just for the sake of Art. That had been the result of his mother's influence, of course. Very early on Natalie had decided that the commune offered little in the way of stimulation or advancement for her, and she'd abandoned it, taking the nine year old Dylan with her. Using a loan from her father she'd set up her first seaside shop that sold everything for the beach. She'd ended up owning a chain of such shops, one in every coastal resort in the south west. It was her ethic that had influenced Dylan much of his life. Now he saw the wisdom of his father's words. Too late!

Or was it really wisdom? Dylan remembered something else: a test his father had once set him. Bernard had always asserted that at the centre of the artist's turbulent soul was a vacuum; and in that airless void was permanently lodged a sliver of ice that never thawed. It was this sliver of ice, suspended in a still, calm centre, that allowed the artist to be completely dispassionate; so that even when he was enduring the most intense experience, his mother's death, for example, a part of him would be scrupulously recording every nuance of his personal reactions to it, as well as all of the attendant circumstances: the nature of the light; who was present in the room; the exact arrangement of the furniture. It was also this sliver of ice, Bernard maintained, that would make the artist, if caught in a house fire, decide to save his paintings rather than his child.

"Would you be able to do that?" Bernard had demanded. "Would you be able to save your work instead of your child?"

Dylan had been horrified by this proposition: he knew he'd always save the child first, and told his father so.

"Then you'll never be an artist!" Bernard told him, sadly.

Back then Dylan had felt humiliated, but now he knew he'd simply been emotionally abused. It was clear to him that the artist's much lauded dedication was just the stubborn, selfish, egotistical heartlessness of a monomaniacal obsessive. Which, in fact, was an extremely accurate description of Bernard. Nowadays, if asked the same question by his father, Dylan was certain he'd say: "All Art is that which isn't found naturally in nature. A child is the most natural thing in nature; therefore as an artist it would be my duty to save the child in preference to my paintings, because without the next generation there's no Art and no appreciation of it."

Yet despite being convinced of the correctness of this humane and rational position, Dylan knew that his father would have detected the whiff of specious casuistry in it, and dismissed his son's tortuous justification of the primacy of people over Art as the last refuge of the amateur. That sliver of ice again. And in his bones, Dylan knew his father was right because he'd never been able to give his art priority over everything else. A career in art therapy had promised to combine the best of all worlds; and give him a living whilst allowing him to dwell within the suburbs of Art. But the longer he'd been an art therapist the more he'd realised he couldn't do it by half-measures. His clients were real people with real problems that demanded his constant and fullest attention. The work took everything, and yet instead of making him feel valued and inspired, he found it insufferable that as an art therapist he was forced to watch others paint creatively all day, knowing he would have no time and energy left at the end of it to do so himself. And now that he'd taken on the onerous responsibilities of team leader, his life as a painter seemed more closed to him than ever. Was that why he'd insisted on an office-cum-studio? So that his paintings and art materials could be on display around the room, reminding him who he really was? And that he should have followed his father's advice?

Dylan removed the lid of another big box which he knew contained his own paintings. He lifted each one out, contemplated it with pleasure and then placed it temporarily in the corner of the room. Several of these paintings with their black vertical and horizontal lines and rectangular blocks of intense, vibrant colour reflected some of Mondrian's influence. Others, which juxtaposed and layered a variety of colourful, fluid geometric shapes, were influenced by other pioneers of abstract art, such as Wassily Kandinsky, Theo van Doesburg and Kazimir Malevich. In amongst them were several of Dylan's paintings from an earlier period. Not abstracts, but examples of representational art: pictures that were recognizably of men and women, street scenes, the countryside and the occasional still life. These were heavily influenced by Courbet and Manet.

As Dylan unpacked and inspected his canvases the delicious aroma of beef curry entered his nostrils. It became much stronger when the door opened and Zoe appeared.

'I'm going to open a bottle of red wine,' she said. 'Would you like a glass?'

It was situations like this that convinced Dylan he should never have taken on the role of team leader. Officiousness and admonishment weren't his thing. It was an aspect of the job he least liked.

'I'm sorry, Zoe, but alcohol isn't allowed in the unit when the clients are in residence. I thought you knew that?'

Zoe stared at him, unblinking. 'I do. But they're not here yet.'

'No, but they'll be here soon.'

'I was only going to have one glass. I didn't know Prohibition was back.'

At least she was behaving more like herself. More like her real character. In a strange way he felt relieved. It was so unnatural to see her putting a clamp on her mouth. It made him feel guilty as well as nervous.

He made a helpless gesture and said, 'Well, you know...'

'No. It's OK. You don't have to role-play the heavy policeman. I won't have any. Not even a glass.'

She turned and went over to look at the canvasses which Dylan had propped against one wall of the room. She pointed at one which foregrounded a big blue diamond on a white background. In various places the diamond was bisected by a series of white, red and yellow lines which sectioned it into a set of internal squares and triangles. It had been painted when Dylan had been heavily influenced by the geometric abstraction of Ilya Bolotowsky. 'I always thought this was your best,' she said. And then, grinning, added, 'Apart from your picture of me, naturally.'

He smiled back. 'Naturally.'

'Is that here too?'

He said, 'Oh yes. In one of the boxes.' But he made no effort to find it for her.

Zoe returned downstairs and Dylan began delving in a tea chest containing his personal art materials. A short time later he heard the doorbell ring. He was so certain it meant the arrival of Eric, Toni and the clients that he left the room without even looking out of the window to check.

He was on the final flight of stairs when he realized his mistake. Standing in the hall next to Zoe was Sharon Makepiece.

'Hello,' said Dylan, hurrying down the stairs towards her.

She smiled broadly. 'Hello. Settling in all right?'

'Yes, thanks.'

'I've asked her to stay and have a glass of wine, but she won't.' said Zoe.

What the hell was Zoe playing at? Dylan wondered. The clients would be arriving at any moment. If Sharon hadn't gone by then he'd have to explain to her what they were doing there, and he wanted to do that later, when it wouldn't be such a shock.

Sharon glanced quickly at Zoe and shook her head. 'No, really, thanks but I can't. I have to get home.'

'Dylan tells me you live in the village,' said Zoe.

'Yes, but only in a modest cottage. Nothing like this.'

Sharon opened her bag and produced a set of keys. She handed them to Dylan. 'These spares turned up this afternoon. Thought you'd better have them.'

'Thanks,' said Dylan.

The keys were actually a pretext. After Greg had told her that he'd seen Dylan Bourne moving in to the rectory in the company of a gorgeous, young woman, Sharon had wanted to take a look at this stunning creature herself. The spare keys had provided her with the perfect excuse for dropping round.

'Everyone seems to be turning up with keys,' said Zoe.

Sharon looked surprised. 'Oh?'

'Only Major Roberts,' said Dylan, 'He came round with a spare key to the garden shed.'

'Oh.'

'Yes,' said Zoe. 'He offered to go on doing the gardening.'

'How nice,' said Sharon. 'He's very good at it. I wish he'd do mine for me.'

'Why don't you ask him?' said Zoe. 'He looks like he's at a loose end.'

Sharon smiled. 'Did you take up his offer?'

'No. We have our own plans for the garden.'

'Oh, well, yes, I expect you would.' Sharon was feeling ill at ease. She suspected that Zoe was being deliberately unpleasant towards her. Had she sensed her attraction to Dylan? Sharon was also confused about the nature of Dylan and Zoe's relationship. Were they partners? Lovers? What? Good thing she hadn't accepted the offer of a drink. 'Well, I'd better go,' she said.

'Oh, do stay and have a glass of wine,' urged Zoe. 'Dylan would so like to thank you for getting us moved in quickly.'

'That was your solicitor. I hardly did anything.'

'Why did we pay you all that commission then?'

'Well, I did some things of course...'

'Go on. Stay and have a glass. I'm sure Dylan would love to show you some of his paintings.'

'No thanks, honestly, some other time.'

At that moment Zoe's mobile rang. She whipped it out of her belt and answered. 'Toni!' she exclaimed, 'Where are you?' After listening to the lengthy reply, she turned to Dylan and said, 'They've found the village but can't find Church Lane'. She then started giving Toni directions.

Sharon and Dylan stood around idly, exchanging unsure glances.

'I must go, I've got visitors too,' said Sharon.

'I'll walk you down the drive.'

She gave him a curious glance and fluttered a goodbye wave to Zoe who was still engrossed on her mobile. Without pausing in her conversation, Zoe waved back.

Outside the rectory the dense summer heat was stifling. As Dylan walked Sharon towards the gate, the trees, shrubs and hedges seemed unnaturally swollen and heavy, their lush verdancy almost tropically oppressive. High above them, in the evening sunlight, many house martins darted and wheeled.

Dylan said, 'Look, I really do want to thank you properly for making things go so smoothly. Let me take you out to dinner.'

She stopped dead and stared at him. Her initial pleasure and delight diffusing into embarrassment and fear. 'Honestly, there's no need. I'm very well paid for what I do.'

'It's not just about thanking you. There are some things I need to talk to you about.'

She was aware that something profound was happening. 'What things?'

'I can't go into it now. Let me take you out to dinner tomorrow night.'

Sharon looked flustered. 'But... Zoe... I mean... won't she...?'

'It's all right. Zoe's not my partner. She's a colleague.'

'A colleague?'

'Yes. It'll all make sense when I've explained the situation. I'll book a table somewhere.'

They reached the end of the drive. Dylan looked anxiously up and down the street for the mini-bus. Thankfully there was no sign of it.

Sharon assumed he was looking for her car. Thinking to disabuse him she said, 'It was such a lovely evening I thought I'd walk over.'

'I see.' He didn't want her to linger but he couldn't let her go without a firm answer. 'So, will I see you tomorrow?'

She was very tempted but wondered if she dared. It had cost her a lot when she'd had to refuse his offer of a drink some days ago. But The Woldsman! Word would have got out that they were sitting in the bar together before they'd finished their first drink and it would have been the talk of the village within hours. She could easily imagine what Greg's reaction would have been when the news reached him. But surely he wouldn't resent her going out for dinner when it was for such an innocent purpose? She was sure Dylan wanted only to thank her and nothing more. She'd worked damn hard to ensure the completion took place in record time. Didn't she deserve to be taken out and thanked for it? And then she remembered: it wasn't just for that, was it? He'd said there were some things he wanted to talk to her about. But what? Probably more house purchases. She knew he'd bought the rectory as the nominee of a property company. Presumably the company was interested in buying other large country houses.

She stared at him, unable to reply. Why was he looking at her so hopefully? So expectantly? Perhaps there was something else to it, after all. He'd certainly gone out of his way to tell her Zoe wasn't a problem. He'd said there was nothing between them, she was just a colleague; although it looked like Zoe had other ideas. But if more than dinner was on his mind then he'd already made it pretty clear that nothing was standing in the way. The thought made her courage waver. She was so afraid of hurting and being hurt. So frightened of leaving her comfort zone. But then she rallied. To hell with it. She'd do it. She'd go. Tomorrow would be perfect because Louise had her rehearsal in the village hall. But the thought of Louise made her courage fail again. Every instinct of self-preservation screamed "No!"

She was just about to refuse him when it occurred to her that Greg needn't know. Not if she was careful. And then the thrill of the clandestine; the lure of the authentic emotion; the excitement of the untrodden path made her reckless. This could be the start of the intense, romantic experience that transcended everything and took her to the place where nothing mattered.

'All right. But I must be back before ten.'

'Fine. What time shall I collect you?'

'Come round about a quarter to eight.' Then, in a panic, she added quickly, 'And please don't book a table at The Woldsman.'

Dylan stared at her curiously.

Realising how hysterical she must have sounded, she swallowed and smiled back at him. 'The food's awful.'

'Really? The meal I had in there the other night was OK.'

'Must have been the chef's night off.'

'All right. I'll find somewhere else.'

Events were spiralling out of her control. She had to limit the fallout from this date somehow. Keep it secret. Make sure Greg didn't get to hear of it. She said, 'There's a lovely little restaurant called The Trout. It's at Danethorpe, overlooking the Derwent. You might try for a table there.'

'All right. I will. See you tomorrow.'

She nodded and turned away.

Dylan couldn't believe what he'd just accomplished. As though in a dream, he watched her cross the road and then he turned and went back up the drive. He therefore didn't see Howard Roberts emerge from the drive of Rooks Nest and call to Sharon as she passed by his gate.

After exchanging greetings, Sharon told Howard she'd been visiting his new neighbours. She said, 'I hear you offered to keep doing the rectory's gardens for them.'

Howard looked glum. His rejection had rankled. 'Yes, but they turned me down. Got plans of their own, they said. Understandable, of course. Hope it doesn't affect our chances in Magnificent Britain though.'

A white mini-bus had turned into the far end of Church Lane. Howard glanced at it briefly and said, 'Actually, I can't quite make them out. Dylan and Zoe, I mean. I thought they were a married couple, or what people call partners these days. But now, I'm not so sure. And there seem to be various teenage children and possibly different fathers. It's all very confusing.'

Howard's expression implied that he expected Sharon to enlighten him. She considered whether to tell him that Dylan and Zoe were colleagues, but decided against it. He would only probe further, and she was terrified that she'd say something inadvertently indiscreet about Dylan and it would be passed on to Greg. She knew that Howard and Greg worked hand in glove on the parish council.

The mini-bus slowly passed by them in a low gear. The driver, a young, foreign looking man was craning his neck from side to side, as though looking for his destination. At the windows of the mini-bus were a number of teenage faces, some of which were black or Asian or of mixed race. Sharon and Howard stared at the mini-bus as it slowed almost to a halt by the rectory, and then turned into its drive.

'My God!' said Howard. 'They must be the kids they were telling me about.' They stared at each other in mutual bewilderment. 'But whose children are they?'

'Perhaps they're fostered?'

They watched the mini-bus come to a halt in the rectory's drive. The driver and an older, blonde woman wearing rimless spectacles, got out. The man went round to the back of the van and opened the rear doors. Immediately, teenage girls and boys emerged from the vehicle.

'My God,' said Howard.

At that moment the front door of The Old Rectory opened. Zoe and Dylan came out and stood in the portico, beaming broadly.

Sharon had no wish to be seen by them. 'I must go,' she said, moving quickly off.

'Just a moment!' called Howard, walking briskly after her.

She stopped and turned to him.

'Did you know there would be all those teenagers?'

She resented his tone. 'No. Why should I?'

'Your firm sold them the property!'

The arrival of the mini-bus and its passengers was making the Major deeply apprehensive about the new occupants of the rectory. He now attempted to pump Sharon for more information about the purchasers; but even if the rules of commercial confidentiality hadn't prevented her, she still wouldn't have given him the private and personal details he sought. She considered them none of his business. Besides, Dylan had suddenly become her secret.

'I'm sorry, I really must go,' she said.

Her emotions in complete turmoil, Sharon walked home through the village, suffering by turns bewilderment, regret and anxiety. Had the rectory been purchased not for domestic use but for some commercial purpose? Yet what? And if it had been bought for such a purpose, had she been negligent in some way? She began to castigate herself for not making sufficiently rigorous enquiries about the prospective purchasers. She feared that the sale might have broken or infringed planning laws, or that Parker and Lund had been exploited for money laundering purposes. Although, she quickly dismissed these possibilities as absurd. But what had Dylan meant when he'd described himself and Zoe as "colleagues?" Colleagues in what? And who were Tony and Eric? Two men hadn't got out of the mini-bus. It had been a man and a woman. Was the woman's name Toni? Spelt with an "i"? But why had they arrived with a bus full of adolescents? Were they all related in some way? Was it some kind of extended multi-cultural family they all belonged to? What was going on?

She consoled herself with the thought that at least her questions would all be answered by Dylan over dinner tomorrow. But that plunged her into more negative thoughts. She was already regretting her acceptance of his invitation. Especially after successfully managing to evade his offer of a drink in The Woldsman last week. But this invitation had been so unexpected and so impossible to reject without seeming churlish, she'd been unable to refuse. Besides, her curiosity had been aroused. Nevertheless, she knew she should have kept her head and told him firmly "No". She dreaded what would happen if Greg somehow found out about it. She was glad she'd managed to persuade Dylan to take her somewhere other than The Woldsman!

And so she walked on, her mind and feelings in a flux; apprehensive at the way things seemed to be turning out. Yet, despite this, her heart seemed to be soaring with an intoxicating sense of expectation. She had an inexplicable feeling that something extraordinary was about to happen, and soon.

CHAPTER TWELVE

Sharon spent a restless night troubled by vexing dreams. She kept waking up, convinced she'd been mad to accept Dylan's dinner invitation. By early morning she was sure that a lot of potential trouble could be avoided simply by calling him to cancel. She even got as far as picking up the phone but immediately abandoned the idea before she'd punched in his number.

Anyway, why shouldn't I go? she asked herself.

Even at work, her concerns that Greg would somehow find out about her dinner date kept destroying her concentration, making it impossible to give her full attention to important tasks. Greg was immensely possessive. He was unlikely to accept her innocent explanation and there was bound to be a terrible row. Besides, she wasn't entirely convinced that Dylan's invitation didn't have an ulterior motive. She'd often caught him staring at her in a way that could only mean one thing. And then there was that Zoe person. Dylan had said she was only a colleague, but if so, why had she behaved like a bitch? Any woman could see that Zoe's familiar and proprietorial attitude towards Dylan showed she'd got the hots for him.

There was also the problem of how Louise would react. Her behaviour had shown remarkable improvement in the weeks since Mrs Henshall had given her and Jade a good talking-to. Jade no longer appeared to be bullying Louise, and both girls seemed to be much happier.

Louise hadn't said a word recently about leaving Leefdale and starting a new life. She was too preoccupied with her part in "Oliver". But it was obvious to Sharon that Louise hadn't forgiven her entirely for breaking her promise: the child's resentment was still there, only masked by a cold civility that was deeply upsetting. However, at least they were on speaking terms again. If she told the girl she was intending to go out with someone other than her father, how would she take it? Would she build too much into it? Interpret it as a sign that they'd be leaving Leefdale soon? Sharon was fearful of raising Louise's expectations. And how could she be sure Louise would keep the date with Dylan secret? Would the temptation to get her own back on her mother be too great? Of course, she could always say nothing to Louise, deliver her to the "Oliver" rehearsal, go on the date with Dylan and hopefully return in good time to collect her from the village hall. But that was far too risky. If the rehearsal ended early for some reason or Louise was taken ill, everything would come to light and it would get to Greg's ears. The obvious way out of this dilemma was simply to ring Dylan and cancel. And yet, every cell in her body resisted the idea.

Sharon spent half the morning agonising, and then at eleven o'clock she made her decision: she would ring Dylan and cancel. She didn't want her colleagues to overhear the conversation so, on a pretext, she stepped outside. Which was why she was now sitting in her car, clutching her mobile and trying to think of the most plausible reason for cancelling that wouldn't sound like a lie.

She accessed the phone's address book for the number of The Old Rectory, but although her thumb hovered over the "Call" button she got no further.

How often, she asked herself, had she been out to dinner with an attractive man in the last ten years? Hardly ever, although several had asked her. On those rare occasions when she'd accepted someone's invitation she'd always kept it secret from Greg, but her concern for his feelings had ensured that nothing had ever come of it. And how many times had Greg taken her out to dinner? Twice in all the time she'd known him, and then only because Pam had taken the children to stay at her mother's! On both occasions she and Greg had driven to a distant restaurant on the other side of the county in separate cars, and he'd been so jumpy and furtive all evening it was no pleasure.

Sharon stared at the mobile she was gripping tightly in her hand and decided that her life definitely had to change. It was totally unreasonable of Greg to expect her to live like a nun. If he discovered she'd been out with Dylan: well, too bad. As for Louise, if she really wanted her to dump Greg and leave Leefdale, she'd have to get used to other men being in mum's life. Anyway, maybe if Louise was told about Dylan it might convince her that life was going to change for the better.

Sharon knew this mundane dinner date with Dylan was an important test, and the way she responded to it could have important implications for the rest of her life. Which is why she locked the mobile, returned it to the pocket of her business suit and got out of the car. When she arrived back in the office she headed straight to her desk.

'Mr Bourne called while you were out,' Karen told her.

'What did he want?'

'Wouldn't say. I asked if he wanted to leave a message but he said it wasn't important and he'd ring back.'

Perhaps he'd called to cancel? Sharon was surprised at how disappointed this possibility made her feel. She turned her attention to her computer and the complex problems that had arisen with a property's shared access. Now that she'd decided to go ahead with Dylan's invitation, she felt more sanguine and capable of doing any amount of work. She hated it when anything prevented her from being focussed. Even if Dylan had called to cancel their date she still had the consolation of her career.

Ten minutes later the phone on her desk rang. It was him. He told her that he'd booked a table at The Trout. It had an excellent view. It was by the window overlooking the river. His voice seemed to be caressing her ear.

'I'll pick you up at seven forty-five,' he said.

'Could you make it seven-thirty? I have to be back before ten.'

'Fine.'

'On second thoughts...'

'What?'

She was about to tell him not to call for her: that she'd meet him at The Trout. But something was making her feel reckless. 'It's all right. Nothing.'

The call ended. Karen and Tracey exchanged a knowing look.

'You kept that pretty quiet,' said Tracey.

'Yes, a real dark horse,' said Karen.

'It's nothing,' said Sharon. 'He's taking me out to dinner to thank me for speeding up the completion.'

'I know how he could thank me,' said Tracey. 'And it would be a lot more fun than that.'

****

Sharon arrived home at six and went straight into the kitchen to preheat the oven to 200 degrees for Louise's pizza. She then went upstairs. As she approached Louise's bedroom she could hear her repeating one of her lines from "Oliver" over and over again, each time with a different emphasis. Sharon knocked and went straight in.

Louise was sitting on her bed, script in hand. She didn't look up.

'Hello, Lou. Had a good day?'

Louise shrugged. 'All right.'

Louise had only recently resumed speaking to her mother civilly again, but her tone was still sulky and resentful. It upset Sharon who rarely held grudges for long.

'Where's your behaviour report?'

Louise reached into her satchel, which was beside her on the bed, and retrieved a small exercise book. She handed it to her mother.

Sharon opened the report in a state of some apprehension. She was therefore relieved and delighted to see that Mrs Henshall had assessed Louise's behaviour in every lesson that day as excellent.

'Have you seen this?' Sharon asked.

'Yeah.'

'Well done,' Sharon said, replacing the book in the satchel. But Louise's attention still remained firmly fixed on her script.

Sharon sat down on the bed, next to Louise. 'Which scene are you working on?'

'My last one.'

'I thought you knew it.'

'I'm not word perfect, yet.'

'I hope you will be by opening night.'

'Of course, I will.'

There was a long pause. Louise remained focussed on her script.

'I'm going out tonight,' said Sharon.

This caught Louise off guard. She lifted her head and gave Sharon a brief, quizzical glance before returning her attention once more to her lines.

Sharon could see that her child was dying to know more but trying not to make it obvious. 'You don't mind, do you?'

Louise stared back at her insecurely. Her mother rarely went out. 'Will you be back in time to collect me?'

'Don't worry. I'll be back before ten. Stay outside the village hall and wait for me.'

'Supposing someone wants to give me a lift?'

'Don't go with them. Tell them I'm collecting you.'

'OK.'

Louise went back to her script. There was a long pause.

Oh, to hell with the selfish little cow, Sharon thought. She stood up. Without looking at Louise she said, 'Tea will be ready in half an hour,' and set off for the door.

'Where?' Louise called after her.

Sharon stopped and turned back. 'Where what?'

'Where are you going?'

'Danethorpe. The Trout.'

Louise put her script down on the bed. 'Who with?'

Sharon decided to come straight to the point. 'A man has asked me to have dinner with him. He wants to thank me for selling his house.'

Louise was now all attention. However, she still said nothing.

Sharon said, 'Do you think I should go?'

Louise shrugged again. 'I don't know.'

'Your dad might not like it.'

Louise tossed her head, indignantly. 'So what? He never takes you out, does he?'

'So you think I should go?'

'Why are you asking me? It's not up to me.'

This was true, but even now part of her hoped that Louise would beg her not to go. There was still time to ring Dylan and cancel. Yet again she was having cold feet. She decided she would only go if it was fated. If Louise was glad she was going.

'Then you don't mind if I go?'

'Well, yeah. I suppose so.'

'Only I won't go if you don't want me to. I know how you get used to me being here all the time.'

'No, go.'

'Then if it's all right with you, I will.'

When Louise next spoke her manner was less hostile. 'Has someone asked you, really?'

'Yes. I've told you. He wants to take me out to dinner.'

'What's he like?'

'Very nice.'

Louise wished she'd listened more attentively when her mother had been going on about her work and the people she'd bought houses for. She could have mentioned some names and seen whether her mum blushed. 'I mean what's he look like?'

'Tall.'

Louise giggled. 'Tall, dark and handsome?'

'No, tall and blonde. But handsome.'

'What's his name?'

Sharon looked serious. 'I'm sorry, Lou, I can't tell you that yet.'

'Oh, come on, mum! Who am I gonna tell?'

'I'll tell you after I've been.'

'You mean if he doesn't ask you out again?'

'Yes.'

Louise turned away and stared sullenly at the duvet. 'OK. Don't trust me then.'

'It's not that, Lou. It's not fair to the guy. He doesn't know anything about you or your dad yet.'

'You haven't told him about me?'

'No. Not yet. I hardly know him.'

'You're not going to tell him about me though, are you?'

'Of course, I am.' Sharon ran her hand through Louise's hair. 'I always tell everyone about you.'

'You won't. You'll be ashamed.'

Sharon was deeply hurt by this assertion. 'Where do you get that idea? I'm going to tell him I've got a beautiful, talented daughter who's going to be a great actress and singer. He'll be really impressed.'

Louise still didn't believe her. Why am I always a big secret? she was asking herself.

Sharon said, 'I'll tell you all about it when I get back.'

'Is he coming here?'

'Yes. He's picking me up.'

'What time?'

'Seven-thirty.'

Louise pulled a face and groaned. 'I won't see him. I'll be at rehearsal. Mrs Henshall wants us there at quarter past seven.'

'I know.'

The child grinned slyly. 'I could always be late.'

'You won't be, because I'm driving you there,' said Sharon. 'Now, I really must get ready. I'll get your tea first, though. It's pizza tonight. I thought it would be quick. You don't mind, do you?'

Sharon went downstairs and put the pizza in the oven. After serving Louise her tea, she went up to the bathroom for a quick shower and then along to her bedroom, where she took out the cornflower blue dress she'd chosen to wear for the evening. She hung it on the door of the fitted wardrobe and then sat at the dressing table in her underwear, applying lipstick and eye shadow while Louise bombarded her with questions about the identity of her mystery date. She deftly managed to field most of them without upsetting the girl. Eventually, she diverted Louise by asking her to choose her jewellery. 'I know, I know,' squealed Louise. She rummaged in Sharon's jewellery box and produced a pair of topaz earrings that complemented the dress perfectly.

At five past seven, Sharon realised that Louise was deliberately delaying her departure. 'I know what you're doing, Louise. Get your coat, now,' she ordered.

'He won't like you if you're an old bag!'

Sharon smiled but she knew Louise was right. It was the nerves, of course. It had been such a long time.

When they pulled up outside the village hall, Sharon was relieved to see that Pam's car wasn't there yet. The last thing she wanted was for Pam to see her all glammed up. That would get straight back to Greg.

Before letting Louise out of the car she said to her, 'And don't say a word to anyone about where I'm going. OK?'

Louise grimaced and gave a long-suffering sigh. 'I'm not stupid, you know.'

Sharon planted a kiss on Louise's cheek. 'I know that Louise. Very far from it. Have a good rehearsal.'

Sharon waited until Louise was inside the village hall and then quickly drove off.

CHAPTER THIRTEEN

When Sharon arrived back at Honeysuckle Cottage she was horrified to find a large mini-bus parked outside it and Dylan standing at the front door. She quickly parked up behind the mini-bus and got out of her car.

As he watched her approach, Dylan experienced alternating feelings of astonishment and admiration. He'd never seen her dressed in anything other than a business suit. Now she was striding towards him wearing a sleeveless blue dress that revealed beautifully tanned arms and an unexpectedly sensual side to her nature. She seemed to be radiating all the warmth and fecundity of summer.

Dylan's own appearance was being appraised by Sharon with huge relief. She'd feared that he might turn up in his faded blue jeans and scruffy old T shirt: the everyday wear which suggested it was his personal mission to prove to the world that he was no-one's fashion victim. However, she was delighted to see that he'd scrubbed up very well. He was dressed in a beige linen suit and a white, open-necked shirt: clothes that complemented perfectly his blonde colouring. As she came up to him, she noticed individual skeins of his hair were gleaming lustrous and golden, as though touched by the low evening sun. He also had that slight saffron hue to his complexion that some blonde men have when the first flush of youth has fled. He'd obviously made a big effort; did that mean it was a real date after all?

He smiled broadly and said, 'Hello. I was beginning to think you'd forgotten all about me.'

'I had to give someone a lift.'

They both stood staring at each other. Neither could quite believe this was happening.

'Aren't we both smart,' he said.

Wryly, she said, 'If I'd known you were collecting me in a double decker bus, I wouldn't have bothered.'

'It was choice between my bike, the white transit van or this.' He gestured towards the mini-bus. 'I chose this because I knew you'd want to travel in style.'

Sharon affected a laugh, despite her anxiety and preoccupations. It was vital that she got him and the mini-bus as far away from Honeysuckle Cottage as soon as possible. It would be a disaster if they were seen by anyone who knew Greg. Fortunately, the Danethorpe road could be accessed from her end of the village so they wouldn't be seen driving through Leefdale. They'd be out in the country before anyone saw them travelling together in such a distinctive vehicle. For a moment she was tempted to suggest that they went in her car, but she instantly dismissed the idea because she knew how rude it would sound. 'Well, I'm ready,' she said, 'let's go. I'll just get my coat.'

Dylan climbed into the mini-bus while Sharon retrieved a light summer jacket from the Passat and then locked the vehicle.

She joined Dylan on the front seat. 'Just drive straight ahead for two miles and you'll come to the Danethorpe road.'

Dylan looked puzzled. 'I thought you reached it from the other end of the village?'

'You can, but this is a short cut.'

He noticed that she was struggling with her seat belt. 'Hang on, let me.'

As he leaned across to assist her she was aware of the brush of his jacket sleeve against her bare arm and the faint musk of his after-shave.

Once her belt was fastened, he said, 'They're a bit awkward, sometimes.' Knowing that his eyes would be mainly on the road from now on he took the opportunity to take one last lingering look at her. Then he gave his attention to the road ahead and turned the key in the ignition.

They set off with Sharon giving directions. Once the village was well behind them, she relaxed and said, 'There really wasn't any need to do this, you know. I was only doing my job.'

Dylan told her it was entirely his pleasure and that she thoroughly deserved to be rewarded for all the hard work she'd done. Then, mysteriously, he added, 'Besides, as I said, it's not just about thanking you.'

'Oh? What's it really about then?'

'I'll tell you later.'

It was clear he wasn't going to tell her yet, so she settled back into the mini-bus's surprisingly comfortable seat and enjoyed the drive. It was an unusual experience for her to be driven by someone else. She was usually the one in control: the one constantly making decisions. It was a relief to pass that responsibility to someone else for a change. It was so long since she'd simply surrendered to life, allowing it to blow her here and there like a dandelion clock in the breeze. When you were as stressed as she was, there was something wonderfully relaxing about relinquishing control and letting go. Even if you were only letting someone else drive.

She asked Dylan how he was settling in at the rectory and listened carefully while he told her about all the re-organizing and cleaning up they'd had to do.

Then he was transparently changing the subject and asking her about her day. Had she sold any houses?

She laughed. 'We don't sell one every day, you know.'

But Sharon was impatient of small talk. She couldn't restrain her curiosity. Something strange was going on at the rectory and she had to know what it was. And why had he asked her out? Was it personal or professional?

Casually, she said. 'This is the mini-bus all those teenagers arrived in last night.'

He looked at her quickly and then back at the road. 'Oh. You saw them.'

'I couldn't avoid it.' She explained that she'd been chatting to Howard Roberts when the mini-bus had appeared.

This was annoying. He'd intended to break the news to her about the inclusion unit during dinner. It hadn't occurred to him that she might have seen the clients arrive.

'They're not all your children, I hope,' she said.

He laughed. 'No. None of them are.' Then, he added, 'And in a way, all of them are.'

'All of them?'

'Yes. Actually, they're the reason I wanted to talk to you.'

'I see.'

So that was it. The reason he'd asked her out wasn't personal at all.

'Perhaps it might be better if I explained while we're eating,' he said.

'Why?'

'Well, if I tell you now, you might ask me to turn back.'

'Is it that bad?'

'It's not bad, it's just that you might be offended.'

They were coming to a T junction. She directed him to turn right, and only resumed speaking when he'd completed the manoeuvre. 'Look, if it's something objectionable I'd like you to tell me right away.'

Her darkly serious face was interrogating him warily.

'I'm sorry. There's no easy way to explain this,' he said. 'That's why I've been putting it off.' He changed up to fourth. 'Look. You know I'm an artist?'

'Yes.'

'I'm also a qualified art therapist.'

'Art therapist? What's that?'

'I use art to help people address their problems.'

Sharon stared at him sidelong, trying to comprehend. 'You mean people with mental problems?'

'Not necessarily, although they can certainly benefit from our therapy. The people I work with find it hard to express themselves verbally. Art therapy enables them to communicate without words. For example, elderly people suffering from anxiety or depression; kids frustrated by learning difficulties; adolescents with behavioural problems. Criminals.'

'Criminals?'

'Sometimes, yes. I've worked in prisons and with people on probation.'

She laughed, nervously. 'I'm not sure I like the way this is going.'

'I told you, you wouldn't.'

'Those teenagers I saw last night. Are they on probation?'

He shook his head. 'No. But they do have behavioural problems.'

'What sort of problems?'

Some distance back they'd passed a sign giving warning of an approaching lay-by. Now Dylan could see it was coming up fast. He braked and pulled into it. When he cut the mini-bus's exceedingly noisy engine, the silence that followed seemed almost unnatural. What a terrible din this vehicle makes, Sharon thought.

'Now that's a view,' said Dylan.

Indeed it was. The lay-by was situated on the brow of a hill where the Wolds halted, brought up fast by the wide plain of the Vale of Pickering. From this vantage point they could see miles and miles of flat, lush farmland through which the River Derwent flowed blindly towards its union with the River Ouse and its ultimate destiny, the great sea. Far distant, on the other side of the Vale, the land rose again to become the North Yorkshire Moors.

'Yes, it's lovely.' Sharon's enthusiasm for the view was tempered by a growing apprehension. Had he stopped because he was going to try it on? And how was she to react if he did? She needn't have worried. His concentration was entirely on the view. It was confirming for him the rightness of his decision to abandon the big city.

'Why have we stopped?'

'I wasn't going to tell you why we bought the rectory until we were having dinner. I didn't want to talk about it while I was driving.'

He looked so earnest and upset Sharon felt sorry for him. 'So, you're not a multi-tasker?'

He smiled, weakly. 'No. Definitely not. Look, you wanted to know about the kids who come to us. Well, they can't fit into mainstream schools. They've all been excluded for disruptive behaviour of some sort.'

'So, they come to the rectory for art therapy?'

'Among other things, yes.'

'What other things?'

'Drama therapy, to help them understand and modify their behaviour. That's where Zoe comes in. She's a drama therapist. And, of course, they still have to be taught the normal curriculum. We have Toni for that. She's a qualified secondary teacher. There's also Eric. He's another art therapist, like me.'

So, "Tony" was a woman. She couldn't help smiling.

He noticed and said, 'What?'

'Nothing. Are the teenagers with you long?'

'Usually about six weeks. But it might be longer if we think it might be beneficial. It takes the pressure off them and their families.'

'So the reason you bought The Old Rectory was because you wanted to set up some kind of school?'

'Not a school. An inclusion unit. It's for young people who've been rejected by school but who still need to be included. The kind of young people society wants to exclude and pretend don't exist.'

'Are they violent?'

'They can be.' He smiled, sardonically. 'As we all can.'

Sharon sat for some time without saying anything. She'd often wondered why a single man had wanted such a large house just for himself, but as he was an artist she'd assumed it was to give him sufficient space for a studio and all his pictures.

'I thought it funny that the rectory wasn't bought by you but some property company,' she said.

'Yes, we set that up specially. Look, I'm sorry I deceived you, but I had no choice.'

She was shocked at his deceit but was certainly not going to let him see it. 'You don't have to apologise. The Corbridges were delighted to sell the property quickly and at such a good price; you were glad to get the property; I was pleased to get the commission. So, we're all happy. There's no problem.'

But there was a problem. She'd been deceived. No-one likes being deceived because it makes them feel foolish and lacking in judgement. It also lowers their opinion of the deceiver, and until then she'd held Dylan Bourne in some high regard. So that's why he'd invited her out: to tell her he'd deceived her over the purchase of the rectory! This was so unexpected she found herself experiencing contradictory feelings of relief and disappointment. She was relieved to discover it wasn't a date in the normal sense, so wouldn't have to extricate herself from a situation that could only have complicated her life even more. However, she was also deeply disappointed because a part of her had hoped that the evening might be a prelude to something else: something nebulous and indefinable; something she couldn't identify but which she yearned for all the same. Her dissonant feelings kept her silent for some time.

Dylan said, 'I'm not surprised you're upset.'

'I'm not upset. I just don't understand why you didn't tell me from the start.'

He shrugged, philosophically. 'Bad experiences. We've tried to purchase properties before and made the mistake of telling the estate agents our plans. A few days later the property would be taken off the market. Much later, we'd find it had been sold to someone else.'

'The agents were probably worried about the effect your unit would have on local house prices.'

'Exactly. So we tried another tack. Next time we didn't tell anyone the real reason we wanted the property. That worked fine. The purchase went through without a hitch, but when we applied to the council for change of use it was always refused. A variety of plausible excuses were given but we knew what their actual reasons were: people objected because they didn't fancy living next door to a place housing difficult teenagers; and, again, the effect it would have on house prices. We had no alternative but to resell the properties.'

Sharon considered this and said, 'I don't understand why you've bought the rectory then. The people of Leefdale will oppose your application for change of use just like everywhere else.'

'Things are different now. There's been a change in the law so any organisation can set up special education centres to help disaffected youth or those excluded by society. That's why they're called inclusion units. The change gives us wide ranging powers and prevents local councils from stopping us.'

'So now you can do what you like?'

'Up to a point.'

'So why couldn't you tell me why you wanted the rectory?'

'The new law doesn't give us the power of compulsory purchase. We still have to buy properties without arousing suspicion.'

'Oh, I see.' Her eyes had widened with sudden insight. 'You think, if I'd known why you really wanted the rectory, I'd have advised the Corbridges not to sell it to you?'

'Wouldn't you?'

Sharon thought hard. 'No. They'd have worked that out for themselves. You see the Corbridges spent a lot of time and money restoring the place. They knew how important it was for the Magnificent Britain contest. They'd have wanted a normal purchaser who'd have treated it like a home and preserved it as it was.'

'In other words, not people like us?'

'They'd probably have preferred to sell it to someone with a family.'

'But our inclusion unit is a family. Of sorts.'

Sharon laughed. 'You know what I mean, a conventional family.'

'I don't know what that is. There are so many different types of families.'

Sharon reflected on this for a moment. 'We'll be late,' she said. 'And I have to be back by ten.'

****

'You take the second exit,' said Sharon.

Dylan negotiated the roundabout, dutifully following Sharon's directions, and within seconds they were driving through Danethorpe.

With a start Sharon realized they'd travelled nine miles but the journey had passed in a flash. 'Go straight on,' she said. 'The Trout's at the end of the village.'

Danethorpe was one of several villages owned entirely by the Budeholme Estate. Before 1843 there'd been nothing but open fields where the village now stood. Then, in order to build accommodation to house his growing army of agricultural workers, the fifth Marquis of Elderthorpe had designated land on the south side of the river Derwent for development. Soon, small terraced cottages for labourers had been built. Semi-detached houses for foremen and other responsible workers quickly followed. Later, a limited number of detached houses were added for senior employees such as the estate manager, professional huntsman and head groom. Finally, in 1849, work was completed on Danethorpe's Church, St Peter's, and its vicarage. Afterwards, no further building was undertaken, and not a single new dwelling added to the village. Danethorpe remained unchanged throughout the remainder of the nineteenth century and the whole of the twentieth. All this Sharon told Dylan as they drove through the village.

Danethorpe's houses were all designed in the same early Victorian style and constructed of exactly the same red brick. Although not unattractive, this gave the village a curiously homogeneous appearance. To Dylan's eyes it was like an expression of uniformity imprisoned in aspic. By contrast, Leefdale with its eclectic styles of architecture ranging from the Elizabethan to the modern was a paean to the virtues of diversity. He could see other stark differences too. Leefdale was a ribbon village which had developed in an ad hoc fashion on either side of a road linking a number of small farms. The farms still existed within the confines of Leefdale, which was why the village was a constant scene of bustling agricultural traffic and activity. It was obvious, however, that Danethorpe had been built to a pre-specified architect's design because all of its identical houses were meticulously positioned around a picturesque village green, with streets radiating off it like the spokes of a wheel. Sharon explained that most of the houses were now second homes or owned by people who commuted miles every day and didn't return until late. This meant that even on a beautiful summer's evening, such as the one they were presently enjoying, the village was deserted and had a curiously subdued and abandoned air, like a suburb on a weekday afternoon. As they drove on, Dylan became aware of another stark contrast with Leefdale: although Danethorpe's gardens weren't neglected and there were one or two hanging baskets here and there, compared to Leefdale it was a horticultural desert. Where was the abundance of topiary; colourful garlands; trailing blooms; floral confections and artful bouquets?

'Well,' said Dylan, 'the Major won't have much competition from this lot.'

Sharon looked at him quizzically. 'Oh, you mean Magnificent Britain. Not every village is as obsessive about it as Leefdale, you know.'

'Evidently not.'

They came to the end of the village and the road bent sharply to the right and went over a hump back bridge beneath which swirled the fast flowing Derwent. After crossing the bridge the road turned sharply left and ran alongside the river.

Almost immediately they came upon The Trout. This was a former coaching inn which in the eighteenth and nineteenth centuries had been a staging post for a change of horses on the old stagecoach routes connecting York, Scarborough and Whitby. Sharon was delighted to see it: she had so many happy childhood memories of the occasions when she'd been taken there by her parents. Subconsciously, this may have been why she'd suggested it. Although, at the time, the fact it was ten miles from Leefdale and there was little chance of running into anyone there who knew her had been its main attraction.

Dylan turned into The Trout's forecourt and steered the mini-bus slowly to the left, following the directions to the car park. This turned out to be filled almost to capacity with expensive vehicles, and Sharon's stress level shot up as Dylan tried to manoeuvre the mini-bus into the only available parking space: a narrow gap between a Jaguar and a Mercedes. Her embarrassment was made worse by the fact that she could see several patrons of The Trout observing Dylan's efforts through the windows of one of the bars with great interest and not a little amusement. She endured her shame silently and berated herself for not insisting on driving them there in the Passat. How humiliating to arrive in a mini-bus! The people in The Trout would be wondering why her date couldn't afford a decent car. She accepted that her attitude was snobbish, but she couldn't help caring about such things and thinking them important. Besides, she'd been hoping and praying that their arrival at the inn would be unobtrusive and go largely unnoticed, not turn into a spectacle.

But further indignities awaited Sharon. Although Dylan had now managed to successfully cram the mini-bus into the restricted parking area, it was obvious that space on either side of the vehicle was so limited it was going to be impossible to open the doors.

'It's all right,' said Dylan. 'We can get out at the back.'

'Oh, for God's sake,' said Sharon.

Dylan looked surprised. 'What's wrong?'

'If you think I'm going to scramble out of the back of this thing in a short dress with all those people looking at me you're mistaken.'

Dylan seemed amused. 'Why should they bother you?'

Sharon glared. 'Because they do! It's undignified. We should have come in my car!'

Good naturedly, he said, 'No problem. I'll just pull back and let you out.'

Dylan started the engine and reversed the mini-bus sufficiently out of the space until Sharon was able to open her passenger door and get out without showing too much thigh. He then drove the mini-bus back into the parking space and exited from the vehicle by the rear. What wonderful entertainment we're providing for everyone, Sharon thought, as she watched him. Even so, it pleased her greatly that she'd at least deprived the leering bastards in the bar of a view of her arse coming out of the mini-bus backwards. Wouldn't they just have loved that!

Dylan joined her, took a deep breath, and stood looking at his surroundings with obvious delight. The car park was positioned close to the Derwent, and although the river was mostly obscured by a thick wall of spreading, full-leafed trees and other vegetation, a gap between a pair of weeping willows gave a glimpse of the water's surface, which was glinting and glittering in the intense light of the evening sun. This constant sparkling was simultaneous with delightful sounds: little sloshings and lappings borne on the still, dry air as the river chaffed its banks; and there were many other liquid murmurings and gurgles, including the occasional plash of a leaping trout; and in the near distance, the faint but continuous roar of water falling from a height.

'Is that a waterfall?' Dylan asked.

'No. A weir.'

They both stood, absorbing the beauty of the location. The lush trees partially screened them against the evening sun, stippling the ground at their feet with its subdued light; and in the background the lilt of occasional birdsong enhanced the river's voice as it soothed and lulled vexed spirits with its promise of perfect peace. Dylan's heart lifted, and he knew that this moment more than any other confirmed to him the wisdom of his decision to leave London far behind.

'Wow. Good choice. What a place,' he said.

Sharon smiled at him happily. 'Yes, I love it.'

He was relieved to see that she was restored to her previously even temper. Her behaviour when she'd shown him around The Old Rectory and again tonight, indicated that she was quite highly strung and, despite appearances, didn't respond well to social pressure. He'd been surprised to see her so discomfited by people simply staring at her, until he'd realised it was caused by her status anxiety. She'd obviously felt that arriving in a mini-bus had seriously lowered her position in the eyes of all the posh, rich people in the inn. Being of a phlegmatic nature himself, such considerations rarely bothered him because he was impervious to those anxieties. It wasn't that he didn't care what people thought: but he generally took the view that very little mattered and nothing mattered very much; particularly when it came to concerns about status and one's relative place in the social order.

As they set off across the car park, towards the inn, Sharon's poise and self-confidence returned. Some of the looks she was getting from those seated inside were most approving. Particularly those she was receiving from the men. Dylan too, was getting his share of admiration from the ladies. This gave Sharon enormous satisfaction. They may have arrived in a mini-bus but compared to the middle-aged, balding, pot-bellied men and their dowdy wives inside The Trout, they were definitely going to be the best looking couple there. And that was something money couldn't buy.

It was a very hot night and all the doors and windows of the inn had been thrown wide open. Even so, as they entered the bar area the warmth generated by many people in a confined space, intensified by the heat from the inn's kitchens, hit them like a blast.

'It'll be cooler on the terrace,' said Sharon, nodding towards the rear of the bar, beyond which was an outdoor area where people were sitting at tables.

'OK. You go out there and I'll fight my way to the drinks. What will you have?'

'A vodka and tonic please. Ice but no lemon.'

There was a big queue at the bar and it took Dylan nearly ten minutes to be served. When he eventually came out on to the terrace, he found Sharon sitting at a table overlooking the river. She relieved him of the two menus he'd been carrying under his arm, and he was able to set their drinks down.

'How did you manage to get a table?' he asked, impressed.

She shrugged, modestly. 'An old couple were about to leave just as I arrived. I saw they were getting ready to go and came and stood over them till they did.'

Dylan took a seat and gazed quickly around the terrace. It was mainly full of people wearing the smart, casual clothes of those who'd come out specifically to dine. Most of the women, like Sharon, were in summer dresses and there were many bare arms and suntanned shoulders in evidence. Several couples, denied tables, were standing. They looked hot and none too pleased. 'I bet you weren't popular with those who've been waiting ages for a table,' said Dylan.

She threw him an insouciant look. 'I saw my chance and took it.'

He nodded. 'You're really quite assertive, aren't you?'

'You have to be, don't you?'

'Dog eat dog, eh?'

She grinned. 'What does it matter? As long as you aren't the one that's eaten.' She raised her glass. 'Cheers.'

'Cheers.' Dylan clinked his glass against hers and was encouraged. It was always such an optimistic, life affirming sound.

Sharon gestured towards his orange juice. 'Don't you drink or is it because you're driving?'

'I'll have a glass of wine with the meal, but that's all. I can't afford to lose my licence.'

They sipped their drinks and relaxed back in their chairs, enjoying the view of the Derwent. The river wasn't as wide as Dylan had expected, but the terrace was positioned at the start of a long, curving bend and so afforded a good view downstream. Upstream he could see the weir. He watched the swallows swoop flat and low over the water in their search for insects, and then soar up in a tight, climbing turn in preparation for the next raid. The current here was strong but not too fast, and there were plenty of expanding rings on the surface where the rising fish were competing with the swallows for flies. Suddenly, out in the middle, an exotic vision of electric blue flying downstream too fast for the eyes to fix on was creating a commotion on the terrace occasioning cries of "Kingfisher! Where? Where?" and lots of pointing.

'Very "Flatford Mill",' said Dylan.

'Sorry?'

'This spot reminds me of "Flatford Mill".'

'Where's that?'

'Suffolk,' he said. 'It's a painting by Constable.'

'Constable? He did "The Haywain", right?'

'I'm impressed.'

'Don't be. It's the total extent of my knowledge about Art.'

'Would you like me to teach you?'

She smiled, and looked down, evasively. 'Thanks, but I haven't the time.'

'You should always make time for Art.'

It was the kind of hot, oppressive evening when just consulting a menu felt like an act of extreme exertion. But they were both hungry and for two relative strangers choosing from the menu provided a shared and neutral context for conversation. They happily turned pages and discussed food and wine.

Afterwards, when the waitress had taken their orders, they talked in a random, gently interrogatory way. Dylan learnt that Sharon had often been brought to The Trout by her parents for Sunday lunch, and for dinner on family birthdays. Consequently, it was evoking strong memories for her. She told him of the advanced qualifications in estate agency she was pursuing in her own time. She spoke of her regret that she hadn't applied to university after A levels, and of her determination to become a highly qualified and successful estate agent. In return, Dylan described his idyllic childhood in rural Dorset, although he avoided any mention of the commune. For some reason, most conventional people always equated such a background with heavy drug taking and orgies. He described his time as an art student in the late 1980s and, because qualifications obviously impressed her, boasted of his MA in Fine Art and in Art Therapy. It seemed to Dylan that the conversation was going well, despite an unpromising start. Although they were as different as chalk and cheese they seemed compatible in many ways. He wondered why he couldn't take his eyes off her and why he was so attracted to her. She seemed to be attracted to him, too. Was there something supernatural at work? Some hidden force? He wondered if he should ask her what her star sign was, but decided she'd think he was a twat. Besides, he was too rational to take such stuff seriously, as so many airheads in the commune had done. Yet, if only he could subtly discover her date of birth, he could work out what her Western and Chinese star signs were. Her numerological number as well.

It wasn't long before their conversation returned to the inclusion unit.

'Who's in charge of it?' Sharon asked.

'I am.'

Knowing she was ambitious and impressed by people who were in authority and obviously "winners", it gave Dylan great satisfaction to reveal that he was the unit's team leader. He described to her the responsibilities of his role, exaggerating its importance and emphasising the managerial qualities required. He was delighted to see she appeared to be warming to the unexpected notion of him as a leader and key decision maker.

'So, who are you employed by?' Sharon asked. 'The government?'

He shook his head. 'Ever heard of Lord Sandleton?'

'No. Should I?'

'He's a big figure in the Art world. Has one of the largest private collections of twentieth century art in the country. He also has a passionate commitment to education. Some years ago he established The Sandleton Trust. It enables disaffected and disturbed youngsters to become healed through art and art therapy. Basically, the idea is that we provide a refuge for them. We take them to a nice place, preferably in the country, and give them lots of art and drama therapy. Other creative experiences too in a stable and supportive environment.'

'Why?'

'To help them understand themselves better so they become more adjusted human beings. Lord Sandleton's belief is that fundamentally we are all creative. But when the creative impulse is thwarted and our lives become devoid of Art, we become anti-social and self-destructive. When we can't create things of beauty we create things of ugliness and violence instead.'

'Is that what you believe too?'

'To a large extent. But I'm more interested in the art therapy aspect. I'm fascinated by the way painting and drawing reveals aspects of the personality which are deeply hidden from the conscious self. That's why I work for the trust. I want to put people in touch with those aspects of themselves they shrink from, so they'll be able to see themselves more truthfully.'

'But where does the money for all this come from? How is it funded?'

Typical estate agent, thought Dylan. I'm talking about Art and all she wants to do is talk about money. 'The money comes mainly from charitable donations, but Charles, that's Lord Sandleton, has put in a lot of his own money too. He's a millionaire. Comes from this area. I'm surprised you haven't heard of him.'

'You don't mean Charles Reynolds, the property developer?'

'That's right. He was recently ennobled.'

Sharon was obviously impressed. 'He owns half the property in Yorkshire.'

'Quite a lot in London, Paris and New York too.'

For the next five minutes they discussed Charles' wealth and influence. Afterwards, Dylan noticed that something seemed to be bothering Sharon. He soon found out what it was.

'You said that these teenagers have been thrown out of school because of their bad behaviour, yes?'

'That's right.'

'What sort of behaviour?'

'Persistent truanting. Bullying. Constant disruption. Assaults on teachers. In one or two cases damage to school property. Even arson.'

My God, thought Sharon. What have I done to poor Leefdale? She felt outraged that he'd deliberately deceived her in order to inflict such disgusting creatures on the unsuspecting residents of their lovely village. What a hypocrite.

'So, they're being rewarded for behaving badly?'

Dylan's face lost some of its relaxed expression. 'I wouldn't put it quite like that.'

'But surely it's unfair that the kids who do the right thing and behave themselves don't get anything, while those who behave like hooligans are rewarded with treats?'

'Treats?'

'Yes. Like going to stay in a lovely house in the country and getting the attention of lots of people. You're rewarding them for behaving badly.'

Dylan hadn't expected this response. He felt his stomach tighten. He hated unpleasantness and, if he could, went out of his way to avoid it. 'They're not being rewarded. We expect them to work hard.'

Sharon's look was uncompromising. 'I'm sure you do. But it's hardly an incentive for those pupils who behave themselves if they get nothing in return; but those who burn the school down get taken on holiday.'

'Coming to us isn't a holiday. Don't think we make it easy for them. If they don't co-operate with us, they're out; so they rarely give us any trouble.'

He was appalled by Sharon's prejudices. It was as though she'd swallowed all the poison pumped out by the right wing tabloids. She obviously thought that people at the bottom of the heap were all undeserving, feckless scroungers; and those, like himself, who tried to help them cope with their bewildering array of problems and difficulties, were simply encouraging them. For a moment he wished Zoe were there. It would have been interesting to have heard her demolishing such selfish, ignorant arguments with her usual mixture of logic and passionate invective. But he doubted whether her combative, brutal style would have worked against this well paid, sanctimonious bourgeoise who spoke only from the ignorance of her secure, insulated lifestyle. He felt very disappointed. He'd assumed that Sharon, being an estate agent, would be a Tory but he hadn't expected such prejudice. He hoped she wasn't a racist too. Perhaps his deception over the rectory had made her angrier than she was prepared to admit and it was manifesting itself in an attack upon the unit's clients. He forced himself to concentrate, and put the logical counter argument to her effectively. Yet, even as he spoke he felt his advocacy to be inadequate despite his strong convictions. He knew he lacked Zoe's passion. 'The children who come to us have terrible histories of abuse and neglect,' he said. 'We're just redressing the balance.'

This cut very little ice with Sharon. She was sick of hearing people blame their anti-social behaviour on their terrible childhoods. She wasn't interested for a moment in what their backgrounds were, only in the terrible things they'd done to other people. Her concern was for the victims. No-one gave a damn about them! She said, 'I'm sure there are plenty of people who've had terrible backgrounds but have also had the strength of character to rise above them.'

Don't get bogged down with abstractions, Dylan told himself. That way you'll never change her mind. Relate it to the real, the personal. Don't antagonize her, educate her. 'If some have been able to rise above their circumstances, that's excellent,' he said. 'But not everyone can, and they're the ones who need our help.' Examples, he instructed himself, give her some examples. 'One of those referred to us was a thirteen year old boy. He was persistently truanting and when he was at school was exhibiting very anti-social behaviour. The school called social services in to investigate. They discovered that the boy's parents had drug and alcohol addictions. They had three children and there were only enough clothes in the house for two of them, so the children had to share. They managed it quite intelligently. One child wore a set of clothes and went to school. The other child wore a set of clothes and went out and stole food. The child without the clothes stayed at home. The next day they'd swap the clothes around. And their role. That's why they were hardly at school two days running, and why, when they got there they'd kick off. The children were having to look after each other and their parents. They didn't find anything strange about it. It's what they'd been doing for years.'

Dylan searched her face carefully, trying to assess the impact his account was having on her; but although she was listening intently her expression gave no indication of what she was thinking. 'Another teenager came to one of our units,' he continued. 'His mother left him when he was just four. Went off with another man. The father raised bull terriers for dog fighting. The boy was raised with the dogs. Treated just like one of them. When the father went to the dog fights, he'd lock the lad in the shed with the dogs who were left behind. The school and social services only discovered what was going on when one of the dogs bit the boy so badly he ended up in hospital. Or perhaps you'd be interested in a sixteen year old girl we helped. Repeatedly raped by her mother's boyfriend. So she ran away, slept on the streets in Birmingham. Fell in with a very bad lot who used her to gratify dozens of men. Now I know that these are the more extreme cases, but I assure you the teenagers who are referred to us aren't being rewarded. The ones who are rewarded are those who have stable backgrounds and normal childhoods to begin with!'

There was a long pause. Dylan could see that he'd shocked her. But he didn't want her putting rumours around that The Old Rectory was full of psychopaths. 'Those are extreme examples, of course. I wanted you to see what some of the children have gone through. You needn't be concerned about any of the teenagers in our unit. They're not dangerous. Most of them have a background of low level disruption in school, that's all, and it's resulted in them being excluded. We're all CRB checked, all highly qualified and experienced and the youngsters love being with us. You've nothing to fear from them. Or our inclusion unit.'

Sharon was feeling slightly chastened. It was occurring to her that she'd led a somewhat sheltered life: also, how lucky she'd been. Even so, she wasn't prepared to accept that she was completely wrong. She still believed adamantly that everybody was free to make their own choices and ultimately could choose to do good or evil. That's why people had to be made to take responsibility for their actions. It was so easy for people to blame everyone else for their bad behaviour and not look to themselves. However, she'd been well brought up and knew it would be rude and unsociable to continue to be argumentative, so she said, 'Well, I'm not saying that what you're doing isn't a very good thing. I admire you for it. I really do. Especially as you're not using taxpayers' money. What the rest of the village will say about your inclusion unit is another matter, though.'

As someone who believed in the virtues of reasonable debate and compromise, Dylan recognised when someone was being conciliatory. It appeared that his horror stories had got through or at least made her think, so he was prepared to let her point about taxpayers' money go, even though he wanted to tell her that he was a tax payer too, and not all taxpayers were Tories or shared their assumptions. Besides, she wouldn't be so supportive if she knew that some of The Sandleton Trust's money came from local authorities.

'So, I'm forgiven for deceiving you?' he said.

Sharon's feelings were so conflicted she was unsure how to respond. She was relieved to find that she'd done nothing illegal or negligent in connection with the sale of the rectory, although she would definitely be warning her superiors about the underhand tactics currently being employed by inclusion units. She could even understand why Dylan had kept his reasons for the purchase secret: she'd have done the same in his position. But the way she'd been personally deceived by him was intolerable. His reason for inviting her out had been a lie. He hadn't taken her to The Trout to thank her for expediting the sale but to expunge his guilt. Her hopes that the evening would mark a new beginning for her and introduce a wonderful, extraordinary happiness into her life, had been reduced to ashes. He'd duped her into mistaking the commercial for the personal and made her feel foolish. For that she couldn't forgive him.

'Well, I don't know,' she said. 'That depends on what effect your unit has on house prices.' Seeing his serious expression, she said, quickly, 'I'm joking. There's nothing at all to forgive. And I really do think your inclusion unit is admirable. In fact, it might be just what my daughter needs.'

Now it was his turn to go quiet.

'You have a daughter?'

She sipped her drink and smiled at him smugly. 'You're not the only one who can spring surprises.'

At that moment the waitress came to tell them their table was ready. They rose and followed her into the restaurant.

****

It was quite early but the restaurant was almost full. As they were led to their table several diners shot them discreetly admiring glances. This didn't surprise Sharon who knew they were a striking couple.

They took their seats. A bottle of Pouilly Fume was awaiting them in the wine cooler. The waitress removed the cork and asked Dylan if he wished to taste the wine.

'No thanks, just pour away.'

Their table was positioned by the window. Through it Sharon could see where the Derwent widened suddenly before the weir. The current slowed as it approached the obstacle; the water was checked and momentarily held before tumbling over in a spray of foam. For some reason she found the repeated action mesmerising but she dragged her attention away to glance quickly round at the other diners. This was such an unusual experience for her that she intended to savour it. The people in the restaurant all looked so relaxed and at ease. Obviously enjoying themselves. Why, she bet some of them dined here regularly once or twice a month. It was all so normal for these people, not something rare and unusual as it was for her. It made her realize more keenly than ever what the relationship with Greg had cost her.

Dylan was talking to her about the linenfold panelling, so she could observe his lovely face without being furtive. Was he to be her saviour? She doubted it. Interesting, though, that despite her goading he hadn't lost his temper. He'd probably be quite easy to live with. An amiable sort. Perhaps too amiable. Too pliant. Like one of those sofas you see in second-hand shops that have been sat on so often the springs have gone. She liked men with more spine. Ambitious, assertive men. She wondered what he'd be like in bed. Good looking as he was, she didn't think, somehow, he'd be very stimulating. Like having sex with a handsome but guilty curate. He hadn't factored in that she might have a daughter, though, had he? Why had she told him that? She hadn't meant to. But there was something about his manner and those frank, watery blue eyes that seemed to invite confessions. Anyway, the shock on his face had given her enormous satisfaction, so much so she felt tempted now to tell him everything; but she cautioned herself against committing such an error. Just get through the evening without revealing too much, and don't agree to any further dates. Presumably, if he was any kind of a man he'd ask her out again. If he did she'd be vague and non-committal. Wouldn't encourage him. Even though part of her longed to do so, if only for the normality of it.

Dylan was still recovering from the astonishing news that Sharon had a daughter. So that's what she'd meant when she'd said she didn't live alone. As he extolled to her the genius of linenfold panelling, a thousand questions were forming in his mind.

'So, how old is your daughter?' he asked, as soon as the waitress had poured their wine and departed.

'She's eleven and her name's Louise.' She told him about her for a while, particularly about her acting talent and her role in "Oliver".

Dylan noted that she made no mention of the girl's father. He thought this strange but didn't wish to appear overly curious.

'You said that our unit might be just what Louise needed,' said Dylan. 'Were you being serious?'

'Half serious. She went through a bit of a bad patch recently.'

Sharon paused. She could see by his expression that he was expecting her to divulge more but she certainly wasn't going to. 'She's not in the same league as your teenagers though, and she's fine now.' In an attempt to steer the conversation in another direction, she said, 'She was very interested in you, by the way. She wanted to know all about the mysterious man who was going to buy me dinner.'

'Really? What did you tell her?'

'As little as possible.'

'I'd be very happy to meet her...'

Sharon was instantly guarded. 'Oh no. I don't want her to know who took me out! I wouldn't want that at all.' She immediately realized how strange this must sound and quickly added, 'You've no idea what the village is like. If I'd told Louise who I was going out with tonight, she'd tell her classmates, and by the end of the week everyone would have us romantically linked.'

'Would that matter?'

'It would to me!'

Was she telling him she didn't fancy him? That he wasn't sexy enough? Probably. And yet, he'd been convinced that wasn't the case. Had their disagreement on the terrace turned her off him? Or perhaps she was jealously protective of her privacy? He said, 'I think my colleagues have already concluded we're romantically linked.' He described how Zoe, Eric and Toni had joshed him before he'd left the rectory to collect her. 'They wanted to know why, if it wasn't a date, they couldn't all come to dinner and apologise. They said it was only fair as they'd deceived you too.'

'That's a good point,' said Sharon. 'Why couldn't they have come?'

He was tempted to say "because I wanted you all to myself" but knew how corny that would sound. He wasn't so sure that he did now, anyway. 'Not possible,' he said. 'Three members of staff have to be with the clients at all times. Anyway, strictly, I was the one who deceived you, not my colleagues. So it's only right I should be the one to apologise and explain why I did it.'

She nodded and sipped her wine. 'So really this is your day off?'

'Yes. We all get a day and a night off each week.'

'And you choose to spend it apologising to me? Even though there's really no need?'

'Yes.'

She saw that this was actually quite a compliment. 'What are you going to do with your other days off?'

'Well, there's a huge area to explore around here. The Wolds, the Moors, the Dales. I was hoping you might show me some of it.'

She smiled and looked down at the table cloth.

The way she finessed away his invitations intrigued him. She really was most evasive; secretive almost. He'd been talking to her for nearly an hour now and hadn't really discovered anything about her except that she was a bit of a bigot who had a daughter. She was very adept at appearing to say a lot without really revealing anything. In an attempt to direct the conversation towards the more personal, he said, 'What made you think that Zoe and I were together?'

'I don't know. Originally, you'd told me you hadn't got a partner. But Zoe was so...' She stopped.

'Hostile towards you?'

'Yes. I got the impression she didn't like me very much.'

'She's like that with everyone. It's her manner. She had a very difficult childhood. Although, I suppose you'd say that didn't count.'

'What was difficult about it?'

'Her mother was Agnes Nutmeg.'

Sharon looked perplexed. 'I'm sorry, that doesn't mean anything.'

'Agnes Nutmeg. Not her real name, of course, how could it be? Actress. Poet. Playwright. Later barrister.'

'No. I've never heard of her.'

Naturally, thought Dylan. 'Perhaps you've heard of Zoe's father? Seamus Fitzgerald? Irish actor and drunkard. More famous for being the latter.'

'Oh yes, I've heard of him.' She reeled off a list of his more famous films. 'How could Zoe have had a difficult childhood with parents like those?'

'You'd be surprised,' said Dylan.

It occurred to Sharon that Dylan might have a thing about Zoe. 'I've obviously misunderstood her,' she said. 'When she was being so nasty to me I thought she was...' She was about to say jealous but stopped herself.

'You thought she was what?' prompted Dylan.

'I thought she was being a bitch.'

He laughed. 'Well, she can be that too.'

Their starters arrived. They ate smoked salmon roulade and sipped the Pouilly Fume. Dylan decided he wouldn't tell Sharon that he and Zoe had once been lovers. It would only complicate matters. Instead, he told her more of his childhood in Dorset but again managed to avoid mentioning the commune. He explained that his father had also been an artist and had encouraged him to apply for a place at the St Martin's School of Art in London.

'But my mother was opposed to it.'

'Why?'

'She was a successful businesswoman. She thought I'd be wasting my time. Besides, she was always opposed to anything my father was in favour of.'

He gave Sharon a brief account of his parents' acrimonious divorce, and of a childhood divided between Natalie and Bernard: term time with his mother; holidays with his father. He then went on to describe how he'd struggled to make ends meet as an artist in the 1990s and had taken qualifications in art therapy, so that he was able to continue painting and earn a living from Art. As he did this it occurred to him how selective people were when trying to present the best impression of themselves. What about all those times when he'd been down and low? Rudderless? Without direction? A frail vessel on a storm tossed sea? How strategic, prescient and inevitable all our choices seem when viewed in retrospect; when, in actuality, they were as arbitrary and haphazard as life itself: all down to chance, coincidence and luck. It's only when looking back that we create the fiction that there was a conscious intentionality to everything we did, rather than admit that throughout our lives we've been pawns of fate and never really in control of anything.

'So you're not a rich artist, after all?' said Sharon.

He laughed. 'Certainly not rich enough to afford The Old Rectory. But I am an artist. I exhibit occasionally and have a modest amount of sales. I don't make a great deal of money. I'm not even as successful as my father.'

'You should have your own gallery,' said Sharon. 'Then you could exhibit all your pictures and sell them too. There are some excellent commercial properties along this coast that would be perfect for a gallery.'

How extraordinary. She hadn't seen one of his paintings and yet she was encouraging him to buy a gallery. No-one had ever given him such unqualified support. It made him feel quite emotional.

Sharon described the properties in Sandleton and Filey that had potential as galleries. But seeing that he obviously had little enthusiasm for the scheme, she said, 'So, what made you move up here?'

He told her that his idyllic Dorset childhood had made cities anathema to him and that he'd always intended to move somewhere more rural.

'I always wanted to get back to the earth. So, when the opportunity to establish the unit in Leefdale came up, I jumped at the chance.'

Sharon watched the waitress refill her glass. She felt relaxed and expansive. The wine had peeled off her inhibitions like a layer of clothing. She suddenly felt the need to tell Dylan about her parents. Her father, a vet; her mother, a nurse. She'd been seventeen and doing A levels when they'd both been killed. She told him about the day when the police came to school to break the news of her parents' accident. She went on to talk about the house she'd shared with them. How full it was of their memories, even now.

'You never thought of selling up and moving on?'

She looked horrified. 'Oh no! I couldn't do that. The house and I are completely compatible. That's so rare. If you find a house that you really feel comfortable in you should stay in it forever.' She took a big sip of wine. 'That's why I love being an estate agent. I get such a wonderful feeling when I find the perfect house for someone. It's like finding them a soul mate.'

'So, a sentimental estate agent?'

Sharon immediately looked offended. 'Selling houses isn't just about making money. There's a lot of satisfaction in it.'

'I'm sure there is,' said Dylan. She was obviously quite thin-skinned. He cursed his flippancy. Her attribution of human characteristics to houses was quite bizarre, but obviously sincerely held. He'd been wrong to ridicule it. He supposed she was now labelling him as insensitive. He said, 'I hope you don't mind me asking but how old are you?'

'I was thirty in January.'

'Early January?'

'The ninth.'

So, Capricorn. What the hell was he doing, trying to work out her birth sign? She laughed and said, 'You're not trying to work out my star sign, are you?'

'No. No.'

'Good, I don't believe in all that guff.'

He calculated she'd probably been nineteen when she'd given birth to Louise. 'Look, I know it's none of my business but you haven't said anything about Louise's father.'

For a moment Sharon was tempted to reveal everything about the background to Louise's birth, and their strange, unconventional relationship with Greg. She felt an overwhelming desire to open herself up to this obviously kind and understanding man. But she knew that way danger lay, and mentally put the brake on her tongue.

'He's no longer around.'

Dylan felt encouraged. 'Do you and Louise ever see him?'

'Yes. From time to time. Look, please, I'd really rather not discuss him. Can't we talk about something else?'

Dylan was taken aback by her forthrightness. 'Right, I understand. OK. What shall we talk about? How about houses? You seem to know a lot about them. How did you get into estate agency?'

'I was very lucky.' She described how she'd managed to become accepted as a trainee by Parker and Lund immediately following her A level exams. 'They didn't even wait for my results,' she said.

'It must have affected things when Louise came along,' said Dylan. He knew his probing was probably unwelcome but couldn't stop.

'It did for a while,' Sharon said, tensely. 'But there was a good child minder in the village. I was able to leave Louise with her during the day and go back to work.' Sharon returned the conversation to houses. 'I love visiting old houses,' she said. 'You know, stately homes. There's some beautiful stately homes not far from here. The best one is Budeholme House. Parts of it are open to the public in the summer and it's got wonderful gardens. They sometimes have concerts in the park there.'

'When?'

'At the end of July.'

'Perhaps we could go to one.'

That same guarded, apprehensive look came into her eyes, and she looked away. What was that all about? 'I love concerts in the open air,' he said. 'I could get some tickets.'

'Well... I don't know. No, I don't think so.'

He could see she was embarrassed. Nevertheless, he said, 'OK, but I've really enjoyed being with you this evening. I'd like to do it again some time. Perhaps we could go for a drink in The Woldsman on one of my nights off?'

She looked horrified.

'I know you think the food's crap but surely the beer's all right?'

'No. I can't,' she said. 'My boyfriend wouldn't like it.'

This was as great a shock to him as the news she had a daughter. 'Well,' he said. 'A double surprise.'

She smiled back at him, enigmatically, but said nothing. He asked one or two desultory questions about the man in her life, which she deflected. By then, a certain awkwardness had entered the conversation. The boyfriend's existence loomed disproportionately over the table and curtailed any further advance into the ever more personal. The main course arrived and they restricted themselves to eating it and discussing bland and uncontroversial subjects.

They were deciding what to choose for dessert when the mobile in Sharon's handbag pinged. She took the phone out and read the text. It was from Louise. She hoped that her mother was having a good time. How were things going?

Sharon said, 'It's from Louise. Her rehearsal's ending early. I'm sorry, can we skip dessert?'

****

Fortunately, Sharon was able to persuade Dylan to return via the short cut, which meant they avoided the village hall. It was still light when they returned to Leefdale. As the mini-bus approached Honeysuckle Cottage, Sharon was relieved to see that the street was deserted.

'Could you drop me here, please?'

'Not the village hall?'

That was the last thing she wanted. It was only ten to ten and if he dropped her off at the village hall now the rehearsal would still be going on, and he'd know she'd lied about it ending early. Also, some parents could have already arrived to collect their children and might be waiting outside the hall. She didn't want them to see her clambering out of Dylan's mini-bus.

'No,' she insisted. 'Drop me here, please. I'd like to walk.'

Dylan thought this was very strange behaviour. 'Are you sure?'

'Yes, really. Just drop me at home.'

Dylan pulled up outside Honeysuckle Cottage. He was tempted to ask her whether the boyfriend was Louise's father. It was a question that had been on his mind since they'd left The Trout. But as she'd made it quite clear her private life was none of his business, he decided not to risk a further rebuff.

He switched off the engine. Sharon turned to him and smiled graciously. 'Thank you for a lovely evening. I'm sorry it was cut short.'

She hung her head slightly, eyes cast down. She'd panicked and lied about the "Oliver" rehearsal finishing early because she couldn't think of another excuse for ending their date. She knew she'd revealed far too much about herself and her personal life, and had been frightened of what else she might divulge.

Dylan nodded understandingly, and continued to gaze at her but she didn't meet his eye. Why did she always look down like that when he said anything personal? Surely it couldn't be coyness? Not at her age? He said, 'Anyway, as we're near neighbours I dare say we'll be running into one another from time to time.'

She nodded. 'I'm sure.'

'I look forward to it.'

'I must go,' she said, reaching for the door release.

'Just one thing.'

She regarded him anxiously. 'Yes?'

'You said that Louise went through a bad patch. If I can help in any way, professionally I mean, please let me know.'

'That's very kind of you but I was exaggerating. There's nothing wrong with her. Now, I really must go.'

She got out of the mini-bus and was relieved to see that the street was still deserted. As Dylan at last set off, she gave the mini-bus a wave and quickly let herself into the cottage. Once inside she went straight upstairs to her bedroom. She took off her high heeled shoes, her jewels and her dress, and pulled on some casual clothes that wouldn't suggest she'd been doing anything at all out of the ordinary. She then set off to collect Louise.

ART THERAPY WITH DYLAN BOURNE

HOMEPAGE

Hi. I'm Dylan Bourne.
Welcome to my website.

ABOUT ME

I'm an artist and art therapist. I studied at the St Martin's School of Art in London in the late nineteen eighties and graduated with an MA in Fine Art. I also have a Postgraduate Diploma from the Institute of Art Therapists and an MA in Art Therapy from the University of Eskhampton. I have worked as an art therapist in day centres for the elderly, prisons, young offenders' institutions, probation centres, and in special education units for adolescents. Most recently much of my work has been for The Sandleton Trust, working with disaffected teenagers whose behaviour problems prevent them from conforming to the school environment and engaging in mainstream education. My special interests in art therapy are the exploration of dreams and the liberation of the client's repressed self.

SO, WHAT IS ART THERAPY?

Being human, we all have a personal history. The journey through life has left some people with intense emotions or painful thoughts which are so overwhelming they make their lives unmanageable. It may be very difficult for such people to express their feelings verbally, either because they're unwilling to confront them or they find it difficult to speak about them.

Art therapy provides a non-verbal way of revealing the thoughts and feelings which are causing conflicts. It can also help to resolve them.

Using various media such as drawing, painting and sculpture, I will encourage you to create images which shed light on your suppressed problems. Then I will help and support you to reflect on the images you've created, so that you can understand and deal with the unresolved issues which the images reveal.

WHAT DO ART THERAPISTS DO?

As an art therapist my overall aim is to increase your emotional well-being and enhance your personal development by effecting change in a safe and supportive environment.

Art therapy is a tool for personal growth and greater self-understanding. It enables people to engage in a conversation with themselves. Hopefully, this conversation will lead you to a greater understanding of who you really are.

My role is to create the conditions in which this conversation can take place. Three elements are involved: me, you and the creative product, i.e. your drawing, painting, sculpture etc.

People who are unfamiliar with art therapy assume that the therapist's job is to interpret the client's creative product "correctly" and then help them deal with the issues which generated it.

Of course, I will always have an interpretative response to your creative product, but my role is to interpret it in partnership with you in an atmosphere of mutual trust. In the course of this we will together negotiate any behaviour or attitude changes you might wish to make to resolve your situation or problem.

I will always try to guide you towards your own interpretation of your art work by respectfully listening to your responses to it and asking appropriate questions. In this way we will explore your suppressed thoughts and feelings together.

This is challenging work which requires skill, sensitivity and flexibility, because individual clients require different approaches.

Often the art therapist is a member of a team liaising with psychiatrists, social workers, teachers, educational psychologists and other professionals.

An art therapist may frequently work in conjunction with a drama therapist. Drama therapy techniques such as role-play, improvisation, re-enactment and other forms of "acting out", either alone or in a group, can help you to express and explore the suppressed emotions, guilt, resentments, anxieties, needs and desires which may be the cause of your conflicts and have already been revealed through art therapy.

WHO CAN BE HELPED BY ART THERAPY?

Art therapy can be of great benefit if you have suffered sexual or emotional abuse; if you are experiencing depression, anxiety, grief or trauma. Perhaps you are a child or a teenager with behaviour problems? Art therapy can help you too.

Art therapy can explore and bring about changes in behaviour and can help transform negative self-images into positive ones: so if you are an addict, a prisoner or an offender on probation, it can be most helpful. It is especially beneficial if you have an emotional and psychological disorder, as it allows you to express feelings which are perhaps too difficult to talk about. Art therapy also permits you to release powerful feelings such as anger and aggression in a safe and acceptable environment.

If you are an older adult, particularly one suffering from Alzheimer's disease or other forms of dementia, or if you have experienced stroke, isolation or bereavement, then you can also be helped by art therapy. Taking part in an art therapy group can reduce your anxiety and isolation, enable you to meet people and make new friends. It will give you the opportunity to reminisce about times past, and explore common feelings and issues associated with ageing.

Art therapy is fundamentally a non-verbal process, so if you have learning difficulties or your verbal skills aren't very good then art therapy can help enormously. It can improve your concentration, help you communicate better and improve your self-esteem.

On the other hand, you may be in the fortunate position of being able to manage your life and have no overwhelming problems. Even so, art therapy can enable you to enjoy the pleasures of the artistic process, explore relationships with others, and enhance your emotional growth and personal development.

So, you see, art therapy can be beneficial to everyone.

DO I NEED TO BE GOOD AT ART?

Absolutely not. No special artistic skills are needed. Art therapy is about creativity, and focuses upon the process and experience of making art.

In an art therapy group you are encouraged to express yourself as freely as you did when you were a child. There is no obligation on you to produce artistically correct paintings or beautiful art work. For some people a scribble can be as big an achievement as a completed picture is for others.

If you feel that you might benefit from art therapy sessions please contact me using the form below.

Best wishes,

Dylan

CHAPTER FOURTEEN

Major Roberts stood at the window of his study contemplating The Old Rectory and bitterly regretting he'd agreed to Isobel's demand for a holiday in the Algarve. During his two week absence, untold damage had been done to the appearance of the rectory's gardens; damage which, apparently, was not going to be repaired by the lazy swine who'd just moved in. Not only had they refused his offer of help to maintain the gardens but appeared to be deliberately neglecting them. He hadn't ruled out the possibility they might even be doing it on purpose to sabotage Leefdale's chances in Magnificent Britain. Now, instead of lifting him out of depression and being good for his spirits, just a glance at The Old Rectory plunged him into despair and despondency. His brooding mind had sought strategies for resolving the situation and failed. It was now obvious to him that whilst Bourne and that Zoe woman rejected his offers of help, there was absolutely nothing he could do.

Or was there?

The previous evening, Greg Maynard had related to him some very disturbing information. According to Sharon Makepiece, The Old Rectory had been purchased by a set of art therapists who'd turned it into some kind of art school for juvenile delinquents called an inclusion unit. This explained many things: the fact that none of the adults living in the rectory ever appeared to venture out to work or had a regular job; the heterogeneous mixture of cultures and ethnicities of their apparent "kids"; and the large number of unwashed white transit vans whose ugly presence littered the rectory's drive.

According to Greg, Sharon was very angry about the fact that the true reason for the rectory's purchase had been kept from her and its former owners, the Corbridges. She felt she'd been tricked into selling the property to Bourne and the other arty types, and was greatly concerned at the damaging effects it was going to have on house prices in the village. Sharon had apparently insinuated that she was even afraid some breach of planning law may have taken place, for which she might be held responsible. It was this last concern of Sharon's which was giving Howard some optimism that the inclusion unit might even yet be stopped in its tracks!

He crossed the room to his desk, picked up his phone and put a call through to the planning department at the local council. The Chief Planning Officer was engaged but his deputy, Norman Fergusson, was available. Howard provided Fergusson with the relevant details and told him he suspected a breach of the planning regulations had occurred. The rectory had been purchased as a domestic dwelling but no application had been received by the parish council for change of use to a so called "inclusion unit".

'That's because it's not necessary.'

Howard was flabbergasted. 'Not necessary? Why?'

'Because normal planning regulations don't apply. Anyone can establish an inclusion unit in any kind of property, even domestic, without applying for change of use. They don't even have to notify us. It's all done centrally. All they have to do is demonstrate to the Secretary of State for Education that there's a need for one.'

'When did this all come about?'

'Earlier this year. It was smuggled in through secondary legislation. A Statutory Instrument. I'm surprised you aren't aware of it. We sent you correspondence about it back in February.'

Howard cast a guilty glance at the pile of unopened envelopes in his in-tray. 'Yes, well, I haven't been quite on top of things recently.' He paused. Embarrassing as it was, the question had to be asked. 'What the hell is an inclusion unit, anyway?'

Fergusson's high-pitched, nasal voice and strong Lancashire accent made him sound irritatingly pedantic and condescending. 'Inclusion units are set up to care for people who've been excluded from mainstream education. They're specifically designed to include young people who are socially excluded. Hence the term, "inclusion units".'

'You mean they're for teenagers who've been expelled from school?'

'As I said, they're intended for anyone who's been excluded from mainstream education.'

Howard exploded. 'You mean they can set up one of these things in the middle of our village and there's absolutely nothing we can do about it?'

'Not if they have government permission.'

'It's an outrage!'

Fergusson said nothing.

'And all they do in them is art?'

'Not necessarily. They can be set up for a broad range of purposes and have all sorts of specialisms. Some are therapeutic; others are vocational and technical. Some do apprenticeships and teach welding, that sort of thing. They're designed to give youngsters a second chance.'

'It rather sounds as though you're in favour of them.'

'I'm a planning officer. They don't require planning approval so I have no professional opinion about them whatsoever.'

'You would if you lived opposite one!'

Howard spent over twenty minutes with Fergusson enquiring about inclusion units. When the call ended he was even more disconsolate than ever. He went over to his in-tray and started opening the unopened envelopes until he came to the local authority's communication advising all parish councils of the possibility of the establishment of inclusion units. He stared at the date despondently. 19th January. Over five months ago. Best to keep that quiet. What was happening to him? Was he losing his grip? Was that why Meakins and some of the others wanted to depose him as chairman?

Howard went over to the study window and stared across Church Lane at the rectory's front garden. Now he knew there was absolutely nothing he could do about it, its neglected state dismayed him more than ever.

THE LEEFLET
The Newsletter of The Leefdale Parish Council
July 2001
Pages 3-4
In the Garden with "The Major"

Well, fellow gardeners, D Day fast approaches. D for Decision Day that is. Friday, 20th July 2001, when the Magnificent Britain judges will inspect every square inch of Leefdale to decide whether or not our village is worthy of a fifth consecutive gold medal!

H Hour will be 11 am, when the judges will assemble in the village hall for refreshments prior to their adjudications. A small number of representatives from the village have been invited and entry is by invitation only. Everyone is welcome to follow the judges as they move around the village, but please do not try to accompany them into any of the gardens of the properties they are inspecting.

The results for the Villages and Small Towns category of Magnificent Britain will be announced at a grand awards ceremony which will be held at Budeholme House on Friday evening. Three members of the Magnificent Britain Sub-Committee have been invited to this event: myself, Greg Maynard and one other, to be decided, who will take the place of the late Walter Marsden. Greg and I are looking forward to the awards with a mixture of trepidation and hopeful expectation.

I took a stroll around the village yesterday and was delighted to see that many of you had responded handsomely to my plea for more hanging baskets. Well done. A big thank you to all those who are doing so much to ensure that our village is a delight to the eye, and achieves its horticultural apogee on D Day.

Even so, during yesterday's perambulations I noticed that there were still some properties with space for another hanging basket or two. If you haven't already done so, I urge you to get to it!

I wish I could report that my stroll around the village yesterday revealed that everything was perfect. Sadly, and most disappointingly, I couldn't fail to notice that there were still a number of properties letting the side down and falling well below the extremely high standard set by the conscientious and hard working majority. I am not going to name and shame the owners of these properties: they know very well who they are and the extent of their neglect. I make no bones about mentioning this, regardless of whether it offends certain people's sensibilities or not.

Now, despite all our gardeners' labour and art we are always in a constant struggle with anarchic nature. As D Day approaches it is absolutely vital we do not allow our standards to drop. At the risk of being accused of being an autocrat, I would ask you all to be particularly vigilant about the following in the run up to D Day:

LAWNS

I advise everyone to water their lawns thoroughly a day or two before D Day. And remember, a good soaking done once or twice a week is better than a light watering done daily. Please try to time your mowing so that on D Day the grass is neither too long nor too short. In either case it will cost us valuable marks!

Under no circumstances should you do any mowing on D Day itself: it will make your lawn look unnaturally shorn, like someone who has just had a drastic haircut! However, if the evening before D Day is a dry one, it will do your lawn no harm to go over it with a light roller.

HEDGES

In this hot, dry weather the soil around hedges requires a good weekly watering to a depth of about 6 inches, which is the equivalent of 1 inch of rainfall. For best results use a soaker hose along the length of the hedge. Repeat watering when the soil becomes dry to a depth of one inch.

Even if your hedges are only slightly overgrown, they will make your whole garden appear untidy. Growth can be prolific, especially at this time of year. Please inspect your hedges regularly and remove any dead branches. Also trim out any intrusive and disfiguring tendrils of new growth that will affect your hedges' appearance on D Day.

SHRUBS

Nothing looks worse than a neglected shrub. Before D Day inspect your shrubs and conservatively prune out any undesirable growth, especially thin and wayward branches and those that rub or twine together. Also remove any broken, hanging or dead branches. This will allow more light into the centre of the shrub and give it a more pleasing appearance. Don't forget to inspect the ground around your shrub for unsightly suckers and ensure that they are removed. Don't do any pruning at the last minute, and certainly not on D Day itself.

WEEDS

Fortunately, apart from one heart-breaking example, most of the gardens I saw yesterday were relatively free of weeds. But it won't do to be complacent. Vigilance is the price we have to pay for a weed free environment. If everyone spends half an hour or so during these long summer evenings removing the persistent intruders it will guarantee Leefdale a weedless D Day! Be particularly aware of them under hedges and shrubs.

If everyone carries out the relatively straightforward maintenance tasks I have suggested above, I am sure we shall have every chance of achieving our fifth consecutive gold medal. Don't forget, if you need assistance to ensure your garden looks its best on D Day please contact Greg Maynard and the Magnificent Britain Support Team. (Tel: 756798). Greg and his dedicated band of volunteers will be only too delighted to come round and help. But only if you wish it. Please do not feel under any obligation whatsoever. You have every right to refuse the support team's offer of help, should you so choose.

Finally, Mrs Phillips, our parish council clerk, informs me that only one name has so far been received to fill the vacancies on the parish council and the Magnificent Britain Sub-Committee. If no other name is put forward for the parish council, a by-election will be avoided. Any proposed co-options will be considered at the next full meeting of the parish council on Wednesday, 11th July, 2001.

All that remains is for me to wish everyone good luck for D Day. May the best village win. And may the best village be ours!

The Major

(Howard Roberts)

CHAPTER FIFTEEN

'Oh no. Who the bloody hell's this!' exclaimed Howard.

Every Sunday it was invariably Isobel and Howard's custom to watch Hymns of Praise on the television. They'd never been enthusiastic church goers and when St Wilfred's, along with three other neighbouring churches, had been mothballed and services transferred twelve miles off to Melthorpe, rather than travel all that way to sit amongst strangers they'd decided that their Sunday devotions could be vicariously served by the TV programme. The advantage of this was that they could enjoy it in the comfort of their own home whilst at the same time tucking in to a late tea. Now, on this third Sunday in July, with a plate of delicious smoked salmon sandwiches and dishes of home-made trifle before them, they'd just settled down to enjoy a favourite hymn, "Lord of all Hopefulness", when their delightful ease was cruelly interrupted by the ringing of the hall telephone.

'You go,' said Howard.

'No, you.'

'It's your turn.'

Isobel shook her head. 'Let's ignore it. They'll leave a message.'

'It might be important.'

'If you're so concerned, answer it.'

'Oh, Isobel!'

'All right! All right!'

Wearing the pained expression of a martyr, Isobel rose from the sofa, muttering. With a baleful look back at Howard, she left the sitting room and went into the hall.

Howard munched his first smoked salmon sandwich and monitored the hymn singers for any attractive women. The location for Hymns of Praise that week was a coastal parish in the Highlands. When the hymn finished, the programme cut to an interview with a local farmer. His name was Sandy, and he explained that when he was working his fields he was constantly aware of God's presence all around him. He said he could understand why the Romans had assumed there was a goddess of the corn, whom they'd called Ceres. The word cereal was actually derived from her name. Did the interviewer know that?

Deciding that he couldn't listen to any more of this tosh, Howard reached for the remote control and pressed "Mute", putting a sudden end to Sandy's pantheistic burbling. In the silence that followed, Howard strained his ears in an attempt to discover the identity of the unwelcome telephone caller, but this was impossible as the door of their sitting room was closed and Isobel, who was in the hall, was speaking even more quietly than usual.

The television congregation now launched into another hymn. Howard turned the sound back on and was delighted to discover that they were singing. "Dear Lord and Father of Mankind." He settled back contentedly to watch. There were some awful old harridans amongst the congregation but some gorgeous lookers too.

Halfway through the hymn, Isobel returned.

'Well?' said Howard.

'It was Barbara.'

That was unusual. Their daughter rarely rang on Sundays.

'What did she want?'

'Not now, I like this one.'

They stayed with the hymn until it finished. It was followed by an interview with a lobster fisherman. He described how he'd been alone on his damaged boat with a storm coming up but was convinced God would never desert him. Howard automatically reached for the remote.

'No, leave it. I want to hear what happened,' insisted Isobel.

'We know what happened,' said Howard. 'God helped him stand up and calm the waves.'

'Don't be so horrible.'

It turned out that the fisherman had been saved by the divine intervention of his mobile phone. The interview ended and the congregation plunged into a specially written hymn by the local scoutmaster.

After several bars of this dirge, Isobel said, 'Turn it off and I'll tell you.'

Howard happily obliged.

Isobel said, 'She's coming tomorrow with the children.'

'That's rather sudden.'

'Peter's gone on some fact-finding mission to Germany. She thought it was a good opportunity to come up.'

'What did you say?'

'I said of course she could.'

'Damn.'

'What?'

Howard's face was turning red. 'Well, it's hardly convenient, is it?'

'Oh, for God's sake. You're not saying she can't come because of Magnificent Britain?'

'It's the final week. I'll be extremely busy. Visitors are the last thing I need.'
'These aren't visitors. It's your daughter and grandchildren.'
'I don't want the additional pressure.'
'But you love them.'

He was on his feet now and shouting. 'You just don't understand, do you? The week after next I'll be delighted to see them. But next week, no. I don't have time for them. Don't you see? It's vital we win!'

Isobel had a sudden suspicion. 'You haven't taken your pill today, have you?'

Howard sighed and reached for another smoked salmon sandwich.

'Go and take it now. At once!'

CHAPTER SIXTEEN

'This reminds me of our estate,' said Mr Carmel, as Sharon's car entered Reed Park.

From the back seat came the voice of Mr Carmel's twelve year old son, Peter. 'No, this is a lot newer. And we've got trees.'

'The developers have put in quite a lot of trees,' said Sharon, gesturing towards a number of forlorn twigs planted at intervals along the street, each one dwarfed by the tall wooden stake which supported it. 'Of course, they have a long way to go,' she conceded.

The Carmels were a couple in their mid-thirties with two young children. They already had a buyer for their property in Leicester, and had been in the process of purchasing a beautiful double fronted cottage at Millingholme, when its owners had unexpectedly taken it off the market. Mr Carmel, a supermarket manager, had recently been promoted to a senior position at his company's branch in Luffield. He was due to start work in a week, and the need to find him and his family an alternative property had now become urgent. The Carmels were interested in several properties but Sharon had recommended that they first view 7, Wilderford Close, a modern, four bedroomed house on Reed Park; one of the many new estates which had recently sprung up around Luffield with the suddenness of fungi, doubling the town's population.

Sharon parked outside number 7. The Carmels got out of the vehicle and stared around them bleakly. Being a new estate, Reed Park lacked mature plants to soften and gentle its stark angles so it had a completed but unfinished air like a builder's model scaled up to the size of reality. The house bricks were bright red and seemed to have come straight from the brickyard, as did the pantiles. The black plastic guttering glinted with dark newness. The UPVC window frames gleamed unnaturally white. As Sharon led them into the front garden of number 7, Mr and Mrs Carmel observed unenthusiastically the islands of coarse grass growing amongst the otherwise bare earth, and stared with dismay at the untreated wooden fencing, which, like a stockade, separated the house and land from its neighbours. This was a long way from the Yorkshire country home of their dreams: certainly nothing like the idyllic cottage in Millingholme over which Mr Carmel was sure they'd been gazumped.

Sharon opened the front door and led them into the hall, and then through to the dining-kitchen, the house's most saleable feature. Mrs Carmel immediately expressed approval of its size and its position overlooking the back garden. This encouraged Sharon to believe that they might make an offer, until Mr Carmel expressed his dislike of dining-kitchens and voiced disappointment that there was no separate dining room.

'There are three reception rooms down here,' said Sharon. 'One of them could easily be used as a separate dining room.'

'But that would make this dining area redundant,' said Mr Carmel, irritably. He'd quite set his heart on the picturesque cottage in Millingholme and, even now, couldn't quite accept he'd lost it.

'He doesn't like new houses,' said Mrs Carmel, with a nervous laugh.

'You do though, don't you mum?' said the Carmel's teenage daughter.

Sharon was in the middle of promoting to the Carmels the advantages of buying a modern house when her mobile rang. Her immediate intention was to switch it off but seeing the number on the digital display she changed her mind and answered.

'Hello?'

'Miss Makepiece?'

'Yes.'

'It's Sally Henshall.'

Something was obviously wrong. The head teacher had never contacted her before on her mobile number.

'Yes?'

'I'm afraid there's been a serious incident with Louise. I'm going to have to exclude her from school for the rest of the week.'

'Just a moment, Mrs Henshall,' said Sharon, and took the phone away from her ear. 'Excuse me,' she said to the Carmels, who were standing around waiting, 'I need to take this call.'

Sharon moved into one of the front reception rooms before resuming her conversation. 'Sorry about that. What's happened exactly?'

'Louise got into a fight with Jade and some other girls, and when Mrs Lucas went to break it up Louise kicked her on the shin.'

'Oh no!'

'I'm afraid so. Will you come and collect her right away? I'm excluding her as from today.'

'You want me to collect her now?'

'If you would please.'

'I don't understand. Are you excluding her just for today?'

'No, the rest of the week.'

'The rest of the week? But it's only Monday.'

'I'm sorry, I've no other option. What she's done is very serious. Are you able to come and collect her?'

Sharon calculated that if she speeded up the viewing she could be at the school within an hour.

'All right. I'm tied up with clients at the moment but I'll be there as soon as I can.'

Sharon's hopes of concluding the viewing quickly were to be disappointed. The Carmels had come all the way from Leicester for the day, and were determined to return there with a new purchase underway in the Luffield area. Understandably, they wanted to spend time in the house, discuss the property and reflect on it. They also had many questions about schools, public transport and a range of other services. Sharon responded to their concerns on automatic pilot. All she could think of was Louise.

At the end of the viewing the Carmel's reaction to the house was still lukewarm. Sharon reminded them that it was a new property, no chain was involved and the purchase could proceed very quickly.

'You could be moved in by the end of August,' she said.

Mr and Mrs Carmel exchanged a look.

'We'd like to see the other properties before we commit ourselves,' said Mr Carmel.

'Of course,' said Sharon. 'But I'm afraid I won't be able to accompany you.'

'Oh!' Mrs Carmel looked crestfallen. 'But you promised to stay with us until we found somewhere.'

'I'm sorry, I've got to collect my little girl from school.'

Mr Carmel resorted to a fierce whisper. 'But you know how desperate our situation is!'

'Anything wrong with your daughter?' Mrs Carmel asked. She recognised the signs that her husband was about to become confrontational.

'She's not very well.'

Sharon stared at Mrs and Mrs Carmel. Their faces were tight with tension. He was facing the anxiety of a new job in an unfamiliar area; his wife was facing the prospect of her ordered life being turned upside down. The children were feeling it too. They stood around, abjectly looking from one parent to the other.

'Don't worry. I'll be back with you as soon as I can,' said Sharon. 'Meanwhile, I'll arrange for my colleague to show you the other properties. We'll find you something you'll like, I'm sure.'

'I hope so,' said Mrs Carmel. 'I'm terrified that if we don't find somewhere soon we'll end up homeless.'

'There's no chance of that,' Sharon reassured her. 'We've plenty of properties on our books to rent.'

****

Sharon eventually deposited the Carmels back at Parker and Lund's just after twelve-thirty. She entrusted them to the cool and reassuring professionalism of Tracey, and then set off at a reckless speed in the direction of Leefdale.

She drove along speculating on all the possible reasons for Louise's appalling behaviour. Yet, as she left the Luffield by-pass to take the short cut through Woldington, images of the Carmels came into her mind. With a sudden insight, she realised that despite their anxieties and insecurities they were a real family and represented something Louise had always been denied. She would never travel with her mother and father to a distant town and view a property in which they might contemplate spending their lives together. Greg was never going to leave Pam and their three children. Not that Sharon had ever expected him to or even wanted it: she'd always been perfectly happy with their arrangement. But now the pressure for domestic normality was coming from Louise. When Louise had been very young she'd accepted it as perfectly natural that her father visited occasionally, and then returned to his own family. Now she'd grown older and was realising that normal family life was denied her and there would never be anything other than duplicity and lies, it was understandable that she wanted things to change. Sharon knew that Louise blamed her for the situation, and she acknowledged that she was, in part, culpable; but consoled herself with the knowledge that there'd never been any intention to inflict psychological or emotional harm on Louise, or make her unhappy. Like so many human situations it had just happened. It was the consequence of drift and indecisiveness; the effect of too much attachment to the past and fear of change.

As she drove on, Sharon's thoughts returned to Louise's exclusion and she castigated herself for not taking her daughter's needs seriously. She'd given Louise a specific promise that the circumstances would change, and then, because the prospect had proved too challenging, she'd bottled it and retreated to her old comfort zone. No wonder the girl's behaviour had gone from bad to worse. And now she'd been excluded.

More practically, Sharon's thoughts turned to what she was going to do with Louise while she was excluded. She'd no wish to leave the girl at home by herself for the rest of the week. But what else could she do? Her only living relatives were in Norwich and she hadn't had any contact with them for months. She couldn't just ring up out of the blue and ask if she could dump her badly behaved daughter on them. Besides, Norwich was miles away. Sharon thought of her small circle of friends. None of them would be able to look after Louise because they all had full time jobs. Nor was it possible for Louise to accompany her to work. It was against company policy. A childminder was out of the question: she'd have to be told that Louise had been excluded and that would be too humiliating; Sharon had no intention of making herself the subject of gossip. Besides, the children being looked after would all be of preschool age and that would only make Louise feel even more rejected. Surely, Sharon reasoned, when she explained all this to Mrs Henshall she'd be understanding and relent?

On impulse she took out her mobile phone. Leaving one hand on the wheel, she dug Greg's mobile number out of the address book and called it. The answering service's synthetic voice told her that the number was unavailable and invited her to leave a message. Sharon was about to do so, and then decided it wouldn't be the kind of message she'd want Pam to inadvertently find on Greg's phone. She ended the call, considered for a moment, and then called Greg's office number. It had been agreed that she'd only do this in an emergency but surely this was an emergency?

The receptionist who answered sounded young and bright. She informed Sharon that Mr Maynard was in conference with clients and couldn't be disturbed. She promised that if Sharon left her name and number, she'd make sure he got back to her before he went to lunch. 'It's all right,' said Sharon. 'It wasn't that important.' She ended the call and drove on, wondering if Greg was fucking the receptionist too. This thought quickly segued into a vengeful fantasy in which she arrived at Greg's firm with Louise in tow and left her at reception. The receptionist would be asked to tell Mr Maynard he had to look after his child as she'd been excluded from school, and Ms Makepiece couldn't help because she was too busy finding the Carmels a suitable family home!

Sharon arrived at Leefdale Primary School just before one and walked hurriedly across the playground towards the school building. Children who'd already finished lunch were standing around aimlessly under the hot sun. On seeing Sharon, several stared and began muttering to each other. One of them pointed in her direction and said quite audibly and ominously, 'That's Louise's mum.'

Sharon entered the school building and found Louise in the corridor, sitting on a chair outside the head teacher's office. The "Oliver" script was in her lap.

Louise looked up as Sharon entered. 'Mum!'

'Don't look so surprised, you know why I'm here,' said Sharon.

Louise gave a defiant shrug of her shoulders. 'So!'

'What happened?' Sharon demanded.

'Jade and the others were picking on me again so I hit them. Like you said.'

'I never told you to kick Mrs Lucas.'

Louise said nothing.

'You did kick her, didn't you?'

Louise remained silent.

'That was wrong, Lou.'

A door opened and Mrs Henshall emerged from the room where she'd been on dinner duty. She closed the door behind her and the appalling din of children's voices and the scraping of tables and chairs receded. Despite her sleeveless summer dress, Mrs Henshall appeared hot and flustered. Perspiration beaded her forehead and glistened on her upper arms. 'Thank you for coming so quickly,' she said.

'I'd have been here sooner but I was in the middle of a viewing,' said Sharon.

'Let's go into my office.' Mrs Henshall turned to Louise. 'Wait here please, Louise.'

Sharon had expected to sit on the other side of Mrs Henshall's desk, but she was surprised to find herself being led to a circular table around which some comfortable chairs had been placed. This innovation had been introduced by Mrs Henshall after she'd attended a recent course where it had been suggested that the circular table was less confrontational because it signified a non-hierarchical, non-intimidatory context for discourse. However, for extra insurance, Mrs Henshall also had her notebook, which she set down in front of her as they took their seats.

'So, what's all this about?' asked Sharon.

'I'm sorry you've had to collect Louise,' said Mrs Henshall. 'But after you hear what happened I think you'll see that I have no alternative but to exclude her.'

Sharon's arms were folded, her chin uplifted and her features set in an expression of fierce implacability.

Mrs Henshall noted Sharon's hostile body language and continued, 'It happened during morning break. Apparently, Louise was playing with Roger Bell. After a while Jade Maynard...'

'Jade again!' exclaimed Sharon, sharply.

'I'm afraid so. Jade, her younger sister Gwen, and another girl called Rose Atkins went over to Louise and Roger and started teasing them.'

'What do you mean, teasing them?'

Mrs Henshall remembered that Sharon had previously objected to her use of the word "teasing" and regarded it as too euphemistic. 'Well, from what I can gather they were goading Louise about her friendship with Roger. They were suggesting that Roger was Louise's boyfriend and that Louise loved him. All that childish sort of stuff.'

'It may be childish but they take it very seriously,' said Sharon.

Mrs Henshall ignored the objection and went on, 'Louise denied that she was Roger's girlfriend but apparently the girls went on chanting "Louise loves Rodger, Louise loves Roger," over and over again. Unfortunately, according to Louise, it didn't stop at that. She says that Jade called out "Louise will be all right with Roger because he doesn't have a dad either".'

Sharon thought of Roger's father, a local farmer who'd been killed in a tractor accident the previous year. 'What a terrible thing to say!'

'Jade denies that she said it.'

Sharon scoffed loudly. 'I don't believe her. It sounds just the sort of thing she would say.'

Mrs Henshall decided to ignore this. 'Apparently Roger slapped Jade hard and ran off. Jade burst into tears. She says Louise then called her mother "a slag" and started punching and kicking her. Louise also scratched Jade's face. Mrs Lucas saw the fight and went to separate them. Jade calmed down but Louise refused to be restrained and started struggling with Mrs Lucas. In the course of this she kicked Mrs Lucas hard on the shin.'

Sharon thought of the many times Louise had complained that Mrs Lucas was always picking on her.

'Couldn't that have been an accident?' asked Sharon.

'No. I'm certain it wasn't. I was in the playground by then and I saw Louise do it. She kicked Mrs Lucas twice in the same place. A huge bruise appeared on her shin. We had to send her straight round to Dr Pargetter for treatment. He immediately sent her for an X-ray. She's now at home and will probably be unable to work for several days.'

Mrs Henshall stared at Sharon reproachfully. Sharon said nothing. She was suddenly ashamed that she'd questioned the veracity of the lunchtime supervisor's story. 'Please tell Mrs Lucas how sorry I am that this has happened,' she said.

'Can you see now why I've no alternative but to exclude Louise?'

'I can see that,' said Sharon, 'but if she's excluded there'll be no-one to look after her. I can't stop working for the rest of the week, and there's no-one I can leave her with.'

Perhaps if she hadn't been having such a terrible day, if she hadn't been suffering so much from the heat, and if an Ofsted inspection hadn't been imminent, Mrs Henshall would have been more sympathetic. As it was, she said, 'I'm afraid that's your problem. This is not the first violent incident Louise has been involved in. I warned you that exclusion would be the next step if it happened again. She's too ready to resort to violence. Now she's injured one of my staff. What kind of message do you think it will send to the rest of the children and their parents if I don't respond appropriately to this latest incident?'

'But she leaves here on Friday. What's the point of excluding her for the last week of term?'

'I'm sorry. She leaves me no choice.'

Sharon fumed silently. 'And what about Jade and the others? Are you going to exclude them?'

'No.'

'Of course not! You won't do anything about the bullies. You're only interested in punishing their victims!'

Mrs Henshall was alarmed by Sharon's vehemence. The circular table's reputation for reducing conflict had obviously been exaggerated.

'Jade and the others were just teasing. I can't exclude them for that.'

'But they were the one's responsible for Louise's violence. They provoked her to it. Have you any idea how much it hurts her when she's taunted about not having a father?'

'Of course, I do,' said Mrs Henshall, 'and I've told the girls concerned that if they do it again they'll be in very serious trouble.' She wrote something down on her notepad. 'I'm also going to write to their parents.'

A lot of bloody good that'll do, thought Sharon. But she kept her anger under control and reiterated the difficulties Louise's exclusion would create both for herself and her daughter.

Mrs Henshall was unmoved by Sharon's entreaties and was adamant that Louise's exclusion had to stand. However, after some negotiation, she agreed not to ban Louise from the school production of "Oliver". She did this reluctantly, and as she privately conceded, not for the best of motives. She knew of no other girl in the school who could play the role of Nancy as well as Louise, and in her absence the production would suffer. 'Louise obviously won't be allowed to attend rehearsals in school during the day, but she will be able to come to evening rehearsals in the village hall,' she said, surprising herself, for she'd never intended to make this concession. She stared at the table. Could it have had something to do with it?

Sharon thanked her profusely.

'Right,' said Mrs Henshall, 'Let's speak to Louise.' She tore a page off her notepad, stood up, went over to her desk and placed the page in the basket marked "For Action". She then left the room and returned a few moments later followed by a subdued looking Louise. However, Louise's expression changed to one of truculent resentment as Mrs Henshall explained that her mother had been given a full account of her disgraceful behaviour and the reasons for her exclusion.

'Your mother pleaded with me not to exclude you,' said Mrs Henshall, 'but I've told her the seriousness of your behaviour leaves me no choice.'

Louise was unable to look at either her mother or Mrs Henshall. She could only stare sullenly ahead. But the girl's countenance brightened visibly when the head teacher told her she could keep her role as Nancy, and would be allowed to attend evening rehearsals of "Oliver".

'Thank you, Mrs Henshall,' Louise said, meekly.

Mrs Henshall went over to her work desk and returned holding a number of text books and exercise books. 'I've set this work for Louise to do while she's excluded. Please make sure she completes it.'

'I will.'

Sharon was standing now too. She took the set work from Mrs Henshall. As they moved towards the door, the head teacher said, 'Oh, by the way, what do you think of my new arrangement?'

Sharon wondered what she was talking about. 'Sorry?'

'The new table and chairs. What do you think of them?'

Sharon remembered that as well as being a parent, she still had a role as school governor. She turned round and looked at the new furniture. 'Oh, I didn't take much notice of them. They're very nice.'

'Yes, they are, aren't they?' said Mrs Henshall.

At the forthcoming governors' meeting Mrs Henshall had intended to give a talk on the psychological rationale for the introduction of her circular table and provide evidence of its effectiveness at reducing conflict. Now she was questioning the wisdom of this. Surely the parent governors would inevitably explain to the rest of the parents her real purpose in using a circular table, and they'd suspect she was manipulating them? Then, whenever she sat a disgruntled parent down to discuss their complaint, they'd assume they were having the wool pulled over their eyes. If they already knew that a specific strategy was being implemented to reduce their aggression it might only succeed in making them angrier, and then the strategy's effectiveness would be nullified! How complicated it all was. Perhaps it would be best if the reasons for deploying circular tables in conflict situations remained esoteric. Known only to herself and her mentors on "The Resolution of Conflict in Schools" diploma course.

As Sharon and Louise left the school building and walked quickly and silently across the packed playground, all the children and lunchtime supervisors stopped whatever they were doing to stare at them. The word had quickly gone round that Louise had been excluded.

As the mother and daughter approached the school gate they came face to face with Jade. Sharon was going to ignore her and hurry Louise on, but suddenly, she felt she couldn't leave without saying something. 'Jade!' she exclaimed, bringing her face intimidatingly close to the girl's own. 'Louise may not have a father to protect her but she's got a mother! Don't you forget that!'

'No,' said Jade, submissively, completely stunned by Sharon's vehemence. Sharon continued on through the gate, tugging Louise by the hand. When they were seated safely in the car she turned to Louise fiercely and screamed, 'What the hell are you trying to do to me!' and then immediately burst into tears.

PART TWO
Monday 16th July 2001
to
Thursday 19th July 2001

CHAPTER SEVENTEEN

'I'm sorry, I'd love to look after Louise but my quota's full.'

Sharon had always thought that Mrs Tomlinson was a most unlikely looking childminder. Not a strand of her coiffured grey hair was ever out of place. She radiated a particular kind of countrified elegance, and always looked poised and unflustered. Today, as she sat on a burgundy armchair in her comfortable sitting room, surrounded by repro wooden furniture, her elegant cream trousers and satin blouse looked absolutely appropriate: as did the delicate drop pearls adorning her ear lobes. Exuding repose, Mrs Tomlinson floated majestically above the domestic tasks and daily drudgery associated with her calling.

Much of her ease and composure was made possible only by the school leavers she employed on a part time basis to look after the children she minded. One of whom was providing lunch for the toddlers in the other room, as Mrs Tomlinson spoke.

'I thought your quota was six,' said Sharon.

Sharon knew this because Mrs Tomlinson was the saviour of Sharon's career. She had looked after Louise from the time she'd been a baby until she'd reached school age.

'Six. That's right.'

To reach Mrs Tomlinson's private sitting room at the back of the house, they'd had to pass the room in which the children were being fed. The door was open and, although Sharon had glanced in briefly, she was sure that only four children had been in the charge of Mrs Tomlinson's youthful assistant. Sharon mentioned this to Mrs Tomlinson now.

'Yes. There are only four in today. Two of them are off because their mothers are ill and can't get in to work.'

Sharon suspected that the childminder was lying but she couldn't be absolutely sure. Mrs Tomlinson was one of those women who rarely looked you in the eye: she always seemed to be examining the carpet, as though on the look-out for coins that had dropped there.

'Why's she been excluded?' asked Mrs Tomlinson.

Sharon gave her a selective account of the reasons for Louise's exclusion, which implied that the girl was a victim of bullying and had been unjustly blamed for standing up to her tormentors. But Sharon was wasting her breath. Mrs Tomlinson was a good friend of a woman called Mrs Sidebotham, who was a good friend of Mrs Lucas, the lunchtime supervisor who'd been kicked on the shin by Louise. After visiting her doctor, Mrs Lucas had telephoned Mrs Sidebotham to tell her all about Louise's attack. Mrs Sidebotham had immediately telephoned Mrs Tomlinson to report the dreadful attack on Mrs Lucas. Mrs Tomlinson had agreed with Mrs Sidebotham that Louise was no better than she should be. She told her that she wasn't surprised to hear that Louise had kicked Mrs Lucas four times. Dragged up, she was. And the mother was a very dark horse. Every man in the village, at one time or another, had been suggested as Louise's father. Very embarrassing for their wives, it must be. At which, Mrs Sidebotham had advanced the view that she was sure Sharon Makepiece was being kept by some rich man. How else had she been able to pay for Mrs Tomlinson's childminding services all those years, which certainly didn't come cheap?

'You were my last hope,' said Sharon. 'There's no-one else in Leefdale I could turn to.' She paused, and then amazed herself by saying, 'I don't suppose you could just take Louise for a few days and forget about your quota? I'd make it well worth your while.'

Mrs Tomlinson raised her eyes and looked at Sharon directly. 'I'd love to help Sharon, I really would. But you're asking me to risk my licence. Word would get out. You know how people gossip.'

'I'm sorry. I shouldn't have asked you. I'm just so desperate, you see.'

'Couldn't you just leave her at home?'

'Not by herself. Not for a whole week.'

As though doing Sharon a huge favour, Mrs Tomlinson said, 'There's a childminder in Scarborough I can put you in touch with. Some people speak highly of her. But don't take my word for it.'

'Oh, no. I couldn't leave Louise with someone I don't know. That's why I was counting on you. She's known you for so long and you've always been so kind to her.'

****

Sharon returned to the car where her daughter was sullenly waiting for her. Earlier, Louise had made it quite clear to Sharon that she'd no intention of being minded by Mrs Tomlinson again and spending the whole week with a lot of babies. But Sharon had been confident that Mrs Tomlinson was the solution, and had insisted on driving round to see her. When they'd got there, she was distraught because Louise had refused to get out of the car.

'Well?' said Louise, as her mother got into the Passat.

Sharon explained the reasons why Mrs Tomlinson was unable to look after her. 'I'm sure the old cow was lying,' she said.

'Good. You ought to be glad. I'd only have run away.'

Sharon was about to say something, but a sound rather like Tchaikovsky's 1812 Overture being played on a glockenspiel told her that her mobile was receiving an incoming call.

It was from Tracey at Parker and Lund. The Carmels had viewed two more properties and rejected both of them. They were very interested in a detached cottage with vacant possession in Longholme, but she was unable to view it with them as she had to take the managing director of Rawlings for a viewing on the industrial estate. Could Sharon get back to the office as soon as possible and take the Carmels to Longholme at three-thirty?

'I'll do my best,' said Sharon. 'But Louise isn't very well at the moment.'

'Don't lie, I'm fine,' said Louise.

Sharon immediately covered the mobile with her hand and glared at Louise. 'Shut up. Do you want everyone to know you've been excluded?'

Sharon returned to her call. Tracey said, 'Couldn't you let Louise sit in the car while you did the viewing?'

'A sick child in the back of my car? How would that look? Parker would really go off on one. You know how image conscious he is. Besides, it wouldn't be fair on Louise.'

'That's true. Poor thing. You'll just have to leave her at home this afternoon.'

'And what about the rest of the week?'

'Is she that ill?'

'She might be. That's why I need to find someone to look after her.'

Sharon assured Tracey that somehow she'd get back to the office as soon as she could, and ended the call.

Louise started complaining but Sharon ignored her. She accessed a number from her mobile's address book and called it.

'Who are you trying to dump me on now?' said Louise.

'Your father.'

Louise closed her eyes tightly and screwed up her face. 'Oh no!'

'Carter and Buxton's. Good afternoon.'

Disconsolately, Louise rested her head against the car's side window.

'Who's calling?'

'Parker and Lund.'

Sharon had no clear idea why she was phoning Greg. She had a vague notion that he might suggest some solution; even offer to help. Perhaps take Louise off her hands for the afternoon so she could sort out the bloody Carmels.

'Hello?' Greg's tone betrayed his perplexity and apprehension.

'It's me. Sharon.'

'Sharon! I thought it might be.' And then, in a whisper, 'I told you not to call me here.'

Sharon told him that Louise had been excluded.

'I know. Pam's already been on. Jade's face is badly scratched and she's covered in bruises.'

Sharon told him about her predicament. She told him that Mrs Tomlinson had refused to take Louise. She told him about the Carmels. She told him about the viewing at Longholme.

Coldly, Greg said, 'What do you expect me to do?'

'I thought you might be able to suggest something. Look after Louise for a while until I can sort something out.'

'What here?'

'Yes.'

'You must be joking. I've got a meeting with our most important client in ten minutes. Leave her at home for the rest of the afternoon. It'll give you a breathing space. You can sort something out long-term tomorrow.'

'No. I'm not leaving her at home on her own. She might get into all kinds of trouble. She could go off and I wouldn't have any idea where she was.'

'Now I'm sure she wouldn't do that!'

Actually, back in April, Louise had done exactly that. She'd gone missing for nearly a whole day soon after Sharon had broken the news to her that they wouldn't be leaving Greg or Leefdale after all. Sharon had spent several anguished hours driving around the locality searching for her. She'd been at the point of reporting Louise's disappearance to the police when she'd remembered a local beauty spot she and Louise had visited several times when the child had been much younger. Louise had always loved the place and it was there Sharon had found her, sitting by the edge of the lake, watching the water fowl and the anglers. As a condition of returning home, Louise had extracted a promise that Greg would never be told about her disappearance.

'I'm sorry I can't be more helpful,' said Greg. He'd ceased to be panicked now and was speaking to her as though she was a customer.

'You'd better go,' said Sharon.

'Tell Louise I'm going to give her a severe talking to when I next see her.'

When he rang off Sharon was in tears. Nobody seemed to care about Louise. What was the point of excluding children when they had nowhere to go?

Louise was sitting up now, alert to her mother's distress.

'Don't cry, mum. Please. Please don't cry.'

CHAPTER EIGHTEEN

Dylan sat back on the old leather Chesterfield and relaxed. Around him, in the art therapy room, were the unit's eight teenage clients. They were standing before easels or seated at tables, concentrating on the images they were creating on cartridge paper with paints or crayons.

On Mondays, Wednesdays and Fridays, Dylan took the afternoon sessions. These invariably followed the same routine. He usually began each session with a warm up in which the clients were asked to produce an image which reflected their current feelings or state of mind. He never asked them to draw anything specific: he wanted them simply to express how they were feeling at that moment or what was uppermost in their thoughts. Afterwards their work would be shared and reflected upon within the group; and, if Dylan thought it would be beneficial, he'd later discuss a client's individual warm up picture with them privately.

Following the warm up, the clients would move on to their next activity which was to produce an image related to a chosen theme. The theme which Dylan had selected for that afternoon was "The plant you would most like to be". He was particularly interested in his clients' self-perceptions, and how their impressions of self could be explored and developed by art therapy. Hence, many of the themes he chose encouraged the expression of self-images: for example, how did the client see him or herself? How did they think others saw them? How would they like to be seen? What were their real selves and their ideal selves? He believed that a picture was always more revealing about a person's feelings concerning their true self than any amount of talk. One image could encapsulate their hidden, subconscious reality: their so-called "felt-self". The client's emerging "felt-self" could then be teased out and sensitively nurtured with more talk and some "acting out", followed by successive cycles of art and drama therapy. Yet it was art that initially created the conditions for exhuming the client's intense, suppressed feelings in the tangible form of an image that could be identified as the "felt-self" which was in conflict with the "conscious-self" and causing problems for the individual.

For example, Liam, who'd been excluded from five different schools, was depicting himself as a pot plant being watered by a woman holding a watering can; Rupa, who had an appalling self-image, was painting herself as a magnificently vibrant sunflower; Amy, who was deeply guarded and suspicious, was drawing herself as a huge, spidery shaped plant that was full of triangular thorns and sharp edges. Tomorrow morning, all the clients' pictures would be reflected upon and discussed at the daily team meeting. Drama therapy strategies would be designed and planned to help the clients actively get in touch with the suppressed feelings depicted in their creative products and help them confront the suppressed conflicts that existed between their conscious and unconscious selves, so that they could be integrated into their whole personality. Art was an excellent way of manifesting the clients' "felt self" but drama provided an active way of physically exploring and developing it. This was Zoe's expertise. And so the process would continue day after day until the client's truly "felt self" would emerge, like a creature from an egg, more assured, more ready to interact with the world, and no longer shamefully suppressed.

Apart from the sounds of the clients working on their warm ups, the room was hushed. Dylan was always astounded at how even the most noisy, talkative and disruptive teenagers would fall silent and reflective as they became absorbed in the images they were creating. It convinced him of the therapeutic benefits of art therapy.

He looked around the room with intense satisfaction. The Corbridges would have been appalled at what had become of their magnificent drawing room. It had been transformed: gone was the period furniture, the opulent fabrics and expensive carpets; their place taken by rough wooden tables, easels and units for storing art materials. Colour in the room came from the clients' pictures, the paints and other art media. Dylan revelled in its authenticity as a workroom.

The tranquil ambience was suddenly and most brutally disturbed by the intrusive ringing of the doorbell. Dylan sighed and shifted in his seat. He knew that Toni was upstairs, taking her break, and so would ignore the sound; Zoe was in the garden and wouldn't be able to hear it; Eric had gone into Luffield. Reluctantly, he roused himself and went to answer the door.

As Dylan left the art therapy room and entered the hall the doorbell rang again, this time its summons was longer, more insistent. Whoever it was didn't like to be kept waiting.

When Dylan swung back the rectory's heavy, front door he found himself facing Sharon Makepiece and a girl aged about ten or eleven.

He hadn't seen Sharon since the night they'd had dinner together, and her lovely, unexpected presence gave him genuine pleasure which produced from him a spontaneous smile. 'Hello.'

Sharon returned his smile, somewhat unsurely. 'Hello. Sorry to bother you.' She placed a hand on the child's shoulder. 'This is Louise, my daughter. The thing is we've got a problem and I think you're the only one who can help us.'

Dylan stared at them, intrigued. He was struck by the similarity of mother and child. Louise was almost a miniature clone of her mother. Was the child the reason for Sharon's call? 'You'd better come in,' he said.

He led them down the hall, past the staircase and into the rectory's large dining-kitchen.

'So, how can I help?'

Sharon hesitated. Desperation had forced her to admit that her problem was one that wasn't going to be solved as usual by her own self-sufficiency. Even though she'd overcome her natural diffidence and managed to persuade herself to approach Dylan for help, she was finding it difficult to ask for it. Now she was actually standing next to him in the rectory's kitchen, the enormity of what she'd done was temporarily depriving her of the power of speech.

'You said I was the only one who could help you,' said Dylan, prompting her.

Urgently, Sharon said, 'Louise has been excluded from school for the rest of the week. I don't want to leave her alone in the house and there's no-one else to look after her. I wondered if she could come here during the day until she's allowed to go back to school.'

'I see.' Dylan was aware of two pairs of similar hazel eyes watching him keenly as he considered the request.

'I'd be willing to pay,' said Sharon. 'Whatever it costs.'

Dylan smiled, reassuringly. 'It would cost very little. We'd just need a small contribution to cover Louise's meals, that's all.'

'Then it's all right? You'll look after her?'

'Well, I'd have to get my colleagues' agreement but as it's only for a few days I can't see them refusing.'

Sharon resisted her urge to hug and kiss him. 'Thank you. Thank you so much. And I'm sorry I said all those awful things about these units, you see, I didn't know...'

'It's all right. We hear those kinds of criticisms all the time. It's only when parents have the problem of an excluded child that they realise the situation's not that simple. Chucking children out on to the streets is no solution.' He turned to Louise. 'My name's Dylan, by the way.'

'I know,' said Louise, 'Mum told me. You're the one who took her out.'

'Louise!'

Dylan laughed. 'Yes, I did. I wanted to thank her for making sure we got this lovely house.' Then, with a subtle change of tone, he said, 'Do you like drawing and painting, Louise?'

'It's all right. I don't mind.'

'She's very good at it,' said Sharon.

'We do a lot of art work here.'

'What is this place? Is it a school?' said Louise.

'No. It's an inclusion unit.'

'What's that?'

'It's for people who can't cope with school and find it hard to fit in. We find that art work helps them with their problems. We do drama too.'

'I like drama. At school I'm in the play.'

'Yes. Your mum told me.'

'She nearly wasn't in it, because of her behaviour,' said Sharon. 'But Mrs Henshall's allowed her to attend the evening rehearsals.'

'That's good.' To Louise, he said, 'Now, do you think you'd like to come here while you're excluded? There's no-one your age in the unit, only teenagers, but they're very nice. I think you'd like them.'

Louise nodded thoughtfully.

'So, would you like to come?'

'Yes.'

'OK. Good,' said Dylan. 'Now, would you like to tell me why you were excluded?'

'I'm afraid that she's been...' Sharon began, but Dylan politely cut her short. 'It really would be so much better if Louise told me herself,' he said. He waited. 'Well, Louise?'

Louise said nothing.

Stung by what she construed as Dylan's slight, Sharon said, 'You see, she won't tell you anything.'

'That's OK,' said Dylan. 'She'll probably tell me when she feels like it. I'm happy to wait till then.'

'I kicked one of the lunch time supervisors,' Louise blurted out, suddenly. 'It was an accident. I didn't mean it.'

'Oh dear,' said Dylan. 'Were they badly hurt?'

'She had to go home.'

'That doesn't sound too good.'

A single tear was forming in the corner of Louise's left eye. Sharon watched, entranced, as it swelled into a clear liquid globe and then slipped over her daughter's eyelid and splashed onto her cheek.

'And how do you feel about that?'

Louise said nothing.

'Do you have any feelings about it?'

'Yes.'

'Do you want to tell me what they are?'

'I feel sorry.'

'I expect you're pretty upset, aren't you?'

Louise's eyes were now brimming with tears.

'Yes,' she whispered.

Sharon opened her bag, found a tissue and handed it to Louise who began dabbing her eyes with it.

At that moment Toni entered the kitchen. She stopped and stared in surprise at Sharon and the tearful child. 'I thought I heard the doorbell earlier,' she said, throwing Dylan a questioning glance.

'This is Toni,' said Dylan. He introduced Sharon and Louise and explained to Toni why they were there.

'Are you OK about that?' he asked Toni, finally.

Toni looked embarrassed. 'Can we have a quick word about it?'

'OK.'

'No, in private.'

'Oh, OK. Let's go in the encouragement room.' He turned to Sharon and Louise. 'Excuse us. We won't be a minute.'

Sharon said, 'Look, I don't want to cause you any problems. I can see it was a stupid idea.'

'There's no problem. Just wait. We'll be back in a moment.'

They left the kitchen and Sharon heard them walk a short distance down the passage and then go into a room. She could hear Dylan and Toni talking, but only indistinctly. However, as their voices rose she caught the odd word or sentence. Louise looked at her. 'I don't think that woman wants me,' she said.

This wasn't quite true. Toni was one of those people who paid tremendous attention to detail. She dotted every "i", crossed every "t" and scrupulously adhered to the rules. She hated being forced out of her routine. She'd no personal objection to Louise attending the unit, but on principle, before the decision was made, she wanted a discussion of the ramifications with every member of staff present. She needed to be reassured that they weren't infringing any rules or regulations. Dylan didn't know her very well, which is why he thought she was simply being obstructive. 'You heard what Sharon's problem is,' he said, when they reached the encouragement room. 'She needs to get back to work, and she can't take Louise with her.'

Toni said, 'All I'm saying is it needs to be fully discussed, by all of us.'

'Is that really necessary? Come on, we can take her in for this afternoon and come to a final decision later, when Eric gets back and we're all together. What's wrong? Are you opposed to Louise coming here?'

'In principle, no. But we have to consider the legal aspects. We don't have a legal contract. There may be issues around money.'

'Are you saying we shouldn't take her in because we won't be getting paid?'

Toni closed her eyes and sighed. 'We have no case notes on her. No multi-disciplinary reports. No authorisation.'

'We have her mother's authorisation.'

'We don't know this child. We don't know what we'd be getting ourselves into.'

'Yes, we do. Sharon's given us the overview. If you want to contact the primary school and liaise with them about Louise, that's fine with me. It'll formalise it, if that's what you want.'

'Yes, but we're an inclusion unit, not a child minding service. We need to be careful.'

'If Zoe agrees we can look after Louise just for this afternoon, are you OK with that? We can come to a final decision about it when Eric gets back this evening.'

Toni was blinking hard behind her rimless spectacles. 'It's a bit messy, don't you think?'

'No, because it's not a formal arrangement. We're looking after Louise as a favour to her mother. Try to see it that way, if it makes you feel better.'

'OK. You're the team leader.'

Dylan and Toni returned to the kitchen. Dylan looked at Sharon reassuringly, 'Everything's all right. I just need to have a quick word with Zoe.'

'You don't want me, do you?' said Louise. She was looking straight at Toni.

Dylan glanced at Toni. Her face was a deepening shade of pink.

'She heard you say you weren't a child minding service,' said Sharon.

Toni said, 'Well, we're not. That's what my concern is. We've been established as an inclusion unit with a specific remit.' Her expression softened as she looked at Louise. 'It's not that we don't want you, Louise. Honestly, I'd be very happy for you to come here for a few days. But we need to get a few things sorted out.' Her expression was defensive as she turned back to Sharon. 'There's a lot of red tape around this kind of establishment.'

'Look,' said Sharon, 'this was a stupid idea. We'll just go. I can find somewhere to put Louise.'

'You wouldn't have come here if you'd had anywhere else to go,' said Dylan. 'Don't worry. I'm doing this as a favour for someone I know. It's no big deal.'

'But it might get you into trouble.'

'How? If all I'm doing is helping a friend?'

Sharon gave him a pallid smile. It was very pleasing to hear him describe her as a friend.

'I'll just go and check it out with Zoe,' said Dylan. 'If she agrees, Louise can stay.'

'Thank you,' said Sharon. Immediately she began to feel apprehensive. Surely Zoe would oppose it?

Dylan strode into the conservatory, opened the French doors and went out into the garden.

After he'd gone they stood around awkwardly. Sharon forced a smile for Toni. 'Dylan said you're a secondary school teacher?'

'That's right. I make sure the kids receive their appropriate dollop of the National Curriculum. The parts of it they can cope with anyway.'

Sharon placed her carrier bag on the kitchen table. 'This is the work the school wants Louise to do while she's excluded.'

Toni removed text books, work sheets and lesson plans from the bag and appraised them professionally. 'Fine,' she said. 'I'll make sure she does this.' She peered at Louise indulgently. 'What's your favourite subject?'

'Drama.'

'You've come to the right place, then. We do lots of drama here.'

Toni began to chat to Sharon about houses. She told her how delighted they were with The Old Rectory. After Sharon had extolled the finer points of Honeysuckle Cottage, Toni revealed that the house her parents had purchased in London for just a couple of thousand pounds in the 1960s was now worth nearly half a million. 'Mum's there all on her own, now,' she added, somewhat sadly.

Dylan returned to the kitchen. 'It's OK,' he said to Sharon. 'We all more or less agree. Zoe will be delighted for Louise to come here.' He looked at Toni and by way of explanation said, 'Zoe managed to contact Eric on his mobile and he's happy for Louise to come too.'

The decision was never really in doubt: Zoe and Toni were deeply antagonistic towards each other and agreed on virtually nothing. Dylan had known all along that he only needed to tell Zoe that Toni was opposed to Louise being allowed to stay, and she'd automatically side with him. And Eric always agreed to anything Zoe asked.

Zoe entered the kitchen. She greeted Sharon with a broad smile and went straight over to Louise. 'You must be Louise. I gather you're going to be with us for a few days.'

'Yes,' said Louise, shyly.

'What's your favourite subject?'

'Drama.'

Toni held Louise's set work aloft. 'You won't have much time for drama, Louise. Not with all this work to do.'

Ignoring Toni, Zoe said, 'So, your favourite subject is drama? Well, we do lots of drama here. But not the kind you're probably familiar with.'

'That's fantastic, Lou, isn't it?' said Sharon. She turned to Zoe. 'Louise loves art and drama. I'm sure she'll be happy here.'

'Good,' said Zoe. She fixed Sharon with a challenging stare. 'So, changed your mind about us?'

Sharon blushed. Dylan had obviously told them what she'd said about inclusion units. 'Yes. I spoke without thinking. I take it all back.'

Zoe placed her hand on Sharon's arm. 'Don't worry about it. Glad we can be of some help.'

'Thank you, we're really very grateful.' She looked at her daughter. 'Aren't we, Louise?'

Louise nodded.

Sharon was disarmed by Zoe's unexpected friendliness and warmth. She didn't know that when Zoe had learnt that Sharon had a boyfriend and a daughter and wasn't the least bit interested in Dylan, she'd downgraded Sharon's level of threat. Even so, Zoe was a little concerned at Sharon's sudden reappearance and slightly worried that Dylan's interest in her might be rekindled, but that hadn't influenced her decision to allow Louise into the unit.

Louise was now telling Zoe about her role in "Oliver". Zoe appeared to be genuinely listening, and was being very nice and kind to Louise. Sharon was surprised, and began to wonder if she'd severely misjudged her. She had. Zoe's great misfortune was that she invariably created a poor first impression which was completely off-putting and prevented people from wishing to know her better. Those who did persevere with Zoe's daunting façade, found that she was a compassionate person with unrealistically high humanitarian ideals. Her goading, sarcastic manner was a panoply for her tender, compassionate nature, which she feared a cynical and unjust world would otherwise destroy.

'So, it's all right if I leave Louise here this afternoon? I've got to get back to work,' said Sharon.

'Sure,' said Dylan.

'And she can come here for the rest of the week? Until her exclusion is over?'

'Absolutely,' said Dylan. 'Now, before you go, you must come and meet the clients.'

Sharon looked at him quizzically. For her the word "clients" always had a specific professional connotation: clients were people who wanted to sell property.

'He means the kids,' said Zoe, acerbically.

Zoe said goodbye and went back into the garden. Dylan took Sharon along to the art therapy room. As they approached the door, she was unsure what to expect. She held Louise's hand tightly and prepared herself for scenes of some disorder and the presence of threatening characters. She was therefore pleasantly surprised to see a number of teenagers standing before easels or sitting at tables, completely absorbed in their drawings and paintings. What she couldn't know was that the moment they'd all become aware Dylan was returning, they'd quickly resumed these positions.

'Listen, everyone,' said Dylan, raising his voice and addressing the room. 'This is Louise and this is Sharon, her mum. Louise is going to spend the rest of the week with us.'

'Hello,' said Sharon. Louise said nothing but hung shyly back behind her mother.

The teenagers stared curiously. A couple nodded acknowledgement. One smiled a greeting.

Dylan explained the theme they were working on and invited Sharon to take a look at their work. Sharon was anxious to set off and return to the Carmels, but, given everything Dylan had done for her and Louise, she felt it would be churlish to just run. With Louise and Dylan at her side, she went from teenager to teenager looking at their paintings. When she'd seen them all she said to Dylan, 'These pictures are astonishing. But do they really tell you what the kids are like?'

'Of course. They represent their ideal selves. If you knew them as we do, you'd appreciate what their work is telling us.'

'And what will you do with them?'

'The paintings?'

'Yes.'

'Discuss them. We talk with the client about the suppressed feelings and conflicts they reveal; we also use the pictures as the basis for more art and drama therapy to explore these conflicts, and give the client a better understanding of themselves and their relationships. This gradually puts them in closer touch with what we call their authentic "felt self", and hopefully enables them to accept it.'

'Fascinating.' And, because she really meant it, she said, heartfully, 'It's so calm in here. So peaceful. Not what I expected at all. I'd love to stay longer but I have to get back to the office to attend to my own clients.'

Dylan said, 'It might help Louise to do some art therapy.'

Sharon immediately became guarded. 'How? How would that help her?'

'Painting and drawing often reveal why things are actually happening. For example, there might be issues between Louise and the woman she kicked on the leg.'

'I know she doesn't get on with her. She's always picking on her.'

'Well, the techniques I use might get to the bottom of it. Basically, it just involves painting, drawing and a bit of talking.'

'Louise is being bullied,' said Sharon, 'I'm sure of that.'

'Really? Art therapy might explain what's going on there too.'

Sharon had certain misgivings about Louise engaging in this, but she thought, 'Hell, it's only a bit of painting and drawing. What harm can it do?'

'I'll see you out,' said Dylan.

Sharon and Louise followed Dylan into the hall. He opened the front door and waited while Sharon said her goodbyes to Louise, kissed her on the forehead and told her to behave herself.

As Sharon stood on the doorstep taking her leave, it occurred to Dylan that here was an opportunity to enhance and extend this sudden renewal of their connection. It was weeks since their unsatisfactory dinner at The Trout, and he'd often thought of her since with a mixture of lust, disappointment and regret. He'd long ago resigned himself to the fact that she had a boyfriend, and was out of his life completely; but now events had magically transpired to propel her straight back into it. 'Do you want Louise to stay and have dinner with us?' he said. 'We usually eat about six-thirty.'

'No thanks. I'll collect her at six on the way home from work.'

CHAPTER NINETEEN

Isobel was standing at her kitchen window. She was watching Howard teaching the grandchildren how to play bowls. Mark and Jessica were at one end of the big rear lawn. On the ground, next to them, was a white jack and several woods. The Major was at the other end, about to bowl his last wood. He slipped his finger into the hole, cradled his right hand under the wood, felt its weight, and prepared to make his run up. 'I think this will surprise you,' he shouted.

Mark looked unconvinced. He placed his hands on his hips and grinned cheekily. 'Bet you can't do it.'

'You just watch me.'

'I bet he does do it,' said Jessica.

At the window Isobel felt a surge of affection for her blonde granddaughter. Only seven but always so loyal.

The Major ran slowly up to the mark and launched the wood, releasing it smoothly. He staggered forward a couple of steps, recovered and stood watching as the wood snaked in a long, long ellipse, first away from the target and then towards it, unbalancing more and more off its axis until finally it lost all speed, momentum and balance and lay down on its side bang next door to the jack.

Jessica was triumphant. 'You see!'

The Major was pleased. He playfully tousled Mark's hair. 'Never say die, Mark. Never say die!'

Smiling, Isobel turned away from the window. She closed it and went and sat down at the kitchen table on which there was a plastic bag of new potatoes, a knife and a bowl of water. Isobel's daughter, Barbara, was sitting on the other side of the table facing her.

Isobel picked up the knife, chose a potato and began to peel it. 'It's so lovely to see Howard enjoying himself,' she said. 'Mark and Jessica lighten him up so much.'

'The new tablets seems to be doing him a lot of good.'

'You think so?'

'Oh yes. He's lost all that dreadful aggression.'

Isobel sighed. 'If only he took them every day.'

'I thought he did?'

'No. He complains they make him drowsy. Which, of course, they do.'

Barbara nodded thoughtfully. 'I can see why he'd hate that.'

'But if he doesn't take them the "black dog" follows him around all the time. It's so worrying.' Isobel stopped peeling the potato. She looked vexed. 'We battle over it every day. At first he wouldn't take the tablets because he said they made him too drowsy to do any gardening. So we agreed he'd garden in the morning and take his pills in the afternoon. Of course, that meant he dozed off every afternoon until well into the evening. But at least he was taking them.'

'Sounds like a good solution.'

'It was, until those dreadful Corbridges put their house up for sale and decamped to Capri. He spent all day maintaining their gardens and didn't take his tablets until the evenings, which made him a pig to live with. And now he's got out of the habit of taking them regularly, he doesn't want them at all.'

'So he hasn't taken one today?'

'Oh yes, he has. I made him.'

'He doesn't seem all that drowsy.'

'He will be, you'll see. He'll be asleep on the sofa soon.'

Isobel placed the peeled potato in the bowl of water and placed the knife down on the table. 'When the rectory was sold I thought that was the end of our problems, but it's only made matters worse.'

Barbara sat up, interested. 'Really?'

Isobel was relieved to see the return of her daughter's usual vigour. When Barbara had arrived with the two children at lunchtime, Isobel had been perturbed by her diminished appearance. Barbara's normally glossy blonde hair was dull and lank and in need of a wash. Her eyes were without lustre, and the verve and panache that normally made her such a vivacious personality had been replaced by an uncharacteristically subdued and negative attitude that was most concerning. As they'd talked over lunch, Barbara's thoughts seemed to veer constantly off at tangents and settle elsewhere. When asked about Peter's fact-finding tour she'd been unusually vague and evasive, shifty almost. Isobel suspected that something was wrong.

'The arty types who've moved into the rectory couldn't give a damn about gardening,' Isobel explained. 'The front lawn hasn't been mown for weeks. The hedges and shrubs are a disgrace. He offered to do the gardens for them but they refused. Didn't want anyone to witness their drug taking, I expect.'

Barbara looked scandalised. 'They don't, do they?'

'I don't know. I hardly ever see them. I wouldn't be surprised though.'

'Poor dad. He was really proud of The Old Rectory.'

'Yes. Ironic, isn't it? After all his hard work it ends up looking like it belongs to someone on benefits.' Isobel sighed heavily. 'But he will keep going on about it, that's the annoying thing. He frets about losing the competition all the time. He's terrified the new owners will destroy our chances of a fifth gold medal.'

'Well,' said Barbara, quietly, 'it's important to him. It always has been.'

In exasperation, Isobel pressed both her wrists down on to the table. Her shoulders hunched. 'You always take his side, don't you? For heaven's sake, Barbara, the village has won the bloody thing four times in a row! What's the point of winning again?'

Barbara went silent, alarmed by her mother's vehemence. She could only gaze at her, shocked.

Isobel's look was immediately regretful. 'I'm sorry, darling, but I've had it up to here.' To indicate the extent of her distress, she raised the potato knife until it was level with her throat.

'I thought there was some talk of dad going back to the psychiatrist?' said Barbara.

'Oh, whatever you do, don't mention that. It sends him completely off the handle. Doctor Draper thinks it best to see how he responds to the new pills first.' Isobel began peeling the next potato. 'Anyway, how about you?'

'Me?'

'Well, you were rather tearful when you arrived.'

Barbara looked away. 'Oh, that was just me being sentimental. Thinking of my beautiful childhood and all that.'

Now Isobel was convinced that something was seriously wrong. She'd known her child in all her moods and this was completely uncharacteristic. Whatever could have happened? Could it be something to do with Barbara's health?

'Are you sure that's all it was?'

'Yes. You and daddy were very wrong to give me such a loving and idyllic upbringing.'

Isobel looked hurt. 'You can't mean that?'

'I do. It ruins you for adulthood. You don't expect to meet so many utter shits!'

'Like whom, for instance?'

'Oh, just people.'

There was a long pause during which Isobel finished peeling the second potato, placed it in the bowl and selected another. 'How long are you staying?' she asked, casually.

'I don't know. I haven't thought about it. Does it matter?'

'No. It's just that you hadn't said and I wondered, that's all.'

'How long can we stay?'

'As long as you want to, of course.'

'Good.' Barbara looked relieved. 'Thanks.'

'When are you expecting Peter back?'

Barbara shrugged and made an evasive gesture. 'I'm not really sure.'

Isobel was beginning to suspect that this story of Peter's fact-finding tour might be bogus. Peter had been an MP long enough for her to know that such things were set up well in advance. Strange then that Barbara hadn't mentioned it once in their weekly telephone conversations. And her sudden arrival with the children was most odd, quite out of character. Their visits were usually planned weeks beforehand.

'Look, if there's something wrong between you and Peter, you will tell me, won't you?'

'Don't be silly. Why should you think that?'

'You don't normally ring up on a Sunday night and announce you're coming the next day. You usually give us more notice.'

'I wanted to surprise you.'

'It did!'

There was another long pause. Isobel finished peeling the third potato and placed it in the bowl.

'And you don't normally come without Peter.'

It was at this point that Barbara could have taken the opportunity to unburden herself of all her matrimonial problems, but she resisted the temptation. She was clinging to the hope that Peter, who'd left her ten days previously to set up home with his best friend's daughter, would reconsider and eventually return.

'Mum, I'm in my thirties. I think it's about time I stepped out of his shadow. Don't you agree?'

At that moment Howard entered from the garden. He was sweating and red faced. 'Those two have exhausted me,' he said. 'I'm off for a short nap.'

Isobel and Barbara exchanged a brief look.

Howard's years of soldiering had given him an instinct as sensitive as a barometer. It was obvious that he'd intruded upon an "atmosphere".

'Anything wrong?'

'No,' said Isobel. 'Why should there be?'

CHAPTER TWENTY

Louise stood in the hall of The Old Rectory, stared at the front door as it swung shut and then listened to her mother's high heels receding down the gravelled drive and into the distance. The door seemed enormous, a huge, black barrier between herself and the outside world which, in some way she couldn't quite explain, seemed to express her feelings. With sudden and astonishing insight, she saw that in the years to come she would think of this door often, would perhaps dream about it, because, even now, she could see it as something significant, something that stood for much more than itself; and she knew that whenever she thought of it she would associate it with the specific feelings she had at that moment.

She listened to her mother's footsteps until they could be heard no more and then turned back into the hall. She looked up at the kind face of the tall, blonde stranger in whose charge she had been left, and wondered what lay in store. Everything felt strange and disorientating. From the art therapy room came the familiar sound of children's voices, just like at school, but these voices were lower in pitch and strangely alien, not like the voices of her classmates at all. They belonged to beings much older, much more rough-edged than herself. There were other sounds too: sounds of chairs being scraped, and the click of things being put down on desks or dropped on the floor; there were also occasional footsteps and the loud tick of a clock she couldn't see but which was very near at hand. And there were smells: familiar smells of paint and pencils and rubbers mixed in with wallpaper and damp; and other smells she couldn't identify: strong and vaguely unpleasant smells, like the stuff mum put paint brushes into when she'd finished decorating. Normally, such familiar sounds and smells would have made her feel secure, but the unaccustomed surroundings made even these normal sensations seem foreign and strange. Now the voices coming from the art therapy room seemed louder and more threatening. It was like being a new girl at school. She felt she was going to cry.

But Dylan was sensitive to her position and very much aware of how intimidating the experience was for her. 'Would you like something to drink, Louise?'

She stared back at him, uncertainly.

To encourage her, he said, 'We've got orange juice, apple juice or cranberry juice. What would you like?'

'Apple juice, please.'

'There's some in the kitchen,' he said. 'Follow me.'

He took a step or two down the hall in the direction of the kitchen and then stopped at the door of the art therapy room. He opened the door and put his head round it, so that he was looking into the room. He said something to those inside and then turned back to Louise.

'Go through to the kitchen, Louise, I'll be with you in a moment.'

He went further into the room and closed the door. Louise continued down the hall and into the kitchen. She could hear Dylan saying things to the kids. They'd gone very quiet. Perhaps he was telling them off. She went and stood next to the huge, American-style fridge freezer, and admired it.

Dylan joined her after a minute or two. He went to a cupboard and produced a paper cup. He smiled at Louise, and said, 'Is it still apple juice or have you changed your mind?'

'It's still apple juice.'

He went to the fridge and poured her the apple juice and handed it to her. 'Sorry it's a paper cup,' he said. 'Saves us a lot of money on breakages.'

The real reason for the paper cups was that several of the children in the unit had a history of self-harm, and as far as practicable were denied access to materials with which they could injure themselves. Dylan could see no possible reason why Louise needed to know this.

Louise's attention was drawn to footsteps in the hall. Toni, the teacher who didn't want her, came into the kitchen. She smiled and said "hello" in a really friendly way, and then she and Dylan began a conversation about something called rotas.

When they'd finished, Dylan said to Toni, 'I'd better get back.' Then he turned to Louise and said, 'Toni will take you through to the encouragement room. It's what you'd call a classroom. You can do your schoolwork in there.'

'OK.'

Dylan smiled again. 'Toni will look after you.'

Dylan left the kitchen and she heard him walk down the hall and then enter the art therapy room.

Toni pointed to the bag containing her schoolbooks. 'OK, Louise, pick up your stuff and we'll go through.'

The encouragement room was next to the stairs and was very much like a classroom, just as Dylan had said. It was full of desks and equipment and was not so different to her classroom at school, apart from there being a white board on the wall instead of a black board. The white board was covered with notes about using capital letters properly, which was strange because the kids in the unit were a lot older than her and ought to have been doing much harder work. Mrs Henshall had taught her about capital letters when she'd been in the infants. She stared at the writing on the white board which had been written in a mauve marker pen. It was a lovely colour.

Toni took Louise to a desk and helped her remove her schoolwork from the carrier bag.

'What would you like to do first, Louise? Maths? English?'

This too was strange. Mrs Henshall never gave you any choice: she just told you what you were going to do.

'We did literacy and numeracy this morning,' said Louise. 'Could I do some science please?'

'Sure.'

Toni found the science textbook and consulted the handwritten notes provided by Mrs Henshall that were paper-clipped to the cover. "Page 26. Revision of the Water Cycle," she said, reading aloud.

Toni turned to the appropriate page in the textbook and spent some minutes going through it, revising the core concepts of the water cycle for Louise. Then she handed her the science exercise book and asked her to answer the questions which were on page twenty seven of the text book.

'I'll leave you to get on with it,' said Toni. 'I'll be back in about twenty minutes to see how you're getting on.'

Toni left the room. Louise opened her exercise book and picked up her pen. But she didn't start writing immediately because she was listening to Dylan's voice which was coming from the art therapy room. He spoke for a long time but the door was closed and it was hard to hear what he was saying. Then some of the big kids were speaking. They were also hard to hear. Then Dylan spoke again. It was like being back at school only it wasn't.

She turned her attention to the questions about the water cycle. It was all so boring. She'd done the water cycle loads of times, and not just with Mrs Henshall. It was a favourite topic of supply teachers. Every time a supply teacher came, they made you revise the water cycle. She knew the water cycle backwards. She could answer questions about it in her sleep. Still, better get on with it. She didn't want to be thrown out of the rectory as well.

The full significance of her exclusion was beginning to impact on her. It had been so unexpected. The shock of her rejection and the way the school had cast her out made her feel tearful. It was crushing to be made so clearly aware that you weren't wanted. But Mrs Henshall had had no choice. She could see that. She'd behaved very badly. Mrs Henshall was quite right to exclude her. If she'd been in Mrs Henshall's place she would have done exactly the same thing.

Hearing footsteps in the hall, Louise assumed that it was Toni returning. She began writing conscientiously. But it was Zoe who entered the room. She stopped and gave Louise a huge smile. 'How are you getting on, Louise?'

Louise wondered how genuine Zoe's smile was. 'All right, thanks.'

Zoe came and stood by Louise's table. 'Oh, you're doing the water cycle.'

'Yes.'

'Do you like science?'

'Yes. I quite like it.'

'Well, it's good to see you're settling in all right,' said Zoe.

'Yes. It's very nice here,' said Louise, continuing to write.

Zoe left Louise and went over to a cupboard which she opened. After searching inside it, she sighed and closed the cupboard door sharply. She'd obviously not found what she was looking for. She came back to Louise and again started talking to her. She seemed to be just chatting, but Louise was guarded. You could never tell with teachers, not even nice ones like Zoe. It could be a trick to make her reveal something. Perhaps she was trying to prise something out of her. Mum had warned her about that on the way to the rectory. She was glad when Toni came back into the room and Zoe started telling her that she was trying to find some thick card. They searched through the cupboards without success and then Toni said she thought Dylan might have stored it in the studio, and they both went out.

Louise had answered six questions and was starting on the seventh, when she heard the door of the art therapy room open. She stopped writing and listened to the sound of the big kids moving out of it and coming down the hall. They all seemed to be going into the room that was across the hall from the room she was in.

A girl suddenly appeared in the doorway of the encouragement room. She was about sixteen and had dark, curly hair, huge hazel eyes and the honey brown skin of a child of mixed race. Louise remembered that her name was Mona, because when she'd first heard it she'd immediately thought of the word "moaner", which was strange because Mona looked really nice and not at all like someone who whinged all the time. That's why she'd remembered Mona's name and no-one else's.

'We're all in the chill-out room,' said Mona. 'It's break time. Wanna come? Dylan sent me to tell you.'

Louise stared at her, surprised. It still seemed strange to hear someone who was a sort of pupil referring to their sort of teacher by their Christian name. She considered Mona's invitation. Toni had said she would pop back to see how she was getting on. Hadn't she better stay where she was?

'Don't you want a break?' said Mona, coming further into the room.

'I don't know,' said Louise. 'That teacher said she was coming back to look at my work.'

Mona looked puzzled. 'Teacher?' Then came enlightenment. 'Oh, Toni. Don't worry about her. She'll check you out later. It's not like school here.'

'OK.' Somewhat apprehensively, she followed Mona out of the encouragement room and into the hall. Shrill, excited voices issued through the open door of the room facing her. She loitered in the hall for a moment preparing herself, and then entered the chill-out room, bracing herself for the awful moment when everyone's eyes would fix on her. But it never happened. One or two of the big kids looked up as she came in, glanced at her briefly and then returned their attention to whatever was occupying them. In a way it was a bit of an anti-climax and she felt oddly disappointed.

The room itself made her feel immediately at ease. It really was a chill-out room: a snooker table was in the centre of it and at the far end, towards the window, a table tennis table had been set up. Around the edge of the room there were a lot of old chairs that looked as though they'd come from junk shops. The largest seat in the room was a huge sofa. It looked like it could sit eight people and was really scruffy. Two older boys were sprawling on it and sharing a bottle of mineral water. They were both laughing hysterically at something or other. She found them slightly intimidating and yet, at the same time, was strangely drawn to them. One was white but the other one looked a bit black or Asian. Both of them were really good looking. Some girls were lying back on big beanbags that had been scattered around. In one corner, two lads were sitting cross legged on the carpet concentrating on a Play Station game.

'Want some?' said Mona, pointing at a coffee table on which there were apples, biscuits, crisps and bottles of mineral water.

Louise took a bottle of mineral water and a few crisps and went and sat with Mona on one of the smaller sofas.

'Did you get slung out of school?' asked Mona.

Louise considered carefully. She was wondering how much it would be safe to divulge. 'Yes. I was being bullied so I fought back and the teachers didn't like it.'

Mona nodded understandingly. 'That's what happened to me.'

'You were excluded?'

'I've been slung out of loads of schools.'

'Wow,' said Louise, genuinely impressed.

'And foster homes.'

'How terrible.'

'Ah, it's nothing,' said Mona. 'If I hadn't been slung out of them places I wouldn't be here.'

Louise said, 'Do you like it here?'

'Yeah, it's all right.'

'I think so too. But don't you miss your mum?'

'Ain't got a mum,' Mona said, matter of factly. 'She ran off when I was a baby.'

Louise was about to ask Mona more, but Dylan entered the room followed by Toni. They both came straight over to Mona and Louise.

'So, Mona's looking after you, Louise,' said Toni. 'That's good.'

Dylan said, 'Toni thinks you've done enough schoolwork for today, Louise. We're going back to the art therapy room in a minute. Would you like to come with us and do some drawing?'

'OK.'

Toni and Dylan chatted to Louise for a while, and then they drifted away to talk to others and eventually went out. Louise wanted to talk to Mona some more about her mother and find out why she'd run off and left her baby, but Mona had moved across the room and was now talking and laughing with three other girls. Louise felt too shy to just go over and join them. She sat drinking her water out of the bottle and kept taking sly, sideways glances at Mona. She seemed so grown-up. She was wearing black trousers and a kind of little black vest. Her arms were bare and there were tattoos on them. There were also lots of piercings in her ears. Louise thought she looked amazing.

Dylan reappeared in the room. He said loudly, 'OK. Time to go back now.'

Reluctantly, everyone got up and headed back to the art therapy room. Louise followed, and in the art therapy room Dylan led her to a table by the window. He went over to a cupboard and returned with A3 cartridge paper and a number of variously coloured pencils, pens and crayons. He set these down in front of Louise and said 'You like drawing, don't you?'

'Yes.'

'I'd like you to draw something. Is that all right?'

'Yes.'

'Do you read comics?'

'Sometimes.'

'Good. Now, what I'd like you to do is think of all the things that led up to you being excluded. Do you think you can do that?'

'Yes. I think so.'

'Great. Then I'd like you to draw everything that happened in the order that it happened. Can you do that?'

'Yeah. OK.'

'I'd like you to draw it in a series of frames, you know, like a strip you'd find in a comic.'

Dylan told her that this was called a storyboard and he showed her how to construct the frames, draw people inside them and write their spoken words in speech balloons.

Afterwards, he again asked her if she was happy about doing this. Yes, she said, she was very happy doing it. It made her feel strange to be asked yet at the same time she liked it. It made her feel good somehow. She was unaware that it was a strategy Dylan consciously employed as a matter of course when dealing with abused and disaffected children. Very often their experience was that of victims who'd had no say in decisions about their own lives. Dylan's objective was to restore their self-esteem by respecting them as persons. He believed they would become more autonomous and mature if given the opportunity to take control of their decisions and own them.

'Now, you're probably wondering why I'm asking you to draw this storyboard. Is that right?'

Louise nodded.

'The reason is that, sometimes, in order to understand why we behaved in a certain way it helps to focus step by step on what we actually did. Then we can think about how, if we'd acted differently at any point, things might have turned out better. It also helps us to see what happened from the point of view of the other people who were there.'

He paused and looked at her and she was discomfited by the earnest look on his face. She returned his gaze guardedly. What was he up to? Why did he really want her to do this? She knew that it was in her interest to co-operate, but she had the same feeling about it she'd had when Zoe had been speaking to her. Could he be trying to trick her into revealing something that mum wouldn't want her to reveal?

As though sensing her suspicions, Dylan gave her a sympathetic smile and said, in a tone of complete understanding, 'Of course, if at any time you feel you don't want to do this you're free to go back to the encouragement room and do some more of your school work. I won't mind, honestly.'

Dylan's words reassured Louise and made her feel certain that he wasn't trying to trip her up. Actually, he was all right, she decided. Normally, when she'd done something wrong and teachers started questioning her about it, the tight feeling in her chest would come and she'd be dying to jump up and rush off: get away as far as she could, anywhere as long as she didn't have to think about it and face the facts of her wrongdoing. But Dylan didn't make her feel like that. His voice was steady and calm; and he was kind and understanding; he just seemed interested in making her feel better, not in telling her off or anything. She liked that. The idea of doing the storyboard appealed to her too.

'I won't be able to draw as good as you,' she said.

'Don't worry about that. Draw stick figures if you want. Just do your best.' He stood up. 'I'll come back in a while to see how you're getting on.'

He moved off, and ambled slowly around the room stopping occasionally to observe a client's work, make a comment or ask a question about it.

Louise found that constructing the storyboard was quite easy. As she steadily became engrossed in the drawing she became calmer and began to feel more at ease. All of her concentration became focussed on selecting the appropriate content for each frame and depicting it economically and effectively. She was determined to describe what had happened from her point of view, and present her actions in the most positive light.

Gradually the art therapy room, the people in it, the world itself, receded; and the only thing that mattered was the large piece of cartridge paper in front of her and the images she was creating freely on it. For the first time that day she felt truly in control of events. She was able to put her own interpretation on what had led to her exclusion and depict it without interference from anyone else. And there was an even greater benefit: Jade wasn't there. She was far away at school, and she didn't have to think about her or worry about what she'd say.

She'd been given a great opportunity to present her side of the story, and, for once, Jade wasn't there to deny it.

As she worked on, Louise began to experience a beautiful sensation, like the one she had when she was acting or singing. She was taking pleasure in the drawing and finding the act of communicating solely through images completely stimulating. So much better than talking because when you talked about it no-one believed you, particularly Mrs Henshall. But there was another feeling too, one that was unfamiliar. Somehow, what she was creating made her feel good about herself. The storyboard seemed to be saying to her, "If you can make something as good as me, there can't be that much wrong with you. Really, you're all right. You're quite OK".

She began to hum "As Long As He Needs Me" very quietly, and for the first time that day felt completely at one with everything.

****

Louise was putting a final flourish to the drawings when Dylan returned to her table. He sat down next to her and stared at the storyboard for a long time. Louise had produced just three frames: frame one depicted her and Roger playing together; frame two showed Jade shouting abuse at both of them; and in frame three Roger had vanished, Louise and Jade were fighting and Mrs Lucas was trying to separate them.

Dylan switched his attention from the storyboard to Louise. Her resemblance to her mother was really quite extraordinary: same hazel eyes, same snub nose, same chestnut hair. But who was her father?

'So,' he said, finally, 'would you like to tell me what the first frame is about?'
'It's me and Roger playing in the playground.'
'Right. Who's Roger?'
'A boy in my class.'
'A friend?'
'Well, sort of.'
'And you're playing a game?'
'Yes.'
Dylan waited for her to go on and tell him more, but she stayed silent.
'Tell me a bit about the game you're playing,' he said.
'It's just a chasing game. You know, like tag.'
Again, Louise became silent. She was waiting for Dylan to compliment her on her drawing. She'd gone to a lot of trouble to make the storyboard perfect and was feeling enormously proud of what she'd created. In fact, Dylan was very impressed with Louise's efforts and could see that she had a genuine talent for art. Yet, he'd decided not to praise her because he felt it would be a distraction. He wanted her to appreciate that the storyboard's content was more important than its form, no matter how aesthetically pleasing that might be.

'Do you and Roger play tag at every break?' Dylan asked.

She shook her head. 'Not always. Sometimes.'

'You and Roger seem to be playing together quite happily.'

Louise said nothing.

'Is that right?'

'Yes.'

'What's Roger like?'

She shrugged her shoulders. 'He's all right.'

'OK. Let's move on to frame two. Another person's joined you and Roger now.'

'Yes.'

'Who's that?'

'That's Jade.'

'Is she one of your friends?'

'She was, but not any more.'

Dylan waited for Louise to expound on this, but it became clear she wasn't going to.

'Right. So just tell me what's happening in this frame.'

'Jade's calling out nasty, horrible things about me and Roger.'

Quietly, Dylan read aloud Jade's speech bubble. "You love Roger because he's got no dad just like you!" When he'd finished, he said, 'And that's what she actually said to you?'

'It's not true!' Louise said, vehemently. She took a quick look round the room and saw that several of the big kids had stopped working and were staring at her. She immediately withdrew into herself.

Dylan was taken aback by the intensity of Louise's feeling. 'What's not true?' he asked.

She meant it wasn't true that she hadn't got a dad. She'd been about to tell Dylan this but she knew mum would be horrified. Instead, she whispered, 'It's not true that I love Roger. I don't!'

Dylan said quietly, 'Why do you think she's saying it?'

'Because she knows it makes me mad. She's always saying that Roger's my boyfriend and I love him. It's not true.'

Dylan pointed to frame two. 'Jade is also saying that Roger's got no dad. Is that untrue too?'

'No. That's true. Roger's dad was killed at work. Something happened to his tractor.'

Dylan was tempted to ask her about her own father but decided it was too early to go there. 'Does Jade often say things like that to you?'

'All the time. She's a bully.'

'Jade bullies you?'

'Yes.'

'Have you told anyone about this?'

'Yeah. But they don't believe me.'

Dylan's gaze returned to the storyboard. 'OK. Would you like to tell me what's going on in the last frame?'

'Jade and I are fighting and Mrs Lucas is trying to stop us.'

'Is that when you kicked Mrs Lucas in the leg?'

'Yes.' Louise looked ashamed. 'I didn't draw a picture of that because you already knew about it.'

Dylan was about to tell Louise that they were doing this for her not for him, but he checked himself and said, 'So this frame is about your fight with Jade?'

'Yes.'

'Would you like to describe how the fight started?'

Flatly, she said, 'I can't remember. It just started.'

'Try to think about what led to the first blow. Can you do that?'

Louise swallowed. The tight feeling in her chest was starting. 'I told you, I can't remember!'

Dylan suspected that this was crucial. He decided to gently press her on it. 'Did you hit Jade first?'

So, he was just like all the others.

'Why are people always on at me?' she demanded, loudly. 'It was Jade who started it! She said those horrible things about me and Roger! Then she hit me!'

This time she didn't care that they were all staring at her.

'It's OK, everyone,' said Dylan, turning round in his seat and addressing the room. 'Go on with your tasks, please.' His attention went back to Louise. 'Please, calm down, Louise. There's absolutely no need for you to defend yourself. I haven't asked you to draw this storyboard because I think it was all your fault. I'm not here to tell you off. All I'm trying to do is help you be very clear about what happened. I'm not trying to blame you, OK?'

Louise looked abashed. 'OK.'

'I'm going to promise you something. This storyboard is confidential. It's your own private account of what happened. I promise you that anything you draw here will be treated with respect and won't be shown to anyone else without your permission. And any discussions you and I have about it will also be confidential unless you say otherwise. Does that help?'

Louise nodded.

'You don't have to talk about your exclusion with anyone, if you don't want to. Not even me. But I hope you will, because drawing a storyboard about your exclusion and talking about it may help you understand why it happened. It might even prevent you from being excluded again. Now, I hope you believe me when I say I'm not trying to blame you. Do you?'

'Yes.'

'Good. Right, I think we'll stop now. But before we do, is there anything you particularly want to ask me or tell me?'

'Yes, I do.' She was suddenly animated again. 'I don't think it was fair of Mrs Henshall to exclude me. It was Jade's fault we started fighting, not mine. She's the one who started it and said all those horrible things to me and Roger. I'm always being blamed for everything Jade does, because her dad sticks up for her and protects her!'

'And your dad doesn't?'

She looked at him warily. Was this another trick? Did he know all about mum and dad?

'I haven't got a dad,' she said.

'Oh yes, you have,' said Dylan.

Relief flooded through Louise. He knew. She didn't have to pretend.

'The one thing we can all be sure of is that we have a father somewhere,' said Dylan. 'Otherwise, we wouldn't be here.'

That wasn't what she'd expected. She felt angry and sick. Disappointed that the awful secret still remained with her and frightened that she'd nearly given it all away!

Although Dylan was unaware of how close he'd come to stumbling upon the truth, he knew from experience that Louise's storyboard was incomplete. He said, 'Louise, tonight I'd like you to go over all the events that led to you being excluded and decide if there's anything you've left out of your storyboard.'

'You mean like me kicking Mrs Lucas?'

'Yes. But it doesn't have to be as big or important as that. Anything will do. Any little thing that'll help make the storyboard clearer to someone who's seeing it for the first time, and doesn't even know you've been excluded.'

Louise looked at him unsurely. 'All right. Why?'

'Because tomorrow I'd like you to draw the storyboard again, but with much more detail. The more frames you can add to it, the better.'

'OK.'

For some reason, the prospect of drawing the storyboard all over again and improving it, filled her with extraordinary pleasure.

****

Sharon arrived at six to collect Louise. The front door of the rectory was opened by Sheldon, a tall youth of about fifteen, with light brown skin and piercing blue eyes.

'Hello, Sharon,' said the youth.

She was surprised that he'd remembered her name. She certainly couldn't remember his.

'I've come to collect Louise,' she said.

'She's in the chill-out room.'

A lovely cooking smell was permeating the house. Sheldon led her down the hall and opened a door to his right. Sharon followed him inside. She couldn't believe the extraordinary transformation which had taken place since the Corbridges' time. Bruce and Ruby's beautiful sitting room had been turned into a seedy youth club. Several teenagers were in there playing table football. Sharon looked around for Louise, and found her sitting on the floor in front of a TV with an Asian boy. They were both intensely absorbed in a Play Station game. The youth who'd led Sharon into the room went over to Louise and touched her on the shoulder. 'Your mum's here.'

Louise turned, saw her mother, smiled and waved.

'Have you had a good time?' asked Sharon.

Louise nodded shyly. The youth next to her sniggered.

'Let's go, then,' said Sharon.

'Oh, mum! Can't I stay and finish this?'

'No. Sorry, we've got to go.'

'Oh, all right!' snapped Louise. She handed over the game console to the boy next to her. 'Bye Khaled. See you tomorrow.'

Sharon took Louise's hand and led her into the hall. As they came out of the chill-out room Dylan came flying down the stairs. 'Hi Sharon,' he called.

'How's she been?' asked Sharon.

Instead of answering her, Dylan addressed Louise. 'How do you think it went? Did you enjoy the afternoon?'

Louise looked at him unsurely. She wanted to come back tomorrow. If she didn't sound enthusiastic they might not let her return. 'Yeah. It was great. Really great.'

Dylan turned to Sharon. 'Louise did some drawing for me. She also did some science. Hang on, I'll get it.' He shot into the encouragement room and returned with Louise's school work. 'You'll probably want to check it,' he said.

Sharon took the carrier bag from him. 'So she's been all right? No problems?'

'Any problems, Louise?' asked Dylan.

'No.'

'You see, it's been fine.'

'So it's all right for her to come back tomorrow?'

'It's OK by me.' He turned to Louise. 'Would you like to come back tomorrow, Louise?'

'Yeah. It's cool.'

'Thank you,' said Sharon. Her enormous sense of relief was bringing her close to tears. She made a herculean effort to suppress them. 'I really don't know how to thank you.'

'No problem. Look, we're just about to start supper. Some of the kids prepare it under our supervision but it's usually quite edible. Sure you won't stay and have some?'

Sharon knew there was more to his offer than mere formal politeness. It made it much harder to refuse him. 'No, thank you. I've got something for us to heat up.'

Louise threw her mother a pleading glance. 'Go on, mum, please. I'd like to.'

'No, Louise. You know I'm expecting visitors.'

'Huh,' retorted Louise, and turned away.

Sharon felt an urgent need to leave. 'I'm sorry,' she said.

'All right,' said Dylan. 'We'll see you tomorrow.'

****

During the short drive home, Sharon asked Louise if Dylan had been pleased with her art work.

'I don't want to talk about it,' said Louise.

'Oh, Lou, don't get all in a huff because I wouldn't stay for supper.'

'It's not that. Dylan says that whatever I draw or paint there is mine and it's private. It'll be treated with respect. I don't have to share it or talk about it to anyone unless I want to.'

'But Dylan saw it, didn't he?'

'Yes.'

'Well, didn't he say anything about it? Whether it was any good or not?'

'It's not like that. It's not like a picture you do in school and teachers say, "Oh, that's good".'

'So Dylan didn't say anything about the drawing at all?'

'No. He just looked at it and then put it away in a big folder.'

Sharon was perplexed, but said no more. Louise turned her head away and stared intently out of the side window. 'And anyway,' she said suddenly, 'it wasn't just one drawing. It was several drawings. Like a comic strip. It told a story. Dylan called it a storyboard.'

'But what was the story about?'

'Mum!'

Sharon knew from Louise's stubborn tone that she'd get no further information out of her. Mother and daughter were silent as the car pulled up outside their cottage.

However, over dinner, Louise was more forthcoming and described everything that had happened to her from the moment Sharon had left her in the rectory. Sharon heard what Zoe and Toni had said to Louise, and her conversation with Mona was described at some length. Louise repeated Mona's shocking information that she'd been left by her mother when she was just a baby, but she refused to relate any of her conversations with Dylan or describe the content of her storyboard. However, she continued to blame Jade for her exclusion and insisted once again that she'd been a victim of her bullying. As she listened to Louise, Sharon became more and more angry on her behalf.

After dinner, Louise took herself up to her room to prepare for her rehearsal. The two performances of "Oliver" were to take place in the village hall that coming Friday and Saturday, and rehearsals were to be held every evening until opening night.

Sharon cleared away the dishes, stayed in the sitting room and finished her glass of Australian red wine. She was steeling herself to receive a phone call or even possibly a visit from Greg.

As she reflected on Louise's reluctance to discuss her storyboard and describe its contents, she became increasingly alarmed. Had Louise used the storyboard to reveal her unorthodox family circumstances? Was that why she didn't want to talk about it?

Emboldened by another glass of wine, Sharon rang the rectory and was eventually passed on to Dylan.

'Hello? Sharon?'

The warmth in his voice was pleasantly unexpected. He sounded genuinely delighted to hear from her.

She said, 'I'm sorry to bother you again.'

'It's no bother.'

'It's just that I was talking to Louise about her comic strip, a storyboard, I think she called it.'

'Yes?'

'Well, she didn't seem to want to discuss it.' Louise paused uncertainly. There was no response from the other end, so she continued, 'In fact, she seemed very secretive about it and I'm starting to get worried she's revealing things in the storyboard that she shouldn't.'

'Things that she shouldn't?'

'Yes, you know, personal things.' Sharon realised that her voice had risen shrilly, but she had to go on. 'Private things about me and... and other people. Because I wouldn't like that. I wouldn't like our family life held up for all to see. You understand that, don't you?'

Dylan realised that bland assurances wouldn't be sufficient. 'There's no need to worry about that, Sharon. The storyboard is just an exercise. It's designed to help people focus and reflect on the events that got them into trouble. They draw the sequence of incidents that led up to their inappropriate behaviour, and this enables them to reflect on ways they could have handled the situation differently. Usually some kind of pattern emerges that they can identify. Then we talk to them about how they can break the pattern, and avoid falling into the same downward spiral over and over again. So today, I encouraged Louise to storyboard the events that caused her to be excluded, and I got her to talk about each frame of the storyboard. It was all about what happened in the playground. It had nothing to do with your family life or anything like that.'

Here Dylan stopped. He wanted to go on to explain that all of the artefacts created through art therapy to some extent reflected the nexus of personal and family connections of the client. But Louise wasn't technically a client, and Sharon was obviously upset, so he concluded that such information would only introduce an unnecessary level of complexity. All Sharon needed was to be reassured that creating a storyboard would produce positive and beneficial outcomes for Louise.

Sharon was somewhat mollified by what she'd heard. She said, 'Sounds a good idea. If it makes her stop and think instead of lashing out, it'll be very helpful. I was just worried that it might have something to do with her life with me.'

'No. We only focussed on the incidents that lead to her exclusion.'

'Oh, good.'

'If you're still concerned maybe we could meet up in The Woldsman later on this evening and I could tell you more about the storyboard technique.'

She immediately shrank at the suggestion. The thought of going to the local for a tête-à-tête with Dylan, although appealing, filled her with consternation. The Woldsman was the centre of the broadcasting network for all village gossip, and all new liaisons were immediately reported. The jungle drums would work themselves into a frenzy if she walked in there with a man. And what would happen if Greg was in the bar?

'I'm sorry, that's not possible. I told you, I've got visitors this evening.'

'Of course, I forgot. Oh well, another time then. How about tomorrow?'

She moved quickly to scotch any further invitations. 'No, it's not necessary. I understand all about the storyboard now, and anyway, you can tell me more about it at the end of the week when Louise has done some more drawing.'

'Sure,' said Dylan. 'Can I say something, though?'

'Yes.'

'Can I suggest that you don't question Louise too much about the art work she does with us.'

'Why not?'

'Well, in my experience asking too many questions tends to inhibit them from expressing themselves freely.'

'Well, I wouldn't want to do that!'

Dylan ignored her sarcasm. 'Just give her time. When she feels confident about discussing the art work with you, she'll talk about it quite happily. And, of course, if she gives her permission, I'll show you all the paintings and drawings she does with us. Anything else I can help you with?'

'No. No. I don't think so.'

'Good. By the way, Jake and Rupa helped cook the meal tonight. It was Moussaka. Toni supervised. She's a great cook. I can't boil an egg, but she's brilliant. They were all sorry you and Louise couldn't join us.'

'Well, as I said, I'm expecting visitors.'

They talked a little longer before ending the call. As she put the phone down, Sharon felt momentary regret that she and Louise hadn't stayed for supper at the rectory. The burden of the secret she was carrying was hiving her off from social life and normal experience. How much more of this self-imposed social isolation could she stand? She dreaded to think what it was doing for her sanity, and where it would all end.

Louise appeared in the doorway. Her face fell when she saw the glass of wine in her mother's hand.

'You'd better not forget to come and get me,' she said. 'I don't want another lift home in Pam's car.'

CHAPTER TWENTY ONE

Barbara's nightmare started on Monday evening as she watched television in the sitting room with Isobel and the children. She was comfort gorging on an extra-large box of Swiss chocolates and Mark and Jessica were demanding their fair share, when the telephone rang.

'Answer it, would you,' said Isobel, who was engrossed in her cross-stitch. 'It's probably for daddy. Tell them he's at a meeting and won't be back until after nine.'

Barbara relinquished possession of the chocolates, went out to the hall and picked up the phone. An unfamiliar cockney voice asked to speak to Barbara Kellingford. Barbara was surprised. Only Peter and Russell were supposed to know she was staying with her parents.

'I'm Barbara Kellingford. Who's this?'

'Terry Bryden, Mrs Kellingford. Chief political reporter with The Source. I just wondered how you felt about your husband running off with a girl of seventeen?'

Barbara's face drained of colour. She slammed the phone down and returned to the sitting room in a state of dazed shock.

'Who was it?' her mother asked.

Barbara was about to say it was a wrong number, but the phone started ringing again. She decided her only course was to lie. 'A horrible reporter trying to get information about some negotiations Peter's involved in. I hung up on him.'

'How did he know you were here?'

'I don't know.'

Isobel looked concerned. 'But how's he got our number?'

Barbara looked distraught. 'I don't know!'

The phone continued ringing.

'That's probably him, again,' said Isobel.

'Yes.'

'You won't be answering it, then.'

'I most certainly will not.'

'It might not be him though. It might be someone for daddy or me.' Isobel went back into the hall to check the phone's digital display. She called the number out. 'I don't recognise that one. It must be your reporter.'

Isobel returned to the sitting room and they all listened to the ringing tone, waiting for it to stop. How the hell did this Bryden man know she was with her parents? And how had he got hold of their number? Unless... An unthinkable and terrifying possibility occurred to her.

'Mum, do something about the phone! I'm trying to watch this!' screamed Mark, positioning himself nearer to the television.

'Piss off!' Barbara shouted at the phone in the hall.

'Disconnect it,' Isobel said, quietly.

Barbara ran back into the hall, pulled the phone lead out of the wall socket and returned to the sitting room.

Immediately her mobile's ring tone was signalling an incoming call. Barbara clasped both hands to her face. 'Oh no!'

In Barbara's bag were two mobiles: one black, one blue. The black one was for everyday; the blue one was used by her and her husband only for emergencies. It was the blue one that was being called.

She picked up her bag, walked quickly out of the sitting room and closed the door behind her. Only when she was safely in the hallway did she take the blue mobile out of her bag and answer.

'Peter?'

'Yes.'

'Where are you?'

'In the car just down the road from the flat. I can't go in. There's a reporter and a photographer camped outside it.'

'Really?'

'Have you been talking?'

'Of course not!'

Aware that loud indignation was entering her voice, Barbara started to climb the stairs. She was heading for the bedroom. Privacy was essential for this sort of call.

'Are you sure you haven't said anything?' demanded Peter.

'Oh, come on!'

'Well someone obviously has.'

'Perhaps Russell did. Have you asked him?'

'We haven't been able to reach him. Besides, he's no longer talking to us.'

That "we" and "us" really hurt. She said, 'I'm not surprised. He's furious. Devastated.' A sudden thought inspired hope. 'Did you say the reporters are outside our flat?'

'Yes.'

'What are you doing there?'

'I came to pick up some more clothes.'

Despair made her silent.

'Barbara? Are you still there?'

She said, 'I thought you might have decided to return home.'

'No. You know we've been through all that.'

'So you're still with Clarissa?'

'Yes.'

'Then why are you ringing me?'

'I wanted to know if you'd been on to the press, and what you'd said.'

'Of course, I haven't. But someone from The Source rang here just before.'

'The Source? My God! What did they want?'

'He was kindness itself. He wanted to know how I felt about you running off with a seventeen year old.'

'Fuck! What did you say?'

'I told him I was delighted.'

'Come on. What did you say?'

'Nothing. I slammed the phone down and took it off the hook.'

'My God, The Source!'

'You can still save yourself. Give her up and come back.'

'I told you I...'

'We can sort it out.'

'No!' His long, exasperated sigh said it all. 'Have you told Howard and Isobel yet?'

'Not yet. I was hoping I wouldn't have to.'

'Well, I think you should.'

'I haven't told the children either.'

There was a pause.

He said, 'I think you'd better tell them too.'

Now she knew it was hopeless. Yet she still couldn't believe it.

'Look... I've got to go. I wanted you to know I've arranged with the Post Office for all my mail to be re-directed.'

'You bastard!'

There was so much more Barbara wanted to say to Peter on the subject of his character, but was unable to do so as he'd already terminated the call. She stared dumbly at the mobile, as though it was a social hand grenade and she was unsure whether or not to pull the pin. Years as a political wife had made her instinctively strategic. The blue mobile she was holding was only ever used by her and Peter. Barbara had insisted on this contingency after Jessica had been taken ill one day and she couldn't get through to Peter because his mobile had been switched off. He'd said it had been unavoidable because he'd been in a meeting and didn't want to be disturbed, but Barbara wasn't fooled. She knew he'd turned it off because he'd been screwing Valerie, one of his latest amusements. The upshot was that they'd agreed to buy another mobile which was to be used exclusively for calling each other in emergencies, and would remain switched on at all times. So far, this arrangement had worked perfectly. But Barbara knew that, great as the temptation was, if she now called Peter back on the blue mobile and started abusing him he might be tempted to switch it off permanently, thereby depriving her of this exclusive and reliable means of communicating with him.

Having considered, Barbara tossed the blue mobile on to her bed, reached into her bag and took out the black mobile. She found the number of Russell Forbes' landline in the phone's address book, and when it appeared on screen pressed "Call". His phone rang several times before she was transferred to voicemail. 'Hello Russell. It's Barbara here. I need to speak to you urgently. Please call me back as soon as you can. Probably best to call me on my mobile. The press seem to have got hold of my parents' number even though it's ex-directory.'

Barbara's next call was to Russell's own mobile. But this was switched off and, again, she was transferred to voicemail. She left the same message as before and was just about to put her black mobile away when she saw that there were fifteen voicemail messages awaiting her attention. She accessed the first message and into her ear poured the coarse, cockney tones of Terry Bryden, the chief political reporter from The Source. After giving his mobile number, he invited her to ring him back and tell him what she thought about her "hubby" running off with Clarissa Forbes. The final part of his message was faux sympathetic. "I mean, it's bang out of order, innit? His best friend's seventeen year old daughter? What a love-rat! Come on Barbara. Give us your side of the story!" Despite the message's humiliating content, Barbara had to smile. Even when they were speaking normally it appeared that The Source's reporters still employed tabloid patois. As a former teacher of English as a Foreign Language, she found that vaguely amusing.

As she suspected, all of the voicemail messages were from Bryden. She took great pleasure in deleting every one of them.

****

Shortly after Louise left for her rehearsal, Sharon went over to the collection of vinyl records which was stored on a shelf in the alcove next to the fireplace. The records had been owned by Archie, her late father. She selected a recording of Tchaikovsky's Violin Concerto and set it to play on her father's music centre which, although it dated from the 1970s, still produced sound of excellent quality. She poured out another glass of Australian red and sat on the sofa, relishing the soothing effect of the wine and music upon her mood. Her father had been a great admirer of Tchaikovsky's work, and when she'd been thirteen he'd told her that the violin concerto was the happiest piece of music the composer had written because at the time of writing it, Tchaikovsky had fallen in love. When her father had told her this, she'd assumed that the object of

Tchaikovsky's affection had been a woman. Now the joyous music was transporting her back to those days of youth and innocence when it was easy to make such naïve assumptions; a byway in time, where, for the moment she was happy to linger, immersing herself in her childhood, and the hours spent in that same room with her parents.

The music ended. She brought her hands up to her face and with the tips of her fingers touched the wet patches around her eyes and cheeks. It's no good, she thought, as she moved across the room to collect a tissue from the box on the sideboard, I must stop hiding in the past. She dabbed at her tears, and forced herself to think of something in the present. Immediately, she thought of her earlier conversation with Dylan, particularly his suggestion that they might meet up for a drink in The Woldsman. The idea of having a drink with him on such a lovely evening seemed very attractive. If only she'd been in a position to take him up on it. An image of her and Dylan sitting together at one of the tables in the pub's garden under a dappling of late evening sunlight came into her mind. She indulged in this happy fantasy for a while, until it was ended by her indignation at the circumstances in her life which prevented her from accepting his invitation.

The telephone rang, making her start. She sprang up from the sofa to take the call. It was Greg. He was about to attend a Magnificent Britain Sub-Committee meeting and was calling from his car which was parked outside the village hall.

'Thought I'd give you a quick call to apologise.'

Sharon said nothing.

'You're not still angry, are you?'

'No.'

'Sorry I wasn't able to be more helpful when you called but the Prentices are our most important clients. I was really stressing about meeting them. You just caught me at the wrong time.'

'Well, I wasn't to know that, was I?'

'No, but we did agree you'd never ring me at the office.'

'I know, but it was an emergency.'

'But you know what people are like. Our receptionist has got a big mouth.'

'I didn't want to ring you at work, but you were the only one I could turn to.'

'Why? What did you expect me to do?'

'I didn't expect you to do anything. I just wanted you to know she'd been excluded. I wanted to share the problem with you because you're her father.'

She heard Greg sigh.

'What did you do with her in the end?'

'I was lucky. I managed to get her into The Old Rectory.'

'The Old Rectory?'

'Yes. They were very kind. They said she could stay there all week.'

The prolonged silence at Greg's end suggested that this information had not been well received.

She said, 'They run a unit there for kids who've been excluded from school.'

'I know what they do.'

'So I thought if they can take other kids why not Louise?'

'Don't be ridiculous. Louise is nothing like the kids at the rectory. They're much older for a start. And they're yobs. Louise has been well brought up.'

The idea of goading him was very appealing. 'They seemed perfectly all right to me. They're very well behaved. Anyway, Louise is staying there till the end of the week.'

'I'm not very happy about that.'

'Really? Then what the fuck do you suggest?'

Again, Greg's silence indicated his displeasure. She knew how he hated to hear her swear. 'Who else is going to look after her?' she went on, vehemently. 'She can't come to work with me, and everyone else I know has a full time job. Mrs Tomlinson won't take her and even if she would, Louise refuses to go; and I'm certainly not leaving her at home on her own all day. She might get into all kinds of trouble. She could go off and I wouldn't have any idea where she was.'

'Now I'm sure she wouldn't do that!'

But Sharon knew differently. 'I don't want to take the chance. So she'll have to go to the rectory, whatever you think.'

'Why don't you call in sick? Take a few days off and look after her.'

'Are you joking? My diary's completely full. Why don't you?'

'What?'

'Take a few days off and look after her.'

'Now you're being ridiculous.'

'Exactly. That's how the suggestion sounds to me!'

Again, Greg sighed heavily. 'Where is she now? Can I have a quick word with her?'

'She's at a rehearsal.'

'How can she be? She's excluded.'

'Not from "Oliver". Mrs Henshall's allowed her to stay in it. Mainly, I suspect because no-one else can do the part. What do you want to talk to her about?'

'I want to warn her not to say anything about you and me to those people at the rectory.'

'Don't worry, she won't.'

'I wish I could be so sure. And I want to give her a telling off for kicking Mrs Lucas. I think she should write to her and apologise.'

'Why? It was an accident.'

'That's not what Jade said.'

Sharon felt a surge of anger on her daughter's behalf. 'Don't you think you should talk to Louise before jumping to conclusions?'

'Pam and I had a long talk with Jade tonight. We asked her why she was taunting Louise for not having a father.'

The irony of such a confrontation struck Sharon forcibly. 'That must have been a challenging conversation for you.'

'There's no need for sarcasm,' retorted Greg. 'Jade swears she's never said anything to Louise about her father. She says Louise is saying these things because she wants to get her into trouble.'

'And you believe Jade?'

'Frankly, yes. Pam and I both think that Louise is bullying Jade.'

'That's ridiculous.'

'You wouldn't say that if you could see Jade. She isn't herself. She's very upset. She just mopes around all day and refuses to go to school. Pam is very concerned. She wanted to come round and see you about it but I managed to divert her. I told her it was just a spat between two ex-friends. Six of one and half a dozen of the other. That sort of thing.'

Sharon said nothing. She was astounded that Greg had so completely taken Jade's side. How could he be taken in so easily?

Greg said, 'Look, I've got to go.'

'All right.'

'Bugger this meeting. I'd like to come round.'

Despite everything, the prospect of his company was attractive. 'Well, why don't you?' she said.

'I think I will. I've been thinking about you all day.'

'In what way?'

Greg described the way his thoughts had been running. It was very clear why he wanted to come round.

'What time does your meeting finish?' she asked.

'Eight-thirty. But I could always leave early.'

'Perhaps you'd better. I've got to collect Lou at ten.'

'OK. I'll leave the meeting early.'

But Sharon's festering thoughts were about to spoil Greg's plans. How could he, she asked herself, have taken Jade's part against Louise without even hearing Louise's side of the argument? Or assumed that Louise had deliberately kicked Mrs Lucas? And how could he compound his insensitivity by exploiting her loneliness and need for physical companionship in order to have another "quickie". He was treating her like a whore: like his bit on the side. That was all she meant to him. She had a vision of herself in ten years' time being in exactly the same position: waiting for him to come round and Pam thinking he was at some meeting or other. This was immediately replaced by an image of herself and Dylan sitting at a table in The Woldsman's beer garden. She saw with astonishing clarity that Greg was the obstacle to all her future happiness, and her vague feeling of generalised resentment towards him was transformed by these insights into an intense and unforgiving anger.

'On second thoughts, don't bother,' she said.
'What do you mean?'
'Leave it for tonight.'
'You don't want me to come round?'
'No. I'm exhausted. All I want is a bath and an early bed.'
He attempted to persuade her to change her mind but she cut him short.
'Anyway, a shag's out of the question. I've started my period.'

CHAPTER TWENTY TWO

Major Roberts thoroughly enjoyed chairing the weekly gatherings of the Magnificent Britain Sub-Committee. He much preferred them to the monthly meetings of the parish council which were difficult to chair because they were always politically contentious. By contrast, the Magnificent Britain get-togethers were generally relaxed and amicable. Being a sub-committee, the membership was mostly co-opted, contained few parish councillors and was relatively small. The members were all experienced and knowledgeable gardeners, had a strong sense of civic duty and were immensely proud of Leefdale's achievements in the Magnificent Britain Competition.

Howard Roberts also looked forward to these meetings for reasons that went beyond the simple pleasure they gave him. The sub-committee's decision-making responsibilities might be limited: encompassing only such mundane matters as the selection of Leefdale's three exemplary gardens; determining potential sites for the planting of daffodils; or deciding the optimum number of hanging baskets to be recommended per property. But the simple act of taking even these petty decisions made Howard feel that he was back in command once more, devising strategy and directing operations. It made him feel purposeful, a master of events; and it defined him yet again as a man of action. For, as he was often fond of saying, what are actions but decisions?

This positive impression of himself was confirmed by the fact that his decisions were never questioned or opposed by his fellow committee members, who were more than happy to trust his judgement in all matters. Previously, he'd only experienced such total authority when he'd been on active service with the army. After his enforced early retirement, life had seemed directionless and uncertain and he'd seemed to exist in a constant state of vacillation which made the simplest decisions impossible. But his work for the Magnificent Britain Sub-Committee had enabled him to find his former authoritative self. The officer self that moved, unassailed by doubt, through a world of comforting certainties in which everyone knew their place and a spade was a spade. The world, in fact, of the past. Before the terrible bleakness and despair had descended.

That evening, as Howard surveyed the faces sitting around him in an anteroom off the village hall, only one person's presence disturbed his well-being and gave him cause for apprehension. This was a woman in her mid-fifties, sitting three places away from him. She had long grey hair down well past her shoulders and exceedingly light blue eyes which observed everyone with a friendly wariness. Her plump cheeks and full, almost sensuous mouth gave her the appearance of a mischievous cherub. Her inappropriately long hair and her long sleeved, maxi-dress were evocative of the 1970s and implied former dalliance with a hippy or counter culture. Indeed, Howard would not have been surprised to have encountered her at an anti-Vietnam war demo or at Greenham Common. On different sides of the fence, of course. The woman was Lucy Birkinshaw, Howard's bête noire: the person with whom for months past he'd engaged in verbal combat via The Leeflet's gardening column and letters pages; and her presence in the room was a cruel reminder to Howard of his bitterest political defeat.

It had happened the previous Wednesday, at the last full meeting of the parish council. In order to fill the vacancies created by Walter Marsden's death, Howard had proposed the co-option of Ed Dayton, a superb gardener and fellow member of the bowls club. Howard had assumed that being his man, Dayton, would be co-opted to both positions without dissent. He was therefore surprised and rather annoyed when Councillor Arthur Meakins proposed that Lucy Birkinshaw be co-opted instead. Lucy Birkinshaw was a relative newcomer to the village and a woman of forthright opinions. Surely, Howard had reflected, it could not have escaped his fellow councillors' notice that she'd conducted an acrimonious correspondence with him in The Leeflet.

Howard had informed the meeting that as there were now two candidates for the position of parish councillor a by-election would have to be held. However, he explained that this didn't preclude one of them from being co-opted on to the Magnificent Britain Sub-Committee forthwith. The matter was immediately put to the vote. To Howard's extreme annoyance the majority of councillors found in favour of Miss Birkinshaw. He'd been out manoeuvred. Obviously, it had been decided beforehand at an informal meeting convened by Meakins in the pub. Howard was well aware that Meakins had been deputy chairman of the parish council in the village in which he'd previously lived, and his suspicion that Meakins was after his position as chairman was strengthened by this ambush. On losing the vote, Ed Dayton's response to his humiliating rebuff was to tell the full meeting of the Leefdale Parish Council that "If they didn't want 'im for gardenin' committee they could stick the by-election for councillor up their arses". He then walked out. Howard formally ruled this as a de facto withdrawal. The by-election was cancelled and Lucy Birkinshaw, by default, was then co-opted on to the parish council. Meakins' triumph was complete. This was why Lucy Birkinshaw was tonight attending the

Magnificent Britain Sub-Committee for the first time in her capacity as the new member.

Howard was determined that no matter how Lucy behaved towards him at that evening's meeting he would be polite and cordial towards her, and would at all times conduct himself in a manner befitting an officer and a gentleman. With this firm intention, he formally drew the meeting to order and apologised for having to hold it in an ante-room because of the "Oliver" rehearsals. He then made a few, brief introductory remarks, gave a eulogistic account of the contribution of the late Walter Marsden, and welcomed Lucy Birkinshaw as his replacement.

Lucy beamed, and in response made a somewhat overlong speech in which she conceded that Walter Marsden was a hard act to follow, and affirmed her commitment to maintaining the highest standards of horticulture in Leefdale. In what Howard interpreted as an oblique allusion to their recent spat, Lucy concluded by saying, 'We all want the best for Leefdale. However, the ways we go about achieving this may differ. I believe we should respect our differences at all times no matter how much we may disagree. If only everyone's point of view was valued it would be a much more peaceful world.'

Howard thanked Lucy for her comments, adding urbanely, 'I'm sure there's nothing in your excellent remarks that any of us could find to disagree with.'

Patronising prick, thought Lucy. Nothing would dissuade her from the view that Major Roberts was an old-fashioned, male chauvinist who felt threatened by strong, confident women.

Thankful that there'd been no embarrassing altercation between himself and Lucy, Howard then proceeded to Item One of the agenda, which concerned the arrangements for the judging of the Magnificent Britain Competition. After thanking everyone for their efforts in securing Leefdale's place in the finals, Howard initiated a long discussion, the purpose of which was to ensure that all the necessary preparations had been made for the great day. He drew this item on the agenda to a close with the following words. 'It is vital that everything goes smoothly. A most important record will be established if we win the gold medal this year. No other village has ever won it five times, let alone five years in succession.'

It was then that Lucy Birkinshaw asked her first question. 'Mr Chairman, I understand that we're going to be the last village to be judged. Is that to our advantage?'

Howard employed his most emollient tone: 'Not if the villages who are seen before us create an excellent impression. In those circumstances, being judged last could make things awkward for us. However, it does give us plenty of time to ensure that every garden in the village is in perfect condition, which, I suppose, is an advantage.' He paused, frowning slightly, 'Which brings us to the second item on the agenda.' He turned towards Greg Maynard. 'Greg, would you give us your Readiness Report?'

'Certainly, Mr Chairman.' Greg diffidently put on a pair of recently acquired reading glasses and consulted a sheet of paper on the table in front of him. 'I'm afraid there are a number of serious failures to report. The first is in "D" Sector.'

'What's "D" Sector?' asked Lucy.

'The area around Elderthorpe Road.'

At the beginning of his involvement in the Magnificent Britain campaign six years previously, Howard had quickly identified poor organisation and lack of co-ordination as the principal reasons why Leefdale often reached the finals but never actually won. One of his solutions had been to divide the village into sectors and to assign to each sector an identifying letter. It was a simple matter then to keep the state of the gardens in each sector under constant review. Patiently and with an appropriate degree of modesty, he explained all this to Lucy. When he'd finished he returned his attention to Greg. 'So, what's the problem?'

'George Sygrove's Lavatera have all failed.'

Edna Phillips, the clerk to the parish council, whose job was to prepare the minutes, ceased taking notes and looked up from her pad. 'Oh no! He had such a lovely show last year.'

'Well, there it is,' said Greg. 'He pruned them well back in the spring like he always does, but there's been little new growth and no buds.'

'Have none of them flowered?' asked Howard.

'Afraid not. George can't understand it. He can only put it down to the late frosts we've had this year.'

'Lavatera should always be pruned at backend,' said Reg Maltby. 'That's what's done it.'

'What's backend?' asked Lucy Birkinshaw.

Howard took great pleasure in enlightening her. 'It's an old East Yorkshire dialect word for autumn.' He referred back to Greg. 'Anyone else reported problems with their Lavatera?'

'No.'

'Right,' said Howard. 'What's George doing about it?'

'He's planted up some new ones. Biggest ones he could find at garden centre. But they're only half the size of those he had last year.'

'That's a pity,' Howard said. 'They're such a feature of his Victorian garden.'

'Aye, and they did a good job of hiding that ugly old shed of his,' said Reg. He was an agricultural labourer in his fifties with a bright red face. Lucy had heard he hadn't much of an opinion of Howard Roberts. She wondered if he might be a potential ally.

A series of screeching, discordant sounds started beyond the closed door of the ante-room. The "Oliver" orchestra was tuning up in the main area of the village hall.

'Bloody din,' said Reg Maltby. 'How are we expected to hold a meeting with that going on?'

'Don't be an old curmudgeon,' chided Edna Phillips.

'It's not ideal, but we'll just have to soldier on,' said Howard. He made a note and looked at Greg. 'All right. What's next?'

'"C" Sector's still giving us problems, of course.'

'Well, that's to be expected,' said Howard.

'Where's "C" sector?' asked Lucy.

'The lazy buggers on Mathieson Walk,' said Fred Birch. He was a turkey farmer who had a slightly drooping right eyelid which always made him look as though he was sizing up a bargain. He'd once employed Reg Maltby in one of his turkey sheds.

'The people there aren't lazy,' said Lucy, hotly. 'There are some beautiful gardens on Mathieson Walk. You're just stereotyping them because it's the council estate.'

'It's not all council now,' said Reg. 'A lot of them took advantage of Right to Buy.'

Greg looked directly at Lucy. 'Have you seen number 17? It's in a right bloody mess.'

'Now, that's still council,' said Reg.

'Number 17 has been unoccupied for months,' said Lucy. 'No wonder its garden's a mess. But that's not the fault of the people on the estate. It doesn't mean they're all lazy, does it?'

Lucy had introduced an alien and unseemly note of discord into their discussion. Looks were exchanged all round the table.

Howard turned to Lucy, and in a polite but patronising voice said, 'I'm sure that Fred wasn't suggesting that everyone on Mathieson Walk was lazy. Were you Fred?'

Fred's shrewd, satirical face broke into a grin. 'Course not. Only having a dig at Reg. No harm meant.'

'Anyway, Number 17 shouldn't be a problem,' said Howard. 'We can deal with that ourselves. Anything else?'

Greg glanced at his notes. 'Sid Arkwright, Dave Higgins and Wayne Strickland have taken no notice of our warnings. Their front gardens are still a tip.'

'Now they're still council,' said Reg.

'What a way to talk about people,' said Lucy.

'We can't afford to be sentimental,' said Sue Rawdon, a woman in her mid-thirties who belonged to one of Leefdale's wealthiest farming families. 'They're going to ruin our chances of getting the prize for the fifth time.'

'Just a moment,' said Lucy. 'This is still a free country, you know. If people don't wish to enter their gardens in the competition it's a matter for them. They shouldn't be bullied into it.'

Howard knew now that his instincts about the woman had been right all along. She was obviously a trouble maker. Probably in cahoots with Meakins, who'd almost certainly insinuated her on to the Magnificent Britain Sub-Committee to sow discord and give its chairman the maximum amount of aggravation.

Howard folded his arms and leaned forward. Looking Lucy straight in the eyes, he said, 'I assure you no-one is bullying anyone.'

'It don't take much to keep a garden tidy, now does it?' said Janet Pinkney, aiming this rhetorical shaft straight at Lucy. Janet was prominent in the Women's Institute, where she and Lucy had often crossed swords.

Edna Phillips' head nodded vigorously in agreement. 'Still, what can you expect from Mathieson Walk,' she said. 'None of them are any better than they should be.'

Lucy's astonished gasp was clearly audible.

Sensing that the meeting was moving in an acrimonious direction, Howard affected emollience. 'Well Greg, you'll just have to appeal to their sense of pride in their community and ask them to get tidying up.'

'That won't do any good' said Reg. 'Dave and Wayne are too busy with harvest. They're working day and night. They've no time for their gardens.'

'Most people in this village work but we still find time for our gardens,' said Greg. 'And there's no reason why Sid Arkwright can't tidy up his garden. He's on the dole. He hasn't done a stroke of work in months.'

'Sid's not on the dole,' said Lucy. 'He's on incapacity benefit.'

'Same thing,' said Greg Maynard.

'No, it's not,' protested Lucy. 'He injured his foot months ago when he was working at Preston's pig unit.'

'Who told you that?'

'He did, in the pub.'

The others laughed.

'Sid'll say anything to get a drink,' said Reg.

'I hope you didn't buy him one,' said Fred.

'Yes, I did,' Lucy said, colouring. 'Two actually. What of it?'

'It's all right, they're only teasing you,' said Howard. He suspected Lucy of being a neurotic and was anxious to avoid conflict between her and the others. 'Now, whatever the reasons, Mathieson Walk mustn't be allowed to spoil our chances in the finals. I suggest that we visit the three chaps concerned and let them know that their gardens are a blot on the landscape; and if they can't be bothered to sort them out themselves we'll put a team together who'll go in and do it for them.'

He's deliberately trying to provoke me, thought Lucy. 'Have you ever done that before?' she asked.

'Only once,' said Howard. 'Usually the threat's enough to motivate them. People don't like the humiliation you see.' He looked from face to face. 'So, is that agreed?'

Everyone except Lucy nodded. Her uncompromising expression told Howard that he was in for a rough ride. She said, 'I'm sorry, but I have to say I'm not happy about pressurising people in this way.'

'Why not? What's wrong with it?' Howard snapped.

Lucy, who'd always regarded Howard as a pompous old fart, was surprised by the dangerous notes in his voice. She couldn't know, of course, that he'd yet again failed to take his medication. However, she recovered quickly and said: 'It'll damage relationships in the village and create an "us and them" mentality between the council estate and the rest of us.'

'It always has been us and them,' said Reg. 'And I should know. I've lived on Mathieson Walk since it were built.'

'Nevertheless...' Lucy began to counter. But Howard, uncharacteristically, interrupted her. 'Lucy, don't you think you're approaching this rather too seriously? I assure you those chaps will be only too glad to have people go round and clean up their gardens for them. Particularly, if they're as busy or as incapable as they claim they are.'

'Aye, I wish someone would come round and tidy up mine for me,' said Reg.

'How can you all be so patronising?' demanded Lucy. 'I would most certainly resent it if people suddenly descended on my garden and started doing things to it without my permission!' She glared at Howard. 'I made my feelings about this quite clear in The Leeflet.'

'But that's the point,' said Greg, irritably. 'They always give us their permission!'

'Only because you harass and coerce them. And we all know how much coercion puts people's backs up!'

'I don't harass or coerce anybody!' Greg protested.

'My experience is that some people only respond to compulsion,' said Howard. He gave Lucy a long, intimidating stare. 'Don't you want the village to win again this year?'

'Of course, I do. But not at any cost.'

'Winning always involves a cost. If we're to triumph again every single garden in this village will have to be in first class condition, and that's not going to happen if a few idlers backslide.'

'If that's your attitude, I'm not surprised some people are so uncooperative.'

'No, Lucy,' Howard said, emphatically. 'Those people are uncooperative because they were born bloody minded!' Ignoring Lucy's disdainful look, he turned to Maynard. 'Now Greg, is that the extent of our problems?'

'I'm afraid not. There's actually quite a big problem in your own sector.'

'Ah, you're talking about The Old Rectory.'

'Yes.'

'If you hadn't mentioned it, I was going to bring it up under any other business,' said Howard.

The casual manner in which the problem of The Old Rectory had been introduced was completely disingenuous. Howard and Greg were strong allies in the microcosmic world of parish pump politics. They'd been on the phone constantly in the past week, complaining to each other about the condition of the rectory's front garden. They both recognised it was particularly problematic because their usual methods of coercion would probably be inappropriate against what were obviously middle class lefties. Their strategy would have to be kept low key.

Howard said, 'The situation, ladies and gentlemen, in the unlikely event that you haven't noticed, is that ever since Mr Bourne and his associates took over The Old Rectory, the front lawn has deteriorated very badly.'

'It's a disgrace,' said Edna Phillips.

'What's it like at the back?' asked Reg.

'Well, it's impossible to see from the road, but we can only assume it's in the same dreadful condition as the front.'

'It is,' said Edna Phillips. 'According to Bill Harcourt, anyway.'

Bill Harcourt was the village milkman. Such intelligence as the inhabitants of Leefdale could glean about the new residents of the rectory came from him, and other tradesmen, who because of the nature of their occupations frequently called at the house or were even able to enter it. Their eye witness reports invariably found their way to the bar of The Woldsman, where, after several pints, they were embellished with a large dash of hyperbole, and disseminated throughout the village. The rumours circulating about the people currently living at the rectory were therefore wild and legion. Major Roberts' concerns about the state of the rectory's front garden now emboldened several at the table to repeat these canards in outraged and sometimes self-righteous tones. Reg Maltby was convinced that the rectory was a refuge for recovering heroin addicts; Sue Rawdon insisted it was a home for young offenders; Janet Pinkney assured everyone that it was the centre of a religious cult.

Howard Roberts listened to their assertions with some amusement. 'Well, I'm afraid you're all wrong,' he said, finally. 'Mr Bourne is an artist, and my understanding is that it's some sort of art school for deprived teenagers.'

This information caused all the other members of the Magnificent Britain Sub-Committee to fall silent. 'Anyway,' Howard continued, hastily moving on, 'the reason why they're here is not important at the moment. The thing is they're neglecting their front lawn. I've already offered to go on caring for the gardens as I did before they moved in, but my offer was rejected.'

The orchestra at last ceased tuning up. 'Thank God for that!' exclaimed Fred Birch. Several of those around the table nodded.

'This Mr Bourne, what sort of a man is he?' asked Reg.

'Difficult to say. I hardly know him. He and the others keep very much to themselves. He's fairly young, about thirty two, and as I said an artist.'

'The thing is, will he listen to reason?'

'I'm not sure. His colleagues seem quite bolshie.'
'Oh. Why?'
'They struck me as rather uncooperative. Anti-authority.'
'What's his name again?' asked Janet Pinkney.
'Bourne. Dylan Bourne.'
'And he's an artist?' said Lucy Birkinshaw, her eyes bright with interest.
'That's right.'
'Never heard of him,' said Janet.
'I don't think he's particularly famous,' said Howard. 'But he must be pretty successful if he's bought the rectory. He won't have much change left out of five hundred thousand.'
'Aye, he must be doing something right,' said Reg.

Greg Maynard was about to inform everyone that the rectory had actually been bought by a property company, for which Dylan Bourne was merely the nominee. But he changed his mind. He'd received the information from Sharon in confidence and he was afraid of compromising both her and himself.

'He's certainly no gardener,' said Howard. 'I first met him when he came to view the rectory with Sharon Makepiece. He told me he didn't have even a window box in his London flat.'

'Ah, he's a Londoner, is he?' said Reg.

Lucy immediately rounded on him. 'What's wrong with that?' she demanded.

'Nothing, no nothing,' mumbled Reg.

The opening bars of "Consider Yourself" struck up, and then abruptly stopped. Mrs Henshall could be heard, giving instructions in a raised voice.

Janet Pinkney said, 'Does Mr Bourne and his friends know that the judges will want to see the rectory gardens?'

'A letter's been sent informing them, but so far they haven't replied,' said Edna Phillips.

Fred said, 'If they're in a bad state it might be better if the judges didn't see the rectory's gardens at all.'

'Can't we enter a different garden in the exemplary category, Mr Chairman?' enquired Sue Rawdon. 'Vera Newbiggin's, for instance. Now her garden's magnificent this year.'

'I'm afraid that's out of the question,' said Howard. 'The closing date for entering exemplary gardens was back in March. The Old Rectory was, of course, in excellent condition at that time.'

Everyone around the table again fell silent. Lucy aside, each was reflecting on the possibility that the poor condition of The Old Rectory's gardens might cost Leefdale the gold medal.

'Mr Chairman,' said Edna Phillips, 'I propose you go and see Mr Bourne again and remind him how important the Magnificent Britain contest is for the village. You could also tactfully offer to go in and tidy up his front lawn for him until the contest is over.'

This was exactly what Howard was hoping would be suggested. However, he tried to appear unenthusiastic. 'I'm happy to do that, but I'm certain he'll only refuse me again and that could make things very embarrassing.'

'Perhaps he might find it harder to refuse if the whole sub-committee appeared on his doorstep,' said Greg Maynard. This was a red herring that he and Howard had previously agreed would be introduced in order for Howard to denounce it as too extreme.

'Hear, hear!' cried Edna Phillips.

'I'm not at all happy about us doing that,' said Howard, on cue.

'Quite right, Major, there's no need for that,' said Lucy, quickly. 'The solution seems very simple to me.'

'What's that?'

'Well, Mr Bourne's obviously been neglecting his beautiful garden. If he won't co-operate, force him to. Bring in a team of gardeners from the village to tidy it up. The same team you're going to put into Mathieson Walk. Surely, The Old Rectory deserves just the same autocratic treatment as the council estate?'

Howard said nothing. He stared at Lucy's scornful, triumphant features. Her sarcasm had found its target and she was relishing it. He knew then that he hated her. It wasn't her sarcasm that he minded. After all, there was always a contradiction between the way some people were treated and the way others were. That was life. What he really resented was her self-righteous, petty point scoring attitude.

He forced a smile. 'I agree. I think we should insist that Mr Bourne and his friends allow a few people from the village to go in and mow the rectory's lawns, trim the hedges and generally tidy things up for the judges.' He stared hard at Lucy. 'After that, we'll leave them alone until this time next year. Just like we do with the people on the council estate.'

'Good,' said Lucy.

Howard had an irresistible urge to slap her face: only violence, he felt, could rid her features of that superior, self-satisfied smile.

With some effort he regained command of himself and said, 'But before we do that, I think I should personally visit Mr Bourne and his colleagues one more time. Just to see if the problem can be resolved by agreement.'

The orchestra launched into the opening of "Consider Yourself" once again. The thin, weak voice of Eddie Arkwright, who played the Artful Dodger was singing along with it. After a few bars the school choir joined in. But they mistimed it. There was hiatus and disarray. They all heard Mrs Henshall bellow "Stop".

Greg made a face. 'This is impossible!'

'We're nearly finished,' said Howard.

There was only one item now remaining on the agenda. Someone had to be appointed to take the late Walter Marsden's place at the Magnificent Britain awards ceremony. Only three members of the committee from a town or village that had reached the finals were allowed to attend. Howard and Greg were assured of their places because the Chair and Vice Chair's invitations were automatic; but, in accordance with the rules, as Walter Marsden was now deceased, his replacement had to be decided by drawing lots.

Edna Phillips gave each participant an A4 size piece of paper on which to write their name. She collected the papers and then compressed each one into a tight ball, so that the name written on it couldn't possibly be seen. Each ball of paper was placed into an odd looking contraption called a hand cranked bingo cage which was used by the caller on village hall bingo nights to mix the numbers up prior to calling them out.

Vigorously, Edna turned the handle on the bingo cage, rotating it many, many times until all the balls of paper were thoroughly intermingled and impossible to identify. She then stopped, opened a small door in the cage and asked Howard to reach inside and retrieve a name.

Howard put his hand into the cage and held it suspended over the paper balls for several seconds while he looked around archly, like some second-rate conjuror creating a moment of cheap suspense. Then he pounced on one of the balls, placed it on the table, opened it out flat and contemplated the name written on it.

Everyone at the table leaned forward in anticipation.

Howard's face was completely impassive as he looked up. 'Congratulations, Lucy!'

There was a long silence.

Lucy Birkinshaw smiled back at him. 'Must be beginners' luck,' she said.

In the background the orchestra started up again. Eddie Arkwright came in perfectly on cue. So did the choir. Everyone sang much more strongly. Musicians and singers all performed in perfect harmony.

CHAPTER TWENTY THREE

Whilst Isobel put the children to bed, Barbara remained alone in the sitting room watching television, but her thoughts were too disturbed to be diverted by the banal programme about improving the saleability of your home. Overhead, she could hear her mother settling Mark and Jessica down for the night. How Isobel loved to play grandma, tucking her two little darlings up with warm drinks and reading to them before kissing them goodnight.

Barbara was grateful for these few minutes of solitude. It enabled her to confront the awful truth that her marriage was dead. As she listened numbly to the television presenter describing how, for very little outlay, a house could be improved to attract first-time buyers, she confronted the reality that her own lovely home, a converted barn in rural Northamptonshire, would have to be sold, the joint possessions broken up and apportioned, and in time the children similarly parcelled out. The knowledge of this inevitable dissolution filled her with dread.

Her other sensation was one of unreality: a sense that this simply couldn't be happening to her. Ten days ago, she'd lived in an intact, predictable world. Now it had all been reduced to chaos and uncertainty.

There was good reason for her bewilderment and disbelief. Peter's affair with Clarissa had not been at all like his others. She'd found out about those through friends, or malicious people in the Party; or he'd confessed them to her when they'd become, as they always did, a burden to him. Being a pragmatist, she'd allowed each of these liaisons to run its course, knowing that familiarity, boredom and Peter's well developed sense of self-preservation, would eventually bring about the affair's inevitable end. Previously, this strategy had always been successful and it had protected her marriage and her children's security. It worked because she was realistic: Peter was very attractive, looked ten years younger than his forty six years, and was successful and charismatic. Being an MP and a shadow minister, he had his own flat in London. He therefore had more independence than most married men, and given his inability to resist the charms of the many young women, both inside and outside the Party, who found him magnetic, it was inevitable that he would stray. But

Barbara tolerated his affairs because she was confident that he would always return to her and the children.

But this thing with Clarissa was unlike any of the others, and had come completely out of the blue! In fact, for the past six months Barbara had been under the impression that his philandering days had finished, so attentive had he been to her, even in the bedroom. She was therefore completely unprepared when, just over a week ago, he'd coolly told her that their marriage was over and he intended to set up home in a rented flat with his best friend's seventeen year old daughter. After this shocking announcement it had been some time before she'd been able to regain command of herself; but having done so, using all the logical reasons at her disposal, she'd at once attempted to convince him of the folly of his intentions. She cited the destructive effect it would have on the children, the damage it would do to his leadership aspirations, and the misery it would create for herself and Russell, Clarissa's father, who had recently lost his wife to cancer. Peter had acknowledged the strength of her arguments but insisted his love for Clarissa was overwhelming. It was then that she'd become hysterical and unleashed at him the insults which were the bitter fruit of her years of humiliation and betrayal. He'd received these philosophically, without retaliation, and so, in desperation, she'd turned to ridicule, beseeching him to consider how the tabloids would react to yet another parliamentary sex scandal: a forty six year old member of the Shadow Cabinet running off and setting up home with a girl more than half his age, who was also the daughter of his best friend. But when he'd still refused to see sense, she'd become more viciously personal. How did he foresee his role in Clarissa's life? Would he be going clubbing with her and her teenage friends? Would he be helping her with her A levels? Did he think she might vote for him when she became old enough? This, and much more. But he remained unmoved. It was then she became truly frightened: she saw that his infatuation had made him impervious even to her contempt.

Shortly afterwards, he'd left home taking with him only a small suitcase. His last words were that he and Clarissa were now going to confront Russell with the news.

Three hours later, Russell had phoned her, stunned and apologetic. Peter and Clarissa had just left. They'd told him everything. He'd had no idea. He didn't know what to say. Had Barbara known about it? He told her of his happiness when Peter had offered Clarissa work experience as his part time researcher. Now he knew why he'd done so. Russell was all incomprehension and disbelief, mortified at the damage that had been done to his friendship with Peter. They'd been friends since university, and had watched each other's children grow. The thought of Clarissa and Peter in bed together, betraying Barbara, revolted Russell. He told her of his relief that Sarah, his late wife, had been spared this. "I've told Peter and Clarissa that I never wish to see either of them again," he said finally. "And now, I feel so empty. As though in some way I'm to blame for this terrible thing that's happened."

She'd tried to persuade him not to take it personally. It wasn't his fault, she told him. He had to stop castigating himself. But Russell was easily prone to bouts of drunken self-pity, and she knew as soon as they'd finished their call he'd be getting very, very pissed. That had been over a week ago. Since then, she'd spoken to him on the phone several times. But the last occasion had been two days ago when she'd told him she was going to stay with her parents in Leefdale, and sworn him to secrecy about her plans. Surely, he hadn't told anyone? But then, if it wasn't Russell, who was it who'd given away her whereabouts? Peter was the only other person who knew where she was. She couldn't believe he'd told the press. Perhaps he'd mentioned it to Clarissa and she'd told someone?

Barbara knew she had to warn Russell that reporters were sniffing about. It would be disastrous if they ambushed him and he said anything damaging or indiscreet. Whatever happened, if there was going to be any chance at all of a reconciliation between her and Peter, it was vital that not a hint of the true extent of the scandal reached the ears of the press. Because, even now, she clung to the hope that they would be reconciled: that Peter, her wonderful, stunning Peter, would come back to her. The thought of telling her parents that her marriage was over made her feel sick. How could she possibly admit that? It was her pride and joy. Peter was the great prize she'd won in the lottery of life. She couldn't just let that go without a struggle. No, she was fucked if she was going to give him up without a fight.

Having satisfied herself that Isobel was still engrossed with the children, Barbara picked up her black mobile and tried Russell on his landline again. She'd already decided that if he failed to answer she'd leave a message on his voicemail warning him not to say anything to the media. The phone in Russell's flat rang for ages, and she was waiting for his voicemail to kick in, when he surprised her by answering.

'Hello.'

'It's Barbara. How are you?'

'Oh Barbara. Hello. Not so good. Not so good at all. How about you?'

He sounded very tired. Or was he drunk?

Barbara said, 'Actually, I'm in a state of shock. I've had a reporter from The Source calling me. They've also been hanging around our flat apparently. Somehow the story's got out.'

There was a long silence at his end. 'Yes. I know.'

'You know?'

'Yes. I'm very sorry, Barbara.'

'What do you mean, you're very sorry?'

'I've done something awful.' He sounded near to tears.

'What? What have you done?'

'I've been so miserable these past few days. Thinking of Clarissa. Thinking of you and Peter. And Sarah.'

'Russell! What have you done?'

'I went out for a very long lunch today. Had far too much to drink and then came back and got stuck into a bottle of brandy. I just sat here thinking about Clarissa and Peter and the way they'd lied to us. I got so angry, Barbara.'

Barbara braced herself for some seriously bad news.

'I'd been drinking most of the afternoon. Then, about four o'clock, I called up a guy I know. Terry Bryden. He's a reporter on The Source. Do you know him?'

'That's the bastard who just called. He asked me how I felt about Peter running off with a seventeen year old girl.'

'Oh, Barbara! No! Oh God!'

She heard a single sob. And then another.

'What did you tell him?'

'Barbara, I'm so sorry. I told him all about Clarissa and Peter. Everything, Barbara. How you and Peter had split up and Peter had moved in with my daughter. Told him what a snake Peter was. I gave him the whole story.'

'Did you tell him I'd gone to stay with my parents?'

'Yes.'

'You gave him their telephone number?'

'Yes.'

'And my mobile number?'

'Yes.'

So that's how the press had known where to find her! When she'd told Russell she was going to stay at her parents' home she'd given him their number because she'd thought he might need a shoulder to cry on.

Barbara couldn't speak. In one utterly selfish stroke, Russell had destroyed any hopes she still had of a reconciliation with Peter. Worse than that, by flushing the scandal out into the tabloid sewer, he'd ruined any chance of Peter hanging on to his Shadow Cabinet post.

'Why, Russell? Why?'

He sighed, miserably. 'I don't know, Barbara. Revenge, I suppose. I wanted to hurt Peter! I wanted people to know how devastated I was. How betrayed I felt.'

'You fool! You've destroyed any hope we might have had of salvaging the situation!'

'I know. I'm terribly, terribly sorry.'

'How could you go to the press without discussing it with me or Peter first?'

'I was drunk, Barbara. Out of my skull. Do you think I'd have done it sober?'

'Russell, you've ruined my life. The one small hope I had was that Peter would eventually come to his senses and we'd get out of this mess with no whiff of scandal.'

Russell's whisper was barely audible. 'I'm so sorry, Barbara. I wish I hadn't done it. I could kill myself!'

Despite everything, Russell's abjectness went straight to Barbara's heart. He was obviously dreadfully distressed. She knew how close he'd been to Sarah and his only daughter. They were his world. Now Sarah was gone, and he wasn't speaking to his beloved Clarissa any more. The last thing she needed at this time was Russell's suicide on top of everything else.

'Russell, it's all right,' she said gently. 'I'm sorry I spoke to you so harshly. I don't blame you for what you've done. You're obviously very depressed and this has come as a terrible shock. You must try to calm down. Drink plenty of coffee. Go to bed with some hot milk and stay off the booze. I'll be in touch soon. And whatever you do, don't say anything more to the press.'

After her call to Russell, Barbara's mobile informed her she now had eleven new messages. They were all from Terry Bryden. She played the first message and heard the reporter's uncouth London voice telling her that the story was going to be all over The Source tomorrow. "Why don't you ring me back? Go on, love. Give the public your side of it."

She was erasing the last of these messages when she heard her father enter the house. She quickly put her mobile away and tried to compose herself. She knew how astute he was, and didn't want him to suspect that anything was seriously wrong.

From the way he came into the sitting room it was obvious he was not in the best of moods. He glanced witheringly at the television. 'Not another bloody property programme! Why don't they hand the television network entirely over to estate agents and be done with it!'

Alarmed by his uncharacteristic vehemence, Barbara sought to mollify him. 'How was your meeting?' she enquired, affecting interest.

This was a mistake. Her words only seemed to agitate him more and immediately produced a rambling tirade about the people who'd moved into The Old Rectory. It seemed that they were doing their best to ruin his chances of winning Magnificent Britain. She listened with growing concern as, in a despairing whine, he complained about the condition of the rectory's front garden. Then, in a furious voice that was full of unstable cadences, he expressed his resentment at the way in which the excellent strategies he'd devised for dealing with the problem were being obstructed by a member of the Magnificent Britain Sub-Committee. A woman called Lucy someone or other, whom he insisted would be held personally responsible if the village failed to win the gold medal for the fifth consecutive time.

'The situation's serious, Barbara,' he said, fixing her with an unnerving stare. 'Something has to be done! If people refuse to co-operate they'll have to be coerced. It's that simple! How I wish I could put all the shirkers into uniform. That would show them! They'd soon buckle to!'

Barbara was becoming very alarmed. She'd never known her father to be like this. It must be what her mother had meant when she'd talked about his "black dog". He seemed paranoid and obsessive, as though the only thing that mattered in the world was the stupid gardening contest. How, she asked herself, as he prowled around the room, could she dump all her own problems on him when he was in such a belligerent and unpredictable frame of mind? Surely, it would only make him angrier? Yet tomorrow, the scandal would be all over The Source and it would inevitably appear in all the news bulletins. If Peter was some dowdy, obscure back bencher, the press would have little interest in him; but he was the darling of the Party: a prominent member of the shadow front bench and tipped to become the next leader. His adultery with a seventeen year old would send the media into a feeding frenzy. She couldn't allow her mother and father to find out about it from the television. Somehow, that night, she had to tell them everything. But just the thought of it made her feel faint, and for a moment she was tempted to pack the children into the car, drive off somewhere and lie low until the looming nightmare was over. But she knew that if she did, her parents would never forgive her. No, somehow, she had to find the strength to see it through.

And then, with a sudden, joyous insight, she saw that Russell's drunken involvement of the tabloid press could actually be her salvation. The story would run for days. Peter would be engulfed in scandal and almost certainly lose his Shadow Cabinet post. He might even be de-selected by the Constituency Party. And all this would be happening when the Party was struggling to retain one of its core seats at a crucial by-election. It would spell the end of his career. And for a man so vain and passionate about politics this would be impossible to bear. Clarissa was still, technically, a schoolgirl. She wouldn't have the maturity to cope with the media's hostility and ridicule. Her relationship with Peter would become fragile, and break. She would leave him, and he would return to his wife and children.

Barbara's positive thoughts were interrupted by Isobel, who entered the room in a state of high indignation.

'Why are you making such a din, Howard? I could hear you at the top of the stairs!'

Howard stared back at her. He seemed genuinely surprised at her manner. 'I was talking to Barbara.'

'You were not talking. You were shouting, and I've only just got the children off to sleep!' She made a loud, angry exclamation and then turned and swept out of the room.

Howard made a face at her retreating back: an expression of hostile resignation and regret.

He and Barbara said nothing and stood listening to Isobel's ill-tempered movements in the kitchen. Drawers were being loudly opened, rummaged through and then slammed. A tap was turned on and off.

Isobel returned holding a glass of water in one hand; the other hand was held palm upwards and clenched into a fist. She opened her fingers to reveal a small, white pill nestling in her palm. She thrust it at Howard. 'Here, take it!'

'I've taken two today.'

'No, you haven't. I've counted the tablets. You've only taken one!'

'I see! Spying on me now!'

'Yes! For your own good! Take it!'

'No! I've told you, I've taken all of them!'

'Don't lie to me!'

'I'm not!'

Isobel let out a huge sigh of frustration. 'You promised me you'd take both pills every day.'

'And I have!'

'Howard, if you go on like this people really will think you're insane!'

The next moment, Howard and Isobel were involved in a full blown row. Distressed and helpless, Barbara could only stand by and watch her parents trade vicious personal insults. Their raised and angry voices seemed somehow to be reflecting her own emotional turmoil.

'Stop it! Stop it!' she cried out. 'It's horrible! You'll upset the children.'

She flung herself full length on to the sofa, sobbing.

Her parents' concern was immediate. They stopped their verbal mauling and both moved towards the sofa, surrounding her protectively.

'Darling, are you all right?' Isobel asked.

'You mustn't mind us,' said Howard, placing a hand on Barbara's shoulder. 'We're just getting old, that's all. Old and crotchety.'

But Barbara continued to sob. 'It's not that. It's nothing to do with you!'

Howard and Isobel exchanged an alarmed look. They were both recalling their private speculations about the potentially worrying reasons for Barbara's sudden appearance with the children.

Isobel said, 'What is it then, darling? You're not ill, are you?'

Recovering her composure a little, Barbara eased herself into a sitting position on the sofa. 'No, I'm not ill,' she said. 'But I'm very, very miserable.'

Then, speaking in a calm, detached voice that was in complete contrast to the turbulence within, she told them of the death of her marriage and described the events that had killed it.

By the time she'd finished her account, both Isobel and Howard were sitting hunched and diminished in their comfortable armchairs, their faces grave and immobile, their eyes registering sympathy and shock. For Barbara had spared them no aspect of the past and present humiliations inflicted on her by Peter. They now knew that his adultery with Clarissa was the latest in a whole series of affairs. Before her there'd been Valerie, Rachel, Yvonne, Gloria, Angela, Jane, Penny, Julia and countless others.

Howard and Isobel sat for some time saying nothing, silently confronting the awful knowledge that over the years their only daughter had been enduring such misery and humiliation at the hands of someone they'd assumed had loved her; a man they'd welcomed and accepted into their family, and whom they'd treated as their own son. Later on, in the privacy of their bedroom, they would recall how Peter had so convincingly played the role of loving father, devoted husband, and idealistic politician, and wonder aloud how they could have been misled by such a charlatan.

'You're absolutely convinced it's all over between you?' Howard asked, finally.

'Yes. He made that quite clear on the phone tonight.'

'No possible chance of a reconciliation?'

'Not at the moment.'

'But if there was, you'd take him back?'

'Of course! I love him!'

'Do the children know Peter has left?' asked Isobel, quietly.

Barbara closed her eyes and shook her head. 'No. I hoped I wouldn't have to tell them.'

'But you'll have to tell them now.'

'Of course.'

'I can't believe he's done this,' exclaimed Howard. 'To run off with a seventeen year old. And his best friend's daughter. It's so humiliating.'

'He's changed so much since he went into politics,' said Barbara, lamely.

No, he hasn't, he's always been a shit! Howard thought. He caught his wife's eye and held her gaze. Isobel had never really liked Peter either, but they'd both tolerated him for Barbara's sake. Howard had several more negative thoughts about his son-in-law and was about to express them, but stopped himself. It would only upset Barbara. Instead, he stood up and said, 'I think we could all do with a drink.'

Immediately, Isobel said, 'You shouldn't. Not with those tablets.'

Howard ignored her. He went over to the drinks trolley and poured out three large measures of whiskey. He handed them round and stood in the centre of the room, gulping the Scotch.

'There's something else you need to know,' said Barbara. She sipped her drink and stared at her parents' solemn faces, as they prepared themselves for yet another awful revelation.

'Russell's been to the press. He's given The Source the whole story.'

'Oh no!' Isobel cried.

Barbara felt a stab of compassion for her mother. She was a shy woman who was fiercely protective of her privacy: a woman who avoided any kind of public fuss, even if it meant refusing to see her own doctor because she didn't want to be a bother.

Unobserved by Barbara, Isobel and Howard exchanged an unusual and deeply apprehensive look. 'The bloody fool!' exclaimed Howard. 'What did he want to go and do that for?'

Barbara was concerned to see her father's face turning a most unnatural shade of red. She knew that he'd nursed a pathological hatred of the press ever since reporters had hounded him and his friends at the time of the famous "incident". 'It's perfectly understandable,' she said. 'When Russell found out about Peter and Clarissa, he was hurt and bewildered. You know how much he's depended on her since Sarah's death. He felt betrayed and embarrassed. He felt he had to do something, so he got drunk and just struck out blindly. That's when he got in touch with The Source. He knows he's been completely stupid. When he told me about it he sounded mortified.'

'Oh, well, that's all bloody right then,' said Howard. He downed his drink.

'This is going to be awful,' said Isobel. 'I can't face it. All our dirty linen will be aired in public. It'll be all over the tabloids.'

'And on the TV,' growled Howard. 'Your husband's done us all a real favour this time!'

Barbara finished her drink. 'Yes, hasn't he? I had to tell you this because you needed to know. Once it gets out we may find the doorstep full of reporters.'

'I do hope so,' said Howard. 'My gun's already loaded.'

Isobel glanced at him nervously. Turning back to Barbara, she said, 'There's no possibility of them coming here, surely?'

'I'm afraid there is. Russell told The Source I was staying here.'

Isobel turned pale. She and Howard exchanged another concerned look. 'So that's why that reporter contacted you on our phone earlier?'

'Yes.'

'They'll have a field day,' said Howard. 'Especially after what he said at the Conference.'

At the last Party conference, speaking on the Fringe, Peter had controversially blamed the country's social problems on its ever-rising divorce rate, and the destruction of the traditional family. He'd received a standing ovation when he'd strongly advocated making divorce much more difficult.

'I'd forgotten all about that,' said Barbara. She began to laugh, hysterically.

CHAPTER TWENTY FOUR

'And if they ask you anything about your dad, tell them you've never met him.'

'I know. Don't keep going on.'

'Well it might slip out. While you're drawing that storyboard thing.'

'How can it?'

Sharon and Louise were sitting in the Passat which was parked in Church Lane outside The Old Rectory. Sharon hadn't yet told Louise that her father didn't want her to return to the unit. Sharon's own feelings about it were conflicted. She knew it was going to make her relationship with Greg acrimonious and she was concerned that Louise would be unwittingly indiscreet. For her part, Louise was astonished that her mother could even think she'd reveal a secret that she'd kept so faithfully all her life.

'Come on,' said Sharon, releasing her seat belt. 'I hope I'm not going to regret this.'

It was a gloriously sunny morning, and as mother and daughter trudged up the rectory's drive the still, hot air seemed palpable: its presence a force that resisted them at every step. It was obviously hot inside the house too, for the big front door had been flung wide open, presumably by the boy who was now hoovering in the hall. Counterpointing the vacuum cleaner's whine was the equally jarring din of a gratingly repetitive pop song being played at full volume inside the house. Dogs also seemed to be barking somewhere.

The raucous noise was putting Sharon's nerves on edge. The argument with Greg had deeply upset her. She felt caught in a Sisyphean trap in which all was dark and without respite. She saw her life stretching before her and no end to it. She would live in Leefdale forever, under the same conditions of secrecy, and nothing would ever change because she couldn't find within herself the will to make things change. She felt overcome and defeated by her own prevarication and inertia.

Sharon and Louise reached the open doorway. The boy who was hoovering looked up and stopped, but he didn't switch the machine off. He was aged about fifteen, rather fat with blonde hair and glasses. He gave them a casual wave.

'Hi Jake,' said Louise.'

Sharon said, 'Could you tell Mr... I mean, Dylan... that we're here?'

Jake switched the vacuum cleaner off, and the noise subsided with a strange collapsing gasp as though the machine was expressing relief. The song that had accompanied the machine's roar was now identifiable: it was Baha Men's recording of "Who Let the Dogs Out?" and was emanating at full volume from the chill-out room. The mysterious noise of barking dogs was now explained: it was on the soundtrack.

Jake went across the hall to the art therapy room and knocked. After a few moments the door opened and Dylan appeared. With a cod theatrical gesture, Jake indicated Sharon and Louise. Seeing them, Dylan's face broke into a huge smile. He stepped into the hall. 'Good morning!'

'Hello,' said Louise.

'I'm sorry I've brought her so early,' said Sharon, 'but I need to be in the office by nine.'

'That's fine. Any time after eight is OK.'

Sharon nodded towards Jake, who'd turned the vacuum cleaner back on and was again deeply absorbed in his hoovering. 'That's what I need,' she said, raising her voice above the din. 'A nice young man to do all my housework for me.'

Dylan laughed and stood aside. 'Come in.'

Louise went straight past him into the hall but Sharon stayed at the front door.

'Actually, I won't if you don't mind. I'm already running late.'

'Well, if you're already late another two minutes won't make you any earlier,' said Dylan.

Sharon hesitated. 'All right. Just for a minute.'

Dylan led them past Jake and on down the hall. Upstairs, the sound of others doing housework could be heard. 'Excuse me,' said Dylan. He ducked into the chill-out room and after a couple of seconds "Who Let the Dogs Out?" stopped. Immediately there were groans from the kitchen, and Mona appeared in the doorway. 'What did you do that for?'

'We're trying to hold a meeting,' said Dylan.

Mona gave Sharon a resentful look.

'It's nothing to do with us,' Sharon assured her.

'No. I know,' said Mona. She went back into the kitchen.

'The staff have a meeting every morning at eight,' Dylan explained. 'We let the clients have music while they're doing the housework.'

'You make them work for their breakfast, do you?' said Sharon.

'That's not very far from the truth. We feel that caring for the house and each other encourages them to take more care of themselves.'

'Good. I approve.'

In the kitchen Mona and Amy were at the dishwasher removing dishes and putting them away in the cupboards. Sheldon was in the utility room loading up the washing machine.

'Hi, Louise,' said Mona.

'Hello,' said Louise. Amy gave her a nod.

Sharon said, 'Louise is very happy today because she doesn't have to wear school uniform.'

Louise smiled. She did indeed look relaxed in her denim shorts and white polo shirt.

'School uniform's crap,' said Amy.

Sharon looked at Dylan, expecting him to admonish Amy for swearing but he said nothing.

'Wanna give us a hand, Louise?' asked Mona.

Louise looked at Dylan uncertainly. 'Can I?'

'Sure,' said Dylan. 'Go ahead.'

Mona found a spare cloth and handed it to Louise who'd joined her at the dishwasher. She told Louise she wanted her to wipe the sink and the draining boards.

'She could hardly wait to get here this morning,' said Sharon.

'Great,' said Dylan. 'So you're happy for her to come?'

'Oh yes.'

'Because last night...'

'Forget last night!' Sharon said, quickly. 'I was just being paranoid.'

'OK. But it's perfectly natural for you to want to protect your privacy. If you're ever bothered about what Louise does here, please feel free to talk to us about it.'

'I will.' She looked into his eyes and felt her own eyes magnetically melding with his. She quickly looked away. 'I really must go. I've got to open the office.'

Sharon planted a kiss on the top of Louise's head, then she said goodbye to everyone and set off into the hall. Dylan followed her. Outside the art therapy room he stopped and said, 'You haven't met Eric yet. Come and say hello.'

Reluctantly, Sharon followed Dylan into the room. A number of desks had been put together to form a large table. Toni, Zoe and Eric were seated around it. In front of them were several paintings and drawings in vibrant colours. On the floor was a stack of portfolios.

'Eric, I want you to meet Sharon, Louise's mum.'

Eric beamed. 'Hi Sharon. So, we haven't frightened you off?'

Sharon laughed. 'No.'

'Good. We're not normally this disorganised. We're having our regular morning meeting.'

'I'm amazed you can work with all the noise going on.'

'We're used to it,' said Zoe.

Dylan began to explain the purpose of the morning meetings. He spoke of the cross fertilization of art and drama therapy, and said that what was revealed through art therapy was developed in drama therapy, but that, conversely, feelings revealed in drama therapy could be explored and developed further through more art. The process wasn't mutually exclusive, it was reciprocal. Sharon found that she was soon only half listening. The room seemed to be affecting her concentration. It was too stimulating. There were pictures everywhere: on easels, on desks and on the walls. Those on the desks and easels seemed to be of plants and flowers. A few were drawn in charcoal and pencil but most had been painted or crayoned using rich, vibrant colours: greens and blues and reds that were too powerful for the eyes. And everywhere there was paint: tubes and drums of colour. It was the most colourful room she'd ever been in. She was overwhelmed by visual stimulation. The sun was streaming straight in through the big, high windows, and its brilliance seemed to be intensifying all the colours in the room and creating a strange halo effect around Dylan, who was still speaking. The faces of the others seemed backlit too, and bathed in light. The room and everything in it was beautiful. But there was also something threatening about it, something disturbing. It seemed to be seducing her, tempting her. She felt slightly giddy.

'And through this continual process of art and drama therapy, we hope eventually to liberate the suppressed "felt-self",' Dylan was saying.

'And help develop a more mature person,' said Zoe.

Suddenly, in addition to the noise of the vacuum cleaner, "Who Let the Dogs Out?" started up again.

Sharon remembered she had a viewing at ten. 'That's very interesting,' she said. 'But I must go, I have to open up the office.'

She moved towards the door. Dylan started to come after her. Halted by a sudden thought, she turned to him. 'You said you needed something for Louise's meals and so on.'

'I'll invoice you.'

Sharon nodded, and quickly left before he had an opportunity to follow her.

As she walked down the drive to her car she felt the sun full on her face, its rays warming her business suit. Instead of shrinking from the radiance, she felt compelled to lift her face towards it as though making an offering of herself. She felt buoyant. Enervated. Unusually empowered and blissfully optimistic. She reached the gate and stood in Church Lane, looking up and down the street. It really was a most beautiful morning. It made her feel as though life was holding out a promise of endless possibilities: there was nothing she couldn't achieve; nothing she couldn't do. All the colours and images in the room and all the noise and activity in the rectory came back into her mind, filling it up and expanding it so that she felt her head was going to burst. She knew something incredibly significant had happened but she couldn't say what it was. And then, the insistent rhythms of "Who Let the Dogs Out?" started up inside her brain. Shit, she thought. It'll be going round and round in my head all bloody day now!

****

Sharon's departure from The Old Rectory was observed with interest by Major Howard Roberts. At the exact moment she exited from the house and began walking down its drive, he was standing at the open window of his study. He'd been there for some time, balefully contemplating the rectory and becoming progressively angered not just by the disgraceful state of its front garden but also by the combined racket of loud hoovering, barking dogs, and ear-splitting pop music issuing at full volume through its open front door and windows. The din was an intrusion into his privacy and violated the sanctuary to which he retreated in search of peace and reflection. Indeed, he'd been in his study since early morning, brooding on Barbara's revelations about the state of her marriage. But now the disgraceful row from the rectory was making considered thought impossible. There was nothing for it: he would have to complain!

If the Major had been of a more sanguine temperament, he might perhaps have acknowledged that due to atmospheric changes sounds were magnified and travelled further on hot days. He might also have conceded that the noise from the rectory was probably caused by thoughtlessness rather than malevolent intent, and could easily be reduced by the simple expedient of him closing his double glazed, soundproofed window. Or he could have waited to see how long the noise persisted before deciding to take the extreme course of making a direct complaint. But Howard conflated conciliation with appeasement, which was why he was standing at his study window silently fuming about the noisy bastards in the rectory. If they could have their doors and windows wide open on a hot sunny day, why the hell couldn't he?

And then, blessed relief, all the noise unexpectedly stopped.

Howard was still debating whether to telephone Dylan Bourne and convey his displeasure, when he was surprised to see Sharon emerge through the rectory's open doorway. He hadn't seen mother and daughter arrive together earlier, and therefore wasn't aware that Louise had been left at the rectory by her mother. He could only speculate that Sharon had called at the rectory on some matter connected with Parker and Lund. It was therefore with some curiosity, and not a little prurient interest, that Howard watched her make her way down the rectory's drive towards her car. Today she was elegantly dressed in a beige business suit and looked particularly gorgeous. As he admired her purposeful stride, Howard found himself wondering, like so many Leefdale males before him, who the lucky chap was who'd fathered Louise. As far as was known, Sharon never mentioned him or provided any indication of his possible identity. Now why was that? Apparently, she'd been no more than eighteen or nineteen when she'd disappeared for several months and then re-appeared with a baby daughter. It had been the talk of the village, so he'd been told, and even now people alluded to it salaciously. Only recently, he'd half-jokingly suggested to Greg that his close association with Sharon in her capacity as school governor and secretary of Community Watch made him particularly vulnerable to village gossip, especially as he was often popping in to see her. He'd had to laugh when Greg's reply had been, "You'd stand more chance with her than me".

Sharon unwittingly provided Howard with a fine leg show as she eased herself into the driving seat of the Passat. But his pleasure in the sight was diminished because, simultaneously, the sound of hoovering, pop music and barking dogs suddenly erupted again and poured out of the rectory at full volume. Unable to tolerate the raucous, jarring din any longer, he grabbed the phone and dialled the rectory's number, which, because of his long association with the Corbridges, he knew by heart.

After many rings the rectory's phone was answered by someone Howard could only assume was one of the juvenile inmates. The voice was female and had a Birmingham accent.

'Yeah?'

'This is Major Roberts here. I wish to speak to Mr Bourne.'

For a moment Scarlett, who'd left off cleaning the upstairs bathroom to take the call, was confused. People at the rectory rarely called Dylan, "Mr Bourne".

'Who?'

Howard decided that the girl was a half-wit. 'Major Roberts.'

'There's no-one called Major Roberts here.'

Was she being deliberately obtuse? 'No. I'm Major Roberts. I wish to speak to Mr Bourne.'

'Who do you want to speak to?'

'Mr Bourne. Dylan Bourne.'

'Oh, you mean Dylan!' Scarlett's voice was full of delighted recognition. 'He's having a meeting. Do you want me to get him?'

Howard sighed, heavily. 'Yes, please. That's the general idea.'

There was no response to this from Scarlett. Howard heard only the sound of the phone being banged down on the telephone table. This immediately acted as a sounding board and amplified the noise of the vacuum cleaner, the awful pop music and the barking dogs. With a pained expression, Howard held the phone at arm's length from his ear.

A few moments later he heard a male voice call out, "Jake, turn it off, I'm taking a call". At this, the sound of the vacuum cleaner abruptly died and the same male voice came on the line and announced that Dylan Bourne was the person speaking.

After they'd both exchanged perfunctory greetings, Dylan said, 'So how can I help you, Major?'

'You already have,' said Howard.

'Oh? How?'

'By turning that bloody hoover off.'

There was a pause at Dylan's end. 'Oh. Sorry. Yes, it is rather noisy.'

'But you could help me even more by stopping all that dreadful pop music too: or, at least, if you must play it, by closing your front door and windows. I'm in my study at Rooks Nest and the din from your house is appalling. I can't concentrate on a thing. I'm not normally one to complain, but on a hot day such as this it really is most inconsiderate of you to make an appalling racket with the doors and windows wide open.'

'Yes, yes, of course,' said Dylan. 'Sorry.'

'And can't you do something about your dogs?'

Dylan was amused. 'I'm afraid not. We don't have any dogs.'

'But I can hear them barking at the music.'

'That's because they're part of the soundtrack.'

'You mean they're on the record?'

'Yes. It's called "Who Let the Dogs Out?"'

'Do people really dance to the sound of dogs barking now? How extraordinary.'

'I'll go and turn it off,' said Dylan.

This was immediately followed by the sound of the phone being placed on the hall table once again. Shortly afterwards, the din in Howard's ear of "Who Let the Dogs Out?" vanished.

Dylan returned to the phone and in his most conciliatory tone said, 'I'm sorry, Howard, for being thoughtless. I didn't realize the sound was carrying so far. I'll make sure the front door is closed when we're doing our housework from now on.'

'And the windows, please.'

Despite feeling that Roberts was being unnecessarily overbearing, Dylan said, 'Sure. The windows too.' Then, in order to move the conversation into a more congenial area, he added, 'The weather's so beautiful at the moment it makes one rather careless about such things.'

'Does it?'

Howard's objectionable tone told Dylan that there was little point in pursuing the conversation. 'Look, I must get back to my meeting. Is there anything else I can do to help you?'

'As a matter of fact, there is. It's to do with the Magnificent Britain Competition.'

'Yes?'

'You do know that the judges will want access to your gardens on Friday?'

'Yes. We read your letter. We're ready for them. We're really looking forward to it.'

You've got a funny way of showing it, thought Howard.

At that moment Isobel, who was in the kitchen, called out that breakfast was ready.

'I'm sorry, Major. I really must get back to my meeting,' said Dylan.

'And I must go down to breakfast,' Howard said. 'But there are a number of matters that need to be cleared up with you before Friday.'

'That's all right. Call round later for a chat. Any time. I'm available throughout the day.'

'I will, don't you worry.'

Howard ended the call, and went and stood by his open window and listened: nothing but silence and the occasional trill of birdsong. Bliss.

Almost simultaneously, Dylan appeared in the open doorway of The Old Rectory. He gave Howard a friendly wave and then self-consciously closed the front door. Afterwards, Howard was most gratified to see him going round closing the rectory's windows.

Howard left the study and descended the stairs in a much improved state of mind. It rather looked as though Dylan Bourne was a reasonable man after all. He'd seen sense about the noise and had been immensely accommodating. So why wouldn't he be equally amenable to the suggestion that Greg Maynard and his team of volunteers should tidy up the rectory's gardens in time for Friday's inspection by the Magnificent Britain judges?

****

When the team meeting ended Dylan came into the kitchen. Louise was standing at the sink. He went over to her and asked if she'd been thinking about her new storyboard.

'A bit. Not much really.'

'Do you want to continue with the storyboard work?'

'Oh, yes. I like doing it.'

'OK. Which would you like to start on first, your school work or the storyboard?'

'That's easy. The storyboard.'

Dylan took Louise along to the art therapy room. He unlocked a metal cupboard in which he kept the clients' work and produced Louise's folder. He asked Louise to get some large sheets of cartridge paper from the trolley, and while she was doing this he took out her first storyboard from her folder and placed it on a desk.

'Take your time over the next storyboard,' he said. 'It should be longer than the first and have more detail. Remember, this isn't about blaming you. I want you to set down exactly what happened so that we can discuss it and consider ways you can avoid those situations that get you into trouble.'

Louise nodded.

'Right. I'll leave you to it.'

After Dylan left, she sat for some moments adjusting to being all by herself in the large art therapy room. The other children were working with Toni in the encouragement room, and she sat for some while listening to them chatting. Mrs Henshall wouldn't have let them do that. She didn't allow her class to talk while they were supposed to be working.

Louise got up and went over to the window. She looked out over the front lawn and across Church Lane to the house opposite where the Major lived. But the sun was reflecting straight at her, so she couldn't remain at the window for very long without screwing up her eyes. She went back to her desk, stood by it and took out a piece of paper from the back pocket of her shorts. It was covered in notes she'd made to herself. Louise had lied when she'd told Dylan she'd only been thinking about her new storyboard "a bit". In fact, ever since he'd mooted the idea she'd been considering how her original storyboard could be enhanced, what new content might be included and how it should be presented.

She sat down at her desk but didn't start work straightaway. She was thinking about what it was she was trying to achieve. It was important that the new storyboard showed that she was in the right and Jade was in the wrong; that she was the victim and Jade was the bully. It was also important that she didn't divulge anything that would upset her mother.

Louise sat and thought for a long time, and then decisively picked up her pencil and began drawing. Almost immediately, she stopped. She hadn't the enthusiasm for the task somehow. It was something to do with the room. Every surface seemed to be reflecting sunlight, and she was more aware than ever of the depth and richness of the colours in the pictures. They were only the big kids' pictures of plants and animals, and things she couldn't quite make out or even recognize, but they all seemed to be demanding her attention and affecting her concentration. Their colours were really pure and vivid and there seemed to be something deep in them that was making them vibrate. It wasn't just the sun on them. They seemed to be speaking a kind of truth. She thought she would love to be excluded the whole time if it meant she could come here to this room every day and do art, and then do drama in the evenings. She loved being in the rectory. It made her feel safe. She studied her original storyboard intently and then picked up her pencil again. Perhaps she shouldn't make herself look too goody-goody this time. That might seem suspicious.

CHAPTER TWENTY FIVE

Breakfast at Rooks Nest was a subdued meal, despite Isobel's efforts to cheer everyone up with a traditional "Full English". Howard, Barbara and the children sat at the big kitchen table while Isobel served bacon, eggs, sausages and mushrooms. The adults were silent and reserved but the children were talkative, demanding that they be taken to the beach and arguing about whether it should be Scarborough or Filey. This eventually drew in Howard and Isobel who, concerned that their grandchildren should have a good time despite the appalling circumstances, immediately agreed that they should be taken to the sea.

Barbara sat toying with her food. She found it difficult summoning up any enthusiasm for the proposed trip because she was sure she could protect Mark and Jessica more easily by restricting them to the house. She was preoccupied with how she was going to get hold of a copy of The Source, yet prevent the children from seeing it on news-stands and in shops while they were out and about. She was certain that the scandal about Peter and Clarissa would make the front page, which meant it would certainly be one of the top stories on the television news bulletins. She consoled herself with the knowledge that the children usually showed no interest in TV news coverage. However, just to make sure they wouldn't be exposed to the news, she resolved to buy some videos that would appeal to them and keep them preoccupied at the danger times. Thankfully, they had no access to the internet. The only computer in the house was in her father's study and he guarded it possessively. Nevertheless, she knew that at some point soon she was going to have to explain to Mark and Jessica the real reason for their father's continuing absence. It was a prospect she dreaded.

Scarborough was eventually selected as their seaside destination. The children were loudly and excitedly anticipating their day when there was a dull thud on the hall carpet.

'Post's early,' said Howard.

'I'll get it!' cried Mark. He jumped up and rushed out of the kitchen.

'It's not the post, it's the paper,' his voice came back from the hall.

'Paper?' said Isobel. Then quickly whispered to Barbara, 'We don't have a paper delivered!'

Barbara was immediately on her feet and preparing to go after Mark, but he'd already returned to the kitchen. He was carrying a copy of The Source. Miraculously, it had landed on the hall carpet in a folded position which had obscured the front page and he'd carried the paper without showing the least interest in it.

Barbara took it from him. One stealthy glance at the front page confirmed her worst imaginings. The banner headline was "Anti Divorce Tory has Teenage Mistress". There were photographs of Peter, Clarissa and herself. She flinched, hastily folded the paper up again and turned to the children. 'You'd better go upstairs with grandma and get ready.'

She nodded towards Isobel who, on cue, scooped up Mark and Jessica by the hand and propelled them out of the kitchen.

As soon as they'd gone, Barbara silently showed Howard the front page. He scanned the contents with horror and then stared into his daughter's moistening eyes. Touching her sympathetically on the cheek, he said, 'Poor darling. I wonder who delivered this filth?'

He left the kitchen to go and peer through the sitting room window to see if anyone was still lurking outside. But he'd only just entered the hall when someone started pounding on the front door. When it stopped, a grating cockney voice shouted through the letter box, 'Terry Bryden here from The Source, Mrs Kellingford. What do you think of this morning's edition?'

Howard ran into the sitting room. Through the bay window he could see two men hanging around the front door. One of them was a photographer. Urged on by Bryden, he snapped Howard's appearance at the window. Howard's response was to treat him to a V sign. He then went straight back into the hall and shouted at the closed front door, 'Go away, you scum. We've nothing to say to you!'

'Is that Mr Roberts? Peter Kellingford's father-in-law?' shouted the reporter. 'How do you feel about your son-in-law and his seventeen year old totty?'

Howard was about to shout "piss off", but stopped himself when he heard Jessica, who was on the landing above, say clearly, 'Why is grandpa shouting at those men?'

'Don't worry, Jessica, it's just a game we're playing,' Howard called up the stairs.

He returned to the kitchen and closed the door. Even so, the rapacious voice of the reporter was still audible as he continued to wheedle and plead for Barbara to go out and talk to him. 'Come on, Mrs Kellingford! Why won't you speak to us? What have you got to lose? Don't you want to give us your side of the story? Russell's told us everything, so what's your problem? Fifty grand for your story. How bad's that?'

'Now I know why the Soviets were so against press freedom,' said Howard.

'How long have you known about Peter's affair, Mrs Kellingford?'

Barbara looked ashen.

'The bastards never give up!' cried Howard.

'Yes, dad. That's just it... they don't. Even when they're investigating some boring aspect of Party policy they're tenacious. They used to ring Peter at all hours of the night. Ambush him on the street. Now they've got their teeth into a scandal about him, they'll never go away.'

Howard's mouth twisted up into a picture of loathing. Then, decisively, he set off out of the kitchen.

'Where are you going?' cried Barbara.

Something in her tone forced him to stop. He turned and replied, 'To get rid of them from my doorstep.'

'No, dad, please don't. They'll only make you angry, and your photo will be in their rag tomorrow with a story about how you threatened them. Please don't.'

Howard's determined expression softened a little. 'All right. But I'm going to call the police.'

'It won't do any good.'

'We don't have to put up with this!'

Barbara reached for her blue mobile phone.

'Who are you calling?'

'Peter.'

There was no reply on his direct line at the House of Commons. She tried calling his blue mobile but that was switched off. This was a devastating blow. They'd promised each other always to keep that channel of communication open, no matter what. 'It's Barbara. I need to speak to you urgently,' she told his voicemail. 'Call me back on the blue mobile.' She then called Peter's other mobile and left the same message.

She placed her blue mobile on the table and turned her attention to The Source. There was a full report of the scandal on pages two and three. Standing side by side, father and daughter read it together. It was worse than Barbara could possibly have imagined. There were several photographs of Peter and herself taken in happier times, one of Clarissa in a bikini and another of a injured looking Russell. There was even a photo of Sarah, Russell's late wife. Peter was characterised as a hypocrite, a love rat, a cradle snatcher and a false friend.

'They've really gone to town,' said Howard, putting his arm around Barbara's shoulder.

A few minutes later the blue mobile rang. It was a London number but not one Barbara recognised. In spite of this she answered. She was convinced it could only be Peter who was calling.

'Hello Barbara, Steve Hawkins here.'

Hawkins was a former milkman who'd founded his own dairy company and was now a multi-millionaire. He was not an MP, but through big donations and utter ruthlessness had worked his way up to a senior position in the Party. He was one of Peter's staunchest supporters.

Barbara was deeply shocked. She and Peter had promised each other they'd never give their blue mobile numbers to anyone else. Why then had he given her number to Hawkins? Another betrayal!

'Hello, Steve.'

'Thank heavens, I've reached you. Peter told me you'd gone incommunicado but were bound to answer on this number.'

'That's because it's supposed to be completely private. Only Peter and I use it. Promise me you'll never give it to anyone else.'

'Course I won't. You can trust me, Barbara.'

How many politicians had she heard say that?

'Good.'

'I was just ringing to say how sorry we all are to hear about your problems with Peter.'

'That's very kind of you, Steve.'

'How are you coping?'

'Well, considering that Peter's affair with his best friend's daughter is spread over three pages in The Source, and I have a reporter and a photographer hammering at my parents' front door, quite well I'd say.'

'Oh God, they've found you already, have they?'

'Yes. And they're demanding I give them a statement.'

'It would be very unwise to do that, Barbara.'

'I know.' Barbara was well aware that the only reason Hawkins had rung was to make sure she was going to keep her mouth shut. 'Don't worry, I've no intention of fanning the flames.'

'Excellent. Now look, I've a meeting with Peter in an hour. As you can imagine we're heavily engaged in damage limitation at this end.'

I'll bet you are, Barbara thought.

'My main worry is Clarissa's father,' Hawkins continued. 'Seems a bit of a loose cannon.'

'He's the one who gave The Source the story.'

'Yes. The editor, Bill Metcalfe, told me. And now he can't be traced. You've no idea where he might be, I suppose?'

'No. But you needn't worry. I don't think they'll get any more out of Russell. He told me he bitterly regretted what he'd done.'

'Well, don't do anything until you hear from me. I'll get back to you as soon as I can with an agreed strategy. But in the meantime, don't say a word to the press.'

Barbara deeply resented Hawkins' high handed manner, but she let it pass. She had other things on her mind. 'Where's Peter now? I've been trying to contact him.'

'I'm sorry, I don't know.'

Lying bastard, thought Barbara. 'Well, when you find him would you ask him to ring me urgently?'

'Of course, I will,' Hawkins said. Then, after making some suitably sympathetic and encouraging remarks, he rang off.

Barbara gave Howard an account of her telephone conversation.

'What a slimy rat,' said Howard. He had a very low opinion of politicians and thought even less of political fixers.

Barbara moved towards the kitchen door.

'Where are you going?'

'To talk to the children. They deserve some kind of explanation for this. And I want to be the one who gives it to them.'

Mark and Jessica's bedroom was at the front of the house. When Barbara arrived there she found both children still in their pyjamas. They were standing at the window, mesmerised by the sight of Terry Bryden and his long haired photographer laying siege to their front door.

Wearily, Isobel said, 'I've told them to get dressed but they're taking no notice of me.'

'Right! If you're not dressed in fifteen minutes we're not going to Scarborough!' warned Barbara.

Mark turned away from the window. 'Why do those reporters keep asking to talk to you, mummy?'

Barbara placed a hand on her son's shoulder. 'When you're dressed, I'll tell you.'

Isobel gave her daughter a look. 'Do you think that's wise?'

'I'd rather they heard it from me,' said Barbara.

'Heard what, mummy?' said Mark.

'When you're dressed!' Barbara insisted.

'What's totty?' Jessica said, reaching for her trainers. 'They keep shouting about totty.'

CHAPTER TWENTY SIX

Dylan spent Tuesdays mainly doing administrative work. Even so, during the course of the morning, he still found time to pop into the art therapy room and cast an eye over Louise's progress with her revised storyboard. Around ten o'clock, Louise sought him out in the kitchen while he was taking a quick coffee break and announced that she'd finished. He returned with her to the art therapy room to see what she'd produced.

When Dylan had seen Louise's first attempt at a storyboard he'd been struck by the fine quality of her drawing. In this respect her second storyboard impressed him even more. The figures were all carefully delineated so that each was a distinctively recognisable character: Jade, small, dark and angular; Roger, chubby, with tousled blonde hair, big eyes and a man-in-the-moon face; Louise herself, tall, long haired, watchful. The overall effect was achieved with skilful economy, each impression of the whole created by a series of tiny yet subtle intimations: for example, the suggestion of a wastepaper bin, part of a fence and some white lines on the floor established the school playground; while Mrs Henshall's office was indicated by the edge of her desk, a glimpse of telephone and some bookcases. Dylan recognised a fellow artist.

Louise's original storyboard had now been expanded to twelve frames. These were highly detailed and involved many more speech balloons. The first frame was without a label and depicted Jade and Roger standing together in the street, arm in arm and smiling. The second frame was labelled "Friday". Louise, Jade and Roger were in the school playground and Louise was adopting an aggressive stance towards Jade. The speech bubble issuing from Louise's mouth said, "Roger's dumping you. He's going out with me now". The third frame, was also taking place on Friday in the school playground, but showed only Louise and Jade. Jade was holding her hands to her face and was evidently crying. Louise was saying, "I told you he fancied me more than you". The fourth frame was again set in the school playground but labelled "Monday", as were the rest of the frames. It showed Louise and Roger now holding hands and Jade shouting at Louise, "You love Roger 'cos he's got no dad like you and his mum's a slag just like yours". In the fifth frame, Roger was crying and Louise was comforting him. He was saying, "I have got a dad but he's dead". In the sixth frame, Louise was standing very close to Jade, aggressively pointing her finger at her and shouting, "Your dad's a slag". The seventh frame showed Jade punching Louise in the face, and in the eighth frame they were both on the ground fighting furiously. In the ninth frame, Mrs Lucas and another lunchtime supervisor had intervened and were trying to stop the fight. The tenth frame showed that Jade and Louise had been separated and were being restrained by the two adults. Mrs Lucas was saying to Louise, "Why are you always upsetting Jade?". In the penultimate frame, Louise was kicking Mrs Lucas hard on the leg and a shriek was issuing from Mrs Lucas' mouth. The final frame showed Louise in the head teacher's office. Mrs Henshall was pointing to the door. In the speech bubble coming from her mouth were the words, "You're excluded!".

Dylan placed Louise's new storyboard beside her first one for comparison, and studied both for a long time. It was apparent to him that, as was often the case, the revised storyboard presented a far more complex version of events. In yesterday's storyboard, Louise had depicted herself as a victim of Jade's bullying, and had been adamant that Jade had been responsible for starting the fight. Now it appeared that Louise had provoked Jade, even possibly tormented her. This admission of culpability was a positive sign, but it was still necessary to discover the reasons for Jade and Louise's animosity. The new storyboard showed that Louise had taken Jade's boyfriend off her. Was that the reason for their quarrel and the ensuing fight? Dylan wondered about the significance of the acrimonious exchanges between Louise and Jade in which they'd called each other's parents "slags". Was that indicative of a deeper conflict?

Dylan had been aware of Louise watching him intently as he studied her new storyboard. Presently, he said, 'This is very good Louise. It gives a much clearer picture of what happened. By the way, you have an obvious talent for drawing.'

She smiled shyly. 'Thank you.'

'Are you happy to talk about it and fill in some of the background?'

'OK.'

'Right. Let's start from the beginning.' He pointed to the first frame. 'Would you like to tell me what's happening here?'

'It's a picture of Jade and Roger.'

'Why are they arm in arm?'

'They're going out together.'

'Oh, I see. They both look very happy.'

'Yes.'

'So Roger was Jade's boyfriend?'

'Yes.'

'How did you feel about them going out together?'

Louise gazed at him warily. 'How do you mean?'

'Did it upset you?'

Louise shrugged her shoulders. 'No. Why should it?'

'Well, Roger was your friend, wasn't he?'

'Yes.'

'I wondered if you might have been a bit jealous that he was going out with Jade.'

'No.'

'You didn't feel that Jade had taken your friend away from you?'

'No. But I knew he liked me more than Jade.'

Dylan studied frame one of today's storyboard again. It intrigued him that Louise had drawn Jade and Roger looking unnaturally happy, and yet had omitted from yesterday's storyboard the information that Roger had once been Jade's boyfriend. She'd also hidden the fact that she'd taken him away from Jade. Had Louise deliberately set out to destroy Jade and Roger's happiness because it had offended her? But why?

He tried another approach. 'Yesterday, you said that you and Jade were once friends.'

'Yes. She was my best friend.'

'How long ago was that?'

'When we first went to school.'

'How did you fall out?'

'I don't know. I can't remember.'

She remembered very well, of course. She'd picked her first fight with Jade in the days following her discovery that they both shared the same father.

Dylan suspected that Louise was "blocking". 'All right,' he said. He pointed to the next frame, the first of the three labelled "Friday". 'Would you like to tell me about this one?'

'This is where I'm telling Jade that Roger's dumping her and going out with me now.'

He said, 'Jade must have been upset to hear that.'

'She was. She cried.'

'How did you feel about that?'

'What? That she cried?'

'Yes.'

Louise looked at him uncertainly. She suspected a trap. 'I don't know.'

'I mean, did it make you feel happy or sad?'

'I don't know. I didn't feel anything.'

'Why didn't Roger tell her himself?'

'Because he's a coward. He didn't want to upset her.'

This was partly true. But Louise could have added that she'd been delighted to tell Jade the bad news herself.

'So he asked you to tell her?'

'Yes.'

'And you didn't mind upsetting her?'

'Huh!' Louise made a scoffing noise deep in her throat. Then said, with a shockingly adult bitterness, 'She doesn't mind upsetting me!'

'In what ways does Jade upset you?'

'All sorts of ways.'

'Would you like to tell me about them?'

Louise paused, remembering her mother's strict warning to say nothing about her father. But surely, she reasoned, it would be all right to repeat what Jade had said? It wasn't as though mum didn't know, was it?

Cautiously, she said, 'Jade's always taunting me about not having a dad.'

This seemed to Dylan to be most significant. In yesterday's storyboard, Louise had shown Jade alluding to the fact that both Roger and Louise were without fathers. It had also been repeated word for word in today's storyboard. Could this be the trigger for Louise's anger? Yesterday, she'd expressed resentment that Jade had a powerful father who protected her, whereas she hadn't. Obviously, Louise had some sort of issue concerning her absent father. He said, 'So Jade often makes fun of you because your father's absent, is that right?'

'Yes.'

'What exactly does she say? Can you remember?'

'She says things like, "Course, you haven't got a dad, have you? Not like me," or she says, "They only gave you the part of Nancy, coz you haven't got a dad". Things like that.'

'How do you feel when she says that?'

Louise shrugged her shoulders, but said nothing.

'When she says those things about you, you feel something, don't you?'

'Yes. I feel upset.'

'And have you told her how upset it makes you?'

'No. She knows anyway. That's why she does it.'

'Have you told your teachers about this?'

'Yes. But Jade always says she didn't say it, and Mrs Henshall always believes her.'

'Always?'

'Yes.'

'Why do you think she believes her and not you?'

'Because she's frightened of Jade's dad. He's the Chairman of the school governors.'

This struck Dylan as a singularly adult observation. Surely it was too cynical to be her own insight? He decided she must be repeating what she'd heard other adults say: her mother, perhaps?

Dylan said, 'OK. When did you and Roger start going out together?'

'Last Friday morning. At break.'

'Just before you told Jade?'

'Yes.'

'So who suggested you go out together? You or Roger?'

'It was me. I told Roger I knew he liked me and asked him if he wanted to go out with me. He said, yes, he liked me more than Jade. So, I said, OK. You can come out with me.'

Dylan now strongly suspected that Louise had deliberately stolen Roger in order to upset Jade.

'So then you went and told Jade straight away?'

'Yes.'

Dylan smiled at Louise and said casually, 'So you like Roger?'

'Not really. Not in that way. But I knew he liked me.'

'It sounds like you said you'd go out with him just to upset Jade.'

Louise said nothing.

'You didn't use Roger to upset Jade, did you?'

'No. He said he liked me.'

'But you knew that if you agreed to go out with Roger, it would hurt Jade?'

'What do you mean?'

'You said, you really didn't like Roger. I was wondering if you agreed to go out with Roger because you knew it would hurt Jade?'

Again, Louise said nothing. She was regretting now that she'd put anything about Roger in the storyboard. 'I said I'd go out with him because he asked me.'

'Even though you didn't really like him?'

Louise stayed silent.

'If someone did that to you, how would you feel?'

'Did what? I don't understand.'

'I mean, would you say using people to hurt others isn't very nice?'

'No, it isn't. But people do it all the time.'

Again, Dylan thought this a particularly cynical view in one so young. He was surprised at the adult nature of her discourse. 'You think people use other people a lot?'

'Some do.'

'Do you say that because you feel other people are using you?'

Louise suspected that Dylan was manoeuvring her into dangerous waters and she considered carefully before she answered. 'No, not me. But people do use people. In "Oliver", Bill Sykes uses Nancy to get Oliver away from Mr Brownlow.'

Dylan decided not to pursue this. He was afraid that if she suspected him of probing too deeply, she might completely clam up.

'OK. Let's move on to the third frame. What can you tell me about this?'

'It shows me telling Jade that Roger fancies me more than her.'

'Do you know why you said that to her?'

'I dunno, but it's the truth.'

'I see that Jade is crying.'

'Yes.'

'Is that because she'd just learnt you were going out with Roger?'
'Yes.'
'What did you feel when you saw her crying?'
'I felt sorry for her.'
'So, why did you say, "I told you he fancied me more than you?"'
Louise was silent.
'Could it have been to hurt her even more?'

Louise said nothing. It was all going wrong. She'd thought Dylan would just accept her storyboard as her version of the truth. She hadn't expected to have to talk about it, and defend herself like this.

'Can you remember what you felt when you said it?'
'No.'

But she could remember. It had made her feel happy knowing Jade was miserable because now Jade knew what it was like to be miserable too. But afterwards, she knew she'd been unkind. She didn't feel sorry for her or anything, but she knew she'd been unkind.

Dylan decided it was time to move on. 'Now, let's look at frames four, five and six together as a sequence, because in these frames things seem to get out of hand, and eventually lead to violence.'
'All right.'
'In frame four Jade is saying that neither you nor Roger has a dad. Has Jade ever said anything like this to Roger before?'
'Not to Roger. But she's always saying I haven't got a dad.'
'I see. And Roger's dad is dead, isn't he?'
'Yes.' Louise pointed to frame two of her first storyboard. 'I told you yesterday. He was killed in an accident.'
'Could that be what made you and Roger friends? I mean, have you ever talked about your fathers?'
'Roger's always talking about his dad. They used to go fishing together. He misses him all the time.'
'Do you talk to Roger about your father?'
'No.'
'Would you like to tell me a bit about your father?'

So mum had been right. He did want to try and make her tell him about dad. And the strange thing was, she felt an overwhelming urge to do it.

'I don't know anything about him. I've never met him. I don't know who he is.'
'But you've talked to your mum about him?'
'No. Never.'

Dylan found this impossible to believe, but he let it pass. He pointed to frame four. 'In this one, Jade is calling your mum a slag and also Roger's mum a slag.'
'Yes.'

'Has she ever said anything like that before?'

'Not to Roger. But she's called my mum a slag lots of times.'

Dylan was intrigued by this new information. Again, Louise had omitted it from her first storyboard. He wondered if it was significant. He also wondered how true it was.

'How do you feel when Jade says that?'

'What? Calls my mum a slag?'

'Yes.'

'I hate her.'

'Do you hate her enough to hit her?'

Louise looked shocked. 'Hitting people is wrong.'

'But do you feel you'd like to hit her?'

'No. It's wrong.'

'But you said Jade calls your mum that word a lot. When she does, don't you sometimes feel angry and want to hit her?'

Louise said nothing.

'You know, it's quite natural to feel that way, Louise.'

Louise nodded.

Very gently, he said, 'And when you feel like that, perhaps sometimes you do hit Jade?'

Louise looked at the floor.

'Have you ever hit Jade?'

Louise shook her head. She fixed Dylan with an unblinking stare. 'No, I never hit Jade. She always hits me.'

Ever conscious of Louise's volatile state, Dylan was unwilling to pressure her further. 'OK. In the next frame, frame five, you appear to be comforting Roger who seems to be crying. He's also telling you that he's got a dad, but his dad is dead.'

'Yes. But I'm not comforting Roger. He's struggling. He wants to get away and hit Jade but I won't let him.'

'Oh, I see. Why did you stop him?'

'I didn't want him to get into trouble.'

'That's good, Louise, very commendable. Have you ever considered doing the same thing for yourself?'

'What do you mean?'

'Protecting yourself from getting into trouble?'

Louise laughed. 'It doesn't matter if I get into trouble.'

'Why ever not?'

'It just doesn't.'

It didn't surprise Dylan that Louise, like many children abandoned by a parent, had a very poor self-image. 'Do you sometimes feel that you don't matter as much as other people?'

She seemed genuinely surprised at this suggestion. 'Yes. Quite a lot of the time.'

'Well, I assure you, Louise, that you matter just as much as anyone else. It's time you started believing that.'

She said nothing, but she was deeply affected. How did Dylan know she always felt other people mattered more than her? That she was a nuisance who nobody wanted?

Something in Louise's expression made Dylan say, 'Look, would you like to take a break from this?'

'No. It's all right.'

But it wasn't all right. She was worried that Dylan's questions were going to reveal the truth about her parents and their weird lives. But amazingly, she didn't care. Part of her wanted him to find out.

'OK. Let's move on to frame six. In this one you seem to be getting more aggressive and you're telling Jade that her dad's a slag.'

Louise nodded.

'Have you ever met Jade's dad?'

Now she really was panicking. The moment of truth was coming closer and closer. How should she answer? She'd already told him that Jade had once been her best friend. How could she lie and say she'd never met Jade's dad? Perhaps it would be best to tell the truth. Dylan would never guess she shared a father with Jade.

'Sometimes.'

'So you know him quite well?'

Louise looked horrified. 'No. No.'

'Then why did you say he was a slag?'

'Jade said my mum was a slag so I said her dad was a slag.'

It struck Dylan as unusual that Louise had used a term which was usually applied to a female.

'Do you understand what the word "slag" means, Louise?'

'Yes.'

'Would you like to tell me?'

'What? What it means?'

'Yes.'

She knew what it meant all right, but she wasn't going to tell him she knew. No way.

'It means a horrible person,' she said.

'So you did it for revenge? Because Jade said your mum was a horrible person, you said that Jade's dad was a horrible person?'

Louise knew that she was just a sentence away from her liberation. All she had to do was explain to Dylan that Jade's father was also her father, and she would be free of the guilt that was binding her. But although the temptation to reveal all was great, she was sure that the consequences would be terrible. She was her parents' secret, and she'd promised them she'd remain silent about it forever. 'I was just trying to get back at Jade for what she said about my mum.'

'So, it's not really true?'

Of course, it was true but she couldn't tell him that her own dad was a slag. Then, suddenly, she saw how she could convince him it was true without putting herself in danger. 'It is true. You see, Roger told me that Jade's dad visits his mum a lot. He's always round Roger's house.'

'I see,' said Dylan. It rather looked as though Louise knew very well what "slag" meant. A terrible sadness invested him. How dreadful it was that children of such a tender age should be the victims of their parents' duplicity. He said, 'But just because Jade's dad visits Roger's mum doesn't mean he's a horrible person, does it?'

Louise shook her head. What was the point? He'd never understand. No-one would ever understand unless she told them the truth: that Jade's dad was her dad too. And she couldn't do that.

Dylan couldn't resist the temptation to be completely unprofessional. 'Have you ever met your mum's boyfriend?' he asked.

Louise felt the panic building again. Was he saying that dad was mum's boyfriend? He must be trying to trick her. She decided he wasn't as nice as she'd first thought. She felt confused. Mum had told her to say nothing about dad. When Dylan used the word boyfriend did he mean dad? Or did he mean boyfriend? 'Mum hasn't got a boyfriend,' she said.

Dylan hadn't expected that. He quickly said, 'Oh, sorry, I must have made a mistake.' His thoughts zigzagged and swirled. Why had Louise denied that her mother had a boyfriend? Was it because she'd never met him? Perhaps there wasn't a boyfriend at all? Had Sharon invented a boyfriend to put him off? Better not pursue it. 'Right,' he said, 'frame seven shows Jade throwing a punch at you.'

'Yes.'

'That must have hurt.'

'It did.'

'And then you hit her back?'

'Yes.'

'Can you think of something you might have done to stop yourself hitting her?'

Louise thought for a moment. 'Walked away?'

'That's one thing.'

'I couldn't. I was too angry. And mum says if Jade hits me I have to hit her back.'

'We can teach you some strategies for controlling your anger and getting out of these dangerous situations. Would you like that?'

Louise nodded slowly. 'OK.'

Dylan pointed at the eighth frame. This was the one which depicted Louise and Jade on the ground, fighting. 'Is this the first fight you and Jade have had?'

'No. We've had others. But not as bad as this one.'

'And who would you say usually starts them? You or Jade?'

'Jade!'

Dylan gave Louise a long, searching look and then waited.

Louise bethought herself. If she seemed too perfect he wouldn't believe her. 'Well, not always Jade. Sometimes I start them.'

Dylan experienced a feeling of achievement. He knew that this disclosure was hugely significant. It was the first time Louise had admitted she might be the initiator of aggression.

'So sometimes you start them?'

'Yes, because she says things about me not having a dad.'

He realised it wasn't such an advance after all. And still she was fixated on the absent father. They moved on to the ninth frame. Dylan asked Louise to describe what was happening.

'This is Mrs Lucas and Mrs Chadbourne. They're both lunchtime supervisors. Mrs Lucas is stopping the fight. She got hold of me, and Mrs Chadbourne got hold of Jade who started to cry.'

'Did you cry?'

'No.'

Louise pointed to frame ten. She said, 'Then Mrs Lucas shouted at me, "Why are you always upsetting Jade?".'

'Is she right? Are you always upsetting Jade?'

'No! She's always starting on me.'

'But you just told me that you sometimes start the fights.'

Louise said nothing. Then burst out, 'Mrs Lucas always picks on me!'

Dylan pointed to frame eleven.

'Is that why, in this frame, you're kicking her? Because she's always picking on you?'

'No. It was an accident.'

'How did you feel when you kicked her?'

'Nothing. I didn't even know I'd kicked her until she shouted and started rubbing her leg.'

'And then what did you feel?'

'Sorry. I felt sorry.'

'Sorry because you really regretted it, or because you knew you were in trouble?'

'Sorry because I didn't mean to do it. It was an accident.'

'It was an accident?'

'Yes. It was an accident! Don't you believe me?'

Dylan said, 'I do believe you. But it doesn't matter what I say or think about the storyboard, Louise. What's important is that the storyboard shows what happened as truthfully as possible.'

Petulantly, she said, 'Well, it does.'

'I know.'

Louise was pleased because he seemed to be saying he believed her. But actually, it was the unconscious truth often revealed by storyboards that he was referring to. He turned back to her storyboard and said lightly, 'Now, let's take a look at this final frame.'

Frame twelve showed Louise in Mrs Henshall's office. The child stood with her head bowed as the head teacher informed her that she was being excluded.

'You look very ashamed,' said Dylan.

'I wasn't ashamed!' said Louise, suddenly defiant. 'I was just upset because I was sure I'd lost the part of Nancy.'

'But you haven't, have you?'

'No. Mrs Henshall said I could do it even though I was excluded.'

'That was good of her, don't you think?'

'Not really. She needs me.'

Again, Dylan was struck by her cynical analysis of adult motivation. He wasn't to know that she was merely repeating her mother's comment. He said, 'Acting means a lot to you, doesn't it?'

'I love it.'

'What's the best thing about it?'

'Being someone else.'

CHAPTER TWENTY SEVEN

When the children were dressed, Barbara sat between them on the bed and placed her arms around their shoulders. Two serious, puzzled faces regarded her.

'You remember yesterday that you asked me why we were going to grandma and grandpa's, and I told you it would be nice to see them while daddy was away for a while?'

'He's not coming back, is he?' said Mark.

Barbara stared at her son, taken aback by his prescience.

'No,' she said, quietly.

'Has he done something awful?'

'Will he go to prison?' asked Jessica.

Despite her emotions, Barbara looked up and exchanged a smile with Isobel.

'No. He won't go to prison. He's decided that he doesn't want to live with me anymore. He's found a new girlfriend. That's what totty means.'

'Who?' demanded Mark.

Barbara paused, unsure how to continue. This was always going to be the hardest part, telling them that their position in their father's life had been supplanted by a family friend so close to their own ages. A teenager whom they'd played with so often, whom they'd trusted and loved.

'Clarissa,' she said.

Their astonishment was obvious.

'It can't be Clarissa,' said Mark. 'She's still at school.'

****

It took Barbara a long time to convince Mark and Jessica that their father had really left them for Clarissa. After their initial incredulity, they began to accept the awful reality and became predictably distressed and tearful. They bombarded their mother with questions. Didn't daddy love them anymore? Where was he now? Was he going to marry Clarissa? Why had he gone off without saying goodbye? Barbara tried to respond as honestly and as sensitively as possible, but the strain was too much for her and soon she, like the children, had dissolved in tears.

Fortunately, in the midst of all this emotion, a diversion occurred which enabled Isobel to temporarily draw the children's attention away from the cause of their distress.

A sizeable crowd was accumulating outside the front door of Rooks Nest. Terry Bryden and his photographer had been joined in the drive by reporters and photographers from several local papers, who also doubled as stringers for the national tabloids and the broadsheets. TV news crews were arriving to complete the media ranks, and the crowd was being swelled even further by curious villagers and other rubber-neckers who were loitering by the gates at the entrance to the drive.

Most of the media people knew each other well, and were veterans of hundreds of such shared sieges. Now, as they milled around in the drive of Rooks Nest, their mood was mostly light-hearted: they idly joshed each other, exchanged gossip and spoke on their mobiles to their editors; they launched periodic assaults on the front door of the house, demanding responses from those inside. They also talked and joked with the onlookers and if any of the locals was discovered to have useful information, he or she was cornered by the pack and ferociously questioned.

'Look,' cried Isobel, who was observing all this from the bedroom window. 'The police are here. Come and look.'

Barbara and the two children joined Isobel at the window. Two police officers were getting out of a patrol car parked at the bottom of the drive. They went over to the large crowd of onlookers which had assembled around the front gates and with commands and gestures ordered them to take up positions either side of the gates, on the pavement. Having cleared the entrance to the drive, the officers then drove up it and turned their attention to the media people and other hangers-on who were laying siege to the front of the house. The officers ordered them all to go back down the drive and join the members of the public in Church Lane. When the media throng had grudgingly complied, and were no longer occupying the grounds of Rooks Nest, the police car returned to Church Lane. The officers got out of their vehicle, closed the gates to the drive and stood guard.

'Well, that's something, at least,' said Isobel.

A moment later Howard appeared in the bedroom. He appeared flushed and agitated, and also triumphant.

'Did you see that?' he said. 'Just one call to Jeff Crawley, that's all it took.'

Jeff Crawley was the Chief Constable and also a member of Howard's golf club.

Howard laughed, slightly hysterically. 'The harassing swine didn't expect that, did they?'

'Well done, dad, thanks,' said Barbara.

Howard's expression changed as he became aware of the tearful faces around him and the emotionally charged atmosphere in the room.

Jessica launched herself at Howard. She threw her arms around his waist and buried her face against his jacket. 'Grandpa! Daddy's run away with Clarissa and he's never coming back!'

'There, there,' said Howard, stroking the child's hair. 'It's not as bad as all that. You'll still be able to see him. You'll see.'

'That's not true. We won't. He's never going to see us again.'

Distress bled out of Howard's eyes. This really was too much! The look he gave his wife and daughter implored their support.

Barbara came over to him, took her weeping daughter in her arms and carried her over to the bed. She sat down, placed the child on her lap and comforted her.

Howard lingered a while, acutely aware of his own inadequacy. Then, he said, 'I've got one or two things to do,' and sidled out of the room.

****

Zoe was in the studio preparing for her next drama session when she realized she'd left a crucial textbook in her bedroom.

She ran out of the studio and took the stairs two at a time. She'd intended to spend just a moment or two in her room, but as soon as she got there she became aware of some noise or disturbance going on outside in the street. Her windows gave her an excellent view of Church Lane and for the next twenty minutes all thoughts of the missing textbook and her morning's preparation vanished. She was mesmerised by the extraordinary behaviour of the reporters and photographers milling around the front door of Rooks Nest; the growing crowd of onlookers at the front gates; and the arrival of more and more television crews. She also observed the efforts by the police to take control and impose their authority on what was becoming an increasingly fraught situation.

But why, she wondered, was the Roberts' home under siege by so many press and media people?

Every bedroom in the inclusion unit was equipped with a television. Zoe went over to hers and switched it on to BBC News 24. She was astonished to see a news presenter immediately appear on screen doing a piece to camera with Rooks Nest behind him. From what she could gather from the man's report, Peter Kellingford, the Shadow Home Secretary, was involved in a big sex scandal. He'd left his wife for a seventeen year old researcher who happened to be the daughter of one of his oldest friends. It appeared that Kellingford was Major Roberts' son-in-law, and Mrs Kellingford was believed to be presently staying with her parents at Rooks Nest. Zoe knew she had work to do but she was so entranced by the drama of it all, she couldn't tear herself away. She was deriving a childish satisfaction from being able to watch the coverage on live television and, simultaneously, with just a turn of her head, witness it happening in actuality, just outside her bedroom window.

Zoe wanted to tell her colleagues about what was going on across the road but she knew Toni was teaching and Dylan was working with Louise on her storyboard. Only Eric was remotely free, finishing his report for Mona's social worker. On an impulse, Zoe went along to Eric's bedroom which was on the same floor as hers but at the rear of the house.

As she entered, Eric rose from the desk at which he'd been writing and came towards her. He stretched out his arms and drew her to him.

She hesitated. It ought to be all right. The door was closed. Everyone else was downstairs. They kissed. He wanted another but she stopped him. 'I told you, that's all finished,' she said.

He looked aggrieved. 'Why did you kiss me, then?'

'Because you look so bloody miserable.'

'If I am miserable, it's your fault.'

'No, it's not. I didn't ask you to leave your wife and kids. I didn't ask you to follow me here.'

'But you told me you loved me!'

'People say all sorts of things when they're about to come. We've already had this conversation. It's over, OK? From now on we're just colleagues.'

A sulky expression formed around Eric's mouth. 'What do you want then?'

'You'll never guess what's going on over at Rooks Nest.' She took his hand. 'Come on. Come and see.'

'No. I'm busy.'

She tugged him harder.

'What are you doing?'

'Trying to cheer you up.'

He thrust her hand away. 'You know what you are, don't you?'

'What?'

'A prick teaser.'

She stared at him with contempt. Then, with laughing eyes, said, 'If I'm the teaser, then you're definitely the prick!'

****

As Zoe descended the stairs, she gently castigated herself for the way she'd behaved towards Eric. She knew it was wrong to wind him up, but he did ask for it. They'd been sharing the same house for nearly six weeks now and she was sick of his possessiveness, his bleating self-pity and his unfair recriminations. But most of all she was sick of his big, lovesick eyes and those long, wounded looks. Really, he was such a child. How she longed to be free of his stifling, embarrassing presence and his constant implication that she was responsible for ruining his life. Why did the men she hooked up with always turn out to be such losers, and blame her for all that was wrong with them? Pathetic!

Zoe had decided she wanted to experience at first hand the extraordinary media event that was taking place on her doorstep. She let herself out through the front door, strode down the drive and crossed Church Lane. What struck her, as she stood on the periphery of the crowd gathered around the gates of Rooks Nest, was the unique atmosphere. Everyone seemed to be quietly anticipating retribution and demonstrating that they had the patience to wait for it, no matter how long it took. There was a sense that they'd been following a quarry which had chosen this place to go to ground, and the thin blue line of police officers was all that prevented these people from finishing it off. The nature of the quarry seemed irrelevant: it could have been a fox or a fugitive from a lynch mob, but all that mattered was flushing it out. She was glad she'd come out of the house to mingle with the crowd. No way could she have experienced this astonishing atmosphere just by watching from her bedroom window. She knew she ought to come away, but she was ashamed to say she was caught up in the suspense of it and wanted to be there when they smoked out their prey. For the moment, however, she was content to stare at the handsome television reporter she'd just seen on News 24, and exchange nods with one or two people she recognised from her daily runs through the village.

Meanwhile, Zoe's striking presence was attracting admiring glances from several men in the crowd, particularly the waiting journalists and photographers who, as usual, were finding the stake-out tedious and boring.

Her arrival certainly hadn't escaped the notice of Terry Bryden who was standing a short distance from her alongside John Carter, his photographer. John wasn't his usual snapper, but a local stringer who normally worked for The Sandleton Examiner. He was only nineteen and somewhat overawed to be on such an important assignment, working with the great and legendary Terry Bryden. Actually, until that morning he'd never heard of Bryden but within minutes of their first meeting Terry had told him how great and important he was.

Bryden dug his elbow into Carter's ribs and nodded towards Zoe. 'Cor, cop a load of that!'

'Very nice,' said John, wistfully. He still lived at home with his mum and dad and hadn't yet managed to lose his virginity. Although, he'd come pretty close to it in Ibiza at Easter.

'Nice? Nice?' said Bryden, with faux incredulity. 'That's more than nice, mate, that is. Just imagine that sittin' on yer face.'

John was feeling out of his depth. 'Yeah.'

'I definitely would, wouldn't you?' leered Terry.

John looked at him, puzzled. 'Would what?'

'You know!'

'Oh, yeah.' John self-consciously deepened his voice. 'Not half.'

Zoe looked particularly beautiful that morning because her whole appearance was bursting with sporty good health. She was wearing stylish trainers and her long, bare legs, tanned the colour of honey, seemed to go on for ages before disappearing into loose-legged, khaki shorts, cut tightly into her thighs. Her full breasts swelled beneath her thin white T shirt. Her long titian hair seemed to spring from her head like a bristling copper halo. Observing the centimetre of lean, bare waist tantalisingly exposed by the gap between her T shirt and shorts, Bryden felt something stir south of his beer gut.

Detaching himself from John Carter, he sauntered casually over to Zoe and stood rather too close to her. She turned and registered his presence with the disapproving look of one whose personal space has been invaded. She then took an involuntary step away from him, and returned her gaze to the drive of Rooks Nest.

'Don't mind me asking, love, but I just saw you come out of that house opposite,' said Bryden. He nodded towards Rooks Nest. 'Do you happen to know the people who live there?'

Zoe gave Bryden more careful attention. She saw an overweight man in his mid to late forties, wearing an awful brown suit that was flecked with faint green and orange hues. His florid tie hung loosely from a striped shirt that was open at the neck. His greying, blonde hair was thick with gel and combed back off his heavily lined forehead in a wavy quiff. His light blue eyes were bloodshot and seemed preserved in formaldehyde.

'Know them? Hardly at all,' Zoe said.

He might have known she'd be posh. 'That's a shame,' he said. 'Only I'm a reporter, see, covering this Peter Kellingford scandal.' He gestured jerkily towards the crowd. 'That's why they're all here. Heard about it?'

Zoe explained that she was au fait with the situation as she'd been following reports on News 24.

Bryden said, 'I was hoping you could tell me something about Kellingford's parents-in-law. But, as you hardly know them...'

'I met his father-in-law once, when we moved in.'

'Major Roberts?'

'Yes.'

'What's he like then?'

'Rather a stereotype.'

'How do you mean?'

'Old-fashioned, military guy. Overbearing. Patronising. Quite anal, I'd say.'

'Overbearing. Patronising. Anal.' Bryden repeated this as though committing it to memory.

Zoe was now enjoying herself. 'I believe he served in Northern Ireland.'

Bryden looked interested. 'Northern Ireland, eh?'

'That's what he said.'

Zoe went silent and gazed aggressively around her.

Bryden said, 'Anything else?'

Zoe racked her brains. 'No, I don't think so.'

'What about his wife and daughter?'

'Sorry. I don't know them. I've never met them.' She suddenly remembered something she'd read in old copies of The Leeflet she'd found lying around. The reporter might find it useful. 'Actually, there is something else. The Major's a big cheese in the Magnificent Britain contest.'

'The gardening competition?'

'Yes. Leefdale stands to win the gold medal for the fifth consecutive year. Major Roberts seems quite desperate to win it. He's putting people under pressure to take part against their will, and they don't like it. It's causing a lot of bad feeling.' Zoe expanded on what she'd read in The Leeflet.

'Well that's very interesting, Miss...?'

'FitzGerald. Zoe FitzGerald.'

Bryden offered her his hand. 'Terry Bryden.'

She took his hand and shook it, noting that it was square and pudgy with thick, coarse fingers. The hand of a pugilist. 'How do you do, Mr Bryden.'

Bryden placed two fingers to his lips, emitted a piercing whistle and gestured to John Carter to join them. John came over, looking at Bryden quizzically.

Bryden turned to Zoe. 'You don't mind if we take a picture of you for our paper?'

Zoe looked at him suspiciously. 'Why?'

'Your information has been very helpful. We might be able to use it. I'd like to give you some credit for it. And you're a lovely looking girl.'

Zoe said, 'So even if I wasn't a lovely looking girl, you'd still take my picture?'

He pulled a face expressing faux indignation. 'Of course.'

Zoe smiled at him. He certainly had a sort of coarse charm. 'Very well.'

'Go on, then,' Bryden said to John.

John raised his camera and focussed it on Zoe. His finger pressed downwards to take the shot. Nothing happened. 'Hang on,' he said, and pressed again. It still failed to work. Perplexed, he lowered the camera and checked it. Bryden glared at him and then turned to Zoe. 'It's his first big assignment,' he explained. 'He normally takes pictures of dogs and cats.'

'Not dogs and cats,' said John. 'Wildlife.'

'Really?' said Zoe. 'What kind?'

He stopped his investigations to look at Zoe. 'The local kind. Deer, badgers, hares.' He delved into his bag and produced another camera.

The new camera worked perfectly. John took several photos. 'You're very photogenic,' he told Zoe.

'All right, enough of the schmooze,' said Bryden.

'Which paper do you work for?' Zoe asked.

Bryden indicated Carter with a nod. 'He normally works for The Sandleton Examiner.' Thinking to impress her, he added, 'But I'm Chief Political Correspondent for The Source.'

Zoe stiffened. 'The Source? That right wing rag?'

Bryden thought she was joking. 'The very one.'

'I don't want my picture in that. It's sexist.'

'It's not sexist.'

'It is. It's full of naked women.'

'They're not naked. Not completely.'

'It's obscene. It degrades women.'

'Half our readership's women,' said Bryden. 'They wouldn't read us if they felt degraded, would they?'

'False consciousness.'

'You mean they're too stupid to understand what they're reading?'

'They're not stupid, they've been brainwashed into thinking they're only sex objects.' Zoe stared hard at Bryden. 'Anyway, I'm not allowing my photo to appear in your disgusting newspaper.' She held her hand out to John 'Give it to me.'

John looked uncertainly at Bryden.

Bryden held out a restraining hand in John's direction. 'Just a minute.' He turned to Zoe. 'That photo is now the property of The Source and we can do what we like with it.'

'I shall sue,' shouted Zoe.

Bryden laughed. 'Plenty have, love. Feel free.'

Everyone around was looking at them curiously.

Zoe was about to scream at the reporter that she was going to complain to the police, but the thought of what Dylan's reaction would be to that sort of behaviour made her decide on a tactical retreat. She turned and strode off, berating herself. How could someone with her knowledge of assertion techniques allow those pigs to oppress her like that? It was all Dylan's fault. Why should she give a shit what he thought?

Bryden and John watched her cross Church Lane.

'Lovely arse,' said Bryden.

John nodded. 'Do you think she'll sue?'

'Let her. We'll just bung her a few quid and stick an apology on the bottom of page thirty four.'

Bryden dug in his jacket pocket and produced his mobile. He held it in one hand and with the other wrote a text: "Major Howard Roberts served in Northern Ireland. See if there's any dirt on him over there. Ask Roy Oates. He used to be on the N.I. desk in the seventies and eighties. He might know something. T.B.".

Bryden then sent the text to Bill Metcalfe, the editor of The Source.

****

When Louise had spoken to him about acting, Dylan observed that it was the first time she'd looked genuinely happy. Was this because acting satisfied a need in her to become someone else? If so, he wondered why that should be. Was it simply that she had a talent for morphing into other people and enjoyed exercising it? Or was there something in her life that was creating so much unhappiness it made her want to get away from herself? Assume a different identity?

He decided that it was an appropriate moment to end the discussion about her storyboards and engage her in a more general conversation. After talking to her about her interest in acting and her involvement in "Oliver", he chatted to her about her life in general. He was surprised to learn that she attended weekly ballet and tap classes in Luffield, and on Saturdays spent all day with the Sandleton Youth Theatre participating in drama workshops. Somewhat vaingloriously, she told him that she was the youngest member of the youth theatre and always had big roles in their end of term productions. She appeared to have few academic interests, although her favourite school subjects were the actors' ones: English and History.

Lowering her voice, as though she was about to reveal a shameful secret, she told him that she loved listening to plays on the radio, and even though her classmates thought her weird, she didn't care. She recounted in elaborate detail a radio play she'd recently listened to about a troupe of travelling players in the Elizabethan period, who'd toured the English countryside performing their shows at a different venue each night. As she tried to recreate for Dylan's benefit the play's atmosphere she became especially animated, and she enthused about the bit when the travelling players arrived at an isolated village or farmstead on a winter's night, and their feet crunched over the snow as they made their way to the place where they were to perform.

Dylan was slightly disconcerted by the rapture shining out of Louise's eyes as she told him how wonderful she thought it must be to move from place to place like that, never staying anywhere for long. It was just how she wanted her life to be when she grew up, she said. Her dearest ambition was to be a travelling player: just like those in the radio play, always moving on.

Louise then surprised him by revealing with unexpected vehemence how much she hated Leefdale, and couldn't wait to leave. He asked her why she felt that way, and was even more surprised when she clammed up and withdrew deeply into herself. She seemed incapable of giving a coherent explanation for her outburst so he said, 'And does your mum feel the same way about Leefdale, as you do?' Her response was a deeply suspicious glance followed by a brooding silence.

Dylan found this perplexing. Extraordinary. Only a moment or so ago she'd been a loquacious, articulate child, expressing her delight in radio plays and openly describing her ambitions; and now she was inhibited and secretive. What the hell was going on?

He said, 'Would you like to join the others for their art therapy sessions this afternoon, Louise?'

'You mean do the same sort of work they do?'

'Similar, yes.'

But that work was for kids who had problems, like the kids in the unit. Was he saying she was like them? She didn't know how to say this without sounding horrible, so she said, 'Isn't that work just for the kids who come here? The big kids?'

Assuming his kindliest expression, Dylan said, 'Anyone can take part in art therapy, you know. So, would you like to join us?'

Her eyes lit up. 'Yes, please.'

'Good. I think you might enjoy it. But before that, would you like to take a short break and then do some maths? Your mother won't be very pleased with me if you only do art.'

Louise set off for the chill-out room but was halted by Dylan calling out, 'Just a moment, Louise.'

She stopped and turned back. Dylan wondered why her default expression was always so wary, so guarded. He said, 'I'd like to show your storyboards to Eric, Zoe and Toni. Is that OK with you?'

This gave Louise a dilemma. She hadn't told her mother what she'd planned to put into her new storyboard because Dylan had promised it would be her secret and no-one else need ever see it. Yet, she was proud of her storyboards and the skill with which she'd created and drawn them. The thought they'd be seen and appreciated by others gave her enormous pleasure, but she feared that displaying them would only invite more difficult questions. And mum might strongly disapprove if she found out: might think she was giving too much away.

Dylan could almost see Louise's mind working. The way she considered all the implications intrigued him. For a child of her age, she seemed incredibly calculating.

She said, 'Why do you want to show them my storyboards?'

'They might be able to help you.'

'How?'

'By suggesting ways you can avoid getting into situations where you might be bullied.'

So he believed her. He actually believed she was being bullied. Louise was jubilant and her gratitude caused her to lower her guard. 'OK. I don't mind. You can show them.'

'Good. By the way, is there anything in these storyboards that Jade might object to?'

She took a long time before answering. 'I don't want you showing them to Jade,' she said.

Dylan smiled at her reassuringly. 'Don't worry. I've no intention of doing that. I just wondered if there was anything in them Jade might say wasn't true.'

'No. I don't think so.'

When Louise had gone, Dylan contemplated both of her storyboards again and spent some time comparing and contrasting them. He then placed them in Louise's folder and locked it away in the metal cabinet. As he did so, he reflected on what the storyboard session with Louise had revealed: most significantly, her dissatisfaction with herself and her restlessness of spirit. Here was someone who seemed to be happy only when she was being someone else, and who yearned to wander endlessly from place to place. Someone who could never be at ease or content with her surroundings, and was constantly in flight from herself. Why? He was sure that Louise had serious emotional conflicts and also had issues to resolve concerning her anger and her self-image. Despite her obvious talents, she seemed to perceive herself as a victim and was deficient in self-worth. Was that why she sought to lose herself in other characters through drama? Could she only tolerate the self she wanted to reject by assimilating it into the artificial construct of a fictional character such as Nancy in "Oliver"? Could she only function by literally fleeing from herself and her circumstances? Was that why she sought refuge in itinerancy and the unpredictability of a nomadic existence? Or was he reading too much into what she'd said? Even so, there was no doubt that Jade was the object of Louise's anger. Was this because she was jealous of Jade? Or was it because Jade kept taunting her about her absent father? Louise seemed deeply affected by not having known her father, but it was unclear why Jade should have intuited this and then used it to antagonise and provoke Louise.

He found himself questioning the wisdom of taking the art therapy work with Louise further. There were good reasons to do so: other art therapy techniques might reveal the cause of Louise's conflicts, and help her explore the underlying reasons for her poor self-image and anger issues. Zoe might even be able to complement this work through one-to-one drama therapy. However, he appreciated that this might exceed what was appropriate in the circumstances, given that Louise wasn't one of their clients. It was almost certain to lead to objections from Sharon who was obviously secretive about her personal life, and sensitive about the identity of her child's father.

This brought him to the nub of the problem. He'd no wish to antagonise Sharon. He was already becoming deeply concerned that his interest in Louise's anti-social behaviour was not purely professional. If he was honest with himself, he knew he'd overstepped the mark in mentioning Sharon's boyfriend to Louise. He'd acted impulsively and unprofessionally because of his intense curiosity about Sharon's personal life, and his need to know what her boyfriend was like. Strange that Louise was unaware of this man's existence. Had Sharon been hiding her boyfriend from her daughter? Did he actually exist? Perhaps Sharon didn't have a boyfriend after all. But if so, why invent one? Again, he found himself reflecting on what Louise had disclosed in her storyboard, particularly Jade's allegation that Sharon was "a slag". Given his own strong attraction to Sharon he found this description of her disturbing in many ways. He remained where he was for several minutes, thinking about it.

Afterwards, he left the art therapy room and went out of the house by the front door. He stood in the drive, delighting in the sensation of the sun's hot rays on his face and the beauty of the day. He was staring pleasurably at the big, expansive trees in Church Lane when he realized something wasn't normal. In the background, there was the constant, low, droning thrum of many voices indicating an unusual amount of activity outside the Major's house.

Dylan's view of Rooks Nest was partly obscured by the various vans parked in the rectory's drive. Curious, he continued on down the drive past these vehicles until he came to the front gate. Now he saw everything clearly. Obviously, some kind of big media event was taking place opposite. But what could it be? Something connected with Magnificent Britain perhaps?

And what was Zoe doing there with those two men? After his initial surprise at seeing her, he realized that she was involved in some kind of animated conversation with them, perhaps even an argument.

He watched Zoe turn angrily away from the two men and set off across the road towards The Old Rectory. Her expression was furious. Yes, there'd definitely been some sort of altercation. Her fury was quickly replaced by a smile when she became aware of him watching her.

'What's going on?' he asked, as she arrived at the gate.

She looked gleeful. 'Guess what? The Major's son-in-law is an MP and he's dumped his wife for his seventeen year old researcher. The daughter of his best friend.'

As she passed through the gateway and joined Dylan in the drive, Zoe continued to expound on the Peter Kellingford scandal.

'Why were you arguing with those two men?' Dylan said.

'Those aren't men, they're tabloid reporters,' said Zoe. She told him about the photograph.

'Will you sue them?' Dylan asked.

'Of course. But it won't do any good.' She glared at Dylan as though he were a much resented super-ego. 'I should have followed my original impulse, seized their camera and stamped on it. Who the fuck do they think they are?'

Dylan groaned inwardly. Why was she always involved in confrontations? He said, 'With all this excitement we'll never get the clients to concentrate.'

'Yes, we will. They'll soon lose interest when they find out it's political.'

'It's nearly time for their break. I think we'll let them take it in the back garden. Maybe have lunch there too. That'll take their minds off what's going on over there.'

'Why do you want to take their minds off it? Surely they should be informed about what's going on?'

Dylan was in no mood to argue. They started walking up the drive towards the front door.

'How did you get on with Louise?' asked Zoe.

Dylan stopped and lowered his voice. 'I'd say Louise was a very unhappy little girl. Do you realize she didn't even know Sharon had a boyfriend?'

'Maybe Sharon hasn't really got one,' said Zoe. 'Maybe she only said that because she thought you were hitting on her.'

****

Isobel and Barbara managed to calm the children down eventually by diverting them with a discussion about whether or not they should continue with the planned trip to Scarborough. Jessica still wanted to go but Mark wasn't so sure. He didn't think it would be much fun without daddy. Barbara was opposed to going because she was concerned about running the gauntlet of the reporters. Her preference was to stay and hunker down until the media feeding frenzy passed. 'And they might follow us,' she said.

'Just let them try,' said Isobel, fiercely.

Barbara was surprised. Her mother was normally a shy and diffident woman. Hardly the sort to take unnecessary risks. 'You really think we should go?'

'Absolutely. Why let those swine spoil our day?'

In the end it was Howard who put the matter beyond any doubt. As Barbara and Isobel were still discussing the pros and cons of the trip, they heard the front door open and then slam. Isobel went straight over to the bedroom window and was quickly joined by Barbara and the children.

'Oh my God!' Barbara exclaimed. 'What's he doing?'

Howard was walking purposefully down the drive carrying his walking stick like a cudgel.

Isobel flung the window wide open and called out, 'Howard! Where are you going?'

He stopped, swung round and looked up at them. He seemed surprised. 'The Old Rectory,' he called back. 'I want to discuss the state of their lawn.'

'For God's sake! Why now?'

'It's no good, Isobel!' Howard thundered. 'I've made up my mind and these bastards aren't going to stop me!'

He turned and strode on, swinging his stick aggressively.

'Have you taken your pill?' Isobel screamed after him. But he ignored her and continued determinedly on.

Barbara gave her mother an alarmed look. 'What shall we do?'

'Do?' said Isobel. 'Nothing!' She moved towards the door. 'We're going to Scarborough. And to hell with him!'

CHAPTER TWENTY EIGHT

Howard's appearance in the drive of Rooks Nest instantly galvanised the press pack into action, sending reporters and photographers scrambling for the best positions around the front gates. As Howard approached, they became frenzied, pressing forward, barraging him with camera flashes and screaming questions at him, the sense of which was mostly lost in the general clamour. But not all: one or two reporters had strong, clear voices that could be heard distinctly.

'Is Peter going to resign?'
'Where's Barbara?'
'Have you met Clarissa?'
'Where are you going now?'
'How d'you feel about your son-in-law, Major?'

Howard's expression was one of complete contempt as he confronted the mob from the other side of his gates. He lifted the latch, swung one gate back and stepped onto the pavement. The media people instantly swarmed around him like bees round an apiarist. The barrage of camera flashes intensified. He responded by raising his stick high and swinging it threateningly about his head.

'Out of my way, you scum! Out of my way!'

Instantly, the press pack fell back. Two police officers came up and stood protectively on either side of Howard.

'I need to visit my neighbours,' he told them.
'That's all right, sir. We'll escort you.'
'It's just across the road.'

Against a background of shouts and yells, Howard crossed Church Lane in the company of the two policemen. The older of the officers made one or two platitudinous observations about the situation, to which Howard barely responded; he was too angry at the position Peter had put him in to engage in small talk. It was Peter's complete lack of principle which enraged Howard most: and whilst in a politician that wasn't surprising, was perhaps even expected, in a son-in-law it was unforgivable. Peter had sacrificed his wife and children for a hot little piece, and betrayed everyone who'd placed their trust in him. Not least his poor constituents. He was nothing but a cheap confidence trickster who was a disgrace to the designation "Honourable Gentleman".

The police left Howard at the gate to the rectory's drive. He lingered in front of it, momentarily overwhelmed by the palpable rage circulating throughout his system. How he wished Peter was there in front of him so he could punch him hard on the nose. How much better that would make him feel!

The brief but welcome fantasy over, he became aware that he was being watched. He turned and looked back at Rooks Nest. Sure enough the police and all the representatives of the media were staring at him expectantly. He made an enormous effort to pull himself together. Of course, he told himself, he could achieve immediate revenge on Peter by going straight over to the reporters and telling them exactly what he thought of his son-in-law. But he was damned if he would give those bastards the satisfaction. The way the press had behaved at the time of "the incident" had made him their implacable enemy forever. Besides, it would soon all blow over: the media would find some other victim to hound and Peter's hypocrisy would be forgotten. He would lose his position as a shadow minister and never get into the government; the teenager would inevitably leave him for someone her own age and that's when he'd come crawling back to Barbara. That would be the perfect time for revenge. That would be the time to tell the man what a twenty four carat shit he was!

Howard opened the gate, passed through it and scrupulously closed it behind him. As he walked slowly up the drive, all thoughts of Peter and his appalling betrayal vanished as he was confronted at close quarters with the reality of the rectory's front lawn. How scrappy and forlorn it looked. Just a few weeks of neglect had produced a pitiful transformation. Instead of being closely cut and standing healthily to attention, the grass was overgrown and exhausted: choked with bindweed, clover and other opportunistic weeds. Large areas of it had been colonised by dandelions, ribwort, thistles and ugly clumps of moss. Nothing, of course, that couldn't be remedied with some expert attention and regular mowing. Stopping and looking all round, he contemplated with dismay the privet hedge that surrounded the front of the property. This too had been utterly neglected and was badly in need of trimming. Its unkempt and unruly appearance unbalanced the perfect proportions of the exquisite building it encompassed. Like a soldier who was badly in need of a haircut, it affronted the very notion of good order.

Halfway up the drive he stopped and stared disconsolately at the lawn again, thinking of Isobel. Why couldn't she recognise how important it was to maintain standards? She assumed his only reason for keeping the rectory's gardens up to the mark was to gain the gold medal again. That would be nice, of course, but it wasn't the only reason he did it, any more than the only reason he shined his shoes was to make them gleam. No, you did these things because the consequences of not doing them were unthinkable: your standards slipped and you let yourself go. And then, where were you? At rock bottom, like those people who lived in squalor, surrounded by unwashed plates, squashed lager cans, and dog faeces on the carpet. No thank you!

He felt rage again welling up within him, its object this time not Peter but the people in the rectory whose neglect had allowed its front garden to deteriorate into such a deplorable state. Immediately he exercised his will, using it, as always, to suppress and suffocate any emotion which he regarded as a threat to his iron self-command. He reminded himself that he'd come to persuade those people to agree to tidy things up, or at least allow him to send in a team to put things right. Leefdale's fifth consecutive win depended on him being conciliatory and controlling his temper. His vital task was to persuade Bourne and his friends that the village's gold medal was contingent on the rectory's gardens remaining in excellent condition. Somehow, he had to convince them that it would be possible to achieve this if they'd agree to relinquish their rights over the gardens for a brief period and accede to all his demands. What could be a more reasonable request? And Bourne appeared to be a reasonable man. How could he not agree? Howard felt an unfamiliar surge of optimism sweeping through him. Everything would be all right. He was convinced of it.

He approached the front door and knocked loudly, hoping it wouldn't be Zoe who answered. He found her manner intimidating. She obviously had no respect for him, no regard, was cynical about his motives. She'd clearly classified him as some sort of Marxist hate figure: the hammer of the downtrodden, a lackey of the imperialists; something of that sort.

Of course, it would have to be Zoe who opened the front door. On seeing Howard her features at once assumed an expression of mild disapproval.

He forced himself to be civil. 'Good morning. Or should I say good afternoon?' He gave her his most urbane smile. 'How are you?'

'All right.'

Undaunted by her surly reply, Howard pushed on. 'May I have a word with Mr Bourne?'

Zoe was amused by his excessive formality. 'He's round the back. Come through.'

She stood aside and admitted Howard into the hall. As she closed the door behind them she said, pointedly, 'Must make sure I close the door properly. Don't want our neighbours complaining about the noise, do we!'

Howard ignored the jibe, and Zoe set off down the hall saying, in a friendlier tone, 'We're all in the garden. We usually take our break there when it's a hot day like this.'

'Good idea,' said Howard, following her.

They passed through the kitchen exchanging more comments about the weather, but when they'd both entered the conservatory Zoe stopped dead and rounded on him accusingly.

'Have you committed a murder?'

The question was so shocking and unexpected that Howard failed to realise she was joking. He stared at her silently, aware only of the loud pounding of his heart. Then, with relief, he understood what she was referring to. 'Oh, you've seen the reporters!'

She laughed. 'We could hardly help noticing.'

'I'm having some problems with my son-in-law,' Howard said, stiffly. 'He's a member of the shadow cabinet. If you watch the television news you'll probably find out all about it. Or, you could get yourself a copy of today's Source. That'll tell you all you need to know.'

It was delightfully cool in the conservatory. All the venetian blinds at the windows had been tightly drawn, giving the place a shady, sequestered air. Howard gazed longingly at the circle of wicker chairs arranged around the wicker coffee table. How comforting it would be to have them supporting his intense weariness. It occurred to him that here would be the perfect place to conduct his potentially difficult conversation with Mr Bourne: it was so secluded, so private and so comfortable. He was about to ask Zoe if that might be possible when he realized that she'd already moved through the French doors and out into the rear garden.

Howard immediately followed her outside. But when he got there so great was the disparity between the scene he was expecting and the sight that actually met his eyes that he took only one step onto the patio and stopped dead. He seemed to be in the grounds of the wrong house. All around him was utter devastation. The Wych elm that had successfully resisted Dutch elm disease for over two decades had had several of its lower branches removed to accommodate a large and ugly tree house. Other trees, some planted many generations ago when the rectory had been newly built, had actually been cut down or hacked so far back they were unrecognisable: Apple; Plum; Cherry; Silver Birch; Ash; Laburnum; Maple; Willow. None had been spared. Surreally, the stumps and ravaged trunks that remained had been augmented by the addition of strange scaffold like structures: lengths of metal, glass and plastic which radiated outwards from the remains of each mutilated tree. One of these structures vaguely resembled a ship, another suggested a kind of robot. But most were unrecognisable as anything familiar at all.

In a state of acute shock, Howard took in the rest of the garden and surveyed the remaining ruins of what he'd once so lovingly nurtured and cherished. In the flower beds, the vividly coloured annuals which at this time of year should have been an absolute kaleidoscope of delight, were suffocated and masked by weeds. The sweet peas, which he'd so carefully tended up until a few weeks ago, were dying off and badly in need of deadheading. Weeds also choked the herbaceous borders and were strangling many of the bushes in the shrubbery. The wonderful greenhouse was empty, its panes grimy and some even broken. But the most appalling sight of all was the rear lawn. Like its counterpart at the front of the house, it was neglected and overgrown: but worse, it was being used as a football pitch! At either end, improvised goalposts had been erected and in front of them large areas of grass had been worn completely away, exposing the dry, bare earth beneath. A game of football was in progress. Several yobs and a girl were chasing the ball, sending up great clouds of dust from the parched and worn areas under their feet. He looked more closely at the goal to his left, sensing something familiar about it. Good God! The Corbridges' lovely statues of Apollo and Demeter were being used as goalposts! He'd failed to recognise them because their Olympian whiteness was all but obliterated by ugly black marks where a muddy football had repeatedly struck them. And Apollo's lyre was gone, too, presumably severed from his hand by a powerful shot. Call themselves artists? These people were nothing but utter philistines!

'Where's Dylan?' Zoe asked. Her question was addressed to Eric and Toni who were sitting around a picnic table on the patio, drinking lemonade.

'He's in the garage, fiddling around with his bike,' said Eric. Both he and Toni stared at Howard with curiosity.

'This is Major Roberts,' said Zoe. 'He's come to see Dylan.'

Eric and Toni exchanged a look. They both seemed slightly embarrassed by this information, aware that any allusion to the events that were occurring simultaneously at Rooks Nest would be a terrible solecism. 'Hello, Major,' said Toni. 'How do you do? Would you like some lemonade?'

'No, thank you,' Howard said, absently. He was unable to lift his eyes from the catastrophic scenes of destruction before him. Until this point, he'd held out some hope that the situation could be salvaged but it was obvious now that Leefdale's chances of winning a fifth gold medal were lost forever. The rectory's gardens were worse than he'd ever imagined and would require months of intense restoration. It would be impossible for them to be rehabilitated by Friday, even if their razing, wrecking owners gave him permission to commence immediately. He closed his eyes and sighed heavily. Every village that reached the final of Magnificent Britain possessed at least one beautiful house with large gardens in optimum condition. Leefdale had once possessed such a house: The Old Rectory. But no longer. The judges would quite rightly mark Leefdale down for failing to maintain its most exemplary garden: the garden which for four consecutive years had put the village way ahead of its rivals. How could the judges fail to penalise Leefdale for this mindless act of vandalism? The whole point of the Magnificent Britain Competition was to encourage people to improve their gardens, not destroy them! What humiliation!

'What do you think of the kids' sculpture park?' Zoe asked.

Howard, who had been miles away in thought, suddenly became aware that the question had been directed at him. He turned to her slowly, his face twisting into a furious rictus. 'A sculpture park? Is that what you call this disgraceful act of vandalism?'

'Vandalism?' Zoe regarded him, incredulously. 'It's not vandalism. It's Art.'

At that moment, Dylan Bourne emerged from the rear entrance to the garage.

'Hello, Howard,' said Dylan, courteously. He could tell from Howard's foul expression that there was going to be trouble.

Radiating vitriol, Howard drew himself up to his full height. All thoughts of conciliation were gone: from now on it was war. 'Mr Bourne. I came here with the intention of trying to persuade you people either to improve the condition of your front garden in time for the judging of Magnificent Britain, or at least to allow some volunteers to do it on your behalf. But now I've seen the extent of the devastation that's been wreaked on what was the finest horticultural display in the county, I... I...' But at this point the preamble to his tirade was halted: the overwhelming intensity of his anger had momentarily deprived him of the power of speech.

Dylan's response was emollient. 'Howard, I realise this has come as a shock but if we explain our reasons for doing it I think you might be able to see...'

'Don't try to placate me, you hooligan!' Howard burst out. 'You've ruined the finest garden in the village and you've cost us the contest!'

'It's not been ruined!' shrieked Zoe, rounding on him. 'You should be praising the kids for their wonderful installations, not slagging them off. All that was here before was a load of bourgeois crap!'

Dylan silenced Zoe with a look and a gesture that desperately urged restraint. He then turned back to Howard. 'She's got a point. The sculpture park is an important feature of our project. It helps the clients to...'

But Howard had already started to move off. He'd suddenly developed an irrational need to make a close inspection of the carnage. Blindly, disbelievingly, he lurched across the patchy grass on which the football game was still being fiercely contested. Muttering incomprehensibly, he barged through the midst of the players who were poised around the goal to his right.

'Heh! What you doin'!' shouted Khaled, the goalkeeper 'Get out the way!'

Sheldon, who, until his exclusion, had been the star player for his comprehensive, unleashed a powerful shot at goal. It was exactly on target but unfortunately was obstructed by Howard who, simultaneously, had dropped to his knees in front of the goal to rake his fingers incredulously through the dry, dusty earth. The ball ricocheted off Howard's thigh, and was immediately pounced on by Amy who cleared it far up field.

Slowly, Howard got to his feet. He was still dazed from shock; still unable to accept the garden's tragic metamorphosis; still aching for the past, for the time before his loss of Eden.

'Oi man, you fucked up me shot. Get out the way, will ya!' Sheldon shouted.

'What did you say?' Howard flung back at him.

'I said get out the fuckin' way, man!'

'Don't call me man, you moron!'

Sheldon advanced towards Howard until their faces were almost touching. 'Fuck you, man! Fuck you!'

'No! Fuck you! Fuck you!' Howard roared back, in a parade ground voice. They stood confronting each other toe to toe. Then, suddenly, Howard turned and ran towards the goal. When he reached it he grabbed one of the goalposts and started wrenching it backwards and forwards as though he was trying to pull it out of the ground.

Sheldon and the other players raced towards him. As they attempted to pull him away from the goal post, Howard turned on them with an outraged roar. Remarkably, he was still holding his stick. He raised it and brought it down hard on Sheldon's head, sending the boy reeling to the ground. Liam, Jake and Khaled dropped to their knees alongside Sheldon to check that he was all right. Khaled was the first one back on his feet, his fists held out ready to avenge his friend. But he was too late. Howard was already on the other side of the lawn attacking one of the sculptures, whacking it with his stick and bawling 'Vandalism!' with every blow.

At first, the inclusion unit's staff had observed Howard's movements across the football pitch with some bemusement. This had changed to concern when Howard and Sheldon had begun to exchange insults. The row had caught the attention too of Mona, Scarlett and Rupa who'd been sitting on the grass by the bushes at the end of the garden. At first, Howard's childish, clumsy attempt to wrest the goal post from the ground had reduced the girls to giggles. But the slapstick atmosphere had changed in an instant with Howard's sudden and vicious blow to Sheldon's head. This violent turn had seemed so unreal and had happened so quickly it took all the onlookers by surprise. Momentarily, they stood rooted, unable to move. Now, as Howard began moving from sculpture to sculpture, attacking each one in turn, the adults sprinted towards him.

Sheldon was still lying on the ground but was fortunately conscious and rubbing his head. Eric dropped to his knees beside him, but the other adults ran on past them towards Howard, who was now attacking his fourth sculpture. Zoe, Toni and Dylan managed to grab hold of him.

'Let go of me!' cried Howard. 'Let go of me, you vandals!'

He tried to struggle free, but Zoe and Toni had him securely in their grip.

'You're the vandal, Major!' Zoe screamed.

'Me?'

'Yes, you! You've destroyed what the kids created. That's what a vandal does!'

Howard went on struggling. 'You must be insane, woman!' he cried. 'To create these stupid sculptures, you and your hooligans have destroyed mature trees!'

'Please Howard, chill! Chill!' Dylan pleaded.

Zoe was enraged. 'I spent hours with the kids designing those structures, helping them choose the right materials, but you had to flatten them without a thought. Just like the military!'

'You flattened the trees, you bitch!'

'Yes, we cut down some trees, but only the small ones. What are you complaining about? There are loads of trees left!'

'Howard, unless you stop struggling I'm going to have to call the police and have you arrested,' warned Dylan.

Howard's face was a picture of defiance. 'Do what you damn well like. But I'll tell you something, you and your little gang of lefties aren't going to stop us winning. The village will punish you for this!'

'You're insane!' screeched Zoe.

At that moment, Sheldon, who'd now recovered from the blow to his head, ran straight up to them and swung a savage punch at Howard's face. If it had landed on his nose it would have broken it, but his left cheek absorbed the full force and Sheldon's fist only glanced the nostril. Everyone stood still, completely shocked. Even Howard had stopped struggling. His hand went up to his nose to cup the blood that was pouring from it.

'You cunt!' screamed Sheldon. He raised his arm to deliver another blow but, just in time, Zoe grabbed it. Sheldon immediately attempted to pull away. Zoe's trained, reflex response was not to resist but to go with him. She placed all of her weight against Sheldon's shoulder and used a safe and secure Thumb Grab Neck Lock to subdue and restrain him. He was unable to free himself from Zoe's grasp, but continued to struggle and swear. In a low and reasonable voice, Zoe assured him that no-one was blaming him for his reaction, that everyone understood why he was angry and urged him to calm down. This initially had little effect, as the adrenalin pumping through Sheldon's nervous system had raised him to an extreme pitch of aggressive excitement. He continued to swear and make threats to kill Major Roberts.

Dylan placed his hand gently on Howard's shoulder. 'Come inside. We'll give you some first aid.'

Angrily shrugging Dylan's hand away, Howard marched off in the direction of the house.

'Listen,' said Zoe, as they all watched Howard disappear into the conservatory. 'If those reporters see him leave here streaming with blood they'll be at our front door like a shot. They'll assume it had something to do with the Kellingford business. Quick! You must go and lock the gate.'

'Right!' said Dylan. He started sprinting towards the house, followed by Eric. They took a short cut through the garage and as they entered the drive they were just in time to see Howard leaving by the front gate. Quickly they ran up to it, slammed it shut behind Howard and drove the bolts home. Through the gate's interstices they saw Howard pause as he prepared to cross Church Lane and head back towards Rooks Nest. But none of the reporters were yet aware of Howard. All their attention was on the Jaguar that was exiting the drive of Rooks Nest. The vehicle sped past in a dazzle of camera flashes. As it turned left into Church Lane and passed him, Howard waved at the occupants: two women and a young boy and girl. The children in the car returned Howard's wave. That was when the press and TV news crews first became aware of Howard. They saw his bloody nose and instantly began streaming across the road towards him. They surrounded him in a state of high excitement, screaming questions and subjecting him to a fusillade of camera flashes. Howard responded by raising his stick, threateningly. Fortunately, the two police officers who'd previously protected him came to his aid and escorted him across Church Lane. Meanwhile, just as Zoe had foreseen, several journalists and two camera crews flung themselves at the gate of The Old Rectory.

'Come on, time to go,' Dylan told Eric. They both turned away and set off up the drive towards the house. They were followed by the noise of reporters pounding furiously on the gate as they fired questions at Eric and Dylan's retreating backs.

'Why's Major Roberts got a bloody nose?'

'Who hit him?'

'Is it to do with his son-in-law?'

Dylan turned and called back, 'Not at all. He just didn't like the state of our garden!' Then, he and Eric continued on towards the house.

CHAPTER TWENTY NINE

'They're still following us!' said Mark.
'Are you sure?' Barbara asked, anxiously.
'Yes,' said Mark and Jessica together.
'It's probably a coincidence,' said Barbara.
'We'll soon find out,' said Isobel.

It had been just a minute or so since Isobel had driven the Jaguar through the gates of Rooks Nest and accelerated it away from the clamouring reporters and blinding camera flashes. As they had turned into Church Lane they'd all been astonished to see Howard standing on the pavement in front of the rectory, waving at them. As they'd returned his wave there'd been an immediate discussion about why he was pressing a handkerchief to his face. Jessica wanted to know why they weren't stopping to pick him up. Isobel had quickly explained that grandpa wouldn't be coming to Scarborough as he was too busy. Jessica continued to complain about leaving him, but Mark, who was staring back at Rooks Nest through the rear window, told her to shut up because two reporters had got into a blue Toyota and were following them.

At first Isobel was incredulous, but a quick glance in her rear mirror told her it might be true. Now, as they neared the end of the road that led out of the village it appeared that the Toyota was still behind them.

'Stop looking out of the rear window,' Isobel ordered. 'And both of you sit well back in your seats.'

A roundabout was coming up. Barbara was surprised to see her mother indicate right and approach it in the right hand lane.

'It's the first exit for Scarborough, isn't it?' said Barbara.

Isobel glanced in the mirror to confirm that the blue Toyota had followed them into the right hand lane. 'Trust me,' she said.

Isobel entered the roundabout and did a full circuit of it. As the road to Scarborough again appeared on their left Barbara expected her mother to take it, but instead Isobel continued on round the roundabout a second time.

'Is the blue car still behind us?' Barbara asked.

Isobel checked the rear mirror. 'Yes, it's still there. It's definitely following us.'

As the Scarborough turn appeared for the third time, Isobel indicated left to take it. A quick look in the rear view mirror told her that the blue Toyota was doing the same. Then, suddenly, at the last minute, just as she was turning into the Scarborough road, she jammed on the handbrake, wrenched the wheel to the right, and u-turned sharply across the oncoming lane, forcing several cars to an emergency stop. She then re-entered the roundabout at speed. The driver of the blue Toyota was taken completely by surprise, and as it was too late and too dangerous for him to do a turn in the road he had no choice but to continue on towards Scarborough.

'Lost him!' Isobel cried. She indicated left and took the next exit, which was the road to Luffield. After travelling a short distance down it, she took the first right: a single track road with passing places. She parked in the first passing place she came to. She opened the window on the driver's side and switched off the engine. All that could be heard was the distant bleating of sheep.

'I don't think they'll find us now. But we'll wait here for a few minutes to be sure.'

'That was very clever,' said Barbara.

'Yes. If you think you're being followed always drive twice round a roundabout. That way you can confirm it. Then pretend you're heading for the first exit and pull out at the last moment.'

'But how did you know to do that?'

'Your father taught me.'

This was not the whole truth. In the course of his army career, Howard had been posted to many dangerous places. Both he and Isobel had received extensive training in various techniques designed to protect them from assassination.

'Did he teach you to do the handbrake turn, as well?'

'Oh, yes.'

'You were brilliant, grandma,' said Mark.

Isobel smiled. 'Thank you, darling.'

They stayed in the passing place for about fifteen minutes, delighting in their escape. Then Isobel set off again, using her intimate knowledge of the area to keep off the beaten track. Her route took her down deserted minor roads that wound between deep Wolds valleys, their sides stippled with exposed chalk and dotted with grazing sheep. Eventually, they came to a T junction and a road sign which showed that Scarborough was fifteen miles away.

'I think we're safe enough now to continue on,' said Isobel, as she cautiously made the left turn.

****

The blue Toyota which had been so skilfully evaded by Isobel was now parked in a lay-by on the road to Scarborough. In the driving seat was John Carter, still in a state of shock, unable to wipe from his mind the image of the Jaguar turning right across the oncoming traffic to shake him and Bryden off. He couldn't stop thinking of the multiple pile up that had just been avoided and of the people who might have been killed.

Next to John sat Terry Bryden, fuming and fulminating because Isobel had so successfully given them the slip.

'Who'd have thought she'd do that?' Bryden raged. 'Who'd have thought it?'

John said, 'Where d'you think they've gone? Do you think they're on their way back to Northamptonshire?'

'How the fuck would I know?'

John swallowed. He was a sensitive young man who was more at home photographing shy and elusive examples of East Yorkshire wildlife such as weasels, barn owls and lapwings. Bryden's aggressive manner and coarse tongue shocked and sickened him. 'Sorry. I said Northamptonshire because that's where the Kellingford's live, isn't it?'

'Use your loaf,' said Bryden. 'Everyone knows that. So why would they go back there? It's the first place the press boys would look.' Bryden took out his mobile, 'I'd better call Bill and tell him the bad news.'

The Source's editor was disappointed and unsympathetic to hear that they'd lost their quarry; but he couldn't resist having a jibe at his chief political correspondent's expense. 'Unlike you to lose an easy tail like that, isn't it? I mean, an old woman? You're losing your grip, aren't you?'

'She's not that old and she drives like Schumacher. Anyway, it wasn't me who lost her. It was that dickhead you've lumbered me with. He was the one driving. He doesn't know one end of a fucking camera from another and he can't even turn a car round.'

'It was a very busy road,' John muttered under his breath.

'Don't worry,' said the editor. 'Powell will be with you just as soon as he's finished the Prince William job.'

Powell was Bryden's usual photographer.

'So what do I do now?' Bryden asked.

Bill Metcalfe said, 'Go back to Leefdale, and wait.'

'What for? They're probably not coming back.'

'Roberts is still there, isn't he?'

'As far as I know.' Bryden told Metcalfe about his chat with Zoe and the curious incident of the Major's bloody nose. 'Looks like someone took a swing at him. Apparently, he's put quite a few backs up in the village. Some people don't like gardening, you know.'

'Might be good background. Follow it up, and add it to whatever you're sending me tonight.'

'Look, I'm not here to cover a fucking gardening contest. I'll be more use in London.'

'No. Stay where you are. There've been some developments this end.'

'Like what?'

'We're being heavily briefed that Kellingford is going to make a statement.'

'Where. When?'

'Tonight, maybe. Possibly tomorrow. Where, we don't know.'

'It'll be in London. Bound to be. That's why I should come back.'

But Metcalfe insisted Bryden stayed where he was. 'Joy and Carl will cover it this end,' he told him.

'Is he resigning?'

'Don't know. They're keeping schtum.'

They discussed how much they should increase the offer to Barbara Kellingford for her story. Bryden wanted to up it to a hundred and fifty thousand but Metcalfe refused to go higher than a hundred grand. They agreed they should offer Major Roberts fifty thousand for his views on his son-in-law. Bryden asked Metcalfe if he'd had a word with Roy Oates yet.

'No,' said Metcalfe. 'He's on a job. I've left a message on his mobile.'

'Well, keep on at him. David Bailey here's got several pics of Roberts as he is now. You'll have them shortly. Show them to Roy. If any mud's sticking to Roberts, particularly from his Northern Ireland days, Roy will know about it and recognise him.'

Metcalfe said he would make it his priority, and ended the call.

'Did you hear that?' said Bryden, putting away his mobile.

Carter shook his head.

'We're to go back to Leefdale and find out why Roberts got a bloody nose.' Noticing that Carter was looking miserable, Bryden jabbed him playfully on the arm. 'Oi! Got the hump, have we? Cheer up, son. I was only joking. You've got to grow a thick skin if you want to get anywhere in this game.'

Carter smiled back at him, wanly. The more he saw of this game, the less he wanted to be involved in it.

'Now,' said Bryden. 'Before anything else I need a pint and a cheese sandwich. Know any decent pubs in this dead and alive fucking hole?'

****

Howard was deeply relieved to be escorted back to Rooks Nest by the police. Once they'd left the frenzied throng of reporters and cameramen behind at the gates and were walking up the drive, he gave the two officers a partial explanation for his facial injuries and made a formal complaint of assault. The older of the officers told him that neither of them could follow up his complaint as they'd both been instructed to guard the gates of his house. However, the constable promised to report the incident and assured Howard that other officers would be assigned to investigate. Both constables advised Howard to seek medical advice which he brushed aside, assuring them that his injuries weren't as serious as they looked.

As soon as Howard was safely inside Rooks Nest, he went straight to the bathroom to inspect his wounds. His left cheek was very red. He touched it gingerly. It felt slightly tender but he didn't think the cheekbone had been cracked or broken. He hoped he wasn't going to have a black eye. It would be most humiliating to appear in public with one, especially during the judging of Magnificent Britain. Noting with some concern that his nose was still dribbling blood, he gently pressed the bridge of it. Nothing seemed to be broken there either. He went downstairs and returned with some salt. He applied salt water to his grazes, and sat in his study compressing his nose with his fingers for several minutes until the bleeding had completely stopped.

His anger had partially abated since the confrontation with Sheldon, but now, as he sat nursing his wounds, violent and disturbing images inundated his mind. The morbid reflections that accompanied them acted like an accelerant, inflaming him once more into fury.

It was bad enough that his son-in-law was a thoroughly selfish bastard who couldn't care less about his wife or children, but what was really insufferable was that Peter's philandering was now public knowledge and the family's name was being dragged through the tabloid mud. Even worse, because of the actions of that reprehensible arsehole, Barbara and the children were being subjected to unimaginable distress. And they weren't the only ones! Rooks Nest was besieged and the reporters camped on the doorstep were evoking for him and Isobel memories of the worst days of "the incident". Furthermore, the beautiful, precious gardens of The Old Rectory had been desecrated and turned into some sort of squalid amusement park, taking Leefdale's chance of a fifth consecutive gold medal down the drain with them. As if that weren't enough, he was suffering physical and mental pain from a savage attack by a foul mouthed, undisciplined thug.

Howard raised his head towards the ceiling. 'You bastard!' he shouted at the oblivious and indifferent God that was taking such delight in torturing him. 'You bastard!'

Temporarily, this spontaneous if irrational outburst of anger made him feel a whole lot better. But the recollection of the teenager's fist thumping him in the face now forced him to recall the sequence of events which had led to the attack, and he was immediately filled with apprehension. It was clear that in the circumstances he'd not conducted himself well. It was therefore imperative that he got his side of the story clear in his mind before the arrival of the police. He began to rehearse what he would tell them. The most vital thing was to make sure they understood that the young thug had attacked him first by deliberately kicking the football at him when he was on the ground inspecting the appalling condition of the lawn, and therefore in a most vulnerable position. It was also essential to stress that there'd been plenty of adult witnesses to this.

But recalling the presence of the witnesses reminded Howard that everyone had seen him lash out with his stick and beat the thug about the head. He knew it had been done in self-defence but that might be disputed. Best to play it down a bit. Make little of it. Yes, he'd over reacted when he'd hit the boy, but it had clearly been self-defence. The natural and completely explicable action of someone who'd sustained sudden and unexpected trauma. The boy had attacked him first, hadn't he? Deliberately kicked the football at him from close range. And then all the thugs had joined in and started manhandling him so he'd no option but to defend himself with his stick, which was why he'd been punched in the face. He had a right to defend himself, hadn't he? Yes, that's how he would play it.

But he'd barely assured himself of the moral justification for his actions, when mortifying recollections of his own manic attack on the sculptures wiped all thoughts of righteous superiority from his mind. He had to admit that it had been completely over the top. Nevertheless, any reasonable person would surely accept that it had been a perfectly understandable reaction in the circumstances. Certainly, any horticulturalist who'd seen the wanton destruction of the rectory's beautiful rear garden would have understood the reasons for his anger and violence. Even so, it was hardly the behaviour expected of a former military officer, one whose life's training had conditioned him to control his emotions under intense pressure and consider the consequences of every action. Doubtless, that Zoe cow would make the most of it. Indeed, it was probable that all the rectory's lefties would conspire to present his actions in the worst possible light. His conviction about this caused him another surge of apprehension.

He began to speculate on the whereabouts of his wife and family. Had they gone to Scarborough or had they decided to go elsewhere? If only Isobel were there with him. Why had she left him like this to face everything alone? Why hadn't they waited for him? Had they no concern for his welfare? Hadn't they seen he was holding a handkerchief to his face? Why had they just thrown him to the dogs?

He considered ringing Isobel on her mobile, but instantly dismissed the idea. What would be the point? It would only alarm her. Once she knew he'd been assaulted she'd insist on them all returning from Scarborough, or wherever it was they'd gone, and he'd be the one responsible for ruining the children's day out. That would be very unfair on Mark and Jessica. The poor things had already gone through enough.

He could feel himself sweating and starting to feel peculiarly unwell. Immediately, he recognised these symptoms as intimations of an incipient anxiety attack. At all costs he had to prevent images of "the incident" returning. Even if it meant taking those damn doctor's pills.

He went into the kitchen, opened a drawer and took out the packet of anti-depressants. He poured himself a glass of water and was swallowing a pill when the front doorbell rang.

He went into the sitting room and peered through the front window. A police patrol car was in the drive. He went closer to the window and was relieved to see PC Wheatcroft and WPC Scargill standing at the front door. Howard knew them well: as chairman of the parish council he'd attended numerous meetings with each of them, and sought their advice regarding various policing matters.

When Howard opened the front door, the two police officers greeted him warmly.

'You were quick,' said Howard, as he led them down the hall.

'We were in the vicinity,' said WPC Scargill.

Howard showed them into the sitting room and invited them to take a seat. Fascinated, he watched PC Wheatcroft ease his massive six foot four frame into an armchair which instantly seemed to shrink to half its size. Howard had once jokingly remarked to Greg Maynard that the best thing for any criminal apprehended by Wheatcroft would be to leg it. They'd easily outrun the overweight PC.

'Looks like you've been in the wars, Major,' said Wheatcroft.

Howard said, 'Yes. All in all, Neil, it's been a hell of a day.' He surveyed both of them quizzically. 'I suppose you know all about my problems with my famous son-in-law?'

Scargill and Wheatcroft both nodded. 'Hard to miss it,' said Wheatcroft.

'I can't begin to imagine what you're going through,' said Scargill.

Howard felt curiously moved. It seemed such a long time since anyone had spoken to him kindly or sympathetically. He felt on the edge of tears. Ridiculous.

Neil Wheatcroft was holding a notebook and a pencil. 'But, as I understand it, your complaint has nothing to do with that. You're alleging an assault?'

'That's right.'

'And this assault took place across the road at The Old Rectory?'

'Yes. About half an hour ago.'

'Tell us what happened,' said Yvonne Scargill.

Howard laughed bitterly. 'Where to begin? I don't suppose you realize it but the rectory's been turned into a home for juvenile delinquents.'

'Yes, it's become an inclusion unit,' said Scargill. She was a Geordie, whose fundamental attitudes had been formed by her initial policing experiences patrolling the rough housing estates in Gateshead. She respected Howard, but had reservations about his attitude. She'd long ago decided that if not actually a snob, he was certainly condescending towards his social inferiors.

'Ah, so you know about inclusion units?' said Howard.

'It's our job to be aware of any developments on our patch,' said Scargill.

'I'm sure that the people who dreamed these units up were very well intentioned, but they failed to take into account the affect they'd have on the communities they were dumping them on.'

PC Wheatcroft laughed. 'When did politicians ever stop to consider the effect of their actions, eh?'

Howard was about to agree with him when he remembered that, in his own humble way, he himself was a politician.

'Have the people in the inclusion unit been giving you problems?' asked Scargill.

'Look,' said Howard, 'the people at The Old Rectory can give themselves all the fancy names they wish, but in my view they're a complete waste of space.' He then went on to give his reasons for visiting the rectory. 'My intention was merely to persuade Mr Bourne and his colleagues to keep their gardens in optimum condition, so that Leefdale would have the best possible chance of winning Magnificent Britain'. He described how shocked he'd been by the devastation visited on the rectory's rear garden. 'So, you see, by then I'd realized it was hopeless.'

When the Major had finished, Wheatcroft lowered his notebook. 'So, Howard, how did you come to be assaulted?'

'I was down on the ground inspecting the appalling damage to the lawn when one of the teenage yobs deliberately kicked a very heavy football at me.'

'Do you know his name?' asked Wheatcroft.

'No. I'm sorry, I don't. We weren't exactly introduced.'

'Can you give us a description of him?'

'Yes, I think so. Black. Well, not completely black. Mixed race. And about fourteen or fifteen. Quite big for his age.'

'And that's how you sustained the injuries to your face?' said Scargill.

'No. The ball hit me in the stomach, not the face.' Howard pointed to the graze on his cheek. 'I got this when he punched me.'

Wheatcroft tut tutted sympathetically. 'He punched you too, did he?'

'Yes.'

'How did that come about?' asked Scargill.

'I was badly winded by the ball. When I got to my feet I had to lean on the goal post for support. I was just getting my breath back when the thug and his friends started to manhandle me. I managed to ward them off with my stick, and get away from them by making my way to another part of the garden. It was there, by one of those ridiculous tree sculptures, that the mixed race thug caught up with me and punched me in the face. Fortunately, some of the staff managed to subdue the hooligan and I was able to escape and report the assault to your colleagues.'

'I'm sure it was a most unpleasant experience for you,' said Scargill.

Again, her kind words brought Howard close to tears. He could only nod.

'Were there any witnesses to the assault?' Scargill went on.

'Yes, there were witnesses to both assaults. The one with the football and the punch to the face. All the staff saw them, but they'll probably deny it.'

'Why do you say that?'

Howard smiled knowingly. 'In my experience people like that stick together.'

'Do you have their names?'

'Whose names?'

'The names of the staff.'

'Only two of them. Dylan Bourne and a young woman called Zoe. A communist I'd say. Certainly, very left. Very subversive.' WPC Scargill wrote the names in her notebook.

'How many staff were there?'

'Four, I think. Besides Bourne and Zoe there was another young man and woman.'

'Who else was in the garden?'

'My attacker's friends who were playing football with him, and there were some teenage girls at the end of the garden. They may have seen what happened. I'm not sure.'

'You didn't mention that there was a game of football going on,' said Scargill.

Howard was perturbed to see that she was now regarding him somewhat differently. Her eyes were no longer radiating absolute trust. Obviously, omitting to mention that the thugs had been playing football had been a major blunder. 'I'm sorry,' he said, with deliberate emollience. 'I thought that was understood.'

'No, it wasn't. Why didn't you say so before?'

'I don't know. I thought I had.'

Wheatcroft shot Scargill a disapproving glance. No need for that, he thought. The old boy's recovering from a vicious attack. Probably in shock. He's bound to be a bit disoriented and forgetting things. She was too quick off the mark was Yvonne. Probably because she was a woman. Felt she had to prove herself. Addressing Howard, he said, 'As they were playing football, is it possible the ball hit you accidentally?'

'Oh no! It was intentional. It was deliberately kicked at me.'

'Was anything said by you or any of the others during these assaults?' said Scargill.

'Yes, the boy who assaulted me was swearing at me the whole time.'

'What were his exact words?'

'Fuck you, man. Fuck you!'

'Anything else?'

'I don't like to use the word in front of a lady,' said Howard.

Scargill smiled. 'That's all right. I'm no lady and I'm sure I've heard them all before.'

'Very well. He called me the "C" word.'

'He called you a cunt?' said Scargill.

Howard found her delivery of the word offensive and suspected she was being subtly insulting. He decided he wouldn't react. Simply nod back at her. Such unattractive uniforms women police officers wore these days. Trousers were obviously more practical but so unbecoming. WPCs had always looked so much better in skirts. Such a shame: Yvonne wasn't a bad looking girl. Definitely had a touch of the Audrey Hepburn's. But so thin faced, her police bowler always looked far too big for her.

'He also threatened to kill me,' said Howard.

Wheatcroft looked up from his notebook. 'He threatened to kill you?'

'Yes.'

'What were his exact words?' said Scargill.

'I'll kill the cunt. I'll kill him.'

'Who did he say this to?'

'To no-one in particular. He was shouting it out when he was being subdued by the staff.'

'I still can't understand why he attacked you,' said Scargill.

Howard was discomforted to see that now both officers were staring at him in the same incredulous, slightly mistrustful manner. He thought of those occasions when they'd all worked side by side together on various policing projects involving the co-operation of the parish council. What a strange and disturbing sensation it was to find himself on the other side of the fence to them. Worse, to be the focus of their suspicion.

'Why did he attack you?' said Wheatcroft.

Howard said, 'I assume he objected to me examining the dreadful state of the lawn.'

'He thought you were in the way and spoiling their game?'

'That possibly may have been in his mind, I don't know. But if that was the case why didn't he ask me to move? If he'd asked me to move, I'd have done so immediately.'

'You didn't provoke him in any way?' said Scargill.

'Certainly not.'

Yvonne's intelligent, grey eyes continued to subject Howard to a searching inspection long after he'd finished speaking. There was silence in the room apart from the sound of Wheatcroft's pen moving across the page of his notebook.

Howard said to Scargill, 'It sounds as though you don't believe me, Yvonne.'

She smiled, indulgently. 'Of course, we believe you, Howard. You're a respectable man who's a leader of his community. But we have to do our job, and asking difficult questions is part of it. You must be aware of that from your own experience in the military.'

Howard nodded, but said nothing.

Wheatcroft said, 'It's all right, Howard. You're not the one on trial here. You've obviously been the victim of a most unpleasant assault. We're not going to allow anyone to push you around. I think we have enough for charges to be brought. And don't you worry, they will be.'

****

'And you've definitely not got a headache?' said Toni.
'No,' said Sheldon.
'Still not feeling dizzy or seeing stars?'
'No.'
'Do you feel sick?'
'No.'

For the past half an hour Sheldon had been sitting on an upright wooden chair in the kitchen, gingerly applying a cold compress to a large bump on his temple. The bump had rapidly increased in size within minutes of Major Roberts' ignominious exit from the rectory. The compress had been supplied by Toni, who had a certificate in First Aid.

'Take the compress away for a moment, I want to look in your eyes again,' Toni instructed. She bent down until her face was level with Sheldon's and was relieved to see that his pupils still weren't dilated.

'Any double vision or blurring in your eyes?' she asked.
'No.'

His anxious, vulnerable expression evoked her sympathy. She held up a straightened index finger and asked Sheldon to follow it with his eyes as she moved it across his field of vision describing a letter "H". He appeared to be able follow it without difficulty.

Toni stood up. She addressed Dylan and Zoe, who were also gathered around Sheldon and regarding him equally anxiously. 'Well, I don't think he's concussed, but I don't like the look of that bump. I think we should get him to A & E as soon as possible.

'I ain't goin' to no hospital,' said Sheldon.

'Shh,' said Toni. She took Sheldon's hand which was holding the compress and guided it gently until it was back in place on his forehead. 'Try to stay quiet and still.' She looked at Dylan and Zoe. 'Can we discuss this privately?'

'No,' said Dylan. 'I don't think we should have private discussions about Sheldon, or make any decisions about him in which he's not involved.'

'I agree,' said Zoe.

'Yeah. You have to do what I want,' said Sheldon.

'We most certainly do not,' Toni told him. 'You're a child. We are adults who are responsible for your welfare.' She was flushed now, and obviously angry. Turning to the others, she went on, 'We are in loco parentis as regards Sheldon. Acting in the place of his parents. I don't think he's seriously injured but we can't be sure until he's been medically examined, and I don't want to take the risk. It would be completely irresponsible if we didn't take him to hospital.'

'No, no hospital,' Sheldon insisted.

Zoe said, 'It's all right, Sheldon. We're not going to force you to do anything you don't want to.' She addressed Dylan. 'He seems all right. Maybe we should wait for an hour or so and see how he gets on.'

'We need to tell the police that Major Roberts has committed a vicious assault on one of our children,' said Toni. 'They need to arrest him.'

'I don't want no police,' said Sheldon.

'Don't forget, Sheldon punched the Major,' said Zoe. 'If the police are involved they'll arrest Sheldon.'

'No police, please,' pleaded Sheldon.

'Stay cool, Sheldon,' Dylan said, quickly. 'Calm yourself.' He sighed heavily. 'Look, there's no way we can keep the police out of this. Everyone saw the Major was injured when he left here. He's probably called them himself.'

'No police!' cried Sheldon.

'Dylan's right,' Toni told Zoe. 'The police could be here any minute. We need to get Sheldon to hospital before they come.'

'Maybe the Major won't press charges,' said Zoe.

'Even if he doesn't we have to inform the police and social services. We have to cover our backs.'

'We can't just think of ourselves,' said Zoe. 'We have to consider what's best for Sheldon.'

'I'm not putting my teaching certificate on the line for anyone,' said Toni. She looked around desperately. She was clearly frustrated. 'God, I hate discussing this in front of...' Realising that she was losing control she took command of herself. 'If Sheldon's condition gets worse, if he gets seriously ill or even dies, I'm not going to be held responsible. Our careers will be over.'

Sheldon swallowed hard. 'Dies?'

'Aren't you being rather over dramatic?' said Zoe.

That's rich, coming from you, thought Dylan.

'We need to think about this carefully and not panic,' Zoe continued. 'And we need to pay attention to what Sheldon wants.'

'I'm ain't gonna die, am I?' said Sheldon.

'I don't know,' said Toni. 'That's why we need to get you to hospital.' She turned to Dylan and Zoe. 'Sheldon's a child. He's not capable of acting in his own best interests.'

'I don't wanna die,' said Sheldon.

'We need to take him to A & E,' insisted Toni. 'That's what he needs.'

'Yeah, call an ambulance!' cried Sheldon.

'What do you think, Dylan?' said Zoe. 'You're the team leader.'

Dylan stared at them irresolutely. He wasn't completely sure, but instinctively felt they shouldn't call an ambulance. It didn't seem urgent enough. His preference was to drive Dylan to hospital himself; call the police on his mobile, explain why he was at A & E, and make the complaint about Major Roberts.

Sheldon had removed the cold compress from his forehead and was standing now. 'I want an ambulance!' he shouted at Dylan.

Dylan was about to tell them what he'd decided and the reasons for it, when there was a sudden noise in the hall. It was Eric emerging from the art therapy room where he'd been taking the clients for a session. He ran down the hall and into the kitchen.

'The police are at the front gate,' he burst out. 'They're trying to get in!'

****

PC Wheatcroft said, 'And this is the goal post the Major was trying to pull out of the ground?'

'That's the one,' said Dylan. 'That's why it's got a lean on it.'

'And it's right here that Major Roberts hit Sheldon with his stick?'

'Yes.'

'And you saw that?'

'Yes. That's when we knew things had got out of hand, and we had to intervene.'

'Who else saw the Major hit Sheldon?' asked Scargill.

'All of us. All the staff.'

'And the kids,' said Zoe. 'Don't forget the kids.'

'All the kids saw it?' said Scargill.

'Yes. They saw everything. Do you want to talk to them again?'

'Not at the moment,' said Wheatcroft. 'Later maybe.'

When WPC Scargill and PC Wheatcroft had arrived at the rectory, they'd quickly established that Sheldon was the boy who'd punched the Major. Sheldon had readily admitted doing it but indignantly protested his innocence, insisting that Major Roberts had struck him first on the head with his stick. Not only did Sheldon's raised bump appear to provide indisputable evidence of this, but his account was supported by Dylan, Zoe and Toni.

Dylan expressed concern at the alarming nature of Sheldon's head injury. He told the police officers that he'd just been about to drive him to A & E. This prompted WPC Scargill to use her personal radio to call an ambulance. She also requested a pre-cons check, which soon revealed that Sheldon had no previous criminal convictions. Both police officers had then sent Toni and Zoe out of the kitchen while they questioned Sheldon. As Sheldon was a minor, Dylan was allowed to remain. The interview with Sheldon ended when the ambulance arrived, although by then it had already become abundantly clear to

Scargill and Wheatcroft that Major Roberts had given them a somewhat selective and partial account of what had actually transpired.

While the paramedics examined Sheldon and assessed the extent of his injuries, Scargill and Wheatcroft questioned all the members of staff including Eric. They also interviewed the clients in the art therapy room. This was done in order to clarify Sheldon's somewhat incoherent account and confirm its veracity. When the officers had finished they were in possession of an entirely different version of events from the one presented to them by Howard. It appeared that Sheldon had accidentally, not deliberately, kicked the ball at Howard, and that Sheldon and Khaled had actually asked Howard to leave the pitch beforehand. Everyone was adamant that the ball had struck Howard on the thigh and not in the stomach, and that he'd not leant on the goalpost for support, but had attempted to wrench it out of the ground. There was unanimous agreement that Howard had brought his stick down hard on Sheldon's head, causing him to fall down; also, that Howard had tried to damage several of the sculptures. Zoe had vociferously asserted that Sheldon had been provoked into punching Howard when he saw his own sculpture being attacked.

After being questioned in the chill-out room, Dylan, Zoe and Toni were then asked to accompany the two police officers into the garden for an examination of the locus in quo and to answer any additional questions. Which is why they were all now gathered around the goal post that Howard had unsuccessfully attempted to wrench out of the ground.

'And after the Major hit Sheldon he attempted to damage the sculptures, is that right?' said Scargill.

'He did damage them,' snapped Zoe. 'Have you any idea how long it took me and the kids to construct them?'

Wheatcroft pointed at the discoloured statues of Apollo and Demeter that were still serving as improvised goalposts at the other end of the pitch. 'I can't see any sculptures, except those,' he said.

That's because you're a philistine, thought Zoe. With an encompassing gesture she indicated the kids' sculptures. 'I'm talking about those installations. Those abstract conflations of the organic and the inorganic. Those juxtapositions of nature and artefact.'

Scargill suppressed a giggle.

Zoe led them from sculpture to sculpture indicating where Howard had damaged them, in some cases extensively so. She stopped by the sculpture that closely resembled a robot. A blue metal pole and a length of red rubber tubing were on the ground surrounded by many fragments of plastic. 'Just look at this,' said Zoe, forlornly. 'It's so hard to create but so easy to destroy. The man's a maniac.'

'We'll send a SOCO round to photo them and make an audit of the damage,' said Wheatcroft. He looked at Dylan, remembering that he was the one who claimed to be in charge. 'Could you make sure that the damage stays just as it is until our SOCO's been?'

'Sure,' said Dylan.

Zoe pointed at the robot. 'By the way, this is Sheldon's sculpture,' she said. 'Good, isn't it?'

No-one said anything.

'This is where you restrained the Major, then?' said Wheatcroft.

'Yes,' said Dylan.

'And who did that?'

'The three of us did.'

'You should have seen him,' said Toni. 'He'd completely lost it. Ranting and roaring.'

Wheatcroft said, 'Where was the other chap while this was going on? The one who's taking a class right now?'

'Eric?' said Toni. 'He was on the ground looking after Sheldon.'

'So how come Sheldon punched Major Roberts?'

Toni said, 'Sheldon was just getting to his feet when he saw Major Roberts attacking the robot. That's when he ran over and hit him. The Major was lucky. It could have broken his nose.'

Wheatcroft made a note in his book. He then turned to Zoe. 'Major Roberts says Sheldon threatened to kill him.'

Dylan, Toni and Zoe exchanged uneasy looks. They all knew how bad that sounded.

Zoe said, 'Yes. But he didn't mean it. He was very angry. He'd lost it.'

Wheatcroft looked sceptical. 'Really? Major Roberts says Sheldon would have hit him again if you hadn't prevented him.'

'That's right. I had to restrain him. But Sheldon was badly provoked from the start. No-one likes being called a moron.'

Wheatcroft smiled wryly, and said, 'I've been called a lot worse than that in Luffield on a Friday night.' He returned his notebook to his pocket. 'That's all for now. Would you three mind going back into the kitchen for a few minutes? My colleague and I need to discuss a couple of things.'

'I hope you're not going to arrest Sheldon,' said Zoe.

'Just go and wait in the kitchen,' said Wheatcroft. 'We'll be with you in a minute.'

Recognizing a look spreading over Zoe's face that meant certain trouble, Dylan took her arm and ushered her and Toni into the house.

Scargill and Wheatcroft watched their retreating backs.

'Well,' said Wheatcroft, 'this is bloody embarrassing, isn't it?'

'It certainly is.'

'The Major must have gone apeshit when he saw the state of this garden.'

'Aye, but that doesn't excuse what he did.'

'As for those so-called sculptures,' Wheatcroft vaguely indicated them with a sweep of his arm, 'they're such a mess. I couldn't even see where the damage was. Could you?'

'No.'

'They all look like a car crash to me.'

'Even so,' Yvonne said, 'Sheldon must have been right pissed off when Howard started weighing into his robot.'

They both laughed.

'I wished I'd seen that,' said Wheatcroft.

Scargill nodded vigorously. She was unable to stop laughing. 'We shouldn't, you know!'

'No!' said Wheatcroft, and laughed again even more loudly.

When they'd both regained control of themselves, Scargill said, 'Still if Sheldon was trying to defend his art work that could count as mitigation.'

Wheatcroft said, 'Yeah, but it's hardly Art, is it? I mean it's not even sculpture.'

'That's what they said about the Angel of the North, mon.'

Wheatcroft said, 'So, what do you think?'

Scargill looked serious. 'I think that by a clever series of omissions, Howard's been telling us a load of porkies.'

'I agree. It's clear Sheldon didn't deliberately kick the ball at Howard. And it was Howard who assaulted Sheldon first.'

'Yes, he kept that quiet, didn't he?'

'But Sheldon held his hands up to punching him.'

'Yeah.'

'So, what do we think? Actual not grievous?'

'Oh yes. Definitely not grievous.'

'With intent?'

'No, I don't think so. No intent.'

'Come on then,' said Wheatcroft. 'Let's go and tell them the good news.'

****

Louise stared at the practice sheet and tried hard to remember whether it was the dividend or the divisor that you turned upside down and whether or not you cancelled before or after you multiplied. It was all so confusing, even though Toni had demonstrated how to do it many times on the whiteboard and worked though several examples with her before lunch.

Louise had missed the violent altercation between Major Roberts and Sheldon. When it had occurred she'd been sitting in the encouragement room, just as she was now, struggling with the division of fractions. She'd heard the Major arrive and Zoe show him into the conservatory. She'd been very shocked to hear Zoe ask him if he'd committed a murder. Grown-ups said the weirdest things.

After that, there were no more voices so she'd assumed Zoe and the Major had gone out into the garden where all the others were taking their break, lucky things.

The window of the encouragement room that overlooked one side of the rear garden was slightly open. Louise had completed the division of just one more fraction when she'd heard some terrible language and a lot of shouting outside. A bit later, she heard someone walk quickly through the kitchen and down the hall and then the front door had slammed. It was like a radio play.

She'd gone back to her desk and tried to concentrate but there was too much noise from people all talking and shouting at once. She could hear Sheldon in the kitchen using some terrible swear words, and Zoe and Toni were trying to calm him down. It seemed that Sheldon and Major Roberts had had some sort of row.

After a few minutes, Zoe had come into the encouragement room and asked her to go out into the garden. She said they were going to have an early lunch out in the open. When Louise had emerged from the encouragement room with Zoe she saw Sheldon sitting in a chair in the kitchen. He had a huge bump on his head, and Toni was at the sink wetting a cloth.

In the garden she'd sat under the trees at the far end with Mona and the other girls. They'd given her a detailed account of what had happened. She couldn't believe that nice old Major Roberts had used such terrible swear words. They were awful and Sheldon's were even worse. How funny to think Major Roberts used swear words like that. And adults were telling you all the time not to use swear words, too. Had Major Roberts really hit Sheldon on the head with his stick? And had Sheldon really punched him? But it had to be true because everyone was saying it and she could see the damage to the sculptures. And Sheldon had a great big bump on his head. That was what Mrs Henshall called evidence.

After lunch, Eric had taken all the clients into the art therapy room. Toni had told Louise that she'd done insufficient work on fractions and asked her to return to the encouragement room to complete the practice sheet. Louise decided that she didn't like Toni very much. She wasn't like the other grown-ups in the unit. She was like Mrs Henshall, a real teacher, and she was very strict.

Louise had found it hard to concentrate on the fractions. There was so much noise and coming and going. First, she could hear Toni, Dylan and Zoe in the kitchen trying to help Sheldon and arguing about whether to take him to the hospital. Then the police arrived and were asking lots of questions. And then the ambulance people came and they were talking to Sheldon. They seemed quite worried about him. Again, sitting in the encouragement room and hearing it all was just like listening to a radio play.

It was a shame she'd missed all the real excitement though. She'd never seen a proper fight between older people. She wished she'd been there to see Major Roberts and Sheldon hitting each other. Mr Evans at the Youth Theatre was always saying that sometimes life is life and sometimes life is drama. She'd never really understood what he'd been on about until now. This was really dramatic. And yet, in a way she was glad she'd been in the encouragement room when it had happened. If she'd actually seen Sheldon and Major Roberts hitting each other she was sure mum wouldn't have let her come back to the rectory any more. She'd have said it was too rough. That was the last thing she wanted. The Old Rectory was so much nicer and more interesting than school. So, she wouldn't tell her mother about the swearing and violence unless she asked her, and then she could say she didn't know anything about it. She was doing her maths in the encouragement room when it happened.

But even if mum refused to allow her to come back to the unit, she'd only be excluded until the end of the week. She'd do "Oliver", and afterwards it would be the six weeks holiday. And next term she'd go to secondary school. But before then, she'd hopefully have left Leefdale for good. She didn't know how it would happen but she was sure it would. It was like a presentiment. She loved that word. She often had presentiments and sometimes they came true. It wouldn't have mattered if she'd had a normal mum and dad like everyone else. But she hadn't. So she was never going to give up until she and mum left Leefdale for ever. Never. Never.

Now she could hear the voices of Toni, Dylan and Zoe. They'd returned from the back garden where they'd been with the police. But the police hadn't come back with them. Louise regarded her worksheet with distaste. Five more fractions to do. Dylan had promised that when she'd finished she could go into the art therapy room with the others and do some painting. Perhaps she should go into the kitchen and ask Dylan if she could do that now. Rupa had told her that when Dylan took you for art therapy he asked you to paint pictures that expressed how you were feeling at that moment; or showed how you felt about things in your life. In her mind she'd been thinking up lots of pictures she could do to show how she really felt about things. The thought of painting them thrilled her. And when was she going to do some drama? Zoe had said they did lots of drama.

Yes, she would go and ask Dylan if she could go into the art therapy room. She stood up and went over to the half open door. She was about to open it fully and walk into the kitchen when she heard the voices of the policeman and the policewoman in the conservatory. They were returning to the kitchen.

Louise ran back to her desk and started working on the next fraction.

****

When Scargill and Wheatcroft returned to the kitchen they found Dylan, Zoe and Toni deep in discussion with the paramedics.

'We want to whip Sheldon into Scarborough for an X-ray,' explained the female paramedic. 'Just to rule out a hair-line fracture.'

'Fine,' said Wheatcroft. He moved closer to Sheldon, who was still sitting on one of the kitchen chairs. Sheldon gazed up anxiously at Wheatcroft's sudden, looming presence. He was clearly intimidated by the constable's penetrating stare. 'Sheldon Smith,' Wheatcroft said, 'I am arresting you on suspicion of committing the offence of actual bodily harm against Major Howard Roberts. You do not have to say anything but it may harm your defence if you do not mention when questioned something which you later rely on in court. Anything you do say may be given in evidence.'

'You can't arrest Sheldon,' said Zoe. 'He's going to hospital.'

'No problem,' said Wheatcroft. His attention remained fixed on Sheldon. 'Now Sheldon, you're going to be taken to Scarborough Hospital for an X-ray. I shall be going with you in the ambulance. If they don't want to keep you in hospital you'll be taken to Luffield police station for further questioning. That's because you've been arrested. You may then be charged. Is that clear? Do you understand?'

Sheldon nodded. He looked very frightened.

Zoe's outrage at Sheldon's arrest was palpable, as though a physical object had penetrated her chest and was crushing her from inside. It was obvious that Sheldon had been provoked by Howard Roberts beyond endurance. She'd thought the officers had accepted that as a given. Several adult witnesses had testified that the Major had brutally struck Sheldon with his stick. His injuries were so bad he was being taken to A & E, and yet he was the one who was being arrested! She knew the best policy was to keep quiet, but as she desperately struggled to control her anger the injustice of it all made her want to burst.

'How dare you arrest Sheldon,' she cried. 'He's just a kid. Major Roberts is a grown man. He should know better. He smashed Sheldon over the head with his stick. He attacked Sheldon's sculpture. What Sheldon did was wrong but it's perfectly understandable. You shouldn't be arresting Sheldon, you should be arresting Roberts.'

'If Sheldon is charged, he'll have the opportunity to make his case in court,' said WPC Scargill.

'But why are you arresting Sheldon?' Zoe demanded. 'It was the Major who started it. He assaulted Sheldon. We've all told you that!'

'Howard Roberts has made a complaint of serious assault against Sheldon,' said Scargill. 'And Sheldon's held his hands up to it. We've no choice but to arrest him.'

'But he hit me with a stick for nothin',' Sheldon protested. 'Just 'cos I told him to get out of the way of the goal.'

Wheatcroft said to Scargill, 'I'll go with Sheldon in the ambulance. You go and see Major Roberts. Then join me at the hospital.'

'Yes, go on, run along,' sneered Zoe. 'Go and report to your commanding officer.'

Scargill said, 'My commanding officer's the chief constable, lass.'

'Is she always like this?' Wheatcroft asked Dylan, fixing Zoe with a look. Dylan looked sheepish and shrugged his shoulders non-committally.

'Yes! She's always like this when she sees something that's totally unfair!' Zoe shouted. She then launched into a furious tirade against the officers, castigating them for arresting Sheldon and accusing them of being in Major Roberts' pocket.

Dylan observed Zoe's outburst with increasing alarm. He was concerned that she'd end up being arrested too. He went across to her and placed his hand on her shoulder. 'None of this is helping anyone. Least of all Sheldon.'

'You're quite right, sir,' said Wheatcroft. He addressed Zoe. 'You should listen to your boss. He's talking sense.' Then, turning back to Dylan, he said, 'Sheldon's a juvenile so you'll have to come with us.'

'To the hospital?'

'Aye. And afterwards to the station.'

Scargill placed a hand on Zoe's arm. 'We're only doing our job,' she said, in a gentle, placating tone. 'And if there are charges to be made, they will be.'

Zoe dismissed this with contempt. 'Sure!' She turned to Dylan. 'I want to come with you.'

'No,' said Dylan. 'This has been a very disturbed day and we need to keep things as normal as possible for the clients. Stay here and take your drama session as usual. That'll do more good.'

Zoe scoffed. It occurred to her that Dylan would be the last person she'd rely on to defend her human rights.

'Come on, lad,' said the male paramedic to Sheldon. 'Let's go.'

Sheldon rose from his seat, and assisted by the paramedics began moving out of the kitchen and into the hall.

Dylan started to follow but Zoe took a step towards him, barring his way. 'I insist on going with Sheldon,' she said. 'Too many young people have died in police custody.'

'Now listen here, Miss,' said Wheatcroft. 'We're taking him to Luffield nick and nothing's ever died there except the station cat.'

Zoe didn't look convinced.

****

Ever since the police officers had left Rooks Nest, Howard had been wandering through the house asking himself how it was possible that in the space of just a few short hours his life had disintegrated into chaos and uncertainty. And how he missed Isobel! She rarely left his side and now that she'd gone every empty room seemed like a massive rebuke for his stupid, reckless actions.

He entered his study and went straight over to the window. He stood there staring at the familiar fabric of The Old Rectory, hoping that it would compose and settle him, but circumstances now prevented him from deriving any pleasure or solace from the sight of it. The rectory's unkempt and neglected air and the media people milling around his own front gate reminded him too painfully of recent humiliating events and of his own uncharacteristic and inexcusable behaviour.

He thought again of Isobel and how much he loved her, needed her; and once again berated himself for stupidly ignoring her always sensible advice. On today of all days there'd been absolutely no necessity for him to have approached those in the rectory. What had possessed him to go over there in the middle of a media frenzy and put himself on offer? And why hadn't he taken his pill? If he'd followed Dr Draper's instructions and taken it, none of this morning's appalling events would have occurred. He wouldn't be staring out of his study window contemplating whether or not his arrest was imminent. He'd be at Scarborough making sandcastles with his grandchildren. For he was no fool: although the police had accepted his version of events, he knew they were bound to find plenty of witnesses at The Old Rectory willing and eager to dispute his account of the violence and disorder. And what would he do then? He stared at the rectory walls and tried to imagine what was taking place behind them. What were those people over there saying about him?

Howard became aware that one of the photographers by the gate had raised his camera and was focussing it on the study window. He wondered what on earth the man was doing, until it occurred to him that photographers had telescopic lenses. By then it was too late. There was a flash like a sudden, single glint of sunlight reflected by glass or metal. And then the photographers were all doing it: pointing their cameras and flashing away.

Howard shut out the unseemly spectacle by pulling down the blind. He turned from the window and went and sat at his desk, considering what to do. And then, for reasons he could only attribute to the anti-depressant he'd recently taken, he felt suffused with analgesic balm; tranquillity seemed to be irrigating through him; equanimity was returning. He now had the absolute certainty that whatever happened, all would be well. As the effects of the pill increased he was able to reflect on his position quite dispassionately, as though the dreadful experience he was undergoing was academic and of purely theoretical interest. This made him feel entirely positive about his situation. There was no reason at all to suppose the police wouldn't accept the veracity of his version of events above all others. Why would they take the word of a bunch of thugs and hooligans in preference to that of an officer and a gentleman: a valiant and highly respected member of the community? And even if they didn't believe him, what did it matter? No harm would come to him, he was sure.

The return of his equilibrium was now producing an unassailable confidence and composure: the perfect conditions for the restoration of his fragmented will. He could sense his strength returning as he no longer felt so utterly defenceless against despair. The countless shards into which his will had been shattered were re-forming, regrouping, uniting again into a single unity, an iron resolve for one purpose only: revenge on the inclusion unit. The example of his hero, Winston Churchill, came to mind. His study of the great man's life had taught him that if you wanted to achieve your aims and yet remain true to your own self, you must never have any truck with shabby compromise: that great illusion and last refuge of those with no stomach or will for the fight. Instead, you ploughed on and gave your enemies no quarter. Yes, striking that yob had been wrong, but he was damned if he was going to admit that to the police. Quite the contrary. If he was to retain his credibility in the face of all those witnesses who'd doubtless be rolled out to traduce him, then it was vital for him to go on the attack with a pre-emptive strike.

Howard straightway went into action. His first telephone call was to Mrs Phillips, the clerk to the parish council. He told her that having now seen for himself the condition of The Old Rectory's gardens, he was so devastated by their deplorable state that he wanted her to organise an extraordinary meeting of the full council for that evening. Although she grumbled about the shortness of the notice, he managed to persuade her to make the necessary arrangements and inform all the parish councillors personally.

After his call to Mrs Phillips it occurred to Howard that a court injunction might be a possible way forward. It would put those at the rectory on the defensive and force them to comply with the wishes of the Magnificent Britain Sub-Committee. It might also swing the public behind his case, and make them antagonistic towards the people in the inclusion unit. He decided to telephone his solicitor.

Robert Armitage was in consultation with a client but he rang back fifteen minutes later. Howard informed him that he'd made a complaint of assault against a youth and that the police were investigating. However, he carefully avoided any mention of his own attack on Sheldon. After receiving Armitage's professional advice regarding the assault, Howard described the appalling state of The Old Rectory's gardens, and enquired about the feasibility of obtaining an injunction against Dylan Bourne and the other residents.

'To do what?' asked Armitage.

'To get them to restore the gardens to their previous condition.'

After asking Howard several questions, Armitage said, 'I'm sorry, but as the rectory's gardens are privately owned I suspect that any attempt to obtain a court injunction to force the owners to do their gardening would have only a negligible chance of success.'

There'd been a smile in Armitage's voice and Howard, who was in no mood for levity, suspected that his solicitor was taking the matter far too lightly. 'This is no joking matter, Robert. Their neglect could cost the village its gold medal!'

Armitage had long ago assigned Howard to the "difficult client" category. Raising his eyes to heaven for the benefit of his secretary, he said, 'In order to get an injunction you'd have to prove that whatever the people in the rectory were doing was interfering with the quiet enjoyment of your land, and therefore constituted a private nuisance. It appears to me, that that is not the case. Therefore, any application for an injunction would fail and would be a waste of time and money.'

'It's certainly a nuisance to me,' said Howard.

'How?'

'It's a bloody eyesore.'

'That doesn't make it a nuisance. You can't obtain an injunction simply because your aesthetic sense is offended. The level of nuisance must be of a much greater degree than that.'

'Everyone in the village will say it's a public nuisance when Leefdale loses Magnificent Britain.'

Armitage had long found that the solution for dealing with litigious clients was pedantry. 'Quite possibly. But to describe neglecting a garden and cutting back trees as a public nuisance would be technically incorrect. If the interference doesn't extend beyond the boundaries of The Old Rectory it doesn't constitute a nuisance to the public. Now, if the people in the rectory were producing unacceptable levels of noise, for example, that could be construed as a public nuisance.'

'They are very noisy,' said Howard.

'Ah,' said Armitage. 'Now that could be a justification for an injunction. Does the noise extend beyond the grounds of The Old Rectory?'

'Yes, I could hear it in my study.'

'What sort of noise is it?'

'Loud hoovering and even louder music.'

'At night? After eleven pm?'

'No, just during the day. This morning, in fact. But they soon stopped when I complained.'

'It only occurred once and that was this morning?'

'Yes, but it may occur again at any time.'

'But the noise stopped when you complained?'

'Yes.'

'Well, if it only occurred once and they've been co-operative and stopped it I don't think you have a case. To get an injunction you'd have to show that the noise was protracted, severe and continuous, and they refused to reduce it despite your complaints.'

Armitage suggested that Howard's best course might be to ring the Department for Education, apprise them of his complaints about the inclusion unit and see what they had to suggest. 'There might be some grounds for revoking their licence,' he said, hopefully. He then abruptly terminated the conversation and rang off as he was already late for lunch with his mistress.

Howard immediately rang the Department for Education in London to see if there was any way he could apply to have the inclusion unit's licence revoked. After being passed from extension to extension, he was eventually able to speak to a woman who had responsibility for inclusion units; she merely confirmed that the inclusion unit at The Old Rectory in Leefdale had been established with the Department's approval. Disappointed, Howard spent several minutes complaining to her about the state of The Old Rectory's gardens.

'I'm sorry, but the Department would only withdraw the inclusion unit's licence if it failed an Ofsted inspection,' the civil servant told him. 'Failing to mow the lawn or trim hedges might give Ofsted Inspectors health and safety concerns. But that particular unit isn't due for an inspection for some time.'

'But they've cut down several mature trees!'

'Again, that's not something we could automatically revoke their licence for. But you could complain about it to the Forestry Protection Officer at your local council. In certain circumstances they can take action through the courts but it usually only results in a fine.'

Thanks for nothing, thought Howard, and abruptly ended the call.

His next phone call was to Greg Maynard's office. He was hoping to tell Greg about the extraordinary meeting and discuss tactics. Disappointingly, he was told that Greg was not on site.

Howard was just about to try Greg's mobile number when the doorbell rang. For a moment hope triumphed over common sense and sent Howard hurrying down the stairs in the expectation that Isobel had returned. But when he reached the hall a quick reflection put an end to such wishful thinking. Why would she be ringing the doorbell when she had a key?

Howard changed direction and shot into the sitting room. Taking care to ensure that he couldn't be observed, he stealthily stole up to the bay window and glanced through it at the caller.

It wasn't the familiar, reassuring figure of Isobel standing on the doorstep but WPC Scargill. Howard took some time to observe her, searching for some subtle alteration in her appearance that might suggest her arrival heralded the imminent removal of his liberty. But her demeanour appeared normal and there was no indication on her countenance that anything was amiss. Howard lingered rather too long watching her. Now her expression did change, and her lips pursed together in an impatient thin line as she pressed the doorbell once again, keeping her thumb in position for several seconds. Howard moved quickly to answer the door.

'Hello again, Howard,' said Yvonne. Her accompanying smile implied that all was indeed going to be well and he had nothing to fear. However, he found that he now neither minded nor cared. This was because his medication was effectively nullifying his emotions and making him feel unnaturally detached and elated, as though he were connected to nothing in the world and not affected by anything in it. 'Come in, dear,' he said. 'Come in.'

He led her into the sitting room and indicated that she should take a seat. As she sat on the sofa he noticed for the first time that she was carrying a rather large but empty transparent polythene bag. Speculating silently on its purpose, Howard took a seat opposite her in an armchair.

'So,' he said, 'what do you think now you've seen the damage to the rectory's gardens for yourself?'

'Well, I don't know what they were like before but they certainly look neglected. The trees seem to have been hacked about quite a bit. I can see why you got angry.'

'Angry?' Howard snorted. 'I was furious.'

Yvonne nodded, understandingly. 'You'll be interested to know that we've arrested the youth who assaulted you. His name's Sheldon Smith.'

'You've arrested him? Excellent. That'll teach him a lesson. Nowadays people seem to think they can behave as they like. Well, they've got to learn they can't assault decent, law abiding people and expect to get away with it.'

'I heartily agree,' said Yvonne.

'I suppose he denied it.'

'Actually, he didn't. He admitted it.'

'He admitted it?'

'Yes.' Yvonne caught Howard's eye and stared. 'Well, he could hardly deny it. Too many witnesses saw him do it.'

There was a pause, during which Howard considered Scargill's remark for its potential implications. It appeared to be entirely innocent, but he was on the lookout now for any utterance or nuance that might indicate he had cause to be concerned. Was she warning him that he'd be a fool to lie?

Yvonne went on, 'Sheldon's been taken to Scarborough Hospital to have his injuries assessed. Neil's gone with him.'

'He has injuries?'

'Yes.'

'Are they severe?'

'I can't say. The paramedics wanted him X-rayed to rule out a skull fracture.'

A skull fracture. This was bad news for Howard, indeed. Was it just his imagination or was she observing him rather more closely than usual? Looking for his reaction, perhaps?

'I see,' he said.

'If Sheldon isn't kept in hospital, he'll be taken to Luffield to be formally charged.'

'Good.'

Yvonne said, 'I noticed a walking stick in your umbrella stand in the hall. Is that the one you had with you at the rectory?'

This unexpected question warned Howard that despite Sheldon's arrest, he himself might not be completely out of the woods. 'Yes,' he said, cautiously.

'I need to see it.'

'Why?'

'Could I see it, please?'

This was not a question from Yvonne, but a command.

Howard attempted to rise from his armchair. 'Of course.'

But Scargill was already on her feet. 'It's all right. Stay there. I'll get it.' She left the room and went into the hall. With the careless insouciance that comes from a sense of complete detachment, Howard heard her extract the stick from the umbrella stand. Everything that was happening seemed disconnected from him, and taking place at a great distance.

WPC Scargill returned carrying a chestnut walking stick with a curved handle. She examined it all the way down to its rubber ferrule. She then placed it in her transparent polythene bag and sealed it up. 'I'll need to keep this as evidence,' she said.

'What on earth for?' said Howard.

'The thing is, we've talked to all the people who witnessed Sheldon's assault on you and they tell a very different story to the one you do.'

'Oh?'

'All the adult witnesses say you weren't leaning on the goal post to recover your breath. You weren't even hit in the stomach by the ball. They say you were angry and trying to pull the goal post out of the ground.'

Howard scoffed loudly. 'They would say that, wouldn't they?'

Yvonne's stare was keen and unblinking. 'I don't understand. Why would they say that?'

'Oh, come on Yvonne, you can see what kind of people they are.'

'No, I can't. What kind of people are they?'

'The kind of people who'd destroy a beautiful garden. The kind of people who'd attack a respectable man.'

'The witnesses say that the youngsters weren't attacking you. They were attempting to stop you pulling the goal post out of the ground.'

'They're lying!'

'What, all of them?'

'Yes.'

'So, you deny you were pulling the goal post out of the ground?'

'Of course, I deny it. It's not true. I was leaning on it.'

Yvonne held up the evidence bag containing the walking stick. 'All the witnesses say that Sheldon's head injury was caused by you hitting him over the head with this stick.'

Deny it, Howard told himself. Just deny it.

'They were surrounding me. Manhandling me. I had no choice but to defend myself.'

Scargill's eyes were two tiny beads of scepticism. 'Why didn't you tell us that you hit Sheldon with your stick?'

'I did tell you. I said I warded them off with my stick.'

'You didn't specifically mention that you'd hit one of them over the head.'

'I didn't realise I had.'

'But now you admit it?'

'I have no recollection of hitting anyone in particular over the head. As I said, I warded them off.'

'Why didn't you tell us you attacked the sculptures?'

Howard saw clearly that the game was up. With all those witnesses ranged against him, there was no point in denying it. He experienced a great sense of weariness, a desire for it all to be over. But once the lie has been commenced it must be sustained to the bitter end. Suavely, he said, 'Didn't I mention that?'

'No.'

'Strange. I thought I had.'

'No. You didn't.'

'Well, I'm still in a state of shock, you know.'

'You admit that you did attack the sculptures?'

'I may have prodded them a little with my stick.'

'One of the sculptures you damaged was Sheldon's. He says that's why he punched you.'

'All I did was prod it with my stick,' Howard protested. 'Does that excuse him for attacking me?' He pointed to the bruise on his face. 'Do you think I inflicted this on myself?'

'Sheldon has admitted the assault, and will be charged. But all the witnesses say you hit Sheldon with your stick first. It was only afterwards that Sheldon punched you, when he saw you damaging his sculpture.'

'I've told you. They're all lying.'

'Then you deny assaulting Sheldon Smith with your stick, before he punched you?'

'I didn't assault anyone. I was defending myself.'

'So why are all the witnesses contradicting you?'

'Because they're in league with each other! They're all trying to cover up for that young thug!'

Scargill found it difficult to contemplate Howard without feeling contempt. Why was it that however high or low they were, however clever or stupid, they all thought they could pull the wool over the eyes of the police? You'd think those of a higher class would be different, but not a bit of it. The public all expected police officers to keep the sewer clean but if any of them personally fell into it, they lied through their teeth, refused to admit to any wrongdoing and always put the blame on someone else. They all disgusted her.

Scargill said, 'I'm sorry, Howard, we have several witness statements that corroborate Sheldon's claim that you assaulted him with your stick before he assaulted you. They say you were furious about what had been done to the back garden, and stumbled into a football match that was going on. You were accidentally hit on the thigh by the ball when you obstructed Sheldon Smith's shot. You then became involved in a swearing match with Sheldon. This made you lose your temper, and you tried to uproot the goalpost. When Sheldon and the other players tried to stop you, you struck him over the head with your walking stick, knocking him to the ground. You then attacked several of the sculptures in the back garden, including Sheldon's which is why he punched you.'

As Howard listened to Yvonne Scargill's account, he had the sensation that she was talking about someone he knew and ought to be concerned about. But her words were coming from the other side of some intangible barrier, a vacuum perhaps, which insulated him from her. Or was everything muffled because it had been covered in cotton wool? Or there'd been a heavy fall of snow? Was that why he felt so sleepy?

WPC Scargill stood up. 'This is terribly embarrassing, Howard, but I have no alternative but to arrest you.'

'Arrest me?'

'Yes.'

Howard sighed, and shook his head disbelievingly. 'You can't do that. I'm the chairman of the parish council. Your job is to protect people like me.'

'No, Howard, my job, is to arrest people who I suspect have committed a crime.' WPC Scargill took out her notebook and pen. 'Howard Roberts, I am arresting you on suspicion of committing the offences of actual bodily harm and criminal damage. You do not have to say anything but it may harm your defence if you do not mention when questioned something which you later rely on in court. Anything you do say may be given in evidence.'

Howard said, 'Criminal damage? What criminal damage?'

Scargill noted Howard's comment in her book. Then she said, 'Criminal damage to the sculptures which are the property of the Leefdale Inclusion Unit.'

'You've seen what those people have done to the rectory's beautiful trees and you charge me with criminal damage?'

There was a long pause while Scargill made a note of this.

'Do you have anything else to say?'

Flatly, Howard replied, 'I'm not saying any more until I've spoken to my solicitor.'

'Very well. Now will you please accompany me to Luffield police station?'

'Yes, but first I need to ring my solicitor!'

'We'll arrange for that at the station.'

Howard gave her an imploring look. 'Please Yvonne, at least let me telephone my wife and daughter to let them know what's happened. You've seen that baying mob out there. This is the worst thing that could possibly happen to my family at a time like this. They've gone to Scarborough to get away from it all. If they get back and I'm not here, they'll be sick with worry.'

'All right,' said Scargill. 'You can make one call.'

Howard went to his blazer which was draped over the arm of the sofa. He reached into his inside pocket and took out his mobile phone. He found Isobel's mobile number in the address book and pressed "Call". Almost immediately he heard the theme tune from the BBC rural soap "The Archers" coming from the next room. Howard was seized by a sudden anxiety. "The Archers" was Isobel's favourite radio programme, which was why she'd chosen its theme for her ring tone.

'That sounds like her phone,' said Howard.

Followed by Scargill, he left the sitting room and went through to the dining room. There, on the console table was Isobel's mobile. It was being charged. Obviously, she'd left in such haste, she'd forgotten it.

'Yes, that's hers,' said Howard. He terminated the call and "The Archers" theme abruptly died.

Howard said, 'My daughter's with her. I'll call her instead. Is that all right?'

Scargill nodded.

Howard began to search through his phone's address book for Barbara's mobile number.

CHAPTER THIRTY

If only Peter was here to help them, thought Barbara.

She'd been watching Mark and Jessica's attempts to build a sandcastle for nearly an hour. It was an ambitious structure, like so many of the sandcastles their father had helped them build on other beaches in happier times. Inspired by these previous examples, the children had constructed a huge mound of sand from which they'd attempted to fashion a central keep surrounded by crenelated battlements. There was a real moat too which they'd hoped would eventually become filled with sea water, via a channel dug all the way down the beach to meet the incoming tide.

Yet it was a pale shadow of the illustrious sandcastles they'd built in Cornwall or the South of France, with daddy alongside to guide them. They lacked the patience and the art necessary for such an ambitious task. As they watched their inexpert structure subside and collapse into a formless heap of sand, frustration and the inevitability of failure caused them to become fractious and squabble. Barbara made no effort to rise from her deck chair and go to their aid. Mark and Jessica had already made it clear that only daddy's help was wanted, not hers.

Here, for the first time, on the sands at Scarborough, she could no longer evade or deny the reality of Peter's absence. It was intensified by the packed beach and the crowds of families lounging or playing games close by; everyone seemingly relaxed and carefree, content to gambol in swimsuits or minimum clothes under a liberating sun; or doze and be caressed by the delightfully cool breeze coming off the sea. A perfect day. It was so redolent of other perfect days at the seaside she found herself expecting Peter to appear at any moment triumphantly bearing ice creams, as he always did. But no, that wasn't going to happen again. She saw that her future would be comprised of many situations like this: their very normality only compounding her sense of loss.

She and her mother had discussed this and many other aspects of Peter's treachery as they'd sat close by Scarborough's jolly harbour, soothed by the relentless uncurling of the waves and watching Mark and Jessica's growing frustration with their sandcastle. They'd talked the topic into the ground now;

and as there were no more examples of Peter's sexual betrayal to mull over and condemn, or suppressed resentments to ventilate, they'd fallen into silence. Isobel had returned to her novel leaving Barbara alone with her thoughts, which, at times, were suicidal. Her constant impulse was to call Peter to tell him where they were, what the children were doing and how desperately they all missed him. Surely the guilt of what he was doing to them would make him want to return?

Barbara searched in the bag by her side and found her blue mobile phone. A quick check revealed that Peter hadn't called or left a message; but the mobile had been switched on all the time, so she knew that anyway. Next, she turned her attention to her black mobile. She switched it on and saw that she had twenty three voicemails and several texts. Twelve voicemails alone were from Terry Bryden, demanding an interview. Nearly all the rest were from family and friends expressing sadness and regret at the disintegration of her marriage. There was also a message from Steve Hawkins asking her to call him urgently. But it was the last voice message that had her sitting forward in her deck chair.

"Hello Barbara. I do wish you'd switch your phone on. What's the point of having a mobile if you don't have it switched on? This is a message for you and mummy. I'm sorry to tell you that I've been arrested. Some ridiculous accusation of assault. I'm supposed to have hit one of those yobs at The Old Rectory. Anyway, I'm being taken to Luffield police station. I've no idea how long I shall be kept there or whether I'll be locked up or anything. Hopefully, I'll be back home fairly soon. Try not to worry. Love to you all."

'Oh my God!'

Barbara quickly pressed the replay option and thrust the mobile at Isobel. 'Listen!'

She watched her mother's face express shock and panic as she received the message.

'Arrested?' cried Isobel. She handed back the mobile and jumped up from her deck chair. 'The stupid man! The stupid, stupid man!' She began to bundle the thermos and other picnic items into a bag. 'We must go to him. This is terrible. It'll bring everything back. We must go to him!'

'Yes. But whatever we do, we mustn't alarm the children. They've had enough shocks for one day.'

Barbara outlined her ideas for a plan of action. Then, after stressing to her mother the necessity for them both to remain composed, she walked briskly but calmly down to the edge of the sea where Jessica and Mark were now paddling, having abandoned their sandcastle in disgust. They turned at her approach, surprised, yet pleased to see her. She took them both by the hand.

'Time to go home,' she said.

'Why?' Mark demanded hotly.

'Oh, mum! We've only just come!' cried Jessica.

She overcame their protests and led them up the beach to where Isobel was waiting. Twenty minutes later, they were all on their way to Luffield.

****

After a quick lunch consisting of a pint and a pork pie at a roadside inn, Bryden and Carter returned to Leefdale. As they arrived in Church Lane the first thing they commented on was the police car parked outside the gates of The Old Rectory.

Bryden and Carter got out of the car and mingled with the substantially increased press pack who were hanging around the gates of Rooks Nest. Bryden lost no time before he began pumping other journos for information about what had been going on in his absence.

Contrary to popular belief, reporters from rival newspapers who are physically thrown together at one location in pursuit of the same story often share gossip or information. Real scoops apart, journalists usually have access to more or less the same facts. It's the angle the story is written from and the paper's house style that makes it distinctive. For that reason, in the tabloid world, Terry Bryden was supreme.

After ten minutes of conversation with other reporters, Bryden had gleaned that Major Roberts' nose had still been bleeding when he'd returned to Rooks Nest. The word was that he'd been involved in a punch up with someone inside The Old Rectory because he'd taken exception to the state of its gardens. Bryden also learnt that after returning home, Major Roberts had been visited by two coppers. After about twenty minutes the officers had left Rooks Nest and gone straight to The Old Rectory, which was why the police car was now parked outside it. Bryden was also told that The Old Rectory was now known to be one of the new inclusion units for deprived and difficult teenagers. It was possible one of the kids had taken a pop at Roberts. No-one had the faintest idea where Mrs Kellingford and her children had gone or whether she was coming back to Rooks Nest. But there were plenty of rumours flying about.

Given what Zoe had divulged to him about the Major's obsession with Magnificent Britain, it seemed very likely to Bryden that Roberts had lost his rag over the state of the rectory's gardens and ended up in some sort of brawl with the people at the rectory. However, he'd no intention of sharing what he'd learnt from Zoe with his rivals, although he did appreciate he had to provide them with something as a quid pro quo in return for the information they'd given him, so he let it be known that he'd followed Mrs Roberts' car as far as the turn off to Scarborough but she'd managed to give him the slip.

This tit bit was of little interest to the throng of reporters gathered around Bryden. As the chief political correspondent of The Source, the paper which had broken the story of the Kellingford scandal, they were sure he knew far more than he was letting on. They badgered and badgered him with questions.

He managed to avoid answering them but in the end, to keep them all quiet, he decided to throw them a bit of red meat. 'I understand Peter Kellingford is going to make some kind of statement soon. Where or when I can't say.' As this was common knowledge, it was received with derision.

With John Carter in tow, Bryden strolled over to the two police officers who were guarding the gates to Rooks Nest. He tried hard to pump them for information but none was forthcoming. The two officers simply stonewalled him by remaining silent and smiling enigmatically throughout his questioning. Bryden was disgusted with their attitude and lack of co-operation. It was not what he was used to. He considered offering them a "drink". However, his instinct told him that they were both completely straight, so he didn't push it.

A few minutes later the sound of an approaching ambulance siren raised Bryden, John and the rest of the media pack to a pitch of eager anticipation. This was heightened as the sound became louder, indicating that the vehicle was only streets away.

The ambulance turned into Church Lane and parked up behind the police car in front of The Old Rectory. Instantly, reporters, photographers and camera crews swarmed across the road towards it.

Two paramedics emerged from the ambulance, and were immediately besieged by a shouting, jostling crowd demanding to know who was injured and how it had happened. The ambulance crew ignored them and forced their way over to the gate which had been unbolted by Toni. She held it open just wide enough for the paramedics to squeeze through, and then quickly closed it against the tide of media people who were pressing against it. Calmly, she shot the bolts home, padlocked them and escaped up the drive with the paramedics, leaving the media pack crammed up tight against the gate, shouting and bawling out questions. Under a non-stop barrage of flashlights, the vast bulk of PC Wheatcroft advanced upon the gate and ordered the crowd to move away from it. 'You're causing an obstruction,' he bellowed. 'If you impede the work of the emergency services, I won't hesitate to arrest you.'

Some heeded his warning and peeled away. But several reporters and photographers remained where they were, riveted by the sight of Sheldon, Mona, Amy and others at the art therapy room windows. They'd been watching the mayhem throughout and were now energetically making V signs at the great British Press.

There was a brilliant discharge of camera flashes as images of their defiance were captured again and again on film. In this, the teenagers were only too keen to co-operate and provide even more egregious examples of bad behaviour. Their rude gestures were brought to an end by Eric, who suddenly appeared and moved them away from the windows and closed the blinds. Members of the press pack who were still at the gate responded to this with a round of applause.

After ten minutes or so when nothing dramatic seemed to be happening, several of the media people, including Bryden and John, drifted away and returned to their former positions outside the gates of Rooks Nest. Here they stood, kicking their heels and speculating on what the next development would be.

They had to wait nearly an hour to find out. Accompanied by paramedics, Sheldon appeared in The Old Rectory's drive, holding an ice pack to his head. He was closely followed by WPC Scargill, PC Wheatcroft, Dylan, Toni and Zoe.

Once again, the press pack swarmed across Church Lane towards The Old Rectory and arrived at the gate just as Toni was opening it.

As soon as Sheldon, the two paramedics and PC Wheatcroft left the sanctuary of the drive and stepped out on to the pavement they were surrounded by reporters demanding to know the name of the youth who was being escorted to the ambulance, whether or not he'd been arrested, and whether Major Roberts was being arrested too. Sheldon attempted to respond to the reporters but was quickly silenced and put into the ambulance by Wheatcroft and the female paramedic. The back doors were slammed shut by the male paramedic, who then got into the ambulance and drove off at speed with the siren going.

Immediately, the media people, like a flock of starlings with one mind, wheeled through 180 degrees and swept down on WPC Scargill, who had left the rectory at the same time as the others and was now getting into the police car. Their questions were all essentially the same: 'What the hell's going on?'

'Get out of my way,' Scargill shouted, as she struggled to prise the car door open against the pressure of the media throng. Only when she threatened to taser them did they move back and allow her to enter the vehicle and close the door. She started the engine and sounded the horn. The reporters took no notice. They continued to surround the car, blocking its path.

Without warning Scargill reversed. Slowly at first, and then more quickly. This cleared the reporters away from her rear, who fell back, anxious not to have their toes run over. She then shot forward at speed, sending those crowded around the car's bonnet scattering for their lives.

The press flock quickly regrouped and wheeled again as one. This time they flung themselves upon the rectory's gate, turning their fire on Toni and Zoe who'd slammed it behind WPC Scargill as she'd left. Protected by the high, solid gate, both women mocked the reporters. Then they turned, walked briskly back up the drive and disappeared into the house.

Meanwhile, Scargill had driven across the road to Rooks Nest. Her colleagues opened the gates for her and she drove on up the drive. The press pack's feverish attention was now no longer on the rectory but focused once more on Rooks Nest.

Twenty minutes passed. Bryden reported in to his editor with the latest account of developments and again complained bitterly that he was wasting his time in Leefdale and ought to be covering the story in London. But Bill Metcalfe was adamant that Bryden had to remain where he was.

Interest quickened amongst the waiting representatives of the media when Howard and Yvonne Scargill suddenly emerged from Rooks Nest. Cameras greedily lapped up images of Major Roberts locking his front door with WPC Scargill standing by her police car, waiting patiently.

Along with everyone else, Terry Bryden watched her drive Roberts out of Rooks Nest and turn left into Church Lane. The cameras of John Carter and all the other photographers were red hot as they shot photo after photo.

When the police car had disappeared from sight, Bryden went over to the two police constables standing at the gate. 'I don't suppose you'd tell me where Major Roberts is being taken,' he said.

'You suppose right,' said the shorter of the two coppers. 'We wouldn't.'

'Has he been arrested?' asked Bryden.

Both officers stared fixedly ahead, as though Bryden had no corporeal existence.

'Come on, you must know,' said Bryden. 'Where's he being taken?'

'You'll have to wait until you read about it in your own paper,' said the taller constable. Both PCs caught each other's eye and laughed heartily.

Despite having a skin like a rhinoceros, Bryden was a vain man with an exaggerated sense of his own self-importance. Like so many of his type, he was happy to make cruel jokes at the expense of others but deeply resented being the butt of jokes himself. 'Come on,' he said to John. 'Let's go back to the car.'

Once they were inside the Toyota, Bryden said, 'If this was London, I'd soon know what was going on.'

'Oh?'

'Yeah. I've got loads of contacts in the Met who'd tell me.' He grinned cockily, showing nicotine stained teeth. 'For a bung, of course.'

John looked shocked. 'You mean you pay them for information?'

'You bet. How else do you think I get it? Some of them are on hefty retainers.'

John's look was reproving. 'But that's illegal, isn't it?'

Bryden tut tutted. 'You really are as green as fucking grass, aren't you?' Seeing John's wounded expression, he laughed. 'Loads of coppers are bent. It's just a question of finding out their price.'

'Oh, no. I don't think that's true,' said John. 'Not round here, anyway.'

Bryden sighed heavily. 'Yeah, well, maybe this place is the one exception. That's why they've told us fuck all.' He went on complaining bitterly about the lack of police co-operation, and then sat brooding in silence for several minutes.

Suddenly he said, 'Drive down the road a bit, will you.'

John complied, and after they'd travelled several hundred yards along Church Lane, Bryden told him to stop. John parked the Toyota outside a bungalow. Like all the other dwellings in Leefdale its walls were festooned with hanging baskets in glorious bloom. Bryden regarded them balefully. 'The people round here must want a job.'

John thought this remark most uncharitable. He was beginning to despise Bryden for many reasons, but most of all the man's appalling cynicism and contempt for goodness. 'Who cares,' he said, 'it's a beautiful village.'

Bryden shot John a quick, sideways glance but said nothing. After a pause, John said, 'Why have we stopped here?'

'I want to hack Barbara Kellingford's phone,' said Bryden. 'And I can't very well do it under the nose of Mr Plod. Mind you, the cops round here probably wouldn't have a fucking clue what was going on.'

'Neither have I,' said John. 'What do you mean, hack her phone?'

'Get into her voicemail and listen to her messages.'

John regarded Bryden quizzically. The man was always joking so it was hard to know when he was being serious.

'How can you do that?'

Bryden winked. 'It's easy, if you know how. A lot easier than getting into her knickers.'

'But how? How do you do it?'

Bryden shook his head. 'Oh, no. I'm not telling you that. It's a trade secret. It wouldn't do for everyone to know.'

'It's illegal, isn't it?' said John.

Bryden said, 'Well, it's not strictly kosher but I ain't losing any sleep over it. We're all at it.' He looked at John satirically. 'How do you think we get all those celebrity stories? D'you think they email them to us personally?'

John doubted that all reporters were at it. Bryden was probably exaggerating again. He said, 'I don't think reporters on The Sandleton Examiner hack phones.'

Bryden scoffed. 'Course they don't. I'm talking about real newspapers, not fucking parish magazines!'

Bryden took out his mobile phone. 'Get yours out, as well,' he told Carter. 'You're going to help me.'

'Help you? How?'

'I just want you to dial Barbara's number.'

'Oh, no. I'm not going to do anything illegal.'

'Listen prick, we've got no choice. Barbara's disappeared with her mum and her kids. She might be in Scotland for all we know. Her old man's shat all over the carpet and is unreachable. And we think her dad's been nicked for some kind of punch up with a black kid only no-one will confirm it. We'd have a great story here, if we weren't in the fucking dark. I need you to help me hack Barbara's phone. We might just find out what the fuck's going on.'

John was in a dilemma. Perhaps Bryden was right: perhaps hacking phones wasn't illegal, perhaps it was standard practice. After a long pause, he said, 'I'm not breaking the law for anyone.'

Bryden looked exasperated. 'I'm not asking you to break the law. All I'm asking you to do is ring Barbara Kellingford's mobile. I'll do the rest.'

'But I'll be helping you.'

'No-one'll know.' Bryden's expression suddenly changed. 'And it'll stop my editor phoning your editor to demand you be sacked.' He gave John a long, hard stare. 'Got it?'

Somewhat unsurely, John said, 'If he did that I'd tell my editor what you tried to make me do.'

Bryden's upper lip curled into a snarl. 'I'd deny it. Your word against mine. And I'm the political correspondent of The Source. Who the fuck are you? A bloke who takes pictures of badgers.'

John knew it was possible that Bryden was bluffing but he didn't want to take the risk of finding out. Not when his dad was out of work and mum's part time job paid only a pittance. They all depended on the extra cash his job on The Examiner brought in. Reluctantly, he took out his mobile.

'Good boy,' said Bryden. He held his own mobile phone out towards John. A number was showing on its digital display. 'That's Barbara's number. Phone it.'

John keyed the number in and pressed "Call".

'Is it ringing?' Bryden asked.

'Yes.'

Immediately, Bryden pressed "Call" on his own phone and connected to Barbara's number. He was put straight through to her voicemail. He pressed another key and a robotic female voice asked for the pin. He keyed in the most likely set of default numbers. "Pin not recognised" came back the robot. He keyed in a different sequence of numbers. Still they weren't accepted. He noticed that he was sweating more than usual. Had she changed her pin from the manufacturer's default and personalised it? With a certain amount of desperation now, he keyed in a further set of numbers. "Welcome to your voicemail," said the voice of the female robot. "You have twenty three messages".

Bryden listened to each message. Some were from himself or his editor offering Barbara a hundred thousand pounds if she'd agree to give The Source exclusive rights to her story. Other messages were from friends and relatives commiserating with Barbara about the breakdown of her marriage. Bryden made a careful note of the names and content and then deleted them. This was to deny phone hackers from rival papers access to these messages. Now that he knew the names and opinions of Barbara's friends, some of whom were very well known, he intended to trace and interview them. Even if they proved uncooperative or unable to provide further information, he knew that the messages they'd left on Barbara's voicemail would spice up the final spread with insightful gossip.

'I've been put through to her voicemail now,' said John, panicking. 'What shall I do?'

'Nothing, just hang on. Don't end the call till I tell you.'

Bryden continued listening. A message from Steve Hawkins beseeching Barbara to ring him back urgently was particularly interesting. Far too interesting to be allowed to fall into the hands of anyone else. It too was deleted.

Next up was the message from Barbara's father, telling her that he'd been arrested. As he listened to it, Bryden stiffened and sat higher in his seat. 'Yes!' he cried, and punched the air.

The message ended. Bryden turned triumphantly to John. 'We've just struck fucking gold!'

****

'I don't think I can cope with the police station,' Isobel whispered to Barbara as she parked at Tesco's in Luffield.

'I'll deal with it,' said Barbara. 'You can take the children shopping and I'll go and sort dad out.'

Isobel looked immensely relieved. 'Would you? Thank you, darling. It's just that I hate...'

Barbara cut her short. 'I know. Don't worry. Leave it to me.'

'What are you whispering about?' demanded Jessica.

'We're not whispering,' Barbara said quickly. 'Grandma wants to take you shopping.'

'Why couldn't we go in Scarborough?'

Mark joined in, 'Yes, why couldn't we? We could have stayed on the beach and gone shopping later.'

Isobel removed the ignition key and handed it to Barbara. 'Here, you'd better take this in case you get back before we do.'

'What about you?' said Barbara.

'It's all right. I've got a spare.'

'Aren't you coming with us, mummy?' said Mark.

'No.'

Both children began to protest loudly.

'I have business in Luffield,' explained Barbara.

'Can't we come with you?'

'No. You'll find it very boring. Now have a good time with grandma.'

She opened the car door and got out.

'Something's up,' said Mark, as they watched her walk off.

'It'll be something to do with the divorce,' said Jessica.

****

Luffield police station was located in Hirings Street. It was a small, Edwardian building constructed of attractively weathered red brick. Barbara arrived there just after three-thirty. She took a deep breath and forced herself to open one of the shabby entrance doors. Immediately, she found herself stepping straight into a tiny reception area which contained a number of plastic chairs. She was the only one there. She approached a desk which was sealed off behind metal and glass. On a small ledge in front of the glass was a button and next to it instructions to ring for attention. Barbara pressed the button and waited. No-one appeared. She pressed again. After she'd pressed it three more times, a tall, burly looking policeman, middle-aged and sporting a fierce moustache came through a door behind the glass window. Barbara explained who she was and why she was there.

'Oh, yes. Take a seat, please.'

Barbara sat down and prepared to wait. The officer disappeared behind the door from which he'd emerged. In the second or so before it closed after him, Barbara caught a glimpse of a green tiled corridor which presumably led into the bowels of the building. She tried to imagine the scene behind the door, but couldn't. She felt reduced to childhood again. As a young girl she'd often had to sit waiting for adults who were behind closed doors getting on with whatever strange business they were up to, and from which she felt helplessly excluded. That's how she felt now.

Her eyes kept darting towards the entrance, hoping for someone else to walk in. She was surprised to be sitting all alone in this dinky little police station, its walls covered with crime prevention posters. Obviously Luffield was a low crime area. How absurd then that her father should be in a place like this. He was no criminal.

At that moment Barbara felt more alone than she'd done at any time in her life, except perhaps when she'd gone into labour. Now, as then, she longed for Peter to be there, providing her with comfort and support. Surely if he knew what a terrible situation she was in and how distraught she was, he'd sympathise and relent? She fished out the blue mobile from her bag and called him. She was perturbed when she was put straight through to his voicemail, which meant that his phone was either switched off or engaged. That was never supposed to happen. She left a brief message urging him to call her as soon as possible.

Barbara was sure that Peter's other mobile phone, the one he used for his everyday business and social calls, would be switched off to avoid unwelcome attention from the media. She called the number anyway. Sure enough she was taken straight to voicemail. She recorded a similar message to the one she'd left on his blue mobile and then rang the House of Commons direct line. It rang and rang and eventually was answered by Joyce, Peter's secretary. Joyce told her she'd no idea where Peter was. He'd gone into hiding, and wasn't answering his mobile phone.

'All I know is he had a meeting sometime during the morning with Steve Hawkins.'

'Right. I'll try him,' said Barbara.

'I was very sorry to hear about your marital problems,' said Joyce.

'Yes, thank you,' said Barbara. 'It's obviously a difficult time at the moment.'

Joyce continued making sympathetic remarks, until Barbara was close to tears.

'Actually, Joyce,' she said, finally, 'I'd find your sympathy much more acceptable if I didn't know that you and Peter had an eighteen month affair.'

There was a stunned silence at Joyce's end.

'You didn't think I knew that, did you?' said Barbara, and ended the call.

Barbara's next call was to Steve Hawkins, who'd now left four text messages on her blue mobile requesting her to return his calls which, on principle, she'd been ignoring.

'Ah, Barbara, good. I've been trying to reach you all afternoon.'

'I know. Sorry I haven't returned your calls. I've been somewhat preoccupied.'

'Have you spoken to Peter?'

'I've tried but he's made himself unavailable.'

She heard Hawkins sigh.

'Well, I don't suppose he'll mind me telling you this. The thing is there've been some developments.'

'Oh?'

'Yes. Peter's been thinking things over and he's decided for all sorts of reasons that his future lies with you and the children.'

Relief surged through her. Could it be true?

'What do you mean?'

'He wants to come back to you and the children. Start all over again.'

Barbara struggled hard to confine her joy. She wanted Peter back more than anything in the world. Nevertheless, she didn't trust Hawkins, and she certainly wasn't going to let him think she was a pushover.

'Bit late for that now, isn't it?' she said.

'Don't you want him back, Barbara?'

She ignored the obvious trap. 'Have you been putting pressure on him?'

'Me? Not at all. You know me Barbara, a person's private life is his own affair. No. Peter made the decision entirely on his own. Frankly, I think he's realised he's been a bloody fool and he's regretting the effect it's going to have on you and the children. And, of course, the harm it's doing to the Party.'

'Nothing to do with next week's by-election then?'

Hawkins laughed, uneasily. 'Absolutely not, I assure you. Anyway, I'm not the one who should be discussing this with you, you need to talk to Peter. I know how hurt you must be, but I think for everyone's sake you should consider his offer.'

'I'll certainly do that.'

'You see, before Peter can go public on this he has to be sure you'd take him back.'

'I understand. But how can I get in touch with Peter? He's not answering any of his phones.'

'I'll get him to call you. Oh, and please, don't switch your mobile off. I'll need to speak to you again after you've spoken to Peter.'

'OK.'

They said goodbye. A call came through immediately on the black mobile. A number she didn't recognise. She thoughtlessly answered and found herself talking to Bill Metcalfe, the editor of The Source. He at once tried to inveigle her into giving an interview for £100,000 so she cut the call straightaway. It rang again. Seeing Metcalfe's number appear on the digital display, she switched the phone off.

A short time later the police officer returned to the sealed off area. He was followed by a very short young man who looked like a clerk. The officer opened a metal door next to the desk and the young man passed through into the reception area and approached Barbara.

'Hello,' he said. 'Are you Major Roberts' daughter?'

Barbara involuntarily rose to her feet. 'Yes?'

'I'm Alex Ryecart. I'm a Legal Executive with Armitage's. I've been advising your father.'

'Oh God! How is he?'

'He's fine. The police are releasing him on his own recognizance.'

'What does that mean?'

'He's been released having promised to attend all court proceedings and on condition that he doesn't leave the area.'

'He's got to go to court?'

'Yes. He's been charged with actual bodily harm.'

Barbara's legs felt suddenly unsteady. Coming on top of everything else, this was the last straw. 'Oh no. Poor dad! When will he be set free?'

'Right now. He's just collecting his things.'

'His things?'

'The police took away his keys and wallet, that sort of thing, while he was in the cells.'

'Cells? He was in the cells?'

'Not for very long.'

'Is he going to prison?'

'I wouldn't have thought so. If he pleads guilty, he'll probably just get a fine.'

At that moment Howard appeared in the sealed off area accompanied by the moustachioed policeman. He opened the metal door and allowed Howard out with an incongruously warm 'Bye now, Howard.'

'Bye, Ken,' said Howard, as the door clanged behind him.

Barbara went straight over to her father.

'Dad. Are you all right?'

Howard took her in his arms. 'Yes, yes, of course. I'm fine.'

As he released her, she noticed that his cheek was bruised and there was a slight cut on his nose.

'You're hurt.'

'It's nothing. Just a bruise.'

'I'll take you to minor injuries.'

'That's not necessary.'

'You need an X-ray.'

'Please don't fuss. The police surgeon said I'm perfectly all right. I just want to get home. I've a meeting to prepare for.'

'A meeting? Not tonight, surely?'

At that moment Barbara's blue mobile rang. It was still in her hand and she answered immediately. It could only be him.

'Hello, Peter.'

'Barbara. I gather you've been speaking to Steve Hawkins?' Peter's voice seemed to fill the room. It had that distinctively breathy tone he always employed when he was attempting to cajole or obtain a favour.

'That's right.'

'Barbara, I've been such a fool.'

Embarrassed and concerned for her privacy, Barbara was about to step outside to take the call when Howard came up and shouted loudly into the phone, 'Yes, you bloody well have, haven't you, you moron!'

Ryecart started as though he'd been shot.

'Who was that?' Peter's voice came back.

Barbara crossed the room to get as far away from her father as possible. 'Peter, I can't talk at the moment. Something terrible's happened. Daddy's been arrested.'

'Arrested!'

'Yes. I'm collecting him from the police station in Luffield right now, so I can't possibly talk. Call me when we get home.'

'Has Steve Hawkins spoken to you?'

'Yes. Call me in about an hour.'

And without waiting for his response, she ended the call.

'Where's Isobel?' Howard said, pathetically.

'She's taken the children shopping. They know nothing of your arrest and we must keep it that way.'

He looked deeply pained. 'Of course.'

Barbara and Howard left the police station arm in arm, accompanied by Ryecart. As soon as they emerged on to Hirings Street, they were confronted by two men. There was a series of blinding camera flashes and a cockney voice was shouting at them.

'Have you been charged, Major?'
'Who hit you?'
'Was it that black kid?'
'Did you hit him?'
'Why did you do it?'

Barbara recognised the voice immediately: it belonged to that bastard Terry Bryden. Panic and terror instinctively made her grip her father's arm more tightly, and hurry him away from the ambush.

Ryecart kept up with them and attempted to remonstrate with Bryden, who was now running alongside them in the gutter delivering a stream of non-stop questions at the top of his voice.

'Where's that black kid?'
'Is he in the nick?'
'Has he been charged too?'
'Got a nasty bump, hasn't he?'
'Did you do that?'

Meanwhile, the photographer had managed to get in front of Barbara and Howard. He'd turned to face them and was running backwards taking shot after shot. Despite being disorientated and dazzled, Barbara could see other pedestrians halting in the street and turning round to stare in amazement at the extraordinary spectacle.

'Enough!' Howard suddenly cried out. He stopped dead and rounded on Bryden, shouting, 'If you don't stop hounding us, you bastards, I won't be responsible for my actions. Now, fuck off!'

Barbara had never in her life heard her father use those words. She feared that he was going to lose his temper and do something violent that might again lead to his arrest. She gripped Howard's hand even more tightly and increased her pace almost to a run, tugging him along behind her. 'Come on, dad!' she urged. 'We're nearly at the car. We'll be safe then. Just a bit further.'

But Bryden and Carter were still keeping up with them. Bryden now turned his verbal assault upon Barbara:

'Why don't you give our editor a ring?'
'Don't you want a hundred grand?'
'That's what you'll get for your story.'
'Don't worry, we'll do the writing.'
'All you have to do is talk to us.'
'A hundred grand, Barbara.'
'Come in handy after the divorce, won't it?'
'There'll be a divorce, won't there?'

It was a relatively short walk down Hirings Street to Wednesday Market. To Barbara it had never seemed longer because never before had she walked down that street molested and harassed at every step by a reporter and a press photographer. Even so, although she felt violated and abused she was no longer panicked and fearful. The predominant emotion surging through her now was hatred: not just hatred for Bryden and his photographer but for Peter and Clarissa, whose selfishness and treachery had caused all her misery.

'Nearly there now,' she told Howard, encouragingly. They had arrived in Wednesday Market, and were about to cross Luffield's main street.

But the lights on the pelican crossing were against them and the traffic was too fast and too heavy to risk jaywalking. With a feeling of profound despair, Barbara saw that until the lights changed they were trapped and at the mercy of Bryden and his photographer.

Bryden seized the opportunity to step up his attack. He sidled up close to Barbara and almost conversationally dropped his poisonous questions into her much abused ears.

'How long's Peter been banging Clarissa?'
'Must have been a terrible shock.'
'How did you find out?'
'It's not the first time he's done it though, eh?'

Barbara was close to tears and her urge to slap the coarse, insensitive features of the goading, cocksure bastard was overwhelming. But she ordered herself not to respond, and gripped her father's hand ever tighter. She noticed that even the photographer's expression seemed sympathetic and appalled, and he'd stopped taking photographs.

'How are the children taking it?'

Bryden's constant needling was at last too much for Barbara. Her chest heaved and the faintest of snatched sobs escaped her iron defences.

To the astonishment of the other pedestrians waiting at the crossing, Howard swung round at Bryden, shouting 'Wash your mouth out, you scum!' He seemed about to lunge at Bryden and would have done so had Barbara not pulled him away. 'Take no notice, dad,' she pleaded. 'Ignore them.'

'All right, all right,' said Howard. But it went against the grain.

Fortunately, Bryden's baiting ceased temporarily when he realised that John Carter was no longer taking photos.

'Why have you stopped?' he demanded.
'I thought we'd got enough,' said John.
'You can never have enough,' Bryden snapped back.

The lights changed to green and Barbara bundled her father across the road. With Ryecart following, they shot down a snicket which led to Tesco's car park. Barbara's heart lifted when she saw that Isobel and the children were already inside the car, anxiously watching their progress.

Carter was taking photographs again; and as Barbara and Howard reached the Jaguar the camera flashes, which had been intermittent, now became almost continuous.

Barbara glanced quickly at the intent faces of her mother and the children, and then wrenched open the rear passenger door. Hurriedly, she steadied Howard and helped him into the vehicle. She tried to close the door on him but this was difficult because the photographer was trying to steal a group shot of Howard and the children, who were beside him on the back seat.

'Make sure you get plenty of shots of mum and the kids,' she heard Bryden call out.

That's when Barbara lost it. She raised both arms to shield Mark and Jessica from the camera. 'Not my children, you bastard! Fuck off! Fuck off!' she screamed. 'Leave us alone!' She pummelled John's chest with her fists, wrenched his camera away from him and flung it to the ground. He went to pick it up and she kicked him hard on the thigh. He immediately lost his balance and fell in a heap on the rough tarmac.

'You fucking bitch!' shouted Bryden. 'He's only doing his job!'

Carter grabbed his camera and jumped to his feet, but Barbara had already slammed the rear passenger door and was slipping into her seat at the front. It took but a moment for her to get inside and slam her door, but not before the photographer had sneaked a quick shot of her sitting alongside Isobel.

Isobel had anticipated what was required and already had the engine running. Before Barbara could fasten her seat belt, the car was accelerating away with a shriek of protesting rubber.

In the nearside mirror, Barbara saw the camera flashes as the photographer grabbed his last images of their retreat.

'Well done, Barbara,' said Howard.

'Are you all right?' said Isobel, indicating left.

'Yes, I'm fine.'

But Barbara was not all right. Her breath was coming in gasps, her pulse was racing and the adrenalin was taking her head off. With trembling hands, she took out her blue mobile and made sure it was switched off in case Peter called. She'd no wish to talk to him in front of all of them.

****

Bryden and Carter watched the Jaguar leave the car park, signal left and join the traffic on Luffield's main street.

'What now?' asked John. 'Shall we go after them?'

'No. Let's go back to the cop shop and see if they've charged Roberts with anything.' He reflected for a moment, and then added, 'Or that black kid.'

'No need for that,' said Ryecart, who'd just come up and joined them. 'You'll get nothing out of the police. But I can tell you all you want to know.'

It was rare that Bryden was surprised. He looked at Ryecart dubiously.

With a wink, the solicitor's clerk said, 'As long as you make it worth my while.'

CHAPTER THIRTY ONE

'Where did they come from?' asked Isobel, as she took the Malton road. She was referring to Bryden and the photographer. Barbara had been describing how she and Howard had been pursued and persecuted by them all the way to the car park.

'They were waiting for us when we came out of the doctor's,' said Barbara.

'Why were you at the doctor's, mum?' said Mark.

Taking his cue from Barbara, Howard said, 'I was the one at the doctor's. Your mother was collecting me.'

'Are you all right?' said Isobel, slowing for the roundabout. 'I'm sorry I didn't come to meet you. I had to look after the children.'

'Don't upset yourself. Barbara coped perfectly. And the doctor said I was fine.'

'You managed to see one?'

'Oh, yes. They sent for him.'

Isobel immediately understood. 'Good.'

Jessica looked concerned. 'What have you done to your face, grandpa?'

'Is that why you had to go to the doctor?' said Mark.

Howard treated both children to a rueful smile. 'Yes. I've been a very silly boy. I didn't look where I was going and had a rather nasty fall.'

'Did it hurt?'

'Quite a bit. But the doctor says no real harm was done.'

'How did it happen?'

'I told you, I had a fall.'

'Yes, but where did you fall?'

Barbara and her mother exchanged an anxious look.

'I tripped and fell in the drive,' said Howard.

'In the drive of the house across the road?'

'No. In our drive.'

'Oh. I thought it happened in the house across the road.'

For the first time, Howard looked guarded. 'Why do you think that?'

'They saw you holding a handkerchief to your nose as you left the rectory,' said Isobel. 'Now children,' she quickly went on, 'you must stop pestering grandpa with your questions. He's had a nasty shock.'

Howard smiled fondly at Mark and Jessica. 'I was just blowing my nose,' he explained.

Mark's voice rose with the suddenness of insight. 'Grandma, you knew grandpa would be at the doctor's, didn't you? That's why you made us come to Luffield.'

'Yes,' said Isobel. 'We knew grandpa had had an accident of some kind. But we didn't say anything because we didn't want to upset you.'

'Mummy, why did you break that man's camera?' asked Jessica.

'I didn't break it. Anyway, he was taking our photographs without permission.'

'Do you need permission to take someone's photo?' said Mark.

'It's good manners to ask first,' said Howard.

Mark said, 'Is that why you were swearing at him and kicking him, mummy?'

'He was swearing too,' said Jessica, indignantly.

Mark gave her a superior look. 'But mummy's always telling us not to swear.'

'Your mother was defending you. All of us,' said Howard. 'That's why swearing was permissible.'

'Is that why you said "Well done" to her for knocking down that photographer?' said Mark.

Howard said, 'Yes. I'm very proud of her.'

'Thanks, dad,' said Barbara.

Jessica said, 'Just like grandma defended us.'

'Oh? How?' said Howard.

'Bryden and his photographer tried to follow us to Scarborough,' said Barbara, 'but mummy gave them the slip.'

'The roundabout manoeuvre,' said Isobel.

'Ah,' said Howard.

'Grandma was brilliant,' said Mark.

'Yes, but it was very scary,' said Jessica. 'Like when you swore and kicked that man with the camera.'

Barbara mentally shuddered. How she wished she could have spared them it. All of it!

Mark had a logical mind, which is why he suddenly said, 'Grandpa, where's your car?'

Just like his dad, so sharp he'll cut himself, thought Howard. 'Still in the drive at Rooks Nest, I hope. I came to Luffield by taxi.'

'Why?'

'In case I had concussion.'

Mark nodded sagely, although he wasn't quite sure what concussion was.

Both children stared at their grandfather, slightly puzzled. They had a suspicion that something important was being kept from them, but couldn't think what it might be.

Presently, Mark said, 'How did that reporter and photographer know you were at the doctor's? Did they follow you, like they did us?'

'They must have done,' said Howard.

'Then why didn't you tell the taxi-driver to drive twice round the roundabout like grandma did?'

'For God's sake!' Barbara exploded, 'Stop asking all these stupid questions!'

'Barbara,' admonished Isobel, gently.

Howard turned to his two grandchildren. 'Your mother and grandmother have taught you both a valuable lesson today,' he said. 'Do you know what it is?'

Mark and Jessica shook their heads.

'Well, you saw what they did to that reporter who was trying to harm us. That took courage. But it's what you must do when somebody tries to bully or hurt you. You must never, never give in and let them get away with it. You must always stand up to them. I hope you'll remember that.'

'For heaven's sake, Howard,' said Isobel, 'there are far less traumatic ways they could have found that out.'

The journey back to Leefdale was an uncomfortable one for the adults. In their different ways all three were recovering from the shock of Howard's arrest and their bruising encounter with Bryden's oppressive methods. Nevertheless, they had to remain patient and keep the children amused with light-hearted talk about the trip to Scarborough, the failed attempts at building the sandcastle, and the presents Isobel had bought for them in Luffield. Yet all the while the adults' thoughts were elsewhere, running like a deep vein of reality beneath the trivial and commonplace. Howard could think of nothing but the incidents which had led to his arrest and charge, and of the court appearance that loomed ahead of him. Every time he looked at the back of Isobel's grey head he thought of the pain and anguish she would have to endure because of his stupid actions, and he sought desperately to think of a way she could be spared. He wanted to admit his mistake, beg her forgiveness and plead with her to help him. Isobel, meanwhile, was driving on automatic pilot while her mind struggled to come to terms with the irrefutable reality of her husband's arrest. Her head was full of questions and she was impatient for answers. Uppermost in her mind was whether or not he'd been charged. Only her innate caution and good sense stopped her from putting her foot down and breaking the speed limit so that they could get home sooner and she could find out exactly what had happened to Howard in the rectory. As her beloved grandchildren chatted with Howard about their day, she found herself becoming more and more irritated and longed for them all to shut up. How could people be talking about such banalities? Didn't they realise her life was falling apart?

Barbara's emotions were pitching and tossing too: alternating between hope, indecision and despair. Having told her mother and father about the misery of her marriage and Peter's serial adulteries, she wondered how they'd react when she revealed that he'd offered to come back and she was minded, no, not minded, desperate, to accept. Surely they'd think her a complete fool? And wouldn't they be right? She wanted to believe otherwise, but she'd a strong suspicion that he'd made the offer not because he genuinely wanted to return but because he was responding to Party pressure and political expediency. In which case, shouldn't she let him sweat for a while? Stall and tell him she wasn't in a position to make a decision because she'd been too badly hurt? That would serve him right, wouldn't it? How dare they all treat her like a door mat? Yet at other times her heart soared with optimism at the possibility of his return, and she wanted to tell everyone, especially the children, that everything was going to be all right again. But a second later this would be tempered by her great fear that if she did announce his return and for some reason it didn't happen she'd look abject and pathetic. What to do? What to do? She longed for the time to pass so that she could be at home, privately talking to Peter, finding out what his true feelings for her were.

And so they journeyed on towards Leefdale: each adult absorbed in their own secret reflections and torments, whilst outwardly talking quite normally and contriving a tolerable reality for the children.

It could be just the end of any other day, thought Isobel as the car entered Leefdale. But today wasn't just any other day. Momentous things had happened. Leefdale had never looked lovelier, yet its ordered beauty and ruffled gaiety were such a contrast to her own disordered and distressed inner state that the streets and houses of the rural idyll seemed to be mocking her and exacerbating her pain. She recalled all those other ordinary days when she and Howard, returning from a drive somewhere, had passed through the village on their way home. How she wished today was one of those other ordinary days, when she'd been deliriously happy with her ordinary, uneventful life but hadn't realised it, and Leefdale's calm beauty had reflected her own serenity so perfectly she hadn't given it a moment's thought.

Isobel turned the car into Church Lane, and conversation in the vehicle ceased immediately as everyone focussed on the band of reporters still milling around the entrance to the drive. They'd diminished in number since the morning but there were still enough of them to intimidate the occupants of the Jaguar. As the car stopped to allow the police to open the gates, the press pack swarmed around it, pounding on the bodywork and yelling out their predictable questions. There was a fusillade of camera flashes, which intensified as Howard displayed his contempt by raising his arm high and making the traditional two fingered gesture of defiance at those pressing up against the vehicle's windows. Isobel accelerated hard and they were quickly through the gates and away, speeding up the drive.

When they'd parked, Howard and the children got out of the car first, so Isobel was able to say to Barbara quietly, 'Has he been charged?'

Barbara was shocked by her mother's appearance. In the last few hours she seemed to have aged ten years. Her delicate features were pinched and drawn, her normally luminous light blue eyes clouded with unhappiness. Barbara placed a hand on her mother's arm. 'Yes, with assault.'

This was what Isobel had been dreading. But now that the uncertainty was resolved, she found herself experiencing only relief.

'The solicitor says if he pleads guilty he'll probably just get a fine,' Barbara added, reassuringly.

Barbara and Isobel entered the house. They'd barely taken a few steps down the hall when Mark ran up to them and said, 'Can we watch the news to see if daddy's on it?'

'Yes, please, please, let's,' begged Jessica.

Barbara had no intention of agreeing to this but rather than face a confrontation, she said, 'I'll think about it.'

Satisfied, Mark and Jessica said no more but bounded upstairs to their bedroom to keep watch on the reporters.

The three adults went into the kitchen and stood around awkwardly. Then Howard closed the door and in a low voice explained that he'd been charged with the offence of actual bodily harm. He went on to describe the events that had led to his arrest. He left nothing out and gave his account objectively and unemotionally, as though he'd been an observer of the incident and not a direct participant. But when Isobel and Barbara's repeated requests for further information forced him to give a more detailed account of his actions, his voice faltered and he showed signs of distress. His interrogation and the time he'd spent in the cells had obviously affected him. He unreservedly acknowledged his guilt, accepted that his conduct had been unacceptable and made it clear that his intention was to plead guilty.

'You bloody fool!' Isobel cried. "This is what comes of not taking your pill!'

Howard stared at her wearily. 'Please Isobel, not now. I don't need it. This has been one of the worst days of my life.'

Tears appeared in Isobel's eyes. She went towards him and squeezed the top of his arm comfortingly. 'You poor darling. I feel so sorry for you.'

She and Howard continued to discuss the awful events of the day. Barbara, unable to bear it any longer, started to unpack the shopping and put the groceries away in the fridge and the cupboards.

'I think we could all do with a strong cup of tea,' said Isobel, when further discussion seemed pointless. She carried the kettle to the sink and began to fill it. The small actions that give life its solidity resumed.

Howard had been sitting at the kitchen table. He now stood up and said, 'I'd better go and get ready.'

'Ready for what?' said Isobel.

'My meeting.'

'What meeting?'

'Before I was arrested I arranged an extraordinary meeting of the council.'

Isobel turned the tap off and turned to stare at him incredulously. 'Not tonight, surely?'

'Something has to be done about the rectory. If it isn't, the village will lose the gold medal.'

Isobel reset the kettle in place and switched it on. 'That's the least of your worries, I should have thought. Really Howard, tonight of all nights!'

'I can't get out of it now. Not that I want to.'

Isobel sighed heavily, opened a cupboard and reached for cups and saucers.

Howard went to a drawer, opened it and took out his packet of medication. He self-consciously popped a pill into his mouth. Then he went over to the sink, filled a glass with water and carried it out of the room.

When he'd gone Isobel collapsed on a chair and put her face in both hands. 'You know what I'm terrified of, don't you? That this will make him dwell on the other business and trigger off a massive depression.'

'He's taken his medication so he should be all right.'

Isobel removed her hands from her face and stared at her daughter intensely. 'You don't understand. Your father's a perfectionist. That's his nature. When things go wrong he blames himself. Then he goes on castigating himself until he drives himself insane with remorse and regret.'

Barbara hesitated and then said, 'Was that what actually tipped him over the edge?'

'What do you mean?'

'Was that what caused his nervous breakdown? For years now you've both referred to it as "the incident" but never actually told me what it was.'

'I did. I did tell you.'

'No. All you ever said was that it was a mission that went wrong.'

'That's all I know. That's all he's ever told me.'

'Where was the mission? Where was he when it happened?'

'I don't know. It's no good asking me anything about it because I know no more than you do. It's all classified. Top secret.'

Isobel got up and went over to make the tea. Barbara picked up a bottle of red Burgundy and started to uncork it.'

'Don't you want any tea?' asked Isobel.

'No. I need something a little stronger. Like some?'

'No thanks.'

Barbara poured a glass for herself and sat down at the kitchen table. 'I've been told that Peter wants to leave Clarissa and come back to me.'

Isobel stopped attending to the tea things and stared.

Barbara described the telephone conversation she'd had with Hawkins.

'Why didn't Peter tell you himself instead of using the messenger boy?'

'He tried, but he rang at the completely wrong moment. The police were just releasing dad. I told him to call back.'

'Taking his time about it, isn't he?'

'I told him to call back in an hour.'

Isobel's expression was cynical. 'What's brought on this turn around?'

Barbara shrugged. 'Pressure from the Party hierarchy? The reality of life with a teenager? Shame? Who knows?'

'Is he being serious?'

'I'll know when he calls me.'

'And if he really is serious? Then what will you do?'

Barbara said nothing. What she wanted was the nightmare to end, for normality to be restored and for her old life, unsatisfying as it was, to continue.

'Could you forgive me if I did take him back?'

Isobel looked astonished. 'There's nothing to forgive you for!'

'All right. Put it this way, could you and dad forgive Peter? After what I've told you about him? That's the important thing.'

'Darling, why should it matter what we think? It's what you want that matters.'

'Tell me. Please!'

There was a long pause. Then decisively, Isobel said, 'I don't think I could ever forgive him. In fact, I would personally find it very difficult simply to be civil to him. But I would try for your sake. As for your father, he's behaving so unpredictably these days, there's no way of telling how he'd react if Peter walked through the door this minute.'

Barbara said, 'Thank you at least for being honest.'

'You want him back, don't you?'

'It's all so humiliating.'

'Of course. But you want him back? That's what you want? What you really want?'

Barbara drained her glass. 'Yes.'

'Despite all he's done to you?'

'Yes.'

Isobel placed tea bags in two cups. 'I've always known he was a bastard, you know.'

'How?'

She smiled lugubriously. 'You don't credit me with much insight, do you?'

'You could tell?'

'A mother's intuition.'

'He wasn't always a bastard,' said Barbara. 'Politics made him one.'

Privately, Isobel conceded that this was probably true. When she'd first met Peter she'd put him down as a rather boring accountant. She hadn't appreciated the fires of ambition and lust that raged beneath his bland, insipid surface. But the untrustworthiness had always been there, and she'd suspected it would one day result in him being caught with his hand in the till. She'd certainly never expected him to end up as a Machiavellian Don Juan. Obviously, for some women power was a potent aphrodisiac, even when exercised by a weak man like Peter. None of these thoughts could possibly be shared with her daughter. Instead, she said, 'Politics certainly made him more argumentative.'

'Of course,' said Barbara. 'It's the art of war without physical combat.' She sipped her wine and gave Isobel a direct look. 'Anyway, even though he is a bastard I can't bear the thought of life without him.'

There was another long pause. There was so much Isobel wished to say, but she was trying hard not to respond.

Barbara said, 'I still love him, you see.'

'Then you must take him back and to hell with what anyone else thinks!'

'But that's the point, I do care.' She gazed at her mother abjectly. 'What would you do, if you were me?'

Isobel was so angry about the way her son-in-law had treated her daughter she wanted to kill him, but she didn't feel it would be appropriate to say so. Instead, she said, 'If your father had treated me in the same way Peter's treated you I'd have put all his clothes in the drive, changed the locks on the house and refused ever to have contact with him again.'

Barbara nodded slowly. 'And have been unhappy for the rest of your life?'

Isobel shook her head. 'Better to walk alone than walk with a fool.'

Barbara said nothing. She sipped her wine, engrossed in thought.

Isobel poured hot water onto the tea bags and added milk. 'I'll take these up. I want to talk to daddy.'

Hastily, Barbara said, 'Don't tell dad we might be getting back together. At least, not until I've spoken to Peter. He may have changed his mind. He seems to be changing it every five minutes.'

'Well, just make sure it's changed for good this time,' said Isobel, and she went out.

Barbara was pouring herself another glass when she remembered that the blue mobile was still switched off. She took it from her bag, switched it on and saw that she'd missed four calls, all from Peter. She called him and he answered immediately in a tone that was petulant and vexed.

'Why's your phone been switched off? I've been calling and calling.'

'I was in the car and didn't want anyone else to hear our conversation.'

'But we agreed we'd never switch the blue phones off.'

'Yes, a promise you broke first. And we agreed we'd never give anyone else those numbers and you gave mine to Steve Hawkins.'

'That was an emergency. He had to speak to you and you weren't responding to your other mobile.' Then, realizing that this was not the tone appropriate for his purpose, he adopted a more conciliatory one, 'Anyway, what's happened? You said Howard had been arrested.'

'Yes. For assault.'

She described the circumstances surrounding her father's arrest and was unnerved to hear her voice trembling. At first Peter was most sympathetic. Then he reverted to his characteristic solipsism, seeing his father-in-law's predicament only in terms of its consequences for himself. 'Fuck! The media will be delighted. What a wealth of material we're giving them! They'll just love this.'

'Don't you ever think about anything other than yourself?' she said harshly. 'Don't you ever think about what others are going through?'

There was silence at his end. Then he said,' 'I'm sorry, darling, I'm overwrought. How are Mark and Jessica?'

'Devastated. What do you expect?'

'How much have you told them?'

'Everything.'

'They know about Clarissa?'

'Of course. Why shouldn't they? The rest of the country does!'

She heard him sigh. 'The poor darlings. I know I've let you all down. I feel totally ashamed of myself.'

'So you should. You've made our lives unbearable. We're under siege. There are scores of reporters at the front gate and they all want to know what I think of your hot totty!'

'That's how it is outside the flat.'

'Which flat?'

'Clancy Road.'

Barbara was surprised. The flat in Clancy Road was Peter's London base which he shared with a fellow MP. 'What are you doing there?' she said. 'I thought you and Clarissa had found a flat somewhere?'

'I came back to pack. I hope to be with you by eleven.'

'Eleven? Eleven tonight?'

'Yes.'

'So it's true. You do want to come back?'

'Yes. Look, I'm sorry you heard it from Steve Hawkins and not me, but I really do. I miss you so much, Barbara.'

She didn't respond immediately. She'd already decided that he could return but she certainly wasn't going to make it easy for him. She was sick and tired of being taken for granted.

'I'm sorry, but I'm totally bewildered. Just over a week ago you were telling me that Clarissa was the person you wanted to spend the rest of your life with. She was so important you were prepared to dump me and the children and put your career at risk. Now you want to ditch her and come crawling back to me. Are you having some kind of a breakdown or something?'

'No.'

'Well, that's what it sounds like.'

'I've come to my senses, that's all. The thing with Clarissa was a massive infatuation. As soon as I moved in with her I realised what a terrible mistake it was and how much I loved you and the children. Barbara, I care for you and the children more than anything else in the world.'

'What a pity you didn't realize that before you left us!'

'I know. I've been a fool. But what's done is done and we are where we are. Please Barbara, don't punish me anymore. I want to be with you and the children.'

Despite herself, she was affected by his contrite tone. 'And you've told Clarissa this?'

'Yes.'

'And how was that received?'

'She was very understanding. She appreciates my feelings. She agrees that it was a terrible error for us to move in together.'

'You should have just gone on deceiving me, is that it?'

A note of desperation entered his voice. 'Just tell me you'll have me back Barbara, please!'

'I'm sorry, I'm not sure that would be the right thing to do.'

'Of course, it is. You know it is.'

She was surprised at how satisfying it was to have him at her mercy; to be in the dominant position where her agreement was crucial to his happiness. It made a nice change. Of course, as soon as she capitulated and caved in, her advantage would be lost. She decided to protract his misery a little longer and discover how much she could make him grovel. It would be her revenge.

'Peter, stop pressuring me. Just think how it would look. How could the public respect someone who changes their mind so easily about an important thing like this?'

'I don't care what the public thinks.'

'All right, what about mummy and daddy? Don't you care what they think?'

'I do. But I'm ready to face them.'

She decided to put him out of his misery. 'Well, there's no need for that yet. If we are to get back together I don't want it to happen here at Rooks Nest. It'll be too embarrassing. I'll drive Mark and Jessica back home and we'll meet you there.'

There was a pause while he thought about this. 'I'm not sure that's such a good idea.'

'Why not? It would halve the journey for you.'

Again, he was quiet for a moment. 'The fact is that Steve Hawkins and the Press Office want me to announce that you and I are getting back together at Rooks Nest. They thought it best if I made a statement with you and the children and my in-laws around me.'

Barbara had a sudden intimation of evil.

He finally broke her long silence. 'I know how it must seem.'

'You want to use us as a photo-opportunity?'

'Of course not!' He was struggling to keep the irritation out of his voice. 'It's just that if the presentation is right then the media will quickly draw a line under everything. We need to create the impression that things have returned to normal.'

'And whose plan is this? Steve Hawkins? The Press Office? Or yours?'

'I understand why you're cynical but...'

'Just a moment!'

Mark and Jessica had come into the kitchen.

'When are we going to eat?' said Mark. 'We're really hungry.'

'Who are you talking to, mummy?' asked Jessica.

Barbara lowered the mobile and offered it to her. 'It's daddy. He wants to say hello.'

Jessica snatched the phone from her mother's hand and clamped it to her ear. Mark immediately went and stood next to his sister. He bent his knees and brought his face close to the mobile so that he too would be able to take part in the conversation.

'Daddy! Is it really you?' cried Jessica.

'Hello, dad!' called Mark.

Barbara clearly heard his reply.

'Yes, darlings, it's me.'

'We're really, really missing you!' Jessica told him.

'Yes, we are! We are!' said Mark. 'Have you really left us to go and live with Clarissa?'

Peter's laugh was quite audible. 'No, of course not. I only went to stay with her for a couple of days.'

'Mummy said you'd gone forever,' said Mark. 'She said you loved Clarissa.'

'Mummy was mistaken.'

'Are you going to see us again?' Jessica asked.

'Of course.'

'When?' Mark demanded.

Jessica said, 'Yes, when?'

Barbara was not pleased to hear him say 'You'd better ask mummy.'

Jessica looked up and caught her mother's eye. 'Daddy says we have to ask you when we're seeing him again.'

Now they were both looking at her, beseechingly. She knew he was probably using her, perhaps all of them, but the look in her children's eyes made the answer easy. 'I thought we were seeing him tonight.'

Jessica squealed. Mark exclaimed 'Yes!' and punched the air. Then both children were shouting down the phone 'Tonight! Mummy says we're seeing you tonight!'

CHAPTER THIRTY TWO

'Don't be a fool!' cried Isobel. 'Explain the mitigating circumstances and plead guilty. Tell them you were provoked.'

'But I'm not guilty,' said Howard, quietly. 'It was self-defence. Why should I plead guilty when it was self-defence?'

'Because no-one will believe you, you stupid man. And then you'll go to gaol. Barbara said the solicitor told her that if you plead guilty, you'll probably get off with a fine.'

'Ryecart's not a solicitor, he's a solicitor's clerk and he knows nothing. If I plead guilty, I'll almost certainly go to gaol. If I plead not guilty, there's a good chance I'll get off.'

'To hell with you then!' Isobel flung at him. 'But you needn't think I'm coming to visit you!' And with that she strode out of the bedroom, banging the door loudly behind her.

Howard closed his eyes and emitted a long, long sigh which expressed decades of disappointment and regret. Then, he shrugged, said aloud to himself, 'Oh well,' and continued getting ready for his meeting.

Afterwards, he stood at the bedroom's open window seeking solace for his bruised mind in the beauty of his extensive rear garden and the high, green wold which rose beyond it. It was one of those summer evenings when the earth itself seemed to be exhaling its delights, and the scent of many roses wafted towards him through the still, balmy air. The exquisitely delicate fragrances of the blooms affected him like an opiate, producing a sudden lifting of his mood and granting some respite from the despair which had descended after the traumatising events of the day. He breathed deeply of the anodyne aromas and wallowed in the nostalgic evanescences they evoked: his parents' magnificent rose garden in Surrey; the perfect summers of his childhood; the delightful days spent working alongside his father learning how to nurture and coax the cherished plants into bloom. How he grieved at the passing of those long vanished days of security and peace.

He'd begun to think Isobel would never go back downstairs. She'd seemed determined to cross examine him again and again on every aspect of the alleged assault. It hadn't helped, of course, that he'd told her he'd changed his mind and no longer intended to plead guilty. Quite naturally, she'd wanted to know why he'd suddenly decided he was innocent. His justification that he'd been provoked beyond endurance by the destruction of The Old Rectory's gardens and the attitude of the football playing yobs, had failed to convince her. She'd insisted he describe in detail what had happened at the rectory: particularly how Sheldon Smith had come to be hit. It was quite obvious she didn't believe his account. She'd then told him that the police must have thought him guilty otherwise they wouldn't have arrested and charged him. This had made him exceedingly angry, and he'd only prevented himself from losing his temper by a strenuous exercise of the will.

He lingered at the window for several minutes, appreciating the oriental simplicity and elegance of the garden's design: deriving, as usual, quiet satisfaction from the islands of rose beds separated by expanses of perfect lawn; the walls and trellises adorned with climbers and trailing ramblers; the gently rising hillsides all around that provided the garden's heavenly setting. He was proud to be the architect of this glorious creation: the person solely responsible for the existence of each fragile stem and delicately enfolded bloom. He felt he'd every good reason to feel such pride in his own artistry and self-evident achievement. Only rose growers knew how hard it was to produce superb specimens in hostile alkaline soil. Some groups of roses tolerated chalk and were relatively easy to grow in it. But others, such as the ramblers, floribundas and hybrid teas required constant nursing and attention if they were to take root. On hearing he'd planted these groups of roses, many gardeners in the village had doubted that his plants would ever achieve maturity. It had been most gratifying to have proved them all wrong.

Yet even the beauty of the roses could only lift his spirits temporarily. He left the bedroom and slunk across the landing to his study, drawn there irresistibly to spy like a fascinated child on the reporters still camped outside his front gates. But he could bear to watch his tormentors for only a moment or two. The sight of The Old Rectory curdled his thoughts; and the awful recollection of his recent behaviour there forced him to retreat from the window knowing he'd never be able to look upon that magnificent residence again without a sense of shame. He went over to his desk and sat on the huge, black-and-chrome swivel chair that always seemed more appropriate to the office of some city tycoon than the study of a retired army officer. He sank on to it gratefully, relieved to be alone.

Of course, he was guilty. He accepted that. He'd deliberately struck the boy first. That was indisputable. And yet, even now, as he sat staring at the blank wall across from his desk, he was still convincing himself that he'd acted in self-defence. Hadn't the boy deliberately kicked the ball at him in an intimidating and threatening manner? Hadn't the boy's aggressive posture, his clenched fist, his hostile movements, suggested an imminent attack? In such circumstances surely no-one could be blamed for instinctively lashing out with their stick?

But try as Howard might, retrospectively, to transform these dubious justifications into an explanation for his behaviour that would convince the Luffield magistrates of his innocence, he still knew himself to be a liar. Why then, he asked himself, did he persist with such a fiction?

His answer was that of the charlatan down the ages. Because it was human nature. Because most people, when charged with wrong-doing will deny it and try to wriggle out of it. It was self-preservation. He was no different to others. Why should he claim any moral superiority? And so, reasoning in this way, he deluded himself that his dishonesty was perfectly acceptable.

He decided he'd put his version of events to Greg Maynard to test how it would stand up in court. Some years previously, when Howard had found himself increasingly involved in parish council matters, he'd arranged for an additional ex-directory telephone line to be installed in his study. Thankfully, none of the press had discovered its existence. He used it now to call Greg Maynard's work number.

Greg had already received a message from Mrs Phillips about the extraordinary meeting to be held that evening; but he was predictably shocked when Howard told him he'd been arrested and charged with causing actual bodily harm and would probably be appearing in court the following week in Luffield.

'It was self-defence,' Howard told him. 'Purely self-defence. After all, a man has a right to defend himself when he's being threatened by a bunch of yobs, hasn't he?' He then went on to selectively describe the appalling condition of the rectory gardens, the circumstances in which he'd been attacked and the severity of the assault, eliminating any details which didn't support or justify his actions. 'So, you see, I'm completely innocent. That's why I have to plead not guilty.'

'I'm sure I'd have responded in just the same way if the little bastards had tried it on with me,' said Greg.

'Thank you, Greg. I'm sure that's what any reasonable person would say.'

'However...' Aware that he was encroaching upon a sensitive area, Greg paused.

'Yes?'

'I'm just wondering how the assault charge will affect your position as chairman of the parish council.'

'Why should it?'

'Aren't you supposed to resign as a parish councillor if you face criminal charges?'

Howard assured him that this was definitely not the case. He then went on to describe an elaborate strategy he hoped Greg would help him to implement at that night's meeting. If successful it would ensure he retained his position as chairman despite any moves which might be made to oust him. It would also characterise his rival, Arthur Meakins, as a cynical and unfeeling opportunist, if he should be so foolhardy as to demand Howard's resignation. The strategy was also designed to ensure that Greg's controversial and distasteful plans for dealing with the problem of The Old Rectory could be carried out without any suggestion that Howard, in his capacity as chairman, condoned them. They discussed their intended machinations at some length, until pressure of work forced Greg to end the call.

Howard felt more confident than ever that he could get away with a "not guilty" plea. It was enormously encouraging that Greg had unquestioningly accepted his version of events, and had even suggested that he'd have responded in exactly the same way himself. However, Howard's optimism was immediately blighted by the recollection that this was not the first time he'd justified violent action with a claim of self-defence. In an effort to get away from the distressing thought, he turned his attention to the Parish Councillors' Handbook. Unfortunately, his hands were shaking so badly it was impossible for him to concentrate. He slammed the book down on the desk, pressing hard upon it with rigid hands to steady himself, but this couldn't dispel the images impinging on his mind. He reached for his notebook and a pen and tried to arrange his thoughts in preparation for the forthcoming meeting, but the awful memories made it impossible. Recently they'd plagued him less frequently, due, in part, to the medication he was taking. But he knew only too well that no medication could ever remove the horrific flashbacks entirely from his consciousness. They were the visual detritus of an experience that had given him severe mental trauma, and no matter how vigilantly he repressed its memory, the images associated with it had an ineluctable power to resurrect themselves without warning, which was why he lived in constant fear of their return. It was impossible to anticipate what stimulus would release their latent energies: it might be a sound, a smell, a single word, the chance appearance of evocative scenery, even one of his own thought processes. Anything might trigger the images off. There was a terrifying unpredictability to their sudden appearance and the consequent totality of their invasion and possession of his mind. The only thing to do when it happened was to submit to them until they ceased. It was the only way to extirpate them. Until the next time.

Most vivid of them all was the byre. The byre. The image of the ancient cow shed was always the first to pour into his mind. The byre. Nestling in the valley, with densely wooded hills rising steeply around it and the gleaming Lough Erne in the distance. The byre. Disused. Dilapidated. Its stones weathered by centuries of callous seasons. Its tiles coagulated with moss. Its door timbers swollen and cracked. The byre. No longer used as a cow shed now the farmer had forsaken beef for dairy and built a spanking new milking parlour further on down the valley. The byre. Neglected. Unvisited. A perfect hiding place.

He closed his eyes, sat back in his chair and submitted to the image of the byre as it had looked that morning when his platoon approached it in two transit vans, bouncing along the valley bottom on a road that was no more than a track winding between the hills. In the leading vehicle were himself, holding the rank of captain at that time, and a corporal and four privates. In the second vehicle were five privates and a sergeant. He thought how innocuous they might have seemed: a party of estate agents, property developers and surveyors perhaps, come to evaluate the potential locked up in the stones of the ancient cow shed, with an eye to converting it into self-catering apartments for tourists wishing to visit this magnificent landscape of hills, loughs and islands. But this was 1982. Few tourists came to Northern Ireland, for they were frightened of being blown to pieces by the Provos. No theodolite or any other kind of surveying equipment was carried by the men in these Land Rovers; the byre would have to wait until the late nineties for that, when after the Good Friday Agreement the green shoots of tourism would accelerate the conversion of farm buildings. But on this mild, October day in 1982 these men, bumping along in their vans towards the byre, were in British Army uniforms and armed with self-loading rifles, Sterling sub-machine guns and a Bren.

The tip off about the byre had come from a reliable and respected intelligence source. An undercover SAS man who'd insinuated himself into a position of trust within the ranks of the supporters and sympathisers of the Provisionals. Inadvertently, he'd been allowed a brief glimpse of a map revealing the location of arms and supply dumps close to the border. The byre's location was one of four that he'd committed to memory, before the map had been removed from his sight.

As soon as the byre came into view, Howard gave the order for the vans to stop. For the next ten minutes the byre and the hills around it were kept under intense observation through binoculars. Only when he was satisfied that he was not leading his men into an ambush did Howard give the order for the vehicles to move on. They approached the byre slowly and pulled up some fifty metres from it. Howard ordered all the men, except the drivers, to get out of the vehicles. He placed two men on the track to keep a look out in both directions and positioned the corporal and another man to cover the hills for any activity. He then ordered the sergeant to take four men and obtain access to the byre with the minimum of damage. If the byre was an arms dump there was no point in letting the IRA know it had been discovered.

Howard watched warily as the sergeant and his men moved towards the cow shed. They approached the door. It was chained and padlocked but the staple securing the end of the chain to the door frame was old and rusted. It took very little effort to prise it free. Then, with the sergeant leading, they all entered the byre. After some minutes had elapsed the sergeant returned to report that he could see no obvious signs of arms or explosives. There was just some old farm gear and a pile of sacks.

'I'd better take a look,' said Howard.

He was surprised to find that the interior of the byre was quite dry. As he moved across the stone floor he detected a faint loamy smell, which was not unpleasant. The roof was low and oppressive and the only light source was the small amount of daylight entering through the open doorway. Even though this was augmented by the beams of the infantrymen's torches, much of the place was in gloom, and occasional furtive scuttlings emanating from the darkest corners indicated the presence of small rodents. The torchlight also revealed several old farming implements. These had been hung on the walls or propped against them with such obvious care and attention they might have been exhibits in a museum of agriculture. Made principally of wood, they obviously belonged to the period long before the introduction of mechanisation. Howard prowled around the cramped space, inspecting them. His experience of farmers was that they were hoarders: not from meanness but because their occupation taught them prudence and not to take anything for granted. One day, these tools might be needed again. Farmers also revered tradition and the experience of previous generations. Perhaps that's why some ornamented the walls and ceilings of their farmhouses with ancient scythes, harness and primitive devices for the gelding of young bulls. This farmer was obviously no exception. There was nothing unusual here.

Or was there?

In the centre of the byre was a huge pile of sacks, stacked to a height of nearly two metres and occupying much of the available floor space. He approached the pile, and as he drew closer the smell of earth and stale organic material intensified in his nostrils. The sacks looked innocent enough, but something about them aroused his suspicion. He studied the pile carefully. They'd not been stacked perpendicularly, edge to edge. Rather, it looked as though they'd been carelessly strewn one upon another. Something could easily be hidden underneath them.

Over the ensuing years, Howard had brooded on that mound of sacks frequently. During that time the force of its malevolence had intensified until it had become an object of morbid fascination and horror for him. But latterly, it had come to possess the latent majesty and menace of an iceberg. He could now only regard the sacks fatalistically. It was something to do with the innocuousness of their existence, silently stacked in that remote, unlit place, lying in wait, drifting inexorably through time towards him, until the moment of his tragic, inevitable collision with them. Thinking about them always caused him to wonder what other inanimate objects were sitting innocently out there, unknown and unconnected to him, waiting to strike; like the iceberg and the Titanic.

He had given the order for the pile of sacks to be carefully dismantled. This was a delicate and nerve racking operation. If there was anything hidden underneath the sacks such as arms or explosives, there was always the possibility that they might be booby-trapped.

During what seemed an age, the sacks were peeled apart, one by one, to reveal, finally, at the centre of the pile, two bags: one containing plastic explosive, the other, timers and a tool box. The faces of his men were triumphant at this discovery. Then their expressions changed to one of resignation. They were well aware that as the byre had now been confirmed as an explosives dump it would have to be staked out. This was verified by Company HQ when Howard, at a safe distance from the explosives, had reported their find over the R/T.

He immediately ordered the two vans to be driven off down the track. They were to be secreted a mile away amongst woodland, their drivers to await the order to return. He ordered the bags containing the explosive and timers to be returned to their hiding place and re-covered with the sacks. When this was done he ensured that the door was shut and made secure, with the chain and padlock placed in position as before. He then ordered his men to new positions. The sergeant was to take three men and lug the Bren and its ammunition up the hill, east of the byre. There, they would establish a firing position amongst the conifers and beeches. The rest of the platoon were deployed to various positions on the hill to the west. Satisfied that the byre's entrance was covered from both of these positions, Howard joined his men on the hill to the west.

It looked like they were going to be in for an uncomfortable and futile twenty four hours. Howard knew that on the rare occasions when the IRA had been ambushed at their supply dumps, it had usually been accomplished on the basis of intelligence information about a terrorist operation that was already afoot and for which the Republicans required arms or explosives. It was most unusual for a platoon simply to stumble upon a group of Provos with their hands full of guns and Semtex.

That's why, when the white van appeared within less than forty minutes of the platoon members taking up their positions, Howard should have been alerted to the fact that all might not be as it appeared. But so great was his elation at seeing the van that he overlooked all other considerations. He felt he'd been incredibly lucky.

Through binoculars, he watched the van advance up the track. As it drew near to the byre, the driver swung the vehicle round and then reversed it so that its rear doors were positioned directly opposite the cowshed's entrance. The rear doors of the van were then opened from inside. Immediately the strains of Blondie's "The Tide is High" blasted out, shattering the serenity of a landscape that until then had been silent apart from birdsong. Four men scrambled out of the back of the van. They went straight to the door of the byre and put a key in the padlock. The door opened and they went inside. The driver remained in the cab, his head bobbing in rhythm to the music from the radio.

There was no activity around the byre for several minutes. Then the four suspects emerged, each carrying a number of sacks which they tossed into the back of the van. The four men went straight back into the byre and continued to remove more sacks and load them into the van. From his high vantage point, Howard watched the suspects' labours and strained his ears to listen to what was obviously jocular, good natured banter passing back and forth between them. He was impressed by their audacity. If they were Provos they were going about their business without a care in the world and with no apparent fear of discovery. Yet, one thing puzzled him. If they'd come to collect the explosives, why not simply leave the sacks in the byre? Why load them into the van? Was it being done to confer some legitimacy to their illegal activity? The only other explanation was that they were legitimate farm labourers innocently engaged in transporting sacks. But he dismissed this possibility. He was sure the men under observation were Provisionals, but he didn't want to confront them until he'd obtained conclusive proof. And he would have that only when the suspects had removed the explosives from the byre and were holding them in their hands. Only then would he give the order to move in.

Three of the men unexpectedly ceased working and lingered around the back of the van, lighting cigarettes and talking. Suddenly, there was a loud shout from the fourth man who was still inside the byre. The three others strolled over to the open doorway and then went in to join him. For several minutes there was no activity, just the driver bobbing his head to the radio, which was now playing "Come on Eileen," the Dexys Midnight Runners song. Several more minutes passed, and then all four men emerged from the byre. Two of them were carrying the bags of explosives and timers. The bags were set down on the ground near the back of the van and all four men stood around them, talking animatedly and gesticulating at the bags. The oldest of the four raised an arm and began pointing towards the track. Meanwhile, another of the men had bent down and was starting to open one of the bags.

Howard decided it was time to begin the engagement. He gave the order to break from cover and advance. With guns fixed, all the infantrymen, except the sergeant who was manning the Bren, emerged from their positions and started running downhill towards the byre. The suspects were taken completely by surprise. They stood absolutely still and stared as the soldiers came to a halt and surrounded them at a distance of about twenty metres: those who had come from the eastern side standing well apart, so as not to impede the Bren's line of fire.

'Stand absolutely still. Make no attempt to resist!' Howard commanded.

The suspects obeyed and remained still, staring back quizzically at the soldiers.

It was at this point that the tragedy occurred. One of the suspects made a sudden movement with his hand towards his inside pocket. Assuming that the man was reaching for a weapon, Howard instantly opened fire with his Sterling sub machine gun. Almost at once, a simultaneous reaction occurred: every infantryman opened fire on the suspects; this was followed by a burst from the Bren which raked the suspects and their van. The suspects dropped immediately.

There was a moment of total unreality. Four bodies lay prone on the ground whilst cutting the air around them like a piece of Welsh flint, the voice of Tom Jones was singing "The Green, Green Grass of Home". This surreal anthem drew the soldiers' attention to the van. The driver had kept the engine running throughout. Now he shoved the vehicle into first gear and accelerated hard. The van's tyres screamed as it roared off down the track pursued by the platoon's bullets.

Howard rushed over to the fallen men. They all lay silent and still, bleeding from terrible wounds. He saw that one of them was just a boy, fifteen or sixteen at the most. The man who'd caused the panic which had resulted in the burst of fire, lay with his right hand under his jacket, as though still in the act of reaching for his inside pocket. Howard pulled aside the man's lapel. This revealed the man's hand. His bloodstained fingers were gripped not around a weapon, but a piece of cheap, lined paper, a scrap torn from a notebook. It had some writing on it. Howard gently prized the dead man's fingers apart, extracted the piece of paper and examined it. It was streaked with blood from wounds in the man's chest. The blood had mingled with the blue ink, blurring the words but the message was unmistakable.

"Take 80 large sacks only. If back within a month, no charge."

The note was unsigned. A terrible, sinking feeling appeared in Howard's chest as he read it. The note confirmed the innocence of the men's activity. At that moment the corporal reported to him that all of the suspects were dead and none had been carrying arms.

Howard immediately retreated from the vicinity of the explosives and informed Company HQ on the R/T that there'd been a serious incident and there were four casualties. He requested the urgent attendance of a clean-up squad. He also provided a description of the fleeing white van which included its number.

Within twenty minutes, a Lynx and two Sea King helicopters appeared. An army medic pronounced the men dead at the scene and the bodies were quickly removed. Howard travelled back with them in the Lynx.

He spent the afternoon in a lengthy de-briefing with Lt Col Anderson, his commanding officer, and then wrote out his report on the incident, which he handed in to Anderson that evening. Later, after a good dinner and several drinks, Howard joined his fellow officers in the Mess to watch the 9 o'clock News. To pre-empt criticism, Anderson had gone on the offensive with a series of interviews for the media. In his interview for the television news bulletin, he'd reported that a substantial cache of IRA explosives had been found, four suspected terrorists had been killed and that the man who owned the building where the explosives had been stored was still being questioned. After the broadcast, all of Anderson's fellow officers congratulated him on the deft way he'd sidestepped the reporter's more searching questions. At 22.30 hours, Howard retired to bed. He felt unusually calm and observed himself to be experiencing no sensation of stress.

The following morning things were not looking good: allegations had begun to trickle out on radio, television and in some of the newspapers that none of the dead men had been connected with the IRA. They were being described as innocent farmworkers who'd been sent to the byre to collect some sacks that their employer had arranged to borrow from his neighbour. Furthermore, family members of the farmer who owned the byre were insisting that he'd never had anything to do with the IRA, and had absolutely no knowledge that the byre was being used as an explosives dump. They suggested that as nobody ever went near the byre it was quite feasible that the IRA had decided to risk using it to store their explosives temporarily. As if this wasn't bad enough, the van driver had managed to escape over the border. When interviewed at a secret location in Eire, he'd asserted that the troops had opened fire without reason and that the men's deaths were the result of the British Government's "Shoot to Kill" policy. He'd also been adamant that neither he nor any of his workmates were connected with the IRA, and insisted they'd simply been sent to collect some sacks for their employer. He claimed that a note existed which would prove this.

Howard was ordered to attend the company commander at 1400 hours. When he arrived in Anderson's office he found three other men present. They were in their mid to late thirties and all wore dark civilian suits. The lieutenant colonel introduced them. They turned out to be a major and two captains from Special Investigations Branch. This disconcerted Howard. He knew then that his command of the operation at the byre was under investigation.

Anderson explained to Howard that the three SIB officers had read his report of the previous day's operation and had spent all morning making a thorough inspection of the byre and its locale. Would Howard mind answering a few questions?

The three officers from the SIB questioned Howard relentlessly for over two hours. He answered their questions honestly, all the time wondering if this was the prelude to a court martial. The questions concerning the actual shooting were particularly rigorous and intense. Howard admitted that he'd been the first to open fire and explained that he'd only done so because he'd seen one of the suspects reaching inside his jacket for something, which he'd assumed was either a gun or a grenade.

'And you only realised that he was reaching for the note when you examined his body?' said one of the SIB captains.

'Yes.'

'So you opened fire purely as a defensive reaction?'

'Yes.'

The SIB captain held up the bloodstained note.

'What do you think this note means?'

'That the men were sent to collect sacks,' said Howard.

'And not explosives?'

'Possibly not.'

'Rather a good pretext, don't you think?'

'I suppose so.'

The interrogation ended at 16.30 hours. As he left the room Howard saw the SIB man placing the bloodstained note into a briefcase. He never saw it again.

In the days immediately following the shootings of the four farmworkers there had been demonstrations across the county. The demonstrators demanded justice for the relatives of the Fermanagh Four and an end to the alleged "Shoot to Kill" policy. As a consequence of these demonstrations and the controversy surrounding the killings, the inquest on the Fermanagh Four was delayed for nearly a year. When the first hearing was eventually held it was immediately adjourned for a further six months. In all, the inquest was adjourned on eight separate occasions over a period of nine years, and then abandoned. Public Interest Immunity Certificates issued by the Attorney General ensured that neither Howard nor any member of his platoon ever had to appear in court. The relatives of the dead men pursued their claims for justice through the courts as far as the House of Lords, without victory. Six years after the shootings Howard took early retirement on medical grounds.

The medical problems had begun within a few weeks of "the incident", the euphemism by which Howard always referred to the killing of the Fermanagh Four. He began to experience severe headaches that disabled him for hours, sometimes whole days. These were often accompanied by or alternated with alarming palpitations, anxiety attacks, and an enveloping depression that closed around him like a fog. The direct consequence of these ailments was that he became mentally far less alert. At Sandhurst, as an officer cadet, his decisiveness had been identified as his most positive characteristic. Now, he found himself vacillating over the simplest operational decision, and was well aware that his men were reluctant to accompany him on routine missions because they regarded him as a liability. He'd seen the looks that had been exchanged between them whenever he gave an order. He knew they no longer respected his judgement.

Then the recurring, blood soaked image began. At any time, without warning, his mind would become dominated by a vision of the farmworker reaching inside his jacket for the note that would confirm he and his men were at the byre simply to load sacks. This action, the hand going to the inside pocket for the note, was repeated inside Howard's head over and over again, until the intolerable repetition of the blood soaked image with its implicit accusation that he'd abused the innocent, trusting simplicity of the man, finally brought Howard to a state of complete emotional collapse. His loss of grip was clear for all to see. Whether alone or in company he'd frequently break down, overwhelmed by unmanageable grief, the symptoms of which were tearless sobs which seemed to be torn right out of his soul, and a bizarre, keening sound which suggested the pain of a mother grieving for a dead child. This protracted and mournful lamentation particularly disturbed and unsettled anyone within earshot. On hearing it, Lt Col Anderson referred Howard to the medical officer. He was given medication and immediately relieved of his patrol duties.

In the weeks that followed, Howard had several interviews with an army psychiatrist. Early in 1983 he was adjudged unfit for active service, promoted to the rank of Major and transferred to a Royal Army Ordnance Corps depot on the mainland. There, he was given responsibility for ration supply and procurement and took overall command of a number of desks. For some years, with the assistance of medication, he was able to discharge his new duties more or less successfully. But in 1987, despite the medication, his depression returned with increased severity: again he became unable to make simple decisions or carry out undemanding tasks. He took early retirement on medical grounds and received a full pension. He was forty four years old.

****

Mark finished his orange squash and said, 'I still think we should go and tell the reporters.'

Barbara stared at her son across the kitchen table with a heavy heart. Since speaking to their father, Mark and Jessica had become increasingly fractious and Barbara had been shocked and saddened by their hostility towards her. They'd swallowed Peter's denial about his involvement with Clarissa; and now believed that he'd never loved her and had never deserted his family for her. Consequently, they were convinced that their mother had been lying to them all along. This not only made Barbara feel like a victim of the most egregious injustice, it also placed her in a terrible dilemma. What was she to do? Insist she'd been telling them the truth and destroy their respect for their father? Or pretend she'd made a terrible error and confirm that he was guiltless of any misconduct? Neither course was attractive but in the interests of harmony she'd decided to allow them to go on thinking that it was all her mistake. Selflessly, she'd explained that there'd been a terrible misunderstanding on her part and apologised for making them unnecessarily unhappy.

If she'd thought it would end there she was mistaken. Mark had immediately suggested that all three of them should go down to the reporters at the front gate and tell them that daddy was coming home; that he'd never intended to marry Clarissa and it was all mummy's fault because she'd got everything wrong. Jessica was keen to do this too, and had immediately supported her brother.

Fortunately, Barbara had managed to talk them out of this dangerous idea. She'd told them that they weren't to do anything without speaking to daddy first. She'd then attempted to divert them with orange squash. But periodically both children kept returning to Mark's suggestion, and now Barbara was intensely worried that they might defy her and slip out to speak to the media.

'Why can't we?' Mark persisted.

Barbara said firmly, 'Daddy wouldn't want it. I've told you, he doesn't want any of us to speak to the reporters.'

Mark sulked for a moment, then said, 'All right. But can we please go upstairs and tell grandma and grandpa?'

'Tell grandma and grandpa what?' said Isobel, entering the kitchen. Both children looked up, laughed, and spontaneously left the table and ran over to her.

'Daddy's coming back to us,' squealed Jessica.

'Yes, he's coming here tonight!' said Mark.

Jessica began twirling round and round, intoning 'Daddy's coming back tonight' over and over, like a mantra.

Isobel looked quizzically at Barbara.

'Stop that Jessica, you'll make yourself sick!' snapped Barbara. Then to her mother, she said, 'He'll be here sometime after eleven.'

There was an almost imperceptible pause as Isobel accommodated herself to this information. 'That's wonderful!' she said, exaggerating her enthusiasm for the children's benefit.

'Yes, isn't it?' said Barbara. Suddenly she felt guilty about allowing Peter to return to Rooks Nest without obtaining her parents' agreement in advance. At the very least it was awfully bad manners.

'Let's sit down,' said Isobel. 'I want to hear all about this thrilling news.'

They took seats at the table, and the children excitedly recounted their conversation with their father. At the end of this, Mark said, 'So, you see, mummy got it completely wrong. Daddy was only staying with Clarissa for a few days. He wasn't going to marry her.'

Isobel gave her daughter a long look, but Barbara remained impassive.

'So, grandma, can we go and tell the reporters?' pleaded Mark.

'I've said no, Mark,' said Barbara.

Isobel said, 'Tell the reporters what?'

'That mummy got it wrong. Daddy's not marrying Clarissa. He's coming back here tonight.'

Isobel was genuinely horrified. 'Certainly not. Daddy wouldn't like that at all. And neither would grandpa.'

'Why not?'

Isobel decided it would be more sensible to divert the boy. 'Why don't you both go up and tell grandpa that daddy's coming tonight? I'm sure he'll be surprised.'

'All right,' said Mark, instantly pushing his chair back and standing up.

When the children had left, Isobel said quietly, 'So, he's coming here tonight. Does that mean he's coming back for good?'

'Apparently so.' Barbara gave a bitter little laugh. 'Until the next time.'

'What about Clarissa?'

'She's joined his long list of casualties.'

'Serves her right. Perhaps next time she'll think twice before stealing another woman's husband.'

'Oh, come on, mum. She's not much more than a child. She was no match for a serial adulterer like Peter.'

'That's very understanding of you.'

Barbara regarded her mother fiercely. 'I don't always feel so generous. Sometimes I want to kill her!'

Isobel looked anguished. 'Oh darling, do you think you've made the right decision? Taking him back, I mean?'

'I don't know. I wasn't going to, but he sort of got the children to blackmail me into it. I'm sorry, I know it's going to be very embarrassing for you. I should have asked you and daddy if it was all right before I agreed he could come here.'

Isobel grasped Barbara's wrist and gave it a squeeze. 'Don't be silly. It won't be easy for us but we'll cope. What's really bothering me is this pretence that he's done nothing wrong. The children seem to think you deliberately lied to them about the reason he left.'

'I know, but what can I do? It's going to be difficult enough as it is.'

'You could tell them the truth.'

'No. Least said, soonest mended, I think.'

'Why on earth does he want to come here, anyway?' asked Isobel. 'Wouldn't it be better for you to get back together at home? If I was in his position the last people I'd want to see would be my in-laws. If he's expecting a warm welcome from Howard he'll be disappointed. And he'll have to run the gauntlet of all those reporters.'

'Ah, well,' said Barbara. 'I was intending to talk to you about that. The reporters are one of the reasons he wants to come here.'

Isobel looked at her curiously. 'Really?'

'Yes. He wants to make a statement to them.'

'What kind of a statement?'

'I'm not sure. To admit what he's done was stupid and apologise for it, I think.'

'My God. How embarrassing! How humiliating!'

Barbara watched the predicted look of horror spread over her mother's face as she finally registered the full impact of what had been said. This was not the moment to tell her that Peter wanted to deliver his statement not only with his wife and children standing alongside him, but his unfortunate in-laws as well.

****

To Howard's welcome and profound relief, the bombardment of distressing images provoked for whatever reason by his brain had now ceased. Yet, as always, he was left with a feeling of infinite emptiness, as though there was a bleak void at the centre of his being. He wasn't alarmed. He knew from experience that the sensation always passed.

He rose from his seat in front of the computer and went over to the window. Although he knew it was emotionally damaging to him and bad for his blood pressure, he remained there staring malevolently at the group of waiting reporters and photographers gathered around his front gates. He recalled with great bitterness how some of their colleagues in Northern Ireland and in the British Press had ruthlessly tried to discover the name of the officer who'd been in command of the platoon which had shot the Fermanagh Four. He knew for a fact that several tabloid journalists had approached men in the regiment's lower ranks and offered them vast sums for the name. Fortunately, as far as he knew, no-one had ever succumbed to their bribes, but, of course, one could never be sure. Shortly after the killings two members of his regiment had been abducted and murdered by the IRA. Their bodies had borne evidence of torture, and as both soldiers had known he'd been in command of the platoon at the time of the killings he continually wondered what they'd told their captors before they'd died. He'd always assumed they hadn't revealed his name, as over the years no-one had attempted to booby-trap his car or shoot him on his way to a meeting of the parish council. But he still remained in fear of it happening. Which was why he was now excoriating himself for revealing to that Zoe woman that he'd served in Northern Ireland. What was so stupid was that he'd done it purely for the pleasure of antagonizing her. Hadn't been in complete control of his emotions. He was damn sure he wouldn't have said a word if he'd taken his pill.

The sound of children's footsteps hurrying up the stairs brought him away from the window. Mark and Jessica were excitedly calling for him. He went out on to the landing and arrived there at the same time as the children.

'Grandpa!' burst out Mark. 'Daddy's coming! He's coming here tonight!'

'Yes. It's all been a mistake,' gabbled Jessica. 'Mummy made a mistake. Daddy was only meant to stay at Clarissa's for two nights but mummy thought he'd gone to marry Clarissa!'

Howard was staggered, but he recovered quickly. 'How lovely,' he said. 'And he's coming here tonight?'

'Yes! Yes!' shrieked Jessica. 'Can we stay up to meet him?'

'They won't let us do that,' said Mark, knowingly. 'He won't be here till midnight.'

Jessica grasped her grandfather's hand. 'Please!'

Howard ruffled Jessica's hair. 'Oh, I think we might let you stay up, if you want to. As it's such a special occasion.'

Mark and Jessica almost exploded with happiness.

CHAPTER THIRTY THREE

Sharon was in an ebullient mood as she entered Leefdale and drove towards Church Lane. A number of factors were responsible for this but principally beautiful Leefdale itself. The village's strenuous preparations for the finals of Magnificent Britain had created a picture of horticultural perfection. Sharon felt like cheering as she steered the car past dwellings and street furniture ornamented by a smothering extravaganza of organic colour that streamed over windowsills and lintels, ascended porticos, clung to walls, curled around lamp posts, embraced a telephone box, overflowed wheelbarrows, twined between railings, encircled street signs and ran on and on in a tender, juicy, fleshy, moist, succulent rainbow river of blooms. Everywhere there were exquisite examples of the gardener's art. Sharon felt she'd entered paradise. In fact, she was sure that if such a place as Heaven existed it would look exactly as Leefdale did now on this gloriously sunny evening in July.

Her blissful mood was also enhanced by her overwhelming feelings of gratitude to the people at the inclusion unit. It had been a wonderful piece of good fortune that they'd been there to look after Louise during her period of exclusion. As Sharon made the turn into Church Lane this thought seemed to penetrate her heart and overwhelm it with gratitude for Dylan's kindness. She'd spent most of the day at the Luffield Industrial Estate taking a consortium of potential purchasers to view a large commercial property. This would have been extremely difficult, if not impossible, if she'd had to look after Louise at the same time. All this made her feel doubly indebted to Dylan and those at the rectory.

But the main reason Sharon's spirits were so buoyant was that she'd made a sale! Amazingly, thanks to her, the mothballed factory on the industrial estate had been purchased for a massive sum: an extraordinary achievement given that the property had remained unsold for nearly a year. Her personal commission was going to be enormous and she'd felt like celebrating with someone.

The triumph of the sale had made her slightly reckless. There was a bottle of champagne which had been chilling in her fridge for weeks, waiting for a good reason to be opened. It occurred to her that as Louise would be at her "Oliver" rehearsal, she could invite Dylan round to Honeysuckle Cottage to celebrate her success. It would be risky, and Greg would be furious if he found out; yet the thought of Dylan's kind, understanding eyes, his lovely earnest face, his interesting conversation, and his overall niceness was encouraging her to reach out to him in a more personal, intimate way. After all, it was obvious he was attracted to her: he couldn't have made it clearer. Otherwise, why else did he keep asking her out? And what if it was just sex he was after? What was wrong with that? Anyway, she felt reckless enough to risk it.

Of course, if she'd wished, she could have stayed and celebrated with the three men representing the consortium that had bought the factory. They were staying overnight at The Lamb Hotel and had invited her to have dinner with them. But she had a good idea what they'd really had in mind as all three of them had been eyeing her up all day. She wasn't going to pretend that her powerful sexual allure hadn't helped her cement the deal. After all, everyone in business operated a bit sexually, didn't they? But she wasn't going to delude herself that three rich, powerful guys had committed to the purchase of a million pound site just because she had nice legs. Even so, when they'd asked her to join them for dinner she was concerned that she might have given off some wrong signals. Their eager faces had been most disappointed when she'd told them she had a partner and a daughter waiting for her.

But during the drive home the prospect of being on her own for most of the evening after such a successful and stimulating day, made her feel quite flat. She was even beginning to regret she'd turned down the offer made by the purchasers of the factory, impractical and dangerous as it might have been. It was then that she'd had the audacious idea of inviting Dylan round to help her celebrate. At once she'd dismissed it as an absurd notion, for all the reasons that were drearily familiar to her. Yet, as the miles between Luffield and home reduced, the enticing image of Dylan and herself relaxing in the sitting room of Honeysuckle Cottage, chatting and drinking champagne, kept insinuating itself into her mind. There were other images too: fantasies of herself and him naked, which were completely compelling and, despite her best efforts, refused to be censored. But to turn such desires into reality she knew that when she collected Louise from the rectory she'd have to contrive to get Dylan alone. The possibility that she'd actually manage to do this with Zoe and all the others around was so unlikely it made her scoff out loud. Immediately, she felt daunted and depressed. How was it possible that she'd all the confidence and assertiveness in the world when it came to doing deals with those sharks in commercial property, yet making changes to her personal and domestic life filled her with such apprehension? The thought angered her. For God's sake, she told herself, stop thinking about it, just bloody well do it!

As soon as Sharon turned into Church Lane she saw that something unusual was going on. Why, she wondered, were there so many vehicles parked in the street? Why was a large crowd gathered outside Rooks Nest? And why were there all those cameras? Were they making a film? Sharon's working day had been long and hectic and at no point had she been near a radio or TV news broadcast. She was therefore completely unaware of the personal, domestic and political drama that was engulfing Major Roberts and his family.

She parked outside The Old Rectory, switched off the engine and sat back in her seat, staring at the crowd. As well as police officers, she could see hordes of photographers and people carrying TV cameras and microphones. There were plenty of reporters too. She knew they were reporters because she recognized one or two who worked for the Luffield papers. But why were there so many of them, and what were they all doing there? Surely it couldn't have anything to do with Magnificent Britain? She noticed that the gates to Rooks Nest were firmly shut. Why was that? Isobel and Howard only closed them when they went on holiday.

The arrival of Sharon's car outside The Old Rectory had not gone unnoticed. Everyone in the crowd was raising and turning their head and staring intently in her direction, like grazing bullocks suddenly disturbed by the approach of a human. She began to feel slightly unnerved by their long, predatory stares and pointing fingers. She quickly got out of the car, locked it and hurried over to the rectory's gate, which, she realized was closed. This was unusual too. Glancing back over her shoulder, she was concerned to see that some members of the media crowd were no longer just curious about her arrival, they were crossing the road and purposefully heading towards her.

She grabbed the gate and tried to push it open but it wouldn't budge. Shit! It was locked or bolted or something. Obviously because of the presence of the reporters. She whipped out her mobile phone, but by the time she'd accessed The Old Rectory's number and pressed "Call" she was surrounded by a pressing, shoving, jostling mob; flashlights were dazzling her and a multitude of questions were being bawled and shouted into her ear.

'Do you work here, love?'

'What's happened to the kid with the bump on his head?'

'Is he your kid?'

'Has he been charged?'

'Where's Major Roberts been taken?'

It was deeply disturbing to be pressed up against the gate by an elbowing, shoving horde of big men (they were mainly men) shouting and ranting about things she couldn't understand. She'd never been in such a situation before. She felt like their cornered prey, and she'd be torn to pieces if she didn't give them what they wanted.

They continued to squash up against her, their harsh, deep voices rasping out their incomprehensible questions. Microphones were thrust in her face like knives. The whole situation was ugly and threatening, almost feral; and yet she sensed there was something undeniably thrilling and dramatic about it too. The reporters' single minded pursuit of their own needs was turning the ordinary and everyday into something primitive and elemental. In a quiet village street, the universal struggle for existence was being enacted. All that mattered was the primacy of their will and the capture of the prize. For the prize was the truth, and they were exercising their freedom to find it and manipulate it to their own ends.

Sharon was repelled by the reporters' rapaciousness, their callous self-interest, their latent violence. Yet she refused to be intimidated by them. Just a couple of hours ago she'd demonstrated that she was more than a match for anyone. Hadn't she recently imposed her will on three large, equally intimidating men who in their way wielded far more power than any of the pathetic specimens harassing her? Hadn't she rejected the derisory offers for the mothballed factory made initially by those three, rich, arrogant men? Hadn't she inveigled, cajoled, persuaded, haggled and finally forced them to buy it on the best possible terms for her client? Didn't that show what she was made of?

'Stop it, you're blinding me!' she shouted. 'Get off! Get away!'

The crowd fell silent.

'What are you doing here, Sharon?'

The familiar face and voice belonged to a reporter from The Luffield Advertiser. Some weeks ago he'd interviewed her for an article about property prices in East Yorkshire.

'I've come to collect my daughter, if you and your friends will let me.'

She immediately saw that this was a terrible mistake. Her admission only seemed to galvanize and incite the press pack further. They milled and surged around her with renewed zeal, and their shouted questions became a roar. Now she really was frightened. The situation had such potential for a complete loss of control.

'Sharon, is it? Sharon who?'

'What's your daughter doing in there?'

'Do you know the kid who's been nicked?'

Fortunately, the phone in the rectory which had been ringing all the while was at last picked up. Sharon was overjoyed to hear Zoe's voice repeating 'Hello'.

'Zoe, it's Sharon. I've come to collect Louise but I can't get in and the gate's locked.'

'Hang on. I'll be right out.'

'There are loads of reporters here, and I can't get away from them.'

'Oh, my God!'

'Is Louise all right?'

'Yeah, she's fine. I'll be with you in a second.'

A few moments later the front door opened and Zoe appeared. She ran down the drive, and opened the gate just wide enough to allow Sharon through.

Several of the reporters tried to stop the gate closing by jamming it with their own limbs.

'Help me!' cried Zoe, pressing her body against the gate. Sharon joined her and pushed hard. Together they forced the gate shut. Despite the crowd's protests Zoe quickly re-bolted and padlocked it.

'Sorry, I took so long answering the phone,' said Zoe, as she and Sharon walked briskly up the drive. 'We're in the back garden.'

'You look like you're under siege. What's going on?'

They entered the house. As Zoe led Sharon down the hall and into the kitchen she explained the reasons for the media's presence.

Sharon was shocked to hear of the Kellingford's marital problems. She'd met Barbara and her husband on a couple of occasions when they'd visited Leefdale, and had always thought them the epitome of a happily married couple. But when she'd originally been introduced to them there'd been something about the way Peter Kellingford had looked her lecherously up and down, like a piece of fresh meat, that made her suspect he had a roving eye. But a seventeen year old! Really! And then it hit her: she'd only been a year older than that when she and Greg had first had sex.

Sharon said, 'Poor Howard. He'll be devastated.'

Zoe looked stern. 'I couldn't care less. For some reason Roberts took it into his head to come over here and physically attack us because he didn't like our sculpture park.'

Sharon was finding it difficult to keep up. 'Sculpture park? What sculpture park?'

'Come and see,' said Zoe, stepping into the conservatory. She went over to the open French doors and passed through them, into the garden. Sharon followed.

'This sculpture park,' said Zoe, with an expansive gesture.

On each of Sharon's recent visits to the rectory the blinds in the conservatory had been tightly drawn. She'd therefore been unaware of the radical alterations to the rear garden. Speechless, she now surveyed the appalling damage and was as shocked by it as Howard had been. Her first thought was that it had probably knocked £10,000 off the rectory's value. 'I'm sorry,' she said. 'What am I supposed to be looking at?'

'The sculptures,' said Zoe. She pointed to each installation in turn, annunciating what it was called. Afterwards, she said, 'The kids made them. With a bit of help from me, of course. So what do you think?'

Sharon was deeply embarrassed. How could she possibly tell her what she really thought? The "sculptures" looked like some experiment in modern art that had gone disastrously wrong. They were the sort of weird constructions her primary school teacher had allowed the class to make out of used cornflakes packets, tin foil pie cases, plastic straws and other bits of junk. The materials used in Zoe's sculpture park were more robust and durable and everything was on a much bigger scale, but the result was just as much of a mess and nothing to do with sculpture at all. It was disgraceful that so many lovely trees had been hacked about to create such monstrosities. Howard must have had a nervous breakdown when he'd seen them. She found herself staring at the soiled and distressed statues of Apollo and Demeter. Why were they there? To act as some sort of example of what real sculptures were like? Or because they were old-fashioned and fuddy-duddy and made a good contrast with the modern stuff?

'Not what you expected, eh?' prompted Zoe.

Sharon chose her words carefully. 'No, it isn't. But they're very unusual.' She pointed towards Apollo and Demeter. 'I suppose you got the idea from the Corbridges' statues?'

'Oh, they're just goalposts,' said Zoe, dismissing the god and goddess with a wave of her hand. Sharon stared back at her, truly perplexed.

All this time Louise had been sitting on the ground at the end of the garden with Mona and Rupa. Now, alerted by Rupa to Sharon's arrival, she stood up and began walking towards her mother.

Zoe described how incredibly stimulated the kids had been by the process of creating the sculptures, and how engaged by it they'd been.

'You said Major Roberts physically attacked you because of them,' said Sharon.

'Not me personally.' Zoe described Howard's crazed reaction to the garden's improvements; his vicious assault on Sheldon and his savaging of the sculptures. In the middle of her tirade, Louise came up. 'You're late, mum,' she said, 'I'll be late for rehearsal.'

'Shh,' cautioned Sharon. She wanted to hear the whole of Zoe's account.

Zoe went on to describe how Sheldon, provoked beyond endurance, had punched Howard and how she'd been forced to restrain and subdue him.

Now Sharon understood the thrust of the reporters' questions. Her face was a study in concern. She turned to Louise. 'Did you see all this?'

'No. She was in the encouragement room,' Zoe said, quickly.

'I was doing my maths,' said Louise.

Sharon was hugely relieved. 'Well, that's something.'

A gleam of mischief appeared transiently in Louise's eyes. She was tempted to say that Mona and the others had told her exactly what Sheldon and Major Roberts had done, and she'd heard quite a lot of what had been going on when she was in the encouragement room. But she quickly thought better of this and said nothing. She didn't want her mother to stop her returning to the rectory.

Sharon thought for a moment and then said, 'I'd better have a word with Dylan.'

Zoe said, 'You can't. He's at the police station now with Sheldon. Sheldon was taken there after they let him out of hospital. He's probably going to be charged with assault.'

This was dreadful news for Sharon. Now she wouldn't be able to ask Dylan to come round and share her bottle of champagne. She was reluctantly becoming convinced that her decision to allow Louise to be looked after by those in the unit might not have been such a great idea after all. The buoyant mood in which she'd entered Leefdale earlier was rapidly deflating.

'The police took the Major away too,' said Zoe. 'I don't know whether he'll be charged.'

Sharon turned to Louise. 'Where's your schoolwork?'

'In the encouragement room.'

'Go and get it please.'

'She can leave it here overnight, if you like,' said Zoe.

'No thanks. I'd like to take it home and check it.'

Louise skipped into the house to retrieve her work. Zoe and Sharon followed her. As they entered the conservatory, Zoe said, 'I know what you've heard has shocked you but it really was the Major's fault. Many of the kids have emotional and behavioural problems. They couldn't cope with him coming over here and behaving in that oppressive, bullying way.'

'I left Louise here thinking she'd be safe,' said Sharon.

'She was safe. All the kids were. Until the Major arrived.'

'Yes, but it must have been a terrible shock for Howard when he saw the state of the garden.'

'What's wrong with the garden?' Zoe said, sharply.

Sharon had just completed a deal involving the sale of a seven acre site for nearly a million pounds. She wasn't in the mood to be intimidated by Zoe. 'Well, it's hardly the garden that was sold to you by the Corbridges, is it?'

Zoe stared at Sharon defiantly. 'No. It's a much better garden now. Besides,' she added, moving on into the kitchen, 'the only permanent thing is change'.

Sharon followed her. She was growing more and more convinced now that Greg was right and the rectory wasn't the proper place for their daughter. Perhaps she wouldn't allow her to come back tomorrow. Besides, she certainly didn't want to run the gauntlet of those reporters again.

Zoe and Sharon stood in the kitchen waiting for Louise. For a while, neither of them spoke. Each, in their different ways, found the other intimidating. To Zoe, Sharon appeared to be the epitome of poise and assurance: a woman possessed of an innate assertiveness that Zoe knew she'd never attain despite all those drama workshops and years of training. Even the way Sharon dressed was assertive. Today, she was wearing a beautiful lightweight business suit in cool, stylish beige. Under her jacket was a pearlescent, white silk top that shimmered and gleamed with every subtle alteration of her body position, or shift of weight from one high heeled shoe to another. A single, milky string of opalescent pearls encircled her neck like a ring of tiny, white, glistening eggs: imparting to her throat a subtle sheen. And today there was something even more potent about Sharon than usual. What could have given her that gleaming eye? That triumphalist look? The confidence which exuded from her like a strong musk? Zoe would have been truly astonished if she'd known that the sale of a disused factory on a bleak industrial estate was the reason for Sharon's enhanced charisma.

But it wasn't just the way Sharon looked that Zoe found intimidating: it was what her presence signified. Every time Sharon entered the rectory, she brought in with her the values of another world. A world redolent of haggling and deals and money; a world where everyone's motives were questionable and no-one trusted anyone else because everybody was on the make, financially, socially, sexually. Zoe abominated this world. She also feared it because she knew that gentle, sensitive men like Dylan found it a powerful aphrodisiac and were seduced by its sexy, meretricious representatives, such as Sharon. That's why, when Zoe had discovered that Louise was denying all knowledge of her mother's boyfriend, she'd upgraded Sharon's level of sexual threat to "severe".

For her part, Sharon was equally intimidated by Zoe's fresh faced, natural beauty which needed absolutely no adornment. Zoe's sparkling eyes, flawless skin and toned body spoke of the superiority of her rigorous diet and exercise regime; and the example of her rude good health and physical fitness made Sharon feel as active as a couch potato. She was willing to bet that Zoe didn't spend loads of time making herself attractive, as she did. Zoe was one of those women whose perfect complexion and distinctive hair colouring made her look gorgeous regardless of what she wore, even if it was only an old grey track suit; and nothing could conceal her relaxed and confident sexuality. Sharon had observed on several occasions the stimulating effect Zoe's daily runs through the village were having on Leefdale's males. Particularly the younger ones. No wonder then, when she was standing next to her in a business suit, Sharon felt ridiculously overdressed and artificial, as though she was always posturing and trying too hard. And then there was Zoe's effortless intellectual superiority: her high mindedness and purity of ideals which made Sharon feel petty and superficial. That's why she was always unconfident and nervous in her company, afraid she'd say something wrong or stupid and Zoe would instantly put her down or make her the butt of her waspish wit. Just being in Zoe's presence impressed on Sharon the magnitude of the mistake she'd made when she'd decided not to apply to university. But the thing that made her feel most uncomfortable of all was her suspicion that Zoe would do anything to stop her possessing Dylan Bourne.

Disingenuously, Zoe said, 'I hope today's upsetting events haven't persuaded you to stop bringing Louise here.'

'Well, naturally I wouldn't want her to come if I thought she was going to be exposed to more violence.'

'Of course, that's for you to decide.' Zoe didn't want Sharon to see that she was encouraging her to keep Louise away, and so she went on, 'but if Major

Roberts hadn't struck Sheldon and tried to destroy the kids' sculptures, there wouldn't have been any violence at all.'

Louise now appeared in the kitchen carrying her school books. She'd delayed her exit from the encouragement room so that she could eavesdrop on her mother's conversation with Zoe. She looked at Sharon anxiously. 'I can come back tomorrow, can't I?'

This was not a decision Sharon wanted to make in front of Zoe. She attempted to divert Louise. 'Listen, when we get outside there'll be reporters, photographers, even TV crews at the gate.'

'I know,' said Louise.

'They may try to get us to speak to them. Whatever they say we're going to ignore them and get straight into the car, OK?'

Louise nodded her head seriously, but her eyes sparkled. She seemed excited by the prospect of media attention.

'If we're quick we might be able to avoid them altogether,' said Zoe. 'Let's go and check them out first.'

Zoe led Sharon and Louise into the drama studio. Through the windows they had a clear view of the drive and part of Church Lane. Zoe was relieved to see that there were no longer any members of the press pack loitering around the rectory's front gate. She explained her plan of action in detail to Sharon and Louise.

'Let's go for it,' said Sharon.

They all moved to the front door. Zoe opened it and Sharon and Louise followed her outside. As soon as she was in the drive, Zoe sprinted towards the front gate with the others close behind her.

When Zoe reached the gate she quickly unbolted it and opened it just sufficiently for Sharon and Louise to squeeze round it. Then, with a loud clang, she closed it after them.

The noise alerted the media crowd gathered around Rooks Nest. They stared hard at Sharon and Louise, and some, bored with long periods of inactivity and desperate for any diversion, made to rush across the road towards them. But Sharon was already directing her key fob at the Passat and unlocking the doors. It took only a moment for her and Louise to get safely inside. Sharon quickly started up the car, revved the accelerator and sped off just as the press were arriving. They all fell back in disarray.

As the car sped away, Louise twisted herself round in her seat to stare at the receding reporters.

'Do you know why they're there, mum?' she said.

'Yes. Do you?'

They'd turned out of Church Lane now, and the reporters could no longer be seen. Louise turned to face the direction of travel and gave her mother her full attention. 'None of the grown-ups would tell me what was going on but

Mona and Scarlett did. They said Major Roberts' son-in-law left his wife and ran off with his secretary. He's an MP. That's why all the reporters are here.'

Sharon smiled to herself. 'Yes. That's about right.'

As Sharon was reverse parking outside Honeysuckle Cottage, her mobile pinged. She reached for the phone and read the text: "Emergency meeting of PC at 7. Hope u can make it. G."

Sharon had no desire to round off her triumphant day by sitting in the audience at a parish council meeting listening to Greg and a lot of others sounding off about petty local issues. It made her terribly depressed and low spirited to think that that was all there was on offer by way of a celebration. There was no chance she and Dylan would share that bottle of champagne now. It had been a dangerous idea anyway. Even if Dylan had accepted her invitation, the bubbly might have gone to her head and she'd probably have made a fool of herself. Much better not to. She didn't need any more complications. Besides, she needed a clear head. In view of everything that had happened she'd have to think very seriously about whether or not she allowed Louise to return to the rectory.

As they approached their front door, Sharon said to Louise, 'Before you go to rehearsals I want you to tell me everything you saw and heard at the rectory today. Particularly if at any time you felt unsafe.'

CHAPTER THIRTY FOUR

At Rooks Nest everyone was sitting at the big table in the kitchen. The evening meal had just been consumed.

Mark's eyes suddenly focussed on the clock on the shelf above the Aga. 'It's nearly time for the news,' he said. 'Can we go and watch it, grandma? Daddy will probably be on it. I want to hear them say he's coming back to us and it was all a mistake about Clarissa.'

Isobel looked unsure. 'Well, I don't know dear...' She looked to her daughter for rescue.

Barbara gazed at her mother's anxious, troubled face and again felt pure hatred for Peter. What torture this must be for Isobel, who fiercely protected her privacy and loathed the very idea of being talked about. Now she was having the lurid details of her family's most sensitive, private affairs beamed into everyone's home. What right had Peter to humiliate them all? What right had he to give them all this pain and force them to make such impossible choices? Barbara's stomach turned over when she thought of the dreadful scene there'd be when Isobel and Howard found out what she'd agreed on their behalf and without their permission. What on earth had made her promise Hawkins that? Why should Peter get off scot free, yet again? More importantly, why should her own children be allowed to blame her for what that bastard had done? And be allowed to go on believing that it was she who'd wronged him? Here was a wonderful opportunity to vindicate herself. 'I don't see why they shouldn't watch the news,' she said.

Isobel looked astonished. 'Are you sure? But you said...'

'I know. But now I think they should watch it.'

'Right,' said Isobel. She stood up. 'Let's go through, then.'

Mark and Jessica rushed ahead of her into the sitting room. Isobel lingered by the kitchen door and said quietly to Barbara, 'I don't think this is a good idea. The children will find out he's been lying to them.'

Barbara stared at her mother coldly. 'Yes. I hope so.'

'But just before you said...'

Barbara cut her short. 'They've got to find out what their father's like sometime.'

Howard pushed back his chair and stood up. 'But surely, they're far too young. It'll do them untold damage.'

'Peter should have thought about that before he ran off with Clarissa. Still, he can make amends to us all tomorrow, can't he?' She nodded towards Howard and then turned back to her mother. 'Have you told him why Peter's really coming here tonight?'

Isobel looked pained. She'd been putting it off because of her fear of Howard's reaction.

'No.'

'What are you talking about?' demanded Howard.

Barbara said, 'Peter's coming here to give a statement to the press.'

Howard looked perplexed. 'I thought he was coming here because you and he were getting back together?'

'He is. But his advisers feel it's the perfect opportunity for him to make a public apology and draw a line under things. He'll make the statement at the gates with me and the children alongside him. Mea Culpa, but all is forgiven, that sort of thing.'

Barbara was about to go further and break the news to her parents that their presence alongside Peter would be required too. But she was stopped by her father's next remark.

'I see. It's all been decided, has it? No question that your mother and I should have been consulted?'

'I'm sorry. I should have asked. But I was desperate to get him back, you see.' Her voice faltered. 'For the children. That's the only reason I agreed.'

Howard nodded, understandingly. 'So he's not man enough to face the music on his own, he wants his poor, humiliated wife and his innocent children as human shields, does he?'

'It's what he's been advised to do.'

Howard's glare was terrifying, as though his features were being consumed by the savagery of his contempt. 'What an abominable little shit we've allowed into this family.'

'Please dad. Please...'

'I know, I know. It's not your fault.' Angrily he flung himself in the direction of the sitting room. 'Come on, let's go and watch the bloody news!'

In the sitting room, Mark and Jessica were struggling for possession of the television's remote. Isobel strode over and took it from them. 'Now unless you sit quietly and behave, you won't be seeing this!' The children immediately fell silent and went and sat on the sofa in front of the TV.

The news coverage was just as Barbara had expected. The Peter Kellingford scandal was the bulletin's top story. The newsreader announced that there'd been calls for Peter to resign his Shadow Home Secretary post, following disclosures in The Source that he'd left his wife and children for seventeen year old Clarissa Forbes, his part time researcher, a sixth former and the daughter of his best friend.

Then it was straight over to the TV station's political correspondent. His report included video footage of Peter and Clarissa leaving the entrance to the block of flats where, according to the voice over, they'd set up home together. There were then shots of them fighting their way towards their car through a jostling mob of reporters, photographers and camera crews, before driving off at high speed. According to the correspondent, the couple hadn't been seen since and had now gone to ground. This footage was followed by a short interview with the editor of The Source, who revealed that the story had been broken to the newspaper by Peter Kellingford's closest friend, Russell Forbes, who was Clarissa's father. He'd done so because he'd recently lost his wife to cancer and had been disgusted by Peter's betrayal of trust. There was then footage of Steve Hawkins, leaving Party headquarters and waddling to his car, followed by another baying press pack. Barbara noted that, to his credit, Hawkins remained calm and refused to be drawn, repeating over and over that he never made comments on an individual's private life.

Then it was back to the studio, where the newsreader explained that Mr Kellingford had been accused of hypocrisy in some quarters, even by MPs from his own party, because he was a strong supporter of marriage and had recently suggested that the institution would be strengthened if divorce was made more difficult to obtain.

The newsreader then handed over to the political editor who was "live" in East Yorkshire. In a direct report to camera, he explained that he was standing outside the home of Mrs Kellingford's parents, where the MP's wife and children were staying. He also reported that Labour MPs and ministers were calling for Kellingford's resignation. He quoted a government minister who'd said it was pure hypocrisy for the Shadow Home Secretary to be opposed to civil partnerships for gay people, who wished to have their loving, caring relationships legally recognized, when he'd disloyally walked out on his wife and children for a girl almost thirty years younger than him. Silently, Barbara could only agree.

At this point, Mark and Jessica became very excited because the political editor's report was being broadcast with Rooks Nest clearly shown in the background.

'Grandma, that's your house!' Mark cried out in sheer wonder. 'That's Rooks Nest, look!'

Jessica clapped her hands. 'That's where we are now. That's where we are now! It's on the telly.'

Barbara was greatly moved by Mark and Jessica's thrill at seeing Rooks Nest live on television. It reminded her that they were only small children, and she felt ashamed of her decision to allow them to watch the squalid news report on their father. Yet, at the same time she was delighted that they'd at last see it was Peter and not she who'd lied to them.

'There are unconfirmed reports that a statement will be made by Peter Kellingford tomorrow on his political future,' said the political editor. 'But with a by-election coming up for the marginal seat of Winterton this couldn't have come at a worse time for the Tories. That's why several in Kellingford's own party are calling for his resignation.'

Immediately, the newsreader in the studio said, 'And there's been a separate development involving Kellingford's father-in-law, hasn't there?'

The political editor looked gleeful. 'That's right. Earlier today Howard Roberts, or Major Roberts as he is known, visited a house across the street called The Old Rectory. This is one of the government's new inclusion units. It's understood he went there to complain about the state of their garden and was involved in some kind of altercation. When he emerged a short time later it was obvious he'd received an injury to his face.'

The political editor was replaced on-screen by images of Howard leaving The Old Rectory holding a handkerchief to his face.

'Good God!' exclaimed Howard.

Mark and Jessica turned to gawp at him.

The political editor continued, 'Some time later a youth from the inclusion unit was taken away by ambulance under police escort. Major Roberts was also taken away by the police.'

Now there were images of Howard being driven out of Rooks Nest in a police car. Howard stared at the TV screen disbelievingly.

The narrator's voice continued, 'Police have so far refused to comment. All they will say is that a juvenile and a middle-aged man have been interviewed in connection with the incident.'

The newsreader thanked the political editor and remarked that it had obviously been a day full of incident. She then moved on to another story.

Howard switched off the TV and turned to Barbara. 'I hope you're satisfied.'

Jessica and Mark stared at Howard.

'You said you fell over, grandpa,' said Mark.

'That's right.'

'But they didn't say you fell over. They said you were taken away by the police.'

'Why was that boy put in an ambulance?' asked Jessica.

'Where did the police take you?' said Mark. 'Did they take you to the doctor?'

Howard ignored the children's questions. He and Isobel looked at each other gravely.

'I'm sorry, said Howard. 'I hoped there wouldn't be any pictures of me.'

'What are we going to do?' said Isobel.

Howard said, 'What do you think?'

'Oh no. I can't face it.'

'What else can I do?'

'What's going on?' said Barbara. 'What are you talking about?'

But Isobel only shook her head and dabbed at her eyes furiously with a tissue.

'Why didn't they say it was all a mistake?' said Jessica.

'Because it wasn't,' said Mark, in a fierce voice. 'Daddy lied to us. They said he set up home with Clarissa.'

Howard turned on Barbara. 'I told you it was wrong to show them that. It was entirely inappropriate.'

Barbara said nothing. She was already regretting her decision. Mark and Jessica could see now they'd been lied to by both their father and their grandpa. Would they ever trust an adult again?

Barbara moved over to the sofa and took her children in her arms. 'Daddy did lie but only because he loves you and wanted to protect you,' she said. She gave them both a tremendous hug.

'You didn't get it wrong, did you, mum?' said Mark. 'He really did run off with Clarissa, didn't he? The man on the news said they set up home together.'

Barbara's eyes filled with tears. 'Yes, darling, he did. But he's left her now and he's coming back to us tonight, and that's all that matters, isn't it?'

'Why didn't they tell us that on the news?' said Jessica, as though wondering aloud. 'I don't think he's coming back after all.' She started to cry.

Barbara hugged her more tightly. 'He is, I promise you. He'll be here tonight. They didn't say anything about that because no-one except us knows. It's our secret.'

So great was the tension in the room that the sound of Barbara's mobile phone made everyone start. She jumped up and headed for the kitchen. Mark and Jessica followed her.

Barbara picked up the blue mobile from the kitchen table and checked the incoming number. It wasn't Peter's. What the hell was going on?

'It's all right, it's not daddy,' she told the children, who were hovering expectantly at her side. They stared at her sceptically. They'll distrust all adults now, she thought. 'Really, it isn't him,' she said, and took the call.

'Barbara?' It was the voice of Steve Hawkins.

'Yes?'

'Have you been watching the news?'

'Yes.'

'So have I. Dire, wasn't it? I really feel for both of you.'

'I feel numb. Sick to my stomach.'

'Yes. Those left wing bastards at the BBC really stuck the knife into us.'

'Why not, when Peter's made it so easy for them?'

'Now Barbara, the important thing is not to be negative. If our strategy works, and I see no reason why it shouldn't, the nightmare will soon be over.'

'Really?'

'Absolutely. I've just been speaking to Peter. He tells me you've agreed to a reconciliation and he's on his way to your parents' house.'

'Yes.'

'That's wonderful!'

'Yes, isn't it?'

Barbara had spoken cuttingly. During the pause that followed, she almost laughed as she visualised Hawkins struggling to decide whether or not she was being sarcastic.

'Naturally, I'm immensely pleased for you both,' he said. 'Now, you're absolutely sure about this?'

'About what?'

'About taking him back.'

'Of course.'

'Only, the thing is, I'm just about to issue a press release. It'll announce that Peter will be making a statement from your parents' house tomorrow. It will confirm you're both getting back together. I'm sure you appreciate we'll all be left with egg on our faces if it turns out not to be true.'

'I've no intention of backing out, if that's what you're suggesting.'

'Excellent. And your parents are willing to appear with you and Peter and the children for the benefit of the media?'

Barbara took a deep breath. 'Yes, they're perfectly happy about that.'

'Marvellous. Now, the press release will announce that Peter's statement will be made at 11am. Not too early for you all, I hope?'

'No. That's fine.'

Hawkins gave her one or two further details about the arrangements, including the information that Bill Carr, the Party's press officer for the Northern Region would be arriving early the following morning to rehearse Peter's statement and liaise with the press. He then attempted to bring the call to a close.

But Barbara, who throughout the conversation had felt like a sheep being skilfully manoeuvred into a pen by a prize winning border collie, decided she'd had enough of Hawkins' effortless display of Party management. It was time to show him he couldn't take her docile compliance for granted. Fortunately, the children, having grown bored, had returned to the sitting room, so she felt able to express herself with total freedom.

'And all this will save Peter's job, will it?'

'Well, that's the intention.'

'I saw on the news they're calling for his resignation.'

'Labour always do that. It's just a knee jerk reaction.'

'I've been around political circles long enough to know that. The difference this time is that it's our side who are charging him with hypocrisy and calling for him to go. I'm concerned it might stick.'

Hawkins emollience was almost palpable. 'That's why, Barbara, it's so important for us to swamp the media with images of him back in the bosom of his family. Surrounded by his wife, his kids and his in-laws. It'll all make sense when you read the statement.'

'I hope that you and the whips have frightened him shitless!'

'Now Barbara, you know very well I can't...'

But she cut him short. 'I said, I hope you've frightened him shitless. Because if he ever humiliates me like this again I will not be taking it so philosophically!'

And giving Hawkins no chance to reply, she ended the call and switched off the phone.

****

While Barbara was occupied on her mobile in the kitchen, Howard and Isobel were grimly discussing the implications of the day's events. However, they were forced to stop when Mark and Jessica returned to the sitting room. Howard left, and went straight up to his study where he made a call on his ex-directory landline. It was answered immediately.

'Secateurs, please,' said Howard. There was a long pause, and then a male voice said 'Secateurs here.'

'It's me again,' said Howard. 'Did you see the bulletin?'

'Yes.'

'It's far worse than I feared.'

'Yes.'

'You're going to have to act fast.'

'Yes.'

Howard and the man discussed various arrangements and Howard ended the call. He'd just replaced the receiver when the sound of the Dam Busters' March filled the study. It was the ring tone on Howard's mobile which was lying on his desk. He didn't recognize the number so didn't answer but waited until the ring tone ceased and the voicemail symbol appeared on the digital display. He then played the message which had been left: "Hello Major, Terry Bryden, chief political correspondent of The Source here. I expect you're wondering how I got hold of your mobile number? Well, I'm not about to divulge the secrets of the journalist's art, so you can wonder on. My editor and I would really appreciate it if you'd give us your angle on your son-in-law's antics. There's fifty grand in it for you, Major. Better still, could you persuade that lovely daughter of yours to accept our very generous offer for her story? A hundred grand. Not bad, I'm sure you'll agree.'

Bryden gave his number and asked Howard to ring him back as soon as possible. Howard's response was to immediately delete the message and switch off the phone.

CHAPTER THIRTY FIVE

John Carter arrived in The Woldsman just after six-thirty. For the past two hours he'd been at The Sandleton Examiner, developing and wiring off his photos of the Kellingford scandal to the picture editor of The Source.

John looked to the far end of the oak beamed pub where Terry Bryden was sitting at a table. Bryden was using one hand to hold a mobile phone to his ear; the other hand was greedily forking pie and chips into his mouth. Occasionally, he put down his fork and took a sip from a rapidly diminishing pint of Theakston's. John stayed where he was for a moment, watching Bryden with grotesque fascination: everything about the man, even his table manners, was coarse and uncouth.

As John approached Bryden's table he heard him exclaim, 'Wonderful! That's marvellous! Brilliant!' Obviously, the information he was receiving was putting him in a very good mood. John wondered how long it would last after he'd told him his own news.

Bryden finished his call and placed the mobile on the table beside his plate. 'Wanna drink?'

'No thanks, I'm driving.'

'That's a good excuse. Sure you ain't in the AA?'

John smiled politely, and sat down.

'That was Metcalfe,' said Bryden. 'He's spoken to Roy Oates who used to cover Northern Ireland when you were in short trousers. Roy's given us some information about Roberts that's dynamite.'

'Like what?' said John.

'Sorry lad, top secret. Too sensitive for the ears of little boys,' Bryden leered. 'Let's just say it'll be enough for me to put the squeeze on the galloping major's bollocks and get a good story out of him.'

John was horrified. It rather looked as though blackmail was another of the techniques in Bryden's armoury of dark arts.

John said, 'Did you try Roberts on his mobile?'

In return for five hundred pounds, Ryecart, the solicitor's clerk, had provided Bryden with much useful information about Howard Roberts, including the Major's mobile phone number.

'It was switched off,' said Bryden. 'I left a message. He'll talk to me in the end, though. It's in his interests.'

John stared at him determinedly. 'If you're expecting me to help you hack his phone, the answer's no.'

'Blimey. The worm's found some balls.'

'I'm just telling you I'm not doing it, that's all.'

'No need. I've already had a go. Up in my room with the spare mobile. You see, you're not indispensable.'

'Did you find out anything?'

'Not a thing. The bastard's changed the default.' Bryden grinned. 'I love the hypocrisy of you self-righteous shits. You won't soil your own hands with my methods but you're dead keen to find out if I dug up any dirt!'

Bryden forked in several more chips and took another big drink of ale. Speaking with his mouth full, he said, 'Anyway, it's not all bad news. According to Metcalfe, Clarissa's dad is so pissed off about Kellingford shagging his virgin daughter, he's agreed to give us the full story. You know, how he's been betrayed; how he's not only lost a wife but now a daughter as well; how Kellingford's destroyed their lifelong friendship. All the usual sentimental bullshit.'

'I don't think that's sentimental,' said John. 'I should think he must be very hurt.'

'Yeah, well, the hundred grand we're giving him will make him feel a lot better.'

John laughed. 'You really have a very jaundiced view of human beings, don't you?'

Bryden shook his head. 'Not really. It's just that time after time they keep proving me right. How can I help it if they always fulfil my worst expectations?' He pushed his plate towards John. 'Have a chip.'

John regarded the uneaten remains of his mentor's meal distastefully. 'No thanks.'

'Had your tea?'

'No.'

'Get some. In this game you never know when you'll have time to eat. Grab a bite while you can.'

'I will.'

Bryden took another swig of beer. 'So, did the photos come out all right?'

'Most of them.'

Bryden's eyes narrowed dangerously. 'What do you mean, most?'

'You're not going to like this.'

'I'm sure I'm not. Have you fucked up again?'

'No. One or two didn't come out, that's all.'
'Which ones?'
'Those of the girl.'
'Which girl?'
'Zoe, I think her name is.'
'The lovely redhead from across the road?'
'Aye. That's the one.'
'What, none of them came out?'
'No. Not one.'
'Fuck me. Why didn't they come out?'
'They were over-exposed. You saw the trouble I was having with the camera.'

Bryden sighed and screwed up his face. 'Show me.'
'Show you what?'
'Are you thick? The photos that didn't come out.'
'I can't. I destroyed them.'
'Well go and print some more.'
'I can't. I destroyed the negs.'
Bryden looked amazed.
'I shredded them,' said John.

'Oh nice! That's very nice!' Bryden breathed deeply, and then drained his glass of bitter. When the glass was empty he didn't replace it on the table but held it in his hand speculatively, as though deciding whether or not to have another. After a long, inner struggle he put the glass down. 'You shouldn't have shredded them. Our picture desk could have rescued enough for the story.'

'Not those negs,' said John. 'There were no images at all.'

'Listen dickhead, never destroy negs no matter how crap they are. Something can always be salvaged. Besides, Zoe threatened to sue to get them back. It's gonna look very fishy if it gets out we destroyed them. People will wonder why. It'll probably increase her out of court settlement by thousands.'

John looked shocked. 'Sorry. I hadn't thought of that.'

Bryden lit a cigarette with a match. Afterwards he blew the match out and stuck the charred matchstick into the detritus remaining on his plate. He said, 'Still, I expect Zoe will be more than pleased. She never wanted us to use those pics anyway. I'd go round and tell her if I were you. She'll be so grateful she'll probably give you a blow job.' He blew smoke in John's face. 'Got any more good news for me?'

'No,' said John, smiling boyishly.

'I've got some for you,' said Bryden. 'Ever been to a parish council meeting?'
'No.'

'Well, there's a first time for everything, as the bishop said to the virgin. We're going to one.'

'We are? Why?'

Bryden nodded in the direction of the crowded bar. 'The landlord and the other carrot crunchers over there tell me there's an urgent one tonight. The word is they're gonna turn Roberts off the parish council for duffing up that black kid. It's our chance to ask the Major a few questions.'

'OK,' said John, with little enthusiasm.

Bryden picked up his mobile and searched the address book for a number. When he'd found it, he pressed "Call" and handed the phone to John. 'But first, I want you to talk to our picture editor. You can tell him yourself why he won't be getting the pics of that gorgeous redhead with the big tits I promised him!'

****

Howard always arrived at parish council meetings early. However, given the day's sensational events, he expected the extraordinary meeting to have a much greater attendance than usual and assumed that everyone present, councillors and spectators alike, would be anticipating his appearance with that mixture of fascination and schadenfreude which is often characteristic of the public's response to a scandal. So, to minimise his embarrassment he ensured that he arrived in the hall only a minute or two before the meeting was due to begin.

Howard's instincts had been correct: the hall was packed. Most of the councillors had turned out for the occasion, even those who rarely made an appearance. All the seats for the public were taken and people were standing on every side of the room. With disquiet, he saw that some of those bastards from the press were there too.

Howard walked nervously down the centre aisle separating the rows of public seats and made his way towards the front, where all the parish councillors were seated at a long table mounted on a dais. As soon as they became aware of his presence the councillors stopped talking and stared at him for several seconds before resuming their conversations. Obviously, he and his family's problems were the subject on everyone's lips. Looking neither to the left nor right, Howard continued on down the aisle ignoring the audience's stares. He went round the back of the dais, stepped on to it and took his usual seat in the centre of the table next to Mrs Phillips, the clerk. He exchanged greetings with her and all the councillors who were seated around him. Was it just his imagination or had several of them avoided his eye when they'd returned his greeting? Had one or two actually looked away in embarrassment? Even the normally sanguine Mrs Phillips seemed disconcerted: she fidgeted uneasily in her seat and seemed absorbed in the notebook and agenda sheet in front of her. The sombre, expectant atmosphere around the table extended to those sitting on the chairs put out for members of the public. Howard recalled the many parish council meetings he'd attended in that hall when every seat had been empty. Greg had obviously done an excellent job of publicising the meeting at short notice. Or did the unprecedented increase in attendance have more to do with the scandal of Barbara's matrimonial problems and his own recent brush with the law? For there was no doubt that everyone in the village would by now be aware that he'd been arrested. Was that what had enticed them from their televisions to sit on uncomfortable, hard backed chairs? Not civic responsibility but simple good old-fashioned curiosity? Some no doubt expected him to resign. Was that why they'd come?

Howard opened the meeting by thanking the clerk and councillors for attending at short notice. He also extended his thanks to the members of the public for their presence. He confirmed that the meeting was quorate, as there were more than three councillors present, and asked the clerk if there were any apologies.

Mrs Phillips read out the fairly short list of names of those unable to attend. When she'd finished Howard stared unblinkingly around him, radiating presence.

'Now,' he said, 'I suppose you've all seen the reporters camped outside my house, hoping to interview my daughter?'

He glanced from side to side and saw his fellow councillors nodding uneasily. Apart from Greg, who'd already been primed, they'd all been wrong footed. They hadn't expected such frankness from Howard at such an early stage, and seemed unsure of the appropriate response.

Staring hard at Terry Bryden who was sitting in the front row, Howard went on, 'Indeed, I see that we have some representatives of the press here this evening. I want to warn you that if any attempt is made by you to disrupt this parish council meeting with irrelevant questions or by taking photographs without consent, I will request Police Constable Wheatcroft...' here Howard gestured towards the back of the hall where the policeman, having just entered, was now standing... 'to remove you.' All heads quickly turned to the back of the hall to take in Wheatcroft, and then everyone's attention was back on Howard. His expression remained stern. 'I'd also remind members of the public that they are only admitted to these proceedings as observers and are not allowed to take part.'

Howard now addressed his fellow councillors. 'You may have thought I convened this extraordinary meeting because of my own personal problems. However, you'd be wrong. As you can see, there's only one item on the agenda: Item One, The condition of The Old Rectory's gardens.'

Howard felt his right hand shake slightly. To steady it he forced his palm down onto the table-top and continued, 'Earlier today, as instructed by the members of the Magnificent Britain Sub-Committee, I called at The Old Rectory to remind Dylan Bourne and his colleagues how important the Magnificent Britain contest was for the village, and also of the rectory's crucial role in ensuring our fifth consecutive gold medal. My intention was to ask them if they'd be prepared to tidy up the rectory's gardens in time for the judging.' He paused. 'But I never got that far.' His features assumed an expression of disgust. 'Ladies and gentlemen, nothing could have prepared me for the scenes of devastation that met my gaze.'

He described in detail the deplorable condition of the lawns and the herbaceous borders; the ruination of the greenhouse; the erection of goal posts; the destruction of healthy trees to create bizarre and inappropriate "sculptures". He was delighted to find that his account was frequently interrupted by exclamations of astonishment and outrage from most of his fellow councillors and several members of the public. He brought his sorry report to a close by saying, 'And when I attempted to remonstrate with those responsible for these appalling acts of vandalism against the most beautiful gardens in our village, I was physically attacked.' He pointed to the bruise on his cheek. 'Yes, assaulted!'

This was received with incredulity and shock. Several people cried out 'No!' and 'Disgraceful!'

Here, Councillor Arthur Meakins, a bald, bespectacled man, seized his opportunity: 'Mr Chairman, I'm sure that everyone would agree that the condition of the gardens in The Old Rectory is a matter of enormous concern. However, on a point of order, I have to say that there are several rumours flying around the village, one of which is that you, Mr Chairman, have been arrested and charged with assault on one of the young residents of the inclusion unit which has been established in the rectory. It would be very helpful for all of us if you could confirm or deny this.'

Howard caught Greg Maynard's eye. 'Unfortunately,' he said, speaking with great solemnity, 'that is indeed true.'

Arthur Meakins licked his lips and without revealing a trace of his deeply felt glee, continued. 'Thank you for clarifying the position. Given the circumstances might it not be appropriate for you to resign your position as chairman of the parish council? And perhaps even as parish councillor, until the charge has been dealt with?'

Howard was elated. Meakins had walked straight into the trap. Now he could show everyone what an opportunistic little shit the man really was, and at the same time rally their support.

'I'm sorry, Councillor,' said Howard, fixing Meakins with a malevolent stare, 'I don't quite understand. Are you saying I should resign as chairman and as a parish councillor?'

Meakins blinked unsurely behind his bi-focals. 'Well, yes.'

'Because I've been arrested for defending myself against a violent mob?'

At once there was an outraged cry from Greg of, 'Withdraw, Meakins! Withdraw!' The cry was immediately taken up by other councillors.

Meakins looked around nervously. He was far less confident now. 'I was only suggesting you stepped down until the assault charge is dealt with.'

Howard adopted a tone of complete reasonableness. 'Obviously, I was aware that rumours about the assault on me were circulating in the village. But

I'd quite naturally assumed I enjoyed the full support of the council, particularly in view of the problems we face at the present time.'

'You can be assured of my fullest support, Mr Chairman,' exclaimed Greg Maynard, decisively on cue. This was immediately followed by several cries of, 'And mine!' and 'Hear, hear!' from many of the councillors and members of the public.

'Thank you, Councillor Maynard,' said Howard, graciously. 'Thank you, all of you.' He stopped to glance quickly at Meakins, who was looking somewhat deflated, and then continued, 'However, Councillor Meakins raises legitimate concerns which must be addressed. Let me therefore assure all members of the council and the public that I have consulted the Parish Councillors' Handbook on this very matter. It confirms that a councillor only faces disqualification when he has been convicted of a crime. I have not yet been convicted of the charge against me and do not expect to be. I shall be pleading not guilty and would remind you that a person is still innocent until proven guilty in this country.'

'And long may it remain so!' thundered the landlord of The Woldsman from the back of the hall.

'Thank you!' said Howard. He looked pointedly at Arthur Meakins. 'I'm sure you'll agree therefore, that there's absolutely no need, at present, for me to resign from any of my posts?'

Meakins nodded grudgingly.

'Now, are there any more points of order?'

Nobody spoke.

Howard smiled suavely. 'Then I propose that we move on. I am well aware that in the month since our last meeting serious concerns have been raised about The Old Rectory's change of use. It's gone from a dwelling house to a home for anti-social teenagers, otherwise known as an inclusion unit. Several councillors have expressed the view privately to me that there's been a blatant infringement of the planning laws. Indeed, I intended to raise the matter at next month's meeting. However, events have somewhat overtaken us. The appalling state of the rectory has made it imperative for me find out what redress is available to the parish council. For example, could we apply to have the inclusion unit closed down? I'm very sorry to tell you that there's absolutely nothing we can do. It appears that the owners of The Old Rectory are not doing anything illegal.'

Again, there were exclamations of astonishment.

'Yes. I was as surprised as you are. Apparently, a few months ago a new piece of legislation was smuggled through Parliament using a statutory instrument, and is now law. As a result, blanket planning permission is automatically available to anyone who wants to set up a unit to provide alternative education for youngsters aged between thirteen and eighteen who, for whatever reason, have been expelled from mainstream education.'

'Surely they'd still have to apply to the district council for planning permission to change the use of the property?' observed Councillor Rawson, a retired butcher.

'No,' said Howard, firmly. 'The statutory instrument specifically permits the district council's planning procedures to be bypassed. If anyone wants to set up one of these inclusion units, all they have to do is apply to the Secretary of State for Education. I'm told that they usually get a decision within fourteen days.'

'Without having to tell the local community what their plans are?' said Councillor Betty Hildreth, a thin faced woman who ran a bed and breakfast.

'So it would appear.'

'But the Corbridges must have known what these people's plans were when they sold them the rectory!' asserted Councillor Meakins.

'Not necessarily,' said Howard. 'There's no requirement on those setting up an inclusion unit to divulge that there'll be a change of use. That's the devious part of it.'

'You said it was done by statutory instrument?' said Meakins.

'That's right.'

'Then how did we miss it? Surely, as a parish council we should have been notified.'

Howard had been anticipating this. 'Unfortunately, responsibility for that has to be laid at my door. Every week, I receive huge volumes of information about changes to the law, which I draw to the council's attention. I'm afraid that this one passed me by. All I can do is apologise.'

Looks were exchanged between the councillors but no-one said anything. The implication was clear. The problems with the rectory were all Howard's fault because he hadn't been up to the job.

Meakins considered whether he should move a vote of no confidence in Howard but knowing he was unlikely to be supported, immediately dropped the idea. Best to wait until later when the circumstances might be more propitious. Instead, he contented himself with saying, 'That's most regrettable, Mr Chairman. If we'd known about these inclusion units we might have been alerted to their danger and been in a position to oppose the one at the rectory.'

'I doubt it,' said Greg, riding to Howard's defence. Hoping he sounded sufficiently casual, he went on, 'I was talking to Sharon Makepiece recently. As you know, she works for the estate agents that sold the property to Mr Bourne and his associates. She says Bourne never said a word about his real reason for acquiring the property. He gave her the impression he was simply an artist looking for somewhere to paint.'

At first, nobody responded to this remark and Greg found himself feeling like an embarrassed fourteen year old, as he always did, on the rare occasions when he mentioned Sharon's name in public. Fortunately, after a long pause, his point was taken up by Councillor Rawson.

'So, Bourne sneaked his inclusion unit in under the radar, eh? And he won't be the only one, I'll be bound. It's the thin end of the wedge.' Rawson turned his reddening, glaring face upon Howard. 'Mr Chairman, I'm very concerned about the effect this will have on house prices in the village.'

'So am I,' said Howard. 'That's one of the reasons I've convened this extraordinary meeting. As you know, we, as a parish council, are entitled to take legal proceedings. This new inclusion legislation has not yet been tested. I therefore propose the following resolution.' He paused to consult his notes, and then continued, reading aloud, 'That Leefdale Parish Council, after taking legal advice, apply for an injunction to prevent the owners of The Old Rectory from using their premises as an inclusion unit.'

'Seconded, Mr Chairman,' said Greg Maynard, immediately.

A short debate followed on the merits of the resolution. Lucy Birkinshaw was the only councillor who opposed it.

'Mr Chairman,' she said, 'I really can't see the point of trying to get an injunction if the law already says that people are legally allowed to set up inclusion units.'

'It'll be a test case!' said Greg Maynard, shortly.

'But we could spend lots of time and money only to discover that the people at The Old Rectory are doing nothing illegal,' Lucy insisted. 'Besides, I've not heard about this new inclusion legislation before but it sounds rather a good idea.'

'You won't think it such a good idea when the value of your house falls by twenty thousand,' exclaimed Bernard Rawson.

'That's right,' said Councillor Brigham, an elderly farmer. 'People will think twice about purchasing when they see this lovely old village overrun with young thugs from Leeds and Bradford.'

'You should see the way they walk about already, as though they own the place,' said Mrs Phillips.

'And look what they've done to the rectory,' said Councillor Hildreth.

Howard said, 'It's certainly very unpleasant living opposite the Rectory now. It used to be one of the pleasures of my life.'

'I definitely think we should obtain legal advice, Mr Chairman,' said Greg Maynard. 'And if the advice is to go for an injunction then that's what we should do. But as far as the Magnificent Britain contest is concerned, it'll be too late. They're coming to do the judging on Friday, and no amount of injunctions will get anything done about The Old Rectory by then. What we need is for a group of villagers to go round there and kick some arse. Get those yobbos and backsliding trendies to clean the place up in time for the contest. Force them if necessary!'

At this there were loud cries of agreement from some members of the public.

'Here's another idea,' Maynard continued, 'We could organise a blockade of the rectory. Ask tradesmen to refuse to deliver anything or do work for them until they tidy the place up.'

This suggestion received even more enthusiastic support from the hall.

Lucy Birkinshaw appeared to be the only dissenter. 'What's the good of a blockade?' she demanded. 'All they'll do is drive into town to get what they want.'

'Yes. But it would inconvenience them no end,' said Councillor Brigham.

'And show them that they aren't welcome here,' said Councillor Meakins.

'There's another thing we could do to improve our chances with Magnificent Britain,' said Greg, who was now carried away with self-righteous indignation. 'On Friday, when the judges go round, we could organise a big protest outside the rectory. When the judges see how outraged we all are at the state of it they might take that into account and not penalise us for it.'

Howard was gratified to see that this seemed to be the most popular suggestion so far with Greg's growing band of supporters.

'It's a great idea, Greg' said Arthur Meakins. 'But it's Tuesday now. How are we going to organise it in time?'

'Why not a special edition of The Leeflet? A side of A4 telling the village about our plans for dealing with The Old Rectory and urging everyone to attend the demonstration on Friday?'

'And tell the local press and TV people. They're bound to be interested,' said Councillor Brigham.

'Excellent idea,' said Arthur Meakins. 'Let's pass a resolution, set up a committee and get on with it.'

'Just a moment,' intervened Lucy Birkinshaw. Staring hard at Greg Maynard, she said, 'Am I the only one who thinks that your suggestions are disgraceful? I won't be a party to the victimisation of these people. It's all getting out of proportion. After all, we're only talking about one property. All right, the rectory garden is in a mess but the rest of the village looks lovely. Why do we have to persecute these people? If they don't want to play, they don't want to play, and that's their privilege. Live and let live. That's what I say.'

One or two heads began to nod in agreement. Howard began to be concerned that by pressing the case too hard Greg was going to ruin it. He decided it was time to speak.

'Let me assure you, Councillor Birkinshaw, that as long as I am Chairman of Leefdale Parish Council it will never authorise any activity that would involve the intimidation or victimisation of any of our fellow residents. Nor would I allow The Leeflet to be used for those purposes. I understand that the condition of the rectory arouses strong feelings, but the proposals that Councillor Maynard makes are entirely outside this council's remit.' He turned towards Maynard who already knew what was coming. 'I'm sorry, Greg, but there is no way that I can accept your suggestions for a blockade or a demonstration, however well intentioned, as a formal resolution. The council has no powers in that respect.' Howard treated everyone around the table to one of his urbane looks. 'However, as private individuals, you are all free to take whatever action, within the law, you think appropriate for enhancing our chances of winning Magnificent Britain and gaining the gold medal. That's entirely a matter for you.' To make his meaning absolutely clear he paused and smiled unequivocally. 'Now, if there's no other business I propose to bring this meeting to a close. As you may appreciate, I've had a long and trying day, and I need to get home as soon as I can to support my family.'

There was no other business, and after thanking everybody once again for their attendance, Howard brought the meeting to its end. As he stood up to leave, he was delighted to hear Greg inviting everyone to his home to discuss the arrangements for Friday's demonstration outside The Old Rectory.

Howard strode out of the village hall pursued by reporters. Once outside, PC Wheatcroft escorted him to the police car in which, for his protection, he'd been brought to the meeting. Howard was then driven swiftly back to Rooks Nest. He was feeling happier than he'd felt all day.

CHAPTER THIRTY SIX

As soon as Howard had left for the parish council meeting, Barbara set up a video of "The Wind in the Willows" for the children to watch in the sitting room while she and Isobel talked in the kitchen. Barbara got stuck in to her bottle of red wine and was surprised to see Isobel, who seldom drank alcohol, attack Howard's sherry with the zeal of a seasoned drinker. They sat around the kitchen table discussing the state of Barbara's marriage for some time, before Isobel finally turned the conversation to her concerns about Howard.

'He's decided he's going to plead not guilty now,' she said.
'No! Why?'
Isobel made a frustrated gesture. 'Because he thinks he can get away with it.'
'But he said he was going to plead guilty because he hit the boy first.'
'Yes. Now he says it was self-defence, and any reasonable person would say he was justified.'
'But if he pleads not guilty and the court thinks he's lying he could go to gaol.'
Isobel looked fearful. 'I know. Try telling him.'
They both fell silent, alone with their apprehensions.
'Do you have the number of The Old Rectory?' Barbara asked suddenly.
'Why?'
'Do you have it?'
'It's in Howard's address book, I suppose.'
'Where's that?'
'Up in the study. What do you want it for?'
'I thought I'd call them up. Ask them if they'd consider dropping the charges.'
Isobel's face was a picture of alarm. 'Oh, I don't think we should do that!'
'Why not?'
'Isn't that the same as interfering with witnesses or something?'
'All we'd be doing is asking them to consider dropping the charges.'
'But why should they?'

Barbara stood up and took hold of her mother's hand. 'Come on, show me where this address book is.'

They went up to the study, and Isobel quickly located the little black book in one of the desk drawers. 'It'll be listed under Corbridge,' she said. She found the appropriate page, handed the book to Barbara and then sat on Howard's chair while Barbara dialled the number.

It was Eric who answered. 'Hello, Leefdale Inclusion Unit.'

She could hear a lot of people talking noisily in the background. 'Is that The Old Rectory?'

'Yes.'

'Could I speak to Mr Bourne, please?'

'Who's calling?'

'My name's Barbara Kellingford. I'm Major Roberts' daughter.'

There was a long pause. 'Just a moment.'

Meals in the rectory were served in two shifts because the kitchen table could only seat six. Barbara had telephoned during the second shift for supper. She heard the man who'd answered the phone bawl out, 'Dylan, it's for you. Someone called Barbara Kellingford. She says she's the Major's daughter!' All the loud background conversation stopped. A few seconds later, she heard Dylan's voice for the first time.

'Hello. Dylan Bourne here.'

'Mr Bourne, I'm sorry to disturb you so I'll come straight to the point. I'm calling to see if it's possible for you to drop the charges against my father.'

Dylan was staggered not only by the nature of her request but her directness. 'I see.'

She was unsure whether his guarded reply was a flat refusal. 'You do know he's been charged with causing actual bodily harm?'

Dylan did know this. He'd returned from Luffield police station with Sheldon just half an hour ago. After a further interview by the police in which he'd again admitted striking Major Roberts, Sheldon had been offered a police caution. Dylan had advised him not to accept it if Roberts was going to get off scot free. WPC Scargill had assured them that Howard Roberts would definitely be charged with actual bodily harm. Dylan was then able to advise Sheldon to agree to the police caution and he'd accepted it. Dylan saw no reason to reveal any of this to Barbara Kellingford.

'Has he been charged?' said Dylan. 'We'd assumed he had, but didn't know for sure.'

'The thing is my father has serious health problems. My mother and I are frightened that the stress of appearing in court and facing a possible prison sentence will make his condition worse. Might even kill him.'

Dylan considered his response. 'I understand your concern but I really don't see what we can do about it. It's in the hands of the police now.'

'I just thought that if my father apologised you might be able to speak to the police and say you were happy to drop the charges.'

'It really was quite a serious assault, you know,' said Dylan. He described graphically Howard's attack on Sheldon. As Dylan spoke, Barbara became aware that an abstract reality was suddenly becoming shockingly corporeal. Sheldon was an actual boy: a real human being whom her father, without provocation, had savagely hit about the head with his walking stick. The thought of it made her ill.

'Believe me,' said Dylan, 'we're all very sorry that things have come to this.'

'I'm sorry too,' said Barbara. 'It must be deeply distressing for all of you. But I'm sure it wouldn't have happened if my father had taken his medication. He's on anti-depressants, you see.'

She began to complain about her father's unnatural obsession with the gardening contest and how it had affected the family. 'That's why the state of the rectory's garden made him behave so out of character. We're all very anxious about the effect this is going to have on his reputation and his health.' Her tone became slightly tearful. 'Really, this is the last thing any of us need right now: particularly on top of all the personal problems I'm going through. I suppose you know about those?'

'Yes, it's been hard not to miss them. I'm sorry to hear you're having a bad time.' He thought for a moment. It was unlikely that anything could be done but he hated to leave her without hope. 'Look, I'll tell you what, I'll talk to Sheldon and I'll talk to the other team members. Then I'll call you back. That's the best I can do.'

'Would you? Oh, thank you.'

'I'm not promising anything, though.'

'No. I understand.'

Dylan asked for her number. Barbara said, 'Because of the press who keep harassing us, we're not answering any of our usual phones. I'll give you my very private mobile number. It's the one number they haven't got hold of, yet. Promise me you won't give it to anyone else, please?'

'I promise.'

Feeling somewhat guilty she gave him the number of the blue mobile. Afterwards, remembering that Peter had been the first to violate the number's privacy, she had a very satisfying sense of redress.

'Well?' enquired Isobel fearfully, when the call was finished.

Barbara assured her that Mr Bourne was going to do his best to get the charges withdrawn, although she didn't hold out much hope of this.

'Mr Bourne seemed rather nice,' said Barbara. 'Let's keep our fingers crossed.'

****

After the meeting of the parish council ended, many of those present lingered in the village hall. They were reluctant to leave until they'd gossiped about the proceedings and the other events of what had been a truly remarkable day.

The reporters had quickly identified Councillor Meakins as Howard Roberts' main political rival. As soon as Howard had left the hall the press turned their attention to Meakins, besieging him with questions and encouraging him to admit that in his view Chairman Howard Roberts ought to resign.

Like so many politicians, whether professional or amateur, Meakins was most susceptible to the media's blandishments. Before long, his expressions of support for Major Roberts in "this trying time and period of great personal difficulty" were being qualified by his serious doubts as to whether the Major could continue in office, given the extent of the scandal that was enveloping him.

Bryden briefly joined the other journos questioning Meakins, hoping to elicit from him some background dirt or bitchy comments, but he soon saw that Meakins was too parochial and circumspect to be of any real interest. Bryden's real prey was Councillor Maynard, who was obviously Roberts' puppet. He appeared to be about to depart and needed to be nobbled quickly.

Detaching himself from the throng around Meakins, Bryden caught up with Maynard as he walked towards the door and placed a hand on his arm.

Maynard spun round. 'Yes?'

Bryden said, 'You seem to know Major Roberts pretty well. In fact, you seem quite thick with him.'

Maynard's face was impassive. 'That's right. We've served together on the parish council for several years. But before you go any further let me tell you you're wasting your time. I don't tittle-tattle about my friends and colleagues to the media.'

'Very noble, I'm sure,' said Bryden. 'But that's not what I want. I'd like you to pass a message on to him.'

'Why can't you do it yourself?'

'Because the Major's not answering his phone.'

'I'm not surprised. For some reason he detests the press.'

Bryden bared his teeth. 'Those with something to hide usually do.' He took a card from his pocket and offered it. Greg didn't take the card but regarded it suspiciously. 'What's this?'

'My card. It's got my mobile number on it. The message for Roberts is on the back.'

'I told you, you're wasting your time.'

Maynard started to walk off. Bryden grabbed his arm again. 'It's in his interests, I assure you. He won't thank you if you fail to pass on my message.'

Maynard jerked Bryden's hand away and turned to go, but Bryden again urged the card on him.

Greg stopped and considered. Supposing it really was important? He took the card out of Bryden's hand, turned it over and silently read the message. Afterwards, he looked perplexed.

'Don't worry,' said Bryden. 'He'll know what it means. Just make sure he gets it.'

****

'So, what shall I tell the Major's daughter?'

Dylan forked some sausage and mash into his mouth and stared expectantly around the kitchen table. Sharing supper with him were Zoe, Toni, Mona, Khaled and Sheldon. Sheldon looked quite recovered. The bump on his head had greatly diminished. Dylan had been explaining to them all the reason for Barbara Kellingford's call.

Before anyone could reply, the telephone in the hall rang.

'That's probably her again,' said Zoe. 'Putting the pressure on!'

Dylan frowned and put down his knife and fork. 'I'll get it.'

It wasn't Barbara Kellingford but Sharon Makepiece. He could tell from her first few words that she was greatly agitated.

'Dylan? I've been thinking about Sheldon and Howard Roberts. Louise has told me all about it. I'm sorry, I know you've gone out of your way to help us but I can't let Louise be exposed to such violence. If that's going to happen I don't think I should let her come back to the rectory.'

Dylan wasn't surprised. He'd already learnt from Zoe that Sharon was greatly upset by what had happened and probably wouldn't be allowing Louise to return.

He said, 'Louise wasn't exposed to any violence. She was in the encouragement room doing her maths when all the unpleasantness was going on.'

'I know. But don't you see? She was there when it happened. She heard all the swearing and then the others filled in the gaps for her. I've been horrified by what she's told me.'

Dylan found himself wondering if Louise, with her flair for the histrionic, had overdramatised her description of the events. 'Is Louise saying she didn't feel safe and doesn't want to come here anymore?'

'No. Not at all. In fact, she doesn't seem all that bothered by what happened. But I am. I left her in your care because I thought she'd be safe. and I thought you'd look after her. And now this has happened.'

As Sharon continued airing her concerns Dylan automatically began to apply the "Four Stage Breathing" technique he'd learned as a child from the elderly Taoist in the commune. He immediately felt calmer. 'Sharon, I can assure you that we were looking after Louise. But none of us expected Howard to behave as he did. It surprised all of us. You do know he attacked Sheldon first, don't you?'

'Yes. It's not like him at all. He's normally such a reasonable man. He must have been provoked beyond endurance.'

'Not intentionally by us. He was already upset because of his daughter's marriage problems and the media circus camped outside his house. Then he came over here, saw the way we'd transformed the gardens and flipped.'

'That's understandable. I've seen the rear garden and it looks like a bomb's hit it. Magnificent Britain is Howard's life. He must have been devastated.'

'Yes, but that doesn't justify him beating people around the head with his stick.'

'I didn't suggest it did.'

Realising that he was becoming drawn into an increasing conflict with her, Dylan paused. Seeking to elicit her sympathy, he said, 'You know he's been charged with assaulting Sheldon?'

'That's terrible. Poor Howard. I feel so sorry for him.'

All her sympathy seemed to be with the Major. Dylan began to grow annoyed. 'Yes, it was all very nasty,' he went on. 'He hit Sheldon so hard it knocked him to the ground. He had to be taken to hospital to be checked over.'

'Poor boy. Is he all right?'

Her reply mollified Dylan somewhat. 'He's a little shaken but otherwise fine.'

'Has he been charged with assaulting the Major?'

'I'm sorry, I can't discuss that with you. It's confidential. Sheldon's one of our clients.'

There was a long pause. Finally, Sharon said, 'If only I knew what to do.'

Years of working with people in situations in which they'd revealed to him the most vulnerable, secretive and complicated aspects of themselves had made Dylan acutely sensitive to subtle nuances of vocal tone. Something ineffable in Sharon's voice told him she hadn't called just to discuss Louise. She was clearly deeply conflicted about something else. His perception was entirely accurate. The reasons for Sharon's call were complex. After Louise had gone to her "Oliver" rehearsal, Sharon had sat alone paralysed by indecisiveness. She'd been horrified at Louise's account of the violence that had occurred and was quite naturally concerned for her daughter's welfare. The teenagers at the inclusion unit, she decided, were obviously not normal. If they were normal they wouldn't be in the unit. Perhaps they were all unstable and capable of violence. In which case it was her duty to protect Louise from any potential harm, and the best way to do that would be to prevent her going anywhere near the rectory again. However, for the past couple of days Louise had seemed happier than she'd been for ages, and this was almost certainly the effect of the inclusion unit. Louise looked forward to going there and Sharon could easily understand why she wanted to continue until the end of the week. Sharon knew that if she insisted on keeping Louise away from the place it would only antagonise her and embroil them both yet again in more conflict.

All evening Sharon had been receiving texts from Greg demanding to know if Louise had been at the rectory when the violence had occurred, and if she'd witnessed it. Sharon hadn't replied to any of these but was certain that the next time she saw him there'd be an almighty row. He'd only be satisfied if she stopped Louise going to the rectory. Yet, to take such an extreme step would probably sever her connection with Dylan forever, and despite Zoe's obvious jealousy and hostility towards her, this was not at all what she wanted. Besides, if she stopped Louise going to the rectory it would appear ungrateful to the people there who'd done so much for her and her daughter. They were the only ones who'd been prepared help them out when no-one else, including Louise's father, had given a damn. And of all the people in the unit, Dylan had helped them the most. He really seemed to care. The more Sharon thought about it, she was persuaded that the most sensible course would be to stand up to Louise and refuse to allow her to return to the rectory for her own good. Yet the girl was so wilful and stubborn. Sharon dreaded how she would react. And where else could she take Louise at such short notice that would make her as happy as she was at the rectory?

And so Sharon had sat in her cottage deliberating and brooding resentfully about the way her life, which just a few hours ago seemed to have been going marvellously, was now transformed and ruined by other people's acts of senseless violence. And then, because essentially she was a positive person, it had occurred to her that she could either give in and be brought low by this or she could refuse to be daunted and rise above it. That's when she'd decided to ring the rectory to see if Dylan had returned from the police station with Sheldon. She felt the need to talk to him, hear once again the sound of his voice. She wouldn't be able to explain to him the real reasons for her dilemma, but she had a kind of blind faith in his capacity to resolve matters of the human heart and a feeling that just by talking to him her problems would be resolved. And, who knows, perhaps he might suggest going to The Woldsman for a drink as he usually did, and then she could tell him about her triumphant sale of the factory, and he might be persuaded to come round and drink a glass or two of champagne with her. It was worth the risk, wasn't it?

Dylan, of course, was unaware of the nature of Sharon's dilemma, but he had his own reasons for not wanting the fracas between Sheldon and Howard to affect his relations with her. He sincerely believed that it was in Louise's interests for her to be looked after by the inclusion unit while she was excluded from school. Yet he was honest enough to acknowledge that his main motive for desiring this was his irresistible attraction to Louise's mother and his need to maintain frequent contact with her. Somehow he had to persuade Sharon to keep bringing Louise back to the rectory, but if he was to do this, Sharon needed to be reassured that the girl would be safe.

He said, 'Look Sharon, I'm absolutely certain that the ugly incident with Howard Roberts won't be repeated. There's no reason at all for him to come back here again.'

'But it still puts me in a difficult position. I know Howard quite well. If I continue to bring Louise to the rectory he might think I'm being disloyal to him.'

'Frankly, I don't think he was even aware that Louise was here.'

Sharon was being disingenuous. Greg, not Howard, was really her main concern. Tempted as she was to allow Louise to return to the rectory, she had no wish to go into battle with Greg over the issue. There was no way she could explain that to Dylan.

Dylan said, 'But if Louise doesn't come here, where will she go?'

'I don't know. There isn't anywhere else.'

She sounded almost pleased to admit this. Encouraged, he said, 'If Howard knew that, I'm sure he wouldn't think you were being disloyal. Simply expedient.'

'That's possibly true. But there's another reason I'm not sure I ought to bring her back.'

'Oh?'

'I don't think I'm up to running the gauntlet of all those reporters again. It was harrowing.'

Again, Dylan was reassuring. 'The last time I looked there were far fewer of them hanging around. I'm sure that by tomorrow it'll all have blown over and they'll be gone.'

'I hope so.' She described being intimidated by the media crowd when she'd arrived to collect Louise.

He expressed his sympathy, and said, 'If you get here early enough you'll probably avoid them.'

He sensed he was winning her round and to encourage her, went on, 'You know, it would be a great shame if Louise stopped coming here. She's made such progress at confronting her problems.'

'What problems?' Sharon demanded, sharply.

He remembered how protective she was about her privacy. Had he gone too far? Quickly, he said, 'The problems she has with managing her anger. We've been unpicking the events that led to her exclusion, and the next step is for her to learn some techniques that'll help her avoid getting into more trouble.'

Sharon was encouraged by this. At the same time she was concerned that Dylan was probing Louise's inner conflicts. She didn't like the sound of that. God knows where it might lead. She said, 'Perhaps she should come back tomorrow then. I'll think about it. If that's all right.'

'I think it would be in her best interests, Sharon. Particularly if she is keen to come back. Your concern is natural but I promise you she'll be perfectly safe.'

'Can I think about it? And let you know?'

'Certainly. You might ask Louise what she wants to do, too. Sometimes you have to encourage people to make their own decisions.'

Sharon laughed. 'Really? If only it were that easy.'

'Why? Is there a particular decision you're having problems with?'

Sensing danger, Sharon said, 'No. I was just talking generally.'

Dylan decided not to push it. 'You know, Sharon, I'd really hate it if this horrible incident was to come between us.'

His choice of words surprised her. 'So would I,' she said. 'It shouldn't though, should it?'

'No. Not at all.'

Wasn't it time he asked her to go for a drink? Perhaps he wasn't going to? Not surprising, when she'd refused him so often. If only she could have explained why! She told him about her extraordinarily successful day and how disappointingly it had ended. She was just plucking up courage to ask him to come and have a glass of champagne when her opportunity was lost, destroyed by loud knocking at her front door. Her heart jumped as she immediately assumed it must be Greg.

'I've got to go,' she said. 'Someone's at the door.'

It occurred to Dylan that this was just an excuse because she thought he was going to ask her out for a drink again. No way. He'd been rejected too often. 'Yes, I've got to go too,' he said. 'I was in the middle of dinner when you called.'

He told her that he'd expect to see her and Louise early in the morning and if they didn't appear he'd understand why. Then he ended the call.

****

When Dylan returned to the kitchen, his thoughts still full of Sharon, he sensed there was a bad atmosphere brewing around the table: everyone had fallen silent.

Toni had thoughtfully placed Dylan's meal on the Aga's hot plate to keep warm in his absence. He thanked her, retrieved it and sat down to eat.

'That was Sharon,' Dylan said. Briefly he described the nature of his conversation with her.

'Sounds as though her sympathy's all with Roberts,' said Zoe.

Dylan swallowed a mouthful and said, 'That's understandable. She's known him for a very long time. She says his violence was totally uncharacteristic.'

'Not for the military,' said Zoe.

'That's right, you've got it,' said Eric. He'd recently joined them in the kitchen and was sitting on one of its work surfaces.

Dylan said, 'Fortunately, I think I've persuaded her that Louise will be perfectly safe here.'

'Why fortunately?' said Eric.

Dylan regarded him with some irritation. 'Because it's in Louise's interests, of course,'

Eric, Toni and Zoe exchanged brief looks. This didn't escape Dylan who knew that behind his back the three of them joked about his thing for Sharon.

Zoe said, 'If Sharon has concerns about Louise's safety, she should keep her away.'

'I agree,' said Toni.

'Look, I'm the team leader and as far as I'm concerned if Sharon wants to bring Louise back tomorrow, she can.' Dylan took a sip of water. 'Anyway, what shall we do about Barbara Kellingford?'

'We've been discussing that while you were deeply absorbed on the phone,' said Zoe.

'And?'

'I'm against it,' said Toni. 'We could be accused of conspiring to pervert the course of justice.'

'You haven't explained why you think that is,' said Eric.

'Oh, come on,' said Toni. 'She's trying to get us to drop the charges. How do we know the Major didn't put her up to it?'

'We certainly have to be careful,' said Dylan. 'Particularly now Sheldon's accepted a police caution.'

'Sheldon's against it too,' said Zoe. 'And whatever we think, it's really down to him. He was the one who was attacked.'

Dylan said, 'So you're against it, Sheldon?'

'Yeah.'

'Why?'

'I want respect.'

'I understand that you're angry but sometimes vengeance isn't the best response,' said Zoe.

Sheldon shrugged indifferently.

Dylan held Zoe in a steady gaze. 'You're not against it, then? You think we should go for some kind of reconciliation?'

'I don't know. Part of me thinks that Major Roberts' daughter is just trying to get her dad out of a hole.'

'But?'

'I think the discussion's academic in one sense because the police have charged him, and that's the end of it as far as we're concerned. But I do think there's scope for building bridges with the Major. Maybe we could invite him over here to meet us so he could get to know what we're really about. Maybe we could engage him in some therapy. He might benefit from it if he's only being treated with anti-depressants.'

The truth was, having followed the Kellingford scandal on TV, and seen the way the reporters had laid siege to Rooks Nest, Zoe was feeling rather sorry for Barbara. She might be a Tory but it was awfully bad luck for her to have such a rat of a husband, and have the situation made even worse by a deranged and violent father. The man needed help.

'Yes, but we shouldn't do anything until his case has been heard,' said Toni.

'I agree with Zoe,' said Eric. 'I don't condone what Roberts did but our changes to the gardens must have been a big shock for him. I mean we've got to live with these people.'

'The Major's our neighbour and he's obviously got a lot of health issues,' said Dylan, 'common humanity demands that we reach out to help him. We can't pass by on the other side.'

'Hang on a minute!' said Toni. 'I'm not happy with the way this is going. This is an inclusion unit. We're not a walk-in art therapy set up. We've got a remit to operate with specific clients. We've already taken on Louise.'

'How about you, Sheldon?' said Dylan. 'I know you're against dropping the charges but how would you feel if the Major spent some time with us?'

'Not happy.'

'No?'

'No way. He should be caged.'

Eric said, 'You know, Sheldon, a lot of people might have said that about you after the things you got up to. Punish him. Don't try and understand him. It's a waste of time. Just punish him.'

'So?'

'That means you wouldn't be here.'

Sheldon said nothing.

'I think that's a rather patronising attitude,' Zoe told Eric. She turned to Sheldon. 'But Eric's right in one respect. The reason you're with us is because people bent over backwards to help you, despite what you'd done. Revenge, whether it's by the state or individuals doesn't solve anything. It only makes things worse.'

'That's right,' said Toni, staring at Sheldon, severely. 'Look at the police: they could have charged you, but instead they offered you a caution because they didn't want to see you go to gaol.'

'Now, I think that's a bit simplistic,' said Zoe.

Sheldon looked thoughtful. 'I still think he should pay. He didn't show me no respect.' Looking directly at Toni, he said, 'If I'd hit the Major first with a big stick, them cops wouldn't have offered me no caution. They'd have sent me to a young offenders'.'

Dylan set his knife and fork down on his empty plate. 'OK,' he said. 'I'll get back to Mrs Kellingford and tell her there's nothing we can do for her.'

****

When Sharon opened her front door she had a shock: the person standing in the open doorway wasn't Greg, but his wife.

'I just thought I'd pop round and check that everything's all right,' said Pam, smiling.

Sharon suspected that this wasn't just a polite enquiry. 'Why?' she said. 'Shouldn't it be?'

'Well, you know. After what happened to poor Major Roberts at the rectory today.'

'Oh, I see.'

Sharon composed herself, invited Pam inside, and closed the front door.

'Did you know, he's been charged with assault even though he was only defending himself?' Pam said, as they moved into the sitting room.

Sharon was struggling to understand the purpose of Pam's visit. 'Really? Major Roberts has been charged?'

'Charged with actual bodily harm. He told Greg himself. He's pleading not guilty, of course.'

What does she want? Sharon wondered, as she as took the sofa and Pam eased herself into a chintzy armchair.

'Is Louise all right?' asked Pam.

'Yes. She's at rehearsal. Is Jade all right?'

'Oh yes, fine. She's at the rehearsal too. But is Louise all right? It must have been a terrible thing for her to see.'

'What do you mean?'

'The attack on Major Roberts by those yobs at the rectory. Louise was there when it happened, wasn't she?'

'Yes, but she didn't see anything. It happened in the garden. Louise was inside the house doing her school work.'

Pam looked disappointed.

Sharon went on, 'And, as I understand it, Major Roberts lashed out first. He lost his temper and cracked one of the kids over the head with his stick. The boy had to go to hospital.'

Pam smiled presumptuously. 'You won't be letting Louise go back there though, will you?'

Now Sharon understood why Pam had come to see her. Masking her resentment, she said, 'Why not? She's just got settled.'

'Yes. But it's not safe. They're not decent people like us. I'm sorry, but I have to say this to you, Sharon. How could you let Louise get mixed up with all those low lives?'

'Louise is very happy there.'

Pam pulled a face. 'Oh come on, Sharon. You can't let Louise go back to a place like that. Greg's very upset. He's heard from Major Roberts exactly what happened and it sounds awful. Howard was trying to defend himself and was punched in the face by one of those yobs. That's why he hit him with his stick.'

'Has Greg sent you round?'

'Greg? No. Of course he hasn't. But he's concerned. Just as I am. Greg said he sent you a text about the parish council meeting and you didn't reply. So I thought I'd pop round and see if everything was all right.'

Sharon said, 'Oh, I see. Thanks for your concern. Tell Greg I'm sorry I didn't reply. I couldn't face another meeting. I've had a very exhausting day.' She treated Pam to a smug smile and added, 'Profitable though.'

Sharon spent some time telling Pam about the sale of the mothballed factory. Knowing how avaricious and impressed by large sums of money Pam was, Sharon mentioned several times that she'd sold it for a huge price and would be receiving a substantial commission.

Pam pointedly ignored Sharon's boasts. 'I suppose Greg and I both feel a bit guilty about Louise's exclusion,' she said. 'I mean, it was six of one and half a dozen of the other but poor Louise was the only one who got excluded.'

'Yes. Mrs Henshall treated Louise very unfairly.'

'If they apologise and promise to be nice to each other, perhaps Mrs Henshall will let Louise come back to school?'

'No, she won't do that,' Sharon said, decisively. 'Mrs Henshall's adamant that Louise must be excluded for the whole of the week.'

'Anyway, all this nonsense must end. We must get the girls to make it up somehow.'

'Is it nonsense? I don't think it is. I think Jade's bullying Louise.'

'Jade? Oh no, Sharon, I don't think so.'

'She keeps tormenting her. She keeps taunting her about not having a father.'

Pam shook her head. 'I've talked to Jade about that and she denies it. She says it's Louise who's bullying her.' Observing Sharon's incredulous look, Pam continued emphatically, 'Yes. Louise is the bully. I wasn't going to mention this but, apparently, she keeps calling Greg and me slags. It makes Jade very upset.'

'Jade's jealous because Louise got the part of Nancy in "Oliver". That's why she bullies her.'

'No. I don't believe that.'

'That's what Louise says.'

Uncharacteristically, Pam seemed lost for words. 'Oh well, whatever's going on we must get to the bottom of it and sort it out.'

Sharon said, 'Anyway, it won't be a problem after this week. Once they've left the school.'

'They might be in the same class at Luffield.'

'Lou's not going to Luffield. I'm arranging for her to go to the High School in Sandleton.'

'Really?'

'Yes. Better for all concerned.'

There was a long pause. Sharon was sure Pam was dying to ask her who Louise's father was. Just like everyone else in the village. I'd love to see your face if I told you the truth, she thought.

Pam said, 'You're not really going to let Louise go back to the rectory, are you?'

'Why not? She's nowhere else to go.'

Pam sighed regrettably. 'I'd offer to look after Louise myself if I didn't have to work. I do know a couple of people who work part time, though. One in the mornings and one in the afternoons. I'm sure that between them they'd be willing to look after Louise for the next couple of days. Would you like me to ask?'

Well intentioned as it was, Sharon was horrified by Pam's suggestion. It would be humiliating for Louise to be pushed from pillar to post in that way. She suspected Greg's hand in it somewhere. 'Thank you very much for your offer but I couldn't possibly impose Louise on complete strangers.'

'Margaret and Joan aren't strangers. I've known them for years. They're lovely people. If I had to choose between Margaret and Joan and the rectory, I know who I'd choose. Margaret and Joan every time.'

Sharon was beginning to get seriously annoyed. She resented Pam's intrusion into her personal and domestic life and her deeply patronising attitude. What right had Pam to tell her what was best for her daughter?

Pam had read Sharon's expression. 'I know you think I'm interfering. But I'm only trying to help. I know how difficult life is for single mothers.'

This really was too much. What the hell did Pam know about single mothers? But before Sharon could reply there was a knock at the front door. Pam had made Sharon so angry she didn't stop to consider who it might be. She marched straight across to the door and wrenched it open.

She was shocked to find Greg on the doorstep, staring at her resentfully. 'Why didn't you come to the meeting? Didn't you get my text?'

His tone was too intimate: too nakedly personal. She couldn't afford to let him go on in this vein and compromise both of them. She had to let him know that his wife was round the corner, sitting on the sofa. 'Funnily enough, I was just telling Pam what an exhausting day I'd had, and couldn't face another meeting.' She stepped aside, allowing Greg to enter and then closed the door behind him.

Clearly the last person Greg expected to find in Sharon's sitting room was his own wife. His face registered complete astonishment. However, he quickly recovered. Stepping further into the cottage and looking straight at Pam, he said, 'Hello. I didn't expect to find you here.'

Brightly, Pam said, 'I've been trying to persuade Sharon not to send Louise back to the rectory.'

Greg looked at Sharon unsurely. The situation was as embarrassing and uncomfortable for him as it was for her. He returned his gaze to Pam. 'And did you?'

'What?'

'Manage to persuade her?'

'No.'

Sharon needed to change the subject quickly. 'How was the meeting?' she asked Greg.

'More villagers than usual. But I think we all know why. Nothing like a scandal to get people interested. And, of course, they all expected Howard to resign. But you know him. Wouldn't give them the satisfaction. Lots of reporters there, too.'

Greg now embarked on a long and tedious account of what had transpired at the meeting. Pam quickly cut him off. 'Do you find this parish council stuff interesting?' she demanded of Sharon. 'Only it bores the pants off me.'

Sharon laughed. 'Me too. I only go because I'm secretary of Community Watch.'

Looking directly at Sharon, Greg said, 'The mood of the meeting was quite ugly. Lots of people are very, very angry with your friends at the rectory.'

'They're not my friends,' said Sharon. Pointedly, she added, 'But they've all been very kind to me and Louise. They agreed to look after her when no-one else would.'

Greg said, 'Leefdale people feel that Howard has been treated appallingly by those low lives. They've trashed the rectory and beaten him up. Did you know that?'

'I heard what happened and it wasn't like that at all!' Sharon related her own version of the incident and explained that Louise had been doing her maths when the violence had occurred.

Until this point Greg had been about to divulge to Sharon his plans for boycotting the rectory and organising a demonstration outside it for the benefit of the Magnificent Britain judges. Now, he decided that would be unwise. She might be tempted to pass it on to that long streak of piss, Bourne. 'You've obviously only heard their side of it,' he said. 'But I think you should know you'll find yourself very unpopular in the village if you decide to take Louise back to the rectory after all that's happened.'

Sharon's emotions were already combustible: now Greg's words were like a match to tinder. 'I'm going to let Louise be the judge of that,' she said.

'What do you mean?' said Pam.

'I'm going to let her decide.'

'But she's only a kid.'

'If she's happy to go back there, I'll let her.'

'She's not mature enough to make a decision like that,' said Greg.

Sharon thought of all the reasons Louise had given for wanting to return to the rectory: particularly her love of the stimulating artistic atmosphere, the friendliness she'd encountered and the kindness she'd received. All reasons Sharon had rejected as insufficient to justify Louise's return, in view of the lack of safety. But the interference of Greg and Pam in a decision that was a matter for her alone was intolerable. She said, 'Look, today I negotiated a property sale worth nearly a million, so don't tell me I can't decide what's in my daughter's best interests!'

'Come on, Greg,' said Pam, standing up. 'She's obviously not going to listen to reason.'

'Yes. It would be a good idea if both of you left,' said Sharon. 'I've had an exhausting day and I'm very het up.' She shot Greg a dangerous look. 'I might say things I'll regret.' The fear in Greg's eyes told her he understood.

Greg and Pam exchanged a look. 'Yes, we'd better go,' said Greg. 'I've got to give Howard a ring. And I've asked some people to come round for a meeting later.'

Pam was clearly put out. 'Oh no! What tonight?'

Ignoring her, Greg said, 'Goodnight, Sharon. If you think what happened at the rectory today was bad, it's only going to get worse. People are in a very unforgiving mood. Dylan Bourne and his friends could cost us the gold medal, and we're not going to let them get away with it. I wouldn't let a daughter of mine go back there. It might not be safe.'

Before Sharon could reply, Greg had opened the front door and Pam was following him out on to the street.

CHAPTER THIRTY SEVEN

Mark and Jessica's determination to stay awake until their father arrived was strong but their need for sleep was stronger, and by ten o'clock both of them had succumbed and were fast asleep on the sofa. Howard helped Barbara carry the children up to their bedrooms and left her to get them ready for bed.

When Barbara returned to the sitting room, Howard was nursing a glass of scotch and regaling Isobel about the planned demonstration outside The Old Rectory. When he'd finished, Isobel said, 'I don't think that's a good idea at all. It'll only draw the judges' attention to the appalling state of the rectory. Why not just hurry them past it?'

'Because the whole idea is to elicit the judges' sympathy. Then they won't penalize us.'

Isobel turned to Barbara, 'Did they get off again all right?'

'Yes. Fast asleep in seconds.'

'Oh, I think you've had a text.'

Barbara's expression became concerned. She went across to her handbag, took out her blue mobile and checked it. Sure enough, the message symbol was on the display. The text was from Peter. She read it quickly.

'Oh no,' she said. 'Peter's been delayed. He won't be arriving until at least one.'

Isobel and Howard had already agreed that it would be sensitive and considerate if neither of them were present at Barbara's reconciliation with Peter. At least, this was the ostensibly unselfish reason they'd decided to use as a pretext to avoid meeting him until the last possible moment. The thought of welcoming him into their home again after what he'd done filled them with anguish.

Isobel stood up and said, 'Well, if you don't mind, daddy and I will go to bed. Anyway, I'm sure you won't want us around when Peter arrives. You'll want time on your own together to heal the breach.'

This was the moment Barbara had been dreading. All evening her stomach had been churning as she'd prepared to tell her parents that they were expected to join her and the children at Peter's side when he read out his statement to the media. She knew they'd be furious that she hadn't even consulted them, let alone sought their permission. There would be a terrible scene, she was sure, but better to get it over and done with now. It would be wrong to tell Peter, when he finally arrived, that he'd have to break it to them personally; and coming from him, it would be for her parents the final straw.

'I appreciate that, mum. You're right. It'll be an ordeal for me. Thank you for being so considerate. You too, dad.'

Howard stood up. 'Well, goodnight. We won't ask you to pass on our love to Peter, if you don't mind. I think you can understand why.'

He went up to Barbara and gave her a long hug. He then kissed her on the cheek and set off for the door.

'No, please don't go yet. There's something I have to tell you.'

They both stared at her curiously.

There was no easy way to say what she had to tell them except to come out with it at once. 'I've done something I shouldn't. I've promised Peter and Steve Hawkins that when Peter makes his statement to the press tomorrow we'll all be standing alongside him. Not just me and the children but you two as well.'

Barbara didn't appreciate the significance of the look that passed between her parents. They were both acknowledging the extreme danger that Barbara's action had placed Howard in.

'I don't understand,' said Isobel. 'You said that Peter wanted you and the children at his side when he makes his statement. You didn't mention anything about us being there too.'

'That's because I told you only half the truth. Steve Hawkins insisted Peter wouldn't make the statement at all unless you and dad were standing alongside him. So I had to agree to it.'

'But why? Why do we have to be there too?' Isobel cried.

'To show that you forgive him. To show that we're all reconciled. Steve said it was absolutely vital for us all to be there if Peter's career was to be saved.'

Howard said, 'So Peter expects us to be there when he humiliates himself in front of all those reporters? Well, he can go and whistle. The very idea of doing that on national television with all those people baying at us is unthinkable.'

Barbara's look was beseeching. 'Please, please, you must. If we can draw a line under all this, it will all go away. I just want this nightmare to end.'

Isobel knew that Barbara was asking for a very simple thing, and it would appear totally unreasonable to refuse when her daughter's happiness was at stake. Yet, refuse she must. Isobel had always known the danger she and Howard faced because of his connection to the killings of the Fermanagh Four. It was why, over the years, they'd been forced to move from one house to another and live in different parts of the country. Why they'd always been required to keep a low profile, and when necessary disappear without warning, cut themselves off socially and sever ties with all their friends.

As more and more years passed since "the incident", Howard had become confident that his connection to the killings, or even the fact that he'd served in Northern Ireland, would never be discovered. And so, he and Isobel had begun to think themselves secure. So secure, that when they'd moved to Leefdale after their many previous moves, Howard had been emboldened to take up a life of voluntary public service: first as a parish councillor and then as the village's principal organiser of Magnificent Britain. Initially, fearing the enormous danger even moderate amounts of local publicity might expose him to, Isobel had opposed Howard's decision. Every time he appeared in public she was convinced that the past would catch up with him and they'd have to move to a new home and start their lives all over again. On the rare occasions Howard's name and photograph had appeared in the local papers or on the Magnificent Britain website, Isobel had trembled for his safety. For her own safety too. Yet, she'd been prepared to risk it, to allow some degree of normality to return to their lives. And now her daughter and son-in-law had unwittingly propelled Howard into the national spotlight. If the IRA had the slightest inkling of the Major Howard Roberts they were looking for, Howard's appearance on the television news had already made him a marked man. She prayed that it had gone unnoticed. But Barbara's rash promise would put paid to all that. For Howard to stand alongside a disgraced MP on national television tomorrow, without appropriate security, could make him an easy target for those who sought revenge and now knew where to find him. It really was too bad. Just as she and Howard had at last settled into something resembling an orderly life, they'd have to up sticks and move on again. All because of the publicity her daughter's philandering husband had exposed them to. It was unbearable. Isobel was filled with anger: more so, because she couldn't tell Barbara the reason for it.

'I'm furious with you, Barbara,' Isobel cried out. 'You had absolutely no right to tell Steve Hawkins we'd appear with Peter tomorrow. It's so humiliating. Everyone will be laughing at us. We'll be humiliating ourselves on our own doorstep.'

'If you don't agree to it, the press will say you haven't forgiven him.'

'But that's it,' said Howard. 'We don't forgive him. We can never forgive him.'

'But mum, you said you would forgive him, for my sake.'

'I've changed my mind.'

'But if you refuse to stand with us, Peter may not make his statement. He may go straight back to London. Think what that'll do to Mark and Jessica.'

'Don't put pressure on your mother.'

Barbara rounded on Howard. 'Well, you don't exactly help in that respect, do you? Did you think hitting that poor boy with your stick would be helpful? Did you think being charged with assault was just what we needed at this moment?'

'Yes,' said Howard. 'But at least I can keep my trousers on for more than five minutes, which is more than can be said for that sainted bloody husband of yours.'

'Howard,' said Isobel, rebuking him. 'Please, please. I can't bear any more of this unpleasantness.'

'Then stop refusing me,' Barbara said, coldly.

Howard shouted, 'We're not going to do it, Barbara, and that's that!'

At that moment they all paused, aware that upstairs in Howard's study the telephone was ringing.

'Quickly Howard, answer it before it wakes the children,' said Isobel.

Howard's study was in complete darkness. He switched on the light and went straight over to the phone on his desk. As he picked it up he saw that his hand was trembling.

As he'd expected, the call was from Greg. He apologised for ringing so late, and explained that after the council meeting he'd invited a number of people round to discuss arrangements for Friday's planned demonstration outside the rectory. He assured Howard that they'd be well prepared and to expect a sizeable crowd.

'Pam wasn't best pleased to have all those bodies in our sitting room,' he said. 'Particularly as she had to make drinks for them all.'

Greg went on to congratulate Howard on his handling of the parish council meeting and his success at foiling Arthur Meakins' attempted coup.

Howard's irritable and volatile mood was telling him to bring the conversation to an end. He was impatient to get back downstairs and smooth things over between himself and his daughter. Which was why he suddenly said, 'Look Greg, I'd love to talk to you about this but it's been a hell of a day and I'm yearning to get to bed. If you don't mind I'll say goodnight.'

'Of course,' said Greg. 'But before you go, I have a message to pass on to you.'

'Oh? Who from?'

'A reporter called Terry Bryden.'

'Stop right there. I'm not interested in anything that man has to say.'

'I thought that would be your response, but it's a very curious message. It intrigued me.'

'Go on then. What did the bastard want to tell me?'

'Hang on,' said Greg, 'he wrote it on the back of his card.' There was a brief pause at Greg's end. 'Here we are: "Tell Major Roberts I want to talk to him about our mutual friends in Fermanagh".'

A crater suddenly seemed to have appeared in the depths of Howard's stomach. Forcing himself to remain calm, he said, 'I see. You're right. That is very strange.'

'You've no friends in Northern Ireland, have you?'

'No. None.'

'Ever served there?'

'Never.'

'Thought not.'

As casually as possible, Howard asked, 'And was that all he said?'

'No. He said it was in your interests for me to pass the message on and you wouldn't thank me if I failed to do it. Something like that.'

Howard paused, trying to organise his racing thoughts.

'Do you want his mobile number?' said Greg. 'It's on his card.'

With faux insouciance Howard said, 'Certainly not. I've no intention of ringing him. This is just a stunt. As you well know, every reporter in the country would like to talk to me or a member of my family at this moment.'

'You're right. What shall I do with the card?'

'Tear it up.'

As soon as his conversation with Greg was finished Howard sat despondently at his desk with his head in his hands. He'd been puzzled when the messages from Bryden had suddenly started appearing after 4pm. Very few people possessed his private mobile number. Ryecart, the solicitor's clerk, had been the only one in months to have been given it. Surely he hadn't divulged it to Bryden? Just proved you couldn't trust anybody. Naturally, he'd deleted Bryden's messages, and now wished he hadn't. But he'd had no choice except to tell Greg to tear up the card. Couldn't have him knowing that he'd responded to Bryden's message.

Howard's mobile was on his desk, being charged. He picked it up and checked to see if Bryden had left any more messages. Fortunately, he had. Howard listened to all three of them. Each one requested Howard to call Bryden back. He made a careful note of the mobile number and called it. Bryden responded almost immediately.

'Mr Bryden?' said Howard. 'Greg Maynard's just given me your message.'

'Oh, hello, Major. Just a minute.'

From the background noise it sounded as though Bryden was in a pub or a hotel. The Woldsman, perhaps. Howard heard him tell someone that he had to take a call. There was a series of unidentifiable sounds and then, finally, one that sounded like the opening and closing of a door.

When Bryden spoke again, he said, 'Sorry about that but I thought what I had to say to you was best said in the privacy of my room.'

'You needn't have bothered, Mr Bryden. I simply called to tell you that you're wasting your time.'

'If that was true you wouldn't have bothered to call. Come on, admit it. My message has spooked you, hasn't it?'

'Not at all. I rang to tell you I didn't understand a word of it. It makes no sense to me, whatsoever.'

'Don't give me all that crap. I have it on the best authority that you were the officer in charge when the Fermanagh Four were shot. You were the one who ordered the men to be killed.'

The injustice of the accusation outraged Howard, but without admitting his involvement he was powerless to refute it. All he could say was, 'I've never been anywhere near Fermanagh. I've never even served in Northern Ireland.'

'Your neighbour says different.'

'Which neighbour?'

Bryden could have protected his source. But Zoe had threatened to sue. He had no reason to save her arse.

'The gorgeous redhead who lives just across the road from you.'

So that's how he knew! How stupid he'd been. What had possessed him to divulge his secret to virtual strangers? But he knew very well why, and he cursed himself like so many before who've ruined themselves through petty vindictiveness. He said, 'She's mistaken and so are you.'

But Bryden knew that Howard was lying. He had it on impeccable authority that Captain Howard Roberts and Major Howard Roberts were the same man.

'Listen Howard,' said Bryden. 'I'm only going to say this once. A veteran Northern Ireland reporter has told me that in the nineteen eighties a number of Provisionals captured two British soldiers from your regiment. Under interrogation, they confessed to being in the same regiment that killed the Fermanagh Four. They also said that the name of the officer who was in charge of the platoon that killed the four men that day was a Captain Howard Roberts. And guess what? My colleague found that a Captain Howard Roberts from your regiment was promoted to Major soon after the Fermanagh Four were murdered.'

'Howard Roberts is a very common name. There are hundreds of us in the British Army.'

'Bollocks!'

'Your Northern Ireland reporter has obviously been making things up.'

'Oh no. He got all his information from an informer. A double agent. Interestingly, this informer was gunned down in the street in Islington just a few days after passing on his information about you. The police said he was the victim of an IRA internal feud. His killers were never found.'

Howard involuntarily shuddered. Everything Bryden was saying was entirely credible. He said, 'Is there a point to this fantasy?'

'There certainly is, old son,' said Bryden. 'If you're prepared to give us your side of the Peter Kellingford story and persuade your daughter to give us an interview, we'll keep your connection to Northern Ireland and the Fermanagh Four out of The Source. But if you refuse to play ball, your identity and your part in the killings will be spread all over our pages. I'm sure you're aware that the van driver who witnessed the killings has been in hiding ever since. He says if he saw the officer again who opened fire that day he'd definitely be able to identify him, so I'd be very afraid if I were you. Lots of people in Northern Ireland read The Source, you know.'

Howard recalled the images of himself leaving The Old Rectory which had been shown on TV earlier. You're too late, my friend, the damage has already been done, he thought. 'If all this was true, why would I expose myself to press and television reporters? It may have escaped your notice but I was all over the television news tonight.'

This was something which hadn't occurred to Bryden. He took a long time to reply. 'I don't know. Maybe you got careless, or maybe you think you're invulnerable or that everyone's forgotten.'

Howard knew that the only way out of the mess he'd created for him and Isobel was for them to disappear again: perhaps this time even change their name, something which had been unnecessary so far. But Bryden had him by the balls. If he printed everything he knew in The Source, it would make it that much harder to achieve a new incarnation. Obviously, it was the interview with Barbara that Bryden wanted most. Howard knew he was being blackmailed to secure that. He said, 'Your story about me is so absurd that if a word of it appears in print I won't hesitate to sue for libel. However, that doesn't mean I have no wish to help you. In the messages you left, you offered a hundred thousand for my daughter's story. Does that still stand?'

Bryden saw exactly what Roberts was doing. 'Oh yes. And we'll bung you fifty thousand for your story too. No-one in our paper's management need know the real reason you came across. They'll assume it was for the cash. So your secret will remain completely safe.'

Until the next time, thought Howard. He said, 'Obviously I'll have to discuss this with my daughter. It might take some time to convince her.'

'That should be an interesting conversation,' said Bryden. 'Wish I was a fly on the wall.'

'I'll call you again tomorrow,' said Howard.

'Oh no. You've got until midnight. If I don't hear from you by then, the story about you and the Fermanagh Four that's sitting in my computer will be emailed to my editor. He's all ready to publish it in the next edition. I've only got to give him the go-ahead.'

'If you do that you'll be signing your own death warrant,' said Howard. 'I strongly advise you not even to contemplate it.'

'What you gonna do? Sue me?' sneered Bryden.

'I'll call you as soon as I've spoken to my daughter,' said Howard. He ended the call and without pausing even to think he placed his mobile on the desk, reached for the landline and dialled a number. His call was answered almost immediately and he asked again to speak to Secateurs. This was an agreed code-name. It wasn't assigned to any specific agent but was responded to by anyone on shift charged with protecting Howard's interests as a vulnerable former officer in the armed services.

'Secateurs speaking.'

Howard recognized the woman's voice. Agents' names were never revealed so he'd christened her Eileen, simply because she sounded like an Eileen he'd once known. He knew that details of his last communication with Secateurs were already showing on Eileen's computer screen. She'd therefore be aware of his unease about the press and TV exposure he'd recklessly brought upon himself, and also of his request for appropriate action.

Howard said, 'The situation's gone to condition red.' He then related to Eileen everything Bryden had used to threaten him.

****

As Howard approached the door of the sitting room he could hear Isobel talking loudly. He paused before entering and stood in the hall, listening. Isobel was still berating Barbara for the promises she'd made to Hawkins without permission.

Isobel stopped talking abruptly when Howard came into the room. She looked up at him and said, 'You've been a long time. Who was it?'

'Just Greg. He wanted to talk about the meeting.' Howard turned to his daughter and said, casually, 'Oh Barbara, I'm afraid the telephone may have woken the children. As I passed their room I heard voices. I think you ought to check they're all right.'

Barbara sighed heavily, stood up and left the room. As soon as she'd gone Howard looked at Isobel and said, 'We're in real trouble.' Quickly he gave her a salient account of Bryden's blackmail attempt and of his own subsequent conversation with Secateurs. Isobel listened gravely as he recounted the advice he'd received, and explained his own plan for dealing with the situation.

'I knew we'd have to move on,' said Isobel, bleakly. 'As soon as I saw you on the news, I knew it.'

'Yes.'

'If only you'd taken those bloody tablets,' she snapped.

'I know.'

'You really are the limit, Howard.' Nevertheless, she agreed to the plan he proposed even though she was opposed to it heart and soul.

'Bryden has left us no choice,' Howard said.

Hearing footsteps descending the stairs, they fell silent.

'They were both fast asleep when I got there,' Barbara said, entering the room. She sat down on the sofa and went on, 'I wish I could change your minds about standing shoulder to shoulder with Peter tomorrow. It's very important not just that Peter comes back to us but that everyone sees he's been completely forgiven by the whole family. I know it's a difficult thing for both of you to do after all that's happened, but please, please, change your mind. You wouldn't be doing it for me and Peter, but for Mark and Jessica.'

'Actually, your mother and I have talked things over,' said Howard, 'and we've decided we will join you tomorrow after all.'

The tension in Barbara's face vanished and was replaced by a beaming smile of gratitude. Simultaneously, her eyes filled with tears. 'Thank you. Oh, thank you!' She stood up and came over to Howard and embraced and kissed him. Then she went to the sofa, bent over her mother and hugged her too.

'We're only doing it for you and the children,' said Howard.

Barbara was wiping away her tears with the knuckles of one hand. It touched Howard deeply to see the extent of his daughter's gratitude, even though it made it harder for him to say what he knew had to be said next. He exchanged a look with Isobel, and then ploughed on. 'But in return, we'd like you to do something.'

Barbara stopped drying her eyes. Her stare was a mixture of surprise and curiosity, 'Oh?'

'We'd like you to be interviewed by Terry Bryden.'

'What?' Now her face was all incredulity.

'We want you to give Bryden the interview he's been begging for. I'll be giving him one too.'

Barbara stood in the centre of the room, her mouth slightly open, shocked into silence. Finally, she said, 'I heard you the first time but it's so incredible, I can't believe it. Why? Why do you want me to do that?'

'I'm afraid I can't tell you.'

'You can't tell me?'

'No.'

'But why?'

'Because I can't. You'll just have to trust me.'

Barbara's eyes narrowed. 'So it wasn't for me or the children you agreed to stand with us tomorrow. It was to get me to do an interview with Bryden?'

'No, that's not true. We'll stand with you even if you refuse. But your mother and I would be very grateful if you'd call Bryden and tell him you're willing to give him an interview.'

'Me? Call him?'

'Yes. I wouldn't ask you if it wasn't vitally important.'

'But I can't. I've promised Steve Hawkins I won't speak to the press.'

'You won't have to. Just call Bryden and tell him you will. Please Barbara, just do it for us.'

Now Barbara looked thoroughly bewildered. 'I'm sorry dad, you've completely lost me.'

Isobel cried out, 'Oh, for God's sake Howard, tell her the truth. I'm sick of all these lies!'

Barbara looked from one to the other. 'What truth?'

Howard shot Isobel a venomous glance. 'You won't be satisfied until you've dragged it out of me, will you?' He sighed and sank into the nearest armchair.

'All right. I'll tell you. I was a long time upstairs because I was on the phone to Bryden. He sent a message via Greg. Bryden's found out that I served in Northern Ireland.'

Barbara said nothing. Her father's revelation, although a surprise, provided no clarity. She was still confused. She said, 'I didn't know you served there. You never said.'

'No. We kept if from you, to protect you. That's why I want you to keep it secret.'

'You don't want me to tell anyone?'

'No.'

'Not even Peter?'

'No. Not even Peter.'

'All right. When were you there?'

'In the late 1970s and the early 80s.'

Barbara's thoughts were roiling. The 1970s and 80s. So that was why she'd been sent to all those expensive boarding schools that made her so unhappy. That's why her mother had always been vague about where daddy had been posted. She said, 'I wondered why mummy never went with you, as she usually did.'

'It was far too dangerous for either of you. We lived virtually under conditions of siege. We couldn't risk the lives of our loved ones.'

'But why is your service in Northern Ireland of interest to Bryden? And why do I have to give him an interview?'

Howard hesitated.

'Tell her,' said Isobel.

'When I was in the province I made a terrible mistake and a number of innocent men died.'

'You can't be completely certain they were innocent,' said Isobel, calmly.

'I'm bloody sure they were!'

Howard paused, aware that a harshness had entered his voice which had to be eradicated. In a more propitiatory tone, he said to Barbara, 'All you need to know is that it was an accident. But there are still some very dangerous people around who've never forgiven the British for it, and if they knew I'd been involved they might seek me out and kill me. Kill all of us.'

'God!' said Barbara.

'That's why we were so unwilling to stand next to you and Peter tomorrow in front of all those press and TV people.'

'But now you're willing to do it. I don't understand.'

'It doesn't matter now, because we're moving on.'

'Moving on?'

'Leaving Leefdale. It's what we always do when the past rears its head in any way. Haven't you ever wondered why we moved house so many times?'

'No. I just thought you were restless spirits.'

'Huh!' exclaimed Isobel.

'Bryden's blackmailing me,' explained Howard. 'Unless he hears by midnight that you and I agree to give him an interview, it'll be splashed all over The Source that I served in Northern Ireland and I was the officer in command at the time of... of the accident.'

'Bastard,' said Isobel.

Howard and Isobel both looked towards Barbara expectantly. Nobody said anything while Barbara deliberated. After what seemed an age, she said, 'But I can't give Bryden an interview. I told you, I promised Steve Hawkins I wouldn't say a word to the press. Can you imagine what will happen if Peter makes his statement and then people read an interview I've done with Bryden in The Source? I'll seem completely disloyal and it'll undo everything Peter and the Party are trying to do, which is to draw a line under the bloody thing.'

Isobel said, 'She doesn't understand, Howard, you haven't made it clear.' She rounded on Barbara. 'Don't you see, you selfish little fool, unless you agree to be interviewed by Bryden, The Source will reveal that your father was the senior officer present when the Fermanagh Four were shot!'

'Isobel!' cried Howard.

'She's got to know sometime!' Isobel gave Barbara a caustic look. 'If you don't promise Bryden an interview and he publishes his filth, we'll be looking over our shoulders for the rest of our lives. We protected you from all this for years. It's why we sent you to all those boarding schools so you'd be safe. And because after the shootings your father had a nervous breakdown. Every time we thought the IRA were on to us, we had to move on. Why do you think we moved from Cornwall to Shropshire and then to Hampshire and now here? And now, just as we've settled and become established in this beautiful place we have to move on again. And it'll always be like that unless you give that scum Bryden his interview.'

Barbara's lip trembled. 'But if I speak to Bryden it'll destroy all the Party's plans. He'll write all kinds of lies about what I've said. He'll distort everything. I gave Steve Hawkins my word I wouldn't speak to the press.'

Barbara began to sob uncontrollably. Howard went up to her and placed his arms around her shoulders. He stared fondly into her eyes. 'You won't have to give Bryden an interview, darling. And neither will I. We just want him to think we will. I'm stalling him. Playing for time.'

'But you said if we don't give him the interviews he'll publish all that stuff about you and Northern Ireland.'

Isobel said, 'No. You see, Daddy's got friends...'

'No, Isobel. No! She mustn't know any more. It's too dangerous!' He turned back to Barbara and his tone softened. 'I promise you, neither of us will have to give that scumbag an interview. Now will you agree?'

Barbara nodded. 'All right.'

Howard took his mobile out of his trouser pocket, located Bryden's number and called him. The call was answered almost immediately.

'Mr Bryden?'

'Ah, Major. I thought it wouldn't be long before you got back to me.'

Howard said, 'You probably know that Peter Kellingford is making a statement tomorrow at eleven.'

'That's right. Outside your place, we're being told.'

'After Peter's made his statement, Barbara and I will answer all your questions.'

'I need to hear that from Barbara herself, otherwise I'm not spiking my copy.'

'Very well,' said Howard. He passed the phone to Barbara. 'He wants to hear it from you.'

She took the phone. 'Barbara Kellingford speaking.'

'Hello Barbara. Nice to hear your voice. I understand you're happy to talk to us now.'

'I'll talk to you but I wouldn't say I'm happy about it.'

'Never mind. The hundred grand will cheer you up.'

'Where do you want to do the interviews?'

'I thought your dad's place. Rooks Nest. I'll have a photographer with me, by the way.'

Howard nodded agreement.

'Very well. My father will contact you tomorrow to make the arrangements.'

'You do realise what'll happen if you back out, don't you?'

'I've no intention of backing out. Nor has my father.'

'Good. Is your husband there with you?'

'No. He hasn't arrived yet.'

'So he's coming tonight? What time will he be there?'

'I honestly don't know.'

'What's in this statement he's making?'

'I haven't a clue.'

'Come on. You must have some idea.'

'Honestly, I don't. I'm the last to be consulted about such things.'

'Is Peter leaving Clarissa, and coming back to you?'

Barbara looked uncertainly at her father.

Howard shook his head, vigorously.

'That's a question I'll answer fully tomorrow, Mr Bryden, along with all the others. But right now, it's late. I've had a terrible day. My head is splitting and I have two fractious children to put to bed.'

Barbara offered the mobile to Howard. He took it from her and gave her the thumbs up.

Howard said, 'All right, Bryden, you've got all you're going to get from us tonight. I'll tell the police to allow you and your photographer into Rooks Nest immediately after Peter's statement. Now, do I have your absolute assurance that no lies about me and Northern Ireland will be printed in your rag?'

'What do you mean lies? The Source only prints the truth.'

'Do I have your absolute assurance?'

'Sure. That's the deal. Just as long as we get your stories.'

'You will.'

'I don't suppose Kellingford would give us an interview too?'

'Don't push your luck,' said Howard. He ended the call and regarded Barbara and Isobel with satisfaction. Then, at Isobel's insistence, Howard spent the following ten minutes explaining to Barbara why, even though their interviews with Bryden would never take place, nothing about his connection to Northern Ireland or the Fermanagh Four would ever appear in The Source.

****

Barbara rubbed her face with make-up remover, plucked some tissues from the box on the dressing table and briskly wiped off her make up. Then she stood in front of the fitted wardrobe's full length mirror and ran a brush back through her hair. She was pleased to see that the blonde haired woman in her thirties who looked back at her seemed in good spirits. A combination of the wine and Peter's return.

She listened to Peter moving about in the bathroom, making his preparations for bed. She heard him turn on the shower; that could mean one of two things: he was refreshing himself for a night of sex or he was postponing the awful moment when he found himself completely alone with her.

Barbara removed the rest of her clothes and then stood admiring her nakedness in the mirror. She wasn't in bad shape for a woman of her age. She'd kept her body toned by twice weekly visits to the gym. Girls half her age would have been proud of it. And what a good idea to cut her hair short. It had taken years off.

She decided not to put on her nightdress. When he got into bed and discovered she was naked he'd be in no doubt about what she had in mind. She allowed herself to become aroused by the thought of his large, powerful body possessing her, his mouth eager for hers, his tongue deep in her throat. She splayed her hands and slowly pressed them against the softness of her inner thighs and stroked them, gently at first, and then more intensely: she flexed her fingers and traced the tips of them slowly upwards towards the tender, yearning flesh between her legs. With a gasp she yielded, opening herself to the exquisite, probing touch of her fingers; and in the mirror, saw her mouth open too in a wide gape as all sensation focussed upon that single, moist point of delicious pressure.

'Beep, beep!'

In a terror of discovery, she withdrew her hand and looked in all directions for the source of the intrusion.

It was Peter's mobile phone. He'd left it in his jacket on the bed.

Emptied now of all desire, she went over to the jacket and took out the mobile. It was his blue one. She held it in her hand. There was a new message. She was about return it to his jacket pocket but suddenly changed her mind. She quickly reassured herself that he was still showering, then accessed the phone's in-box. It was a text message.

"Is it really awful? C U tomorrow. Me 4 U Luv C"

She stared at the phone numbly, aware only of the significance of her discovery and the lingering odour on her fingers.

She snapped into action. She went over to the door of the en-suite bathroom and listened. The shower was still running. She went back and stood next to his jacket. She began delving through the phone's in-box, looking for saved messages. There were no saved voice messages, but the text messages that she read told her conclusively that Peter had no intention of coming back to her. He and Clarissa were planning to continue their relationship after his reputation as a family man had been restored.

Trembling, she replaced the phone in the inside pocket of his jacket. Then she hastily got into bed.

She heard him turn off the shower and a second or two later the door of the en-suite opened. Peter switched the light off and came into the room. He was naked, towelling himself. The sight of his nude body, once so familiar but unseen for so many days was a shock.

'God, that's better!' he said. He finished drying himself, then threw the towel to the floor.

Her expression told him that something was wrong.

'What's the matter, darling?' he said.

'I don't know. I suppose I'm shocked. I never thought I'd ever have you in my bed again.'

'You're pleased though, aren't you?'

'If it's really over, yes.'

'Darling. trust me. It really is over.'

He bent his body towards her. Their lips came together in a brief, passionless kiss and he joined her in the bed. They switched their bedside lights off. In the darkness she felt him turn on his side and she snuggled up to his back. Despite everything, it was still the greatest pleasure to feel the solidity of his naked body against her. They lay like this for some time, she planning her revenge.

She placed her hand on his thigh and then moved it up caressing and squeezing the fullness between his legs, working on him until she stirred him into firmness beneath her fingers.

'Not a good idea,' he said. 'We'll wake the whole house.'

'No, we won't,' she said. 'I can be really quiet.'
'Well...'
'Go on. I've been looking forward to it.'

She went down under the duvet and kissed his hard, taut flesh and traced her tongue in long, licking movements along its length. He groaned, and she felt him grow even firmer and took him into her mouth.

Suddenly he extricated himself. He rolled on top of her and his head went down between her legs. She felt the bristles of his chin on her inner thighs, and then his moist tongue at the crossroads licking and probing. This was most unusual. Was he hoping that this would satisfy her? Get him off the hook of fucking her? Not that it mattered. She cared nothing for him. He was just a piece of flesh pleasuring her, as functional as her own finger.

She cupped her hands around his head and pressed him to her ever tighter. She closed her legs around him in a vice, suffocating his head between her thighs. She was enjoying his humiliation. He'd always said how much he despised this.

Then, when she was sufficiently aroused she cried out in a hoarse whisper, 'Now, Peter. Now. Fuck me. Fuck me really hard!'

CHAPTER THIRTY EIGHT

'You're early,' said Zoe, as she unlocked the gate of The Old Rectory for Sharon and Louise.

'I wanted to avoid the reporters,' said Sharon.

Zoe swung back the gate and glanced across at Rooks Nest. The road in front of the gates was deserted except for a solitary police car with two very bored looking officers inside it. 'What reporters?' she said.

Sharon and Louise passed through the gate. Louise went on ahead up the drive towards the house, but Sharon stood around waiting while Zoe closed the gate and re-set the padlock. When she'd finished, Zoe said, 'I'm surprised you're here.'

'Why?'

'I sort of got the impression from Dylan you'd decided not to bring Louise back.'

'Oh, no. I just wanted to think about it, that's all.'

They walked up the drive in silence until Sharon said, 'Is Dylan around? I'd like to speak to him, if possible.'

'He's still getting up. He's got the 7.30 bathroom slot so he should be nearly ready.'

'You take the bathroom in shifts?'

'Have to, with so many of us. Fifteen minutes each. The joys of communal living.'

Sharon made a face. 'I'd hate it.'

Zoe gave her a sideways look. 'Yes, I suppose you would.'

They came to the vehicles parked in the drive. Sharon noted that the white mini-bus had been carelessly parked and half of it was encroaching onto the lawn. She was sure Major Roberts wouldn't have approved. As they manoeuvred themselves past the vehicles to get to the front door, Zoe said, 'Actually, I'm surprised you and Dylan have anything left to say to each other.'

'Why?'

'Well, you were on the phone for ages, last night.'

Bloody cheek, thought Sharon. They'd arrived at the open front door. She stopped and turned to Zoe. 'We were discussing my concerns about what happened here yesterday.'

'Really? He seemed to be doing a lot of laughing.'

Sharon's eyes glittered, maliciously. 'Oh, that was just me going on about my million pound sale and the huge commission I hope to make.'

Zoe's smile was equally malicious. 'Are you boasting or complaining?'

When they'd passed over the threshold and were in the hall, Zoe turned to Sharon and said, earnestly, 'You know, if you've got real concerns about Louise's safety perhaps you should keep her well away from here.'

Why had Zoe said that? Sharon wondered. She was about to respond but at that moment Dylan appeared at the top of the stairs. He wished Sharon a delighted, 'Good morning' and bounded down. Arriving in the hall he gave her a broad smile and said, 'Is Louise with you?'

Zoe said, 'She's in the kitchen.'

He continued to gaze at Sharon, warmly. 'So you decided to allow her to come back. That's great.'

In fact, Sharon still had reservations about returning Louise to the rectory, but she was damned if she was going to allow Greg and his wife, or anyone else, to influence her decision. She said, 'Yes. I talked it over with Louise and she tells me she loves it here and feels absolutely safe. She said she wants to keep coming back.'

'Good.'

'I'm sorry we're so early.'

'That's all right.'

'I wanted to avoid the reporters.'

'And did you?'

'There aren't any. Just as you said.'

Dylan smiled. 'Probably still sleeping off their hangovers.'

Sharon laughed.

To Zoe's dismay, throughout this short exchange Sharon and Dylan's pure delight in each other's presence was obvious. As they stared into each other's eyes, the intense attraction that passed between them flashed and crackled like an electrical arc connecting two points. It made Zoe feel excluded and jealous. She said, 'The media will be back at Rooks Nest soon. According to "Today", Kellingford's going to make a statement from there at eleven.'

Without taking his eyes off Sharon, Dylan said, 'That should be interesting. Perhaps we'll all watch it.' His look towards Sharon became enquiring. 'Do you object to Louise watching it with us?'

Sharon smiled and shook her head.

'Good. I'm really glad I've managed to assure you that Louise is safe here. What happened yesterday with Major Roberts was a complete one-off. No-one could have predicted it.'

'It's getting late,' said Zoe. 'We need to start our meeting.'

Sharon said, 'Zoe's been telling me that if I have any doubts I should keep Louise away.' The displeased look Dylan shot at Zoe didn't escape Sharon. 'But I'm sure you're giving her the best standard of care,' she added, quickly.

Coolly, Zoe said, 'I was just pointing out to you it was a decision only you could make.'

'I certainly know that, after what happened yesterday. I've already had people pressuring me to stop Louise coming here.'

'Who?' demanded Dylan.

'Just a few neighbours who are angry about the state of the rectory and fear it'll cost them Magnificent Britain. Some said if it did I wouldn't be forgiven, almost treating me like a collaborator which is absurd. It's only a gardening contest.' Then, looking pointedly at Zoe she went on, 'But, I don't give in easily to that kind of pressure. If I make up my mind to do something, I'm not easily deterred. That's what assertiveness is all about, isn't it?'

Zoe looked bemused. 'Good for you,' she said.

'I visited your website,' said Sharon, 'and found it most useful.'

Zoe smiled at Sharon graciously. 'I certainly don't think you need any help from me in that area. But it's there if you want it.' She looked at Dylan. 'Now, I really think we should get on with our meeting.'

****

The anticipated sexual fireworks with Peter had turned into something of a damp squib. Afterwards, Barbara had found it impossible to sleep. She'd tossed and turned all night, while her incredulous brain attempted to accommodate itself to the reality and magnitude of Peter's double cross.

All her hopes that the nightmare had finally ended and her domestic life might at last be returning to some vestige of normality, had been completely dashed by the content of the texts she'd seen exchanged between Peter and Clarissa. The message was clear: her husband was deceiving not only her and her family, but the public too. He was making all the right noises about returning to her and the children, but had no intention of actually doing so. Even worse, he'd planned to keep not only his wife and family in ignorance of the deception, but the whole country as well, so that he could present himself as the penitent sinner and hang on to his job.

Certainly, his conscience hadn't prevented him sleeping. All night he'd lain alongside her snoring loudly. Poor Clarissa, she thought, that must have been a shock. Finally, when Barbara could tolerate his despised presence no longer, she'd slipped quietly out of bed, put on her dressing gown and gone down to the kitchen to make herself a cup of tea. She was surprised to find her mother already there, fully dressed.

'We heard him arrive,' said Isobel. 'He was very late, wasn't he?'

'Well after one,' said Barbara. She knew what was coming next but had no intention of relating to her mother any of her private discussions with Peter, and so quickly changed the subject. 'Where's dad?'

'In the garden doing something with his roses.' Isobel took advantage of Howard's absence to launch into a catalogue of complaints about him. She told Barbara he was still insisting on pleading not guilty to the actual bodily harm charge, which she considered absolutely stupid. He was also refusing to take any medication until the afternoon because he was concerned that he might become drowsy while Peter was reading out his statement to the press. But her greatest cause for angst was that Howard had arranged for them to leave Rooks Nest by the weekend.

Barbara was shocked. 'So soon?'

'The people who protect Howard have told him it's advisable for us to disappear without trace as soon as possible. They can't guarantee our safety otherwise.'

Barbara could say nothing. Words seemed futile. All she could do was stare at her mother with a stricken face. One by one the familiar cornerstones of her life were being removed. Everything was in a state of dissolution. For the first time she saw with absolute clarity that impermanence was truly life's most characteristic condition.

Isobel was in torment. Tears formed in her light blue eyes and spilled over onto her cheeks. 'Look what Peter's done to us!' she cried, and a single sob wrenched itself out of her. It looked like she was going to lose it and break down completely but at that moment Howard's footsteps in the utility room announced his return from the garden. Struggling to regain her composure, Isobel turned away to make the tea.

Howard joined them, and they all sat around the kitchen table drinking tea and discussing their apprehension at their imminent appearance before the press. At one point, Isobel said to Barbara, 'I wish you'd told Peter "no". I wish you'd told him we wouldn't do it. But then I remind myself it's for you and the children and when it's over, at least you'll have Peter back and the children will have a father again.' She gave Barbara a pitiably wan smile. 'The only thing is, I'm so nervous about it I don't think I'm up to doing a full breakfast. Will cereal and toast be all right?'

Isobel's touching faith was unbearable for Barbara. She wondered how she could possibly keep all she knew to herself. How could she stand by and allow Peter to deceive everyone? But she had to. Had to! She felt the necessity to comfort her mother and so comfort herself. She went over and took Isobel in her arms and gave her a big hug. 'Don't worry. Toast and cereal will do just fine.'

'There'll be some fruit too, of course,' said Howard.

Shortly after this Howard and Isobel started bickering. Barbara could stand it no longer. Carrying the cup of tea she'd made for Peter, she left the kitchen and headed back to the bedroom. She'd expected to find him lying flat on his back snoring, but as she climbed the stairs she was surprised to hear her children's excited voices, interrupted occasionally by Peter's sleepy baritone. When she entered the bedroom she found Mark and Jessica jumping up and down on the bed, bombarding Peter with embarrassingly direct questions. He was parrying these with a mixture of bemusement and bland re-assurance. The children's most urgent concern seemed to be to establish that daddy had really come home for good. Barbara watched him lie to them, and her heart became a dagger.

'Ah, tea,' said Peter. 'Just what I need, thanks.'

'What's happened to the home you set up with Clarissa?' asked Mark, suddenly. His innocent tone was curiously at odds with the worldliness of the question, and for the first time Peter's assurance deserted him. His panicked look appealed to Barbara for support. Deciding it was time to intervene, she set the tea down on the bedside cabinet and took the children off to get ready.

The family's forthcoming appearance before the media provided Barbara with the perfect opportunity to show the world the lovely children that her husband had deserted for Clarissa. She wanted Mark and Jessica to look their best and insisted they wear their smartest clothes. This was met with much resistance, particularly from Mark. The thought of wearing his grey suit with its long trousers, a long sleeved shirt and a tie filled him with horror. 'But why? I'll be so hot,' he whined.

Jessica said, 'Yes, why? Why can't we just wear our shorts?'

'Because today is a very special day,' said Barbara.

'Why's it special?' said Mark. 'Because daddy's come home?'

'Partly. Daddy will tell you all about it after breakfast.'

'But why can't you tell us now?'

'Because it will come better from him.'

She left them to finish dressing and returned to the bedroom. Peter was snoring again and he hadn't even touched his tea. But that didn't matter. Nothing mattered, now she knew what she had to do.

****

The morning meeting of the inclusion unit's staff initially passed without discord. They spent nearly an hour discussing the issues arising from the products of the previous day's art therapy and agreed upon a programme of complementary art and drama activities for the day ahead.

Dylan then produced Louise's two storyboards for consideration. After they'd been studied and analysed Dylan gave an account of his conversations with Louise. A discussion followed. There was general agreement that Louise was presenting unconscious hostility to her absent father, and was conflicted about her relations to other people's fathers. Dylan supported this view, and revealed that in his discussions with Louise he'd detected indications of transference as he'd occasionally felt he'd been the object of her suppressed hostility towards her absent father.

Eric drew attention to Louise's expressed need to become someone else and her wish to be in constant flight from reality, which was idealised by her ambition to become an itinerant actor. What, he asked, or whom, was she in flight from? There was obviously deep conflict, perhaps even trauma, associated with this because of the way she'd been prepared to discuss it with Dylan up to a point and had then clammed up. Eric also expressed his disappointment that the only evidence available was her storyboards: it would have been helpful if Louise had done some drawing and painting in the form of warm ups and discrete art therapy themes. This would have facilitated the surfacing of her pain and blocked feelings in the form of recognizably archetypal images.

Toni believed that from the evidence of the storyboards, Louise was definitely being bullied. Drawing on her years of experience as a teacher, she said it was quite common for girls approaching or experiencing puberty to say and do appalling things to each other and make insulting sexual remarks about each other's parents. Louise was obviously a victim. She had a poor self-image and was socially embarrassed by her missing father. Toni suggested that Jade intuitively understood this and used it to provoke and emotionally bully Louise.

Zoe disagreed. From the evidence of the storyboards and Dylan's accounts of his conversations with Louise, it appeared that she had an almost pathological desire to hurt Jade physically and emotionally. It was as though she couldn't forgive Jade for possessing a father when she didn't. Zoe postulated that Louise could be a passive-aggressive: someone who presents themselves as the victim in order to put the blame on another, who is then wrongly perceived to be the bully.

Dylan provisionally accepted Zoe's analysis but stated that his own impression was that Louise sought to project herself as someone distinctly separate and different and seemed to delight in this. He cited the way she relished listening to radio plays even though her classmates regarded it as weird; also her ambition to be a travelling player. He wondered if her lack of affinity and empathy with others indicated psychopathic tendencies. He also alluded to her extraordinarily objective and cynical perceptions and the adult nature of her discourse. She was an outsider with an idealised vision of a missing father; indeed, her childhood was the stereotypical template for an artist manqué, particularly with all her extracurricular dancing and theatre activities and her unusually singular and intense commitment to becoming an actor. At this, Zoe reminded him that an absent parent wasn't a precondition for being a performer: lots of actors had grown up in households where both parents were present. At an early age, she'd had a burning ambition herself to become an actor, nourished and encouraged by her actor father.

'So,' said Dylan, at an opportune moment, 'how should we progress this?'

'I think Louise would benefit greatly from drama therapy,' said Zoe. She sat up in her chair and looked at the others in turn, as though daring them to disagree.

Dylan said, 'How exactly?'

Zoe explained that Louise was ideally suited to psychodrama because of her acting background. The key to unlocking her conflicts and allowing her to act them out lay in her core attitudes to Jade, which were aggressive and hostile. Zoe suggested that crucial scenes from Louise's storyboards could provide concrete examples for enactment. The older kids could become "auxiliary egos" and take the parts of significant people in Louise's personal drama. As the scenes were played out, Louise could show the auxiliaries how figures like Jade, Roger and Mrs Lucas really moved, spoke and acted, by giving them feedback until the scene from the storyboard was being enacted in the way Louise actually recalled and visualised it.

Zoe went on to describe the psychodrama techniques available in much more detail and then said, 'The kids are very accomplished at being auxiliaries and taking part in enactments now. Although, in Louise's case, I'd start with Monodrama techniques. No auxiliaries. Just a one-to-one with Louise and some chairs. Each chair could represent a different part of Louise's psyche. She could move between them to express different aspects of herself. Or she could imagine that someone with whom she is in conflict is sitting in the chairs and act out her suppressed feelings and hostilities towards them. For example, Jade, her mother or her absent father. She obviously has deep antagonisms towards him.' She paused, and then added, 'And the boyfriend too, of course.' She glanced quickly at Dylan. 'I'm surprised you didn't mention him.'

Everyone was now looking at Dylan.

'What's that?' said Eric.

Dylan said, 'Sharon told me she has a boyfriend but Louise denies it.'

'Ah,' said Eric.

There was a pause. Everyone waited, but Eric didn't elaborate.

Toni looked at him quizzically. 'Ah, what?'

Eric smiled. 'Ah, Louise possibly finds her mother's relationship with any man threatening.'

'Louise could explore those issues through enactments too,' said Zoe.

'I still don't understand how all this helps, Louise!' exclaimed Toni.

Zoe sighed. 'Louise is exhibiting aggressive behaviour because of intense feelings of hurt and anger caused by past experiences: notably rejection by her absent father. Louise identifies these feelings as negative and tries to reject and suppress them. But because she's unable to address them they're being expressed as frustration, hostility and rage. If, within the security of an accepting and supportive group, Louise can role-play and act out the experiences and circumstances which are associated with her negative feelings, she might be able to release and normalise them. They can then be acknowledged and accepted as something part of herself and not alien to it. Her conscious self will gradually come to understand that human beings can have a range of different feelings that are both negative and positive, and there's no need to be ashamed of them or to reject or suppress them. On the contrary, she should express them to herself and others.'

'That's all very well, but what would it achieve practically?' said Toni.

'Louise should begin to feel more comfortable with herself, which should reduce her hostility and aggression. You may not think that very important but I think it's crucial. And by role-playing her conflicts over and over with other kids who have similar conflicts to her own she'll acquire strategies for dealing with them. In time, she might be able to deal with those crisis points that are the triggers for her aggression and violence without automatically lashing out. Is that practical enough for you?'

Toni appeared unconvinced. 'I think that's far too sophisticated for a child of Louise's age. Are you really suggesting she should be role-playing with teenagers?'

Condescendingly, Zoe said, 'It sounds more complicated than it is in practice, but I assure you it works. You ought to sit in on some of my sessions sometime. Even take part.'

'No thanks.'

'Why not? Everyone can benefit from acting out.'

Toni scoffed. 'Not in front of the clients, thank you.'

'I'm sure you have issues just like everyone else.'

Toni's eyes narrowed. 'What are you suggesting?'

Dylan could see where this was going. Quickly, he said, 'Zoe, I support everything you say about Louise but I think your claims are rather ambitious.'

'Well, I'm not suggesting it'll happen overnight.'

'Of course. But I don't think Sharon would allow Louise to do it. She's so protective about her privacy.'

'Yes. Funny that,' said Zoe. 'I mean, what's she afraid of?'

Dylan stared at her and said, quite pointedly, 'We all have things we'd like to keep to ourselves, don't we? My feeling is that drama therapy for Louise would be a step too far. After all, we're simply looking after her while she's excluded, that's all.'

Zoe's look was scathing. 'So why did you start doing art therapy with her?'

'All she's done with me so far are the storyboards.'

'Frankly, I can't understand why we're even discussing Louise in this meeting,' said Toni. 'She's not one of our clients and we've no remit to work with her. Besides, she's got plenty of school work to do. Her understanding of fractions is non-existent.'

'School work won't address her emotional issues,' said Zoe.

'I'm not convinced she has any.'

Zoe was genuinely shocked. 'Really? I think her storyboards reveal that she has plenty.'

Toni wasn't easily going to abandon common sense. 'If we're that concerned about her why don't we just refer her to social services? Or the educational psychologist?'

Dylan shifted uneasily in his seat. 'I don't think her behaviour is so extreme that we need to do that.'

Eric nodded.

'Sharon certainly wouldn't like that at all,' said Zoe, glancing at Dylan.

Dylan turned to Eric. 'What do you think?'

Eric said, 'I'm sure that Louise would benefit from drama therapy. However, I think it would be wrong to initiate a programme for her. She's only going to be with us for a couple more days.'

Dylan and Toni were astonished. Eric always agreed with Zoe.

Zoe fixed Eric with an imperious look. 'I'm sure I could find time for some one-to-one with her. And she could easily be included in my psychodrama groups.'

'Yes. But it might her make her confused and resentful to receive professional attention that stops suddenly at the end of the week. It could do her more emotional damage.'

'In which case, so will art therapy,' said Zoe.

Eric shook his head. 'No. I don't think so. Art therapy isn't so direct. It's oblique. Reflective. It's not confrontational. It enables people to express their deepest emotions through images and artefacts which mirror their inner states. It seeks to reduce conflict not encourage it. I don't think art therapy will do Louise any harm.'

Zoe's look was contemptuous. 'All art can do people harm, if misapplied.'

'Are you suggesting I don't know what I'm doing?'

'You don't know anything about drama therapy, that's for sure.'

'I know as much about it as you know about art therapy!'

Toni looked shocked. It was getting rather nasty. Dylan decided to intervene. Genially, he said, 'I think it's very kind of you to offer to give up your precious time and expertise for Louise, Zoe, but I don't think we should take advantage of your good nature. Particularly as it won't be possible to do any effective work with Louise in the time available.'

Zoe stared at him, impudently. 'Is that a decision?'

'I'm sorry?'

'Is that your decision? Only it's often hard to know whether you've made one or not!'

Toni gasped.

Before Dylan could respond, there was a loud knock on the door of the art therapy room.

'Dylan!'

It was Rupa's voice. She was shouting.

'Yes?'

'It's my turn for the bathroom, but Liam won't come out.'

Toni stood up. 'I'll deal with it.' She set off for the door.

Eric stood up too. His gaze lingered for several seconds on Zoe, but strangely she didn't seem to notice. Was she perhaps deliberately avoiding eye contact with him? Dylan couldn't be sure of this, any more than he could interpret Eric's look which was full of strange subtexts.

Eric turned to Dylan. 'Well, if there's nothing else?'

'No. You go ahead. We're finished here.'

Eric went out. Zoe watched him go.

When the door was closed, Dylan said, 'What was all that about?'

'What?'

'You and Eric. It seemed to be getting rather personal.'

It was personal. How could she tell Dylan that Eric was still hoping for a physical relationship, even though she'd made it quite clear to him that there was nothing doing? How could she tell Dylan that was why Eric was being so petty?

She said, 'I don't think Eric really sees any benefit in drama therapy.'

'Really? I thought you said he was very supportive?'

'He's one of those people who says supportive things just to get on side with you.' She shot Dylan a hostile look. 'Maybe you're one of those too.'

He strove to avoid another potential conflict. 'I've always accepted the close association between the two therapies. You know that.'

'Then why won't you let me work with Louise?'

'I'm surprised you even suggested it.'

'Why?'

'You saw how hard I had to work to persuade Sharon to bring Louise back here after what happened yesterday.'

'What's that got to do with it?'

'Oh, come on. You know this is nothing about drama therapy. This is all about you and Sharon.'

Zoe looked astounded. 'What?'

'Why did you tell Sharon that if she had misgivings she should keep Louise away from here?'

'Because she was very upset about yesterday's violence. I didn't want her to think she was under any obligation to bring Louise back.'

'Really? I think you were deliberately doing your best to persuade her to take Louise away.'

Zoe got to her feet. 'What nonsense! You're being ridiculous.'

'Am I?'

'Why would I want her to keep Louise away?'

Dylan said nothing. The accusation didn't need to be verbalised. She was jealous. They both knew it.

Zoe decided that the time for frankness had arrived. 'The only reason you want Louise to keep coming back here is because you're obsessed with her mother.'

'Obsessed?'

'Yes. Sexually obsessed. That's why you're doing so much art therapy with Louise. You're using Louise as a proxy to unlock Sharon's secrets.'

Dylan affected disbelief and shook his head. 'That's an outrageous accusation and totally baseless. It's very clear to me what you were doing earlier. You were setting me up to tell Sharon that Louise needed drama therapy.'

'Setting you up? What an extraordinary thing to say. All I want to do is help, that's all.'

'No. You knew it would infuriate Sharon if she thought her private life was going to be put under scrutiny in your drama sessions.'

'That's ridiculous. Your infatuation with that woman is making you paranoid.'

'I'm paranoid!' Dylan made a scoffing noise in his throat.

Zoe knew she'd gone beyond the bounds of what was professional or appropriate but she couldn't help herself. She said, 'We often discuss it, you know. Toni and Eric and I.'

'What?'

'You're obsession with that philistine. We can all see you're besotted with her but none of us can understand why.'

This wasn't strictly true: knowing something of Dylan's childhood, Zoe had early on formed the theory that Sharon was Dylan's mother surrogate.

'Sharon's no philistine,' Dylan said.

'Oh come on. She's got no interest in art or theatre. The only things she reads are property details. But you're so infatuated with those scissor legs, you can't see straight.'

'Even if I am, what's it got to do with you?'

'Because I can't bear to see you throw yourself away on that capitalist. All she cares about are big property deals and loads of money.'

'Some people are impressed by that.'

'Really? Well, I'm not. If you take up with her, she'll kill your art stone dead.'

'Kill it? She's trying to get me my own gallery!'

Zoe was shocked. So they'd got as close as that. But how? When? What opportunity had they had? 'You really haven't a clue what I'm talking about, have you?' she said, turning and heading for the door. And then, as her hand grasped the door knob, she stopped.

Hadn't she just been lecturing everyone on the dangers of repressing your feelings because it twisted you up inside and turned you into something you weren't? She'd been living and working in Dylan's presence for weeks now, knowing that there was no future in their relationship, yet hoping for some sign from him that there might be. She'd become more and more frustrated: unable to express to him how she felt; suppressing the very essence of her personality; rejecting the spontaneity in herself that she advocated for others in order to be the kind of person he wanted and admired. All in the hope that he might recognize her true worth and reward her with the radiance and warmth that had once been hers. Every day was a complete torment for her. Feeling herself so attracted to him, feeling so in love and yet knowing it wasn't love: it was something she pursued in order to feel good about herself again. And it made her feel so degraded. She knew she couldn't go on repressing and rejecting her natural impulses without doing herself serious emotional harm. The more she refused to recognize and acknowledge her very deep feelings and resisted expressing them, the worse it would get.

Her decision made, she opened the door and crossed the hall and went into the drama studio. A number of cushions lay scattered randomly on the floor in front of the improvised stage. The kids sat on these cushions during drama sessions or when they were being the audience to enactments.

She picked up one of the smaller cushions and, supporting it by the palm of one hand, raised and lowered it slightly, as though estimating its weight. Then, she clutched the cushion to her chest and with both arms wrapped protectively around it she returned to the art therapy room.

As Zoe entered, Dylan was still sitting in his seat pouring over Louise's storyboards. He looked up, and his expression showed that he couldn't quite believe that she was advancing across the room towards him with a cushion clasped to her bosom in a tight embrace.

She came right up so that she was standing directly in front of him. She said nothing but there was a look in her mesmerising eyes he'd never seen before. He was staring at her, quizzically. Curious. Wondering what she would do next.

Suddenly, she raised the cushion above her head and in a sudden, swift movement whacked him hard on the forehead and face. He felt more shock than pain but instinctively raised both arms to fend off the flurry of blows from the cushion that were now raining down on him from all sides, thumping his arms, head, face and chest.

Laughing, he fought her off. 'What are you doing!'

But she went on clouting him furiously. The ferocity of the blows and the intensity in her eyes made it clear she wasn't doing it for fun. She didn't stop until he managed to wrest the cushion from her and was holding it high above his head, out of her reach.

She made no effort to retrieve the cushion, but sat down calmly on the nearest desk and stared at him expectantly. She seemed quite composed, almost serene. He, meanwhile, continued to hold the cushion aloft.

'Have you any idea how funny you look?' she said. 'If any one comes in they'll wonder why you're holding that over your head.'

Dylan slowly lowered the cushion until it was at waist level, but he held on to it firmly.

Zoe said, 'That was the empty chair exercise. The one in which you imagine the person you have a conflict with is sitting in the empty chair, and you hit them with the cushion to disclose your hostility to them. Only the chair wasn't empty. The person I have the conflict with was sitting in it.'

'And it's made you feel better?'

'Much. It didn't hurt, did it?'

'No. It was a bit of a shock though. And I'm very confused.'

She said, 'Why do you think I was so keen to get the job here and work with you again even though you'd dumped me?'

He looked surprised. 'I must admit, I've often wondered.'

After a long pause, she said, 'I came here to be near you.'

'Yes. I thought that might be it. But why, when you knew it was so hopeless?'

'I took the job because I couldn't believe that after all we had, you'd throw me over. I wanted to prove to you how wrong you were. I hoped that in time your feelings for me would return and I'd be myself again. I thought I could persuade you that I wasn't the terrible stereotype you accused me of being. It's so awful when someone who you think is your soul mate, your friend, the person you're going to spend your life with, goes and throws you over like that.'

She went on explaining to him how wretched she felt, how abject. Unless they could get back together and restore their relationship to what it had been before, she'd go on forever feeling worthless, and that her whole life was pointless. She explained that she'd never felt like that before. If this was love, they could keep it.

Dylan didn't think it was love. He believed it was her extreme reaction to rejection. When he'd split with her it had awakened other feelings, long suppressed. Feelings in relation to the massive rejection she'd experienced at the age of twelve when her adored father, the actor, had walked out on her mother and never spoken to either of them again.

He wondered if he should offer her his professional services as an art therapist to help her address her issues. But knew that would come across as deeply insulting, if not humiliating. Zoe was a co-therapist. And the transference difficulties would be daunting.

Instead, he said, 'I hate knowing that I'm the cause of so much pain and distress. But this isn't the appropriate time to discuss it, you know.'

Zoe got up. 'You're right. Anyway, I feel a lot better about things now. It's a great exercise, the empty chair. You should try it sometime. I'm sure you'd benefit.'

He held out the cushion towards her.

She took it off him and grinned. 'OK. Don't take my advice. You'll be the loser.' She turned and he watched her cross the room and leave, closing the door behind her.

When she'd gone he expelled all the remaining air in his lungs in a long, heartfelt "phew". Thank God the Community Watch had come round that night, otherwise he'd have ended up in bed with her.

CHAPTER THIRTY NINE

'Why do we have to wear these hot clothes, daddy?' said Mark. 'Mummy says today's a special day. What's special about it?'
Peter looked enquiringly at Barbara, who was sitting opposite him. 'Haven't you told them?'
'No. I thought I'd let you have that pleasure.'
Breakfast was proving to be an even greater trial than Barbara had imagined. Looking at the subdued and pensive faces around her at the table, she felt immensely weary and depressed. Having left Peter to get ready, she'd brought Mark and Jessica down to the kitchen as soon as they were dressed. Howard and Isobel had attempted to be sociable and put aside their differences for the children's sake, but it was clear they were completely daunted by the prospect of the public ordeal that awaited them. When Peter appeared some time later and wished his in-laws a guarded "good morning", Howard barely raised his head from his cereal and simply muttered his response. Isobel returned Peter's greeting quite civilly but in a martyred, long suffering, intensely bitter sort of way, so that her "Good Morning, Peter. I hope you had a good journey", seemed to have come direct from a Greek tragedy. As breakfast progressed, Howard and Isobel made no attempt to disguise their contempt for their son-in-law and their attitude towards him became one of polite malice. They either ignored him completely, consuming their cereal and toast without speaking, or made perfunctory and indifferent remarks as they passed him the butter and marmalade. Even Peter's facility for glib small talk was inhibited by their barely concealed hostility. He was reduced to consuming his toast in penitent silence.
Mark and Jessica, who'd expected an atmosphere of joyful celebration around the kitchen table, were puzzled and disappointed to find that the adults sharing breakfast with them were subdued and, at times, oppressively quiet. They tolerated this and the clothes that were making them hot and uncomfortable for as long as young children could reasonably be expected to. Then, finally, despite their mother's warning that under no circumstances were they to ask their father any questions at breakfast, particularly about Clarissa,

discomfort forced Mark to ask why they were wearing insufferable October clothes in a July heatwave.

Peter paused before answering his son's question. He was struggling with the challenge of providing an answer that would be acceptable to an audience that was disparate and, in part, intensely hostile. An explanation of the day's significance was required that would be simple and credible for Mark and Jessica, without making Barbara and her parents think he was trying to deny his responsibility for the scandalous situation he'd placed them all in.

'It's special because at eleven o'clock we're all going to do something together,' he began.

'Are we going out?' said Jessica.

'Only as far as the gates.'

'Oh.' Jessica looked disappointed.

'Yes, we're all going to stand together at the gates. You and Mark, me and mummy, grandma and grandpa.'

'But there are reporters at the gates,' interrupted Mark. 'That's why we aren't supposed to go there.'

'Shh. Let daddy finish,' said Barbara, who, despite everything, was savouring Peter's discomfort.

'That's why today's so special. Today I'm going to speak to the reporters. I'm going to explain my behaviour in recent days, and I'm going to apologise for some of the mistakes I've made.'

'Like setting up home with Clarissa?' said Mark.

Peter's voice rose angrily. 'I did not set up home with Clarissa!'

Everyone looked shocked. No-one moved. There was an embarrassed silence.

'I stayed with her for a few days, that's all,' Peter continued defensively, his voice returning to its normal, quietly spoken level. 'She needed my help.'

And so Peter went on, using all his politician's arts of persuasion and equivocation to depict his appalling behaviour as selfless concern for the well-being of others. As Barbara observed him camouflage the truth from his own children; conceal his real intentions behind pompous double-speak; assert his commitment to decency and integrity and generally present himself as misunderstood, she became angrier and angrier. Only she knew the full extent of his subterfuge. Only she knew that he was just going through the motions and felt no compunction about using his family as supporting players in the huge act of deception he was about to practise upon the nation. And only she knew that once they'd all dutifully and loyally accompanied him to the gates and stood shoulder to shoulder with him while he attempted to end the shitstorm with a public apology, he'd be straight back to Clarissa to resume his affair. It made her sick at heart to think that she'd even contemplated involving her children and her parents in all this. But now they'd committed to assist him unknowingly in this massive confidence trick, and the announcement about his forthcoming statement had appeared in the newspapers and was, even now, being broadcast all over the airwaves, she knew there was absolutely nothing she could do to stop it. As she stared across the table at Peter's well-groomed head and conventionally handsome features, and heard him explain with all his fluency and easy affability why it was such a special day, she wondered, if in addition to being a serial adulterer he was also some sort of psychopath.

Convinced that he'd answered Mark's question to everyone's satisfaction without doing serious damage to his standing, Peter stopped speaking.

Mark sighed. 'Yes, but when can we change out of these clothes?'

'Probably about half past eleven,' said Barbara.

Howard smiled satirically at Mark and Jessica. 'You'll easily put up with your discomfort as long as you remember that you're doing it for daddy's sake. You see children, when an important man behaves as disgracefully as your father has, he not only has to say sorry to his family, he has to apologize to the whole nation. That's why he needs us to help him face the press.'

'Howard,' exclaimed Isobel, horrified.

Howard took a bite out of his toast and munched it unconcernedly. 'Well, it's true, isn't it?'

Isobel's lips tightened into a thin line. She got up and went over to a kitchen drawer, opened it, and produced Howard's box of medication which she slammed down on the table. "Take one!' she ordered.

'Certainly not,' said Howard, calmly. 'I've no intention of falling asleep in front of the world's media.'

'Are they sleeping pills?' said Mark.

Barbara could take no more. She pushed back her chair and stood up. Tightening the cord of her dressing gown, she said, 'I'm off to get ready. Carr will be here any minute. I can't meet him like this.'

She left the kitchen, went up the stairs and straight into the bedroom. Once inside she paced up and down several times and then locked the door.

Peter's jacket was hanging on the back of a chair. She went over to it, reached into the inside pocket and took out his blue mobile. She found Clarissa's number in the address book and sent her the following text: "Hi Clary - awful - had to screw B last nite - she gagging for it - but I could only think of U while we did it - Me 4 U 4 ever luv - P

She sent the text and then went off to shower.

****

Bill Carr, the Party's press officer for the Northern Region, arrived at Rooks Nest just after half past nine. He was a large, forceful man whose presence seemed to fill the house, and he exuded a calm resourcefulness forged from years of dealing with the rough old trade of politics. He was accompanied by a tall, young woman in her twenties with honey blonde hair and almond coloured eyes. Carr introduced her as Tanya, his assistant. Barbara was piqued to see Peter's eyes brighten with interest the moment he saw her. Why did he always have to make it so obvious?

Carr called all the adults to a meeting in the sitting room. He told them that he'd already spoken to the huge media crowd assembled at the front gates and confirmed for them that the Shadow Home Secretary would be making a statement at eleven. He then outlined the planned sequence of events. Just before eleven, Peter and the family would take up their assigned positions outside the front door. Together, they'd then move down the drive until they were about a yard away from the gates. Peter would read out his statement. If the reporters asked questions, Peter was not to answer them. No-one was to say anything to the media. After the statement was read, the family would return immediately to the house.

'I'm very unhappy about not answering questions,' said Peter. 'The whole point of this is to convince everyone that the matter is closed. How can I convince them if I refuse to speak freely?'

Carr sighed heavily. 'Peter, if you start answering questions you're going to give those vultures masses of copy for tomorrow's editions and create a sensation on every national news bulletin. My job is to limit the damage. Just deliver your statement, smile while they take the pictures and stay schtum. Then we'll be fine!'

'Oh dear,' said Isobel, 'the whole thing sounds very stressful.'

'If you follow my advice, it won't be,' said Carr. He looked hard at Peter. 'All right?'

'But if I'm not frank and open with them, they'll assume I'm deceitful.'

'They already know you're deceitful. The object of this exercise is to kill the story stone dead. The only way to do that is for you to make a statement of contrition, surrounded by your understanding and forgiving family.'

'Huh!'

Howard was the one responsible for the scoff. Carr looked at him warily. He knew he was flaky and had been charged with actual bodily harm. He said, 'You sound sceptical, Major.'

'That's because I am.'

'Howard,' said Isobel, reprovingly.

Howard flapped a dismissive hand at her. 'Now Isobel, we both know that this whole exercise is a sham.' He turned to Carr. 'We don't understand Peter's behaviour and we certainly don't forgive it. We're only going through with this charade for the sake of Barbara and the children. That's why we're going to grit our teeth and get on with it.'

Carr looked relieved. 'In that case, you'll be fine,' he said. 'The art of politics is to make people think you agree with something when you're diametrically opposed to it.'

Barbara knew that this was the moment when she ought to speak out. Here was the perfect opportunity to confirm that the whole thing was a sham, denounce Peter as a liar and reveal that after the fake display of family unity he'd be going straight back to his teenage mistress. But the thought of the consequences of this and the damage it would do to Peter and the Party was daunting, which is why she hesitated.

'What sort of questions will the reporters ask?' said Isobel, desperate to divert everyone's attention away from Howard.

Carr said, 'They'll want to know how you all feel about Peter running off with a seventeen year old; if he's truly been forgiven; whether his change of heart has anything to do with next week's by-election. That sort of thing. Just use your imagination. And the more you say, the more they'll keep the story running. They want a scalp, and they'll only be satisfied when they get it. So say nothing.'

Barbara said, 'But surely Peter should be given the opportunity to talk to reporters and convince them he's given up Clarissa for good?'

'No need,' said Carr. 'That's what he'll say in his statement.'

Barbara persisted. 'But if the press ask Peter if he's really left his mistress and returned to us and he refuses to answer, won't it look as though he's lying?' She turned to Peter and, looking him straight in the eye, said, 'We don't want them to think you're lying, do we?'

Peter reddened, and nodded gravely.

'They won't, said Carr, 'as long as he responds to all their questions in exactly the same way, and says nothing.'

'All right,' said Peter. 'You've convinced me.'

Given the magnitude of the lie that was about to be perpetrated, Barbara knew it was morally reprehensible of her to keep silent. Do it now, she told herself. Speak out. But all she could do was say, 'Whatever you advise, Mr Carr. But I'm perfectly happy to tell them what I think.'

'Me too,' said Howard.

Carr regarded father and daughter nervously. 'I'm sure they'd be delighted to hear what you all really think. That's why it's vital you keep your mouths shut. Just smile and ignore everything they ask you. It's the only way for Peter to survive.'

Peter reached into the inside pocket of his suit and produced a folded sheet of paper. 'This is my statement,' he said, offering it to Carr. 'I wrote it last night. Would you like to give it the once over?'

Carr took it, read it silently and then handed it back, saying, 'It's too long and full of excuses. It won't draw a line under anything.' He turned to Tanya. 'Give Peter his statement, please.'

From her thin briefcase, Tanya produced a single sheet of A4 and handed it to Peter along with a dazzling smile. Peter thanked her with a smile of equal radiance, and silently read what was on the sheet of paper. It didn't take him long.

'It's very short,' he said.

'It admits you made a mistake and you apologise,' said Carr. 'What more is there to say? The aim is to close this thing down not to make it run and run. Now, can we rehearse, please?'

Carr began to coach the four adults for their ordeal. First, he arranged them in their respective positions. Peter and Barbara stood hand in hand and mimed holding the hands of their children. Howard was placed on Barbara's left; Isobel on Peter's right. Together, they were all made to advance over the sitting room carpet, which represented the drive, until they came to a halt at the sideboard, which represented the gates. Peter then read out his prepared statement. As Tanya videoed the whole thing on her camcorder, Carr called out various instructions such as "smile more", "be more relaxed", "look at each other more fondly".

'Good,' said Carr, when they'd been through the actions a couple of times. 'Now, Peter, when you've finished just say, "Thank you very much", put the statement in your pocket, then pick up the little girl...' He turned to Barbara. 'What's her name?'

'Jessica,' said Barbara, frostily. She'd already told him the children's names twice.

'Jessica, that's it. OK, Peter, pick up Jessica in your arms, and then turn and slowly carry her back up the drive. Oh, and don't put her down until you get back into the house.'

'Why does he need to do that?' asked Barbara.

'We need to show Peter's caring side, of course.'

Having established the sequence, they rehearsed it many times with Tanya videoing it and Carr role-playing the press pack. He flung a non-stop barrage of crass and humiliating questions at them, which they all dutifully ignored. When the rehearsal was finished, Tanya played back the recorded footage on the camcorder. They all gathered round to watch the tiny screen.

Despite herself, Barbara was impressed. Peter was an accomplished performer, and she could see that his appearance before the press was going to be commanding. He read his statement most plausibly with just the right combination of dignity, culpability and regret. She knew now that there was no question of her speaking out and branding him a liar. After all, what purpose would it serve? It certainly wouldn't send Peter back into her arms. It would probably only drive him further and further away. Besides, even if she exposed what Peter was really up to, she suspected Carr would insist on them continuing with the public deception. It was easy to work out the grounds he'd use to justify it: he'd argue that it was too late to pull out of making the statement now; that to do so would appear amateurish and incompetent, and most people would be assuming Peter was lying anyway. Did she really want to derail her husband's career? Ruin the Party's chances at the by-election? Finally, he might remind her that this was politics they were involved in, not a truth symposium. And of course, he'd be right. So instead of speaking out she decided to say nothing, play the long game and hope that Peter would come back in the end.

'OK,' said Carr. 'It's coming. I think we'll do it with the children now.'

****

Peter Kellingford's impending statement had been much publicised on radio and TV, and everyone in the inclusion unit was anticipating it with varying degrees of pleasure and excitement. For example, Jake, who'd never shown the slightest interest in current affairs before, had become completely absorbed in every aspect of the Kellingford scandal and now never missed a news bulletin. Amy and Rupa were so thrilled by the gathering media circus that was again materializing below their bedroom windows, they'd refused to come down to breakfast. While Zoe had made it quite clear she was eagerly looking forward to hearing the excuses "that Tory hypocrite" was going to come up with, to save his job and his neck.

With everyone in a state of febrile expectation, it was obvious to Dylan that very little meaningful work would be done that morning. He decided it would be in everybody's best interests to suspend the normal timetable until the distraction was over. Fortunately, all his colleagues were just as keen to watch Kellingford make his statement as the clients were, and happily agreed with his decision. So, after breakfast Dylan called everyone into the art therapy room. Only Louise was absent: she was in the encouragement room doing her schoolwork.

Dylan explained that it would be pointless asking everyone to try to concentrate when such distracting, historical events were happening right on their doorstep. This statement was being substantiated, even as he spoke, by the presence of a large and growing crowd which was visible through the room's windows and was inevitably claiming his audience's attention. Reporters, photographers, TV crews and many curious onlookers could be seen, milling around the gates of Rooks Nest and overrunning Church Lane. If the windows of the rectory hadn't been double glazed, the din from outside would have been deafening.

A huge cheer went up from the clients as Dylan announced he was suspending the timetable for the whole morning, so they could all watch Peter Kellingford MP make his statement to the media.

At this point Mona and others asked if they could go over and mingle with the crowds so that they could watch the whole thing close up, as it happened. A collective groan of disappointment came from the clients as Dylan shook his head. 'You know I can't possibly allow that,' he told them. 'Anyway, you'll get a much better view from the top of the house. As a special favour I'm going to allow you to see it all from my office.' He went on to explain that there was a television in there so they'd be able to watch the events at Rooks Nest on TV and, simultaneously, live as they happened. He was pleased to see that the novelty of this seemed to appeal to most of the clients. However, he was quick to remind them that the office was also his studio and warned them not to touch his art materials and canvasses.

At this point, Jake said, 'This MP guy. He's a dirty old man, right?'

Dylan allowed time for the laughter to subside. 'That's another thing,' he said. 'You all know very well why the Shadow Home Secretary is making his statement. But I don't want to hear any of that sort of talk in my studio, particularly when Louise is there with us. She's only a child. I expect you to be grown-up about this, otherwise you'll be brought down here to the encouragement room for a maths session.'

What to do with Louise had presented Dylan with a problem. Although Sharon had given permission for her daughter to watch the Kellingford statement, Dylan knew very well the sort of lewd comments that would be passing between the clients, and, whilst recognizing that he oughtn't, indeed couldn't, police their private discourse, he didn't want it to reach Louise's ears. He'd discussed these concerns with his colleagues. Toni had volunteered to work with Louise on her maths and English in the encouragement room until about fifteen minutes before Kellingford was due to speak. This offer was gratefully accepted. After all, how could Sharon possibly object? Louise had been excluded. Hadn't Sharon told him in The Trout that children shouldn't be rewarded for bad behaviour?

Just after ten, Dylan unlocked the door of his office-cum-studio and ushered everyone inside. As they poured into the room a few of the clients gave Dylan's canvasses the briefest of cursory glances, but most ignored them. Their main interest was to obtain the best position at one of the studio's two big sash windows, and, almost immediately, everyone was jostling for a place. The outlook from these windows provided an excellent overview of Church Lane and the crowd laying siege to Rooks Nest. Reporters, photographers and TV crews had priority and were already in position directly in front of the gates. Several of those watching from the rectory expressed surprise at seeing so many of the photographers standing on stepladders and boxes: anything that would elevate them and give them a better shot. There was also a huge multitude of curious onlookers now gathered in Church Lane, which was dense with tightly packed bodies and had been sealed off at both ends by several police cars.

Dylan, Zoe and Eric had just joined the clients at the windows, when an older woman of striking appearance appeared in the street below and approached the gate to the rectory's drive. She tried the gate and finding it wouldn't open, gazed up at the rectory's windows. Seeing that several people were standing on the top storey, looking out, she started beckoning them to come down, presumably to open the gate.

'Who's that?' said Amy.

Jake took a long look. 'A reporter?'

'No, she's too old,' sneered Amy.

'Quite a lot of older women have jobs as reporters, you know,' Zoe told her.

Eric said, 'I wonder what she wants?'

'Want me to go and find out?' said Khaled.

'No, I'll go,' Dylan said, quickly. He suspected that Khaled, like the others, was just waiting for the opportunity to do a bunk over the gate and join the crowds around Rooks Nest.

'I'll come with you,' said Zoe.

'Why?'

'She may be a reporter. I don't think any of us should speak to a reporter without witnesses. Look what a mess I got into when I spoke to that guy from The Source.'

Zoe was speaking from the heart. She deeply regretted revealing to Terry Bryden so much about Major Roberts.

Dylan was about to tell her he was perfectly capable of dealing with reporters alone, but thought better of it. 'All right,' he said. 'Come with me.'

When Dylan and Zoe arrived at the gate, the woman was pressing her nose hard up against it.

'Mr Bourne?'

'Yes.'

'I must talk to you. I'm Lucy Birkinshaw. I'm a parish councillor and member of the Magnificent Britain Sub-Committee.'

'You say that,' said Zoe. 'But how do we know you're not a reporter?'

Lucy laughed. 'The only time I appear in print is in The Leeflet. Perhaps you've read one of my letters. I'm usually locking horns with Major Roberts.'

Zoe moved closer to the gate until her face was on the same level as the woman's. 'Lucy Birkinshaw. Yes, I've read your letters. So, what's the name of your house?'

Lucy's response was almost playful. 'You are a distrusting girl. But not a great security guard. Anyone who's seen my letters would know where I live.'

'Maybe. But what's your address, anyway?'

'I live in a tiny Victorian house at the end of the village called The Burrow.'

'A lovely name for a house,' said Zoe. 'That's why I remember it. But where did you live before Leefdale?'

'Northampton. But again, anyone who's read The Leeflet could tell you that.'

Dylan and Zoe looked at each other, uncertainly.

'I can see that neither of you believe me,' said Lucy. 'But I can easily prove my identity.' She unzipped the money belt strung at her waist and produced a plastic card which she passed to Zoe through the bars of the gate.

It was a bank debit card. Zoe took it and read aloud, 'Lucy C Birkinshaw.'

Zoe looked at Dylan and said, 'I think she's all right.' She passed the card to Dylan. He checked it, and handed it back to Lucy, saying, 'I'll let you in.'

Dylan unlocked the padlock, swung the gate open, and allowed Lucy to enter the drive. 'Can't be too careful with all these reporters about,' he said, closing the gate behind her and padlocking it again.

'I understand,' said Lucy, who was returning the card to her money belt. 'It must be dreadful feeling under siege.'

Dylan and Zoe now had the opportunity to observe Lucy more closely. Dylan saw a tall woman in late middle age, whose iron grey hair was worn defiantly long. Large, light blue eyes, iridescent with integrity, illuminated her fleshy, archetypically maternal face. Her height was accentuated by a flowing maxi dress inspired by a William Morris design of densely entwined leaves and flower heads in various shades of blue. The dress had long, loose sleeves and was cut square and low at the neck. Sandals peeped out from under the hem, giving a glimpse of Lucy's toenails, which were varnished in navy blue. Worn high on Lucy's neck was a black, velvet choker, enhanced at intervals by seaweed fronds in silver filigree; and glistening at its centre, like a teardrop, was a transparent blue topaz pendant. Wraparound rings in the shape of birds, snakes and flowers adorned her fingers. She had an aura of the nineteen sixties about her: a suggestion that the colours and forms of all art were derived from nature and embodied in her, and that she, like all life, had originated in the sea.

Her appearance evoked for Dylan memories of his careless, blissful childhood in the commune. There, in the care of women who'd looked and dressed so much like Lucy, he'd romped on summer days amongst fields of wheat the colour of yellow ochre; or played with friends on a patch of grass encircled by cradling vans, tents and tethered horses. She reminded him too of those long, hot evenings he'd sat in the gathering dusk watching the licking candle flames, smelling strange tobacco fumes and listening to his father and others playing Dylan songs on their acoustic guitars and fiddles. He found himself strangely moved to be reminded of this time of unquestionable trust, when he'd received nurture and support from an extended family of strangers with whom he shared no blood ties. He counted himself very lucky indeed to have had such a childhood.

Zoe, on the other hand, saw a laid-back looking woman with honest eyes and a wryly indulgent expression who had the patient mien of an aging earth mother or sympathetic infants' teacher. Under Lucy's kind, benevolent gaze she felt all her suspicions about her evaporating like dew on a sunny morning, and introduced herself.

Lucy smiled at both of them. 'This is much more civilised than talking through the bars of a gate.' She nodded in the direction of Rooks Nest. 'I see the siege is well under way again over there. Let's hope when the son-in-law's offered himself up as a sacrifice to the tabloid God we'll all get some peace.'

Zoe and Dylan laughed.

'I've heard about your problems with Howard Roberts, of course,' Lucy said, 'but I can't say I'm surprised. He's always on a rather short fuse.'

'Yes, it was all very unfortunate,' said Dylan.

'Did he really hit that poor boy?'

'Why do you ask?' said Zoe.

Lucy shrugged insouciantly. 'Just curiosity. The thing that makes us all human.'

Dylan said, 'I'm afraid I can't discuss it. It's in the hands of the police.'

'That's what I thought,' said Lucy.

Dylan said, 'So, how can I help? You said you wanted to talk about something.'

'I felt I simply had to come and speak to you.' She described the enormous anger in the village at the state of the rectory's gardens and the great fear that their condition would affect Leefdale's chances in the Magnificent Britain contest. She also told them how annoyed people were that the rectory had been sold to the inclusion unit, because it was feared its presence would affect people's house prices and lower the tone of the village.

'Outrageous,' said Zoe.

'Exactly,' said Lucy. 'And don't think I didn't tell them so.' She looked around her. 'I can't see what they're all complaining about. This garden looks perfectly charming. Just a little overgrown, that's all.'

You haven't seen the back, thought Dylan.

'Anyway, last night there was a special meeting of the parish council to discuss the grievances and a lot of hot air was exchanged. But after the meeting, a parish councillor called Greg Maynard...'

'We've met him,' said Zoe. 'A nasty piece of work.'

'Quite,' said Lucy. 'Well, last night he held a meeting in his home which was very well attended, and they decided to organise a boycott of deliveries to the rectory.'

'It's not been very effective, then,' said Dylan. 'We've had our milk and fresh meat delivered as normal this morning.'

'I'm glad to hear that, but it may simply mean that the delivery people haven't been got at yet.'

'No sweat. We'll just shop more frequently in Luffield, that's all. We'll be inconvenienced and the tradesmen will lose money.'

'What's the point of it?' said Zoe.

'They want to send you a message. Some of them think it'll force you to leave Leefdale, or, at least, tidy up the rectory gardens and restore them as they were.'

'Never!' cried Zoe. 'What we do with the gardens is our own affair. Anyway, there's nothing wrong with them.'

'Good for you!' said Lucy. 'But here's another thing. As you know, the Magnificent Britain contest is being judged on Friday. At the meeting, it was decided to mount a demonstration outside the rectory as the judges go round the village.'

'Why?' said Dylan.

'Maynard and the others feel that if they can show the judges how strongly the villagers disapprove of the state of your gardens, they might be prepared to overlook them and award Leefdale the gold medal, regardless.'

Zoe shot Dylan a resentful look. 'I told you we should never have come here!'

Dylan ignored her. Through his conversations with Louise the name Maynard had become familiar to him over the past couple of days. Now it was appearing in a new but no less revealing context. 'Greg Maynard. He's the father of Jade Maynard, isn't he?'

'That's right.'

'And he's the one behind all this?'

Lucy smiled, knowingly. 'Ostensibly yes, but Major Roberts is the real brains. He has to hide behind Maynard because as chairman of the parish council he can't be seen to be acting like a thug.' Lucy's face registered concern. 'What will you do? Evacuate the rectory on Friday?'

'Why should we?' demanded Zoe.

'For the sake of the children. The demonstration could be very upsetting for them.'

'We'll give the matter serious thought,' said Dylan. 'But someone will have to be here anyway, while the judges go round.'

Lucy seemed relieved. 'I'll do everything I can to stop the demonstration, but I'm only one amongst many, and my opponents are very powerful.'

'That doesn't matter,' said Zoe. 'Bullies have to be stood up to and the best way to defeat them is with their own strength.'

'Ah, like Gandhi, you mean?'

Dylan decided that Lucy would make a very useful ally. He said, 'While you're here why don't we show you round the unit and introduce you to the clients?'

Lucy looked at him blankly.

Dylan exchanged a quick look with Zoe. 'I mean, the kids.'

Lucy beamed. 'I'd like that very much. I told the council last night what a wonderful idea I thought these inclusion units were.'

Dylan said, 'Let's go then. And when we've finished perhaps you might like to join us watching the Shadow Home Secretary deliver his statement on News 24.'

'Well, that's very kind of you,' said Lucy, struggling for a legitimate reason to refuse. 'But I'd much rather be in the crowd outside Rooks Nest when history is made.'

CHAPTER FORTY

Two minutes before 11am, the front door of Rooks Nest opened. First out was the Honourable Peter Kellingford MP, formally dressed in his finest Savile Row pin stripe with a white shirt and blue silk tie. At his appearance there were immediately shouts of "Here he comes!" from those crammed around the front gate and a general surge forward by the crowd. He advanced confidently into the merciless sun's broiling glare with Jessica just behind him, her hand clasped in his. She was wearing sandals and a burgundy coloured dress, and as she bounced through the doorway beaming enthusiastically, she exuded the happy child's confident expectation that whatever was about to happen could only be exciting and fun.

Next through the open doorway was Barbara, looking cool and elegant in a long, white summer dress with three-quarter length sleeves. She was bare legged and wore flat, gladiator style sandals. Following her was Mark, looking hot and resentful in his grey suit, blue shirt and school tie: full of the embarrassment of the growing boy forced to hold his mother's hand in public, for Barbara had him in a vice-like grip. Tugging the reluctant Mark behind her, she took her place alongside her husband with a determined tilt of her chin that suggested she was more than ready for whatever vicissitudes life or the media had to throw at her.

Next to step out on to the drive was Howard, looking very debonair indeed in his navy blue blazer, cavalry twill slacks, crisp white shirt and military-looking tie. He also sported a panama hat, worn low down on his forehead, shielding his eyes. But it equally could have been to hide his face. Unsurely in his wake came Isobel, wearing a honey coloured frock and two strings of pearls. She looked strained and drawn and was blinking fiercely.

Once outside the house, the little party lined up religiously in the positions which Bill Carr had so meticulously choreographed for them. They shuffled into their places self-consciously, as though assembling for a family photograph. When they'd composed themselves sufficiently and were ready, Peter gave the agreed signal and they set off walking in formation down the drive towards the gate.

The media crowd was now in a high state of animation. There were shouts and indignant cries as reporters, photographers and TV crews struggled and jockeyed for the best positions. Cameras were focussed through the bars of the gates, boom mics swung, flashlights flashed.

As Peter and his party neared the gates, they were all astounded by the sheer tumult that greeted them as incomprehensible questions were bawled simultaneously from every reporter's throat.

The family halted at a huge bank of microphones which Carr had positioned at the end of the drive, just a couple of yards from the front gates.

'Good morning, everyone,' said Peter. 'Thank you for coming.'

In his hand he held a single sheet of A4 paper. He held it aloft for everyone to see. 'I have here a short statement I should like to make.'

The camera flashes didn't stop, but Peter was an accomplished politician and he had the confidence to wait for those corralled behind the gates to fall silent before he began to read.

'For some days there has been much media speculation about the state of my marriage. Just over six months ago I formed a relationship with Clarissa Forbes, my researcher. That relationship has now ended. As you can see I have returned to my wife and children. Both they and my parents-in-law have forgiven me, and have been immensely understanding about my lapse. I am grateful to them all for their support at this trying time. As a married man and the father of young children, I accept that I was totally wrong to enter into the relationship with Miss Forbes. Unfortunately, I was the victim of an infatuation. It's not the first time that an older man has been fatally attracted to a much younger woman, but fortunately, I have realised my mistake in time and have apologised to my family...'

'And why haven't you apologised to Clarissa!'

All eyes went to the man who was responsible for this angrily shouted demand. He was pressed up against one of the gates. Barbara experienced a shock of recognition. It was Russell Forbes, Clarissa's father.

Barbara immediately looked to Peter for his reaction. He was staring at Russell, utterly at a loss. Blinking at the orgy of flashlights.

'Don't you think she deserves an apology, Peter?' Russell ranted. 'After all, she's only seventeen, she's pregnant, and you've dumped her!' He turned to the jostling, frenzied mob of reporters squashed up behind him; the photographers and TV camera crews who were frantically attempting to get him into frame. 'I'm Russell Forbes, by the way, Clarissa's father.' He turned back, pointing at Peter. 'And that bastard was once my best friend!'

The camera flashes fused into a wall of white light as Russell attempted to climb over the gates, and was immediately restrained by a police officer.

It was then that Barbara spoke. 'It's all right, Russell. You don't have to worry about Clarissa. Peter's going back to her. This is all a sham.'

Barbara's every word was amplified by the microphones.

'Barbara,' cried Peter, looking at her horrified.

'I've been reading their text messages,' Barbara called to Russell. 'They're planning to carry on as they did before, behind my back. But this time they're going to be more careful.' She turned back to Peter, slapped him across the face, then grabbed the children and ran back up the drive towards the house. Isobel followed, running after her. Peter turned to Howard. 'Howard...' he began.

'Clarissa's pregnant. Is that true?'

Peter looked down at the ground. 'Yes.'

'And you never had any intention of returning to Barbara and the children?'

'No'

Howard punched Peter on the jaw.

'Oh!' roared the crowd.

Peter lay on the gravel, feeling his jaw. Howard shook his head despairingly at him, then turned and went back up the drive towards the house.

The camera flashes were orgasmic.

****

'This is going to get out of hand,' said Eric.

The teenagers in Dylan's studio were still reacting hysterically to the violence they'd just witnessed in the grounds of Rooks Nest. The commotion had begun restlessly with the appearance of Russell Forbes; it had erupted when Barbara had slapped Peter; and now, after Howard's punch to Peter's jaw, it was at its zenith. The clients were shouting; pointing; squealing; gesticulating; laughing; screeching; making strange noises; pushing; shoving; and getting more and more worryingly physical and uncontrolled. It was as though today's violent behaviour by the adults over at Rooks Nest had released all of the kids' latent emotions associated with Sheldon and the Major's attacks on each other yesterday.

The sash windows had been opened and the racket in the room was intensified by the noisy crowds in the street, which the microphones in the drive of Rooks Nest were picking up and amplifying through loudspeakers. If that wasn't enough, the television was still switched on. Live pictures were being shown of Peter Kellingford MP addressing a febrile media through the bars of the Rooks Nest gates. Over these images the voice of a commentator was excitedly recounting all of the incredible events that had just occurred.

'We should get them downstairs,' said Toni.

Dylan gazed anxiously at an easel supporting his treasured painting in the style of Theo van Doesburg. Sheldon and Liam were "high fiving" worryingly close to it. 'You're right,' he said.

'They won't like that,' said Zoe. 'They don't think it's finished yet.'

'Too bad,' said Dylan. He started ordering the clients to go down to the chill-out room. This was met with a huge groan and aggressive body language. Undeterred Dylan, Zoe and Eric started to separate the clients and steer them out of the room. Mona, Scarlett and Liam were compliant and moved off immediately. The others were being more obstinate.

Seeing that Louise was still standing at the window, Toni went over to her. The child didn't look up, but kept her attention riveted on watching Peter Kellingford addressing the press. The microphones were still functioning and everything he said could be heard clearly.

Toni said, 'You'll have to come downstairs now, Louise.'

Louise remained staring out of the window. 'Oh,' she said, petulantly. 'Do I have to?'

'Afraid so. Your mother wouldn't like it.'

Louise turned away from the window to look up at Toni. Her eyes were luminous with excitement. 'But something else might happen. I don't want to miss it.'

'No. You must come away. You shouldn't be seeing this.'

'But it's so exciting,' said Louise. 'It's like a play.'

****

When the catastrophe occurred, Carr and Tanya were in the Roberts' sitting room watching Peter's statement being carried live on BBC News 24. They exchanged horror-stricken glances and cries of disbelief as Carr's carefully constructed plan to bring the media frenzy around Kellingford to an end disintegrated into soap opera and farce.

Initially, everything had seemed to be going perfectly to plan: the adults and children had got into position without a hitch; they'd all moved as one down the drive giving the impression of a united, quintessential middle class family. Peter had delivered his speech with just the right note of dignified remorse. Carr was looking forward with anticipation to receiving the congratulations of the Great Man himself. And then, for a complete control freak like Carr, who was paranoid about unstage-managed encounters with the press, it became the stuff of nightmares.

At first, they'd heard only a voice in the crowd demanding to know why Peter wasn't offering Clarissa an apology. Immediately the images on the TV screen had become blurred as the camera operators struggled to get the man responsible for the interruption into focus.

The man continued interrupting, asserting that Clarissa was pregnant and Peter had dumped her. By now the News 24 camera had got him into frame, just as he announced who he was.

All the blood had drained from Carr's face. 'My God! It's Clarissa's father!'

From then on it was downhill all the way. Carr and Tanya could only hold on to each other for support and cry "No! No! No!" as live on TV, Barbara told Russell Forbes, the press pack and millions of viewers that the demonstration of remorse and repentance they thought they were hearing from Peter, was in reality a complete sham because he'd every intention of going back to Clarissa. Revelation had piled on revelation, until the whole cynical fraud was exposed.

Carr broke into a cold sweat as he visualised the embarrassing images that would be replayed endless times on mainstream television for the next 24 hours; the pics that would be in all the newspapers; the damaging stories accompanying them. And it wouldn't just end there. Far into the future, when broadcasters wished to present striking examples of political nemesis or the most embarrassing moments ever experienced by a politician live on TV, they would always reach for the Peter Kellingford "moment of truth" clip.

But it was getting worse. Barbara was slapping Peter across the face. Now she and Isobel were breaking ranks, pulling the children after them, and running up the drive towards the house.

'It's a fucking shambles!' exclaimed Carr.

Now the cameras were on Howard as he stepped towards Peter. They heard him ask Peter if Clarissa was pregnant. They heard Peter's reply. Then Howard's fist was striking Peter in the face.

'He's only decked him!' cried Carr.

They watched Peter fall to the ground. They watched Howard turn, sorrowfully, and walk away from him. They watched the camera flashes that were more brilliant than the sun. They watched Peter lying on the ground rubbing his jaw.

'You've got to do something. Get out there!' cried Tanya.

'Come with me!'

Tanya hesitated.

He grabbed her hand. 'Come on!'

They rushed out of the sitting room. As they entered the hall they almost collided with Barbara, Isobel and the children who were standing there in shock.

'How could you? How could you?' screamed Isobel.

Carr was completely perplexed by this question, until he realized it was being addressed to Howard, who'd just come in from the drive and was standing framed in the front doorway.

Howard stepped further into the hall. He was trembling and white with rage. Ignoring Isobel, he went up to Barbara. 'My poor darling,' he said. 'This is awful. My heart bleeds for you.'

'How could you hit Peter in front of all those people?' Isobel screamed. 'Are you insane? Are you a madman?'

'I make no apology!' Howard retorted.

'Why did you hit daddy?' Mark asked him.

Howard was resolute. 'Because he deserved it.'

Carr was so beside himself with anger, he couldn't speak. He could only point his finger at Howard and splutter, 'You! You!'

'Oh, you too,' said Howard, facetiously. 'And by the way, if you want to save your boy I suggest you get down to the front gates, pronto. He's started talking to the press. Just the thing you wanted to avoid, wasn't it?'

Carr took Tanya's arm. 'Come on.'

They both ran out on to the drive and were immediately brought to a halt by what confronted them. It was true. Peter was talking to the reporters. He was pressed up close to the gates, responding to their questions. Meanwhile Russell Forbes was still trying to climb over the gates to get at him. Fortunately for Peter, Forbes was being restrained by two police officers.

Carr and Tanya exchanged a horrified look and then hurried on down the drive.

****

'You see, Russell, I love Clarissa. Anyone can fall in love.'

'It's not love, Peter, it's lust. And you're just an old letch.'

'I didn't intend it to happen. But you can't predict who you'll fall in love with.'

'You make me sick!'

Dylan had finally managed to persuade all the clients to leave his studio and go downstairs. Zoe, however, remained at the window, gazing at the gates to Rooks Nest through which Peter Kellingford was talking to Russell Forbes and the representatives of the media. He explaining to them why no-one should be judging him too harshly. But he obviously wasn't convincing Russell Forbes one bit. These embarrassing exchanges were being loudly relayed around Church Lane by the microphones set up in the drive, which no-one had switched off. They were also being broadcast to the whole country on BBC News 24.

As Zoe was observing what was going on across the road and simultaneously listening to the amplified conversations on TV, her attention was drawn to a tall, well-built man in his forties and a younger, blonde woman, who'd emerged from Rooks Nest and were walking leisurely down the drive. They went up to the big bank of microphones near the gates, and the man appeared to pull a plug or switch, because instantly all sound diminished as transmission became dependent solely on the TV crews' mics.

Via the television, Zoe was aware of the man and woman muttering something indistinctly to Kellingford which sounded like a plea for him to return to the house. But it was incomprehensible because it was drowned out by the angry protestations of the watching crowd. However, it was apparently effective because Kellingford moved away from the gates, and escorted by the man and woman, walked back up the drive and went into Rooks Nest.

Zoe stayed by the window, reflecting on the scenes she'd just witnessed. The kids had thought them amusing but she'd found them profoundly disturbing. It was clear that Howard Roberts was deeply stressed by his daughter's domestic problems and the fact that they were being played out in the public arena. No wonder he'd behaved so violently yesterday. He clearly had many suppressed emotional issues, which under conditions of extreme social pressure manifested as aggressive behaviour. He was plainly in need of therapy, and she felt ashamed of the way she'd provoked him when they'd first met. That had been childish and immature. And how wrong she'd been to speak about him in that disparaging way with that snide shit from The Source. She decided that if there was any way she could possibly help Howard Roberts, she would.

Zoe watched the police restrain Russell Forbes who was making yet another attempt to climb the gates to Rooks Nest. His shocking intervention during Kellingford's statement had been almost comic, but as a former actress she knew how fine the line was between comedy and tragedy. It was impossible to imagine the emotions of a father who'd only recently lost his wife to cancer, and whose teenage daughter had become involved in a sordid political sex scandal.

But Zoe's greatest empathy was for Barbara Kellingford. A woman who'd clearly been prepared to forgive her husband and take him back and who'd been publicly humiliated for it in the cruellest way possible. A wife who'd been betrayed and practised upon by the husband she'd trusted. The man had obviously been plotting to deceive her all along and had hidden from her the fact that his teenage lover was pregnant. Zoe knew it was vulgar solipsism on her part, but her identification with Barbara's humiliation was reflected to a lesser degree in her own relationship with Dylan. Like Barbara, she'd put her trust in a man who wasn't worthy of her. How stupid women were to abase themselves for such worthless men. Men who abused the trust reposed in them and treated it with humiliation and contempt.

Everyone had left the room now except Dylan. He came up to Zoe, and said, 'We're all going to have an early lunch out in the garden. I need to lock the room up. Are we done here?'

****

The police had finally succeeded in pulling Russell Forbes off the gates to Rooks Nest. They were now providing him with protection as he was escorted through the crowd to a waiting Mercedes by a triumphant Terry Bryden.

Having been deprived of Peter Kellingford MP, the throng of reporters and camera crews now besieged Russell, jostling each other for position as they milled around him, flinging questions like darts.

'You're wasting your time with all these questions, boys,' crowed Bryden. 'Mr Forbes is now under exclusive contract to us. If you want his story you'll have to read it in The Source.'

The crowd surged around the chauffeur driven limousine. Carson, a reporter from one of The Source's tabloid rivals, was positioned right next to the vehicle. As Bryden struggled to open the door for Russell, Carson said, 'Nice one Terry, you set him up to do that, didn't you?'

'Not me,' said Bryden, 'That's unethical.'

Russell appeared to be about to say something but was prevented by Bryden. 'Inside!' he commanded, and placing his hand protectively over Forbes' head, he forced him into the back seat of the Mercedes. 'Move up,' Bryden barked. Russell shuffled along the seat to make room for Bryden, who followed him in and slammed the door shut. Bryden then banged twice on the roof of the vehicle and it shot off at speed.

It may have been unethical, but the ambush by Clarissa's father had indeed been set up by Bryden. After obtaining from Russell the number of Peter Kellingford's everyday mobile phone, Bryden had immediately hacked it and discovered that Clarissa was pregnant. He'd revealed this to Russell who, in a shocked and depressed state, was ripe for manipulation and had readily agreed to announce Clarissa's pregnancy live on television during Kellingford's statement. Shrewdly, Bryden had suggested to him that this would not only create a sensation, it would destroy the MP's career and so provide Russell with his revenge. This was the bait Russell couldn't resist. He'd been picked up from his flat in West London that morning at 4am, and driven straight up to Leefdale. Once there, Bryden had positioned the anonymous Russell up against the bars of the gates of Rooks Nest, hiding him in plain sight, with strict instructions for him to deliver his bombshell at the appropriate moment, when Kellingford was well into his speech.

Bryden was elated. 'Your timing was wonderful, Russell. Perfect. "Don't you think Clarissa deserves an apology, Peter? After all, she's only seventeen, she's pregnant, and you've dumped her!" Ha, ha, ha!' Bryden slapped his thighs and laughed enthusiastically. 'Fucking brilliant. And if it wasn't for you, no-one would have known Peter and Clarissa were not only double crossing Barbara but the great British public as well.' Bryden was hysterical with laughter now. 'What a cunning stunt, if I say so myself. What a fucking brilliant piece of journalism.' He broke into uncontrollable laughter again. 'And then she slaps him around the face!' He was helpless now with mirth. 'And then, to top it all, the Major goes and smacks him in the gob! Ha, ha, ha!'

An unwelcome thought brought a sudden end to his laughter. That useless twat Carter better not have fucked up the photos again. It would cost a fortune to buy them off the paps.

The Mercedes turned out of Church Lane and sped through Leefdale's main street. However, it had only travelled a few hundred yards when Bryden ordered the driver to stop.

'Why have we stopped?' said Russell.

'This is where I get out.'

'I thought you were coming with me to London?'

The Source had arranged for Russell to be put up in a London hotel. There, in a penthouse suite, a team of reporters had been assembled to ghost his account of the traumatic events which had turned his life upside down, estranged him from his daughter and destroyed a twenty five year friendship. They would be working around the clock to have the feature ready for serialization in The Source over the coming days.

Bryden said, 'I've got to stay here and do some interviews.'

Russell was sitting hunched forward in his seat. Now it was over, he deeply regretted his actions. He was sure Clarissa would never speak to him again. Not after he'd humiliated her by revealing her pregnancy to the world. And Barbara's revelations had come as a complete shock. He'd absolutely no idea Clarissa and Peter were deceiving everyone. He'd thought Peter really was returning to his wife and abandoning Clarissa because she was pregnant. He certainly hadn't expected Barbara to slap Peter. Or Howard to hit him, either. In front of the whole nation. It had all been just too awful!

To Bryden, he said, 'I can't believe I've done what I just did. On live TV as well. I should never have gone along with it. I shouldn't have let you talk me into it.'

Bryden gave him an incredulous look. 'Listen pal, don't try and guilt trip me. You talked yourself into it. When I told you the plan you jumped at it. You said you'd do it just to stuff the bastard, even if we weren't offering you more cash.'

'Yes, but I didn't expect it to turn out like this.'

'It ain't my fault you've got no imagination.'

'Nevertheless, I don't think I should take it any further.'

Bryden's eyes narrowed dangerously. 'What do you mean?'

'I don't want to humiliate Clarissa or my friends any more. I think I'm going to have to withdraw my co-operation with The Source.'

'You're not going to help us with the feature?'

'That's right. I'm sorry.'

'Well, I hope you've got very deep pockets. You signed a contract with us, remember?'

'You'd sue me?'

'No choice.'

Russell fell silent.

From his inside pocket Bryden took out a hip flask. He offered it to Russell. 'Take a drink, while you think it over,' he said. 'I need to make a call.'

Bryden took out his mobile and called Howard Roberts' mobile number. There was no reply. He left a message on Howard's voicemail asking him to return his call urgently. Bryden's next call was to his editor. It was answered by Stella, Bill Metcalfe's assistant.

'Hello Stella, where's Bill?'

'He's on the sixth floor.'

'Oh.'

There were only five floors in The Source's building. "The Sixth Floor" was code for the proprietor's Georgian residence in central London, just a few streets away from The Source.

Sheila congratulated Bryden on the success of his ambush, which everyone in editorial had watched on TV. They discussed the shambolic scenes at the gates of Rooks Nest and speculated on Peter Kellingford's future. Bryden told Stella that he was still attempting to set up the interviews with Howard and Barbara, which would now be an absolute gift. 'I'll leave a message on Bill's mobile,' he said. 'But if he doesn't pick it up ask him to call me as soon as he gets back.' He turned his head towards Russell and stared at him coldly. 'Tell him Forbes is getting cold feet about the feature.'

'I only said I was thinking about it,' Russell hissed.

Bryden had just ended his conversation with Stella, when his ring tone announced an incoming call. It was Howard Roberts.

Bryden's tone was affectedly friendly. 'Hello, Major. Thanks for getting back. Congratulations on giving that love-rat what he deserves. How does it feel?'

Howard said, 'I hope you won't think me rude but I prefer not to answer that question. In fact, neither Barbara nor I will be answering any of your questions. We've decided there's no necessity for us to talk to a blackmailing swine like you at all.'

'What?'

'You heard me.'

'This is very sudden. Why? Why the sudden change of mind?'

'Ask your editor.'

Bryden sat up erect in his seat. 'Listen, don't fuck with me. I think you're overlooking what's at stake here, pal. We had a deal. If you shit on it, I'll make sure everyone knows your little secret. It'll be a three page spread. You'll be looking over your shoulder for the rest of your fucking life.'

'Talk to your editor,' said Howard.

'What do you mean talk to...'

But Howard had ended the call.

There was a long silence as Bryden struggled to come to terms with this unexpected turn of events.

Russell looked at Bryden nervously. 'I've been thinking it over, Terry. You're right. I've signed a contract. I can't back out now.'

Bryden regarded him sourly. 'Excellent. I'd hate to give Bill Metcalfe two bits of crap news in one day.'

Russell smiled, relieved. 'You said you wanted to know if I had any photos that would do for the feature. I have but they're back at my flat. I'll have to pick them up before I go to the hotel.'

'Sure, Russell. Anything you need, just tell the driver.'

Russell went to return the hip flask but Bryden held up a hand. 'That's all right. Keep it.' He turned his attention back to his phone, found Bill Metcalfe's mobile number and pressed "Call".

****

'Why's Uncle Russell gone in the car with that reporter?' Mark asked his grandmother. 'Does he know him?'

'I don't know, dear,' said Isobel. She searched for the most innocuous explanation. 'He's probably giving him a lift home.'

Isobel was sitting on the sofa in the sitting room of Rooks Nest. She was positioned between Mark and Jessica and had her arms around both of them. For the past five minutes they'd been watching News 24. On screen were live images of Russell Forbes' departure with Terry Bryden in the limousine.

'But we did. I assure you, we did,' said Tanya, speaking into her mobile phone. She was standing at the end of the sofa, keeping one eye on the television and trying to reassure her caller that the reason for the humiliating fiasco which had just been witnessed by millions was neither her fault nor Carr's.

'Grandma,' said Jessica. 'Mark says Clarissa's having a baby.'

'No, I didn't,' said Mark.

'You fibber! You did.' She appealed to Isobel. 'He said that's what pregnant meant.'

Isobel put her hands up to her face. Behind her palms she could feel warm tears starting. Why was she expected to answer such questions from her innocent grandchildren? Why had she been subjected to such total humiliation? Was she ever to hold her head high in public again? Many such painful reflections surged across her consciousness.

At the far end of the room, Carr, Peter and Barbara were standing by the cabinet in which the best glassware was kept. They were all talking heatedly in very low voices.

'So you did know that Clarissa was pregnant,' said Carr.

'Yes,' said Peter. He was still nursing his jaw.

Carr's fists were tightly clenched. 'Then why did you keep it from me?'

'How was I to know Russell was going to ambush me like that?'

'But you could have told me, couldn't you?' demanded Barbara. 'Hadn't I a right to know? How could you let us all go through that charade knowing she was pregnant?'

Peter glowered at her. 'You're the one to blame for this shambles.'

'Me?'

'Why did you have to say anything? Why didn't you just keep quiet?'

Spiritedly, Barbara said, 'That's what I intended to do. Even when I found out you were going back to Clarissa and were lying to all of us, I didn't say a word. I kept quiet for your sake.'

'You should have just stuck to the script, and said nothing,' said Carr.

'And I would have done,' Barbara shouted. 'But when Russell told the whole world Clarissa was pregnant something inside me snapped.'

Isobel had suddenly appeared at her daughter's side. She jabbed her finger towards Peter. 'If you knew all the time that this rat had no intention of coming back, why didn't you tell us before we went out there?'

'Because I was trying to save his career!' Barbara cried.

'Well, he's not worth it. You should never have put us through all that. It was so undignified. So humiliating. With the children there too. Awful!'

And then they were all shouting at each other at once. Peter bawled at Carr that he'd never intended to deceive anyone, but had been forced to do so by senior figures in the Party. Carr insulted Peter's competence and accused him of making him look stupid. Isobel howled at Peter that he was an untrustworthy, duplicitous swine and she wished Barbara had never met him. Barbara yelled at Peter that she was glad Russell had spoken out because it had forced her to tell the truth, and now everyone knew what a charlatan her husband was.

Mark and Jessica watched in fascination, dismay and disbelief as the grown-ups' voices rose higher and higher and tempers were suddenly lost. The adult world seemed to have gone completely mad. Only Tanya was aware of the children's distress. She ended her call and went over to the sofa, stood behind it and placed her hands consolingly on Mark and Jessica's shoulders.

In the middle of all the uproar there came a loud knocking on the front door. Still shouting at Peter, and backing out of the room, Isobel went to answer it. Meanwhile the row continued.

'Why couldn't you stick to the script, you silly bitch!'

Peter squared up to Carr. 'Leave Barbara alone, you thug. She's had a terrible shock.'

'Oh yeah? And who's responsible for that, then? Eh?'

Peter's response was to grab Carr around the throat and force him back against the wooden cabinet full of glassware. The cabinet tilted and there was the sound of glass scraping against glass.

'That's my best crystal!' exclaimed Isobel, who'd just returned to the room. She went straight over to Peter and Carr, pulled both men apart and anxiously checked the cabinet for damage.

PC Wheatcroft and WPC Scargill had entered behind Isobel. A hush fell as they now stood looking disapprovingly around them, as though they'd unexpectedly encountered a fracas in a pub.

The silence was interrupted by the sound of "Land of Hope and Glory" emanating from Carr's jacket pocket. He whipped out his mobile phone and answered the call. 'Yes, yes, you're absolutely right,' he said, obsequiously.

Isobel went straight across to Barbara. 'No damage to the Waterford Crystal, thank goodness. But the police have come for daddy. I've told them he'll be down in a minute.'

'Why do they want him?'

'They won't say.'

Barbara glanced at Mark and Jessica. 'Oh God. The children mustn't be here.'

Isobel went out into the hall and called up the stairs, urging Howard to hurry down.

'Of course,' said Carr, speaking into his mobile. He took the phone away from his ear and held it out towards Peter. 'It's him!' he said, in an awed whisper, simultaneously raising his eyebrows.

Peter looked visibly shaken. He took the mobile from Carr and went out of the room to take the call.

Tanya caught Carr's eye and gave him one of her approving looks. She was always impressed by his close connection to power.

Isobel returned from the hall and went straight over to Mark and Jessica who were still on the sofa. 'I want both of you to go upstairs to your room, and stay there until you're told you can come down.'

'Yes,' said Barbara, who was now also by the sofa. 'Go up and change into something cooler.'

'But I want to stay with you, mummy,' wailed Jessica.

'Darling, you must do what grandma says. Please.'

'We want to see what happens on the TV,' said Mark.

'You've been complaining all morning about how hot you are in those clothes. Well now's your chance to change into something cooler.'

'Why don't I go with them?' said Tanya.

Isobel said, 'Would you, Tanya? That would be so helpful.'

'Are you sure you can cope with them?' said Barbara.

'Oh yes. I worked as a nanny in Switzerland during my gap year.' She addressed the children. 'Will we be able to see the reporters from the top of the house?'

'Yes,' said both children together.

Everyone's attention was on Howard as he now entered the room. Despite all that had happened, he looked completely undaunted, almost jaunty. He went straight over to Mark and Jessica. 'Hello you two,' he said. 'How about a game of bowls?'

The two children responded enthusiastically.

Isobel was outraged. 'How can you possibly suggest playing bowls at a time like this?'

Howard said, 'The perfect thing, I should have thought. A pleasant diversion after all the awfulness.'

Isobel looked in the direction of Wheatcroft and Scargill. 'Anyway, there's no time. They want to talk to you.'

'Really?' Howard turned to the children. 'I'm very sorry, but it looks like our game will have to wait.' Looking intensely wearisome he went over and joined the two police officers.

Mark and Jessica were bitterly disappointed, and didn't hide it.

'I tell you what,' Tanya said to them, 'I've always wanted to learn how to play bowls. After you've changed, perhaps you'd show me?'

The children were instantly appeased. They got up and tugged Tanya out of the room.

'Don't forget, Tanya, we'll be leaving soon,' Carr called after her. He glanced up at the TV and immediately wished he hadn't. Images of Russell Forbes' ambush were being replayed, accompanied by the studio anchor's gloating commentary. Yet again Carr watched Russell drop his bombshell; Barbara slap Peter; Howard punch Peter. He now knew exactly what people meant when they said they wanted the ground to open up and swallow them. This was not the outcome he'd expected when he'd been appointed as a safe pair of hands to detoxify the Kellingford affair. And now the Dear Leader had indicated that his job was on the line!

The screen suddenly went blank. He turned and saw that Barbara had the remote in her hand. 'I don't think we need to see that all over again, do you?' she said.

Howard was now in earnest discussion with the police. 'But I was provoked,' he was saying. 'I'd just found out my son-in-law had lied to us all. The bastard had never intended to return to his wife and children and his mistress was pregnant. Of course, I hit him. Any father would.'

Wheatcroft looked genuinely sympathetic. 'I'm sorry Howard, but you did it in front of a significant number of witnesses.'

'About half the country,' said Scargill. 'And it's on video.'

'I'm not denying it,' said Howard.

Wheatcroft said, 'Howard Roberts, I am arresting you for committing the offence of actual bodily harm...'

'Not again,' Howard sighed.

'Against the Honourable Peter Kellingford MP...'

Howard laughed. 'Honourable!'

'You do not have to say anything but it may harm your defence if you do not mention when questioned something which you later rely on in court.'

'Yes, yes,' said Howard.

'Anything you do say may be given in evidence.'

Howard regarded him frankly. 'Actually, I do have something to say. Given what that shit's done to my daughter and the rest of us, he's going to get off rather lightly, in my view. So I don't regret hitting him. Don't regret hitting him at all.'

Scargill noted this in her book.

'Very well,' said Wheatcroft. 'Is that all?'

Howard nodded.

'You can't arrest him,' said Isobel, going up to Wheatcroft. 'It was only done in the heat of the moment. You saw yourself what pressure we were all under out there.'

'I'm sorry, Mrs Roberts, it's too late for that. The whole country saw it.'

Barbara said, 'Aren't you going to arrest me too? I assaulted Peter first. I slapped him, remember?'

'You aren't released on bail, pending trial,' said Wheatcroft. 'Your father is. We can't just ignore it.'

'If it was down to us,' said Scargill, 'we'd just be treating it as a domestic that got a bit out of hand and needed an informal caution. But a man's just punched an MP on live TV. We'll be publicly hung out to dry if we don't take some action.'

Howard placed his hands on Isobel's shoulders. 'They're only doing their job.' He turned to Wheatcroft. 'I suppose you'll be taking me to Luffield?'

'That's right.'

Addressing Barbara, Howard said, 'Will you ring Armitage and tell him I've been arrested and taken to Luffield police station. And insist that it's he personally who comes to advise me. It must be Armitage himself and not that little toad, Ryecart.'

'Hang on dad, I've got an idea.'

Her intention was to find Peter and ask him to stop Howard's arrest. But at that moment, Peter entered from the hall. He was holding the mobile in his right hand and looked poleaxed. Barbara ran over to him.

'Peter, you must do something, daddy's been arrested for punching you!'

Peter looked straight through Barbara. He walked past her and handed the mobile back to Carr.

'He's just relieved me of my portfolio,' he said, incredulously.

Howard laughed loudly. 'You've been sacked. Good job! You'd make a terrible Home Secretary.'

Wheatcroft said, 'Come along, Howard.'

Peter suddenly realized the significance of what Barbara had just said. 'Where are you taking him?'

Barbara said, 'I told you. He's been arrested for punching you.'

Peter treated Scargill to a display of his charm. 'Oh, now look here, there's no need for that is there? It's a family matter.'

But Scargill was impervious to any man's charm. 'I'm sorry, it's too late for that.'

'But I'm never going to press charges. And if I'm called to give evidence I'll say Howard was provoked beyond reason. I expect most of the country would agree with that. And they'd probably approve of what he did to me, too.'

Wheatcroft and Scargill exchanged a look.

'Just give us a moment,' said Wheatcroft. He drew Scargill aside and they both engaged in a bout of animated whispering. When they'd finished, Wheatcroft addressed Peter. 'In view of your refusal to press charges, sir, and the unusual circumstances surrounding this case, we've decided to consult a superior officer before we proceed. It could well be that this might turn out to be a public interest matter. We need to take advice.'

When the officers had left, Barbara thanked Peter for postponing her father's arrest. 'At least you've done one decent thing today,' she said.

Peter gazed at her abjectly. 'I know you won't believe me, but I'm deeply ashamed of what's happened.'

Brusquely, Howard said to Peter. 'Good. And so you should be. I'm grateful for what you said to the police just now. It shows you're at last taking some responsibility for the mess you've caused, but don't think it changes my feelings about you one jot. If the press ever give me the opportunity to express my opinion of you, I shall tell them exactly what I think!'

Barbara's hands flew up to her face. 'My God. Bryden. I'd forgotten about him.'

Howard said, 'You don't have to worry about him anymore.'

'You've told him the interview's off?'

'What interview?' demanded Carr.

Howard was signalling to Barbara to keep quiet, but she couldn't care less now. She wanted Peter and Carr to know she was no longer their creature. 'The interview with Bryden,' she said. 'He's a reporter with The Source.'

'I know who the bastard is,' said Carr. 'He's the one who set up the ambush for Peter.' He regarded her suspiciously. 'And you agreed to talk to him?'

'I'd hardly say agreed.'

Carr gave a strange little jolt of indignation. 'God's teeth. Why won't you people let me handle the press? That's my job. I'm the press officer. I'm the one who authorises interviews.'

'You overreach yourself, Carr. I don't take my orders from spinmeisters,' said Howard.

Carr ignored him. He was still concentrating on Barbara. 'Didn't Steve Hawkins tell you not to go anywhere near the press?'

'Yes, he did.'

'Then why did you say yes to Bryden, for God's sake?'

'He forced us to.'

'No, Barbara,' said Howard. 'You must keep quiet about this.'

Carr gave Barbara a sharp, quizzical look. 'Us?'

This time Barbara stayed silent.

'What's going on?' said Carr.

'Ah, I see it all now,' said Peter, taking a step towards Barbara. 'I wondered why you didn't seem all that surprised to see Russell. You set it up with Bryden, didn't you? You knew Russell was going to be there all the time. You knew he was going to ambush me and reveal that Clary was pregnant.'

'It wasn't like that at all,' Barbara cried, indignantly. 'I was as surprised as you were. I hadn't the faintest idea Russell was going to be there. It was a complete shock. To all of us!'

But Peter was convinced he was on to something. 'Not to you. You knew Russell was going to be there and tell everyone Clarissa was pregnant.'

'How could I have known that?' demanded Barbara.

'Because Bryden told you.'

'How would he know she was pregnant? Did you tell him?'

Peter was incensed. 'Of course not! Russell must have told him.'

'No.' Barbara insisted. 'Clarissa and Russell aren't speaking. And if Russell had known she was pregnant he'd have told me.'

'Bryden must have found out somehow. Anyway, you knew I was going back to Clary, didn't you? How could you have known about that?'

'Because of her text messages. On our mobile phone. The mobile phone only you and I were ever supposed to use!'

'And that's how you knew she was pregnant. Her text messages.'

'No. She never said anything about being pregnant in the texts.'

Peter considered this. 'You're right, she didn't. But she left voicemail messages about it on my other phone.'

'I never checked any messages on your black phone.'

'I don't believe you.' He turned to Howard. 'That's why you punched me, isn't it? You were set up by Bryden to do it.'

'If I'd known you'd betrayed Barbara with all those women I'd have punched you a lot sooner,' said Howard.

'What women?' said Carr.

'His cock's too big for his trousers,' said Howard. 'Perhaps you should issue a press release about it.'

At this moment PC Wheatcroft and WPC Scargill came in. They had plainly heard Howard's last remark because they were having difficulty keeping their faces straight.

Peter marched over to them. 'Good, you're back. I want you to arrest him after all.'

Scargill looked put out. 'I wish you'd make up your mind, sir. The last thing you said was that you didn't want to press charges.'

'That was before I knew he'd deliberately planned to hit me.'

There was a long pause. Wheatcroft said, 'Is this true, Howard?'

'Of course, it's not true. It was a completely spontaneous response!' He turned to Peter. 'Not everyone is as duplicitous and calculating as you!'

'We've had a word with our DI,' said Scargill. 'He says we're not to proceed any further until he's discussed the case thoroughly with the CPS.'

'No action can be taken until then,' said Wheatcroft.

Barbara said, 'Peter, if you have dad arrested, I'll tell everyone what my life's been like with you all these years. The press. Anyone who'll listen. Is that what you want?'

'Why should I care? Your plot with Bryden has ruined me.'

Barbara was outraged. 'How dare you suggest that we were in league with Bryden? We detest the man. Mummy and daddy didn't even want to stand out there with you. I begged them to do it to save your career. And they agreed to it even though their lives were in danger.'

'What danger?' said Carr.

'From the IRA.'

'Is this true?' said Wheatcroft.

Howard said, 'I never comment on military matters.'

'But I do!' screamed Isobel. 'And I'm telling you, it is true!' Now all of her suppressed anger was vented on Peter. 'Because of your philandering we're in such danger we're going to have to move out of our lovely home and go God knows where.' She broke down in tears. 'It really is too much. Too much!'

Peter's face had contorted into a rictus of remorse. 'My God. I've made such a bloody mess of everything!'

There was a sound very like a sob as he walked quickly out of the room.

Everyone stood looking after him, astonished.

****

'Unless Roberts is in the boot, I don't think he's been arrested,' joked Bryden.

He and John Carter were standing outside Rooks Nest watching the departure of PC Wheatcroft and WPC Scargill, the only two figures visible inside the police car which had just sped through the opened gates and was now setting off down Church Lane.

After sending Russell Forbes on his way to London, Bryden had walked back through the village to re-join Carter. When he'd arrived in Church Lane, he'd received the anticipated joshing from his rivals about his ambush of

Kellingford. None had expected to see him again: they'd all thought he'd be off celebrating. But that was the farthest thing from Bryden's mind. Whatever his failings as a human being, he was a first class newspaperman; and his years of experience told him that there were still plenty of story possibilities to be mined from the Kellingford scandal. For example, he knew that if Kellingford departed Rooks Nest alone, that would confirm he'd never had any intention of returning to his family and was going back to his teenage mistress. But if Kellingford left with his wife and children that would be an even bigger story, and the readership's sympathy could then be directed towards Clarissa Forbes, the dumped and pregnant teenage mum. Either way, The Source would sell millions more copies. There was also another reason why Bryden had returned to keep watch on Rooks Nest alongside Carter: he hadn't altogether given up hope that he'd eventually get his interview with Howard Roberts and his daughter.

Bryden's mobile started vibrating. He fished it out of his jacket pocket and saw that it was Bill Metcalfe who was calling. At last!

Metcalfe was characteristically upbeat and laconic. 'Hello, Terry. Congratulations on the ambush. Brilliant stuff. Watched it on TV with the boss. He was delighted. Pics come out OK?'

'Yeah.' He shot Carter a look. 'No fuck ups, I'm told.'

'Listen, we're getting very credible reports here that Kellingford's been sacked. Although, of course, it'll be presented as a resignation.'

'That's no surprise. Did you get my message? About Roberts and his daughter pulling out of the interviews?'

'No worries. They're not needed now. We've plenty of stuff already, and if Kellingford leaves the Shadow Cabinet the story's dead.'

'Dead? That's ridiculous. We've got enough on Roberts to keep this stuff running till next week. Not to mention all those ex-squeezes of Kellingford's we've signed up. Tarts as well.'

'Ah, well, I was coming to that.'

Bryden detected something unusual in Metcalfe's tone: an uncharacteristic hesitancy or prevarication.

'I'm afraid we're going to have to spike it.'

'Spike what?'

'The Roberts story. And the Kellingford stuff too.'

'What the fuck's going on?' rasped Bryden. 'When I told Roberts just now he could expect a shitstorm, he didn't seem unduly bothered. He told me to talk to you. Why was that?'

The long pause convinced Bryden that something was definitely wrong. Metcalfe lowered his voice. 'Listen, I shouldn't be telling you this. I've just spent the morning with the boss and two very scary individuals who were at great pains to convince me it wasn't in our interests to print anything about Howard

Roberts or his activities in Northern Ireland. They told me to lay off Kellingford too.'

So Metcalfe had been got at. That's why Roberts had been so confident.

'And I'll tell you something else.' Metcalfe's voice had become a whisper. 'Roy Oates is dead.'

'Dead?'

'Yeah. Went under a tube train this morning. Bank Station. The official line is it was suicide. But I'd say the Security boys' hands were all over it. Oates knew too much. You know how he shoots his mouth off when he's pissed.'

Bryden struggled to take all this in. 'Christ! If the spooks topped him they must have moved fucking fast. Did Roberts tip them off?'

'No idea. Why? Did you mention Oates' name to him?'

Now it was Bryden who went quiet. He recalled he hadn't mentioned Oates' name at all, but he had told Roberts that the information about his connection to the Fermanagh Four had come from a senior reporter. He decided there was no necessity for Metcalfe to know that. 'Why would I tell Roberts where I got my intel? I'm not a fucking rookie, you know.'

'Good. I'm sure you wouldn't want Oates' death on your conscience.'

Bryden quickly passed on. 'Russell Forbes is on his way to the hotel. Do you want me to close the ghost job down and send everyone home?'

'No, Russell's complete account will be very useful. Let's get all the dirt on Kellingford we can but not publish. At the moment it looks like he's going to stay on as an MP. He'll probably return to the Shadow Cabinet at some stage. If he stays in politics it might be useful to have something on him, in case we need to call in a favour.'

They returned to the subject of Oates and exchanged a few reminiscences about him. Then Metcalfe said, 'Where are you now?'

'Still on the doorstep.'

'Has Kellingford left yet?'

'No. Not yet. I'm waiting to see if his wife and kids leave with him.'

'What about Roberts? Has he been arrested?'

'Not so far.'

'I'm sure he will be. He was bang to rights. Tell Carter to get pics of anyone who leaves. But you, I want back here.'

'You do?'

'Absolutely. There's the by-election next week, and now probably a reshuffle.' Metcalfe lowered his voice again, this time to a whisper. 'By the way, how many others up there know Roberts served in Northern Ireland?'

'I dunno. One or two. Why?'

'The spooks wanted to know. They want me to provide a full list of their names. Email it to me asap.'

'No.'

'What?'

'I said no. They can do their own dirty work. Tell them to go and fuck themselves.'

Metcalfe first pleaded then threatened, but Bryden was adamant.

'Terry, I don't think you appreciate...'

'Oh, I do appreciate. I appreciate very well. I'll talk to you about it when I get back.'

And with that, Bryden ended the call.

John Carter stared at him quizzically, but said nothing.

Bryden said, 'If anyone asks, you don't know a thing about Major Roberts. Particularly where he served in the army.'

John looked bemused. 'Why?'

'Because it might save your life. You know nothing about him, understand?'

'All right. But how could it save my life?'

Bryden ignored the question. 'Metcalfe wants me to go back,' he said. He gave Carter his instructions, then held out his hand. 'You're a good snapper. If you ever want a full time job at The Source, I'm sure our picture editor would take you on.' They shook hands. 'But my advice is not to bother. You'll be happier here taking pictures of dog shows.'

'Supposing I want more out of life than that?'

'That's your choice, son. We're all free agents.'

****

Barbara ascended the stairs at the lowest nadir of despair. Her world had collapsed. Everything in it had been ruined. What little hope she'd had of restoring the balance of forces in her life and returning to her normal state had vanished. The news of Clarissa's pregnancy was decisive. There was no way that Peter could abandon his teenage mistress now. There were limits, even for a charlatan like him. Barbara knew she'd have to start visualising a life without him. But the thought of starting all over again with someone else was deeply anathema. She'd no appetite for it. All she wanted was her old way of life restored.

She was halfway up the last flight of stairs when she heard Peter's voice in their bedroom. He was talking loudly to someone on his mobile. She crept up the remainder of the stairs, tip-toed across the landing and stood outside the closed bedroom door, listening. It was quite clear that Peter was speaking to Clarissa. He seemed to be having a hard time persuading her that the text she'd received purporting to be from him, had actually been sent by Barbara. 'But I never sent that text,' Barbara heard him say. 'Why would I send you a text like that? It's abusive. It was that cow, I expect. She's the one who's done it!'

Barbara winced as she heard herself referred to in this way. But if you listened in at keyholes, she told herself, you had to expect to hear some unpleasant truths. Undaunted, she listened on. It now seemed that Clarissa was accusing Peter of breaking his promise not to tell her father she was pregnant, a charge Peter was vehemently denying. 'I never said a word to Russell. I haven't a clue how he found out. Are you sure you haven't told someone?' This was followed by a very long pause as Peter listened to Clarissa's reply. 'Well you must have told someone,' he continued. 'How else could Russell have known?' Clarissa now seemed to be suggesting that it was Barbara who'd told Russell, because Peter said, 'No, I was right next to her when your dad blurted it out. It came as a complete shock to her. She could only have known you were pregnant if she'd heard your voice message, but she doesn't know the pin for my black mobile.' This didn't seem to appease Clarissa, because her recriminations continued. Peter and Clarissa, like so many of Terry Bryden's other unfortunate phone hacking victims, could only assume that their most guarded secrets had been betrayed by those closest to them. The possibility that their personal, intimate voicemail messages could have been accessed by a representative of the free press and cynically exploited for profit, was so fantastical it would never have occurred to them.

Barbara was aware that Peter's tone had suddenly changed to one of peevish resentment. He was clearly blaming Clarissa for his sacking from the Shadow Cabinet. 'But you don't seem to understand what a catastrophe this is for me! I've lost my job. My career's ruined.' Clarissa's response suggested that she was more concerned with her own plight, for it forced Peter to quickly reassure her with, 'Of course, I'm not going to desert you, darling. You're having our baby.'

For the first time since her brutal public humiliation in front of the media, Barbara felt some cause for hope. She recognised in Peter's voice a familiar timbre, one she'd heard on so many other occasions when his current fling had run its natural course. This particular voice quality told her that he was tiring of the relationship with Clarissa, and it no longer held the strong attraction for him it once had; that as well as boring him she'd become a burden and he now regarded her as being more trouble than she was worth. Heartened, Barbara opened the bedroom door without knocking and went straight into the room.

'I've got to go now,' Peter told Clarissa. 'I've got to pack. Bye. Love you.'

He looked at Barbara, expectantly.

'Do you really?' said Barbara.

'What?'

'Love her?'

Peter ignored the question. 'What do you want?'

'You've really fucked up this time, haven't you?'

He nodded, sadly. 'Come to gloat?'

'Not at all.' It was a big gamble but she had to take it. 'You know, there's still a way you can salvage the situation.'

'Really? How's that?'

'Is Clarissa really pregnant?'

'Do you suppose Russell would have told the world if she wasn't?'

'Tell her to get a termination.'

He shook his head, vigorously. 'No.'

'She's young. She'll soon get over it.' She gave him a long look. 'After all, I had to.'

'And you've never forgiven me for it, have you?'

'After the termination you can issue a press release. Announce that as well as resigning from the Shadow Cabinet, you're stepping down as an MP.'

'Why should I do that?'

'Because, if you don't, it's goodbye for ever. And this time I mean it. I love you and I want you back, but the price is giving up politics. If you won't there's no future for us together.'

'You'd take me back? Despite all the public humiliation? You don't care what people would say?'

'I told you, I love you. I don't give a damn what the world thinks.'

'I'm sorry. You're asking too much.'

'It's your choice.' She turned and made to go.

'No, wait. Everything's going so fast, I can't think. I can't make a decision as important as that in five minutes.'

The ring tone on Barbara's blue mobile went. 'I hope this isn't Clary,' she said.

But when she answered, it wasn't a voice she recognised.

'Is that Barbara Kellingford?'

'Yes?'

'It's Zoe Fitzgerald here. You don't know me. I work in the inclusion unit in The Old Rectory. How are you?'

'I'm fine.'

'I want you to know how sickened I am by what went on this morning. I saw it all and my heart went out to you. You didn't deserve such public humiliation. Your husband is obviously a deceitful arsehole. A complete male chauvinist. You should leave him. He's a total user. And your father has clearly got mental health issues. He violently attacked one of the children over here and damaged their sculptures. He desperately needs help.'

'How did you get hold of this number?'

'Dylan Bourne gave it to me.'

'But I gave it to him in confidence.'

'I know. He wouldn't give it to me at first. But I forced it out of him. I told him you needed our support. He's a very kind man so he gave it to me.'

'How typical,' said Barbara. 'Men are so pathetic they can't even be trusted with a telephone number.'

'You're not going to take your husband back, are you? After all he's done?'

'That's none of your business.'

'Look, I appreciate how raw you must be feeling, but you really need the opportunity to reflect on your situation with a professional. I'm a trained psychotherapist and I can see that you're in a very abusive relationship...'

But Barbara cut her short.

'Listen, you don't know anything about my life and I don't intend to discuss my problems with you or anyone else. I don't need advice from a complete stranger who knows nothing about my situation, and who is, presumably, touting for business. How dare you patronise me.'

Zoe was undeterred. 'Naturally you're suspicious of everyone at the moment. I assure you I'm just ringing to give you my support and the benefit of my professional experience.'

'Well, that's very kind of you. Now piss off!'

Barbara terminated the call and switched off her mobile.

'Who the hell was that?' asked Peter.

'Someone from The Old Rectory.' She gave him an account of what Zoe had said.

Peter looked affronted. 'Really. The cheek of some people!'

CHAPTER FORTY ONE

After the morning's excitement it took the clients a long time to settle back into the inclusion unit's normal routine. A picnic lunch in the rear garden helped to calm their unsettled spirits, and afterwards they were soon amusing themselves playing football or just sitting and chatting under the shade of those few trees which had escaped Zoe's transformation into sculptures.

During lunch, Dylan took the opportunity to hold a consultation on the patio with his colleagues. It was decided that the incidents over at Rooks Nest had been so disturbing it would probably be best to scrap the timetable for the afternoon and use art and drama therapy to enable the clients to work through their emotional responses to the traumatic and violent scenes they'd witnessed. Dylan suggested that it would be helpful if all the staff took part and worked with the group. Not only would this provide extra support for clients whose behaviour might still be in a volatile and unpredictable state, it would also give them the opportunity to ventilate their feelings with a number of adults who'd witnessed the same violent incidents as themselves. 'It might encourage them to go beyond the superficial and reflect on their reactions to the experience more profoundly,' he said. Zoe agreed. 'It could also benefit us,' she said. 'I'm sure we've all been affected by the distressing things we've seen today.'

Zoe requested that Louise be included in the group session too. Eric demurred. He felt that the presence of Louise might inhibit the older children from expressing themselves.

'We can't just send Louise home without an opportunity to engage with what she saw,' Zoe said, sharply.

'I agree,' said Dylan.

'I thought you were opposed to Louise doing drama therapy,' said Toni.

Dylan sighed, patiently. 'She won't be doing drama therapy. She'll only be joining us for the art segment. When the group moves on to drama therapy, Louise can return to her school work.'

Zoe looked displeased. 'But that'll deny her the opportunity to explore her feelings in relation to the art.'

'I don't want Louise going anywhere near drama therapy for the reasons we've already discussed,' Dylan said, firmly.

'I agree with Dylan,' said Eric. 'Given the age difference between Louise and the clients it would be inappropriate for her to join them for drama therapy.'

Zoe rebuked Eric. 'You used to call them "kids" not "clients".' She looked pointedly at Dylan. 'Must be catching.'

'For God's sake,' Eric muttered under his breath.

Dylan's proposals were accepted, and after lunch everyone assembled in the art therapy room. The dramatic events of the morning were discussed at some length and then Louise and the clients were asked, as a warm up exercise, to create a picture which reflected how they were thinking and feeling.

Everyone set to work. Soon the room fell silent and its ambience became one of intense concentration. As Dylan and his colleagues moved around observing the work in progress, it was clear to them that the momentous events of the morning were at the forefront of every clients' consciousness. Amy had drawn a huge fist which was clenched and raised to strike a blow at the large crowd besieging it. Khaled's picture was of a young man standing alone with his hands covering his face, as though unable to accept what he was seeing. Jake's image was of an androgynous figure lying prone on the ground surrounded by photographers brandishing their cameras like weapons.

Only Louise's picture appeared totally unconnected with the violent and dramatic scenes enacted earlier. Her drawing was of a young girl swimming under the water of a pond which had frozen over. Above her, on the ice, people were skating unaware of the swimmer beneath. The skaters were wrapped up in colourful winter coats, hats and scarves, and were of various ages ranging from the very young to the elderly. The familiarity existing between them suggested that they were members of the same family. By contrast the girl under the ice was wearing jeans and a T shirt, and her feet were bare. Her arms and legs were frozen in mid-stroke and her long hair trailed in floating tresses behind her. The skaters looked jovial and happy but the girl's expression was resigned, almost serene, and her big eyes were as empty as those of her only companions, a pair of grey fish.

The image affected Dylan profoundly. He interpreted it as an archetypal expression of loneliness and psychological dissociation. The swimmer was hived off from other people and their ordinary activities by a thin, membrane of ice: literally frozen in an unnatural state. The image was also redolent of solitary confinement, suspended animation, even death. The girl was entombed in a cold watery world with only the dead eyes of fish for company. Yet above her on the ice there was warmth and movement, life was going on and people were full of animal spirits, enjoying themselves quite normally, completely oblivious of her situation. Implicit in the picture was also the notion of liberation through exposure: the possibility that one day the ice would melt and the girl would be revealed to the world. Until then she'd continue to suffer, and the people who could help her would remain too absorbed in their own selfish amusement to notice. But who or what was creating the barrier between her world and theirs? Was the girl's detachment from reality of her own making or caused by others? Most importantly, was this how Louise really felt about herself?

Louise was seated at a desk working intensely, quite oblivious to Dylan who, for some time, had been looking over her shoulder observing the movements of her coloured pencils. He was admiring the skill with which she used just the white space of the cartridge paper to suggest the blades of the skates, the film of ice, and the swimmer beneath. He was also wondering what to say, or indeed if anything needed to be said. He decided to limit himself to one or two remarks.

'Is this really how you feel about today?'

Louise looked up from her work, almost irritably, as though she was annoyed to have her concentration interrupted. 'Yes.'

'And that's how you feel about what happened at Rooks Nest?'

She seemed perplexed. 'No. Not at Rooks Nest.' She looked at him anxiously. 'Have I done it wrong? You said we had to show how we feel today.'

Dylan remembered that this was the first time Louise had done a warm up exercise.

'Don't worry, nothing's wrong,' he said. 'So this is how you really feel today?'

'It's what I feel like every day.'

'I see.' If that were true Louise's life must be extremely bleak indeed. 'What do you think will happen to the girl?' he asked.

'I suppose she'll either die or find some way of smashing through the ice.'

Dylan nodded. There was so much more he wanted to ask her about the picture but decided it could wait until tomorrow. He moved on to look at Mona's work.

Dylan knew that the experiences of the past couple of days had put everyone into a subdued and negative frame of mind. In order to combat this depressed mood an upbeat, positive subject for the rest of the afternoon's session was essential. When the warm up period was finished, he called everyone together and announced that the afternoon's theme was to be "A Happy Event".

After some discussion everyone got down to work. Louise took much longer than anyone else to get started, but once begun she worked quickly as though possessed of a flowing, continuous inspiration. Her picture was of the "I'd Do Anything" scene from "Oliver". Nancy, her character, was centre stage, surrounded by Fagin, the Artful Dodger and Fagin's gang, and they were obviously all singing. The characters were so realistically drawn that Dylan had no difficulty recognising the context. Louise asked for powder paints thickened with PVA glue, and painted the whole scene in bright, primary colours. Watching her, Dylan was again impressed with her skills as an artist: particularly the way she depicted the effects of stage lighting with an impressive use of light and shade.

When it was time for everyone to share their work, Zoe suggested that they all move into the drama studio where they might use their paintings as a basis for discussion and acting out. Looking across the room directly at Dylan, she said, 'I assume Louise won't be joining us?'

Zoe's obvious ambush sent a surge of irritation through Dylan. Hadn't he made it clear to her that Louise wasn't to do any drama therapy? He was about to reply to her with a definite "That's right" when he found that Louise had looked up and was staring at him. Seeing her stricken yet oddly malevolent expression, he immediately thought of the girl trapped under the ice. 'I suppose on this occasion it'll be OK,' he said.

They all carried their pictures into the drama studio. Louise had never been in there before and she took in everything with great interest. In many ways it was rather like the studio at the youth theatre. There was a small stage constructed of rostra and a number of hard, straight backed chairs set around the edge of the room. But there were other things in there that she'd never seen in the youth theatre studio: art materials, puppets, cuddly toys, lots of cushions, musical instruments; and on the walls many strange pictures done by the big kids.

As the adults entered the studio, Louise heard Dylan say to Zoe, 'Start with "A Happy Event" and don't forget what I said about Louise.' Louise was disturbed by this, especially as there was a harshness in his voice she'd never heard before. She wondered what it could mean.

Zoe asked everyone to sit on the carpet in one large circle with their pictures in front of them. Louise was surprised to see all the grown-ups sit down in the circle too. Zoe went over to a set of drawers, opened one and took out a large smooth stone about the size and shape of a goose egg. It was painted bright blue and decorated with patterns of red, green and yellow zig-zags.

Zoe held up the colourful object for Louise's benefit. 'This is the "truth stone", Louise. We pass it round the circle and when it comes to you, it gives you the right to speak about your picture, but only if you wish to. Before you start speaking I'd like you to hold your picture up and show it to us. You can say anything you like about it, as long as it's the truth. You might like to tell us why you chose to draw it; why it's important to you and so on. I might ask you some questions about your picture but you don't have to answer them if you don't want to. If at any point you feel uncomfortable and don't want to say any more, just pass the stone to the person on your left. The stone will keep going round the circle until it eventually comes back to you. That'll give you the opportunity to speak again if you want. But remember, you can only speak when you have the stone in your hand; and if you'd rather not say anything at all, just pass the stone on. Any questions?'

Louise shook her head.

Zoe gave the stone first to Rupa. When Rupa had originally started at the inclusion unit she'd been pitifully shy, and if the truth stone had ever come into her hands she'd treated it like a hot piece of coal and immediately passed it to her neighbour in the circle. But gradually, the stone had emboldened her to overcome her diffidence and given her the courage to speak out. Today she clenched it tightly in one hand, staring at it with intense concentration as though she was communing with it, absorbing its liberating power and being fortified by it.

Using her free hand, Rupa held up her picture. It showed a street of terraced houses. Two girls were standing on the pavement outside one of them. One girl was larger than the other and they were both looking at a parked car with their arms raised in welcome. Rupa explained that the two figures in the street were herself and her sister, Shamita. The people in the car were Aunt Debbie and Uncle Dave. They'd come to collect her and Shamita because their mother had been sent to prison and they had no-one to look after them. 'Mum and dad were druggies,' said Rupa. 'Dad left us a long time ago. When mum went to prison I had to look after Shamita. But I couldn't, so dad's brother and his wife said we could live with them. When they came it was a happy event because they lived in a nice house on the edge of Leeds. They gave us lots of nice food and looked after us properly.' Rupa's eyes became downcast. 'But we couldn't stay. I don't know why. They took us away.'

Zoe asked Rupa a number of questions and then the stone was passed on to Khaled. Without looking at it or speaking, he passed it straight on to Mona. Her "Happy Event" was a picture of a school journey to the Lake District she'd been on when she was eleven. She described it briefly, and then passed the stone on to Jake. His picture showed him being picked up by the mini-bus which had brought him to Leefdale. Louise thought it was rather sad that that was the only happy event he could think of. The stone continued on round the circle. Louise observed that not everyone spoke when the stone was in their hand and they quickly passed it on, but some spoke for quite a long time about their pictures.

She wished all of them would pass the truth stone on without speaking because she couldn't wait for it to come to her. In this she was disappointed, as most of the big kids spoke in some detail about their pictures, and when the adults got the stone, even though they hadn't done any pictures at all, they talked on and on about what they would have drawn.

At last the stone was in her grasp and she had the authority to speak. She held up her picture with her free hand and showed it to the circle. 'This is me playing Nancy in "Oliver". Dylan told me you're all coming to see it on Saturday.'

Everyone looked at each other. This was the first they'd heard of it.

'It was meant to be a surprise, Louise,' said Dylan, awkwardly. His face had acquired a pink hue.

Eric and Toni exchanged knowing smiles.

Zoe said, 'Tell us more about the picture, please, Louise.'

'Right, well, in this scene we're all singing, "I'd Do Anything".' With the hand that held the truth stone, Louise pointed out the various characters in her picture, named them and described their parts in the show. She ended by saying, 'It's based on "Oliver Twist" by Charles Dickens.'

'And is that why it's a happy event?' prompted Zoe.

'Yes, I love being in "Oliver". But also because my mum and dad are sitting together watching me.' Louise put the truth stone down on the floor so that she could indicate her mother and father in the picture. Her finger pointed to two figures seated in the audience. 'Here, you see.'

Louise's depiction of her mother was so lifelike that Dylan recognised her immediately. But the male figure seated next to her was vague and amorphous, almost a cypher without any distinguishing features: no eyes, nose or mouth.

'I've never known who my dad is,' Louise went on, 'so, if he was there in the audience next to my mum it really would be a happy event.'

Zoe saw that Louise's picture was the expression of a wish fulfilment. She said, 'So this happy event hasn't actually happened. It's something you'd like to happen?'

'Yes.' Louise looked towards Dylan. 'You never said it had to be for real, did you?'

Dylan shook his head.

Zoe said, 'Why's it so important that your dad's there? If you don't know him and haven't seen him before? Why isn't it enough for you that your mum's there?'

Louise picked up the stone and felt it throbbing in her hand, urging her to tell them that if mum and dad were sitting together watching her in "Oliver" it would be an acknowledgement by her dad that she was his daughter. But she couldn't say that, no matter how much she wanted to, because mum would be horrified. Besides, she'd just told everyone in the circle that she'd never met her dad. Had never known him. And the stone in her hand was reminding her that she had to tell the truth. So, in order to say something that was true, she said, 'Because if he was there it would show he loved me.'

Zoe said, 'What would you say to your dad if he were here?' She pointed to an empty chair. 'If he was here now, sitting in that chair and you could say anything you liked to him, what would you say?'

Yes, what would she say to him? So many of Louise's suppressed resentments towards her father clamoured for expression. I'd say I can't stand what you've done to me all my life. I'd say how do you think I feel when you come to our house behaving like my dad and yet outside the house I'm nothing to you? I'd say I can't go on lying like this and I'm longing to tell the truth to Jade and Gwen and Ian. I'd say that unless you admit to everyone you're my dad I never want to see you again!

The truth stone in Louise's hand was urging her to say all this, but to do so she'd have to confess that the dad she denied knowing, actually saw her regularly and was Jade's dad too. That would be terrible. And so the padlock on her tongue remained.

Everyone in the circle was watching her now, expectantly. 'I don't know,' she said. 'I don't know what I'd say to him.' And with that she passed the stone on to Dylan.

When everyone had been given an opportunity to talk about their pictures, Zoe retrieved the truth stone and held it up for everyone to see. 'Now, I'm going to send the stone around the circle again. This time you can make comments or ask questions about anything you saw or heard the last time it went round.'

Louise raised her hand. 'Do you mean questions or comments about other people's pictures of "A Happy Event"?'

'That's right.'

Zoe handed the truth stone to Liam. Louise expected him to pass it straight on just as Khaled and he had done before. Instead, he grasped it firmly and said, 'I haven't ever seen my dad either.'

Zoe exchanged a look with Dylan. This was a real breakthrough. Liam had never once said anything during the truth stone exercise. Dylan shook his head imperceptibly at Zoe. She instantly understood. He was telling her not to comment or question Liam. It was sufficient that he'd said something at last.

Even if Zoe had wished to pick up on Liam's revelation, it was too late. He'd already passed the stone on to Scarlett.

Scarlett took the stone and said, 'Nor me. I ain't got no dad, Louise. I've never seen him. I think he lives in Bristol.' She quickly passed the truth stone on to Amy.

Louise was starting to feel tears building behind her eyes.

Amy said, 'Me too. I've never seen my dad. My mum says his name is Pete, though.'

Louise could stand it no longer. 'You're taking the mickey out of me,' she said, angrily.

'No, I'm not,' protested Amy. She sent an appealing look to Zoe. 'I'm not!'

'You are. You're all making fun of me.' Louise started to cry.

'Why do you say that, Louise?' asked Zoe.

'They're saying they've got no dad because I said I've got no dad.'

'But it's the truth,' said Zoe, calmly. 'We know it's the truth because they were holding the truth stone in their hands when they said it.'

Louise looked at Liam, Scarlett and Amy. 'Is it the truth? You've really not got a dad?'

The three teenagers nodded.

'Sorry,' said Louise. She wiped the tears from her eyes with her fingers.

Toni stood up and walked over to Louise and handed her a tissue from her pocket. 'It's clean,' she said.

Zoe decided she had to divert Louise. She said, 'You really like playing Nancy in "Oliver", don't you? What do you like best about it?'

'Everything really.' Her tears were suddenly forgotten. 'I love being her because she's so strong and funny. And I love all the singing and dancing too.'

Amy was still holding the truth stone. She said, 'What's your favourite song, then?'

'From "Oliver"?'

'Yeah.'

'That's easy. It's one that Oliver Twist sings called "Where is Love?"' Louise adopted a confiding tone. 'I'd really like to play the part of Oliver more than Nancy. I could too. I know all the songs in the show.'

Amy threw Louise a challenging look. 'OK. If you're so clever, why don't you sing it?'

Zoe was straight in. 'That's not very kind, Amy.'

Amy shrugged.

'Go on, Louise, sing "Where is Love?"' begged Mona. Her pleas were quickly taken up by the other teenagers, including Amy.

'All right,' said Louise. 'But I'll have to stand up.'

'Go ahead,' said Zoe.

Louise got to her feet. She took a few seconds to compose herself and then, suddenly, the room was full of the sound of her extraordinary singing voice. With perfect pitch and despite having no accompaniment, she launched into the song in which the orphaned Oliver asks whether he will ever find his mother or discover true love. From this tall, slender child came a voice that was full of unusual power and purity, and seemed to belong to an angel. Everyone was transfixed. It was as though the workhouse boy was actually in the room with them, his plangent, yearning plea for affection penetrating and rending their hearts. Mona and Amy were in tears. Zoe was on the edge of them. Even Dylan, who despised sentimentality, was deeply affected by Louise's seamless display of technique and feeling. He had no doubt that he was in the presence of a potentially great artist.

Louise finished the song and there was a long silence as though a spell had been cast on everyone. It was broken by a sudden, spontaneous burst of applause that quickly reached a crescendo and took many seconds to die.

Afterwards, Zoe said, 'That was lovely, Louise. Beautiful. So moving.'

There were murmurs of agreement all round.

Louise seemed consumed with happiness. 'Thank you.'

When Louise had resumed her place in the circle, Zoe said, 'I was an actress once, you know.'

Louise stared at her with renewed interest. 'Were you?'

'Yes.'

'Why aren't you an actress now?'

'Well, it's very hard to earn your living at it, so I gave up.'

'But don't you miss acting?'

Zoe was intimidated by Louise's probing, earnest stare. She certainly did miss acting. Every single day. 'Sometimes,' she said.

Louise looked horrified. 'I'd never give up. Never.'

'Not even if you were hungry or had nowhere to live?'

'Never,' said Louise. 'If you give up there'll never be a chance you'll act again. But if you don't give up, there's always a chance you can do it.' Her expression became very fierce, very determined. 'I'm never, ever going to give up!'

The child's total commitment to her art and unshakable determination to persevere made Zoe feel diminished in so many ways. She had started off with such similar dreams and they'd all ended in failure. And now here was an eleven year old reproaching her for throwing in the towel.

Zoe took the truth stone from Amy and said. 'OK. I'm going to send the stone round the circle again. This time I want you to talk about your other picture. The one that shows how you felt about what went on at Rooks Nest this morning. I'm looking for a possible protagonist to do some acting out.'

Dylan saw that they were moving into the area of drama therapy, something he didn't wish to expose Louise to, given the content of her warm up picture. Looking at the child, he said gently, 'I'm sorry, but this part of the session isn't for you.'

Again from Louise came the sharp, stinging look of hurt and disappointment.

Zoe said, 'Can't she just stay and look at everyone's pictures?'

'No.' He looked across at Toni. 'Would you take Louise through to the encouragement room and start her on some school work, please?'

CHAPTER FORTY TWO

'It was amazing! You should have been there! Everyone kept rushing from the TV over to the window to be sure it was really happening just across the road. We couldn't believe it. When the Major came out everyone booed, it was like, you know, being at a pantomime. But we all went quiet to listen to the MP. When he said he was going back to his wife, Zoe said, "Poor cow!" and then when that man called out that his daughter was pregnant everyone went like "Wow!" and "Oh no!" and Dylan went "How humiliating for her." Then, when the wife said the whole thing was untrue and he was never gonna go back to her, he and his girlfriend were just gonna go on like before only not tell her, well, everyone went hysterical. And then, when the MP's wife slapped him there was loads of noise, people shouting and laughing, and loads of flashlights. Well, there were flashlights going on all the time but even more then. When the Major hit the MP there was like a massive riot, and in the studio everyone was shrieking and laughing and dancing about saying it was just like when he hit Sheldon. Liam went "The man's an animal!" and Sheldon went "Yeah but the slimy rat deserved all he got cos he dumped out on his pregnant girlfriend". But they all said the Major was crazy. Zoe said he needed courses in anger management. Then the MP started telling the people at the gate how sorry he was. But I didn't see what happened after that because Toni made me go downstairs with the others. Then it was time to eat lunch. We had it in the garden.'

Louise stopped speaking, grinned and with her fork speared a chip from the plate on the table in front of her.

Greg had listened to Louise's account with increasing anger. He'd had a terrible day. The Gorsedale Farms business had been lost because of constant complaints about undelivered spares, and when he'd returned home he'd been met with nothing but griping from Pam and Jade. On his way to a Finance and Personnel meeting of the school governors he'd dropped in on Sharon and Louise, hoping to extract from them some sympathy for his awful day. Instead, he'd had to listen to Louise's animated description of the extraordinary and disgraceful events which had occurred at Rooks Nest.

'It was so funny,' Louise said, and giggled.

Sharon smiled. 'It sounds it. I wish I'd been there.'

It infuriated Greg to see Sharon and Louise treating Howard's woes and misfortunes as a joke. Both of them had changed so much recently. They seemed to be slipping away from him. He was sure it was something to do with those people at the rectory. They were an appalling influence. He'd been filled with anxiety ever since he'd learnt that they were looking after Louise. There was something sinister and underhand about the way Dylan Bourne and the rest of them had clandestinely established themselves in the village. He was terrified that their meddling would uncover his secrets and disrupt his comfortable, well-ordered life.

'Is that what they're teaching you at the rectory?' asked Greg. 'To make fun of people's misfortunes?'

Louise looked surprised and slightly shocked. 'I'm not. It was just a laugh.'

'Well, I don't think you should have been watching it. Not a child of your age.'

'How could you stop them watching it?' said Sharon. 'It was going on just across the street. Anyway, they showed it on the news. Every child in the country must have seen it by now.'

'Well, I wouldn't have watched it. Howard Roberts is a friend of mine. He's done a lot for the village. It would be very wrong for me to take pleasure in his troubles.'

As Greg said this Sharon was wondering how she could ever have found someone so pompous, attractive.

'Oh! Come on!' she said. 'No-one knew it was going to turn out like that. And you've got to see the funny side of it. The whole country's laughing at them. I only wish I'd been there instead of watching it on the news.'

'Then I must have no sense of humour because all I saw was the humiliation of an entire family.'

Sharon was about to say something but stopped. It suddenly occurred to her that public exposure and humiliation were the things Greg feared most. It was why he could only regard the televised shambles at Rooks Nest as a tragedy.

'Anyway, you can't go on Friday,' Greg told Louise.

'Where?'

'The Old Rectory. You can't go there on Friday.'

'Why?'

'There's going to be a demonstration.'

Sharon said, 'Yes. Dylan told me about that when I collected Louise.'

He'd actually told her that he hoped the clients would be taken on a day trip on Friday to avoid the demonstration and Louise would be welcome to join them.

'Oh, so he knows, does he?' Greg was disappointed. He'd hoped the demonstration would have been a nasty surprise. He regarded Sharon gravely. 'I hope you told him Louise wouldn't be there on Friday.'

'I said I'd think about it.'

Greg couldn't conceal his incredulity. 'What is there to think about?'

Sharon was still deciding whether to keep Louise away from the rectory on Friday because she was naturally concerned for her safety and had no wish for her to be upset by the demonstration. But she'd been reassured by Dylan's intention to organise a day out for the kids. At least Louise would be spared the ordeal of watching her own father demonstrating. Nevertheless, Sharon still hadn't come to a firm decision. Greg could have persuaded her not to allow Louise anywhere near the rectory on Friday, had it not been for his autocratic and dictatorial manner which was riling her intensely. He was putting pressure on her, just as he'd done last night. She knew he'd give anything to prevent Louise returning to the rectory and she was determined not to be intimidated by him.

Louise was staring at Greg resentfully. 'I still don't see why I can't go to the rectory.'

'Because it could be very unpleasant,' said Greg. 'The people at the rectory have made themselves unpopular because of the state they've allowed the place to get into. It's probably going to cost us the Magnificent Britain contest. There'll be lots of insults and unpleasant things being shouted. You don't want to be on the receiving end of all that, do you?'

'I don't care. They're my friends.'

Greg snorted. 'Friends! Your friends!'

'They're all right!'

Sharon said, 'I don't see what you hope to achieve.'

'What? By the demonstration?'

'Yes.'

'We're hoping that when the judges see the strength of public outrage at the state of the rectory they'll overlook it and still give us the gold medal.'

Sharon was genuinely appalled by his attitude. 'And for that you're happy to frighten vulnerable children?'

Greg said nothing. He looked vaguely uncomfortable.

Sharon said, 'I hope you're not planning any unpleasant surprises for those in the rectory.'

'What do you mean?'

'Last night you told me it wouldn't be safe for Louise to go there.'

'I only meant that when feelings get high, things can kick off.' With a slight sneer, he went on, 'Don't worry, Dylan and his friends are all perfectly safe. It'll be a peaceful demonstration.'

Sharon saw no reason to tell Greg he'd be wasting his time as there wouldn't be anyone there on Friday. 'Good. There are some very nice people at the rectory.' She stared at him resentfully. 'And they were the only ones who'd take Louise in when no-one else was interested.'

She quickly turned her attention back to her daughter. 'But perhaps your dad's right, Louise. It might be awful for you.'

'No it wouldn't!'

'Think how I'd feel knowing you were in there while I was outside demonstrating,' said Greg.

Louise's lips formed into a tight, wilful line. 'I'm still going!'

'Now, Louise,' said Sharon.

'No you're bloody not,' said Greg. 'And if it had been up to me you'd never have gone there in the first place.'

'Oh, and where would you have taken her?' Sharon said quietly.

'Anywhere but the rectory.'

'But that was the only place that would take her. You were no help. What would you have done?'

'What could I do? I had a meeting with a very important client.'

'You didn't want to know!'

They carried on with their recriminations for several minutes. Louise stared at them wondering why she'd been brought into the world when she was obviously such a terrible nuisance to everyone. Why were people always arguing about who was going to look after her? She longed to be grown-up and independent so that people would stop rowing about her, and she could get right away from them all. No-one would miss her. They'd all be a lot happier if she wasn't around.

Finally, tiring of the bickering, Sharon said, 'If Louise isn't going to the rectory on Friday where is she going?'

'I am going to the rectory,' Louise insisted. 'I like it there.'

Greg ignored Louise. 'Can't you call in sick or something?' he asked Sharon.

'I can't take the day off. I've got three viewings on Friday.'

'Then she'll just have to stay at home. It'll only be for one day.'

'I'm not leaving her alone all day. Why can't you take her into your office?'

'Don't be ridiculous.'

'It'll only be for a day. Tell your receptionist you're helping out a neighbour.'

'Now you're being childish. Why not take up Pam's suggestion of Margaret and Joan? They'd look after Louise.'

'Yes, I'm sure. And regard her as morally inferior because she's been excluded.'

Greg said nothing. More and more, Sharon was saying things that were entirely out of character. She was obviously being brainwashed by the people in the unit.

Louise regarded Greg artfully. 'If you didn't go to the demonstration I could go to the rectory.'

'Don't be silly. I have to go to the demonstration. I'm organising it.' He sighed and shot her a vindictive look. 'Thanks for getting us into this mess!'

'Me?'

'Yes, you. Who else? How could you kick poor old Mrs Lucas on the leg? And not once, but twice. You know, when your mum told me that's why you'd been excluded, I was ashamed.'

'Why? No-one knows I'm your daughter.'

Greg looked staggered but quickly recovered. 'I was ashamed because despite everything you're my flesh and blood. How could you kick her? She was only doing her job.'

'It wasn't all Louise's fault,' said Sharon.

'Oh? Whose fault was it then? Jade's?'

'Jade started it!' cried Louise.

Sharon said, 'Jade and the others were bullying her.'

'Jade's the one who's being bullied.' He glared at Louise. 'She's refusing to go to school because of your bullying!'

'No! She's bullying me! She keeps winding me up about not having a dad.'

'No, Louise, I've questioned Jade about this and she absolutely denies it.'

'Well, of course she denies it,' said Sharon.

Louise said, 'Jade's always saying "You haven't got a dad. And you know what they call someone who hasn't got a father? A bastard." That's what she says. She's always saying it.'

Greg shook his head. 'Jade swears that's not true.'

'Oh yeah, and you'll always believe Jade, won't you? I hate you. I hate you. You don't love me. You only care about Jade and Gwen and Ian cos they're your real kids. Your proper kids. Well, mum and me are leaving Leefdale. I hate it here and I hate Jade! We're going and we're never coming back. Then you'll be happy. You'll never have to see me again!'

Greg stared at Sharon, his eyes full of questions.

'Be quiet, Louise. We're not going anywhere.'

'But you said. You promised.'

'What's she talking about?' Greg demanded.

'Not now, Louise! That's enough!'

Greg experienced a feeling of acute fear. He suddenly saw it was possible that he could lose both of them. 'You're wrong, Louise. I do care for you. I care for you just as much as Jade and Gwen and Ian. It would make me very unhappy not to see you again.'

'I think I can see a way out of this,' Sharon said suddenly. 'When you see Mrs Henshall at the meeting tonight, tell her I formally approached you in your role as chair of governors. Remind her we're both school governors and it'll make things difficult between us if Louise is inside the rectory while you're demonstrating outside it. Ask her if, in the circumstances, she'll allow Louise to return to school on Friday. She always listens to what you say.'

'I don't know,' said Greg, uneasily. 'It might seem…'

'Like what?' snapped Sharon, flashing him a dangerous look.

'All right,' said Greg. 'I'll give it a try.'

Louise's face had a stubborn, recalcitrant look. 'I'm not going back to school on Friday. I'm going to the rectory.'

'You don't have a choice, Louise!' shouted Greg.

'Yes, I do. I'm going back to the rectory. Lots of people there don't have fathers! Just like me!'

Greg looked amazed. 'What's all this about not having a father? I'm your father, Louise!'

'Then why don't you admit it!'

Louise jumped up and ran over to the door. When she reached it she turned and gazed back at Greg with the malevolent eyes of a snake. 'Everyone at the rectory really loves mum, you know. They think she's so nice. Dylan even took her out a few weeks ago.'

Greg looked quickly at Sharon.

'He didn't take me out. Not in that way.'

'Yes, he did,' insisted Louise. 'He took you out.'

'Yes. But it wasn't a date. He took me out to dinner to thank me for helping them get the house.'

'That was very nice of him,' said Greg.

Sharon gave Louise a long, reproachful stare. How could she be so disloyal? She'd promised never to tell Greg about that night out with Dylan. But a sudden insight neutralised Sharon's anger. This was obviously Louise's retaliation for the broken promise about leaving Leefdale. 'Go and get ready, Louise. You'll be late for your rehearsal,' she said.

Louise consulted her watch. 'Yeah.' She looked at Greg. 'Don't suppose you're gonna come and see it now?'

'Well you're wrong there. I'm coming on Saturday night.'

'So's mum,' said Louise. 'That's good. You'll both be in the audience.'

'I'm going on Friday night, too,' Sharon told Greg.

'So's Pam. It's a shame it's only going to be on for two nights after all that work.'

'What do you care?' said Louise. She turned her back on them and strode disdainfully out.

'Don't just walk out without saying goodbye to your dad,' Sharon called after her. 'Where are your manners?'

'It's all right. She's pissed off with me. She'll get over it.'

Sharon got up from the dining table and carried the plates from the meal over to the dishwasher.

'Where did Dylan take you then?' Greg asked.

Sharon opened the door of the dishwasher, knelt down and began placing the dirty plates inside it. 'The Trout at Danethorpe.'

'Hm, expensive. He must be worth a few bob.'
'It was very nice of him.'
'Of course. And he did it out of the goodness of his heart.'
'He just wanted to thank me.'
'Fuck you, you mean.'
Sharon gave an exasperated sigh.
'I'm not stupid, you know. If it was so innocent why didn't you tell me?'
Sharon stood up, slamming the door of the dishwasher.
'Because I knew you'd react like this!'

Greg said nothing. The news that she'd been out with Dylan explained everything. Why she'd been behaving so coolly towards him recently. Why she'd taken Louise to the rectory without trying to find somewhere else to go. Louise obviously liked it at the rectory, probably saw this Dylan character as some sort of father figure. It might even explain why Louise was talking about leaving, and why she'd been transferred to the High School in Sandleton. His torrenting thoughts led him to one conclusion.

'You only went out with Dylan once?' he said.
'Yes, once. That's all.'
'Are you screwing him?'
'No'
'You're lying.'
'If I was shagging him, you'd be the first to know.'
'Thanks. Does he know about us?'
'No. But I told him I had a boyfriend.'
'He doesn't know I'm Louise's father?'
'No'
'You're sure?'
'Of course, I'm sure.'
'Well, that's something.'

Sharon placed her hands on Greg's shoulders 'You see Greg, that's the problem. All this secrecy. All this abnormality. It's poisoning everything. It's killing Louise and it's killing me too. What Louise said just now is the truth. We're leaving Leefdale.'

'When?'
'As soon as I can.'
'I see.' Greg pondered this. He was obviously shocked. 'I thought you couldn't bear to leave this house?'
'I can't. But feelings are more important than things.'
'But all your feelings are tied up in this house.'
'I'm sorry, Greg. Things have been going wrong between us for ages. I've been dissatisfied with our arrangement for a long time.'
'That's a strange word to use.'

'Well, what else is it? It's not a relationship. It's not even an affair. We never go anywhere except to meetings.'

'You weren't complaining the other night.'

'That's just it. The sex is all that's left and there's not very much of that.'

'Are you asking me to leave Pam?'

'You know I never expected that. Perhaps I should have, I don't know. All I'm saying is that things can't go on as they are. When I went out with Dylan that night to The Trout, I realised it was the first time for years I felt normal. Just another couple out for the evening. You've no idea how good that felt.'

Her words told him what he already knew: that their relationship had run into the ground. He'd been stupid to think that their present set up could continue indefinitely. It offered her no social life, no stability, no emotional support. He saw clearly that an arrangement which for years had been so comfortable and convenient for him, offered her only aridity and social isolation.

He got up from the table and turned to face her. 'Yes. I can see it's no life for you being tied up with me.'

'No. It isn't.'

And yet, he wanted to believe that there was a lot more to it than that. Something was going on between her and that bloody artist, he was convinced of it. He said, 'But we were all right until those people at the rectory came.'

'No, Greg. We haven't been all right for some time.'

He sighed. There was a long pause. He looked tired, defeated. 'So, what are you going to do? Put this place on the market?'

'Yes.'

'So your mind's definitely made up?'

'Yes.'

He seemed about to say something, but stopped. His eyes were moist. 'I'd better go to that meeting,' he said.

'Yes.' She kissed him lightly on the cheek. 'Don't forget to ask Mrs Henshall if Louise can come back on Friday.'

Greg nodded. 'End of a perfect bloody day,' he said and left.

Almost immediately afterwards, Louise came down the stairs and into the room.

Sharon stared at her, wondering whether her daughter was sophisticated enough or calculating enough to deliberately engineer conflict between herself and Greg. She said, 'I know what you're up to.'

'What?'

'Trying to cause trouble between me and your dad.'

Louise looked shocked. 'I wasn't.'

'You told him about Dylan taking me out.'

'Well, he was being horrible to you.'

'But you promised me.'

'Promises don't mean anything.' Louise gave her a sideways look. 'You should know that.'

'You did it deliberately, didn't you?'

Louise looked away. 'No.'

'You did. You thought we'd have a row.'

'No, I didn't.'

'And then you thought I'd tell him we were leaving.'

'No, mum.'

'Well, it didn't work. I'm not leaving here, Louise. Not for a long time. You'll just have to get used to it.'

****

Peter Kellingford was entirely alone when he drove away from Rooks Nest just after 3.30pm. This was all the proof the waiting media needed that he was returning to Clarissa. The TV journalists duly reported his solitary departure in their final pieces to camera before thankfully driving off with their crews. Many of their print media colleagues had already left to phone in or email their stories about Kellingford's presumed return to his mistress. Some were in their cars and following him at high speed to London.

By late afternoon, the many onlookers and media people who'd been milling around the gates of the house since the early morning had nearly all departed. A few, hopeful photographers and a couple of TV crews hung on for another hour or so, hoping to capture Mrs Kellingford's sad departure with her two children. But, by early evening it had become obvious to even these persistent souls that Barbara wouldn't be leaving that day, and they too eventually drifted away. The attention had now switched to London where Peter Kellingford was expected to tender his resignation that evening.

By 7pm the road in front of Rooks Nest was deserted except for a lone police car with two officers inside it. It was parked directly in front of the house's gates to deny any other vehicle access to the drive.

At 8pm a sleek, black BMW four door sedan turned into Church Lane and glided to a stop behind the parked police car.

Two men in dark suits were in the front of the BMW. The driver got out and looked all round before going to speak to the driver of the police car. After a brief conversation, the BMW driver returned to his car. The police car started up and drove off and the BMW immediately pulled forward to occupy the space vacated by it. An identical BMW then came into view and parked up behind the first one. It was also manned by two figures in dark suits.

'Our new protectors,' Howard remarked to Isobel and Barbara. The three of them were standing at the window of Howard's study where they'd been observing the new arrivals.

'At last,' said Isobel, heatedly. 'I feel so much safer with the experts in charge.'

'Yes,' said Howard. 'Wheatcroft and Scargill are good officers in their way, but hardly the people for this job. They're not even armed.'

The family trio stared in silence at the men in the vehicles as though they were expecting something dramatic to occur, even though it was apparent from the men's understated but alert manner that they were merely on a routine protection assignment. All were white and in their twenties or thirties with dark, cropped hair. The only unusual thing about them was that they all wore ear pieces.

Barbara stole a quick glance at Isobel and Howard, who continued to be transfixed by the presence of the black BMWs. She was reflecting that twenty four hours ago the possibility that she and her parents could even have had such a conversation would have struck her as absurd. Now she accepted it as normal.

For years she'd thought she'd known these people, but it was quite clear she'd never known them at all. Her mother, that reserved woman who enjoyed the theatre, cooking and cross stitch, now, surreally, had to be reconfigured as someone who could drive twice round a roundabout to prove she was being followed, and who, with the proficiency of an accomplished stunt driver, could do handbrake turns across oncoming traffic to evade her pursuers. She stared at her mother's strained and aging face, fascinated by the stippling of fine lines around her disapproving mouth. It had been truly heroic of her to endure the consequences of her husband's past for so long without divulging his involvement in the deaths of the Fermanagh Four. She wondered what other secrets there were locked away inside that elderly stranger's head.

Similarly, this person who was called her father, who was he, really? Barbara had always assumed he was a man who lived for his roses, and had retired early after doing some rather routine job in the army. Yet now it transpired he'd been at the forefront of operations in several theatres of war, and had been involved in one of the more infamous episodes in that long, sorry saga known as "The Troubles". He was obviously hugely important because people were prepared to go to great lengths to protect him. His powerful friends in high places could force newspaper editors to pull their reporters' stories on his behalf; could summon up the resources to provide round the clock armed protection; and organise his transfer to a safe house in a totally different area of the country or abroad. She experienced a surge of love for him as she thought of what he'd done to protect her from that Bryden bastard, and how cleverly he'd out-manoeuvred him. But, of course, he couldn't have done any of it without the help of his protectors.

Barbara recalled a conversation she'd once had with Peter during which he'd told her that everyone thought that government ministers had real power, but in reality they had very little: not even the Prime Minister. The people who had the real power in the country operated in the shadows, were part of a deep state that few people even knew existed: and its members were always ready and available to go into action at a moment's notice, should the realm be threatened. The problem was that the higher up the food chain your career propelled you, the more you came into contact with such people without knowing it.

One of the men in the front BMW was drinking water from a bottle. Barbara found herself wondering how long their shift would last, whether or not they'd brought sandwiches with them and how they managed the business of going to the lavatory. The knowledge that such people were there to protect the lives of her and her family made her feel secure, yet also, more vulnerable than at any time in her life. How could their presence be so hugely comforting, yet at the same time give her such a feeling of unease? Could it be because it dramatically underscored the enormous danger they were all in?

CHAPTER FORTY THREE

Just after 8 pm, Dylan held a meeting in his studio with Zoe, Toni and Eric to discuss how the unit should respond to Friday's planned demonstration outside the rectory. He began by stating that he was guided entirely by the need to maintain and protect the welfare of the clients, and that this took priority over all other concerns. He reminded everyone that the clients were vulnerable young people and any decisions taken in respect of the demonstration should always be informed by this fact.

There was complete agreement with his remarks. Encouraged, Dylan continued, 'On Friday, I think we should take the clients for a trip somewhere. Perhaps to the coast, Filey or Scarborough. Or there's Flamingo Land, or the art gallery in Hull. I'm sure we could organise something that would keep them away from here until the demo was over.'

Dylan's proposal was met with silence. He looked from colleague to colleague but their expressions were impossible to read.

'What about Louise?' said Toni.

'I assume she'll come with us. With Sharon's approval, of course.'

Zoe said, 'So your solution is to run away?'

'It's not running away.'

'Of course, it is. Someone's oppressing you, so you run away. What kind of a message does that send out?'

'This isn't about sending messages. It's about protecting the clients.'

'It's capitulation.'

'Why do you have to use such bellicose language?' said Dylan. 'Capitulation is what you do in war.'

'Well, what's this, then? If someone stands outside your home harassing you and intimidating you and you run away, that's capitulation.'

With studied patience, he said, 'All I'm suggesting is that we remove the tension from the situation by taking the clients away for the day.'

'Exactly. Running away. Why don't you have the balls to stay and fight?'

'I'm sort of inclined to agree with Zoe,' said Eric. 'I think we should stay here on Friday, but for different reasons. If we take the kids away for the day they'll miss a marvellous learning opportunity. If we keep them here we can engage with them about the demo's purpose. Explain why it's happening. It could be a wholly positive experience if handled the right way.'

'Only if we encourage them to resist,' said Zoe.

'Really, said Toni, 'you do talk such rot. How can they be expected to resist? They're children.'

Zoe hadn't spoken to Toni since their earlier confrontation that morning. She stared at her frostily.

Dylan said, 'I'm sorry, Eric, but I don't think you appreciate how fragile and delicate the egos of these young people are. The kind of pressure they'd be subjected to by a noisy and possibly aggressive demonstration could cause them to regress to previous inappropriate and anti-social behaviours. That would undo all the good work we've done with them so far.'

Toni said, 'Surely, if the work we've done with them is that good their egos should be sufficiently developed to withstand a few people with placards shouting at them.'

'Now you're the one talking rot,' said Zoe.

Dylan's expression was long suffering. 'Please, can we keep the discussion on a professional level and not personalise it,' he pleaded. Turning to Toni, he said, 'If you'd worked with young people as long as I have, you'd know their apparent confidence and maturity is deceptive. Anything which threatens their safety and security could undo their progress in an instant.'

'All right,' said Toni. 'But suppose we do take the kids out for the day, the demonstration might go on right into the night. What if we return from our day out and find that the demo's still going on? That won't do the kids any good will it?'

'She's right,' said Zoe. Eric nodded.

Dylan said, 'I'm sure it won't go on into the night because Lucy Birkinshaw said its purpose was to influence the Magnificent Britain judges and by the evening they'll be long gone. Anyway, I'll have to stay here all day to let the judges in to inspect the gardens. If you phone before setting off back, I'd be able to tell you if the coast's clear or not.'

'That all sounds rather furtive and cowardly to me,' said Zoe. 'Anyway, if this demonstration goes ahead, I think we'd be perfectly entitled to refuse those judges access to our property. Why should we co-operate with a mob of fascists when they're putting vulnerable children under such duress?'

'There's no evidence that the judges are fascists,' said Dylan, 'and we can't stop them inspecting our gardens because we've already agreed to it.'

'That was before we knew there was going to be a demo. And if it wasn't for Lucy we wouldn't have known anyway. We'd have woken up on Friday to find it on our doorstep and we'd have been totally unprepared.'

'But Dylan's right,' said Eric. 'After all we've got to live with the people here. Refusing the judges entry would only antagonise the locals even more. Look at it from their point of view. Before we moved in, the rectory was their pride and joy and won them four gold medals. The gardens were in perfect condition when we arrived and we've totally neglected them.'

'That's my fault,' said Dylan. 'I've been so busy.'

Eric was one of those people who never pass up an opportunity to lay blame. 'Yes, and you refused the help that was offered by the Major to maintain the gardens, cut the grass and so on. And then we went and ruined the beautiful trees by hacking them all back. To the people of Leefdale it must have looked like vandalism.'

Zoe was incensed. 'We didn't ruin the trees and it wasn't vandalism. It was a creative project. A sculpture park.'

Eric snorted. 'That's your rationalisation of it, but that's not how it looks to the people here.'

'So what should we have done?' demanded Zoe. What she despised most about Eric was his ability to change sides when trouble threatened. She'd decided some time ago that lurking beneath those amiable, obliging features was a weak man of extremely bad faith.

Toni said, 'Eric's right. We should have tried to help the villagers more. Cooperated with them and helped them achieve their fifth gold medal.'

Zoe shook her head vigorously. 'That means they'd have been imposing their values on us. Influencing our decisions and determining what goes on inside this unit.'

'It would have prevented the situation we're in now.'

'No. They'd never have agreed to the sculpture park and they'd have gone ahead with their demo regardless.' Zoe rounded on Eric. 'You were very much in support of my sculpture park at first. But now you want to make it personal!'

'It's not personal.'

'Of course, it is.'

'No, I supported your sculpture park in ignorance. I hadn't any real conception of what you intended to do.'

That wasn't the real reason you supported me, thought Zoe. But she wasn't going to be so crass as to spell it out in front of Dylan and Toni. 'I made it very clear what was involved,' she said.

'I didn't realize it would mean destroying healthy trees,' said Eric.

'They haven't been destroyed. They've just been altered, that's all.'

Eric's wide, fleshy mouth curled petulantly. 'Well, I wouldn't let my garden get in such a state.'

Zoe treated him to one of her thin, sarcastic smiles. 'Then why aren't you at home looking after it?'

The heated and at times bad tempered discussion continued. Finally, in exasperation, Dylan said, 'All right, it's quite obvious that none of you agree with my proposal, so what do you suggest?'

'I think we should just go on as normal,' said Toni. 'I'll take their literacy and numeracy sessions on Friday morning, and in the afternoon they can have their usual art and drama therapy.'

Eric and Zoe expressed agreement with this.

Zoe said, 'At least that would teach the kids you don't give in to bullies.' She gazed pointedly at Dylan. 'And not to run away as soon as someone starts oppressing you.'

'OK.' said Dylan. 'You all seem to support Toni's idea, so on Friday let's go on as normal. But I'll contact the police and insist they give us plenty of protection.'

Eric and Toni thought this an excellent idea.

'I think you'll find that the police's sympathies will probably be with the demonstrators,' said Zoe.

'What's your evidence for that?' said Toni.

'They all share the same conservative mind set.'

'Well, whatever their mind set they still have a duty to protect us,' said Dylan. 'Now, as we've decided we're going to remain here on Friday, I have an idea which might address the village's concerns about our gardens. It might even placate the demonstrators.'

Briefly, Dylan outlined his plan.

'You're not serious,' said Zoe.

He stared back at her, earnestly. 'Yes, I am.'

'But that's still capitulation. As bad as taking the kids away for the day. You'll still be caving in to mob rule by bigots!'

'No,' said Dylan, 'It's called meeting people halfway.'

Eric said, 'I think it's an ingenious plan, Dylan. Well done.'

'So do I,' said Toni.

Zoe looked rather cross. 'It'll make us look stupid. We'll be admitting we're in the wrong.'

No-one spoke. Dylan's plan was put to the vote. Only Zoe voted against it.

'Obviously we're going to need some equipment,' said Dylan. He glanced at Eric. 'Would you go into Luffield tomorrow morning and get it? I'll write out a list. You can take a couple of the clients with you to help.'

'OK.' said Eric. 'I'll take Mona and Liam.'

There was a knock on the door of the studio.

'Come in,' called Dylan.

It was Khaled. He was grinning from ear to ear. 'There's a guy down at the gate who wants to talk to Zoe.'

'Oh?' Zoe thanked Khaled and went across to the window and looked out. Standing in Church Lane was John Carter.

Dylan joined Zoe at the window. 'Who is it?'

'That photographer from The Source.'

'Wonder what he wants? Like me to come down with you?'

'No thanks. I can handle him,' said Zoe.

****

Zoe strode down the drive brimming with curiosity yet very much on her guard. That morning she'd held her nose extremely hard and bought a copy of The Source from Leefdale's general store. The coverage of the Kellingford scandal was a disgrace, but she'd been relieved to see that none of the photographs taken of her were in the paper. So what could the photographer possibly want? Had he come to tell her that her threat of legal action had convinced them not to publish?

She approached the gate. Through the spaces between the bars she was able to make out his lanky, stick-thin figure and large mop of long black hair. This, with his tight blue jeans and white T shirt, gave him the curiously dated look of a seventies rock star. The last time she'd seen him he'd been encumbered with cameras and photographic equipment. Without them he looked more adolescent, almost callow. She told herself not to let her guard down. The last encounter she'd had between him and his colleague had been emotionally bruising.

'Hello,' she said, 'I thought I'd seen the last of you.'

He swallowed, and said, 'Hi.'

Now that just the gate was separating them, she could see from his anxious, strained expression that he was quite nervous.

Through one of the gaps between the bars he pushed a large, buff coloured envelope towards her.

'What's this?'

'The negatives of the photos I took of you yesterday.'

She made no attempt to take the envelope but stood considering. Why was he giving them to her? Was this some kind of trap set by Bryden to get him off the hook?

'What's the catch?'

He looked shocked. 'There's no catch. I don't think The Source has any right to print these photos without your consent. They're your negatives so I'm giving them back to you.'

Her expression softened. 'Does Bryden know about this?'

'No. I told him that the film was useless. I said it was over-exposed and didn't come out so I shredded the negatives.'

That's why there'd been no photos of her in The Source this morning! She accepted the envelope and opened it. Inside there were several negatives and a set of contact prints.

'I ran some contacts off so you could choose some for ten by eights if you wanted.' Shyly, he added, 'They're very nice photos of you, by the way.'

He was right, the contact prints were excellent. If she'd still been an actress she'd have had ten by eights made of all of them to send in with her CV when applying for castings. She regarded him suspiciously, 'Are you telling me the truth? Bryden didn't get cold feet because I threatened to sue, did he?'

'It's nothing to do with Bryden. Like I said, I told him the negs hadn't come out and I'd destroyed them.'

'But why? I don't understand.'

He was looking at her incredulously. 'Because it was the right thing to do.'

'Wow! A tabloid photographer with integrity.'

He turned and walked away.

Fuck! Her stupid, crass insensitivity. Why was she such a sucker for the glib remark? She pressed her face against the gate and called to him. 'No, wait! Wait!'

He came back.

She said, 'That was a stupid thing to say. Sorry. I really appreciate what you've done. Thank you.'

For the first time, he smiled. 'I'm not a tabloid photographer. I was with The Source because the paper I work for in Sandleton is owned by the same company. I was told to help Mr Bryden out because his usual photographer was on another job. I've never worked with him before. Actually, I can't stand him.'

She laughed. 'I see. Sorry, I've forgotten, what's your name?'

'John. John Carter.'

She held up the negatives . 'Well, thank you very much for these, John. I'm really grateful.' She had a sudden idea. 'We can't really talk with this gate between us. Would you like a cup of coffee? I'll get a key and let you in.'

He didn't seem very keen. 'It's all right, really. I've got to be going.'

'Sure?'

'Yes.'

But he seemed reluctant to go.

She said, 'Don't you want any money?'

'What for?'

'The photos. The negatives.'

He looked embarrassed. 'Oh, no. It's nothing.'

He was already regretting refusing the coffee. She didn't seem too much older than him, but she was probably very experienced. And so gorgeous. What amazing eyes. He had a sudden image of her naked. Wouldn't it be fantastic if she was the one who... He wondered if he dare ask her to go for a drink.

Zoe was thinking along similar lines. Tomorrow was her day off and she was intending to spend it in Sandleton. Perhaps she should ask him to join her for a drink after work. He was such a lovely guy. Surely he deserved something in return for his integrity? But he was so young. No more than nineteen or twenty. She didn't want to be accused of cradle snatching.

'I'd better be going,' he said.

'OK. Thanks again.'

'You're welcome.'

They said their goodbyes. Zoe turned and set off back towards the house, smiling. She was walking along the drive but her heart was climbing stairs. Despite all the shit she encountered daily, it took only one act of kindness to restore her faith in human nature.

****

After Louise left for her rehearsal, Sharon forced herself to go up to her study and do some further work on the long essay she was writing for her advanced estate agency qualification. The study was Sharon's favourite room in the house. It had previously belonged to her late father and, apart from the introduction of her personal computer, remained much as it was at the time of his death. The room was her sanctuary and she liked nothing better than to shelter beneath its low oak beams and blockade herself behind its dark book cases, which in places rose from floor to ceiling. The cossetting familiarity of the wine coloured curtains and matching lampshades; the winged armchair's tartan upholstery; the ivory coloured sofa's plump satin cushions; the deep piled Axminster, all reassured her and made her feel totally secure. For this was the room in which Sharon felt the presence of her parents most strongly. She was always conscious that her writing desk, a former dining table, was the one at which her father had sat and typed his invoices; and when she relaxed in the winged armchair she never forgot that he'd once sat there too, drawing on his pipe, searching for elusive inspiration. The Georgian escritoire which she now treated with the reverence appropriate to an antique, had been used by him to write his reports and personal letters. When she looked at the big sofa it was hard not to recall herself and her mother sitting on it side by side, talking of this and that, childishly savouring their brief and audacious appropriation of the male's exclusive domain whilst father was out on his rounds.

All around her were these repositories of fond and cherished memories. On her writing desk, on certain bookshelves and on the escritoire stood many framed photographs of her parents, including the most cherished: the one taken on their wedding day. Archie, her father, bespectacled, his hair already thinning, smiling wryly but obviously ill at ease in his morning suit. Mary, her mother, dark and serious even on this happiest of days, virginal in her white Victorian style wedding dress. (Both the dress and the morning suit were now carefully preserved in Sharon's loft). There were also photos of the many holidays the little family had shared: Sharon aged two in her swimsuit, Archie and Mary holding her by each hand as they posed for the beach photographer on some stretch of Cornish sand; Sharon aged ten standing with her mother, looking up at the Eifel Tower; and a teenage Sharon, standing slightly apart from her parents on the shores of Lake Como, glowering with embarrassment into the camera held by the Japanese tourist who'd intruded on their privacy and kindly offered to take a snap of the family group. This was a particularly poignant photo, as the tour of the Italian Lakes was Sharon's last holiday with her parents. There were many other photos too which Sharon had liberated from the anonymity of albums and lovingly framed, and which now cluttered every available surface in the room. And then there were the artefacts collected by her parents on their holidays and little jaunts. Archie's passion was for clocks and there was an abundance of them in the room: cuckoo clocks, table clocks, bracket clocks, carriage clocks and mantel clocks from Geneva, Rome and the salerooms of London, Lincolnshire and Yorkshire. Mary collected oil paintings wherever they went, those on the walls of the study being of mountains they'd visited: Snowdon; the Eiger; Mount Etna and King Arthur's seat. (Although Archie had often jokingly chided Mary that this last did not merit inclusion as it was "no more than a wee hill".) Then there were all father's hardback books which he'd allowed Sharon to borrow as soon as she could read fluently, and were like old friends. And so many other items: vases, jugs, pots, a two-handled drinking vessel, a music box; all encrypted with unique associations and personal memories that only she could access. The study was not only her retreat but also her parents' mausoleum; and whenever she entered it, as now, the thought of violating this shrine to their memory by putting it on the market and showing it to potential purchasers who would later haggle over price and be the cause of its dispersal made her feel quite ill.

She sighed, and seating herself at her desk attempted to apply herself to the complexities of Section 11 of The Landlord and Tenant Act 1985, which set out landlords' obligations to make repairs: a must for anyone contemplating a career in lettings agency management. And yet she found it impossible to concentrate. Something momentous had happened: she'd told Greg that she intended to leave Leefdale! She'd actually expressed to him her deep dissatisfaction with the cul-de-sac that was now their relationship. She couldn't believe that her life had reached this turning point, although she was glad it had. What she'd shared with Greg hadn't been love but a power relationship. Once, it had been mutually beneficial but not any longer. She knew it was a cliché but if she was to develop as a person it had to end.

Yet every treasured object in the room seemed to be casting doubt on her ability to carry this through. She was still unsure whether she possessed the necessary emotional resources to make such a profound change and break completely with the past. That's why she hadn't given a specific date for leaving, had left it nebulous and vague. It was also why she hadn't told Louise what she'd done. The girl wouldn't have believed her anyway, but Sharon couldn't bear the humiliation of breaking her word a second time. At least Greg now knew her direction of travel. Naturally, he'd try to dissuade her. She recalled the mortified look on his face when he'd learned of her intentions; his expression told her that fulfilling them would take all her courage and determination. Even now, just sitting in her precious study and thinking of the day when she'd have to give everything up, made her want to forget the whole thing. But she knew now that her present life was impossible. If she was ever to have a chance with men like Dylan she had to end the thing with Greg. The knowledge that she'd made a start down that road terrified her. Yet it thrilled and excited her too.

She forced her attention back to her studies and was reading Section 11 of the Landlord and Tenant Act for the third time when there was a loud knocking at her front door.

As she briskly descended the stairs she wondered if her visitor was Pam, come to harangue her again about sending Louise to the rectory. If so, she'd tell her where to get off.

For a second, she didn't register that it was Greg standing in the doorway. His arrival, so soon after leaving, was unexpected and the cowed, peevish looking figure who greeted her seemed like someone else. His glance was wary, his eyes hooded.

'You were quick,' said Sharon, as she let him in.

'Quick? It's well after nine. Anyway, it was a short agenda.'

He followed her into the sitting room and they each took a seat. Sharon asked him if he'd spoken to Mrs Henshall about Louise.

'Yes, but she won't wear it. She said even if she was minded to have her back on Friday, which she isn't, the paperwork's been submitted so it's too late to reverse the decision now.'

'Didn't you explain that you'd be in the demonstration and that would make things difficult for her?'

'Of course.'

Actually, he'd seen no reason to mention it. He'd been concerned that Mrs Henshall might wonder why his presence at the demonstration should create difficulties for Louise. He was terrified that anyone should suspect a connection and conclude that the child was his.

Sharon sighed heavily. 'Well, that's that.'

'If it's any consolation, Sally Henshall's convinced Louise is in good hands. She says there's a perfectly competent and highly qualified teacher in the unit.'

'Yes, Toni.'

'She said she's spoken to her and is happy with what she's providing for Louise.'

'That was good of her!'

There was a long pause.

Greg was in a deeply emotional state. He was preoccupied with the thought that she might be leaving him forever. Throughout the meeting with Mrs Henshall he'd been unable to think of anything else. Afterwards, he'd popped into The Woldsman for a quick one which had quickly developed into two. Now he wanted to tell her how he felt but couldn't find the right words. He wanted her to know he loved her and Louise and would do anything to stop them both leaving. He wouldn't mind what she did. He'd give her all the freedom she wanted. As long as she and Louise stayed. He said, 'So what will you do with Louise now? Keep her here on Friday?'

She considered. 'You said your demonstration would be peaceful?'

'I'd hope so.'

'So if Louise was in the rectory she'd come to no harm?'

His eyes narrowed suspiciously. 'Probably not.'

'Then there's no reason she shouldn't go there on Friday if she wants to?'

'It's your decision.'

'No, it's Louise's too.'

He stared at her resentfully. 'But how will it look?'

'What do you mean?'

'If Louise is seen in the rectory people will say you're supporting those wankers and you approve of what they've done to the place.'

'Why should I care what they think?'

'Well, you should. People are already saying you're the one who brought them here.'

She laughed. 'Me?'

'Yes. You sold them the rectory without checking who they were. Why they really wanted the place.'

'It's a good thing I'm leaving then, isn't it?'

'You don't really mean that, do you?'

That crushed expression. She knew now why she hadn't recognized him. He looked whipped, beaten. She was suddenly afraid, and said nothing. She felt she was already losing heart. Was this as good as it gets? All there'd ever be? Supposing her hopes about herself and Dylan were just an illusion? That she was reading too much into things?

He said, 'After the meeting, Mrs Henshall and I had a word. She thinks there's a way for you to continue as a school governor next year without having a child in the school.'

She thought, he hasn't realised, has he? He just doesn't get it.

'Is this your doing?' she said, sharply.

He looked surprised. 'No, she brought it up. She values the work you've done for the school.'

'Well, that's very kind of the old cow, but she needn't bother. I told you, we're leaving.'

He looked dazed. 'Why? We have a good set up. Why spoil it?'

'Because I'm fed up with living a lie. So is Louise. How long do you expect us to go on like this? Another ten years? Twenty years? I'm only thirty. I want a life.'

'Other men, you mean.'

She made an impatient gesture. 'All right, if you must know, yes, I do want to try other men. You're the only man I've ever been with. And the situation's hardly perfect, is it?'

'If it's other men you want, well, I understand. You're young. You want fun. I won't stand in your way. As long as you don't move away.' His look was desperate. 'Don't take Louise away, please, Sharon. I couldn't think of anything else all through the meeting. Please don't break everything up. I couldn't bear it.'

He got up and came over and bent to kiss her. His face loomed large in her eyes and as his lips sought hers she smelt beer and whiskey on his breath. She could see what he was trying to do but she wasn't going to let it happen anymore. She refused to be held hostage by her own sexuality. He knew it was her weakness and used it to control and dominate her. But no more. It was time she put her foot down.

She pushed him off and jumped up out of the chair. 'No, Greg. Sex isn't the solution any more. Go home.'

He looked incredulous, as though he'd been slapped.

'You really are a cold hearted bitch, aren't you?' he said.

****

When Barbara entered the sitting room Howard and Isobel were seated on the sofa waiting for the start of the BBC's News at Ten.

Isobel said, 'You've been up there for ages. Are they asleep?'

'Just about. I thought they'd never get off.'

'They're over stimulated, poor little things,' said Howard.

Yes, and some of that was down to you, Barbara thought unkindly. After Peter had left for London her father had diverted Mark and Jessica for two hours with numerous games of bowls. Then, after supper, he'd insisted that the whole family played French cricket. Barbara knew that his intention was to tire the children sufficiently so they'd want to go to sleep early, but he'd only succeeded in making them more hysterical and fractious. They'd begged her to let them stay up to watch the news but she'd told them that grandma and grandpa were too upset by the events of the day to allow it.

'They weren't the slightest bit interested in the story I was reading them,' complained Barbara. 'All they wanted to talk about was what happened to them at the gate this morning and Clarissa's baby. It was awful.'

'We should never have allowed them to be used for political propaganda like that,' said Isobel. 'We should have told Peter where to get off the moment he suggested it.'

'I know,' said Barbara. 'It's all my fault. I'll never forgive myself.'

'It's all our fault,' said Howard. 'Hang on, it's starting.'

The visual pyrotechnics that were News at Ten's opening credits had begun. Howard picked up the remote and turned the sound back on.

The top story was Peter's resignation from his position as Shadow Home Secretary. Footage followed of him making his resignation statement in the gathering dusk outside his flat in Clancy Road. Surrounded by reporters, he stated that after recent events he'd concluded that he could no longer stay on in his post and with great regret was stepping down with immediate effect. The statement was short and had the hand of Carr all over it. Barbara was shocked at Peter's tired and defeated appearance. As soon as he'd finished speaking, he quickly retreated into the house to avoid the inevitable media blitz.

Video was then shown of the extraordinary events earlier in the day which had brought about Peter's resignation. The political editor's voice could be heard speaking over images of Peter reading out his statement of apology at the gates of Rooks Nest: "Chaos ensued when Mr Kellingford attempted to draw a line under the controversy of his affair with Clarissa Forbes, his seventeen year old researcher and daughter of a close family friend..."

Barbara could barely bring herself to look at the screen as yet again the mortifying images of Russell's ambush were repeated. As she heard Russell reveal that Clarissa was pregnant, watched herself slap Peter and then rush the children away from the appalling scene, she felt suffocated and wanted to scream. And then her father was punching Peter. It really was too much. Aware that her family's humiliation and shame were being enjoyed and relished by millions across the country, she could endure the spectacle no longer. She jumped up and set off towards the door.

'Where are you going?' cried Isobel.

'To pack. I need to go home!'

****

For the past hour, Eric had been in his room typing up Sheldon's daily report. After Sheldon had been formally cautioned, his social worker had expressed great concerns about his behaviour. She'd felt that as Sheldon obviously wasn't settling into the inclusion unit, he should be returned to Leeds and referred back to the care of the local authority. However, Dylan had argued for Sheldon to be allowed to remain in the unit. The social worker had conditionally agreed to this as long as a formal case conference was convened to consider Sheldon's situation and a daily report was provided on his behaviour and attitudes. As Eric was Sheldon's mentor, this task had fallen to him.

Eric read the daily report through again. Its content and tone were mainly positive. Fortunately, despite the exciting and disturbing scenes over at Rooks Nest, Sheldon's behaviour since being cautioned had been relatively restrained.

Eric made one or two corrections to the report and printed it out. He then placed it in a lever arch file with Sheldon's name on it.

Afterwards, Eric sat on his bed, preoccupied inevitably with thoughts of Zoe. He still couldn't believe that her attitude towards him had changed. His mind was tormented by images of the night he'd gone back to her flat and they'd had sex until dawn. That's what had convinced him he should get out of his miserable marriage and make a new start with her. It really had seemed like the real thing. But then she went and applied for the job at Leefdale without even telling him. What choice had he but to apply for the remaining therapist position that no-one else seemed to want? He should have recognised the signs that she'd grown cold towards him, but he'd been intoxicated by the wonderful sex and was ecstatic that he'd at last found his soul mate. But instead of congratulating him on getting the job and expressing her delight that they'd be together, she'd treated him with a hostility that was almost vicious; all because he'd dared to follow her. He'd been sure that once they were colleagues and working closely together in the unit, she'd eventually thaw out and their relationship would get back on track. Sadly, it hadn't worked out like that. Everything he now said or did seemed to antagonise her. Yet there were occasional moments when she seemed to be offering him hope. Only the other day, she'd kissed him. Although he suspected she'd done this to tantalise him, to punish him for daring to pursue her. Nevertheless, he didn't regret following her to the unit. Zoe was the catalyst that had made him take the decisive action to leave Rachel and the kids. It was hard to keep receiving his wife's accusatory, self-pitying phone calls, and those from the boys pleading with him to return were the worst of all; but his period of duty would be up in a couple of weeks and he'd be able to see them all soon. His life would be just fine, if only he and Zoe could get back to where they were before. It was unthinkable that she'd simply used him for sex.

Eric left his room and crossed the landing. He was on his way to the kitchen to make himself a cup of coffee, but the sound of a voice in a state of some agitated emotion brought him to a sudden halt. It was coming from Toni's room, and she was arguing with someone. Eric thought this strange as he'd assumed everyone else was downstairs. He heard Toni say extremely loudly, 'I've had enough. I'm going to bed now. Goodnight.' A few seconds later he heard a sob and then continuous weeping. This was so untypical of Toni's normal behaviour that Eric was at a loss what to do. Normally, he'd have respected her privacy and gone straight down stairs. But supposing she'd heard some bad news? A death in the family perhaps? He decided he couldn't just pretend that he'd heard nothing.

Eric crept up to Toni's closed door and listened. She was still crying but now in a muffled, muted way, as though she had a hand or handkerchief over her face.

He knocked gently. Immediately, the crying stopped. He heard footsteps moving slowly across the carpet inside the room. When she opened the door he saw at once that his colleague was in considerable distress. She'd taken her glasses off and her eyes were moist and red.

'I'm sorry to disturb you but I heard you crying and wondered if you were all right.'

'Well, obviously I'm not,' she said, sniffing.

'Want to share it?'

She was about to say no, but something in Eric's darkly serious, concerned face made her change her mind. She nodded, and said, 'Actually, you might be able to give me some advice. Come in.'

Eric had never been in Toni's room before. Like his own, it contained a built in cupboard, a bookcase, a writing desk, a television, an easy chair and a straight backed chair. But it had been personalised with pictures, a few framed photographs and various knick-knacks. A small vase of carnations was on the desk. As he'd expected, the room was scrupulously tidy.

Toni sat on the bed and offered Eric the easy chair.

'I suppose you heard me arguing on the phone just now?' she began.

Eric nodded.

'That was my mother. She rings me every night. Sometimes two and three times.'

'Is she lonely?'

Toni looked anguished. 'Yes.'

She explained that her mother was in her late sixties and suffered from a number of health conditions. Several carers visited her during the day to get her out of bed, give her breakfast, and dress her. She received lunch from meals on wheels and supper in the evening. After supper she was entirely on her own. 'And that's when she rings me. Every night, without fail.'

Toni got up and went across to the book case. She picked up a framed photograph and showed it to Eric. 'This is her.'

The elderly woman Eric saw was grey haired, plump and jolly looking. She was smiling into the camera with a great deal of self-conscious conceit. Hardly a martinet, thought Eric. But you never could tell.

Toni carefully returned the photograph to its position on the bookcase. She came back to the bed but remained standing. 'I have two brothers. One lives in Australia and the other's an airline pilot, so they rarely get to see her. Until recently, I always lived at home and looked after her. Then...'

She stopped, obviously embarrassed. 'You don't want to hear all this.'

'Is it helping you?'

'Yes. Yes, I think it is actually.'

'Then why not go on?'

'All right.' She took her place on the bed again. 'As I said, I always lived at home. But a couple of years ago I met a man and we moved into a flat together.

My mother took it very badly and continually put pressure on me to return to her. I resisted, but in the end the stress of it all destroyed the relationship. The man and I broke up. After that, although I was really starting to enjoy my independence, my mother begged me to return home and be with her. I felt so sorry for her and I was at such a low ebb...' Her voice trailed off and she shrugged.

'So you agreed to go back and look after her?'

'Yes. But once you've tasted the freedom and independence of a mature adult it's very hard to reconcile yourself to living like a child in your mother's home again. After two desperately unhappy years of living like that I couldn't take any more. That's why I decided to apply for the job here in Leefdale. Way out of my comfort zone. It's been a whole new life for me and I love it. But it's meant moving hundreds of miles away from my mother. I thought I'd severed all the emotional threads but every night mum rings, telling me how depressed she is and begging me to give up the job and come back and be with her. She's so lonely and helpless I feel terrible about leaving her. I don't think I can hold out much longer. In fact, I'm almost on the point now of going to Dylan and handing in my notice.' Whilst Toni had been recounting this her eyes had never left the floor. Now she looked up at Eric. 'So there you are. That's it. The ties that bind, eh?'

'I know all about them,' he said, heavily.

'There's a novel by George Elliot in which she describes them brilliantly.' She closed her eyes in concentration. 'Let's see if I can remember. Ah, yes!' And then, tentatively, hesitantly, as though recapturing some long neglected memory learnt by rote, she recited, 'If the finest threads that no-one can see are cunningly bound around sensitive flesh so that any movement to break them brings torture, then these invisible threads make a worse bondage than any fetters.' She shrugged, and smiled. 'Something like that, anyway. I learnt the quote for A level.'

'You said I might be able to give you some advice. Do you still want it?'

She laughed, bitterly. 'Like what? Have some art therapy?'

'Only if you feel you'd like to. Anyway, it's probably not necessary because you've already done the hardest thing.'

'You mean by moving away?'

'That's right.' Eric relaxed back in his chair. It was a lot more comfortable than the one in his own room. 'You know, I once had a client in a similar position to you. It took her a long time in therapy to realise that the way she was living, so dependent on her mother for security and emotional fulfilment was infantilising her and was the cause of many of her conflicts and depression. But that's not your problem. You've already faced up to it and done the hardest thing of all, which is to make the decision to leave. Didn't you feel that once you'd made your decision to go, the leaving was incredibly easy?'

'Yes. I did.'

'That's because we agonise for years about a decision but when we actually make it and take the action we can't believe how easy it is. We wonder why we spent so much time procrastinating about it when it was actually so easy and we could have just got on with it.'

Toni frowned. 'But that isn't the problem now. I've taken the decision and left but my mother won't accept it.'

'No, it's still the same problem because you're thinking of handing in your notice and returning to her. It won't cease to be a problem until your mother accepts that the dynamic of the relationship has fundamentally changed. She still sees you as a child and wants to play top dog to your underdog. The challenge now is for you to make her see that you're her equal. When you're speaking to your mother, what do you call her?'

Toni looked bemused. 'Mum, of course. And sometimes mother.'

'And when you talk to someone else about her, how do you refer to her then?'

'Mother. My mother.'

'But she has a name, doesn't she?'

'Yes. Cynthia.'

'From now on, when thinking about her, when referring to her or speaking directly to her, you could try only using her actual name. Cynthia. No mum, or mummy or mother. It will redefine your relationship as adult to adult.'

'Even when we're speaking on the phone?'

'Then more than ever because that's the only contact you're having with her at present. And that's another thing: you could stop taking her calls.'

'And how do I do that?'

'Stop answering the phone.'

Toni laughed. 'I can't stop speaking to her.'

'I'm not saying you should do that. I'm suggesting you take control and set the agenda. Don't allow her to determine when the conversation takes place or how frequently it occurs. You decide when you'll speak to her. Otherwise, turn your mobile off.'

'She'll only start ringing me on the land line.'

'Then tell whoever answers to say you'll call her back. Does she have a computer?'

'No.'

'Then why not buy her one and show her how to use it? Not only can she send you emails but she might find people to communicate with on the internet. She's obviously quite lonely. Does she text you?'

'No.'

'You could teach her how to, next time you go home. You can control your communications with her far more effectively with texts than telephone calls. Make her look forward to texts and emails so that your rare phone calls to her are a significant event. Make it clear to her that there are many other things in your life besides her. You could also contact your brothers and ask them to speak to her more. Whatever you do, you mustn't give in to her emotional blackmail. You've almost achieved your goal of normalising your relationship with Cynthia. To give up and go home to live with her now will set you back psychologically. Whilst it might assuage your feelings of guilt about her, in time it'll only compound your conflicts and frustrations, infantilise you and plunge you into a severe depression. Whatever you do, you mustn't leave here. In the unit you're a fully functioning adult.'

'You make it sound so easy.'

Eric shook his head, sadly. 'Believe me, I know how hard these situations are. I'm at present in the process of separating from my wife. She and the children are constantly contacting me, begging me to return.'

'I'm sorry, I didn't realize.' She looked embarrassed. 'Thanks for the advice. It's very helpful.'

'That's all right.' He stood up. 'I'd better go.'

She stood up too and said, 'Before you do would you mind giving me a hug?'

He looked taken aback, but quickly recovered. 'Of course not. But why?'

'Because it's such a long time since anyone did.'

****

Sharon was about to set off for bed when her mobile indicated that a text had just been received.

It was from Dylan. "If u r awake can u call me?"

She was surprised and curious. Why did he want to speak to her at this time of night? Tired as she was, she had to find out. She called his number and it was answered immediately. He apologised for calling her so late and then went on, 'I just wanted you to know we won't be taking the kids away for the day on Friday after all.'

This was very bad news for Sharon. She couldn't keep the disappointment out of her voice. 'That's a real shame. Why?'

'Zoe and the others didn't think it was a good idea. They felt it would look like we were running away.'

'I see. That's all I need.'

'You sound rather annoyed.'

'Well, it puts me in an awkward position. I hear the demonstration's going to be very unpleasant.'

'That's why I told them we should take the clients on a trip.'

'It sounds like the most sensible thing to do.'

'That's what I feel too. So, presumably you won't want to bring Louise round on Friday? I'll understand if you don't.'

This placed Sharon in a dilemma. She knew that it was in the interest of Louise's safety and well-being for her to be kept away from the rectory on Friday. But then Greg and Pam would have won and she couldn't tolerate that. She said, 'It doesn't really matter what I think. Louise is determined to be with you on Friday, no matter what happens.'

'You've asked her?'

'Of course. If she does come on Friday can you guarantee that you'll do everything you can to keep her safe?'

Dylan spent several minutes attempting to convince Sharon that Louise couldn't possibly come to any harm. 'I've already been on to the police and they've promised to protect us,' he said.

For some reason the mention of a police presence impressed on her the seriousness of the situation with a force she hadn't experienced before. It filled her with dread and she really began to worry about Louise's safety. 'What a shame it is you can't just take them all on that trip.'

'I know, but the others thought it was rather weak.'

'They have a point, I suppose.'

'No, they don't. Some of the children are very fragile. It could be distressing for them to be in the rectory with a demo going on outside.'

He continued complaining about his colleagues. Sharon was surprised at how scathing he was about them. She felt gratified to be entrusted with such frank confidences about the people he worked with, yet she also felt irritated by his pusillanimity. He was a kind man, very sensitive and understanding. But despite that she believed he was weak. Sharon was one of those who refuse to see that strength can reside in finches' wings as well as in the lion's mouth. She said, 'If you think it's right to take the kids away for the day why don't you just tell Zoe and the others it's what you want and order them to do it?'

His laugh came back at her, gentle and soughing. 'It's not as simple as that.'

She wanted to shake him. 'Why not? You're the team leader, aren't you?'

'Yes, but our units are run democratically. Collegiately. We discuss things until a consensus is arrived at. A compromise, if you like.'

'But at the end of the day someone surely has to make a decision. That's what leadership is all about, isn't it?'

'It sounds like you're saying I'm not cut out for leadership.'

'No, I'm not. I'm just saying it wouldn't happen in business. Zoe and the others would be told what to do and they'd just have to lump it.'

'The inclusion unit isn't a business.'

'But you get money from it, don't you? I mean Lord Sandleton wouldn't be doing it unless he got a profit out of it, would he?'

'Well, yes, councils do pay us to take their difficult kids off their hands, and we also get grants.'

'There you are then, it's a business after all. Social entrepreneurship.'

He didn't respond and she was afraid she'd offended him. But he was silent only because he sensed there was a deeper sub-text to her comments and was struggling to fathom what it was.

Sharon said, 'It's just that I was hoping you'd take everyone away for the day and Louise would miss the demonstration.'

'Well, if you're really that worried don't send her on Friday.'

Sharon was growing increasingly tired and concerned that she might give away the real reason she didn't want Louise to be inside the rectory while the demonstration was taking place. She said, 'No, Louise wants to be with you all. Besides, in a way it might be good for her.'

'That's what Eric says,' said Dylan. 'He sees it as a learning opportunity for the clients.'

It struck Sharon that as far as Louise was concerned, Eric might very well be right. 'Well, if those kids haven't seen a demonstration before they certainly might learn something,' she said.

Dylan disagreed. He could see that they might derive something from the experience but it was too high a price to pay for making them upset.

'That man Greg Maynard's behind it, you know,' he said, suddenly. And with an unexpected display of venom, added, 'I think it's despicable of him to intimidate vulnerable young people.'

Sharon wanted to wholeheartedly agree but some lingering, misplaced sense of loyalty to Greg prevented her.

'I don't think Greg and the others see it that way,' she said. 'They're just obsessed with winning Magnificent Britain. I don't think they want to hurt anybody.'

'Really? I wish I could be so sure.' Dylan's tone was so negative Sharon could almost visualize his petulant frown. Suddenly, he perked up. 'Oh, by the way, I've bought tickets for the concert at Budeholme House. I know you've got a boyfriend but I don't suppose I can persuade you to change your mind and come with me?'

Why was her reaction a sudden twinge of fear? Perhaps because it was all going a bit too fast? She'd told Greg she wanted to see other men, but she hadn't reconciled herself yet to the idea of openly cheating on him. Especially with someone like Dylan. Although she liked him and felt sure she could make something of him, she didn't feel he was the life transforming, intensely romantic experience she was yearning for. She said, 'You might persuade me. But what about Louise? I can't leave her alone to go to a concert.'

'It's all right. There's a ticket for her too.'

Oh, how wonderful. A man who was inviting her and her daughter as well. She experienced an overwhelming feeling of gratitude, and, for a moment, mistook it for love. 'That's so thoughtful of you.'

'I just assumed you'd want Louise to come too. Your boyfriend won't mind, will he?'

'No. He hates concerts.' She laughed. 'Anyway, what he doesn't know won't hurt him.'

CHAPTER FORTY FOUR

At 10am the next morning Louise was sitting at a desk in the encouragement room completing a page in her English workbook on the uses of the comma. The clients were all seated at desks around her and were listening to Toni who was revising the twenty four hour clock.

Louise happened to look up and saw that Dylan was standing in the open doorway. He was calling her name.

'Yes?' she said.

'Would you come with me for a moment?'

Happy to be given the opportunity to abandon the many uses of the comma, Louise jumped up and followed Dylan down the hall to the art therapy room. He led her over to a desk in the centre of the room. She was surprised to see spread out on it her picture of the girl trapped beneath the frozen pond.

Dylan sat down at the desk and indicated that she should sit too.

'I'm really impressed with your picture, Louise. It's very fine, indeed.'

She thanked him cautiously, wondering where all this was leading.

'Tell me about it, please.'

Louise thought this very odd. Anyone with half a brain could see what the picture was supposed to be about. 'It's a picture of a girl who's trapped in a pond under some ice.'

'Go on.'

Louise looked at him blankly.

'Tell me about the people skating on the ice.'

'They're the girl's family.'

'They all look as though they're having a good time.'

'Yes. They are.'

'When I spoke to you about the picture yesterday you said it showed exactly how you felt every day.'

'That's right.'

'So are you the girl trapped under the ice? Or are you one of the family? One of those skating?'

It was hard for her to explain because she was both the girl under the ice and one of those skating. She settled for the simple answer. 'The girl under the ice is me.'

'So every day, you feel trapped?'

'Yes.'

'And unable to contact your family?'

This wasn't quite true, but she nodded anyway.

'What's making you trapped? A thing or a person?'

That was an interesting question. What was making her feel trapped? In a way it was a thing, because she couldn't leave Leefdale and being in Leefdale made her feel like she was in a prison. But then again, it must be a person. Two people. Her mother and father. Her mother who wouldn't leave because her father didn't want them to go.

She said, 'It's a person.'

'Do you want to tell me who it is?'

She did. She really did. She wanted to tell him everything but she knew she never would. She wanted to tell him that her dad was Greg Maynard and that he'd fallen out with her mum because she'd told him that Dylan had taken mum out. Perhaps the only way to make happen what she wanted to happen would be to tell Dylan that Greg Maynard, Jade Maynard's dad, was her dad too. Then Dylan might see what was really happening and how awful it was for her and her mum and he might do something about it. But it was just as likely that even if she told him everything he wouldn't do anything about it, and if mum and dad found out she'd told Dylan their most precious secret they'd make her life a misery. So she said nothing: her parents' attitude over the years and their threat of reprisals had established repressive responses and behaviours in her that were automatic.

She stared at Dylan and said, 'Do you like my mum?'

Her searching, vulnerable expression told him that this was more than just a casual enquiry. He took time to consider his reply. A lot obviously depended on his answer.

'Of course, I do.'

'No, I mean really like her. You took her out once, didn't you?'

Dylan smiled. 'It wasn't a date, if that's what you're thinking. It was to thank her for helping us get this house.' He gestured towards the picture on the desk in front of them. 'What do you think will eventually happen to the girl under the ice?'

'I think that one day she'll break free. Smash her way out and join the others.'

'But what about the person who's preventing her. Won't they stop her?'

Louise laughed, suddenly. 'They won't be able to.'

'Why's that?'

'They just won't.'

Dylan decided to leave it there and move on. He made strong eye contact with Louise and said, 'Has drawing the storyboards helped you think about those events that led to you being excluded?'

She stared back at him seriously. 'Yes.'

'Good. Well, there's one more thing I'd like you to do.' He placed a sheet of A3 cartridge paper in front of him, took up a felt tip pen and began to draw. Gradually, the outline of a thermometer appeared. He sketched in the mercury reservoir and calibrated the thermometer from 0-100 in units of ten.

With fulsome admiration, Louise said, 'That's a thermometer. It's really good.'

He thanked her and began to cut out small strips of paper that were more or less the same size. On each strip he wrote a single word: "Jade", "Dad", "Mrs Henshall" and "Roger". On a few strips he also wrote some short sentences, one of which was "You've got no dad". When he'd finished writing, he said, 'This is a "feelings thermometer". It's called that because it measures the strength of feelings. The words and sentences I've written on these slips of paper are called "triggers." Can you think why they might be called that?'

Louise shook her head.

'Think of the trigger of a gun. When you pull it, it sets the gun off.' He pointed to the strips of paper with writing on them. 'In the same way, certain words or sentences can set you off, like the trigger on that gun. That's because you may feel very strongly about some of these words and sentences, the ideas behind them or the actual things they represent. You may feel so strongly that if you hear the words, or see them, or even just think them, they may arouse very angry feelings in you, causing you to lose your self-control and start behaving in ways that are inappropriate and get you into trouble.'

'You mean like, if I think of Jade, I get angry?'

'Right.'

'Or if someone says I don't have a dad?'

'That's it. Now I'm going to leave you alone for a bit, and while I'm gone I want you to think about these words and sentences and then place them on the thermometer where you think they should be. For example, if you feel really strongly about something and think it might make you behave very badly, you should put it at eighty or ninety or even a hundred. And if something doesn't bother you at all or you have only lukewarm feelings about it, you should put it at zero or ten.'

'I get it.'

'Just to be sure I'll give you a little test.'

Dylan picked up the slip of paper on which he'd written Jade's name. 'OK. Where would you put this on the feelings thermometer?'

Without a moment's reflection Louise snatched the slip with Jade's name on it and placed it at 100 degrees.

Dylan said, 'She upsets you that much?'

Louise scowled. 'Yes.'

Dylan pointed to the slip with Roger's name on it. 'How about that one?'

Louise took a little time to consider. She then placed it at 20 degrees.

'Good. I think you've got the idea. Now, you don't have to restrict yourself to just the words or sentences I've written. You can write down any words or sentences that have made you angry, behave badly or upset you in some way in the past.'

He pushed the blank sheets of paper towards her. 'You can write on those if you need to.'

'So I don't just have to use the words from my storyboard?'

'No.'

After Dylan had gone, Louise sat staring at the feelings thermometer and the blank strips of paper. She was trying to think of a way she could use them to suggest that Greg Maynard was her father.

****

Twenty minutes later Dylan returned to the art therapy room. He sat down next to Louise and studied her feelings thermometer. In addition to Jade's name, Louise had placed the following: "Jade's Dad", "My Dad" and "Mum" at the 100 degrees mark. The sentences, "Your mum's a slag", "You've got no dad" and "I must get away from him" had also been placed at 100 degrees.

'Obviously all of these triggers around 100 degrees make you very angry indeed,' said Dylan. 'But is there one that makes you angrier than all the others?'

Louise nodded slowly. 'When I think of Jade. Especially when she says I've got no dad.'

'Why does that make you angry?'

'Because she's got a dad and I haven't.'

'So, you resent her because she's got a dad and you haven't?'

'Only when she says I haven't got one.'

It seemed to Dylan that this could be a simple case of envy. But he knew that simple cases are often far from simple. He said, 'How do you think you could stop Jade making you so angry?'

'Move a long way away from her?'

'But if you can't do that. If you can't move away. How else could you stop her making you angry?'

Louise shrugged her shoulders.

'One way is to avoid being alone with her. Try only to be with her if there are adults around.'

'What, like Mrs Lucas? Mrs Henshall?'

'Yes. And if you can't avoid being in Jade's company and she uses those expressions that upset you, you should say, "I know you're trying to make me angry, but no matter what you say I'm not going to lose my temper, so it's a waste of time". Then you should immediately get away from her. Go and find an adult and complain about Jade's verbal abuse. Tell the adult exactly what Jade's saying to you and why it's upsetting you. Tell them that if they don't make Jade stop you're going to lose your temper and you're trying very hard not to lose your temper.'

Louise had been listening intently. She nodded. 'All right. I'll try that.'

'Good girl.'

Dylan turned his attention back to the feelings thermometer. He said, 'Why did you place your dad at 100 degrees?'

'Because he's not there for me when I need him.'

Dylan's tone was gentle and sympathetic. 'Where is he? Do you know?'

Louise shrugged. 'No-one knows. Not even mum.'

'You've never met him or had any contact with him?'

'No.'

'Would you like to?'

Louise laughed.

'What's amusing you?'

'Nothing.'

Dylan waited, but Louise remained silent. Finally, he said, 'It's interesting that you've placed your mum at 100 degrees. You love her, don't you?'

'Yes.'

'So why does she make you so angry?'

'If it weren't for her, dad would be there.'

'You blame your mum for your dad not being around?'

Louise nodded.

'Is that really fair?'

Again, Louise shrugged.

'You've put Jade's dad at 100 degrees too. Why does he make you so angry?'

'Because I wish Jade didn't have him.'

'You wish Jade didn't have a father?'

'I wish Jade didn't have him as her father.'

Dylan tried to tease out exactly what she meant by this but she refused to engage. He was perplexed. She was clearly using the feelings thermometer to signal covertly that she had some issue with Greg Maynard that was causing her distress. Yet her reluctance to ventilate the matter suggested that she was suppressing her feelings about it, and at some deep level blocking all engagement with it. Could the cause be some acute trauma in connection with Maynard?

Dylan said, 'Do you see much of Jade's dad?'

'Quite a lot.'

'How's that? I thought you and Jade were no longer friends?'

'He comes to see mum.'

Dylan was shocked. 'I see. So he comes round quite a bit?'

Louise said nothing.

'Are you ever alone with him?'

Now she was immediately guarded. 'No. Why?'

'But he comes to your house?'

Louise suspected she'd divulged too much and her mother would be angry. She gave a heartfelt sigh. 'This is boring!'

Now Dylan knew that he was getting close to the truth. 'Is it really boring?' he said, 'Or are you only saying that because it's upsetting you?'

Louise returned his stare defiantly. 'No. It's boring.'

Dylan shrugged and adopted an attitude of great reasonableness. 'OK. Do you want to stop?'

She wanted to stop but she also wanted to continue. 'I don't know,' she said, shaking her head.

Dylan pointed to the sentence, "I must get away from him" and read it aloud. 'Who says this? You or someone else?'

'Me.'

'Who does it refer to, Louise? Who's this "him" you feel you must get away from?'

Louise stood up. 'Can I go now? I've got to finish my page on the comma.'

Dylan was about to ask her if she'd allow him to show Sharon her storyboards, her picture of the girl under the ice and her feelings thermometer; but Louise's uncompromising expression made him think better of it. The girl would only see it as a betrayal of her trust and become suspicious. He said, 'No problem. Go back and join the others if that's what you'd like to do.'

Louise moved towards the door. As she approached it she turned and gave him a long look that he found hard to interpret.

'I don't want to do any art therapy any more,' she said.

He tried not to look hurt. 'That's OK.'

He watched her go and afterwards sat reflecting on what had just transpired. The most extraordinary thing he'd learned was that Greg Maynard was a fairly frequent visitor to Honeysuckle Cottage. Sharon had never mentioned that. Was Louise somehow using the feelings thermometer to tell him that Greg Maynard was her mother's boyfriend? That they were having an affair? After all, she'd already innocently mentioned that Maynard quite often visited her friend Roger's mother. Could Maynard be a regular swordsman who was putting it about all over the village? An image of Sharon and Greg Maynard having sex overwhelmed his mind with tremendous feelings of revulsion and anger. He instantly recognised this as an extreme jealous reaction and willed himself to decentre. If Sharon and Maynard were having an affair it certainly explained Louise's antagonism towards Jade. Could it be that Louise resented Maynard assuming the role of her missing father? Was that why she'd so strongly denied that her mother had a boyfriend? Or could it be something else? And who was this "him" that Louise was desperate to get away from?

Dylan stayed there thinking for some time. He was constructing a hypothesis and like many who do so, was seizing on the facts that seemed to confirm it because those were the only facts he had.

****

'You'd better come down,' said Toni.

Dylan sighed heavily. He'd been about to start on his huge backlog of admin when Toni had burst in to the studio and breathlessly delivered the news that there'd been some sort of spat between Louise and Mona.

'What's it about?' he asked, getting up from behind his desk.

'Louise is saying that Mona's been mocking her about not having a father.'

'Christ!'

As they descended the stairs, Toni explained that Louise had elected to do her school work on her own in the encouragement room. However, at break she'd joined the others in the garden. That's when the row had started. 'It came out of nowhere,' she said.

When they arrived in the garden, Eric was standing with Mona and Louise on the patio. He appeared to be reasoning with both of them. Mona and Louise were facing each other in silent confrontation, their body language speaking eloquently of conflict and hostility. Both appeared brutally self-contained, their facial expressions vicious and pugilistic. Dylan was shocked.

As soon as she saw Dylan, Louise cried out, 'Mona's been abusing me!'

'No I haven't!' protested Mona.

'You have. You were horrible and going on about me not having a dad.'

'I didn't. Why would I say that?' Mona turned to Dylan. Her face was puckered with tears. 'I wouldn't say that to her. Why would I say that? She knows I've got no dad and no mum either. So why would I say that? She's a fucking liar.'

'You're the fucking liar!'

'Both of you stop swearing,' said Toni, horrified.

Dylan wished Zoe was there. She was always so much better at dealing with this kind of thing than he was. 'I'll need to speak to you both, individually,' he said. 'You first, Mona.' He turned to Toni. 'Would you come with us?'

Dylan led Toni and Mona into the drama studio. He was aware he was trespassing on Zoe's professional domain, but he wanted to conduct his investigation there because it seemed more appropriate for the task in hand. It was a place of dramatic interaction where suppressed truths were constantly being revealed. He also hoped to be inspired by Zoe's influence, and the drama studio was where it was at its strongest.

Once they were all seated, Dylan said to Mona, 'OK. Stay calm and tell me everything that went on between you and Louise in the order that it happened.'

Mona explained that earlier she and Liam had gone with Eric into Luffield to get the special shopping that Dylan had asked for. When they'd got back they'd unloaded the things and put them in the shed in the back garden. She said, 'We'd just finished when the others came out for their break. Eric thanked us for helping him. He said we'd done really well. Liam went off to play football, and Eric told me again how glad he was I'd been able to help him and I was always so reliable. Stuff like that. I started to feel a bit embarrassed so I left Eric and went and sat on the bench with Amy. That's when Louise came over and started saying things to me like, "Eric only said that to you because he loves you", and all stuff like that.'

'What did you say to Louise?'

'I just laughed. Then I said don't be stupid. He's an old man and everyone knows he fancies Zoe.'

It was an unexpected remark but Dylan's expression didn't alter. 'What did Louise say to that?'

'Nothin'. She didn't say nothin'. Then after a bit she said somethin' really weird like, "I know you're only tryin' to make me angry but it ain't gonna work 'cos I'm never gonna lose my temper." And then she said, "I'm gonna tell him what you just said". And then she went over to Eric and starts talking to him. In a while he comes over and says, "What's all this you've been saying to Louise about her not having a father? Why you takin' the mickey out of her?" I said, "I'm not. I never said nothin' about her not having a father". But he says "I'm really surprised at you, Mona. You're normally so kind and responsible." And then I got angry and said, "She's a liar. She's makin' it up." And he goes, "No, she's not making it up. She's told me you're trying to make her lose her temper and she's trying really hard not to. She wants me to make you stop it. So I'm asking you now, please Mona, to stop it."'

'Astonishing,' Dylan said, quietly.

'Why?' asked Toni.

'I'll explain later.' To Mona, he said, 'OK. Go on.'

'Well, I got annoyed, didn't I? I wasn't tryin' to make her lose her temper. No way! Why would I do that? She's just a little kid. And I never said nothin' about her not havin' a dad. Nothin'. Then Louise goes, "You're a liar. You did say it! You did!" And Amy goes. "She's not a liar. She never said a word about your dad."'

'Amy was on the bench all the time this was going on?'

'Yeah. So she knew I was tellin' the truth.'

Dylan asked Mona several more questions but none of her answers altered her story in any significant way. Finally, he said, 'OK, Mona. Go back to the garden now with Toni. And stay away from Louise.' To Toni, he said, 'I'd better talk to Amy. Can you fetch her, please?'

As Dylan expected, Amy corroborated everything Mona had said. She was a small, impish figure with a large nose, and her angry avowals of Mona's innocence reminded Dylan of an indignant bird. When she'd left the room there was a long pause, after which Toni said, 'It looks like Louise is jealous of Mona.'

'Actually, I think it's rather more complicated than that.'

He didn't expound any further, causing Toni to wonder, yet again, why he always treated her as though she was intellectually inadequate. If only he realised how much that hurt.

'Right. Let's talk to Louise,' he said.

His tightly clenched mouth and general demeanour suggested to Toni that he was apprehensive at the prospect. She understood why, when she brought Louise to him. Before Dylan had even opened his mouth, Louise said. 'Amy's Mona's friend. She'll say whatever Mona tells her to say.'

Once again Dylan was astonished at Louise's adult ability to attribute cynical motives to the behaviour of others.

'So they're both lying?'

'Yes.'

'But why would they both lie about something so important?'

'Because they don't want to get chucked out.'

'You mean sent away from here?'

'Yes.'

'But we wouldn't do that, Louise. We don't believe in sending people away.'

Louise said nothing.

Dylan said, 'What exactly did Mona say about your dad, Louise?'

Louise avoided his eye. 'I was only doing what you told me to do. You said if anybody starts abusing me about my dad I should go to the nearest adult and complain. You said I should tell them that if they didn't make it stop I'd lose my temper and I was really trying hard not to. You told me that's what I had to do if anyone started saying things about me not having a dad.'

'Yes, I did tell you to do that. But I don't think it was necessary in this case. You see, I don't believe Mona said anything to you about your dad, Louise.'

'She did!'

'No. Mona likes you very much. She'd never do anything to hurt you.'

'You're wrong. She would.'

'If you want us to believe that, you'll have to tell us what Mona actually said.'

Louise took a deep breath. '"You wish Eric was your dad, don't you? That's because you haven't got a dad". That's what Mona said.'

This sounded so plausible that for a moment he almost believed her. He struggled to regain the initiative and wondered what Zoe would do in this situation. And then, instinctively, he knew.

He said, 'You're always accusing people of taunting you about not having a dad, but really that's got nothing to do with it, has it? You just made that up because you're frightened to tell us the real truth, aren't you?'

Dylan was looking at her so expectantly. That must mean he knew. But how could he know? He couldn't know, could he? Had she said too much this time?

'I don't know what you mean.'

Dylan was convinced now that there was only one reason Louise was behaving as she was. Everything pointed to it.

****

Something really needs to be done about this, Dylan thought.

He was standing at one of the windows of the drama studio, gazing out over the rectory's front garden. It was certainly in an awful state. The lawn that for months Major Roberts had so assiduously cultivated to perfection was now unrecognizable. The dehydrated and overgrown grass was knee high and reduced to the colour of straw by the relentless summer sun. Thistles, buttercups, spectral dandelion clocks and the yellowing stems of decaying daffodils were the only flowering plants Dylan recognised amongst the profusion of pretty, opportunistic weeds that had almost obliterated Howard's pride and joy. And both grass and weeds themselves were being slowly strangled by the rapacious bindweed and other coiling, serpentine growths.

Raising his eyes from the lawn, Dylan's gaze took in the rest of the garden. He saw hedges, shrubs and bushes which through his neglect had grown shaggy and unkempt with unrestrained growth. But he honestly felt no guilt: only admiration for the tangle and mess of it all. For him, it was nature's reminder that everything had a claim to exist and that even behind the appearance of the most random, aleatory chaos lay pattern, order and a controlling artistry. Nonetheless, he appreciated that such a view might be regarded as perverse and placed him in an eccentric minority. Worse, might suggest that his love for botanical pluralism and his tolerance for weeds was simply an excuse to justify his laziness and inadequacies as a team leader. For he couldn't entirely avoid the nagging suspicion that the sad condition of the garden really was a consequence of his poor leadership. It certainly hadn't helped that his colleagues had no interest in gardening either. His half-hearted efforts at persuading them to contribute to Leefdale's chances of winning Magnificent Britain had been met with polite resistance from Eric and Toni, and undisguised hostility from Zoe. Of course, if he'd been a real leader, the kind Sharon admired, he'd have refused to accept their refusal. He'd have organised the staff and the clients into teams; assigned one team to the back garden, the other to the front, and given them personal rotas and a list of gardening jobs. Perhaps if he'd been more autocratic the villagers wouldn't have decided that their only redress was a demonstration, which was already making him sick with anxiety. But then again, where would he have found the time to organise all that activity, even if he could have had everybody's cooperation? When he wasn't dealing with the day to day management of the unit, his every other waking moment was absorbed in keeping on top of the admin. He couldn't remember the last time he'd applied paint to canvas, or even made a sketch.

The stark truth was he should have accepted the Major's help when he'd offered it. Still, perhaps it wasn't altogether too late.

Dylan's preoccupations were interrupted occasionally by noises from the kitchen: sounds of voices and laughter, plates and saucepans scraping, tap water being run. With Toni's assistance, Liam and Scarlett were preparing the evening meal.

He remained at the window but it was almost with relief that his thoughts now turned to his conversations with Louise about her feelings thermometer and her picture of the girl trapped under the ice. Like her visual alter ego, Louise was hived off from the real world, her pain and suffering unappreciated by her family. He was more and more certain now why she behaved as she did.

From where he was standing he had a clear view through the rectory's open front gate into Church Lane. The thoroughfare, laying mellow and dappled in the late afternoon sunlight, had returned to its former sequestered privacy. Across the road, the gates of Rooks Nest were still closed, but two sleek, black limousines now seemed to be permanently parked in front of them. The cars looked vaguely sinister. He'd noticed that their drivers never got out, just stayed behind the wheel, alert and watching. Cops of some sort, obviously. It was so strange to think that only yesterday Church Lane had been crammed with people and had witnessed such scenes of extraordinary disorder. Now, it was just another quiet village street. It occurred to him not for the first time that life was nothing but a juxtaposition of such contrasts, each as dreamlike and ephemeral as the other, which was why the artist had such a hard time recording it.

He knew his long reverie at the window had ended when Sharon's Passat pulled up and parked directly in front of the drive. He watched her get out and stand on the pavement. She was dressed in a business suit and looked hot and bothered. He watched her open the rear door of the vehicle, take off her jacket, and place it carefully on the back seat. She locked the car remotely, turned, looked up at the rectory and gave a relieved sigh. Smoothing down her skirt, she passed through the now open gateway, entered the drive and ambled slowly up it. All she carried in her hand was her car key. She looked hot and irritable. A faint film of sweat gleamed across her forehead, and there were creases in her clothes put there by the wear and tear of her busy day, but this only made her seem lovelier. Again, he reminded himself that his sexual infatuation for her was only nature exerting its con trick, inveigling him to breed. Nevertheless, it was proving incredibly successful.

He was sure she was unaware that he was standing at the window, but something in her expression made him take a couple of steps back into the room so that he could watch her unobserved as she moved on tanned, bare legs towards the house. She looked gorgeous in her T shirt and short blue skirt, even though she, like her clothes, had a tired and crumpled look. He'd been on the phone to Rupa's social worker when Sharon had dropped Louise off at the rectory that morning, so he'd missed seeing her then. He now took the opportunity to snatch a quick glimpse of her beauty before letting her into the house.

Sharon was just reaching for the bell push when the front door sprang open. Dylan was revealed standing in the doorway. He was grinning, as though thoroughly pleased with himself for pulling off a successful practical joke.

'Oh!'

She was startled by his sudden, unsummoned appearance. Despite his good looks, she was aware of something gauche and immature about him. A naked callowness, as though a gawky teenager was occupying the body of a grown man.

She gave him a faint smile but didn't look entirely pleased. 'You were lurking behind the front door!'

Sheepishly, he said, 'I saw you walking up the drive. I anticipated you.'

Now she laughed. 'Liar!'

He invited her inside. As she stepped into the hall she was surprised to see him opening the door to the drama studio.

'Let's go in here for a moment.'

Sharon had never been in the drama studio before. At first glance it wasn't very different to the studio at the Luffield Youth Theatre where Louise spent most of her Saturdays. But it had an entirely different atmosphere. There was no clutter, everything was arranged most tidily. Consequently, there was a greater sense of space. She wondered why he'd brought her in here. To be more private? Was he trying to steer her towards a greater degree of intimacy now that she'd agreed to go to the concert with him? Throughout the day her thoughts had been returning with some frequency to his invitation. Each time the thought of it had given her a little frisson of happiness, rather like the warm feeling she had when she remembered she'd a brilliant book on the go and was looking forward to reading more of it.

Dylan closed the door and she knew then he wanted to speak to her privately.

She said, 'This is Zoe's room, isn't it?'

'Yes. The drama studio. But she won't mind. Anyway, she's not here. It's her day off.'

Thank God for that, thought Sharon. She said, 'Have you managed to persuade your colleagues to take the kids out for the day on Friday?'

He looked displeased. 'No, I haven't.'

'Would it help if I spoke to them? I could explain why I think it's the most sensible thing to do.'

Dylan was horrified. 'No. They'd really resent that.'

Sharon's face fell. She was regretting her automatic resumption of last night's easy familiarity. In a thinner tone, she said, 'It was only a suggestion.'

He could see she was piqued. 'Sorry. That was rather rude. It's just that they're professionals and they'd probably resent...' His expansive gesture suggested that whatever it was they'd resent was surely obvious.

She lifted her tanned and glowing face towards him. 'It's all right. I shouldn't be interfering. I'd resent it too if someone told me how to conduct a purchase.'

She wanted to put him at his ease. She was keen to get back to the relaxed intimacy they'd achieved on the phone last night. It seemed to have evaporated and she longed to restore it. Why did he look so anxious? She said, 'I never thanked you properly for inviting Louise to the concert.'

'That's OK.'

She was determined to keep the conversation personal. 'No, it's more than OK. You know, there are plenty of men who wouldn't have done that. You're very special.'

He was delighted to be appreciated but it was only making it harder for him. Again he asked himself if it was worth jeopardising their developing relationship for the sake of his suspicions. But he banished the thought. It was necessary for him to tell her what was on his mind. He said, 'Actually, it's Louise I wanted to talk to you about.'

Sharon immediately suspected the worst. 'Oh God, what's happened? What's wrong?'

'Nothing.' He looked conflicted. 'Well, you'll have to decide, I suppose.'

'What do you mean, I'll have to decide? Now you're really worrying me.'

He told her about the row between Louise and Mona; the various claims and counter-claims each had made and his attempts to resolve the situation.

When he'd finished, Sharon said. 'It sounds like you don't believe Louise.'

Even at this point he was tempted to avoid telling her the truth and simply say that it was hard to know whom to believe. But he had a strong sense of professional responsibility. 'That's right. I'm sorry to say I don't believe her.'

His unexpected frankness shocked her. 'Why not?'

'Because Mona's denied it.'

'But she would, wouldn't she?'

'I believe she's telling the truth. It's highly unlikely she'd goad Louise about not having a father. Mona was abandoned by both her parents.'

'All the more reason for her to take it out on Louise, I'd have thought.'

'There are several children here who don't have fathers. Mona's never goaded them about it.'

'Perhaps because they're too frightened to tell you she's bullying them.'

'I doubt that. We have regular meetings in which people are expected to speak out about issues they're having with others. It's part of the therapy. Besides, as I said, Amy completely corroborated Mona's story. She was there all the time.'

'Her friend backed her up. That's not so surprising, is it?'

'It's possible Amy is lying, of course. But I don't think she is.' He told himself it was essential not to get diverted. 'How many times has Louise accused Jade of goading her for not having a father?'

Sharon looked surprised. 'Jade?'

'Yes. A few times? Several?'

'A few.'

Actually it was rather more than a few, more like a lot, but she wasn't going to let him know that.

'Have any children apart from Jade taunted Louise for not having a father around?'

'If they have, Louise hasn't told me.' Again Sharon was being disingenuous. 'Why do you want to know?'

Dylan chose his words carefully. 'The whole incident with Mona struck me as completely contrived by Louise. In other words, Mona was set up by Louise just like I believe Jade Maynard is set up by her. It's all part of a pattern.'

Sharon's hazel eyes were now black with hostility. 'You're saying Louise is a liar?'

'Yes. I'm afraid I am.' Avoiding her angry stare, he said. 'Have you ever heard the term, "passive aggressive"?'

She shook her head and placed her hands pugnaciously on her hips as though preparing to receive something disagreeable.

Undeterred, he continued. 'I believe Louise claims other children goad her for not having a father because she wants them to be perceived as bullies. Whereas it's Louise who's actually doing the bullying. The passive aggressive uses their fake victimhood to bully others and make everyone feel sorry for them. I believe that's what Louise does to Jade: and today, when she claimed Mona was goading her about not having a father, I knew I was right. It confirmed my belief that Louise is a passive aggressive bully.'

Sharon was outraged. What right had he to say such things about her daughter? 'Rubbish! It doesn't make sense. Why would Louise say children were goading her about not having a dad when they weren't? What could she gain from it?'

'Superficially, to get them into trouble and have them regarded as bullies. But I believe there's actually a deeper reason.'

Sharon felt suddenly uneasy. 'Oh? What?'

'That's the crucial question, isn't it?' He regarded her steadily. 'Louise has an unnatural amount of hostility towards Jade. Can you think of any reason why?'

Sharon could certainly think of a very good reason why Louise might have hostility towards Jade, but she'd no intention of revealing it to Dylan. 'None.'

Her evasive look told Dylan she was definitely hiding something. He said, 'Would you like to tell me a bit about Louise's father?'

Sharon regarded him suspiciously. 'No. I don't think so.'

'OK.'

He continued to gaze at her but said nothing more. She was beginning to feel very uncomfortable.

When the pause became unbearable, she said, 'Why do you want to know about him?'

'Louise seems to have a lot of hostility towards her absent father. I thought if there was some way she could meet him it might resolve a number of issues.'

Meet him? Oh no. She'd have to scotch that idea. Now she was deeply troubled. It appeared that Dylan might be in possession of the whole truth. She wondered how much Louise had told him. Or what he'd say if she blurted out: "But she does meet her dad. She meets him quite often. That's the problem."

She said, 'That's impossible. I only met him once myself. The night Louise was conceived.'

Dylan looked mortified. There. She hoped that was sufficiently shocking to shut him up.

She underestimated his tenacity. He said, 'I think Louise's hostility to Jade has something to do with her missing father.'

'Why do you say that?'

'Today, Louise said she wished Jade didn't have Greg Maynard for a father. Doesn't that strike you as a rather odd thing to say?'

Sharon fought down her panic. 'It does sound strange.'

'Why do you think she'd say something like that?'

Sharon was now sure that Louise had told Dylan everything. But if he knew, why didn't he come out directly and say it? Why was he holding back? Was he taking pleasure from her discomfort? She resolved to get Louise on her own as soon as possible and find out what the hell she'd been saying.

Sharon said, 'Perhaps because Louise hasn't got a father at home she's jealous of Jade who does have one.'

'Possibly.' He took a step towards her. 'Louise seems quite hostile towards you too. I think she resents you for being responsible for her father's absence.'

The appalling irony of Dylan's innocent remark made her almost want to laugh. If only he knew! Obviously Louise had been manipulating him with some sob story about her missing dad, and poor, sweet Dylan had fallen for it. He thought he was so clever. Well, he was no match for Louise. Sharon could see she had no choice but to continue with the charade.

'Well, that's understandable. She blames me for everything. Her dad isn't around so I suppose she'd blame me for that too.' It was essential to move him off this, so she said, 'Where is Louise? She needs to be at the dress rehearsal for "Oliver" at seven.'

'She's in the garden.'

'I'd better go and get her.' She turned and moved towards the door. But Dylan quickly followed and caught her gently by the arm. Other than shaking hands, it was the first time they'd touched. She was disturbed by the novelty of it. She glanced down at his hand on her upper arm, and then gazed questioningly into his eyes. Embarrassed, he removed his hand and took a step back.

He said, 'Before you go there's something else I need to tell you.'

'Oh?'

'Yes. You see, I have other, deeper concerns.'

'What?'

His grave look was making her afraid. 'What?' she repeated.

'Louise tells me that Jade's dad comes round to see you quite a bit.'

Why was this happening? After their talk on the phone last night she'd felt they'd discovered a new empathy and their relationship had entered a much more positive phase. She really didn't need this. She'd already had one hell of a day: most of it spent trying to finalise a completion that had gone wrong because of a missing receipt. And now, the man she'd thought was sympathetic and who offered her a way out of hell was behaving like a suspicious policeman. He'd already accused Louise of being some kind of psychological case who cried "wolf "all the time so that others got the blame for bullying her; and now he wanted to know why Greg came round to visit them too! What the hell had Jade been saying to him? Good thing Greg had anticipated something like this happening and had set up their alibi.

She said, 'That's right. Greg comes round to see me about Community Watch matters. He's chair of the Community Watch and I'm the secretary. He's also chair of the school governors. As I'm a parent governor, he comes to see me about school things too.'

'Does Louise know why he visits you?'

Sharon stared at him incredulously. 'Of course.'

Dylan nodded, yet was perplexed. If Louise knew the reasons Greg Maynard visited her mum, why hadn't she mentioned them? Yet again he had the feeling that he was being subtly manipulated. He said, 'Is Louise ever left alone with him?'

'Alone with him? No. Why?'

But she knew the answer almost as soon as she'd asked the question. Dylan was looking unusually ill at ease. His expression suggested he was finding the conversation painful, almost repellent.

'My God. Are you saying what I think you're saying?'

'I'm afraid I am.'

'But that's ridiculous. How could you think such a thing?'

He immediately went on the defensive. 'Louise exhibits intense hostility towards Jade and seems to have some very strong issues concerning Jade's dad. If he were abusing her that could be the explanation. I'm sorry, this isn't pleasant for me, but I have to tell you about my suspicions.'

So, this was where bringing Louise to the rectory had got her. Greg being wrongly accused of abusing his own daughter because no-one knew he was her dad! Surely, she'd have to reveal Greg's relation to Louise now? Once Dylan knew the truth, his terrible, unjust accusations would be repudiated. He'd see how ludicrous they were.

'What are you saying? That I'm having an affair with Greg Maynard and he's abusing my little girl?'

'I'm just asking if you have any suspicions.'

'Certainly not. Greg Maynard's a respectable married man. I've told you, he comes round to see me about the Community Watch and the school governors. Louise is hardly ever there when he comes round. She's usually in her room and Greg doesn't stop long. I'm not having an affair with him, if that's what you're suggesting. Not that it's any of your business. And what you're accusing him of is absurd.'

'I'm not accusing him of anything. But certain things Louise said made me suspicious. You must see that I'd no choice but to raise it with you.' Almost apologetically, he added, 'I've been agonising all day about whether I should speak out or not.'

Sharon was deeply relieved. So that was all it was then. Suspicions.

'Has Louise actually accused Mr Maynard of doing anything?' she asked.

'No.'

'Then where have you got all this rubbish from?'

'From the art therapy work that Louise has done. And what I've inferred from things she's said.' He related selectively some of Louise's responses to the feelings thermometer. Sharon's contemptuous expression left him in no doubt that she considered his evidence quite lame. To convince her, he said, 'Just the mention of Maynard's name makes her incredibly angry.'

Tell him the truth! Sharon screamed at herself, silently.

She said, 'So, your suspicions are only in your mind. Is that what you're saying?'

'Not exactly. I have a lot of experience working with abused children.'

'Louise isn't being abused.'

'No. But something's going on that concerns me.'

And then he had a gestalt moment. Was Sharon's boyfriend the abuser? Was that why Louise had denied his existence? In an agitated, tumbling voice he said, 'What about your boyfriend? Is she left alone with him a lot? I'm sorry I have to ask you this but I've no choice but to raise it. If I suspect abuse I can't just remain quiet about it.'

Now Sharon saw the way to divert Dylan away from Greg Maynard. She gave an ironic little laugh. 'I'm sorry but I haven't been straight with you.' Her face assumed a frank look. 'You see, I don't have a boyfriend.'

'But you told me you did. That night we went to The Trout.'

'I know. And I wish I hadn't. It's sort of automatic with me. If men are getting a bit too interested I tell them I've got a boyfriend.'

Dylan tried not to appear hurt. 'I see.'

She touched him sympathetically on the arm. 'That sounds awful. It's nothing personal. I told you, it's sort of automatic. I can't help it.'

So that's why Louise was sure her mother didn't have a boyfriend! He felt exceedingly stupid. Disappointed too. And yes, angry. No-one likes to be deceived.

Sharon said, 'Where's this art work of Louise's you were talking about? Can I see it?'

'I'm afraid not. I promised Louise no-one would be able to do that without her permission.'

'Let's go and get it then!'

Sharon stalked out of the drama studio and set off down the hall with Dylan hurriedly following. As she entered the kitchen, Toni greeted her. Sharon gave her a curt and perfunctory 'hello' and passed straight on into the conservatory. Her ill-mannered behaviour was so uncharacteristic that Toni threw Dylan a questioning look. He shrugged his shoulders and hastily carried on.

Sharon hadn't meant to be deliberately rude but her world was breaking up and she was in no mood to be sociable. Disappointment the size of an iceberg dominated her thoughts and temporarily deprived her of the ability to think rationally. She knew now that she'd been a fool to bring Louise to the rectory and seek help from Dylan. Why hadn't she seen that his kindness would gradually start prising the truth out of Louise? Why hadn't she foreseen that it might lead to the exposure of the facts that she and Greg had managed to keep hidden for so long?

She continued castigating herself for entrusting her daughter to the care of the inclusion unit. Fool! It had given Louise the perfect opportunity to exploit all the resentment she felt towards her parents and reveal very private matters to Dylan that were none of his business. Worse, because of that stupid decision, Greg was now unjustly being accused of something unspeakable. Fool! The only way out of the mess was to tell Dylan that Greg Maynard was Louise's father. Then Dylan would see in a moment why Louise hated Jade: because Jade could publicly claim Greg as her father and Louise couldn't, and that was the reason for Louise's anger. Nothing to do with being abused.

So why not just tell Dylan the truth? What did it matter what people thought of her, anyway? But it did matter. She'd deceived everyone in the village for so long. Exposure would be deeply embarrassing, not to say shaming. Her reputation for honest dealing would be lost. How could she continue as an estate agent at Parker and Lund with that sort of local gossip circulating about her? She'd always intended to tell Dylan the truth, but only when she and Louise had left Leefdale; perhaps when Dylan and she had entered into some kind of relationship. Fat chance of that happening now! Why would he want to be involved with someone so duplicitous and dishonest? She'd seen the hurt in his eyes when she'd revealed that there'd never been a boyfriend; and she'd seen him wince when she'd told him that Louise had been the result of casual sex with a stranger. If she told him the truth now, why should he believe her?

Sharon emerged from the conservatory and entered the rear garden with Dylan following closely behind her. Vaguely, she registered that a game of football was in progress. And then she gasped. Chasing after the ball and competing for it as aggressively as any other player was her own daughter! She was obviously enjoying herself and playing with great determination, challenging child after child for the ball, and calling out for it when someone else had possession. She was playing a most physical game: tackling recklessly, kicking other players and receiving kicks in return. Sweat was pouring off her, gluing strands of her lank, dark hair to her face and neck. Sharon was appalled. She rounded on Dylan and glared at him balefully. 'She shouldn't be doing that!'

He responded with a relaxed smile. 'She seems to be enjoying herself.'

'That's not the point. She shouldn't be doing it. It's dangerous. She could break a leg. Anything. She's got a huge part in "Oliver" and tonight's the dress rehearsal. If she gets injured it'll ruin the show. I left her here thinking you'd look after her. Is this how you keep her safe?'

She continued to berate him for neglecting Louise. Her voice was raised and thick with recrimination. Dylan said nothing, even when she was shouting at him. Once he'd recovered from the shock of her verbal attack he stood passively by, reminding himself that her anger was almost certainly caused by her delayed reaction to the shock she'd received when he'd presented her with his suspicions about Greg Maynard.

Sharon's outburst became so loud it stopped the football game. The players all stood around, staring at her.

'Louise! Come here! Come here, now!' Sharon called out.

Louise glared at her mother but didn't move. Afraid of a public confrontation between mother and daughter, Dylan called to Louise, 'Your mum's come to take you to the dress rehearsal. Hurry up or you'll be late.'

Louise's demeanour suddenly changed. She said goodbye to the others and came over, albeit sulkily and dragging her feet.

'Look at the state of you,' said Sharon. 'All hot and sweaty. You'll have to have a shower now, which leaves even less time. Go and get your school stuff.'

'Can't I leave it here?' said Louise. 'There won't be any time for you to check it tonight.'

'No. Go and get it. You're not coming here tomorrow. There's been a change of plan.'

'But I want to come here tomorrow.'

'Well, you can't. There's going to be a demonstration and it's not safe.'

But Louise was obdurate and continued to insist on returning to the rectory. Sharon, who was equally obdurate, insisted that it wasn't going to happen.

In frustration, Louise appealed to Dylan. 'You said you never make kids leave here.'

'That's right, we don't. But if their parents want to take them away there's nothing we can do.'

Sharon's face was taut with suppressed resentment. It was the first time Dylan had ever seen her looking less than beautiful. 'I'd like to see the art work you've been doing, Lou,' she said. 'Will you let me see it? Dylan says I need your permission.'

Louise suddenly became fearful. First her mum had told her she couldn't come back to the rectory and now she wanted to see her art therapy pictures. Why? Had she given away too much? She knew she'd been very stupid. She'd so wanted everyone to know that Greg Maynard was her dad even though she was forbidden to reveal it. That's why she'd tried to convey it in different ways to Dylan with the feelings thermometer. That was how it always was. She wanted people to know Greg Maynard was her dad, but was terrified they'd find out. It was clear that mum was deeply angry about something. She and Dylan had obviously been talking. He'd probably said something to her about that feelings thermometer. That's why mum wanted to see her art work. She wanted to find out what she'd been telling Dylan. But she hadn't told Dylan anything. Well, except that Greg Maynard came round quite a bit. She shouldn't have told him that. No, she shouldn't. What else had she told him? She couldn't remember. She'd better not let mum see that feelings thermometer. Or that picture of the girl under the ice.

Louise said, 'I'll let you see my art work if I can come back here tomorrow.'

'I've told you, you can't!' Sharon turned to Dylan angrily. 'I don't see why I should be asking my own daughter's permission to see something she's painted.'

Dylan said, 'Louise, I'm sorry but we can't let you come here if your mother doesn't agree to it.'

Louise lifted her sweaty, sunburnt face to him. 'You said I didn't have to show my pictures to anyone if I didn't want to. You said they were private.'

'That's true.' Dylan stared at Louise reassuringly. 'But as you won't be coming back here again you can take your art work home with you. Then, if you change your mind in future you can allow your mum to see it. It'll be up to you. Is that OK?'

Grudgingly, Louise said, 'I suppose so.'

'Good.' Gently, he added, 'Now, will you go and collect your school work from Toni? I need to talk to your mum. We'll be along in a minute.'

Louise set off for the house. Dylan watched her go and then gave Sharon a consolatory smile. 'Hopefully, in time, she'll let you see the art work.'

'Thanks for that,' said Sharon. 'I appreciate what you've just done. It was a good solution. And I really do appreciate you looking after Louise these past few days.' She looked suddenly tearful.

Dylan was concerned. 'Are you all right?'

'Yes.' Fiercely, she blinked away the tears that threatened. What did crying ever solve? 'I'm sorry I racked off just now. I don't know what came over me.

But you do understand why I can't let Louise come back? I was in half a mind to stop her coming here anyway, but now I know you're not taking the kids away tomorrow, I don't want her in here with that demonstration going on.'

Dylan looked at her shrewdly. 'That's not the real reason though, is it?'

'Well, now I've found out about Mona bullying Louise, or, as you believe, Louise bullying Mona, that's another reason she shouldn't come back.'

'That's not the real reason either.'

Dylan's eyes locked with hers. She found herself recalling the first time they'd met, when he'd come into Parker and Lund's and asked for the details of The Old Rectory. How long ago that seemed. 'All right, here's the real reason. I left Louise in your care because I trusted you to look after her but all you seem to have done is poke and pry into our affairs. Also, you've accused a good friend of mine of assaulting my daughter without any evidence whatsoever. Just because he comes round to see me from time to time about our voluntary work. But I know he's completely innocent and done nothing of the kind. How could I let Louise come back here after that?'

Dylan nodded, slowly. 'You're right. That is the real reason. Or reasons.' His eyes flickered briefly towards the football game that had now resumed, and then returned to her. 'I suppose we'll have to forget about the concert at Budeholme House now?'

Her mouth dropped open in disbelief. 'Oh, for God's sake! I'd think so. Wouldn't you?'

'I don't see why. I'm only doing my job.'

She couldn't believe his brass neck! 'After what you've accused Greg Maynard of doing, you expect me to go to a concert with you?'

'I don't see why not. If I have suspicions that someone's being abused I have to raise them.'

He couldn't be that insensitive, surely? She said, 'That's why I'm surprised you're giving Louise her folder of art work.'

'Why not? It's hers.'

'Don't you want to pass it on to the police as evidence of Greg's guilt?'

'Why would I want to do that? You've explained why Greg Maynard visits you and convinced me nothing improper is going on. I'm satisfied that Louise isn't in any danger from him or your imaginary boyfriend.'

'You're admitting you were wrong?'

'My suspicions were wrong but I'm not sorry I raised them.'

'So, you won't be reporting Greg to the police?'

'No.'

'That's good. Because if you did you'd be making a terrible mistake.'

She turned and walked quickly towards the house.

PART THREE
Friday 20th July 2001
to
Sunday 22nd July 2001

CHAPTER FORTY FIVE

The next receipted invoice was for heating oil and amounted to £171.68p. Wearily, Dylan typed the details into the spreadsheet on his computer screen. Afterwards he closed his eyes, sat back in his chair and yawned loudly. It was way past midnight, he'd been updating the unit's accounts for over two hours and there was still a stack of invoices that needed to be recorded.

Throughout the day and well into the night the house had been a soundscape of raised voices, domestic activity and loud music but now that the clients were asleep it had fallen eerily silent. After a long and demanding day Dylan knew he ought to be in bed himself, but the early hours were the only time he could be sure he wouldn't be disturbed and could work without interruption at reducing the mountains of paper that kept accruing on his desk.

He was glad to take a moment's break from the tedium even though it meant his thoughts turned inevitably to Sharon and the clumsiness with which he'd told her of his suspicions about Greg. He could have kicked himself for not approaching the situation more sensitively. He shouldn't have been so dogmatic, especially when the evidence was hardly conclusive. Nevertheless, he was certain she was hiding something and there was definitely some funny business going on. But he certainly might have handled it better. No wonder she'd backed out of the concert at Budeholme House.

The sudden sound of footsteps moving across the landing could have been those of Toni or Eric going to the bathroom. Evidently not, because they were keeping straight on and approaching his office. There was a gentle knock at the half open door and then Eric was putting his head round it. 'Can I come in?'

Dylan wanted to say no: he was dead tired, needed to finish his work and was fed up talking to people.

'Sure, come in.'

He'd expected to see Eric in a dressing gown, or at least pyjamas, but he was fully dressed in a pair of well pressed chinos and a turquoise silk shirt. Even when relaxing, Eric always seemed dressed up for a night on the town.

'Still burning the midnight oil?' said Eric.

'Yeah. It's the only time I get to do it.' Dylan didn't take his eyes off the computer. Perhaps if he made it clear he was busy, Eric would realise he was disturbing him and go. 'Zoe back yet?' he asked. He knew she wasn't but Eric was always like a cat on hot bricks about her when it was her day off. Strange, when their professional relationship was so antagonistic much of the time.

'No. Not yet. It's getting kind of late. I hope she's all right.'

'If she's not, I'm sure she'll phone.'

'She didn't happen to mention where she was going, did she? Or what she was going to do?'

Dylan expelled a big, audible breath. Obviously Eric wasn't going to take the hint. 'Zoe's a big, grown-up girl. She's no reason to tell me what she does on her days off. She can stay out all night if she wants to. As long as she's back on duty at seven.'

'Sure.' Eric looked thoughtful. Dylan pointedly turned his attention to the next item of expenditure which was for groceries from a supermarket in Luffield. He began transferring the details to the spreadsheet.

Something was clearly on Eric's mind. He looked awkward and at a loss and clearly had no intention of going to bed. He was mooching around the studio now, looking at Dylan's paintings; moving from easel to easel without comment. Dylan found his brooding presence extremely irritating.

When he'd surveyed all Dylan's art work, Eric said, 'How do you find the time for painting?'

'I don't. When I first claimed this room as my studio-cum-office I decided I'd call it my studio when I was doing my personal painting and my office when I was doing the admin. That was weeks ago, and since then I haven't called it my studio once. I'm beginning to wonder if I ever will.'

It was obvious to Dylan that with Eric prowling around no more work on the accounts would be done. He sighed and started closing down the computer.

Eric said, 'I'm not stopping you working, am I?'

'No. I was ready for bed anyway.'

'Good, because there's something I need to mention. Although I don't know if I should because it was told to me in confidence.'

Oh God, thought Dylan. Now what? He said, 'If you're going to betray a confidence it must mean you've a very good reason.'

'I have.'

Eric went over and closed the door, quietly. He took the only unoccupied seat in the room, which was at the front of Dylan's desk. He then delivered a full account of Toni's troubled relationship with her dominant and possessive mother.

Dylan listened in silence. When Eric had finished, he said, 'How seriously do you take her threat to resign?'

'Very seriously. She's at a crisis. I'm surprised she hasn't handed in her notice already.'

This was a real blow. Dylan liked and respected Toni, even though at times she could be a bit crabby. She was deeply committed to the aims and objectives of the unit and was achieving miracles with the clients.

'I've given her some basic coping strategies,' said Eric. He described the suggestions he'd made to Toni for ameliorating her situation and minimising the inherent conflict triggers.

Dylan said, 'They'll certainly help but it sounds like she'd benefit from a full course of therapy.'

'I agree. But I got the impression she was quite resistant to it.'

'Understandably. She probably thinks it would undermine her authority with the clients.'

'If she goes, she'll be very hard to replace.'

'I know,' Dylan said, regretfully. 'So we must do everything we can to persuade her to stay.'

They discussed the contingency plans that could be made if Toni carried out her threat and resigned. Dylan was hopeful that an agency might be able to supply a local secondary teacher as a temporary replacement until they could fill the vacant position. They continued to discuss strategies that would help Toni resist her mother's attempts to infantilise her. Finally, Dylan said, 'Zoe ought to know about this. Are you happy for me to pass on to her what you've told me?'

Eric looked uneasy. 'I've already told her.'

'I see.'

'No disrespect to you but I thought Zoe might have some helpful suggestions from the assertiveness perspective.'

'I'm sure she would.' There was a barely perceptible hesitation and then Dylan said, 'So you're back on good terms with her?'

'We were never on bad terms.'

It certainly hadn't looked like that to Dylan, but it was late so he let it pass.

Eric stared at his watch. 'It's half past one. I hope she hasn't had some sort of accident.'

'Relax, Eric. You don't have to worry about her. That's my job.'

'But I do worry about her!'

Eric had said this with unexpected force. Realising that his tone was too revealing, he added, 'I was just expressing my human concern for her, that's all.'

'I understand,' said Dylan.

There was a long pause, during which Eric weighed up how much he should tell him. His first instinct was to say nothing, but Dylan was obviously aware that there were issues and, despite all his vacillation and indecisiveness, he was no fool.

'Actually, you're quite right. We are on bad terms. I don't know why I'm denying it.'

Dylan assumed the expression he reserved for encouraging confidences.

Eric regarded him candidly. 'You see, a few months ago I slept with her. It was really no more than a casual affair. At least, that's how she regards it. That's why I'm not supposed to tell anyone about it.'

Dylan said nothing, but not because it was part of his strategy for eliciting confidences. He was genuinely lost for words.

'It meant a hell of a lot to me but afterwards she made it quite clear it was nothing to her and she didn't want us to continue. Apparently, the sex was an unguarded moment on her part. She said she only slept with me because she was at a low ebb after the guy she was in a relationship with dumped her. But she still couldn't get over this guy and move on with someone else, so she was going to make a fresh start, far away from anywhere that had associations with him. The problem was I couldn't accept that because I'd fallen in love with her. When I heard she'd applied to join the unit here in Leefdale I was gutted. I thought I'd apply too. Just to be near her. If we were working in close proximity I thought I might persuade her to change her mind about me.' He gave a hollow, little laugh. 'You can imagine how furious she was when she found out I'd applied to work here too. She accused me of stalking her. So, you see that's why it hasn't been an easy working relationship.'

What exquisite irony! Dylan wanted to laugh out loud. It was like the plot of some silly farce. He said, 'That night we were all in Charles' flat, I wondered if you and she might be an item. You even gave her a lift home.'

'Yes, but I didn't offer her the lift, she asked for it. By then I'd thought it was all over between us. I was really surprised she was being so nice to me. That was the night we started sleeping together again.' Bitterly, he added, 'But now I'm sure it was all done just to make someone jealous.'

Dylan was taken aback but tried hard not to show it. He said, 'So that's why you left your wife?'

'God, no. My marriage to Rachel was finished long before Zoe. And there were two other women before her.' He hung his head slightly, as he added, 'Neither of them worked out either.'

'But you decided to follow Zoe here after spending just one night with her?'

'It was several nights actually.'

'OK. Spare me the details. What I mean is, it sounds a little excessive, don't you think?'

Eric's normally sanguine expression was distorted by misery. 'Yes, but I fell in love with her.'

Dylan nodded, sympathetically.

'Now we hardly exchange a civil word.'

'Yes, it's been obvious for some time that you and she have issues. But I never suspected... What a mess.'

'I know. I shouldn't have followed her here. It's hardly rational, is it?'

'What's love got to do with rationality?'

Eric laughed.

'What's funny?'

'Nothing.'

Eric had actually been thinking of Dylan's infatuation with Sharon, but he wasn't friendly enough with him to be able to mention this comfortably.

Casually, Dylan said, 'Who was the guy Zoe was with before you? The one who dumped her? Did she say?'

'She never told me. But I've always suspected it might be Charles.'

'Charles?'

'Charles Reynolds.'

'Surely not.'

'Yeah. He's always sniffing around her. "And how's my lovely Zoe today?" and all that crap.'

'But he's years older than her.'

'He's got tons of money, though. And he's a Lord.'

'Zoe's never struck me as being particularly materialistic.'

'Take it from me, she is. You don't know her like I do.'

Seeing Dylan's sceptical look, he went on, 'If Charles proposed to her she'd accept him like a shot.'

Dylan still didn't seem convinced.

'I'll tell you why,' Eric went on. 'When we were together I sometimes used to joke about Charles fancying her and how he made it so obvious. I asked what she'd do if he made a move on her. She said he already had and that they'd been out to dinner a few times.'

When the hell was that going on? Dylan wondered. Was that why she hadn't wanted anyone to know about their relationship? Because behind his back she was knocking off Charles and was frightened he'd find out?

'I jokingly asked her if he'd proposed yet,' said Eric. 'She said he hadn't so far but if he did she'd give it a lot of consideration. It was the only way she'd be financially secure and be able to concentrate on her career as an actress and a writer.'

And she was the one accusing him of selling out! Dylan gave an involuntary laugh.

'What's funny?'

'Nothing.' Quickly, he moved on. 'I thought she'd given up her artistic ambitions?'

'Oh, no. That wasn't my impression. She was always saying "It's no good just having a talent. You've got to have a talent for having a talent". I think she meant you've got to do whatever's necessary to protect the artist in you and keep the art alive.'

'No-one knows that more than I do,' said Dylan. 'But I don't have the option of marrying a rich man.'

'Well, perhaps Zoe does. Quite soon after we arrived here, she again made it very clear that we were finished. I was devastated, as you can imagine. I felt like I'd been used, like a man uses a woman.'

'So she did it to you twice?'

'Yes. That's what made me think the guy she was carrying a torch for was Charles. I guess that shortly after she moved up here, he came back on the scene. After all, she's always popping into Sandleton on her days off. Charles has one of his many homes there.'

Dylan stared at Eric's sad, lugubrious face, and contemplated telling him the real reason Zoe had applied to work in Leefdale. Fortunately, what could have turned into an embarrassing exchange of late night confidences was interrupted by the sound of the rectory's front door softly opening and closing. It was barely audible but in the slumberous and somnolent atmosphere of the silent house it seemed noisier and more adrenalizing than the loudest fire alarm. Dylan sprang up from his chair, remembering that he hadn't enabled the security system yet. He was ever fearful of burglars or intruders, especially at this time when the rectory was the focus of so much antagonism.

'Sounds like Zoe,' said Eric.

There were footsteps on the stairs. They listened to them climb all the way to the top floor and then cross the landing. Next came a light knock at the door.

'It's not locked,' Dylan called out softly. The door opened and Zoe put her head round it cautiously. Her eyes darted from Dylan to Eric with a mixture of curiosity and surprise. Also, not a little apprehension, as though she was sampling the atmosphere with some trepidation having stumbled on something unexpected and clandestine. 'Gosh,' she said, 'you two are up late.'

Dylan said, 'The same might be said for you.'

She grinned, suggestively. 'You both look rather furtive. Are you plotting something?'

Dylan laughed. 'No. But Eric's been most concerned about you.'

The knowing tone in which he said this and the insinuating look that accompanied it confirmed her worst fears. So, he knew. Eric had told him. But what had Dylan told Eric?

Eric looked embarrassed. 'Well,' he began, defensively, 'it was getting rather late and we were both getting a bit worried.'

'That's very sweet of you but I'm perfectly all right. I went to York to see "The Seagull".'

'What was it like?' Dylan asked.

'Great production. Truly inspiring. But the traffic on the way back was terrible A lorry spilled its load.'

They exchanged a few more idle remarks about her day in York. Then she said, 'Sorry, but I really must go to bed. I'm dog tired and I've got to be up at seven.'

'Just a minute,' said Dylan. He picked up a piece of folded paper from his desk and offered it to her. 'John Carter called. He wants you to ring him tomorrow on this number.'

'Oh.' Zoe looked surprised but gratified as she took the slip of paper. 'I wondered if he'd call. Thanks.'

Eric was frowning. 'John Carter. I don't know him. Is he a social worker?'

Zoe gave him a crisp smile. 'No. A photographer. Good night.'

After she'd gone they heard her moving around in her room. Dylan and Eric eyed each other awkwardly. It was hard not to imagine her undressing.

Eric said, 'The trouble with this place is there's no bloody privacy!'

He had that strange expression on his face again, but this time Dylan knew the reason for it.

CHAPTER FORTY SIX

'You're not going to sit in your pyjamas all morning, are you?' said Sharon.

Louise was sitting at the kitchen table with a bowl of cornflakes in front of her. Her immediate impulse was to say something unpleasant in response but she checked herself in time. All she wanted was her mother to go to work. She took a spoonful of cereal and, speaking with her mouth full, said, 'There's no need for me to rush is there?'

Sharon had been agreeably surprised by her daughter's reasonableness at breakfast. After the furious row they'd had last night on their return from the inclusion unit, she'd expected Louise to punish her by reverting to her usual tactic of freezing her out completely. But instead of withdrawing into a prolonged and embittered silence, Louise had been pleasantness itself. Perhaps she was seeing some sense at last; she'd certainly been shocked to hear that Dylan thought she was the real bully and not Jade. Even so, it was infuriating and worrying that Louise had refused to say what she'd told Dylan about Greg. But astonishingly the row hadn't affected her subsequent attitude and this morning she'd been chatting quite normally about the success of last night's dress rehearsal, and how much she was looking forward to the opening night.

Sharon said, 'You know very well that if I don't nag you, you'll still be sitting in your pyjamas when I get home.'

Sharon picked up her bag, left the kitchen and hurriedly went out to her car. She opened one of the rear doors, threw her bag onto the back seat and cursed Mrs Henshall. She could understand that it would set a bad example if Louise's exclusion was ended prematurely, but she felt the head teacher could have been rather more understanding of Louise's needs.

Sharon located the road map and checked out the route to Edenholme, the village where she was meeting a potential purchaser to view a substantial property. The viewing had been arranged at the last minute the night before. She glanced at her watch. The appointment was for 9 o'clock and it was already twenty-five to.

Sharon returned in a rush to the kitchen. Louise was still eating her breakfast.

'Don't take the chicken and pasta bake out of the freezer till you're ready to cook it.'

'OK.'

'And don't forget to turn the microwave off.'

'OK.'

Sharon began to search for something in her jacket pockets. 'And don't answer the door to anyone.'

'I won't. Don't worry.'

'It's easy to say don't worry but I am worried. I don't like leaving you alone all day. Sod Mrs Henshall. She's such a cow.'

'What's up? What have you lost?' said Louise, as she watched her mother go through her pockets again, frantically.

'I can't find the piece of paper with the names of the people I'm meeting on it.'

'Does it matter? You know where you're going, don't you?'

'That's not the point. It's so embarrassing if you don't have their names. It looks bad. Shit!'

'Did you put it in your diary?'

Without a word Sharon ran out of the kitchen and back to the car. She returned holding a piece of paper. 'You were right. I put it in the diary. I meant to transfer it later.' She bent to give Louise a quick kiss. 'Right, I'm off.'

'Bye.'

'Now promise me you won't answer the door to anyone.'

'I said I won't.'

'And you'll stay here all day and won't go off anywhere? The pond, for instance?'

'I won't.'

'You won't go anywhere near The Old Rectory, will you?'

'I won't.'

'Promise?'

'I promise.' She smiled happily. 'I'm just going to spend the whole day going over my lines and getting ready for tonight.'

'Good girl, Lou. I'm so glad you're being sensible about the rectory.'

'You're going to be late.'

'Christ. So I am. Look at the time! Bye. I'll be back as soon as I can. Certainly before five-thirty.'

Sharon rushed out of the kitchen. Louise followed her down the hall to the front door. Sharon turned hastily and delivered a quick kiss on Louise's cheek.

'Bye, Lou.'

'Bye, mum. Take care.'

'And you.'

Louise stood in the open doorway and watched her mother get into the car. They exchanged a wave and Sharon drove off.

Louise's eyes followed the car until it was out of sight, and then she slammed the front door and ran upstairs to shower and dress. She had a full day ahead of her.

****

'I'm hoping we can leave for good today,' said Isobel.

Barbara said, 'As soon as that?'

'Yes. These things are arranged quite quickly. It won't please daddy, of course. He wants to hang on here until this evening. He says he can't miss the awards ceremony.'

'But the longer you stay the more dangerous it is.'

'Try telling him that. All he's concerned about is holding up that gold medal. No consideration about how I feel. Because of that appalling husband of yours, your father's face is now the most well known in Britain.'

Isobel paused, half expecting her daughter to join in her condemnation of Peter. But there was only silence at Barbara's end of the line. Isobel hoped that now Barbara had returned home and was living in the house without her faithless husband she wasn't going to lose her contempt for him. She resolved to ring her every day. And then, with a sharp pang, remembered that wouldn't now be possible. 'Supposing the IRA recognised Daddy and connected him to the Fermanagh Four?' Isobel went on. 'One of them might be waiting to shoot him as we go round the village with the judges. It's going to be bad enough as it is with all those people laughing at us behind their hands, nudging each other and enjoying our humiliation. Every time I think of it my stomach turns over.'

'Perhaps the security people will tell him it's too dangerous to stay on until tonight.'

'I hope so. I'm ready to leave now.'

'Have you really no idea where you'll be going?'

'No. All I know is it's a safe house and we'll be staying there until our appearance has changed.'

'What? Plastic surgery?'

'No. Just different hairstyles. Daddy will grow his hair longer. Shave off his moustache. Something like that. We'll both probably wear dark glasses for a while. Hopefully, people will soon cease to recognise us. Unfortunately, we won't be able to tell you where we are for ages.'

'But if I don't know where you are, how will I keep in touch with you? By mobile?'

'No. Our mobiles will be replaced. Our email too. We'll contact you with our new numbers and new email addresses when it's considered safe.'

'All right. I'll just have to wait until you contact us.'

'Yes. I'm sorry.'

'But this is so horrible. You'll miss the house terribly. And that beautiful rose garden. It took dad years to perfect it. I'm so sorry I've brought all this on you.'

'Don't be silly. It's Peter's fault, not yours. Besides, now that it's happened, in a way I'm relieved.'

'How can you say that?'

'Well, I've been dreading something awful would happen one day that would force us to move on. Now it's happened I don't feel so anxious all the time. In fact, I feel quite liberated now I've been released from all the uncertainty. Our enforced move could be very positive for us. What seems to be the worst thing very often turns out to be the best thing. Isn't that what they say?'

'This doesn't sound like you.'

'Really? But what else can I do but be philosophical?'

'I still can't believe this has been going on for years and I knew absolutely nothing about it.'

'Yes, we kept it well hidden, didn't we?'

'But how do you get used to it? All this chopping and changing homes. And living in fear of death the whole time?'

'One never gets used to it. But that's the point. Anyway, we all live in fear of death, don't we?'

'Yes, but not from immediate death. And certainly not from the IRA!'

'Your father says that all life is war: actual war is merely an intensification of hostilities. It's a view I happen to share too.'

'Dear me, you are being philosophical today, mum; and brave. You know, I'm only just starting to appreciate the sacrifices you and dad made to keep Michael and me safe.'

As Barbara talked on, Isobel wondered why her daughter had been speaking to her for several minutes and hadn't once mentioned Peter. Was she starting to get over him already? Somehow, she doubted it. Yesterday, before Barbara had left to drive back to Northamptonshire, they'd had several long, tearful conversations about the failure of her marriage.

Isobel said, 'By the way, Michael rang last night to see how you were. He was surprised when I told him that you'd left and gone home.'

'Is he actually aware of anything that goes on outside that bank of his?'

It saddened Isobel that her two children no longer got on. 'Now that's not fair. He told me he's been following every instalment of the Kellingford saga in The Times.'

'Good for him. I suppose he was delighted to hear of our break-up.'

'Not at all. He sounded very upset. He said he hoped you found someone soon who was worthy of you. I hope so too. As far as I'm concerned the only good thing to come out of this terrible experience is that we now know what hell you've been through all these years. Thank God you've left that bastard.'

There was a long pause. Barbara seemed unusually reticent. Yesterday evening she'd been complaining about some journalists and cameramen that were loitering outside her house. Isobel said, 'Are those reporters still there?'

'Yes. There are more of them now.'

'More?'

'Yes. Rather a lot, in fact.'

'That awful man Bryden's not with them, is he?'

'No.'

'He's probably got more sense. Knows it's a waste of time trying to get anything out of you.'

'Actually, the press aren't here for me.'

'Oh?' Something in Barbara's strained tone made Isobel anxious.

'Look, I wasn't going to say anything as you've got such a lot on your plate but there are going to be lots of stories in the papers and on TV tomorrow, so you ought to know Peter came back here last night. He's left Clarissa and returned to us for good.'

This truly was astonishing news. Yesterday, Barbara had insisted that she'd never have him back.

'Oh, Barbara!'

'I know. It's a shock. After everything I said, too.'

'Did you know he was coming back? Is that why you went home?'

'No. It came out of the blue. But I had a feeling he might come back. He always does.'

'But how can you take him back after what he did to you? After what he's done to all of us?'

'Because he's giving up politics. He's resigning his seat and triggering a by-election. That was my condition for taking him back.'

That's not the answer to the question I asked, thought Isobel. She said, 'But you've been so humiliated.'

'And so has Peter. So now it's time to draw a line under it.'

'He's really giving up politics?'

'Yes, that's why the reporters are here. For the official announcement. From now on he's going to be just a boring accountant.'

'But what about Clarissa?'

'Being quite a nuisance actually. Constantly texting, emailing and leaving hysterical voicemail messages.'

'I meant what about the baby?'

'I don't know. I'd have thought the best thing might be a termination, wouldn't you?'

Poor Clarissa, thought Isobel.

'You're not happy for me, are you mum? That Peter's come back, I mean.'

'Of course, I'm happy for you. If you're happy, I'm happy. And I'm relieved that Mark and Jessica will now have a father to help bring them up. But are you sure you've made the right decision? If a man had done only half the things to me Peter's done to you I'd never have forgiven him. I could never have taken him back.'

'We're all different, mum. If you knew Peter as I do you'd see his wonderful qualities. I've always known that there's a good, kind husband and father there. But since entering politics, he's changed. Besides, people have flaws. If you go through life assuming you're perfect and it's only others who are flawed, you're never going to make a success of marriage or any relationship. That's why marriage is so difficult. But I believe it's worth it in the end.'

'Really? Leopards don't change their spots.'

'Oh but they do, mum. They do. He's changing already. One day we're going to be grandparents and celebrate our Ruby wedding together. We're going to be a comfort to each other in our old age. We're going to stay with each other because marriage lasts a whole life long. You can't just pick people up for five minutes, treat them like a commodity and then change them like a car. Discard them for a new model. It's better to bend than to break, you know.'

And it's better to walk alone than walk with a fool, Isobel thought. But she kept it to herself this time, and said only, 'God knows what your father's going to say.'

****

After breakfast, Dylan called everyone together in the drama studio. He reminded them that today was the day the Magnificent Britain judges would be visiting the rectory, inspecting the gardens and awarding points. He also informed the clients that there was going to be a demonstration against the rectory and explained that he hadn't told them about this until now because he hadn't wanted to alarm them. He warned them that there might be a lot of people outside the rectory and quite a lot of shouting but the gate was locked and there'd be plenty of police to protect them.

'Is that why Louise isn't here?' said Liam.

'Yes,' said Dylan. He saw no reason to elaborate.

'She's chicken,' said Amy.

'Now, now,' warned Toni.

'What will they be shouting about?' asked Scarlett. Her complexion was often pale, but today it was ghostly white, so that her dark eyes gleamed out of it like two shining pieces of coal.

'Some people in the village don't think we've kept the rectory gardens very tidy and it'll stop them winning their Magnificent Britain contest,' said Zoe.

'Are they angry with us?' asked Khaled.

'Yes,' said Eric.

Sheldon said, 'Angry enough to kill us?'

Dylan smiled reassuringly. 'No. But don't worry, I've got a little plan that should make them change their mind. Yesterday, Eric took Mona and Liam into Luffield to buy some tools, and here's what we're going to do with them.' He spent some time describing his plan to the clients. When he'd finished, Amy said, 'When are we going to do this?'

'Shortly before the judges arrive which will be sometime between twelve and one.'

Dylan told the clients that they were to try and ignore the demonstration. Activities would go on as normal. He then sent them off with Toni to the encouragement room.

As the meeting broke up noisily, Zoe came up to Dylan. She looked concerned.

'The milk still hasn't arrived yet. Could this be the start of the boycott?'

Dylan checked his watch. The milk should have been delivered at eight o'clock and was now well over an hour late. 'Could be. I'll give him a ring.'

Dylan went up to his office and called Bill Harcourt's mobile number. When it was eventually answered he was told by Harcourt that deliveries of milk would resume only if Leefdale won Magnificent Britain.

Dylan said, 'What do you mean by that?'

Harcourt didn't answer but rang off.

Dylan knew they'd sufficient milk for two days and they could always pick some up in Luffield. Nevertheless, he was gravely disturbed by the milkman's hostile attitude. Involuntarily, he moved across to the window.

A movement at the gate caught his eye. Louise was rattling it.

That's all I need, he thought. He grabbed a set of keys and immediately left the room, ran down the stairs and let himself out onto the drive.

As he approached the gate he said, 'You know you're not supposed to be here today, don't you, Louise?'

'Yes. Mum said I was to stay at home.'

'So what are you doing here?'

'I've come to apologise to Mona.'

Dylan was staggered. 'Why?'

'I lied. She didn't say what I said she did.'

'I see. So she didn't say anything about your father at all?'

'No.'

'Then why did you accuse her of saying "You wish Eric was your dad because you haven't got a dad", when you knew it wasn't true?'

Louise said nothing.

'Do you know why you said that, Louise?'

'No. But I was horrible to her. And I want to say sorry.'

Tears plopped out of Louise's eyes and ran down her cheeks. Dylan could see that it wouldn't look good if a child was seen standing outside the rectory's gate obviously in some distress. 'All right. You'd better come in and say sorry to her personally.'

He quickly unlocked the padlock. As he pulled the gate back, he glanced across at the two black cars parked outside the gates of Rooks Nest. They'd been there all night. The people in them had to be policemen and he'd been assured by a police inspector that the rectory was in no danger. Even so, he decided it would be prudent to keep the gate locked until the demonstration was over.

When they were in the house, Dylan asked Louise to wait in the hall while he went into the encouragement room. He returned with Mona and took both girls into the art therapy room and closed the door.

Mona looked puzzled.

'Louise has something to say to you, Mona.'

Shyly, Louise made her apology. 'I've come to say I'm sorry, Mona. You didn't say I wanted Eric to be my dad because I hadn't got one. That wasn't true. I made it up. I lied.'

Mona said nothing.

Prompting her, Dylan said. 'What have you got to say to that, Mona?'

Mona turned to him. 'I told you I was telling the truth.'

'And I said I believed you. So, what do you have to say to Louise? Do you accept her apology?'

'Yeah.' Mona suddenly rounded on Louise. 'But don't think that makes it all right.'

'Sorry, Mona.'

Dylan said, 'Does that mean you don't accept Louise's apology?'

Mona had a stubborn, surly look. 'Yeah, I accept it. But I'm just tellin' her don't think that makes it all right.'

Dylan sent Mona back to the encouragement room. When she'd gone, he said, 'You were lying about Jade Maynard too, weren't you, Louise? She's never taunted you about not having a dad, has she?'

Louise looked down. In a voice that was barely audible, she said, 'No.'

'You made all that up to get her into trouble, didn't you?'

'Yes.'

'Have you told your mum this?'

'No.'

'Will you tell her the truth now?'

'Yes.'

'Thank you.' He smiled at her, kindly. 'You'll have to go home now, Louise.'

She looked horrified. 'Can't I stay? Please.'

'I'm afraid not.'

'Why? Why can't I stay? I've apologised.'

'Your mother doesn't want you to. There's going to be a demonstration and your mum doesn't think it's safe.'

Louise knew that wasn't the real reason. Mum was too frightened he'd get close to the truth.

'You shouldn't have come here today, Louise. Your mum's going to be very annoyed. You'd better go home right away.'

'Please, let me stay. If something horrible's going to happen I want to be here with my friends.'

'But your mum thinks you're safely at home.'

'Please let me stay. I won't be horrible to anyone. I won't. Please.'

Dylan thought hard. He didn't want to antagonize Sharon, but on the other hand, if he sent Louise away she might end up wandering the streets, putting herself in danger. On balance she was probably safer at the rectory. However, he didn't want Sharon thinking he'd encouraged Louise to remain there.

'All right,' he said, 'but on one condition.'

She regarded him warily. 'What's that?'

'That you phone your mum and tell her you're here.'

She gave him a joyful smile. 'I will. Thank you.'

She took out her mobile and called her mother.

Sharon answered almost at once. 'What is it, Louise? I'm in the middle of a viewing.'

'I'm at The Old Rectory.'

There was a squawk of dismay from Sharon. 'What are you doing there? You promised me you wouldn't leave the house.'

Dylan was just within earshot so couldn't help listening. He'd expected Louise to explain that she'd come to apologise to Mona, but she said nothing. Dylan found this extremely interesting.

'This is too much, Louise. I thought you were safe at home and now this. I brought you up to be honest but you keep lying all the time. How can I trust you? Why are you doing this to me?'

With a gesture, Dylan indicated to Louise that he wished to speak to her mother. 'Hang on,' said Louise. 'Dylan wants to talk to you.'

He took the phone and said, 'She just turned up at the gate ten minutes ago. She said she'd come to apologise to Mona. I told her she had to go home because you didn't want her here, but she says she wants to stay for the rest of the day. I'm happy for her to do that, if it's all right with you. But if you'd rather she didn't I can run her home in the mini-bus.'

There was discernible tension in Sharon's voice. 'God, I can't take any more of this. I'm in the middle of a viewing.'

'Why don't you think about it and call me back when you're less busy?'

'Has the demonstration started?'

'Not properly yet. There are one or two people hanging around in the street outside. I don't really think there's anything for us to be concerned about. The police have promised me that everything will be under control.'

'Has Louise brought any school work?'

'No. But Toni can set something for her.'

There was a pause at Sharon's end. The decision was hard for her.

'All right. She can stay. I'll come for her as soon as I can, but it won't be until late this afternoon.'

'That's all right. We'll look after her, Sharon. I promise.'

'Thank you.' Sharon sounded quite emotional. 'I'm so sorry about this. I mean, everything...' She stopped. There was a long pause. She attempted to speak again, 'I...' But again she stopped. Even though she was on the phone and miles away he could detect the presence of tears.

'I'm sorry too,' he said.

When she next spoke she'd re-gained control. 'What did she want to apologise to Mona for?'

'I think she'd better tell you that herself.'

He handed the phone back to Louise. Appreciating that she might need privacy for her crucial confession, he said, 'When you've finished come and join us in the encouragement room,' and left her to it.

CHAPTER FORTY SEVEN

Isobel checked the grandfather clock in the hall. Ten minutes past ten. Time they were setting off to meet the judges. How she dreaded the prospect. The mere thought of it made her feel quite sick. In fact, she really was going to be sick! She rushed upstairs to the bathroom.

She reached the sink just in time and bent low over it, retching; palpitating out the sour, liquid mess that was, in part, still recognisable as her breakfast.

Afterwards, when she'd recovered, she washed and dried her face and then moved slowly and gingerly across the landing and along to Howard's study.

He was on the phone when she entered. He was sitting at his desk and responding with passive obedience as though he was receiving orders from a superior.

'Yes, I'll certainly do that. Thank you...'

'Very well. I'm relieved to hear it...'

'I certainly won't...'

Seeing Isobel, he politely terminated the call.

'I've just been sick.'

'I know, I heard you. Poor thing.'

'I told you I felt queasy.'

'You'd better take something before you go. Are you sure you're all right?'

'I'll live.' And then, as an afterthought, she added. 'I hope. Who was that on the phone?'

'Secateurs Eileen. She says that the house will be ready for us today. She wanted us to drive there this morning but I explained I had to go to the awards ceremony tonight. They're going to take us to the house as soon as the ceremony's finished.'

Isobel looked horrified. 'Damn! Bloody Magnificent Britain!'

Howard ignored the outburst. 'Blair and Brown will take me to Budeholme House tonight. Thatcher and Major will be here protecting you until I get back.' The four minders had now acquired political nicknames.

'Did she say where the house was?'

'No. Only that we'll be driving through the night so it must be some way off.'

'Anything else?'

'She told me to shave off my moustache, to be on the safe side. I'll do that tonight when I get back from Budeholme House. Tomorrow, I'm to get my head shaved as well. A number one, I think the yobbos call it. But where or how she didn't say.'

'You'll look like a skinhead.'

Howard shrugged. 'Needs must.'

Isobel ran a hand back through her grey hair. Quietly, she said, 'Howard, look, I know you're not going to like this but I really don't think I can come round with you today.'

Howard had wondered how long it would be before she embarked on the familiar ritual. At every final of Magnificent Britain she'd refused, at the last minute, to accompany him to the judging. Every year he had to reassure and cajole her until she changed her mind: although, he acknowledged that this year there was more justification than ever for her pulling out. Oddly enough, he'd thought he was to be spared her usual attack of cold feet this time, which would have been truly extraordinary given the events of the past few days. But now she was running true to form.

Registering his pained expression, she said, 'I'm sorry. I just can't face walking round the village with everyone looking at us. Not after what happened on Wednesday. They'll all be laughing behind their hands and whispering about us.'

'I know Isobel, I know. But we'll just have to try to ignore it.'

'How can we ignore it? Everyone saw what happened. I don't think anyone in the country missed it. I can't stand another humiliation.'

'But no-one blames you, Isobel.'

'I know, but they pity me, which is worse.' She shuddered. 'No. I can't go!'

Howard rose from his chair and took her hand. 'Please darling, you must come with me. I can't do this on my own. I need you there with me.'

'No you don't. I don't need to be there at all. For years I've been at every judging, standing around like a spare part. I hate it. I've always felt awkward and uncomfortable. And now, after what happened on Wednesday, I'm going to die with embarrassment. All those cameras and journalists again.' Isobel raised her hands to her face at the awful thought of it. 'No, I'm sorry, it's too much.'

Patiently, Howard said, 'Do you think I don't know that? Do you think it's going to be easy for me, when everyone knows I'm due to appear in court on Monday? I know they'll all be talking about me, but I have to go through with it. Lady Brearley and all the other judges expect me to escort them round the village. I'm the chairman of the Magnificent Britain Sub-Committee for God's sake. Please Isobel, don't desert me now. I can't face it without you.'

'It's too dangerous, Howard!'

He looked shocked. For years they'd agreed never to unnerve each other with talk of the threat of assassination that hung over them. Neither of them had ever allowed the possibility of being murdered by the IRA to play on their minds. It would have completely destroyed their morale. And so they'd taken all the necessary precautions, and tried to get on with their lives without thinking about the threat or mentioning it. For how else can the simple routines of everyday life be retained if one is constantly under the terror of death?

'I'm sorry to raise it, Howard, but since your cover's been blown and you're famous in every pub in the country, we've never been so vulnerable to attack. Why else are those men sitting outside our home? It's no good. I'll be thinking of it, expecting it all the time we're out there walking round the village. My nerves just won't stand it.'

Howard took his wife in his arms and hugged her tightly. 'We'll be perfectly safe, I assure you. Blair and Brown will be with us all the time. And Thatcher and Major will be positioned outside the gate to make sure no-one gets in the house while we're out. They're all armed. If anyone tries anything they'll be shot dead.'

Isobel looked up at him, unblinking. Her light blue eyes suffused with sudden defiance. 'You're right. I'm being bloody pathetic. Why should those bastards intimidate us?'

'That's the spirit.' Howard dropped his arms to his sides and said, insinuatingly, 'Besides, if you don't appear with me this year everyone will have something else to talk about.'

'What do you mean?'

'They'll swear our marriage is in trouble.'

This obviously hadn't occurred to her. She nodded thoughtfully. 'Maybe they'd be right.'

His brows puckered with incomprehension. 'Right?'

'That our marriage is in trouble.'

'Is that what you think?'

'Ever since we've been married I've been on show, Howard. I hate it. I thought when you retired that was the end of it. But it goes on. It goes on and on!'

'It's the last time I'll ask you to do this for me.'

'It had better be!'

'I promise you.'

'It's the eyes, Howard. All those eyes on me. I can't stand it.'

'I know what torture it is for you. But just this last time. Please?'

She nodded. Suddenly her chest heaved as she fought back the urge to vomit. Her hand went to her mouth and she rushed out of the room.

Howard stood listening to her retching. It pained him to hear it. He glanced at the clock on the mantelpiece. Nearly half past ten. They were going to be late.

Left alone, he was now forced to contemplate his real fear: that the IRA had worked out his identity and had already despatched a hit man to the mainland. He tried to assure himself that this wasn't going to happen, but was exercised by the knowledge that there were still plenty of dissidents around, despite the Good Friday Agreement. However, he took some consolation that the media were only referring to him as an ex-army officer. In his regiment alone there'd been at least eight men with the same surname as himself. They'd never connect him with the deaths of the Fermanagh Four unless Bryden spelt it out in his article, and he was certain he wouldn't be doing that now. If Bryden had any sense he'd see his colleague's death as a warning. Nevertheless, it seemed completely unnecessary to put Isobel in harm's way by insisting she attend the judging, when he was the one the bastards were really after. Perhaps he'd suggest to her that she should stay behind and give the judging a miss.

The retching from the bathroom continued. Now they really were going to be late. Good thing the judges weren't expected to arrive at the village hall until eleven o'clock.

Howard crossed to the door of his study and closed it. He then drifted anxiously over to the window and gazed across the street to The Old Rectory. Every day he'd watched the rectory's front garden become more and more neglected and unkempt. The grass was now so high it would need to be strimmed or even scythed before it could be mown. The shrubs were completely overgrown and besieged by weeds. But it was the epitome of good maintenance compared to what had been done to the rear garden by that appalling Marxist-Leninist-Feminist woman. He could barely bring himself to look at the rectory's boundary hedge, which under his regular and assiduous attention had resembled a smooth and continuous wall of privet. Now it was an overgrown and shaggy thing, with individual sprigs shooting out of it haphazardly in all directions, each one screaming out for the electric trimmer. Observing the daily deterioration of the rectory's gardens had been a torture. Recently he'd found it harder and harder to go into his study. He couldn't sit or stand anywhere in the room without the rectory's criminal neglect impinging itself on him through the window. Only Greg and his handful of demonstrators gave him any grounds for optimism. How he needed Greg's demonstration to be successful. If Lady Brearley failed to gain admittance to the rectory, there was just a chance that the strength of public feeling might persuade her to award the village the gold medal, regardless.

Suddenly, Greg Maynard's 4x4 turned into Church Lane and parked a short distance from the rectory. Greg got out, followed by three other members of the Magnificent Britain Sub-Committee: Fred Birch, Janet Pinkney and Sue Rawdon. Greg went round to the back of the vehicle, opened the door and started to hand out banners. Good. The demo was starting. Greg had told Howard the night before that he was expecting about forty demonstrators. Howard hoped so.

The door of the study opened and Isobel came in. She looked pale but presentable having washed her face and refreshed her minimal make-up.

Howard said, 'Better?'

'Yes, thanks, but if I feel sick again, I'm coming straight home.'

'Of course.' He moved away from the window towards her. 'Actually I've been thinking. Perhaps you shouldn't come with me, after all.'

'Why?'

Gravely, he said, 'There's no reason we should both put ourselves on offer.'

'Nonsense,' she replied, briskly. 'You're my husband. If you're going to be taken out I want to be with you.'

Howard took her in his arms and lightly kissed her cheek. 'I'm so glad I met you,' he said.

'Come on, we're late,' said Isobel. 'Nothing's going to happen. And tonight we'll be gone from Leefdale forever.'

****

The judging of the finals of Magnificent Britain always followed the same procedure. The judges would arrive in a village and be driven around it slowly, rather like tourists, and would award a mark out of ten for the overall impressiveness of its horticultural display. They would then adjourn to the village hall for refreshments. Afterwards, they'd proceed around the village on foot; this time subjecting everything to a closer examination, awarding marks against more specific criteria such as plant variety and condition; colour intensity; innovative display; artistic arrangement and floral contrasts. In the course of their travels they would rigorously inspect three gardens which had been nominated as exemplary. In the case of Leefdale these were Twinings, a nineteenth century farmhouse with a walled garden; Holme End, a Tudor, timber framed dwelling which possessed the oldest garden in the village; and of course, the gardens of The Old Rectory. Each of these exemplary gardens had been nominated, under the terms of the competition, before the 31st March.

It was ten-forty when Howard and Isobel finally emerged from Rooks Nest and got into the black BMW which, driven by "Blair", had reversed up the drive to collect them. As the car slowed to pass through the gates and turn into Church Lane, Isobel experienced an extraordinary sense of unreality. Could it be that only two days ago huge crowds of thronging, jostling people were blockading these same gates? Just like all the other events of that momentous day, it now seemed hardly possible. A dream.

Greg Maynard and more than a dozen demonstrators were now in position outside The Old Rectory. They waved and shook their placards in solidarity with the Roberts' car as it turned out of the drive and swept off down Church Lane.

'Your demonstration's started early,' observed Isobel.

'It's not my demonstration,' said Howard. 'It's Greg's.'

'People will think it's yours, though. You're so thick with him.'

'I can't help what people think.'

Instead of gladdening Howard's heart, the presence of the demonstrators only depressed him. They were a stark reminder that to win the gold medal for the fifth time the village needed three exemplary gardens and it now only had two.

'I hope you've told Lady Brearley and the other judges that you're persona non grata at the rectory because of the assault charges?'

'Yes. They know I won't be going into the rectory with them. But I'm hoping that those wankers from the inclusion unit will refuse the judges access too. That's another reason for Greg's little demonstration.'

'So you did put him up to it?'

'Not at all.'

If you did, I hope it backfires on you, Isobel thought, and turned to look out of the car window. It was a beautiful summer's day under a perfect blue sky and the village was at its best. Petunias, lobelias and many other trailing plants poured over the sides of the hanging baskets affixed to every house. Even those smaller cottages and terraces that were deprived of front gardens had their frontages embellished with tubs and containers filled to the brim with flowers: roses, clematis, sweet peas, marguerites, lupins, delphiniums, geraniums and many others. The gardens of the more substantial houses boasted large spreading trees in full leaf. Everywhere Isobel looked her sight was ravished by vivid colour.

As the car passed by lush front lawns, punctiliously striped like woven cloth, and bordered with elegantly manicured topiary and shrubs, Howard reflected ruefully that any one of those gardens would serve as a better exemplar than The Old Rectory in its present state.

'The village has never looked better,' said Isobel. Now that she was taking part she was entering into the competitive spirit of the thing. 'I'm sure we'll win.'

Leefdale indeed looked even more perfect than it did on the Magnificent Britain calendar. At once Howard felt a surge of optimism. Perhaps, despite the rectory, the village had a chance after all. But immediately, the thought of the rectory seized him with an intolerable dismay. He tried to think of some analogy to the way he felt. A bride who'd had a bottle of ink poured over her spotless white wedding dress just before the ceremony, sprang to mind. What right had that shower of bastards at the rectory to come to a beautiful village like this and ruin everybody's hard work?'

'Have you taken your pill?' asked Isobel.

'Yes, of course.'

****

'If this keeps up it'll really upset the kids,' said Zoe. 'Even I feel intimidated.'

'I agree,' said Dylan. 'We should have taken them away for the day.'

'No way.'

For some time, Zoe and Dylan had been standing at the window of the drama studio watching the demonstrators assemble outside the rectory's securely locked front gate. Greg Maynard was the only one they'd actually met, although some of the others were familiar faces from the village. Most of these were older than Maynard and were smartly dressed in middle class country casuals. They were holding placards bearing such imaginative slogans as "You Should Be Ashamed of Your Neglect", "Clean Up Your Act" and "Your Vandalism Will Cost Us the Gold Medal".

At first, the demonstrators had been small in number and relatively peaceful. They'd simply stood around on the pavement, holding up their placards and shouting largely unintelligible insults. But since then the crowd had grown larger, and when someone had started chanting "Inclusion Unit Out!" it had been taken up loudly and with gusto and had quickly become an intrusive, repetitive rant.

At that moment another middle-aged man arrived, attached himself to the group of demonstrators and immediately took up the chant. There was something mechanical about the way he slotted in.

'That makes sixteen now,' said Dylan.

'Can't we do something about it?'

'Apparently not. The police say they're entitled to demonstrate.'

'I mean do something about it ourselves?'

'We've agreed what we're going to do.'

'That won't achieve anything.'

The telephone in the hall rang. 'I'll get it,' said Dylan.

Zoe said, 'I'll go and see how the others are getting on.'

When Zoe arrived in the encouragement room she was surprised that even though it was towards the rear of the house, the demonstrators' chanting could clearly be heard.

Eric was sitting at a table with three teenagers and Louise. They were each taking it in turn to roll a couple of dice. Before each throw they called out the number they were predicting and its probability as a fraction of the combined faces of the dice. After the roll of each die there were cries of delight or disappointment. Other teenagers were seated at separate desks filling out worksheets. The noise from the probability group and the constant background drone of the demonstrators combined to make the encouragement room a very noisy place indeed.

'How's it going?' Zoe asked Toni.

'They're very restless.'

Toni explained that for a while the kids had got on with their maths tasks and had been unaffected by the crowd and the noise from outside. But since the chanting had started, they'd lost concentration. Some were lifting their heads at every cry and shout from the street, and others, often in the middle of their work, were getting up from their desks and wandering about, visibly disturbed.

Scarlett came up. She was wearing a pained yet beseeching expression.

'Can I go to the toilet?'

'But you've only just been.'

'I've got the runs.'

'All right, go on.' said Toni, wearily.

When Scarlett had left her side, Toni said. 'They keep asking me if they can go to the toilet but I know they only want to go upstairs to look at the demo.'

Zoe said, 'That's understandable. They feel vulnerable and want to reassure themselves that everything's all right. They're probably going upstairs to check that the gates are still locked and the demonstrators haven't broken in.'

'Surely it's just curiosity?'

'No. It's more than that.'

Zoe explained that given the insecurity and trauma in the children's backgrounds, the situation must appear extremely threatening. She was concerned it would cause them to regress emotionally and start manifesting the kind of disturbed behaviour which had originally occasioned their referral to the unit.

Toni said, 'Yes, I'd hoped that being in here and unable to see what's going on would have made them feel more secure. I didn't anticipate all this noise from outside would penetrate. Perhaps Dylan was right and we should have taken them away for the day.'

Zoe was adamant. 'No. They must learn to cope with such stressful situations. And with our support, they will.'

Toni didn't look altogether convinced. She felt threatened and intimidated and was very glad that there was a high and fairly robust gate between the inclusion unit and the demonstrators. It wasn't an impenetrable barrier, but it comforted her to know that there was at least something to hold back the mob. She was now bitterly regretting that she'd opposed Dylan's plan to take the children away for the day. However, she wasn't going to admit that to Zoe.

At that point Dylan entered the room. He came straight over to Zoe and Toni and said, 'That was the police on the phone. They've promised me they'll be out in force. Don't worry, they'll protect us.'

Sheldon who'd been sitting at a desk close by had clearly overheard. 'Yeah, sure,' he said. 'Sure they will.'

Despite the tension each adult felt, or perhaps even because of it, Sheldon's remark made the three of them burst out laughing.

Afterwards, Zoe gazed around the room. The kids' emotional distress was palpable. 'This noise is very unnerving,' she said. 'No wonder the kids can't settle. I'm going out to talk to the demonstrators. See if I can get them to listen to reason. Once they realise how much their chanting is upsetting the kids, they'll surely be reasonable and stop. They must have children themselves. They wouldn't like to see their own kids upset like these are.'

'I don't think you should do that,' said Dylan. 'The crowd could turn ugly.'

Zoe's face had a stubborn look. 'We've got to set an example and assert ourselves. We've got to show the kids we're not intimidated.'

Zoe and Dylan argued about this for several minutes. Toni took no part.

Finally, in exasperation, Zoe clapped her hands loudly and called for quiet. The clients fell silent and looked to her, expectantly. Zoe was just about to address them when the door opened and Scarlett came in. Zoe waited for her to scurry shyly across the room to her seat, before continuing. She said, 'I know this horrible noise is making you upset so I'm going to go out and talk to the demonstrators and ask them to stop.'

'Do you want us to come with you?' said Sheldon.

'It's very kind of you to offer, Sheldon, but no thanks.'

'You shouldn't go on your own,' said Scarlett. 'There's loads of people out there and they look really mental.'

Toni looked severe. 'I thought you went upstairs to go to the toilet?'

'I did.'

Dylan assured the clients that their presence at the gate wouldn't be necessary or allowed. 'None of you need worry,' he said. 'I'll be going with Zoe.'

'So will I,' said Eric.

'But thank you for offering,' Dylan added.

Zoe set off down the hall with Dylan and Eric following. As soon as the front door of the rectory opened and Zoe and the other two stepped out onto the portico, a great murmur went up amongst those in the crowd. Zoe strode down the drive with Eric and Dylan alongside her, and the chanting increased to a roar.

They'd got halfway to the gate when Zoe stopped and said, 'I don't think you ought to come any further. There's enough testosterone flying around. I think you should leave it to me.'

'Are you sure?' said Eric.

'Perfectly sure.'

'OK. But we're here if you need us.'

'Don't do anything reckless,' said Dylan.

Zoe left them and approached the gate. The crowd reacted as though this was a deliberate provocation and became incensed. Now that they had an individual to rant at instead of the rectory's impervious bricks and mortar, their loathing had found a focus. As well as the persistent, rhythmic chanting of "Inclusion Unit Out", some individuals shouted obscene sexist comments and worse.

As Zoe came up to the gate the demonstrators surged forward, angrily shaking and rattling the bars. They seemed to be under the influence of some drug which had released all the malignity in their natures. She stared into their dead eyes, and confronted by their merciless expressions and relentless anger for the first time felt real fear. It was clear they were motivated by something that was making them insensible to reason. Nevertheless, she had to try to reason with them. They were human beings, like her, weren't they?

'Look, please listen to me,' she called through the bars of the gate. 'This is an inclusion unit. It's where we provide refuge for children with emotional and educational needs. Your demonstration is making it impossible for us to work. We appreciate that you have the right to demonstrate but not in this fashion, please. It's making our children deeply upset. They're vulnerable kids. We're more than happy to discuss your grievances but first would you please stop making this awful noise? All I ask is that you stop this ugly chanting and move away from our gates.'

'Why the bloody hell should we help you? What have you done for us?'

This question was wildly cheered. Zoe looked more closely at the person who'd asked it. Greg Maynard. The Community Watch man she'd had a run-in with on her arrival in Leefdale. The one who'd destroyed all her hopes of getting it back together with Dylan that night. Greg Maynard. The father of Jade Maynard.

The noise of the crowd was now so great she had to shout above it. 'You've got children. How would you feel if your children were in there feeling frightened?'

'My children would never end up in a place like this,' Maynard bawled back.

'All I'm asking...'

But what Zoe was asking for was never discovered. For at that moment an egg thrown by someone at the back of the crowd shot through the bars of the gate and broke on contact with her chest. For a microsecond of arrested time it remained there, motionless: an incongruous mixture of clear and yellow mucous and shards of eggshell splattering her right breast. Zoe looked down at the disgusting stain with horror and disbelief. Seeing it slowly start to coalesce and slip down her T shirt like a string of old man's snot, she clutched her breast and retreated from the gate amidst loud and raucous laughter.

CHAPTER FORTY EIGHT

An empty Bentley was parked outside the village hall. Howard and Isobel stared at it through the windscreen of the BMW and then turned to each other, aghast.

'They're already here!' cried Isobel.

'Damn!'

They both knew they'd committed a terrible faux pas by not being present to greet and welcome the judges. Now they would have to make an embarrassing entrance and give their apologies like children late to school; all the while being scrutinised by those who'd turned up just to see how they'd handle their first public appearance after their much publicised humiliations.

'Come on,' said Howard, undoing his seatbelt. 'Let's face the music.'

But Isobel didn't move.

'What's wrong?'

'I can't.'

'What?'

'I can't go in there. All those eyes on us. I can't face it.'

'Oh yes, you can.' Gently, and to her surprise, he kissed her cheek and stared earnestly into her eyes. 'Tomorrow we'll be far away from here forever. We'll never have to see any of these people again.'

They remained in the car while one of their security officers, the one they'd nicknamed "Brown", went ahead of them to check out the hall. The other officer, "Blair", stayed with them in the car. When Brown was sure that everything was safe and secure he beckoned to Howard and Isobel. They emerged from the car and followed him into the village hall.

The place was more crowded than Isobel had ever known: members of the village hall committee; parish councillors; various hangers on and assorted busy bodies, all were packed in.

As Howard and Isobel entered the room conversations faltered for a barely perceptible beat as all eyes turned towards them and then just as quickly looked away. Some faces were patently disapproving, a few were smiling but most just expressed curiosity. After this almost imperceptible hiatus, conversations resumed.

Lady Celia Brearley and the other judges were standing by a trestle table at the far end of the hall. Howard noticed with great annoyance that they were talking to Arthur Meakins. How he'd be relishing this!

As Howard and Isobel moved down the hall towards the judges, a woman holding a video camera and another woman with a boom mic tracked them. A tall man was trailing the camera crew, quietly issuing instructions. This was the director who'd been responsible for videoing the finals of Magnificent Britain for several years. He nodded at Howard. Howard nodded back, unsmiling. The sight of the video camera had made him feel quite agitated.

Isobel kept her eyes fixed on the table: it was laden with a tea urn, a huge kettle, a catering sized tin of instant coffee and a great number of municipal looking cups and saucers in a depressing shade of off-white. Various spoons were also visible which, although fulfilling a similar function, were revealed by the diversity of their design to have come from different sets of cutlery and had obviously been donated by separate households. There was also a bowl in the same shade as the other crockery, containing several sugar lumps, some of them browning where they'd been splashed with tea or coffee. Isobel shuddered and fought back her need to vomit.

'Lady Brearley, I'm so sorry that Isobel and I weren't here to meet you,' said Howard.

Celia beamed. 'That's all right. Councillor Meakins has been looking after us.'

Meakins smiled. 'My pleasure, Howard.'

Was it his imagination or were they all staring at him apprehensively? No, it wasn't his imagination. The same guarded look was in all their eyes. Obviously they'd seen him on television striking Peter; probably knew he'd struck the boy too. That's why they were giving him that look. They weren't quite sure how mad he was, and whether an innocuous remark would result in them receiving a sock to the jaw. He apologised again even more profusely, aware, as he did so, that it wasn't entirely for his lateness.

'Think nothing of it,' Celia told him briskly, sensitive to his position. 'Anyway, we arrived early. So early, we finished our preliminary drive around the village by half past ten.'

Although Howard had spoken occasionally to Celia on the phone, it had been ages since he'd actually seen her. He was shocked to see that she'd abandoned the practice of highlighting her hair: it was completely white now, and despite her youthful trouser suit and cream silk blouse she looked all of her eighty two years. Her blue eyes were still shrewd and keen but there was a distinct impression of tiredness and strain around them. There was a reason for this, unknown to Howard. The previous evening she'd had a most unpleasant interview with a journalist called Arnie Stidges who'd been trying to inveigle her to take part in a televised interview. Stidges had made some very distressing accusations about her late husband which had greatly upset her.

Howard wondered if Celia and the other judges had seen the demonstration forming outside The Old Rectory. He decided it would be impolitic to ask. He would leave the question until later.

'Let me introduce you to my fellow judges,' said Lady Brearley.

Apart from Celia, two men and a woman were wearing red and gold rosettes bearing the words "Official Judge". The female judge was Kate Smith and she came from Shropshire. She was middle-aged, grossly overweight and the unfortunate possessor of a permanently superior expression. Isobel concluded that this was an accidental impression created by the combined effects of a raised and furrowed brow, plump cheeks, and an unnaturally snub nose. By her bulk, Isobel suspected that Kate had long ago abandoned the more physically arduous aspects of gardening in preference for relaxing on her lawn with a glass of chilled white wine and a large plateful of savouries.

The next judge to be introduced was named Ned Pugh. He was a retired accountant from somewhere in Wales that neither Howard nor Isobel had ever heard of. He was an affable, softly spoken man in his late fifties. The other judge, a tiny middle-aged man called Patrick McSweeney, surprised and startled Howard by delivering his "How do you do?" in a strong Northern Irish accent.

With some trepidation, Howard enquired which part of the province Patrick hailed from.

'County Antrim. Do you know it?'

'No.'

'You ought to visit it. Now that things have calmed down.'

'Yes, we probably will. We've always meant to visit Ireland.'

'Weren't you stationed there at one time?' said Celia.

Howard looked guarded. 'No. What gave you that idea?'

'I'm sorry, I must be mistaken.'

'Yes.'

Howard's clenched teeth and fiercely urbane smile signalled that further conversation on the subject would be most unwelcome. Celia wondered why he'd found it necessary to lie. She was certain that her brother Rex had told her he'd been stationed there. And then she remembered: Rex had told her in the strictest confidence. Oh dear. She'd put her foot in it.

'He's been stationed virtually everywhere else,' Isobel said lightly. This produced polite laughter, which was followed by an awkward pause.

Howard and Isobel knew it was considered bad form to discuss the appearance of one's own village in the presence of the judges, which was why they now stood around searching for some suitably bland subject which would not propel them towards any mention of the competition. Isobel made polite enquiries about the forms of transport Kate, Ned and Patrick had used to travel from their respective parts of the country. As it transpired that all of them (even the Ulsterman) had driven to Leefdale, this topic was quickly exhausted. The conversation moved on to include the virtues of the water garden at Budeholme House, (Howard's contribution); the abandoned railway lines of East Yorkshire, (Ned was a railway enthusiast); and whether The Woldsman served jugged hare, (Kate's enquiry).

Isobel sought some means of escape. 'Excuse me, I must get some tea,' she said, 'Howard, would you like a cup?'

'No thank you.'

Isobel had already noticed that Lady Brearley, alone amongst the judges, was not holding a cup and saucer. 'Lady Brearley, you're not drinking anything. Can I get you some tea or coffee?'

Celia declined. 'My bladder is so weak these days that if I drank anything I'd have to keep stopping at every other house.'

There was uncertain laughter. Isobel smiled graciously and set off towards the tea urn. Lady Brearley's coarseness of manner never failed to upset her. As she chatted rather awkwardly to Mrs Mears, who was in charge of refreshments, she was anticipating, with her customary dread, lunch with the judges at The Woldsman. From bitter experience, she knew it would involve tedious conversation and more of Lady Brearley's crude observations. She was tempted to declare herself unwell and get out of the whole thing, but she hadn't the heart to desert Howard now, not when he so obviously needed her.

Isobel looked around and thought of the dreadful scenes that had taken place in the drive of Rooks Nest on Wednesday. She was sure they were at the forefront of everyone's mind and assumed that some people were whispering to each other about them. Naturally, no-one would ever mention her humiliations directly to her face: they were all pretending none of it had happened and couldn't wait until she'd left so they could gossip about her and Howard with all their usual self-righteousness and sanctimony. Really, the hypocrisy of the British middle class was insupportable; yet, at times like this, how glad she was of it.

While Isobel collected her tea, Howard took the opportunity to work the room. He went round greeting and talking to his colleagues on the parish council and members of the village hall committee. Everyone shook his hand, gave him their best wishes for the final and commiserated with him about the state of the rectory. No-one was ill mannered enough to mention his recent embarrassments. Until that is, he spoke to Ken Bottomley, the landlord of The Woldsman.

'You don't mind me saying this, do you Howard,' said Bottomley, 'but I was jolly glad to see you give that son-in-law of yours what he deserved. It takes a real man to do something like that!'

Bottomley had a very loud bass voice. Howard glanced over to Isobel who was standing with the judges, looking as usual like a fish out of water. Fortunately, she didn't seem to have heard Bottomley's tactless remark.

Howard said, 'Thank you, Ken, I appreciate your support. Now, if you'll excuse me, I must re-join the judges.'

'Ah, Howard,' said Lady Brearley, as he approached. 'If you're ready we're anxious to get started. It's fine now but showers are forecast.'

'Of course,' said Howard. 'But before we start, there's something I'd like to discuss with the four of you.'

'Yes?'

'Er... privately.' He gestured towards a door at the end of the hall. 'Would you mind coming this way?'

The judges exchanged curious looks.

'As long as it doesn't delay us too long,' said Lady Brearley.

Howard led them into an ante-room off the main hall. It was the place where private meetings were held. When it wasn't in use it had a seedy, abandoned atmosphere.

'I'm sorry about this,' said Howard, 'but when you hear what I have to say I think you'll see the necessity for it.'

'You're going to offer us a bribe,' said the Welsh judge, facetiously. There was nervous laughter all round.

'Not quite,' said Howard, smiling patiently, 'though it might come to that.' He paused, and then continued. 'Seriously, did you happen to see some people gathering outside The Old Rectory as you drove round the village?'

'We did actually,' said Celia. 'We assumed it was the demonstration.'

'Ah, so you know about it,' said Howard, immediately put off guard. 'How's that?'

Lady Brearley affected coyness. 'Oh, a little bird told me.'

'I see.' Obviously Lady Brearley wasn't going to divulge how she'd come to hear of it. Sanctimoniously, he went on, 'You know, I tried to dissuade them from demonstrating but feelings in the village are running very high about the state of the rectory.'

Celia looked severe. 'Most unfortunate. A demonstration would be against the very spirit of Magnificent Britain which is to promote harmony not discord.'

'It's not going to get out of hand, is it?' asked the Irish judge.

'Oh no, nothing like that.' Howard frowned. He knew that what he was going to say next would be irregular, and he was anxious about how it would be received. 'As you know, The Old Rectory is one of the three exemplary gardens we've submitted for adjudication.'

'It's the best garden in the village,' said Celia, warmly. Her fellow judges exchanged glances. Because her husband had been the founder of the competition her occasional lapses of protocol were overlooked. Hastily, she corrected herself. 'I mean, it used to be the best garden in the village.'

'Well, it certainly was the best garden when we nominated it back in March,' said Howard. 'But there's been a change of ownership since then and the new people have neglected it very badly. It's completely overgrown, several trees have been chopped down and the back lawn has been turned into a football pitch. It's a disgrace.'

'How very disappointing,' said the Welsh judge, levelly. He was trying very hard to remain impartial as he suspected he was about to be asked to do something unorthodox or disagreeable that might have to be refused.

'Yes, well in the circumstances,' Howard continued, 'I wondered if, even at this late stage, we might submit another garden in place of the rectory.'

This was met with total silence.

Incredulously, Patrick McSweeney said, 'You mean you wish to withdraw The Old Rectory as an exemplary garden and make a substitution?'

'Yes.'

There was another pause, this time even longer, broken eventually by Lady Brearley.

'Oh no!' she said, adamantly, 'We can't possibly do that. It would be unfair to the other finalists. I'm sure they'd object if they learnt that an entirely different garden had been nominated and accepted at the last minute.'

Her fellow judges nodded in agreement.

'But that's so unfair,' said Howard. 'When we nominated The Old Rectory as one of our exemplary gardens we didn't foresee that it would have deteriorated so much.'

'Luck of the draw, I'm afraid,' said Celia.

'There doesn't appear to be anything in the rules to say a substitution can't be made,' said Howard.

'Quite, but that's because the situation has never arisen before.'

Pugh looked indignant. 'Everyone knows what the deadline for nominating exemplary gardens is. You can't make a change after the deadline.'

'Besides,' said Kate Smith, 'presumably the people at the rectory are expecting us.'

'Well, they've been notified, of course,' said Howard, 'but frankly I wouldn't be surprised if they refused you access. They're most uncooperative and the place is in such a state it wouldn't be worth your while inspecting it anyway.'

'We judges will have to decide that,' said Lady Brearley, curtly. Whenever she found herself in a position where she had to make a difficult judgment, she always asked herself what Maurice would have done in the same circumstances. He'd never been a stickler for rules, and had always applied them in the spirit, not the letter: his precepts being fairness and reasonableness, which, she knew, would have surprised many people, particularly Arnie Stidges. Nevertheless, she was sure that her decision to refuse to allow a substitution to be made at such a late stage was precisely what Maurice would have done. She was disappointed that Howard had thought it proper even to make such a suggestion. However, she wasn't altogether surprised. With age, she'd become completely unimpressed with politicians and regarded Howard as a sort of parish pump Machiavelli. In short, she didn't trust him. She'd always enjoyed cordial relations with him and was impressed by his determination and powers of organisation. After all, under his leadership Leefdale had won Magnificent Britain four times. Yet his overwhelming desire to be top dog at every opportunity struck her as low and vulgar, suggesting perhaps a personality defect. He seemed to be using the competition to keep proving something to himself, which, of course, was understandable given that Northern Ireland business back in the eighties, which, dear Rex, God rest his soul, had confidentially told her about. Moreover, she was uneasy with Howard's overweening ambition, which she knew could tempt one to unethical or even illegal acts. His anger at the state of the rectory garden had apparently caused him to assault one of the unfortunate inmates of the place, and now he was pressing her and her fellow judges to bend the rules to his advantage. She wondered if some sort of desire for revenge lay behind it. She and the other judges had already discussed the assaults by Howard, and had all agreed that they would say nothing about them unless he himself raised the matter. She was certain that Major Roberts was the sort of officer Maurice would never have got on with. That's why it was so essential that she and her fellow judges saw the state of the rectory gardens for themselves.

Howard added, 'It's a great pity that a substitution can't be made. If it could I'm sure the villagers could be persuaded to call off their demonstration.'

Lady Brearley appeared deeply offended. 'That rather sounds like a threat.'

'Not at all. I'm just looking for a way to resolve a most volatile situation.'

'You have to be careful, you know,' the Welsh judge told Howard. 'In view of the assault charge people might think you were being vindictive.'

This was the first time anyone had overtly alluded to Howard's arrest. It created some awkwardness.

'Well, of course, you may be right,' said Howard. He realised now that it was futile to pursue his ploy any further. All the judges were implacably opposed to it. It had been a long shot anyway. He'd hoped that the threat of the demonstration might have persuaded them to relent and allow him to substitute another exemplary garden. But they'd seen through his ruse. All he could hope for now was that the demonstration would either prevent the judges from gaining admission to the rectory or would at least make them think twice about it. Better still, Dylan Bourne and his lefty friends would refuse the judges access. In any event, the demonstration would surely spell out to them the depth of antagonism the deplorable state of the rectory had provoked locally, and still might elicit their sympathy.

'About this demonstration,' said Patrick. 'No-one from your Magnificent Britain Sub-Committee is involved in it, are they?'

Howard stared at the diminutive Ulsterman, struggling hard to determine what was implied. Something in the judge's tone warned him that an honest answer would be unwise. 'I don't think so,' he said.

'Good,' said Patrick, 'because if they were involved, the village would automatically be disqualified.'

Howard looked from judge to judge, startled.

Thinking Howard had misunderstood, Kate said, 'It would be in direct contravention of Rule 31 of the competition.' She began to quote, in the disengaged tone of one who has learnt by rote, '"Any attempt, either covert or overt, to influence the decision of the judges will result in disqualification".'

He might have known the fat cow would be able to recite the rules from memory. He wanted to kick himself: how could he have failed to see that the planned demonstration would put the village's chances of winning in jeopardy?

'It's a good thing none of the committee are involved, then,' he said.

'Right,' said Celia. 'If that's all, shall we get started?'

'Of course.'

As they all returned to the main hall, Celia said, 'We thought we'd walk up the north side of the main street first.'

'Fine,' said Howard. 'Are you going to manage to get all the way round the village on foot?'

'Why shouldn't I?'

'Why... your hip... I thought... '

'Oh, it's perfectly all right,' she snapped. 'Come on, let's be off.'

'Before we begin, Lady Brearley, I'd very much like to say a few words to all our volunteers and supporters,' said Howard.

'God! Must you?'

'I think that it would be appropriate.'

Celia sighed. 'Oh very well, but do hurry up!'

Howard drew himself up to his full height. Raising both arms and spreading them out wide, he assumed an attitude evocative of crucifixion. 'May I have your attention ladies and gentlemen?' Conversation ceased immediately, and Isobel began to feel sick again as everyone's eyes focussed on her husband. The combined suspicion, hostility and contempt emanating from some of those giving Howard their rapt attention was palpable. However, he appeared completely unaffected by it. He welcomed the judges and introduced them individually; he briefly outlined the timetable of events; he reminded his audience that they were welcome to accompany himself and the judges around the village, with the caveat that only he and the judges could enter the exemplary gardens. Finally, he thanked everyone for their efforts. All of this was done with an emollience and a confidence which Celia and many others found, in the circumstances, truly impressive. It displayed many of Howard's leadership qualities, and, yet again, Isobel found herself speculating how far her husband might have gone in the army if it hadn't been for "the incident". She felt such pity for him.

As the judges were finally about to set off to begin their adjudications, Howard unexpectedly said, 'I'll catch you up.'

The judges stared at him.

He nodded in the direction of the toilets. 'Need to pay a visit.'

'That's right,' Celia said, with a chuckle. 'Don't want to be caught short!'

Howard turned to move off and realised with dismay that the other male judges intended to accompany him.

'Good idea, I'll come too,' said McSweeney. 'I've had a great deal of coffee.'

'And me,' said Pugh.

Howard cursed silently and set off for the lavatories with Pugh and McSweeney following behind. As soon as he entered the gents he went straight into a stall, closed the door and sat down on the pedestal.

He listened impatiently for the sounds from the urinal area that would indicate that the two judges had finished relieving themselves. Although Lady Brearley was in a hurry to get on with the judging, her impatient haste had not infected Pugh and McSweeney who seemed quite content to take their time. Howard listened with increasing frustration to their relaxed and unhurried conversation and an eternity seemed to pass as they washed and dried their hands.

Finally, to Howard's enormous relief, he heard the entrance door to the toilets open and then close. This sound was followed by the judges' receding footsteps. He waited for a moment or two to establish that absolutely no-one was still in the gents, and then took out his mobile phone to make his call to warn Greg.

Damn! The absence of bars told him that there was no signal. He'd have to wait until he was in a part of the village where the signal was stronger and somehow make the call without alerting the judges' suspicions.

He cursed again and put the phone away.

CHAPTER FORTY NINE

By a quarter to twelve it was apparent that the character of the demonstration had significantly changed. The number of demonstrators had now increased and more people were arriving all the time. The presence of these additional individuals provided the crowd with far greater vocal power to oppress their intended victims. The chants, apart from being very much louder, had now developed into something more obsessively rhythmic and were being delivered with a rapaciousness that was unequivocally violent in its intention. The hard, merciless voices penetrated the rectory as though its walls were made of paper; they terrorised the house and delivered a slashing blow to everyone's emotions. It was now impossible to ignore them, and Toni had long ago given up any pretence of delivering a maths lesson.

All of the teenagers had become extremely rattled. They were constantly shifting about in their seats, unable to settle to anything and some kept demanding to be allowed to go to the toilet even though they'd already been several times. As the noise of the demonstration increased in volume and hostility, the kids' individual behaviours became more and more disturbed. Some of them actually displayed signs of acute physical and mental distress. Jake rolled about on the floor making strange, jabbering sounds. Liam had retreated into a corner of the room and was sitting with his hands over his ears, rocking to and fro. Rupa was hiding under a desk and refusing to come out. Khaled and Sheldon were standing at the side window of the encouragement room, staring straight ahead, their bodies rigid with tension, as though they were expecting the mob to storm the rectory at any moment. Mona was sitting at her desk, her arms clasped around herself for comfort, weeping continuously. At all times, at least one of them was moving constantly about, panicked into involuntary, random movement, as though trapped and seeking escape. Louise had never seen any of them behave in this way before. She suddenly understood why they'd all originally been brought to the unit and it made her frightened. For the first time she questioned whether it had been such a good idea to come there.

The members of staff had all been comforting the children. Now Dylan called them together for a quick discussion about how they should deal with the worsening situation.

'This is hopeless,' said Toni. 'I feel really frightened so God knows what the kids are feeling.'

'Let's take them out to the back garden,' suggested Eric.

Zoe's spirits had been revived by a complete change of clothes. Decisively, she said, 'That will only make them more insecure. The noise will be ten times worse and they'll still feel powerless to do anything about it.'

'We could implement Dylan's plan now instead of later,' said Toni.

Zoe scoffed. 'In this atmosphere?'

Dylan said, 'Zoe's right. It'll be too intimidating for them. It needs to be done just before the judges arrive.'

'It would be better if we took them upstairs to your studio,' said Zoe. 'They'd feel safer and at least be able to see what's going on. It's not knowing that's making them so insecure and frightened.'

The others agreed.

Dylan handed Zoe a key. 'Would you go up and open the studio while I tell them what we've decided?'

'Sure.'

'And open the windows too. It'll be stifling in there.'

Dylan was trying to attract everyone's attention as Zoe left the encouragement room. She sprinted up the stairs to the top of the house, went into her bedroom to get her camera, and then unlocked the door to Dylan's studio. It was fusty in there and had the usual smell of paint and other art materials. She went over to the big windows and looked out. Her gaze was met with the sight of almost a hundred people surrounding The Old Rectory and spilling out across the road. They were all ages and there was a large proportion of women amongst them. Many of the men were young, had skinhead haircuts and wore T shirts. Some wore brutal looking boots. They were all chanting with harsh, metallic voices and vicious annunciation, like an aggressive football crowd: their ugly mouths working mechanically as though they were organs designed not for eating, communicating or kissing but only to express hatred. Standing incongruously amongst them were a number of older, conventionally dressed people, looking almost embarrassed to be associated with such an uncouth crew. Nevertheless, they stood shoulder to shoulder with the others and chanted along enthusiastically, determined to show solidarity. Seeing them all bolted seamlessly together like that, made Zoe realise how easy it was for ugly and inhuman ideas to become irresistible when expressed by the force of a mass of human bodies. And then, with a twinge of guilt, she recalled all the demonstrations she'd taken part in without a care for the feelings or emotions of those she and her fellow demonstrators were protesting against. She dismissed the thought instantly. All the demonstrations she'd been on had been justified.

As she opened the sash of the first window to its fullest extent, several of the demonstrators, alerted by the sudden movement, raised their heads to look up at her. Many of them had the predacious eyes of those who do not regard killing as unthinkable. Some were stripped to the waist, wearing tattoos on their skin like bruises; others were lightly dressed in T shirts and shorts. Despite the intense heat a few even wore hoodies. They reminded her of the more evil English football supporters she'd seen whiling away the time before away games in Italy and France when she'd had the misfortune to come across them on holiday. Of course, their excuse for abusing people in those quiet European squares was that they'd been laggard drunk. This lot didn't even have that excuse. She recognized the particular stench of the English far right, and suddenly felt deeply troubled. She'd attended quite a few protest demonstrations herself, yet at no time during them had she personally felt unsafe. But here, in this quiet Yorkshire village, the presence of such people who were so unpredictable and potentially violent made her feel deeply apprehensive. Particularly after the way they'd treated her at the gate. It had only been an egg they'd thrown, but it could have been a brick, a can of paint, a jar of acid, anything. She'd been planning to take a photo of the demonstration, but now she turned away and retreated from the open window, forced back by all those merciless eyes.

Everyone was now arriving in the studio and going straight over to the windows. Zoe was glad to have been proved right. Now that they'd been released from their internment in the encouragement room the kids' behaviour had returned to normal. They were all milling around the windows, eager to get the best view of the demonstration, and excitedly commenting about the extraordinary scenes in the street below. They made her feel ashamed of the uncharacteristic cowardice she'd just exhibited and reminded her that it was her job to protect them. The solidarity of their presence and the comforting arrival of her colleagues gave her the courage to go over to the other window and open it. And this time when the eyes of those in the street raked her, she stayed at her post, eyeballed them back and faced the bastards down. These appalling people offended every vestige of liberty and equality she believed in; every tenet of her socialism. They must not be allowed to prevail.

Louise watched Dylan, Eric, Sheldon, Mona and Jake take up positions at one of the windows. Mindful of her mother's demand that under no circumstances was she to allow her father to find out she was in the rectory, Louise hung back behind Dylan, using his long body to screen her from the people below. However, there were sufficient gaps between the others at the window for her to get a good view of what was happening in the street without being seen and recognized. She was amazed at the size of the crowd and how cross they all looked.

For a few minutes there'd been a slight reduction in the volume of the demonstrators' hard voiced chanting, but the appearance of all the rectory's residents at the windows instantly revived the crowd's hostility. Incensed, they shook their fists and placards and anything else to hand, and with renewed loathing chanted "Out! Out! Out!"

Still shielded by Dylan and Mona, Louise edged closer to the window until she was looking past them and into Church Lane. From this position she could see what looked like hundreds of people surrounding The Old Rectory and spilling out across the road. They looked very frightening and she recognized only about a dozen people from Leefdale. But where was dad?

Louise saw that many in the crowd were holding home-made placards or banners with slogans on them. Her eye was drawn to one long banner carried high by four people on which was written in block capitals:

"NO-ONE ASKED US IF WE WANTED AN INCLUSION UNIT!"

Other slogans which she was able to read clearly were:

"THE OLD RECTORY IS A DISGRACE"

"CLEAN UP YOUR ACT"

"LEEFDALE DESERVES TO WIN"

"YOU'RE NOT FIT TO LIVE AMONGST DECENT PEOPLE"

"GO BACK WHERE YOU CAME FROM"

What horrible people to write things like that about her friends! But where was her dad? She moved to the other side of the window and positioned herself behind Sheldon so that she could see what was happening in the street below.

There! That was him! Through the tiny slit of space between Sheldon's arm and the window frame, she saw him. Right at the front of the demonstration. Tight up against the bars of the gate. He was screaming and shouting at the rectory: looking so angry and nasty she scarcely recognized him. She felt shocked and yet curiously powerful. So that's why he hadn't wanted her to come to the rectory today!

At that moment he glanced up. She knew there was no way he could see her or even know she was in there, but involuntarily she took several steps back from the window until she was well away from the others and hidden deep within the recesses of the room.

The demonstrators' latest eruption of deafening hostility silenced all those who were the object of it. They could only watch, listen and endure it. Even Zoe was cowed. It is one thing to fight, quite another to simply stand there and be the object of a mob's hate.

'I wish I had a machine gun,' Sheldon suddenly said.

****

Greg was delighted by the number of people who'd turned out to demonstrate. At first there'd been only himself, Sue Rawdon, Janet Pinkney and

Fred Birch standing outside the gates of The Old Rectory. By 10.30 a dozen more Leefdale residents had arrived. Disappointingly, some of these bore news of other villagers who, at the last minute, had developed cold feet and pulled out. Greg resigned himself to a low turnout. Then, just after 11am, to his surprise and delight, six van loads of people arrived carrying their own banners and placards.

No-one knew any of these people, but when he got into conversation with them he learned some were sympathisers who didn't want to see an inclusion unit established in their own villages. He asked them how they'd come to hear about the demonstration and was told that someone from Leefdale had posted it on the internet. The surprising thing was how far these people had travelled: some had come from as far afield as Leeds and Bradford, even Manchester. But Greg was more than pleased to see them: they swelled the size of the demonstration to almost a hundred. There were so many they spilled off the pavement in front of the rectory and out on to the road.

The arrival of the outsiders quickly transformed the whole dynamic of the demonstration. Augmented by the addition of so many extra voices the previously feeble chants of "Inclusion Unit Out! Inclusion Unit Out" now assumed a terrifying power and authority. Nevertheless, pleased as Greg was by the increased level of intimidation provided by the reinforcements, he found their presence slightly disturbing. Although undeniably more effective, the chants were being executed with a merciless oppression and callousness which, to his ears, seemed alien in this quiet village setting. Something possessed these strangers, something very different from the Leefdale villagers. It was obvious in the iron set of their faces, and the uncompromising malevolence which seemed to emanate from deep within them and made them seem almost inhuman.

Yet, their attitude was contagious. Despite himself, Greg noticed that not only he but his fellow villagers were becoming infected with it: Sue, Janet and Fred were all standing much taller; their backs were more rigid; their faces stiffer and their voices harsher. They seemed filled with a sense of purpose which hadn't been there before.

At some point, Greg couldn't be sure when, the crowd's militancy seemed to step up a gear. The chant changed to the more urgent and imperative "Out! Out! Out!" It was shouted with a force that made it seem palpable and bludgeoning, like a weapon blasting the air, and it fell upon the rectory's ivy clad walls like a bombardment. Again, Greg felt slightly alarmed; yet, at another level, he was deeply impressed and heartened. How could the judges possibly ignore this outpouring of public resentment? Surely they'd be influenced by it?

Greg had never been on any kind of demonstration before and he was stirred and liberated by it. It was astonishing how emboldened you became surrounded by lots of other people, all making a huge uproar. The solidarity and support of the crowd empowered you to shout or chant anything, no matter how vile or abusive; because you felt that with all these people behind you, you were no longer subject to the normal constraints of civilised conduct. You were part of something that was elemental and had a volition of its own, like a force of nature. You were untouchable.

Yet, even though Greg was leading the protest, the viciousness injected into the demonstration by the newcomers unsettled him and made him uneasy. The small band of ordinary villagers who'd gathered to protest about a perceived injustice, had been subsumed into a foul mouthed mob that was exuding intolerance from every pore. As he stared at the faces around him, each set in a rigor of uncompromising hatred, their mouths bawling out non-stop venom, he realised with a chill that the strangers who'd joined them were not what they seemed. They were too organised; too relentless; too political! He began to feel apprehensive about the demons he'd unleashed; and now, because he wasn't completely unimaginative, as he chanted and gesticulated with the rest, he did so with a consciousness of the fear, and perhaps even terror, that he and the rest of the mob were provoking in the hearts and minds of the people in the rectory, and he was thankful Louise wasn't in there.

The conviction that his daughter was safe at home made it easier for Greg to justify the ugly nature of the demonstration. Surely, he reasoned, it was understandable that the crowd was so worked up? They'd laboured long and hard all year to get their gardens and properties looking just right, and now because of the appalling state of the rectory all their hard work had been for nothing. How he loathed those liberal wankers in the unit! They'd ruined his relationship with Sharon and Louise and now were ruining the village's chances of winning Magnificent Britain. What right had they to be there anyway? Disaffected teenagers! That was a laugh. Thugs and hooligans more like: thieves and chancers: druggies and pushers. He knew their sort, all right. Probably all from broken homes. What had those teenagers ever done for society? Why should they be allowed to live in a beautiful house like the rectory when it was denied to hard working people like himself? At least he'd have treated it with respect. But could he ever get his hands on a property like that? No, never! All he could afford was a three bedroom cottage, even though he worked hard and paid the government's crippling taxes. Break the law and they reward you with a beautiful house. Trash it and everyone stands by without lifting a finger. What an upside-down world! He glanced at those demonstrating alongside him. Only these people understood his grievances.

Greg's self-righteous attempt to convince himself of the demonstration's moral justification was suddenly interrupted by a movement on the rectory's top floor. The unmistakable figure of Zoe Fitzgerald was opening one of the windows. So, the egg hadn't deterred her.

Zoe's appearance silenced the crowd. They stared at her malevolently, curious to know what was going to happen next. It wasn't long before they found out. Several teenagers and other adults appeared alongside Zoe. She then opened the room's other window and leaned out, defiantly planting her hands on the sill and staring stonily down at the demonstrators.

The eyes of all those in the street were now concentrated on the rectory's upper windows. The sudden and unexpected sight of their enemy now provoked them to an even greater frenzy than before. Animated by an intense and renewed hostility, they beat their placards with their fists, shook their banners, shouted obscenities and smote the rectory with whistles, jeers and boos. As he booed and jeered with the rest of them, Greg was astonished by the power and intensity of his own antagonism. He felt elated by the collective hatred that was being directed towards those at the uppermost windows of the rectory. It was exhilarating to be borne along on such strong currents of feeling. He'd never felt less like an individual or freer of the crushing restraints of his individuality: for there were no individuals now, all were subsumed to the same purpose and all doubt had been dispelled. The tiresome and inconvenient complexities of life had been replaced by the crowd's absolute conviction of its irrefutable rightness, and the necessity of achieving the aims of its uncompromising will. He stole a quick glance at Fred, Sue and Janet who were standing alongside him. He'd known them for years, yet the faces of these reasonable, kind people, now twisted with contempt and hatred, were entirely focussed on their malign purpose and seemed like strangers to him. Did he have that look too?

Those at the windows seemed stunned and deeply affected by the ferocity of the hatred directed at them. They stood absolutely still, staring grimly back at the demonstrators. Again, Greg felt overwhelming relief that Louise wasn't standing at those windows. If she'd been there he'd have felt deeply ashamed, and he didn't want to feel ashamed. He knew what he was doing was inhuman and terrible but it had to be done.

Now the crowd were chanting a new slogan: "Go Back Home! Go Back Home! Go Back Home!" Strange how these slogans suddenly appeared in everyone's mouth. For some reason he was reminded of the flocking together of starlings just before dusk. Yet even though his little demonstration had been hi-jacked and was uglier than he'd ever intended, he felt compelled to chant along and behave as badly as everyone else.

Suddenly, a teenage boy at one of the windows was miming an imaginary sub-machine gun and firing it. The rapid, percussive movements of his hands and arms were utterly realistic, and as he raked the crowd with a fusillade of non-existent bullets his face was twisted into a rictus of murderous intent. The youth's machine gunning fantasy had an electrifying effect on the mob, rousing them to a renewed frenzy. As one they pressed forward, throwing themselves at the gate, gesticulating angrily and roaring abuse at the boy, even though his weapon was merely fashioned out of air and imagination.

Greg, who was at the front of the crowd, worryingly felt the pressure of bodies building up behind him, pressing into his back and forcing him forward.

Suddenly, he realised that along with Fred, Sue and Janet, he was being pinioned against the rectory's gate. He cried out as the vertical bars cut deeply into his chest, but his cry was lost in the roaring of the crowd and went unheard and unheeded; for his cry was indistinguishable from the cries of spontaneous outrage against the grinning youth at the rectory window who, having finished his imaginary enfilade was now standing with his arms folded, delighting in the mob's fury.

The crowd continued moving forward, regardless. Now the pressure on Greg's rib-cage was intense: he could scarcely breathe and his heart was fluttering like an imprisoned bird. Somewhere to his right, Fred Birch was groaning and sliding down the front of the gate; Sue Rawdon was gripping the bars and using her straightened arms to brace her back against the ever onward pressure of the crowd; Janet Pinkney was frantically attempting to climb over the gate but was prevented by the sheer weight of the crowd and was screaming.

And then several voices were shouting 'Back! Get back!'

Greg managed to force his head round a fraction. It was the police. They were diving in amongst the demonstrators, pulling people out of the crowd; flinging them aside and urging everyone to stop pushing. At once Greg no longer felt the pressure on his back. At last he was able to stand up and turn around. Immediately, he collapsed back against the gate, gasping and massaging his chest.

PC Wheatcroft spoke to him. 'You all right?'

'Yes, thanks.'

'Need an ambulance?'

'No, I'll be OK.'

'I want everyone to move away from this gate and stand on the other side of the street!' The order came through a loud hailer and was delivered by a uniformed inspector standing next to Wheatcroft.

This was bad news for Greg. If the demonstrators were moved away from the gate the judges would be able to enter the rectory. He said, 'There's no need for that, is there?'

The inspector gave him a withering look. 'Aye, every need. If things get out of hand someone's going to get hurt. Besides, your demonstration's obstructing the entrance to the rectory.'

'It's not my demonstration, Inspector. It's Leefdale's. It's an expression of the village's anger.'

'Well, whoever it belongs to, it's got to move to a position across the street!'

****

Louise had loved Dylan's studio the moment she saw it. She loved its chaos and she loved its order. She loved the oil paints: those tubes of soothing, aromatic ointments which seemed to be everywhere, their contents squeezed out on to palettes or bits of wood or cardboard, where they lay in glistening whorls of deep, viscid colour, good enough to spread on your bread or dip your chips into. She loved the mixture of smells that entered your nostrils as a single unguent odour: linseed oil, turpentine, size, varnish, oil paint, canvas and wood. She loved to move amongst the easels which stood like small, angular trees, and she loved the huge canvasses supported by them, with their simple, clean, rectilinear designs and their apparently random blocks of intense, vivid colour. She was too young to be able to articulate why, but she knew that all of these beautiful things calmed her and made her feel serene; made her want to stay amongst them forever. It was to these sources of comfort she'd retreated to recover from the shock of seeing her father, his face convulsed with hatred and contempt, leading an enraged and furious mob which had been raised to a frenzy just because her friends had appeared at the studio's windows.

With some concern, Dylan had watched her retreat from the window into the depths of the room. Now, he came towards her and said, 'Is the crowd frightening you?'

Louise looked up at him. Her face was darkly serious, her eyes glistening with suppressed tears. 'Someone in it is.'

He immediately thought of Maynard. 'Someone you know?'

Louise suspected a trap. 'No. Just a neighbour. They were horrible.'

'It's all right, Louise. There's no need to be afraid. No-one can harm us. The gates are strong and the police will stop them.'

Louise smiled back at him, wanly. Dare she tell him the real reason she'd sought escape amongst all his beautiful things? That her father was actually in the crowd down there? That he'd organised the demonstration. That it was the sight of him being so horrible to everyone in the rectory that had made her so upset? How could she tell him that her own father was the cause of all their distress?

Her long silence made Dylan wonder if she wanted to go home. He said, 'Are you sorry you came back to us now?'

Without a beat, she said, 'Oh no. I had to say sorry to Mona. And I wanted to see what the demo would be like.'

Dylan thought this an odd response. 'Did you think it would be like a play?'

She nodded, sadly. 'Yes. I suppose I did. But it's a horrible play.'

'Would you like to go downstairs?'

That was the last thing she wanted. She felt a sudden panic and said, quite forcefully, 'No, I'd rather be up here.'

Dylan said, 'I noticed you looking at my paintings. Do you like them?'

'Yes. They're lovely. I love it here in your studio. It's the best part of the house.' She went across to the easel on which rested his latest work, one greatly influenced by Mondrian. She pointed at it and said, 'What do all these squares and lines mean?'

Dylan laughed. 'If I told you it probably wouldn't make it a better picture. You know, people always think they need to say something about paintings, but sometimes the best thing is to say nothing and just experience them. Anyway, if you'd like to stay here, I'll leave you to it.'

'OK.'

'But please, don't touch anything.'

She was relieved when Dylan left her and moved across to join the others. His honest eyes and searching gaze made her feel like a liar. She drifted from canvass to canvass trying, as he'd suggested, to just experience each one, whatever that might mean. But the ugly clamour from the street was too distracting and it wasn't long before curiosity got the better of her. She felt compelled to see what other dreadful things her dad might do. She also had a perverse need to do something completely unexpected that would change things between them forever. Something that would make it clear to him that, unlike her mother, she'd never do anything he wanted.

Louise returned to the window and again used Sheldon's broad back to screen her from the street. In this position she could continue to observe her father without being seen. She wasn't afraid of being seen by him, but it wasn't time yet. If he saw her too soon it would inhibit him and he'd conceal the extremes of his awful behaviour. She wanted to see what he was truly capable of. It thrilled her that he believed she was safely at home and unable to see what he was up to.

Sensing that Louise was hanging back, Dylan turned from the window and said to her, 'Look, Jade's dad's down there. Do you see him?'

Louise nodded cautiously.

He mistook her diffidence for shyness. 'Come to the front for a better view.'

'No. It's all right.'

'Go on. You can't see anything there.'

'No. It's all right. Thanks.'

Dylan stopped pressurizing her. It occurred to him that if his suspicions were correct and Maynard was abusing the girl she might have good reasons for not wishing him to see her. Was Maynard the person in the crowd who was frightening her? Had his original suspicions about him been justified?

'Why are they being so horrible to us?' Mona wailed. 'What have they got against us? It's not fair!'

Sheldon repeated his wish for a machine gun.

'Stop that, Sheldon,' said Dylan.

'Why?' said Sheldon. 'They wanna kill us, don't they?'

'I understand why you feel like that, Sheldon,' said Zoe, calling across the room to him from her place at the adjacent window. 'It's awful feeling so helpless.'

'That's right,' he called back. 'They need to know we ain't gonna just take it.'

'I feel like going down there and confronting them again,' Zoe said, addressing Dylan. 'Throw the terrible things they're shouting right back in their faces. Why should they be allowed to spread these lies about us?'

Eric looked at her satirically. 'Oh? You've got plenty of spare T shirts, have you?'

'I don't care how many eggs they chuck at me,' Zoe snapped back. 'The egg is a symbol of life. Those people are anti-life.'

'No,' said Dylan. 'If we react like that we'll be doing just what they want. They're trying to wind us up and we mustn't let them.'

'So we just let those Nazis do what they like?'

Dylan sighed, patiently. 'We're going to deal with that, soon.'

'They're not all Nazis,' said Toni.

'Oh no?'

Toni pointed at the crowd of onlookers who'd gathered on either side of Rooks Nest to watch the demonstration. 'No. Look at that crowd across the street. They're not even chanting.'

Zoe said, 'That's because they don't have to. They've bussed in a whole lot of racists to do their dirty work for them.'

Toni shook her head. 'They look quite disapproving to me. I don't think the people who live here are happy with what's going on.'

'Well, let's go down and ask them,' said Zoe.

'We will go down,' said Dylan. 'But later and we won't confront them. We'll stick to our plan.'

'It's too dangerous to go down there at the moment,' said Toni. 'No way can we let the judges in.'

'We must let the judges in,' said Dylan. 'It's the only way we'll win.'

'He's right,' said Zoe. 'The judges need to see what these kids have created. Why should those Nazis stop them.'

'Nazis!' Khaled bawled at the crowd through the open window. 'Fucking Nazis!'

'Khaled!' reproved Toni, looking stern.

Sheldon laughed. 'They can't hear you, man!' It was true: Khaled's shout was lost in the tumult of the crowd below.

Sheldon suddenly thrust both arms through the open window and grasped his hands around an imaginary sub-machine gun. Then, he took aim at the demonstrators and in the back of his throat began simulating the rapid, staccato sounds of machine gun fire as he swung the non- existent weapon back and forth in an annihilating arc of frenzied wish fulfilment, spraying the mob with bullets which existed only in his fancy, until every single one of his tormentors was dead.

The mob's reaction was terrifying. Louise moved closer to the window. Through the narrow spaces between those crowding there, she saw the demonstrators exploding with fury, provoked out of all reason by Sheldon's aggressive mime. They were surging forward: roaring, booing and uttering wild cries. She found herself once again staring into the face of her father who wore his rage like a grotesque mask and was venting his outrage in obscenities at Sheldon and all those standing beside him.

Sheldon's imaginary fusillade ended. Amazed and shaken by the contrast between the pile of imaginary corpses he was contemplating, and the mob's extreme reaction to his childish provocation, Sheldon began to laugh hysterically. 'They shouldn't be doing that!' he cried. 'Man! After what I done they should all be dead!' His laughter sucked the tension out of the room, and suddenly they were all laughing along with him.

As the laughter and the cross talk grew more hysterical, Louise retreated from the window and went deeper back into the room, seeking refuge once again amongst the tubes of oil paint and canvasses. She'd wanted to see how badly her dad would behave, and yet when it came to it, she couldn't bear to look. So instead she was trying to concentrate hard on Dylan's pictures. The strangely soothing arrays of grids with their rectangular blocks of intense reds, blues and greens were apparently arranged randomly: yet within the randomness was the suggestion of some meticulous planning, some soothing and strangely pleasing design which in its stillness and silence produced a chord which was louder than the ugly primeval shouting in the street, and for an instant seemed to silence it. She took up the tubes of oil paint and held them in her hands and murmured the names of the colours printed on their sides. She enunciated them reverently, as though they possessed spiritual or magical properties, were charms or invocations: Raw Sienna; Prussian Blue; Chrome Yellow; Burnt Umber; Lamp Black; Oxide of Chromium; Windsor Green.

But these spells couldn't silence the tumult from the street forever: it broke in upon her consciousness, more intrusively than before, putting an end to her brief illusion of sanctuary. And then she was aware that the nature of the noise had changed. There was still the inhuman hard voiced chanting and shouts of mockery and contempt, but mixed in with these were other sounds, higher in pitch, more urgent and hysterical: the unmistakable cries of pain and fear and panic.

'There's going to be an accident!' she heard Dylan say.

'Good! Good! Good!' cried Scarlett.

'They're so stupid!' said Zoe. 'Someone's going to get killed!'

Louise ran back to the window. Enraged by Sheldon's violent fantasy, the demonstrators were surging forward. Sheldon and Mona were standing together, and through the slight gap between them Louise saw the crowd crushing her dad against the bars of the rectory gate. She saw him struggle and cry out as he collapsed under the weight of bodies, and his face, still jammed against the bars, slid downwards. His mouth was an agonised rictus, his arms useless, pinioned to his sides by the straightjacket of other bodies, so that his hands could only flutter feebly. Her first thought was that it served him right.

And then he was nearly on the floor, his face wedged between two bars, as though his head was prising them apart, and the people behind were sinking down on top of him and she saw he was in real danger.

Oh, no, he's going to die!

Now, seeing the peril he was in and how his strong, powerful figure had become so trapped and helpless, she revolted at the prospect of his death. Her urge was to scream out "That's my dad down there! Do something!" But the years of repression and subterfuge had made the expression of such instincts impossible. She turned the scream in upon herself, and as it expanded inside her skull and filled the universe beyond, she watched the man whom she'd come to know as her father, slowly quashed by the forces which he himself had conjured and orchestrated. And then it was a silent "Thank you God! Thank you God!" because the police were wading in and breaking up the mob and her relief was overwhelming.

She had no concern about being seen now. All she wanted to know was that her dad was alive. She pushed closer to the window until she was standing just behind Dylan and Sheldon. Dad looked a bit shaken but seemed to be reassuring the policeman that he was all right. She watched the police shepherd him and the other demonstrators away from the rectory and into a space which had been created for them amongst the onlookers directly across the street. Once assembled there, the demonstrators resumed their merciless chanting, but the extra distance placed between them and the rectory occluded their oppressiveness and made them less intimidating. They could still be heard, but it was as though they were in another room, with the door slightly ajar.

'OK.' said Dylan. 'Looks like the police have the situation under control. We can go down now.'

He moved away from the window, followed by Sheldon and Mona. The others began to drift away from their windows too. Louise retreated with them, for without the others masking her she was completely exposed to the eyes of those positioned across the street and she didn't want dad to see her. Not yet. But she continued looking out.

Dylan was saying in a loud voice, 'And remember, no matter what these people shout at you, no matter what they do, don't react. Understand?'

All the kids except Sheldon murmured their assent.

'You got that, Sheldon?' Dylan demanded.

'Yeah, yeah.'

'Good. Let's go then.'

He started to move off but Toni's hand arrested him. She said, 'Is Louise involved in your plan?'

This was something Dylan hadn't considered. He frowned thoughtfully.

'Involved in what?' said Louise. 'What plan?'

'Best not to,' said Dylan. He turned to Louise. 'Some of us are going into the front garden. But I know your mum won't like that. So you'd better stay in the encouragement room.'

'She could come with us in the sculpture park,' said Zoe.

Louise said, 'Can't I just stay here for a bit?'

Dylan looked doubtful. 'Why?'

'I just want to stay here and see what's going on in the street.'

Dylan said, 'I'm sorry, Louise, but you can't stay here. I need to lock up.'

Zoe said, 'It's all right, I'll stay with her.'

Dylan looked unsure. But the others were already on their way down and he knew he had to be with them. It was, after all, his plan. 'All right. But when you come down you'll make sure it's locked, won't you? I'm concerned about my paintings. And then there are the health and safety issues. It mustn't be left unlocked.'

'Don't worry. I'll make sure.'

'OK. Here's the key.' Dylan began to search in his pockets for it.

'I've still got it,' said Zoe. 'I unlocked the room, remember?'

Dylan looked immensely relieved. He'd had a sudden panic when he couldn't find the key in either of his pockets.

'Don't stay up here too long, we need you downstairs,' he said brusquely, and left.

Zoe watched him go and wondered if he was all right. It was unlike him to forget something like the key. She'd obviously underestimated the stress all this was causing him.

Louise returned to the open window but she didn't go right up to it. Now that the others had gone and she had no bodies to mask her from the crowd, the space within the window frame seemed huge. She was sure that if she positioned herself directly in front of it she'd be seen immediately and provoke another aggressive reaction from the crowd, which she was keen to avoid. Anyway, now that the demonstrators had been moved back to the other side of the road it was possible to see them without going right up to the window, so she stood off it, slightly.

Zoe was at the other window. Her camera was raised to her eye and she was photographing the demonstrators. As she snapped away she said, 'That's Jade's dad down there, isn't it, Louise?'

'Why does everyone keep telling me that?' demanded Louise, curtly.

Zoe lowered her camera. 'No reason. Just thought you might be interested.'

Louise said nothing. She was wondering if she had the courage to step forward and lean right out of the window.

****

'Of course, Isobel and I can't go round the rectory gardens with you now,' said Howard. 'After my little altercation I'm slightly persona non grata.'

What an extraordinary gift for understatement he has, thought Celia. She'd been told that his assault on the boy had been really quite vicious.

'The yob was the perpetrator. He was the one who started it.'

Why did she automatically disbelieve anything he said? Perhaps because she'd had so many dealings with blackmailers over the years. And Howard was a blackmailer, of that she had no doubt. He was definitely the one responsible for the demonstration which had been oppressing her ears with the noise of its ugly presence all morning: turning something which should have been pleasurable for her into a worrying trial. And he'd tried to use the demonstration to blackmail her and her colleagues into replacing the rectory's garden with a better one! Hadn't he said that if they agreed to his demands he'd call the demonstration off? He was obviously a man who loved to exercise that sort of corrupt power. Maurice would have detested him. And then there was that funny business about Northern Ireland. She was convinced Rex had told her that Roberts had served there. So why deny it? It must be true. Her brother knew the sort of people who had access to such information.

'I had no option but to defend myself,' said Howard.

Celia looked at him, puzzled, and then realised he was still talking about the incident at the rectory.

'He came at me without any sort of provocation. My reactions were instinctive. I just lashed out.'

Celia saw that he was trying to justify himself. How tiresome. She was simply not in the mood for this conversation. For one thing, her hip was playing her up, the consequence of having walked the length and breadth of five other villages in the past week in fulfilment of her judging responsibilities. She was also filled with anxiety. Wherever they'd been in Leefdale that morning it had been impossible to escape the din made by the demonstrators outside The Old Rectory. The chanting was like some vicious mantra for invoking conflict and constantly reminded her that an ugly confrontation might possibly lie ahead. At first, she'd tried to joke about it and laugh it off, but now they were drawing near to the rectory the noise of the huge crowd was increasing by the second and making her feel distinctly nervous. It was such a pity because Leefdale had never looked lovelier: even the telephone box was surrounded by tubs of marigolds and bedecked with hanging baskets ablaze with trailing blooms. The villagers had really excelled themselves. As she and the judges had wound their way through the village, their progress had been delayed more than once by many proud gardeners wishing to engage her on the thought and ingenuity which had gone into the design of their floral displays.

She was about to ask Howard why he was being followed by two men in a large back saloon the whole time, when she realised that he'd left her side. She turned round and saw that he'd dropped some distance back and was making a call on his mobile. He'd obviously interpreted her silence on the subject of his assault as some indication of disapproval.

In fact, Howard had just discovered that his mobile phone at last had a signal and was taking his first opportunity to call Greg Maynard.

****

Louise took a step towards the open window. Through it she could see the tall, rather heavy looking figure of her father standing amongst the demonstrators across the street. They were still chanting. "Out! Out! Out!" Why did they chant the same thing over and over again? It was so stupid.

She had to be careful. Only another step and the angle would be altered and she'd be standing at the open window in full view of those down below. That was what was known as altering the sight lines. She knew all about altering the sight lines from her work at the youth theatre, which was why she was sure no-one standing across the street could see her. She didn't want him to see her yet. She didn't quite have the courage to reveal herself fully. And after what mum had said, she still wasn't sure if she should.

So for the moment, Louise continued to observe her father. It was so interesting to watch him without being seen. A bit like being a spy. But she wasn't going to remain unseen for long. Soon she was going to stand close up to the window and reveal herself. She wanted him to know she was there. She wanted to shock him and make him uncomfortable. She wanted him to know that despite all he'd said, she was in the rectory. She'd no fears, no concerns now about revealing herself because she knew that whatever she did, no matter how outrageous, he'd never publicly acknowledge that she was his daughter. She could stand in full view of the window in complete safety, knowing he'd never say anything because as far as the world was concerned she was nothing to him and he was nothing to her. And by revealing herself she'd be sending him a message: she'd be telling him that he no longer had the right to tell her what to do anymore; that something fundamental had changed and there was no going back. It was the perfect act of defiance. She had to do it. Do it, she urged herself. Go on, do it!

She steeled herself, and then took a big step forward. There. It brought her right up to the open window. But the movement was simultaneous with Greg Maynard taking his mobile phone out of his pocket, talking into it and turning away.

Louise found herself staring at her dad's back.

****

'Greg, listen. I haven't much time. Are you at the demonstration?'

'Can't you hear it?' Greg directed his mobile towards the chanting demonstrators. He wanted Howard to receive the full impact. Returning the mobile to his ear, he said, 'What do you think of that?'

'Sounds like an excellent turnout. Are any TV crews there?'

'Yes, a couple.'

'Damn. Have they got you on video?'

'I don't know. Why? What's up?'

'Bad news. The judges say that if they find anyone from the committee amongst the demonstrators we'll be disqualified.'

'No!'

'Oh yes. Are Fred, Sue and Janet still there with you?'

'Yes.'

'Well, I want all of you to get yourselves out of there. By the sound of it you won't be missed.'

'My God! This is terrible. Where are the judges now?'

'"A Sector." Just past the telephone box.'

'That's close.'

'Yes. So you'd better get a move on. After you leave the demonstration make yourselves scarce. Make sure none of you are anywhere near The Old Rectory. That should allay any of the judges' suspicions.'

'Have they got suspicions?'

'I don't know. But to be absolutely sure I'll nobble Reg Maltby and Edna Phillips and tell them to keep quiet about your involvement. You know what big mouths they have.'

'What about Lucy Birkinshaw? She might blab if she thinks she can get one on us.'

'I know. It's a worry. We'll have to make sure she doesn't get wind of all this. Where is she by the way?'

'No idea.'

'We must keep her away from the judges. Look, I must go.'

'Right then, I'll pull us out of the demo. But people are going to think it's a bit odd.'

'Too bad!'

After Howard rang off, Greg gathered Sue, Janet and Fred together. He quickly explained the situation and the need for discreet flight. They immediately started handing their placards to other demonstrators.

****

Louise had stood framed in the window all the time her dad took his call, but she might as well have been invisible for all the notice that anyone across the street took of her. That's why she was now leaning out of the open window: leaning right out over the sill to make herself more conspicuous. A few demonstrators glanced up at her but most seemed to have their attention fixed on the gate to the rectory's drive.

She was willing her dad to turn round. It must have worked because at that moment he put his mobile away and started talking to Mr Birch, Mrs Rawdon and Miss Pinkney. They all nodded back at him and seemed very grave and concerned. She wondered what he was telling them. It must have been something very important because now Mr Birch and Mrs Rawdon were handing their placards to people around them. Suddenly, she was aware that Miss Pinkney was pointing up at her. Next, dad was looking up too and staring. She never forgot that stare all her long and celebrated life.

'Careful, Louise,' said Zoe. 'You'll fall out.'

****

'Isn't that Sharon Makepiece's daughter?'

Greg felt all the colour drain from his face. Janet Pinkney was pointing up at the rectory. Leaning out of an open window was Louise.

'It is her, isn't it?' pressed Janet.

'Yes. Yes, that's her.'

'What on earth is she doing in the rectory?'

'I believe she's been excluded from school,' said Greg.

'Yes, for kicking poor old Mrs Lucas. And I'm not surprised at all. Rather a surly child, I've always thought. And her mother! Well, now there's a mystery. Disappeared from the face of the earth and returned three months later with a baby girl. No-one ever fathomed out who the father was. Some even suggested it was the vicar.'

'The vicar?'

'Well, the church was closed soon afterwards.'

'We'd better go or the judges will catch us,' said Greg. He gave his placard to the man next to him. 'Look after that will you.'

'Leaving already?' the man asked.

'Aye. Got a number of things to sort out.'

Greg quickly set off down Church Lane towards the main street followed by the other committee members.

Lucy Birkinshaw, who was standing a short distance away amidst a group of onlookers, observed the departure of Greg and his fellow demonstrators with surprise and interest.

****

Louise wondered what Miss Pinkney could be talking to dad about, although from the disapproving way the woman kept glancing up at her, she had a pretty good idea. Surprisingly, after his first amazed stare, dad hadn't looked up at her once. He seemed to be deliberately avoiding her. Treating her as though she didn't exist. Well, that was nothing new. Revealing her presence in the rectory to him had been a big step, but she could hardly expect him to be pleased about it, could she?

She saw Greg hand his placard over to someone in the crowd, and then he and the others were moving off down Church Lane. She watched them reach the end of it, turn into the main street and disappear. Afterwards, she felt an intense feeling of anti-climax. It was a while before she realised the reason for this. It had felt invigorating to reveal herself at the window. It had been more than a dare: more than a piece of mischief. Her action was a gauntlet she'd thrown down: a challenge to her dad's authority and a statement of her own personal freedom. But, in retrospect, she realised she hadn't done it to be daring or challenging at all. She'd done it because she'd hoped to receive a sign from him. Some acknowledgement that a connection existed between them. Some act of recognition that showed Greg Maynard knew her in some way: even if only as the daughter of the secretary of the Community Watch. When she'd appeared at the window, all she'd hoped for was a smile and a wave from him: but he'd just been stony faced and unforgiving.

A sudden and excited clamour went round the demonstrators. Their attention seemed to be riveted on what was happening at ground level: in particular some activity that was taking place in the front garden of the house. By leaning further out of the window, Louise saw the reason for their excitement: Dylan was emerging from the garage followed by Toni, Eric and the clients. They were all carrying various gardening tools that looked very clean and new, as though they'd never been used. Their appearance was greeted by the demonstrators with a mixture of jeers, boos, whistles, cat calls and howls of derision.

'What are they doing?' Louise asked Zoe, who had joined her at the window.

'Humouring the judges with a little gardening. It's Dylan's brilliant idea.'

Louise regarded Zoe unsurely. Why was it sometimes so hard to work out if adults really meant what they said?

Sheldon was the last to arrive in the front garden. He was carrying a hover mower. The appearance of the youth, whose fantasy was quite clearly to machine gun the demonstrators out of existence, enraged his intended victims. They now seized their opportunity to machine gun him with verbal abuse.

'Ignore them,' Dylan called out. 'Just focus on your tasks.'

Everyone immediately got to work. Eric began cutting back the wildly overgrown grass with the strimmer so that Dylan could begin mowing the lawn. Sheldon and Liam raked up the grass cuttings and Khaled collected them in the wheelbarrow for disposal. Toni and Mona trimmed the privet hedge. Rupa, Amy and Jake were down on their knees amongst the shrubs, weeding. Liam and Scarlett swept the drive.

Instead of being won over by all this gardening, as was Dylan's intention, the demonstrators seemed to regard it as a direct provocation. A new chant began somewhere amongst the crowd: mumbled at first, but as it was taken up by more and more people the message became clearly audible:

"Too little! Too late!"
"Too little! Too late!"
"Too little! Too late!"

For some reason that was a complete mystery to Louise, Zoe couldn't stop laughing; but she hadn't time to ask her what she found so funny because at that moment Mona suddenly stopped working, put down her shears, looked up and gave Louise a smile and a wave. Supporting herself by the sill, Louise leaned right out of the open window, beamed and waved back. Her movements attracted the attention of several people in the crowd but she couldn't care less. Her dad knew she was in the rectory now. He'd seen she'd defied him. That was all that mattered.

'Why are you up there, Louise?' someone amongst the bystanders called out.

She recognized the voice. It belonged to the mum of one of the girls in her class. Several other people were shouting questions at her now which she couldn't understand, one of which produced tremendous laughter from the demonstrators.

Zoe said, 'Come on, let's go downstairs. We can make a start on the sculpture park.'

Pausing only to stare at Dylan's unfinished painting, Louise happily followed Zoe out.

CHAPTER FIFTY

'Action!'

At the director's cue the four Magnificent Britain judges and those accompanying them exited the churchyard of St Wilfred's and moved into Church Lane. As they passed through the 17th century lychgate, lovingly decorated with pink and white roses, hydrangeas, chrysanthemums and scented stocks, they stopped to shake hands with another formally dressed group of people which included former members of the Parochial Church Council and congregation. These were the volunteers who, despite the church's permanent closure, continued to maintain the churchyard throughout the year. Many of them had spent every spare moment of the past week enhancing St Wilfred's somewhat austere interior by liberally adorning it with inspired floral arrangements. The volunteers were there today to ensure that the churchyard and the House of God's west door remained open in order that the judges could appreciate their efforts. The people in the rectory might let the side down, but never they!

A professional video camera mounted on a tripod was positioned across the street, directly opposite the entrance to the churchyard. As Lady Brearley and her party came through the lychgate, turned left and moved up Church Lane in the direction of The Old Rectory, the camera panned slowly with them until the demonstrators who were protesting at the far end of the lane also appeared in the shot.

The director allowed the camera operator to continue shooting footage of the judges and the demonstration for several seconds, before calling 'Cut!' However, for some reason, the sound recordist deliberately appeared to be ignoring the director's instruction; she continued directing a boom mic towards the noisy demonstrators, as though collecting additional background sound.

Every year, for the past seven years, the same video company had filmed the judging of the finals of the Magnificent Britain Competition. During those years, many hundreds of thousands of video cassettes and DVDs had been sold, each showing cities, towns and villages across the UK in glorious bloom being inspected and adjudicated. The idea for videoing the final stages of the contest had originally come from Graham Spend, the manager of the

Budeholme Estate, and it had proved to be a money-spinner. Most of the videos and DVDs were sold over the Internet, but they could also be purchased at Budeholme House's own shop along with Budeholme House honey, Budeholme House jam and Budeholme House paté. For Budeholme House was now a substantial brand. So too was Magnificent Britain. The name of Sir Maurice Brearley's obscure gardening competition had become world famous: it was now associated with the highest quality and sold everything from seeds to garden furniture. Celia herself was a brand, a publishing brand, and millions of her ghosted gardening and recipe books were sold annually. Which was why, once a year, Lady Celia Brearley, although now in her eighties, was prepared to don a lapel mic and submit herself to the arduous task of judging Magnificent Britain in front of a video camera. A task she undertook without complaint, even when, as now, the director was on his fourth take and Celia and the other members of her little procession had rehearsed many times moving in and out of the churchyard under a broiling sun.

'Please say that one was all right!' Celia called across to the director.

He smiled and gave her the thumbs up. His name was Brian and he was a ginger haired, bespectacled man in his thirties who looked like a secondary school teacher. In fact, this was what he'd been for five years before bravely abandoning the profession to start his own video production company.

Brian had a crew of three young women helping him: a camera operator, a sound recordist and an assistant who worked the clapper board and was the general "gofer". At present the assistant was helping the camera operator remove the heavy video camera from its tripod in preparation for the next shot.

Brian left his crew and came across the street to join Celia and the others who were standing around irresolutely in front of the lych-gate. 'We're going hand-held for the next one,' he said. 'I want you to walk down the street towards the rectory. We'll be following close behind you.'

Celia thoroughly enjoyed the experience of filming. Not only did it allow her to be the centre of attention, it also partly fulfilled her teenage ambition of becoming a movie star. She may have been in her eighties but her intelligence was still keen, and over the many years in which Brian had videoed the judging she'd collected a significant knowledge of filming techniques and a battery of jargon. She used that to her advantage now.

'I noticed in that last shot that you panned with us until those demonstrators were in the frame and stayed with them in long shot for some time. I thought we'd agreed there'd be no footage of that awful demonstration.'

'Don't worry,' Brian said, reassuringly. 'It'll be removed at the edit.'

'Good.' Giving Howard Roberts a brief, reproving look, she went on, 'The demonstration is an outrage and I don't want it to spoil our beautiful video.'

'You can be assured that'll never happen,' said Brian. He wasn't lying. The official 2001 recording of the finals of Magnificent Britain would contain no mention of the conflict concerning Leefdale's Old Rectory; nor any images of the irregular and unsporting demonstration taking place outside it. But Brian was an artist and artists do chafe at censorship. Having videoed the Magnificent Britain contest for several years, he was damned if he was going to pass up the chance of making a documentary about a real conflict instead of the usual bland and unobjectionable homily to the art of gardening he produced every year. Everyone had to eat, but he didn't want to be remembered just for shooting videos of a flower show.

As soon as Brian had heard that a demonstration was to take place outside the rectory, he'd resolved to surreptitiously shoot as much footage of it as he could get away with. Similarly with the sound. Once people were fitted with lapel mics they soon forgot they were wearing them and were astonishingly indiscreet. Some of the private exchanges in the village hall between the judges and Major Roberts had already proved to be dynamite; although, of course there was no record of the Major's contribution as he hadn't been miked up. But his crude attempt to rig the competition could easily be inferred from the responses of the judges.

Lady Brearley would, as usual, have her wholesome video, but Brian's plan was to edit all of the inadmissible footage into a controversial documentary of his own. It would be an exposé of the antagonisms, conflicts of interest and corruption at the heart of one of Britain's most famous gardening contests. His theme would be the squalid and sordid reality behind the beautiful and beguiling façade. He already had his working title: "Not So Magnificent Britain", and he was hopeful that on the back of this controversial work his name might one day be ranked alongside Grierson or Flaherty. He cautioned himself to watch out for Celia, though. She was a canny old girl. She'd already spotted his crafty long shot of the demo. It wasn't going to be easy to get the footage he needed from under her nose.

When everything was set up and ready for the next shot, Brian called 'Roll sound!' The sound recordist responded with 'Speed!' Brian called 'Roll Camera!' The camera operator responded with 'Rolling!' The assistant called out 'Scene 49 Take 1' and marked it with the clapper. Brian then called 'Action!'

Celia's party set off up Church Lane with the director and crew following them. To their left was the wall of St Wilfred's churchyard which extended alongside the carriageway for several yards. After this it gave way to an area of pasture on which a few sheep were grazing. The pasture ran adjacent to Church Lane for a further hundred yards or so, and ended at a large and very ugly modern agricultural building which obscured the rear garden of The Old Rectory.

Brian's crew knew that he wanted as much covert footage of the demonstration as possible. He'd asked his camera operator to stay tight on the backs of the judges all the way up Church Lane but had instructed her to adjust the angle of the shot from time to time to take in the demonstration. This would give him two versions for the edit: one for Lady Brearley and one for himself.

Celia noticed that the incline of Church Lane was becoming gradually steeper. The increased gradient was requiring extra exertion and badly affecting her progress. She was in considerable pain and beginning to feel very tired. She'd spent the past ten days trudging around all the villages that had made it into the UK final. Last night she'd hosted a demanding reception for the judges and her estate workers, and had been emotionally drained by her meeting with that bastard Arnie Stidges, who'd had the temerity to ask her to take part in a television programme designed to traduce the reputation of her beloved late husband. Tonight she would host the awards ceremony at Budeholme House for the winners in the villages and small towns' categories. Tomorrow she'd have to dash down to London to make a speech at the awards ceremony for the large towns, cities and London boroughs. And on Sunday, she'd be flying to Dublin to hand out medals to the winners and runners up from Northern Ireland and Eire in a joint awards ceremony. This was most important and she owed it to Maurice to be there. That's why, no matter how tired or daunted she might feel, it was essential for her to attend. But she doubted that she'd have the energy to do it all over again next year.

Fellow judge Kate Smith, who was striding purposefully ahead with Pugh and McSweeney, noticed that Celia was having difficulty keeping up and dropped back to join her.

'Are you all right, Celia?'

'Of course! Please don't fuss so!'

Kate's face fell.

Celia chided herself for her appalling manners. She took a deep breath and tried to ignore the agony in her hip. 'I'm so sorry. It's very kind of you to ask, dear.'

Kate reduced her pace in order to stay by Celia's side. They discussed the excellent floral decorations in St Wilfred's and the beautiful condition of the churchyard.

Kate said, 'Such a shame the vicar couldn't have been there.'

Somewhat testily, Celia reminded her that St Wilfred's was without a vicar because the church had been mothballed, as had several other churches in the vicinity. 'Sunday services now only take place at St John's, Melthorpe, because the only vicar in the area lives there and has to combine his ministry with a full time job as a probation officer. That's why he was unable to be at St Wilfred's today! This is the state the Church has now got itself into. It's disgraceful.'

Her ire now fully up, Celia complained that when she was a young woman there was a church in every village and each one had its own vicar and a healthy congregation. She fulminated about the disgraceful decline of the church in rural areas; the closing of schools and post offices; the absence of pubs and butchers' shops. Kate was sorry she'd started the conversation. She'd only meant to make small talk. She wondered why the old girl was so ratty. Talking to herself too. Perhaps it was the onset of dementia.

But the reason for Celia's irascible temper lay just up the road ahead of them, filling her with anxiety and dread. The hard voiced, aggressive chanting of the mob outside the rectory was affecting her nerves, and every step that brought her closer to the demonstration made it more and more intimidating. It was the prospect of a confrontation with this uncertain enemy that was making her uncharacteristically disagreeable. So this was what funk was like, she mused. Now she could understand what Maurice had suffered in the trenches. But it had never been in her nature to be daunted. Doggedly she pushed on towards the rectory, even though as she drew nearer and nearer to it the mob's harsh and persistent chorus fell upon her ears like blows.

'What on earth are they chanting?' Celia asked.

Kate said, 'It sounds like "Too little, too late. Too little, too late".'

'How odd. Whatever for?'

'I don't know.'

'I hadn't expected such a large demonstration,' said Celia.

'There's certainly a lot of very angry people.'

'It's so untypical of Leefdale.'

'Really?' said Kate, naturally assuming that the remarks had been intended for her. But Celia had actually been addressing them to her late husband, Maurice, whose presence she strongly sensed was accompanying her as she moved around the village. Leefdale had been a special village for him. He'd always hoped it would reach the finals. Something to do with the war. The First War, of course. Every young man from Leefdale who'd gone to the front had perished. That was it. It said so on the war memorial, which she'd been admiring earlier in the company of the other judges; in the company of Maurice too. But, strangely, no-one else seemed to be aware of his presence. Every year Maurice had stood with her, side by side in front of the memorial. They'd often remained there for several minutes reading aloud the names of the dead and remembering. Just as they'd stood in front of all the other memorials in all those other villages they'd judged together. Maurice had served, you see. That's why he never forgot.

Shadows passed across her mind as she thought of Stidges, and despite the intense heat, she shivered. She wondered bitterly why Leonard had come back to stir things up again, and then remembered that it wasn't Leonard who was plaguing her but his son, Arnie Stidges. But she'd faced him down too, hadn't she? How dare he make such disgusting accusations about Maurice? And about Rex, too. Well, he'd been put firmly in his place. Like father, like son. Both of them blackmailers. Did he really think she'd be such a pushover? Why was Maurice shaking his head at her? Was he saying that after all this time it really didn't matter? Was that what he was saying? Well, she couldn't possibly agree with that.

'Who? I'm sorry, I don't understand,' said Kate Smith.

'Don't understand what?' said Celia.

Kate Smith regarded her oddly. 'You just said, "You didn't expect me to tell him, did you?" I don't understand.'

'I was talking to...' Celia stopped. She was going to say "My dead husband" but realized how crazy that would sound. 'I was talking to myself. It's what you do when you get old.'

They had passed well beyond the churchyard boundary now, and on their left was the area of pasture. Celia gazed uneasily ahead towards the rectory and the crowds assembled on the pavement opposite. She recalled that Major Roberts had said the people in the rectory were bolshies and probably wouldn't allow the judges in. Oh dear. She did hope there wasn't going to be a scene. She couldn't bear the thought of being refused entry in front of all those dreadful, bawling people. The brute force of their antagonism seemed powerful enough to move a battleship. Her anxiety was intense and she was convinced the demonstration could only end in some sort of riot. There appeared to be two distinct groups: the demonstrators who were lining the pavement directly across the road from the rectory and waving placards and chanting; and on either side of that lot, a large number of bystanders who were standing watchfully and weren't at all animated. However, she was relieved to see a substantial police presence which reassured her a little. There were also a number of camera crews, probably from the regional news people, and also lots of reporters and photographers. Why so many? The media had never taken this much interest in the competition before. Then she remembered. Howard Roberts was accompanying them. After his disgraceful behaviour on television the other day he was obviously the magnet. She felt deeply resentful that he'd had the temerity to make an appearance in public knowing what a distraction his divisive presence would be. The thought made her involuntarily stop and turn round to look for him. She was surprised to see that he and Isobel had dropped far back and were getting into the large black car that had been shadowing them round the village all morning. Of course, he was persona non grata at the rectory so wouldn't be putting his nose in there. She watched the car set off and go past her. It then turned right and passed through the gateway to Rooks Nest. Celia remembered that the Major's gardens were next on the list to be inspected after The Old Rectory. He and Isobel were probably going on ahead to prepare themselves. But who were those people in the black cars? Police? Bodyguards? The Security Service? And why were they protecting Howard and Isobel? Rex would know. But he was dead. So many of the people she'd known were dead.

The chants of the demonstrators were even louder now. But although perturbed by it, Celia refused to be intimidated. If this menacing rabble thought their street protest could influence the judges' decision, they were barking up the wrong tree. Such a lot of fuss and bad temper! It reminded her of the summer's day in 1936 when her father had taken her to a meeting in Corporation Fields, Hull, held by Oswald Mosley and his British Union of Fascists. Her father had been, for a short time, an admirer and supporter of Mosley. She and papa had stood some way off while Mosley addressed the crowd from a coal cart. Surrounding him, like a kind of Praetorian Guard, were his Blackshirts; and surrounding the Blackshirts was a huge crowd of young Jews and Communists. At least, that's what her father said they were. The angry crowd was shouting insults but the Blackshirts remained undaunted and stood very still. Their demonstration of military discipline made them appear much more sinister and terrifying than the vast, threatening crowd surrounding them. It was a vivid memory: Mosley's men dressed in black tunics, wide belts around their waists and grey trousers tucked into black leather boots. Their opponents in scruffy clothes and cloth caps, the men wearing heavy working boots. And just like now the air seemed to shimmer with so many powerful and frightening emotions: and underneath everything was the constant threat of primitive violence and the strange sense that ideas could only be given tangibility by the spilling of blood. Her father had urged her to draw nearer to the meeting, but it was the last thing she wanted to do. Her instinct, as now, was to run away. She recalled remonstrating with her father and pleading with him not to move any closer. Suddenly the crowd had begun pelting the Blackshirts with bricks and other missiles. Only then had her father hurried her away. It was the only meeting of Mosley's she'd attended. Following it, her father expressed himself out of sympathy with the fascists and distanced himself from them. Years afterwards, her mother told her he'd only done so because his Jewish business friends had cut him.

Her preoccupations returned to the present. How you would hate this, Maurice, she thought. You so loathed the mass, the herd. Except, of course when you were drunk. Then you seemed to crave the company of crowds of total strangers. Unaccountably, she found herself uttering these thoughts aloud and immediately stopped. Kate Smith was staring at her again.

Surely the angry clamour was at its zenith? She was close enough now to read the placards. Her old eyes could see the larger writing without too much difficulty. What vile and vicious things were written there! How could a simple gardening contest have unleashed such mindless hatred?

Now that she was close enough to observe the distinctions of dress and facial features that gave each demonstrator their discrete individuality, the crowd no longer seemed an undifferentiated mob. Not that this made them any less terrifying, quite the contrary. There were so many more than she'd expected and every one of them seemed to be choking with hate. She speculated on the effect that the mob was having on those inside the rectory and wondered if they were cowering in various rooms, hiding in lavatories or under beds. How awful it must feel to be the object of such extreme hatred!

The relentless aggression of the mob began to make her feel angry. She'd been told that the rectory had been turned into some sort of home for slum children. Bunny Reynolds' boy was behind it: the one who'd recently been ennobled. Lord Sandleton, he called himself now. Gave them art and drama, regular meals and exercise, so she'd heard. Nothing wrong with that. Jolly good idea. In the thirties she'd often taken baskets of groceries to the tenants in the estate villages when they were having a hard time. The angel of mercy they'd called her. No need for that now: most of those hovels were smart second homes owned by affluent members of the middle classes.

Watched closely by the demonstrators, Celia and her fellow judges advanced until they neared the gate of The Old Rectory. Here they stopped, and all four judges were relieved, at last, to be able to turn their backs on the terrifying crowd. As they gazed through the bars of the gate the first thing that struck them was the number of people who were working hard in the front garden.

'So that's why they're chanting "Too little, too late",' said Pugh. Actually, the demonstrators were now shouting something a great deal more offensive, but he felt it best not to mention that.

'Yes, and I think it's unfair,' said Celia. 'They're at least making an effort.'

The three other judges, always alert to Celia's partiality, exchanged uneasy looks.

'Yes, but we can't allow ourselves to be influenced by sentiment,' said Kate Smith.

Mona, who was trimming the privet hedge close by the gate, was the first to become aware of the visitors' arrival. She stopped clipping and approached the gate. Raising her voice above the din from across the street, she said, 'Those funny things you're wearing must mean you're the judges.'

'We certainly are,' said Kate Smith. 'And those funny things are called rosettes. Do you mind if we come in for a look round?'

'Of course not,' said Dylan, who'd joined Mona at the gate. 'We're expecting you.' He took out his keys to undo the padlock.

Celia was hugely relieved. Roberts was wrong: there would be no dreadful scene after all.

There was a sudden roar from the crowd. Celia and the others turned round involuntarily. They were startled to see a bunch of media people and demonstrators charging across the road towards them. They swarmed around, rasping out questions like demented interrogators:

'Aren't these gardens a disgrace?'

'What are you going to do about it?'

'What do you make of the demo?'

'Will Leefdale win?'

Hastily Dylan opened the gate and ushered the judges through. They were barely in the drive when he slammed the gate hard against those who were attempting to follow. It was done with such speed and force that one or two of the reporters were lucky to escape with all their fingers.

'How are you managing to cope in these impossible conditions?' Celia asked Dylan. 'It must be most upsetting for the children.'

'It is. We considered taking them out for the day but some of us thought that would be running away, so we decided to stay.'

Celia looked at him approvingly. 'That's the spirit. You must always stand up to bullies.'

Meanwhile, outside the rectory, the police were forcing the opportunistic raiding party back across the street, in the process corralling Brian and his camera crew, who, as far as the police were concerned were indistinguishable from other members of the media. As the tightly packed bodies were pushed steadily backwards, Brian yelled out to his camera operator, 'Keep rolling! Keep rolling!' This industry jargon commanded her to keep filming, no matter what. She gave him a quick thumbs up without taking her eyes off the camera and continued shooting.

Brian couldn't believe his luck. He'd now have plenty of close up footage of the demo and also the demonstrators' point of view of the rectory. When he'd got all the shots he needed he'd simply tell the police who he was and demand to be allowed to join Celia. He'd never been so glad to be locked out of anything in his life!

****

Now that the judges were actually standing in the rectory's front garden they were able to fully comprehend the true extent of its neglect. They stood in a group gazing disconsolately around them, their thoughts rendered ineffable by the sight of the undernourished and exhausted grass, the overgrown hedges and shrubs, the borders totally obscured by weeds. It was obvious to every judge that the residents' belated improvements were pathetically inadequate, and an army of volunteers would be required to restore this garden to anything like its exemplary status. And then there were the vehicles: horrible white vans straddling the drive and lawn, even a mini-bus. What a contrast to the Corbridge's solitary and gorgeous red Ferrari, thought Celia. It had provided the perfect complement to an exemplary garden: its expensive, sleek lines signifying affluence, taste and class.

Celia could have cried as she stared at the ruins, recalling how perfect everything had looked at the same time last year. The gardener in her was inclined to agree with the ugly sentiments being expressed by the mob in the street. It really was too little, too late. She dreaded to think what the rear garden looked like. For the first time she understood what had roused Howard Roberts to such violence, and felt some sympathy for him.

She looked at Dylan, who was still at her side, and experienced a spurt of hot anger. How could anyone so young and good looking and so obviously nice have stood by and watched horticultural perfection go to such rack and ruin? How could he call himself an artist, an appreciator of beauty, when, through neglect, he'd destroyed one of the most beautiful gardens in the village? What had been his motivation? Was it just laziness on his part or had it been done out of deliberate vindictiveness towards the people of Leefdale? And was this belated and token attempt to make amends genuine or was he, as the crowd seemed to be chanting now, merely taking the piss?

And yet, the sight of all those young people mucking in and mowing the lawn, trimming shrubs and hedges, weeding and digging out, softened her heart a little. If all their hard work was intended as a conciliatory gesture, well, she would have the grace to acknowledge it as such and reciprocate.

Mona had returned to trimming the privet hedge with a pair of shears. Pugh and McSweeney were watching her crude efforts.

Pugh said, 'It'll take her weeks at that rate. She needs an electric trimmer.'

McSweeney said, 'Anyway, she hasn't the art of it.'

Celia heard them. She looked annoyed. 'No, she hasn't the art, but we have!' She moved awkwardly across the grass to Mona and stood beside her, watching. After a few moments, Mona stopped working. She turned to Lady Brearley and smiled, bashfully.

Lady Brearley took the shears from Mona and demonstrated the correct way to hold them and position herself in order to ensure a straight and level cut.

'I'm sure she's infringing the rules by doing that,' said McSweeney.

Kate said, 'Yes. It's an infringement of Rule 31, I'd say.'

'It's only a very minor infringement, surely?' said Pugh. 'And the garden's such a dump what does it bloody matter, anyway?'

Seeing that Celia was helping Mona, Dylan came over and joined them.

'Do you have any stakes or poles, Mr Bourne?' Celia asked.

'I don't know. We might have something like that in the garage.'

'I was explaining to Mona that if you place stakes in the ground at each corner of the hedge, and run strings tightly between them you'll get an outline of the shape that you want the hedge to eventually become. All you have to do then is cut away everything outside the guidelines and you'll get an even trim all round.'

'Thanks for the tip,' said Dylan.

'It's not a tip,' Celia said, frostily. 'It's a technique. There are lots more little techniques for cutting and trimming hedges. You'll find them in most good gardening books.'

Dylan had the resentful look of one who'd been corrected. 'Right. I'll get one.'

Mona resumed trimming and Celia turned away to contemplate the garden once more.

'I'm afraid it all looks rather a mess,' said Dylan, who felt compelled to offer some sort of explanation.

Celia said, 'Yes. It does rather.'

'You see, managing the unit and working in it full time, as I do, is incredibly time consuming. It leaves me no time for anything else.'

Celia looked stern. 'Then why didn't you accept Major Roberts' help? I gather he offered to maintain the gardens for you shortly after you moved in.'

Dylan looked surprised. 'Oh, but they wouldn't have been our gardens then, would they? You see, no matter how awful it looks, at least it's our awfulness.'

Celia was surprised to find that she had some sympathy for this sentiment. Such a beautiful young man: so frank and engaging and the kindest eyes. She was sure Maurice would have taken to him.

However, she was prevented from responding to his last remark because everyone working in the front garden had now downed tools and gathered around. Dylan insisted on introducing all of them to Lady Brearley and her fellow judges. This took some time.

Afterwards there followed some rather stilted small talk, during which Scarlett asked Lady Brearley if she knew The Queen.

Celia was delighted with the girl's guileless simplicity. She smiled and said, 'I was formally presented to Her Majesty when I was much younger. I've also attended several functions at which she was present, but I can't claim to be an intimate friend.'

This aroused a lot of interest and some of the teenagers wanted to know what the queen was like.

At this point Dylan intervened and said, 'The judges have a job to do, so I think we should let them get on with it.'

Ignoring him, Lady Brearley said, 'The queen has beautiful manners.'

Everyone returned to work. The judges stood looking bleakly all around them. Then, individually, they made an inspection of the garden. Afterwards they gathered together in a huddle.

Pugh spoke first in a low voice. 'This has got to be the worst maintained garden in the village. It's even worse than those on Mathieson Walk.'

'I agree,' said McSweeney. 'No wonder Major Roberts wanted to enter a substitute exemplar at the eleventh hour.'

'Deplorable,' said Kate. 'I've awarded it zero on every criteria.'

Celia knew that the others were right. The condition of the front garden was inexcusable. She desperately wanted Leefdale to achieve its fifth gold medal for Maurice's sake. Leefdale was his favourite village on the estate. But it could only be done on merit. No village with an exemplary garden in such a disgraceful state could ever hope to win the contest. After all, Magnificent Britain was a competition. Sentimentality could play no part in it.

And then she saw the poppies. Strange how she'd missed them. A cluster of red poppies had become established in the centre of the lawn. If the grass had been conventionally short their presence would have been an infestation to be rooted out: but the weeks of neglect had given the poppies the opportunity to establish themselves, and now they were as tall as the overgrown weeds and grasses they'd self-seeded amongst. However, being stronger in colour their gossamer petals dappled the unmown grass with conspicuous daubs of red; and their tender fragility, occurring randomly, without art or design, was a reminder that nature's haphazard, unkempt beauty was still, nevertheless, beauty.

And standing there, amongst the knee high poppies... Maurice! Wearing the uniform of a lieutenant in the First Battalion, North Wolds Infantry. He was pointing to the poppies and saying something she couldn't hear.

'Of course! A weed is only a flower in the wrong place. That must be it. That's what you always said!'

The judges stared at her uneasily.

Kate whispered to Pugh and McSweeney, 'She's been saying odd things all the time. Talking to people who aren't there. It's rather disturbing.'

'It's her age,' said McSweeney. 'Just humour her.'

At that moment Zoe appeared and bounded over to them, full of smiling enthusiasm and lissom loveliness. She introduced herself and said, 'I'm afraid we haven't been able to do much work on the front because we've been so busy at the back with our sculpture park.'

Celia's eyes widened. 'A sculpture park? That sounds exciting.'

'Oh, it is. The kids are really pleased you're coming to see it. They've put so much into it.'

Celia looked around as though she'd lost something. 'Where's Brian?' she said, and pointed towards the lawn. 'I want him to video those poppies.'

'Which poppies?' said Zoe.

Kate, Pugh and McSweeney exchanged more looks. They couldn't see any poppies either.

****

'It's Greg. Louise is in the rectory. I've seen her.'

'Hold on, just a minute.'

Sharon was at Melthorpe, in the middle of her second viewing of the morning. The potential purchasers, a young married couple, seemed much taken with the four bedroomed, double fronted cottage she was showing them, and she'd been in an excellent mood until she'd seen the familiar name on her mobile's display. She excused herself, left the couple to look round and went into the garden to resume the call.

'Yes, I know she's there.'

'You know? But you promised me she wouldn't go back.'

Sharon described at some length the reasons why Louise had defied them both and was now in the rectory. But Greg was in no mood for rational explanations. He'd experienced a profound shock seeing Louise at the rectory's window. As well as a deep feeling of anger at her defiance, he felt ashamed at the probability that she'd seen him behaving in a thoroughly uncivilised, thuggish manner. Conflated with this was his guilt at failing to acknowledge his own daughter, even simply wave at her. It reminded him of the school sports day when he'd been unable to congratulate her fittingly for winning the hurdle race. He'd had to ignore her too at open evenings when he should have been enquiring about her progress; and in May, when Years 5 and 6 were departing for school journey and the children were getting on to the coach, he'd been unable to hug Louise goodbye as he'd hugged Jade. He could express none of this to Sharon, and so instead said, 'Janet Pinkney saw her too. They all did. It's all your bloody fault. You should have made sure she got nowhere near the rectory.'

'I did my best but you know she's got a mind of her own. When I realized she was there I told her to make sure she wasn't seen.'

'She took a lot of notice of that, didn't she? She was standing in the window, bold as brass. You've no idea how I felt seeing her there with everyone howling abuse. She probably saw everything.'

'What do you mean, everything?'

Yes, what did he mean? He was thinking of the terribly aggressive way he'd behaved, but he couldn't bring himself to say it. 'I nearly got trampled to death by the crowd. Janet and Sue and Fred too.'

'God!'

'We would have died if the police hadn't acted promptly.'

Sharon was genuinely concerned for him. 'Are you all right?'

'Yes.'

'Are you sure?'

'Yes. But Louise must have seen it all. It must have terrified the life out of her.'

'I'll ring her and see if she's OK. Look, I've got to go, I'm in the middle of a viewing.'

'Hold on. Don't go. I need to ask a favour.'

'Oh?'

'If anyone asks you, say I wasn't at the demo.'

There was a pause as Sharon speculated on the reasons Greg might be requesting her to do this. 'What have you done?'

'Nothing.'

'There must be a reason you're asking me to lie. Have you hit someone?'

'Certainly not. The thing is, Leefdale will be disqualified if the judges find out members of the committee were demonstrating. So, if anyone asks, swear I wasn't there.'

Sharon was appalled. 'I'm not going to lie for you. If anyone asks me, I'll tell them the truth.'

'Of course. Stupid of me. Why should you help me when you're fucking Dylan Bourne?'

Sharon immediately terminated the call. What was the point?

She returned to her prospective purchasers. They were both delighted with the property and prepared to offer two thousand below the asking price. Sharon told them she'd communicate their offer to her clients. When the couple had gone she locked the cottage and went to her car where she sat wondering what to do. She contemplated ringing Louise but that would mean telling her that Greg was furious at seeing her in the rectory. She certainly didn't want that conversation overheard by Dylan. Perhaps after her last viewing of the day she wouldn't return to the office but would feign a headache and go and collect Louise. After much consideration, she sent her a text: "R u alright? Someone we know tells me he saw u at rectory window. What r u playing at? Will pick u up early as I can."

****

'They're afraid to show their faces,' said Sid Arkwright.

'I'm not surprised, after what he did to his son-in-law,' said Mary Arkwright.

'And don't forget what he did to that boy, Sheldon,' said Lucy Birkinshaw.

All three were standing amongst the onlookers who'd assembled in Church Lane to observe the demonstration and the arrival of the Magnificent Britain judges. They'd just watched the black limousine carrying Howard and Isobel pass through the gates of Rooks Nest and continue up the drive. Earlier, they'd been positioned perfectly to observe the videoing of Isobel and Howard's departure from St Wilfred's church along with Lady Brearley and the rest of the judges. They'd been intrigued to see Isobel and Howard suddenly hang back behind the others, obviously hesitating. From their facial expressions and body language it was quite clear that neither relished going anywhere near the demonstration outside The Old Rectory. Isobel had said something to Howard, and then retaining a semblance of dignity they'd both climbed into the limousine. After being driven the short distance down Church Lane, they'd entered the drive and were now in the safety of their home.

'Not much of a man, is he?' said Sid. 'I mean, the demo was his idea and he's too frightened to put in an appearance.'

'He's a bloody coward,' said Mary.

'Yes,' said Lucy, 'and a dangerous coward too.'

Mary laughed. 'Here they come, the stars of tomorrow.' She was a blowzy looking woman in her mid-fifties with a chubby pink face and dyed blonde streaks expiring amongst her brittle grey hair. A cigarette seemed to be permanently between her lips and in her right hand she tightly clutched a packet of Benson and Hedges and a lighter. She was referring to the self-conscious progress of the Magnificent Britain judges up Church Lane towards the rectory, which was being videoed, as ever, by Brian and his crew.

Lucy and Sid laughed at Mary's quip. The judges certainly seemed a motley bunch. Like some diminutive Pied Piper, the short and merry figure of McSweeney led the way; whilst behind him, towering at least a foot taller, came the dour and guarded looking Pugh. The incongruity in their heights and their contrasting demeanour sent a frisson of amusement rippling through the watching crowd. Following them were the two women: Kate Smith, large and overweight, dragging her feet to keep up with the slow but determined progress of Lady Brearley, whose arthritic hip gave her an awkward, rolling gait. This disparate quartet appeared to possess only one common denominator: the Magnificent Britain Competition rosette which each wore over their heart.

'Lady Brearley's breaking up,' said Sid, sentimentally. He was an obese man in his late fifties. He'd worn his hair very long in his youth when it was fashionable and had kept it that length ever since, even though it was now grey and the crown of his head was completely bald. He wore a grubby white T shirt and an even grubbier pair of grey jogging bottoms that were so long they ended in deep folds around his ankles. His massive beer gut flowed over his waistband like froth over the rim of an overfilled glass. A testament to his six pints a night.

PC Wheatcroft and WPC Scargill were in their police car, slowly shadowing the judges as they advanced up Church Lane. As the little procession approached the rectory the volume of the demonstrators' voices shot up several decibels and their chant changed noticeably in character and tempo. "They're taking the piss! They're taking the piss!" they rasped.

There were just two regional TV crews, a couple of local radio reporters and some hacks and photographers from local papers covering the demonstration. Nothing like the extent of the media presence that had laid siege to Rooks Nest on Wednesday. But now, as the judges halted at the gates to the rectory, some of the media people and demonstrators broke free of their police cordon and as one, surged forward across the road. The photographers suddenly began snapping away. Against the pure radiance of a perfect summer's day, their camera flashes seemed cheap and meretricious. The judges turned towards the source of this sudden disturbance with alarm. Realizing the judges' distress, Dylan Bourne could be seen quickly unlocking the front gate and ushering them into the safety of the rectory's drive. He was slamming the gate behind him just as the local media people flung themselves at it, shouting their questions.

'They've left Cecil B de Mille behind!' laughed Mary.

It was true. The Magnificent Britain video maker and his crew had been mistaken for just another TV unit and denied access to the rectory along with all the others. Now, in the company of the local media, they were being unceremoniously forced by police officers away from the entrance to the rectory and back across the road.

Thwarted in their attempts to nail their prey, one or two reporters now began to sidle up to the bystanders, asking for their responses to recent events in the village. One of these journalists, a sandy haired man with twinkling eyes and a face that bore a permanent look of amusement, was interviewing Bill Harcourt, who'd finished his milk round and was delighted to be able to express to The Sandleton Examiner his support for Major Roberts.

'I told him,' said Harcourt, 'if Leefdale wins gold medal then I'll deliver your milk.'

'So, if Leefdale fails to win the gold medal, you'll blame the inclusion unit?'

'I certainly will.'

'Hey, lad,' bawled Sid Arkwright to the reporter. 'If you want to know summat about the Major, I can tell you!'

The newspaperman turned to Sid with obvious interest.

'And you are, Mr...?'

'Arkwright. Sid Arkwright's my name. Well, you listen to this. There's those of us around here who don't hold with this Magnificent Britain going on. We don't want to stop others doing it but some of us can't be bothered. Or we can't get round our gardens like we used to. I'm on incapacity benefit, you see.'

'I'm sorry to hear that,' said the reporter. All this was much better than he'd hoped.

'Aye, I was injured in an industrial accident. So any kind of heavy work like gardening is difficult for me.'

'I can understand that.'

'Aye, well, mebbe you can but that's not good enough for Major Roberts and all those other busybodies. They come round, heavy handed, without by your leave, and start tidying up our gardens for us. Reckon we're letting side down. Swinging the lead and all that. It's a bloody liberty if you ask me.'

'He's right!' cried Lucy, pushing herself forward. 'I'm Lucy Birkinshaw. I'm on the Magnificent Britain committee.'

'So you know Major Roberts quite well?'

'As well as I want to.'

'And you'd agree with Mr Arkwright, would you, that there's a certain amount of arm twisting goes on to make sure Leefdale wins?'

'Absolutely. As I said, I'm on the committee so I ought to know. You should hear the way some of them talk about those who don't share their enthusiasm for the contest. It's like living in a police state.'

'You've obviously never lived in a police state!' scoffed Harcourt. He was a wizened little man whose face bore a permanent scowl.

The reporter said to Lucy, 'Is that why you're not over there demonstrating with the rest of them?'

'Those folk aren't from Leefdale,' said Sid. 'Most of them we've never seen before.'

'They're political,' said Lucy. 'Rent a mob. The Major and his pal on the parish council have bussed them in from all over. That's because most of us in Leefdale haven't the heart to terrify the poor people in the rectory.'

'I see,' said the reporter. He was scribbling in his notebook furiously. 'And the name of the Major's pal is...?'

'Greg Maynard.'

'That's not fair, Lucy,' said Harcourt. Addressing the reporter, he said, 'You should see what those so called poor people have done to the gardens in the rectory. They've ruined them.'

'They haven't ruined them,' insisted Lucy. 'I've been inside. All they've done is put up some goal posts.'

'That's no crime,' said Sid.

'Yeah. Live and let live,' said Mary.

'They're a bunch of scroungers,' exclaimed Harcourt.

'I suppose you'll be calling me a scrounger, then?' demanded Sid.

The reporter said to Lucy, 'You're rather in the minority over this though, aren't you?'

Lucy bristled. 'The rights of minorities are as important as anyone's.'

'Oh yeah?' said Harcourt. 'What about the rights of the English minority?'

'What English minority? In England the English are the majority.'

'Not for long. England for the English, I say,' said Harcourt.

'He's right. They're letting too many foreigners in,' said Mary.

The reporter returned his attention to Lucy. 'So Major Roberts and this Greg Maynard organised the demonstration?'

'Greg Maynard organised it but it's the Major's idea, you can be sure of that. Maynard does everything the Major tells him. Can't think for himself.'

'Aye, thick as thieves they are,' said Mary Arkwright. 'I'm Sid's wife, by the way.'

The reporter said, 'Major Roberts is possibly facing two charges for assault. Would you say he was normally a violent person?'

'Not usually, no,' said Sid.

'I don't know about that,' said Lucy, darkly. 'Sometimes at committee meetings he frightens the life out of me. The other day he shouted at me really loudly. In front of everybody. It was most intimidating. I think he's got a lot of anger in him. And they do say...' Lucy lowered her voice. 'They do say he gives his wife a bit of a hard time.'

'That's very interesting. And you say he's been sending round clean up squads to tidy people's gardens against their wishes?'

'Only when people ask for help,' said Harcourt, who was now getting indignant.

Sid rounded on him. 'I never asked for any help but I got it all the same!' He returned to the reporter. 'He sent Greg Maynard and his henchmen round to my place when I was out. They just marched in and started rearranging my front garden. They said it was a tip and needed to be put straight. When they'd finished it weren't my garden anymore.'

The reporter said, 'But if your garden's a mess, shouldn't you be grateful to people who tidy it up for you?'

Sid gave him a look that would have cracked cement. 'It might be a mess to them, lad, but to me it's organised. I told you, I'm on incapacity benefit. I arrange my garden so I know where everything is and I don't have to lift heavy things. And they went and changed it without even consulting me.'

'And Sid wasn't the only one who got that treatment!' exclaimed Lucy. 'Shame you can't interview the Major about it.'

The reporter shook his head. 'Some of us tried to interview him as he went round the village but the police threatened to arrest us. The cops in the big black car were most unpleasant.'

'Typical,' said Lucy. 'They're his minders now, ever since that trouble with his son-in-law.' Harcourt was now moving off. She watched him go with satisfaction, before continuing, 'And I'll tell you something else that's deeply disturbing. This demonstration's illegal under the rules of Magnificent Britain.'

The reporter's eyes twinkled even more than usual. 'Really? What makes you say that?'

Lucy was delighted to have the opportunity to explain at some length Rule 31 of the Magnificent Britain Competition which automatically disqualified any town or village that attempted to unfairly influence the result. Afterwards, she said, 'You see, in my view Major Roberts has broken both the spirit and the letter of the rule by his use of coercion and his organisation of the demonstration, both of which are clearly intended to affect the competition's outcome.'

'Lucy's right,' said Sid. 'There was a meeting at Greg Maynard's house the other night. During it Maynard told everyone that the demonstration was Roberts' idea but they were to keep it under their hats because the Major didn't want it known he was involved.'

Sid and Lucy rehearsed their various grievances for several minutes. Afterwards, the reporter said, 'Have you complained about this to anyone?'

'What's the use?' said Sid. 'It's the Leefdale mafia.'

'Sid's right,' said Lucy. 'I've tried complaining but it's a waste of time. They just shout you down.'

Having got his story, the reporter went off to get someone else to corroborate it. When he'd gone, Lucy touched Sid's arm. 'Actually, you know, there's someone we haven't complained to who's a lot more powerful than the Leefdale mafia.'

'Who's that?'

'Lady Brearley and the other judges. When they come out of the rectory we should follow them around the village and at a convenient point complain about the Major's gang re-arranging your garden.'

Sid looked doubtful. 'Oh, I don't know about that.'

Lucy touched Sid's arm again. 'Go on. And I'll complain to them about the way the Major's set up this demo to give Leefdale an unfair advantage. I shall appeal to Lady Brearley's sense of fair play.' She smiled encouragingly at him. 'So, are you with me?'

Sid was beguiled and suborned. He had a weakness for strong, intelligent women. 'Aye, love, all right. I'm with you.'

Mary said nothing. She had a suspicion that Lucy was a troublemaker. And being possessive by nature, she didn't like the way Lucy kept touching Sid's arm.

****

When Sharon arrived outside The Old Rectory just after four she was surprised to see that there wasn't a demonstrator in sight. She got out of the Passat and approached the rectory's gate, which was wide open. She was astonished to see that the front garden had been given a complete makeover. The grass had been cut short and was as smooth as a billiard table, the shrubbery had been weeded, and the hedge, although irregular and uneven, was no longer bursting with straggly overgrowth. Obviously the achievement of Eric and the teenagers who were still going hard at it.

Eric abandoned his weeding and came over. They greeted each other and she expressed her surprise at all the activity and improvements.

'Yes. It was Dylan's idea.' He smiled wryly. 'I don't think it'll get Leefdale its gold medal. But it'll tire the kids out and make them sleep soundly, so that's a bonus.'

'Are they enjoying it?'

'Actually they are. Me too.'

She asked where the demonstrators were.

'After the judges left they got bored and drifted away.'

'Were they very frightening?'

His normally kind face had an unpleasant, scathing look. 'Would you like your home besieged by a howling, racist mob?' He described to her graphically how the demonstrators had behaved and how their behaviour had affected the children. Sharon felt uncomfortable. She suspected he associated her with the forces behind the demonstration.

'Where's Louise? I've come to collect her.'

'She's in the back garden.' He gestured towards the open doors of the garage. 'You can get to it through there.'

'Yes. I know. I sold it to you, remember?'

He smiled broadly. 'So you did.'

Sharon entered the garage. It housed only one vehicle: Dylan's Ariel Red Hunter. She paused briefly to re-acquaint herself with it, but its solitary, curiously forlorn presence gave her a sentimental pang, and she quickly continued on through the rear door of the garage and out into the back garden. Here again there was more gardening activity going on.

Sharon's eye was drawn to an arresting sight at the centre of the lawn. Louise and a ginger haired boy, whom Sharon vaguely recalled was named Liam, were standing by the statues of Demeter and Apollo. There was a bowl of soapy water on the ground at their feet, and they were using it to clean the mud and dirt off of the statue of Apollo. It appeared that Demeter had already received their attentions, because she stood transformed: as white and gleaming as the day Sharon had made an inspection of the rectory to provide an estimate of its purchasing price.

Seeing her mother, Louise briefly acknowledged her and went on cleaning Apollo. Sharon came up to Louise and said, 'Hello Lou. Mind that doesn't fall on you. It looks pretty heavy.'

Liam said, 'It's all right, they're quite stable.'

Sharon had always regarded Liam as different to the other teenagers in the unit. He had a middle class accent and was always scrupulously polite. He was the one she least minded Louise playing with. However, it's unlikely she'd have felt the same way about him if she'd known about his pyromaniac tendencies and that he'd been excluded from his comprehensive for lighting a series of fires.

Sharon took Louise by the hand. 'Come over here, I need to talk to you.' She led Louise a short distance away from the statues and said, 'Why didn't you stay at home and do your lines like you promised?'

'I told you. I wanted to apologise to Mona.'

'You're a little liar. You came here to upset me and dad, didn't you?'

'No.'

'You came here to deliberately show yourself to dad. He's told me all about it.'

'No, I didn't. I came to apologise to Mona.'

'I told you to make sure none of the demonstrators saw you.'

'I just wanted to see what was going on.'

'Why?'

'I don't know, I just did. But it was terrible. You should have seen dad. He was so angry and horrible, like he hated everyone in here. He was really frightening. And all those people were just like him. All shouting and chanting and making us afraid.'

'Well that's your fault. You shouldn't have been here. I told you not to come!'

While this heated exchange between mother and daughter was going on, Dylan had been crossing the lawn towards them. He greeted Sharon and after one or two pleasantries, said, 'Louise tells me she's nervous about this evening but really looking forward to it.'

Sharon said, 'Yes, she really needs to go and get ready. But, before we do, can we have a quick word?'

'Of course.' Dylan folded his arms, and waited.

'No. I mean privately.'

This was unexpected. 'Oh, sure. Let's go in the house.'

As they walked together across the garden, Dylan said, 'Louise has been fine. She's apologised to Mona and they're getting on very well.'

'Yes,' she said.

'Were you surprised when Louise admitted she'd lied?'

'What do you mean? Lied?'

Dylan looked surprised. 'When she said that Mona was goading her about not having a father.'

'I don't understand.'

Dylan found himself becoming irritated. What was so difficult to understand? Speaking slowly, he said, 'Louise has admitted she was lying when she accused Mona of taunting her about not having a father. Mona did nothing of the kind.'

Sharon stopped dead. As she turned to him her dark, beautifully manicured eyebrows furrowed into an incredulous frown. 'She never told me that.'

'But that's why she came here to apologise to Mona, because she'd lied. Mona never said anything about Louise's father. Louise made it all up. Just as she did with Jade.'

'No. Louise told me she'd apologised for saying things about Mona and Eric. Perhaps you misunderstood.'

'No. I was there when she apologised to Mona. Louise made it perfectly clear that Mona didn't say what she was supposed to have said. And Louise told me that Jade didn't say the things she was supposed to have said, either.'

Sharon closed her eyes and her head went down. She sighed heavily. 'Then it rather looks like you were right about her. She's trying to get other kids into trouble.' Almost to herself, Sharon said, 'As if I haven't got enough to worry about.' She gave Dylan a determined look. 'I'm going to have words with her when we get home.'

'Not harsh ones, I hope.'

'What do you mean?'

'Don't you see? Louise has done something extraordinary today. She's admitted the truth, not just to Mona but to herself. She's admitted that she's the bully. It's a huge step forward. That's why I've been praising her all day.'

'You don't think I should tell her off for hiding from me why she apologised to Mona?'

'No. After lying about it for so long it's understandable that she couldn't face telling you the truth. But now that Louise has accepted she has this problem we need to find out why she feels it necessary to behave as she does. We need to know what the basis of the conflict is that's causing her to act in this way.'

Doubtfully, Sharon said, 'All right. If you think it's best, I'll let sleeping dogs lie.'

'That's not what I'm suggesting at all. I think you should talk to her about it. Tell her that you know now exactly why she apologised to Mona and praise her for it. Try to explore with her gently why she feels it necessary to falsely accuse people of giving her a hard time for not having a father.'

'OK,' said Sharon.

They entered the house and Dylan led Sharon into the art therapy room. As soon as they were in there, Sharon said, 'I'm very annoyed. You promised me that Louise would be kept safe and wouldn't be seen by anyone in the demo. But someone I know was in the street. They told me they saw Louise standing at an open window in full view of the crowd.'

Dylan was perplexed. 'I'm sorry, Sharon, I recall promising you that we'd keep her safe, and we have done. But I don't remember promising you she wouldn't be seen by people in the demo. You never asked me to promise that.'

Sharon rubbed her forehead. She seemed confused and agitated. 'No, you're right. I was the one who made Louise promise not to show herself to the crowd. I forgot. I'm sorry.'

Dylan looked at her, concerned. 'Are you all right?'

'Fine.'

He explained how intimidating the demonstration had been and that everyone had watched it from his studio because that had made it less threatening. He said, 'Louise never went near the window when I was there. She hung back in the room. But I had to come down stairs to meet the judges. Louise stayed there for a while with Zoe. Zoe told me that Louise deliberately went and leaned out of the window. She thought it rather strange. It was as though Louise wanted to be seen by the crowd.'

Sharon looked perturbed. 'I see.'

'Are you saying Zoe did something wrong?'

'No. Not at all.'

'Do you want me to fetch her so she can tell you herself?'

'No. That's not necessary.'

Dylan gazed at her searchingly. Why did he always feel that she was keeping something from him? He said, 'You didn't want people in the village to know Louise was in the rectory, while the demo was going on, is that it?'

'Yes. I'm still getting stick about her coming here from people I know. I thought I could cope with it, but it's too much.'

Dylan nodded.

'There's something else.'

'Oh?'

'I haven't slept all night because of what you said about Greg Maynard. Your suspicions about him are way out of line. Louise has never been alone with Greg. I'm always there. He only pops in for a few minutes to collect stuff to do with the Community Watch or the school governors. And he's never left alone with Louise. Anyway, she's in her room most of the time when he comes round. You've completely got the wrong end of the stick.'

Dylan was suitably chastened. He decided that the only way forward was to admit that he'd been mistaken. 'Yes. I obviously jumped to the wrong conclusions. It was just that the feelings thermometer indicated that Louise had some kind of intense conflict with him.'

'Well, she doesn't. He's never been left alone with her. And even if he were, I'm sure nothing like that would ever take place. Greg Maynard is a respectable man.'

He knew he'd been right to alert her to his suspicions, but it probably was insensitive to keep banging on about it. Besides, there might be another reason for Louise's behaviour. 'I'm sorry.'

'So you should be!'

Quietly, Dylan said, 'Actually, Louise drew a very interesting picture this afternoon.' He went over to a desk on the other side of the room where the painting had been left to dry, and brought it back to show Sharon. 'She said she was happy for you to see it.'

Dylan placed the painting, a wax crayon and paint resist, flat down on the desk. It was of open, hilly countryside in which a hot air balloon was soaring up into a clear blue sky. Two figures were in the balloon's basket. Trailing downwards from the balloon was a long rope and at the end of it, a girl was suspended in mid-air like a puppet worked by a single string. Several people on the ground below were staring and pointing at the figure on the end of the rope, and from their frenzied gestures it was evident that they were all suffering considerable shock and distress.

Sharon stared at the picture appreciatively.

'It's rather good, don't you think?' said Dylan.

'Yes. We quite often see hot air balloons around here. People like to take trips in them over the Wolds.'

Dylan nodded. He'd discussed the picture with Louise and she'd admitted that she was the person on the end of the balloon's rope. In some ways it was complementary to the image she'd created of herself trapped under the icy pond. In his experience, when a client created an image of flight it represented their urge for freedom and release from imprisonment. Also aspirations, ambitions. But here the flight was imperfect. Louise was being given a ride by the balloon but not the comfortable, joyride of the passengers in the balloon's basket. She'd had to snatch and grasp at the end of the rope in order to become airborne. Why had she taken such a hazardous course? To escape the onlookers on the ground who might be imprisoning her? In which case the risk might be worthwhile. It was certainly going to be an uncomfortable and perilous ride: the balloon might fly too high; Louise might lose consciousness and fall to earth. Was this a parallel with the loftiness of her artistic ambition? He saw the picture as a metaphor for her present predicament (whatever that was) and the difficult time she was having escaping from it. He communicated none of these reflections to Sharon. After the drama of last night they seemed to be getting on a little better and he'd no wish to antagonise her.

They were both quite close together now, leaning over the table and studying the picture. Her proximity was affecting him so profoundly he was reduced to thinking of her entirely in sexual clichés, as though she were an actress in a perfume ad.

He said, 'Sharon, I don't want to be bad friends with you.' Christ. He was even speaking in clichés, now!

She turned her head towards him slowly, and he felt the lick of her hazel eyes. 'Me neither.' She took a deep breath. 'Would you still like me to come with you to the concert?'

'Of course.'

'That's good. Because I'd still like to come. I'm sure Louise would too.'

'Great. But that won't be for a couple of weeks. Let's have a drink before then.'

'No. Don't rush things. I've a lot to think about.'

CHAPTER FIFTY ONE

Budeholme House, Lady Celia Brearley's Yorkshire residence, was situated ten miles from Leefdale and stood on rising ground overlooking the Vale of Pickering. It was set amidst the Budeholme Estate of approximately seven thousand acres. The estate consisted of five thousand acres of farmland; fifteen hundred acres of woodland and five hundred acres of parkland.

The house was built in 1592 by Barmston Randly on the proceeds of plunder. Randly was a privateer and favourite of Queen Elizabeth I. By the age of forty he'd amassed a considerable personal fortune from his share of captured "prizes": vessels and their cargoes belonging to other nations. In 1597, for his considerable contributions to Elizabeth's exchequer, Randly was created Marquis of Elderthorpe. His descendants maintained the house and extended the estate by further acts of plunder. The second Marquis appropriated large tracts of the American colony of Virginia and earned himself a further fortune from the growing and exporting of tobacco. In the eighteenth century the fourth Marquis plundered common land from the local sheep farmers and enclosed it. The fifth Marquis continued the Elderthorpe tradition into the nineteenth century by plundering human souls from villages in Africa and trafficking them to the West Indies to be sold as slaves.

In 1937 Budeholme House and its estate (but not the title) passed to Maurice Brearley, a nephew of the eighth Marquis. With the assistance of his young wife, Celia, Brearley restored the house and created forty two acres of gardens. These gardens came to be regarded as among the finest in the country. The house's interior was chiefly renowned for its Long Room: a ground floor gallery over two hundred feet long, extending for almost the entire length of the south side of the house. In 1953, Brearley was knighted for services to his country. He died in 1969 aged seventy six. Since his death, not a day had passed when Celia hadn't thought of him and cried.

Budeholme House was normally open to visitors from May until October. Today, however, it had been closed to them all day in order that the Long Room could be prepared for the Magnificent Britain awards ceremony. Whilst Lady Brearley, in the company of her fellow judges, had been trailing around

Leefdale, workers from all over the estate, helped by volunteers known as The Friends of Budeholme House, had been moving large, round tables into the Long Room, covering them with white linen tablecloths, and setting in place the plate and cutlery normally reserved for the wedding receptions, anniversaries and other numerous functions which provided the house with additional revenue. Appropriate wines had been chosen to complement the Budeholme House chef's menu (Pan fried scallops; Rack of lamb; fresh vegetables from the kitchen garden; raspberry coulis. Vegetarian options if preferred). Floral arrangements had been positioned at appropriate points around the Long Room and a small stage had been erected to serve as a podium. Large, free standing electric fans had also been brought in, for the weather was incredibly hot and with well over a hundred guests in attendance it was expected that the heat generated by so many bodies would become unbearable. All this had been accomplished by the time Lady Celia Brearley and her fellow judges had returned from their long and exhausting day. Yet despite being tired, irritable and in great pain, Lady Brearley was still able to summon the good grace to visit the Long Room, pronounce its transformation "excellent", and thank all the workers and volunteers for their splendid efforts.

Just two hours later, the ambience of the Long Room had been transformed yet again by the arrival of the guests. From all over England, Wales and Scotland they came (but not from Northern Ireland, which had caused not a little resentment); three privileged individuals representing each of the Magnificent Britain committees whose town or village had made it to the final. All dressed in their finery: evening dress or lounge suits (evening dress preferred), and all delighted to have gained admittance to the inner sanctum of Magnificent Britain. For what an enormous privilege it was to sit in the very Long Room where, in 1946, Sir Maurice Brearley himself had announced to Lady Celia his intention to relieve the dreariness and tedium of a post war, bombed out, grief stricken, bankrupted, socialist dominated, ration fixated, depressed Britain, by establishing a gardening contest that would get everyone pulling together and digging for victory again. What an honour to be fêted as a guest in that same Long Room: feeling you'd made it at last to the top of society's pinnacle, even if one couldn't actually be at the top table with Lady Brearley and had to break bread with some aggressively competitive, not to say uncouth, representatives from other towns and villages.

Earlier, all the guests had been personally welcomed into this most exclusive club by Budeholme's estate manager, Graham Spend. As the evening had progressed and the delicious courses, complemented by appropriate wines, had come and gone, many had found their dining companions to be not so bad after all. Gradually, the status anxiety and deferential formality had been replaced with something altogether more confident, relaxed and expansive. Liberated by the wine, some had even discovered a savoir faire they were unaware they possessed. For there was something about the Long Room and its multitude of servants that encouraged you to feel ever so slightly aristocratic; and many a guest sitting within its sixteenth century, mahogany panelled walls, observing their dining companions' faces limned and suffused with chivalric romance (an effect of flattering lighting and too much claret) had naturally assumed that their own features were exhibiting similar evidence of superior breeding. They'd looked through the mullioned windows of the Long Room, they'd gazed across vast expanses of perfect lawn, and knowing that all of this went on acre after acre, had allowed themselves to briefly indulge in the delicious fantasy that not only the Long Room, but Budeholme House and the Budeholme Estate in all its entirety really belonged to them. For a few short, blissful, exhilarating moments they experienced the delusion not just of feeling aristocratic but of actually being aristocrats; and they exulted in the transfiguring bliss that only the possession of land, money and position can bestow, regardless of whence it is derived.

The trouble with social climbing, thought Howard Roberts, looking around at the guests on his table, was that no matter how high you climbed you were always meeting the people you thought you'd left behind. Perhaps he would have been more charitable if Lucy Birkinshaw hadn't been sitting with them. What brass neck she had, turning up after what she'd done. It must be a very malevolent God indeed, he concluded, who'd deprived Leefdale's Magnificent Britain Sub-Committee of the late Walter Marsden and allowed the appalling Lucy Birkinshaw to become his replacement.

Lucy was already in place at Leefdale's table when Howard and Greg had arrived together. She'd decided that if she was in position already it would be hard for them to snub her. She was wrong, for Howard and Greg had agreed beforehand that they were not going to speak to her under any circumstances. When she'd wished them a polite good evening neither had acknowledged her. She'd therefore been forced to direct all her remarks to those at the table who were representing the villages of Fiddle and Larch-on-Ouse. This had caused these people some embarrassment. They thought it extremely odd that she was speaking to them yet had barely exchanged a word with her fellow committee members. However, they were too polite at first to mention it, and now, after an excellent dinner with plenty of wine, they were too inebriated to care. They, like so many others in the room, were only interested in finding out whether their town or village was to receive a medal.

Now that the meal was over and the tables cleared, they didn't have very long to wait. Graham Spend had already left the table he'd shared with Celia and other dignitaries and was walking somewhat unsteadily to the podium.

'Now we're for it,' said Greg, who was on his sixth glass of wine.

Spend was a man in late middle age. He had a surprisingly vigorous head of iron grey hair and angular features which gave him the look of a fading matinee idol from the 1950s. When he spoke into the microphone his voice was unexpectedly light. He thanked Lady Brearley for her generous hospitality, and then delivered a paean to both her and Sir Maurice for their achievements at restoring Budeholme House and its gardens and establishing the Magnificent Britain Competition. Spend then delivered several anecdotes which were intended to show his long and intimate connection with the Brearleys. He obviously thought these humorous, but they only demonstrated his pomposity and ingratiating obsequiousness.

Spend's speech may have disappointed in many respects but it had the great virtue of being short. Thankfully, he was soon asking Lady Brearley to come to the podium to hand out the awards.

There was a spontaneous thunder of applause as Lady Brearley covered with some difficulty, and yet great dignity, the short distance from her table to the podium. She wore a full length evening gown in champagne satin complemented by a discreet diamond necklace and diamond earrings. She refused all assistance in mounting the podium, and when Spend relinquished the microphone and she turned to survey those assembled, a smile transformed her wrinkled face and her eyes glittered with the gratification and mischief of those who relish the public's attention. Anyone who had little imagination and was unaware of the enormous demands made upon her by her marriage to Sir Maurice would have assumed that although now old and frail, she'd led a privileged and untroubled life. Nothing could have been further from the truth.

Age, not nervousness, caused the typewritten speech in Lady Brearley's hand to quiver slightly as she started to speak. She began by welcoming everyone to the fifty-fifth Magnificent Britain awards ceremony and described her astonishment at the fact that every year the horticultural displays throughout the UK's cities, towns and villages seemed to get better and better. She reminded everyone that representatives of the thirty six towns and villages who'd reached the finals of the competition were present in the Long Room that evening. In addition, there were specially invited guests who were to receive awards for their personal contribution to Magnificent Britain over the years. Smiling graciously, she said, 'As you can see, we are in for quite a long evening. So I must ask you to keep your acceptance speeches short.'

Celia went on to explain that this was one of the busiest times of the year for her and all of those involved in the competition. 'Tomorrow I shall be in London to present the awards to the winners of the London Boroughs and the UK's major cities. On Sunday I shall be flying to Dublin. There I will be presenting the awards to the winners from Northern Ireland and Eire. This is most important. It will be the first time that people representing villages, towns and cities from both Eire and Northern Ireland will take part in a joint Magnificent Britain awards ceremony. It is a sign of the new spirit of co-operation that has developed between Eire and the Six Counties since the implementation of the Good Friday Agreement. The awards ceremony will be a magnificent achievement not only in itself but because it is fully in accord with the values and spirit of Magnificent Britain. Maurice would have been so proud of it. Firstly because his ancestors owned estates in Northern and Southern Ireland. But most importantly because such a joint ceremony is a marvellous example of the spirit of co-operation Maurice hoped Magnificent Britain would foster and promote. For Maurice, and myself, Magnificent Britain was always intended to be much, much more than just a gardening competition. For Maurice's greatest mission in life was the prevention of conflict.'

There was a flutter of sarcastic laughter from one of the tables in the middle of the room. All eyes turned towards the person responsible: Lucy Birkinshaw. She was finding the notion that Sir Maurice Brearley, a former arms manufacturer and trader, had been instrumental in the development of world peace, deeply ironic. Howard and Greg glared at her. The others at her table tried to distance themselves by fixing their eyes determinedly on Lady Brearley.

Undeterred, Celia returned to her theme. 'Maurice inaugurated the Magnificent Britain Competition for several reasons. The idea came to him in 1946. It was just a year after the Second World War ended. London and our other major cities had been reduced to rubble. Society was fractured. There were shortages everywhere. Life was bleak. Maurice wanted to encourage a sense of community spirit and hopefully create a new world in which such a catastrophe could never happen again. And what better way to do so than establish a gardening contest which would bring communities together and brighten the gloom with that combination of art and science that gives us the beauty of horticulture. The spirit of Magnificent Britain is to promote peace, reconciliation and harmony through gardening.'

Lady Brearley stopped reading the anodyne speech specifically written for her by Graham Spend and looked around the Long Room, seeking Maurice. Having swept the tables her gaze took in the margins of the room around which the waiters and other temporary staff who'd been hired for the evening were standing, waiting disinterestedly for the event to end so that they could go home. But there was no sign of Maurice amongst them. Strange. She was certain she'd glimpsed him earlier, hovering near the representatives from Leefdale. But no, he'd gone. Very well, she would have to continue without him.

'From those small beginnings this competition has grown into a global movement. Countries as diverse as Israel and Syria have their own form of the Magnificent Britain Competition. How proud my husband would have been of this achievement if he were alive. How delighted he'd have been to see so many countries in the world uniting their populations and coming together with other nation states through the common interest of horticulture and a gardening competition. I may be naïve but I look forward to perhaps one day hosting a joint Israeli and Palestinian awards ceremony on the lines of the one I shall be attending in Dublin on Sunday.'

At this point someone said quite audibly, 'If she thinks that she must be bloody deluded.'

The remark had been made by Greg Maynard to Howard Roberts. Unfortunately, Greg was now into his second bottle of wine which had given him a laggard grin and an inability to appreciate the loudness of his whisper.

Raising her voice and directing it towards those sitting at Major Roberts' table, Lady Brearley continued. 'And my greatest inspiration for that ambition must be the wonderful example of the West-Eastern Divan Orchestra. It was founded in 1999 by Argentinian-Israeli pianist and conductor Daniel Barenboim and his friend, the Palestinian philosopher and musician, Edward Said. It includes members from the Palestinian territories, Israel and other Arab countries, and is an excellent example for those of us who believe that the resolution of conflict can best be achieved through art, education and bringing together those with political and religious differences to share the same cultural platforms. It is a great source of optimism. And we must always remain optimistic in dark times. Because with optimism we can achieve anything. Who would have thought that one day we would have a Good Friday Agreement? Or that Magnificent Britain would hold a joint award ceremony in Dublin for the people of Eire and the North? But this is what can be achieved if we work together in the right spirit.'

Every word of Lady Brearley's speech was being captured on video. Brian had set up two cameras in the Long Room. One was focussed on the podium from which Lady Brearley was delivering her speech and would be presenting the awards. The other camera was discreetly shooting footage of the guests.

As Lady Brearley continued with her speech, Howard Roberts stared at Brian malevolently. Like some cruel and tormenting form of synecdoche, the man's bloody video camera seemed to be the part that represented the whole of his misfortunes. First, there'd been all those video cameras recording his exit from The Old Rectory with blood streaming from his nose. An image not only shown on numerous news bulletins but reproduced in virtually every national newspaper. Then there'd been all those video cameras outside Rooks Nest, recording him punching Peter, and convincing the nation that he was nothing but a man with a violent temper who wasn't averse to thumping his philandering, hypocrite of a son-in-law. Next, had been that incident when the slimy rat, Brian, had taken sly shots of him and Isobel as they'd scuttled into the minders' BMW to avoid the demonstrators outside The Old Rectory. It had made him and Isobel look like craven cowards.

And then had come the greatest humiliation of all: Lady Brearley's announcement as they were lunching in The Woldsman, that Lucy Birkinshaw and Sid Arkwright had made serious allegations against him which could result in Leefdale's disqualification from Magnificent Britain. He'd had no choice but to vigorously defend himself and, of course, the whole grovelling performance had been caught on camera by that Brian bastard who, naturally, just happened to be videoing them as they were eating lunch. After that the judges had quite understandably been in a filthy mood. Instead of spending the afternoon selecting the winner and runners up in the small village category, they'd had to investigate Lucy and Sid's complaints, which involved making extensive enquiries and taking several statements, as well as subjecting Howard to a lengthy interrogation. And had Celia protected him? Not bloody likely. She'd even allowed the Brian scumbag to video his interrogation by the four of them, because in her view "a video recording would make an excellent record". He'd had no option but to agree. What else could he have done? If he'd refused he might as well have tattooed a big "Guilty" all over his forehead. Why had God decreed his nemesis to come in the shape of Lucy Birkinshaw?

Howard's gaze returned to Lucy. Had she and that ridiculous Sid Arkwright had their complaints accepted by the judges? Was that why she was looking so smug and self-righteous? Well, he'd never give her the satisfaction of asking her. Not that there was any need. Although nothing had been said or hinted at, Howard was certain it would shortly be announced that Leefdale had been disqualified and the reasons revealed to all the Magnificent Britain luminaries gathered together in the Long Room. Then the shit would hit the fan. Everyone would know that the chairman of Leefdale's committee had tried to influence the result: it would be revealed to the whole of the Magnificent Britain movement that he'd organised the demonstration outside the rectory in which members of his own committee had taken part; and everyone would believe that he'd behaved like a despot, sending gangs into people's gardens to improve them against their wishes because he was obsessed with winning.

'Of course, many people think that because I live in Budeholme House I'm shut away in some sort of ivory tower,' Lady Brearley continued. 'But I wish to reassure all of you that as a guest judge I have visited many urban areas and inner city boroughs and been inspired by all the work they've done and the superb results they've achieved, sometimes in the most unpropitious circumstances.'

Lady Brearley's speech was continuing for far too long in the view of many in the audience who were listening to it with barely concealed irritation and were impatient to hear whether or not their own town or village had won. Howard consoled himself with the knowledge that the smallest villages always had their result announced first. At least it wouldn't be long before he learnt Leefdale's fate.

Greg Maynard refilled his glass. He too was listening to Lady Brearley's speech with only half an ear. However, unlike Howard, his concerns weren't that Leefdale would lose: he'd already accepted that as a certainty. No, he was too preoccupied with his own sense of shame and guilt. Could that person who'd behaved so badly at the demonstration really have been him? Such behaviour seemed to belong to a totally different individual: a man consumed with hatred. It had left him with a tremendous sense of self-disgust, as though he'd taken part in something sordid or obscene. As long as he'd remained convinced Louise wasn't in the rectory and bearing the brunt of the mob's abuse, he hadn't felt it necessary to consider the feelings of those inside the house at all. He hadn't even thought of them as people: just impediments to Leefdale's fifth consecutive victory. But seeing Louise at that window, seeing the look on her face, sensing her revulsion and horror at his actions, had suddenly made him aware that it was sentient human beings that he was doing this to. The shock of this epiphany had remained with him long after the demo had ended, and made him feel the absolute wrongness of what he'd done. Louise's presence in the rectory had personalised it. Even now he couldn't get the image of her appearance at that window out of his mind. It reminded him that the people in the rectory were flesh and blood, and he was deeply ashamed of what he and the other demonstrators had done to them. He was also infuriated that those political activists had influenced him personally to behave in such a thuggish way. He was resentful at Howard too, for inveigling him into demonstrating when it was against the rules. It was like awakening from some nightmare in which he'd dreamt he'd been a guard in a concentration camp, only to be told that the nightmare had really happened and the people he'd murdered had actually died. The only way he seemed to be able to blot any of it out was by constantly filling and emptying his glass.

Lady Brearley's speech ended and was followed by spontaneous and deafening applause: an indication of the relief felt by most people that it was over. Lady Brearley remained on stage but went and took her seat next to a small table on which were displayed the cups and medals coveted by so many of those gathered in the Long Room. Her role now was to hand out the prizes to the lucky recipients.

Graham Spend returned to the stage and unctuously thanked Lady Brearley for her wonderful speech. 'And now, ladies and gentlemen,' he said, 'we come to the principal business of the evening. The annual Magnificent Britain awards for villages and small towns. The first finalists to receive awards are in the small villages' category. It gives me great pleasure to ask Judges Kate Smith, Ned Pugh and Patrick McSweeney to please come to the stage and announce the winners.'

Every year the judges were required not only to announce the winners and runners-up in each category, but also to provide some objective horticultural justification for their often arbitrary and subjective decisions. All this added considerably to the length of the ceremony. As groups of judges clunked on and off the stage, conversations would resume, glasses would be topped up and chairs would scrape as disinterested members of the audience whose awards were in categories to be announced later, took the opportunity to visit the lavatory or go outside for a smoke or a breath of fresh air. It was against such a background of noise that Kate Smith, Pugh and McSweeney arrived on stage.

Graham Spend appealed for quiet. Kate Smith then took her place at the microphone. By profession she was an auctioneer and was used to dominating large crowds. She looked poised and confident in her long black evening gown, which had the additional benefit of making her appear several inches taller and slimmer.

'Before I give you the results in the small village category, I have an announcement to make. I have to tell you that today we received a very serious complaint. As we were adjudicating in the village of Leefdale, we were approached by Ms Lucy Birkinshaw, a Leefdale resident and member of its Magnificent Britain Sub-Committee. She was accompanied by Mr Sid Arkwright, a fellow resident of Leefdale. Ms Birkinshaw made three specific allegations. Firstly, that Major Howard Roberts, the chairman of Leefdale's Magnificent Britain Sub-Committee, was responsible for organising a demonstration against the residents of The Old Rectory in Leefdale. She alleged he'd done this because he was convinced that their neglect of the rectory's gardens would affect the village's chances of winning for the fifth consecutive year. Ms Birkinshaw claimed that the Major hoped the demonstration would persuade the judges to award Leefdale the gold medal despite the rectory's sorry state. Incidentally, all of the judges witnessed this demonstration and we all agree that it was large, aggressive and deeply disturbing. We all felt it to be inimical to the spirit of co-operation and cohesion which Sir Maurice Brearley hoped to promote and encourage when he established this competition.'

Howard faced down the disapproving stares directed at him across the table by Lucy Birkinshaw and the representatives of Fiddle and Larch-on-Ouse. My God, we're for the chop now, he thought. But what did it matter anyway? He'd never be involved in another Magnificent Britain. As soon as the awards evening was over, he and Isobel would collect their bags and suitcases and place them in the boot of their minders' BMW. Then they'd be driven through the night to a temporary safe house. Once installed there he would shave his head and moustache and become unrecognizable as the Major Roberts who'd thumped his son-in-law live on News 24. The incident would fade from memory and people would forget what he looked like. Tomorrow a removal van would arrive at Rooks Nest and those protecting him and Isobel would arrange for all their belongings and furniture to be put into storage until it was time for them to be shipped to their new location, wherever that might be. Rooks Nest would be put on the market and it would be as though he and Isobel had never existed.

'Ms Birkinshaw's second allegation was that four members of the Magnificent Britain Sub-Committee, but not Howard Roberts himself, had actually taken part in the demonstration outside the rectory. These members were Sue Rawdon, Janet Pinkney, Fred Birch and the Vice Chair, Greg Maynard.

'Miss Birkinshaw's final allegation was that coercion had been used by Howard Roberts and other members of Leefdale's Magnificent Britain Sub-Committee to persuade all residents of Leefdale to take part in the competition, regardless of their wishes. She alleged that any resident who didn't participate was subject to compulsion and had their garden improved by force. Mr Arkwright verified this. He described how a gang of men had suddenly appeared at his house a few days previously and begun to tidy up and re-organise his garden without his consent.

'These were serious allegations which, if proved, would have meant that Rule 31 of the Magnificent Britain Competition had been infringed. This rule, as you probably know, disqualifies any community competing in the competition if one or more of its members has intervened directly to influence the result. My fellow judges and I took these allegations most seriously and, as you would expect, made a thorough and extensive investigation. The allegations were put to Major Roberts and he denied them. He assured the judges that it was not himself but the deputy chairman of the Magnificent Britain Sub-Committee, Greg Maynard, who'd planned and organised the demonstration outside the rectory at the behest of a large number of Leefdale residents.'

Howard caught Greg's eye. They'd both agreed beforehand that Greg would have to carry the can for the demonstration.

'Major Roberts produced for us the minutes of the Extraordinary Meeting of the Leefdale parish council held on Tuesday 17th July 2001. These clearly show that he, as chairman, publicly disassociated himself from the planned demonstration and also refused requests by the organisers to use the parish council's newsletter, The Leeflet, to publicly appeal for support for the demonstration. Major Roberts admits that he suspected Sue Rawdon, Janet Pinkney, Fred Birch and Greg Maynard would take part in the demonstration, but insists that they and he were unaware that by doing so they would infringe any of the competition's rules and certainly not Rule 31. He is certain that if any of them had appreciated this they'd have taken no part in the demonstration. This morning, as soon as he realised from his conversations with the judges that Leefdale faced possible disqualification, he immediately contacted Greg Maynard on his mobile phone to establish if he and the others were present at the demonstration. When he learned that they indeed were, he insisted they withdraw from it immediately, which they did. Certainly, as far as the judges are concerned, when we visited The Old Rectory as part of our adjudication we saw no committee members who were involved in the demonstration.

'Major Roberts categorically denies that force was ever used to improve any of the village's gardens. He referred us to his column in the June edition of The Leeflet in which he offered assistance to those in the village who couldn't, for any reason, find the time or energy to maintain their gardens. He told us a number of villagers responded and took advantage of this offer, and a team of helpers was sent in to help put their gardens in order. He insists that at no time was anyone's garden entered unlawfully, without permission or improved without their consent, and those who did receive help in this way were extremely grateful for it. We, the judges, found no evidence to cause us to doubt this. We also investigated the specific allegation by Sid Arkwright, that his garden had been altered without his consent. Our investigations revealed that Mr Arkwright's wife had, in fact, without his knowledge, contacted the Magnificent Britain Sub-Committee and asked for assistance in tidying up the front garden because, in her words, "She was sick and tired of the state of it!"'

This was met with a huge gale of laughter that seemed to blast up and down the Long Room. When it subsided, Kate continued. 'Mr Arkwright was unaware of this when he made his complaint.' Again, there was more laughter. 'When he learnt that his garden had been tidied up at the express request of his wife he immediately withdrew his allegation. In the circumstances the judges have decided that neither Rule 31 nor any of the competition's other rules have been breached and Leefdale has therefore not been disqualified.'

A shocked silence followed this announcement. Expressions of disbelief could then be heard in every part of the Long Room. But no-one was more incredulous than Lucy. She was so horrified at the rejection of her allegations and the evidence in support of them that she didn't even notice Greg Maynard give a whoop of glee and blatantly give her the finger.

Lucy had been prepared to tolerate Kate Smith's ponderous, quasi-judicious account of the investigation because she was convinced it would conclude with the announcement of Howard Roberts' disqualification. Now that it hadn't, she was bitterly disappointed. But she had to ask herself, why was she so surprised? Hadn't her long experience of civil disobedience and passive resistance taught her that when things got ugly the establishment always closed ranks and the first casualty was the truth? Why had she expected it to be any different just because it was a gardening contest?

No wonder Howard couldn't meet her eye and his features even now still bore a revealing look of disbelief. Yes, he knew he was as guilty as hell and was probably still wondering how he'd got away with it! Her only consolation was knowing that he and Greg obviously wished to triumph publicly in their victory over her, but were constrained because all eyes in the room were on their table. Yet nothing altered the fact that she'd lost. She felt humiliated and demoralised. Not just because she'd lost, but because she'd been naive enough to believe that the judges' petty little enquiry into Roberts' wrongdoing would be any less of a whitewash than all those great judicial enquiries that were supposed to change things and deliver justice. Her trust in authority had yet again been misplaced. Once again she'd been proved a fool for placing her faith in the powers that be.

'We're in with a chance now,' Greg whispered to Howard out of the corner of his mouth as he simultaneously gave Lucy the evil eye.

Howard shook his head. Even though, astonishingly, the allegations against him had been thrown out, nothing could change the fact that the rectory's gardens were a complete mess. Between them, Mr Bourne and his friends had utterly ruined Leefdale's chances of another gold medal.

'Quiet please,' Kate Smith was saying. She had a surprisingly commanding presence and the packed room fell instantly silent. 'We now come to the results of the 2001 Magnificent Britain small village category, which is for villages with a population of less than five hundred inhabitants.'

Kate's expression had been serious and grave but now she had a beaming smile. 'Third place has been awarded to a village which throughout the competition has shown consistently high standards of floral decoration and superb examples of riverside horticulture.'

'That's definitely not us,' Greg informed Howard. Leefdale's nearest river was ten miles from the village.

'Would the chair of the Kirkbuchan Magnificent Britain committee please come to the stage to accept their award, which is, of course, the bronze medal.'

There was huge applause during which Howard didn't know whether to be relieved or depressed. At least Leefdale was still in with a chance of first place.

A middle-aged man wearing Scottish evening dress complete with tartan kilt and sporran, moved through the room to the podium. He accepted the bronze medal from Lady Brearley and held it aloft, triumphantly.

'Straight out of "Braveheart",' said Greg loudly, and chuckled. Howard decided that Greg was becoming a liability. At least Lucy had the good grace to keep quiet.

After a brief expression of thanks, the man in the kilt departed with his medal and Kate returned to the microphone. She said, 'The village which has been awarded second place in this category has been specially commended for its outstanding topiary, which is to be found not just in its gardens but throughout the village thoroughfares and greens. We were also impressed with this village's bulb planting initiatives which engaged the whole community, and for the floral displays in its business premises.' She paused for dramatic effect. 'Would the chair of the Weasle Magnificent Britain committee please come up and receive the silver medal, their award for second place.'

There was loud applause as the representative from Weasle, an attractive blonde woman in her late thirties, ascended the stage. She received the award and immediately embarked on a long speech of thanks which was firmly but politely cut short by Kate Smith who, apologising, told her that if everyone who received an award made a speech longer than a minute the ceremony would go on into the early hours of the morning.

Howard was rigid with impatience and apprehension. How he wished she would get on with it. And yet, curiously, a part of him wanted the uncertainty to last forever, so that he could at least be spared the knowledge that Leefdale had lost.

'And now, we come to the award of first prize in this category, the Magnificent Britain gold medal.'

Howard surveyed the demeanour of everyone around his table. The people from Fiddle and Larch-on-Ouse knew they were still in with a chance: they were hunched expectantly forward, their body language expressing hope and dread. By contrast, Greg Maynard was slouching back in his chair. Lucy merely looked politely interested.

'The judges were impressed by the profusion, variety and perfect condition of the floral displays throughout this village. Especially its unprecedented number of hanging baskets.'

At this, Howard experienced a tiny resurgence of hope. Leefdale had hanging baskets in abundance. Could it just be...?

But Howard's rekindled optimism was extinguished by Kate's next remark. 'The judges would also like to commend the choice of this village's three exemplary gardens, which provided such magnificent contrasts in terms of colour and design.'

Now Howard was sure they'd lost. There was no way The Old Rectory deserved to be included in that sort of commendation.

'Special praise goes to Mr and Mrs Marsh of Twinings for their herbaceous borders and spectacular display of sweet peas.'

Howard and Greg suddenly stopped slumping, sat up and looked at each other with mounting joy and incredulity. Lucy's spine seemed to have stiffened. She felt her head go back, her mouth drop slightly open.

Kate continued. 'Also to Mr and Mrs Sedgemoor at Holme End for their authentic Tudor knot garden. However, Lady Brearley has specifically asked me to point out that the judges' greatest commendation goes to Zoe Fitzgerald, Dylan Bourne and the rest of the staff and students at the Leefdale Inclusion Unit in The Old Rectory for their exciting sculpture garden. In the judges' opinion the sculpture garden miraculously combines traditional horticulture and modern materials to create elaborate structures which provide an entirely different kind of horticultural experience.'

'She's taking the piss,' hissed Greg Maynard to Howard Roberts. He started to get to his feet and was about to sarcastically shout out "Hear, hear" when Howard silenced him with a restraining hand on his arm and pulled him back into his seat.

'The village which is to receive the gold medal is no stranger to the award, having received it on four previous occasions.'

Howard, Greg and Lucy knew then beyond all doubt.

'And so, this year's first prize in the small village category is awarded for the fifth consecutive year to... Leefdale, in East Yorkshire!'

There was instantaneous applause, which Kate Smith ignored. Speaking over it, with the assistance of the microphone and an extremely loud voice, she said, 'A truly historic achievement. No village in this category has won the gold medal for five consecutive years. Will the chair of Leefdale's Magnificent Britain committee please come up and receive the gold medal on behalf of their village.'

Howard stood and moved towards the podium with the emotions of a condemned man who'd just been reprieved as the noose was about to be placed around his neck. He moved slowly, as though underwater, with the noise of thunderous applause in his ears. People were on their feet now, applauding, cheering; and as he passed between the tables on his way to the stage, he found himself being thumped heartily on the back by complete strangers as congratulations were bawled in his ear.

As he stepped onto the podium Kate Smith shook his hand and stood aside. Lady Celia Brearley was already on her feet, the perspex case containing the gold medal in her hand. She held it out to him, and as he accepted it, he said, smiling broadly, 'Thank you, Celia, thank you. You've no idea what this means to me.'

I didn't do it for you, she thought. I did it to restore peace and harmony to your village. I did it because Maurice always said Leefdale had suffered enough.

'Congratulations, Howard,' Celia said, smiling graciously. She nodded in the direction of the video camera which was in position in the middle of the Long Room, directly opposite the podium. 'Would you mind showing the medal to the camera?'

'Certainly.' Howard turned around fully, so that he was no longer sideways on to the camera lens and held up the gold medal. The applause increased. He started feeling in his inside pocket for the short speech he'd written long ago, when he'd had good reason to hope Leefdale would win the gold medal for the fifth consecutive time. And then, he remembered: before coming out that evening he'd torn it to pieces. It lay in shreds at the bottom of the wastepaper basket in his study at Rooks Nest. He forced himself to remain calm as he frantically tried to recall its main points.

Celia hadn't noticed his discomfiture: her eyes were on the far end of the Long Room where Maurice had just walked in. How lovely to see him applauding so vigorously.

Howard began his brief speech of thanks but Lucy couldn't bear to listen. To audible gasps, she dramatically rose from her seat and set off out of the Long Room. But to do this she had to pass by Greg's chair. As she did so, he reached out and grasped her hand in a sadistically tight grip. She rounded on him with a scathing look. He stared back at her, eyes heavy lidded with drink and full of gloating triumph. In a loud and drunken slur, he said, 'Well Lucy, we won after all, despite your best efforts to stop us.' Watched by the whole room she jerked her wrist from his grasp and retorted loudly, 'Little things please little minds, Greg! And little trousers, fit little behinds!'

Ignoring the instantaneous laughter, she set off again towards the exit, weaving her way between the tables with every eye in the room following her. What did she care? She could stand it no longer. Her only concern was to get out of there. It was intolerable that the judges had refused to believe what she and Sid Arkwright had told them. They should have made an example of

Roberts and Maynard and disqualified Leefdale. That was what justice demanded. Why did the bad guys always win? Never the good guys? Of course it was wonderful that the kids in the rectory weren't going to be blamed for losing the village its fifth gold medal, but she'd have been far happier to see Leefdale lose, rather than see oppression ignored and dishonesty rewarded. Why was it that people who broke the rules always won and those who played by the rules and expected others to follow them, always lost?

She was quite near the exit now, and her path had brought her close to the podium on which Major Howard Roberts was in full flow with his self-aggrandising speech of thanks. Until that moment her only intention had been to put as much distance between herself and the scene of her disappointment and humiliation as possible. But when Roberts asserted with false modesty that he could take no credit for the gold medal because it was the people of Leefdale who'd won it, yet insinuated it would never have happened without him and his marvellous organisation, Lucy saw red. She stopped and turned slowly to face the podium. Howard hadn't quite finished his concluding remarks, but he stopped and looked nervously at Lucy's tall, imposing figure. In a strained but determined voice, Lucy said, 'The enquiry into my allegations was a disgrace. A complete whitewash. But I'm delighted that Leefdale has won. If nothing else, it means that at least now you'll stop hounding those poor people in The Old Rectory and give them some peace!' Then, with a contemptuous toss of her head she turned away and looking neither to the right nor to the left walked imperiously towards the exit. Her grim expression didn't alter even when Howard resumed the microphone, smiled urbanely and said, 'I apologise for the interruption, ladies and gentlemen. Let no-one tell you that gardening hasn't its fair share of conflict.' There were understanding murmurs, a little wry laughter and more applause.

Lucy came to the double doors of the Long Room which, like all the other doors and windows on this unbearably hot night, had been flung wide open. Still looking straight ahead, and walking in a red mist, Lucy passed out of the Long Room and entered a small adjacent lobby. Here, she turned immediately right, following the route which would eventually lead her to the Grand Entrance Hall and, thankfully, out of Budeholme House. To do so she had to pass through a series of interconnected rooms. As she passed though the Grand Dining Room she was aware that someone was running after her.

'Just a moment!'

She turned and didn't immediately recognise the tall, ginger haired, bespectacled figure. And then she remembered. Of course! He was the video director that Mary Arkwright had laughingly referred to as "Cecil B.de Mille".

'Miss Birkinshaw?'

'Yes?'

'You're the one who made the complaint about Major Roberts, aren't you?'

'Yes.'

'I'm sorry it didn't get anywhere.'

'So am I.'

'My name's Brian.' He offered her his card. 'My contact details are on there. Would you be prepared to be interviewed by me on camera about your complaints? For a documentary I'm making?'

'Why?'

'I'll explain all about that if you agree. It would have to be done privately. I wouldn't want Lady Brearley to find out about it.'

Lucy was intrigued. 'I see.'

He shot a quick, furtive look over his shoulder. 'I've got to get back. Call me, if you're interested.'

Lucy said, 'For what good it will do.'

But she took his card, anyway.

CHAPTER FIFTY TWO

'Eric had no right to do that,' said Toni. 'I told him in confidence.'
'He was very concerned about you.'
'But what I told him was private. He shouldn't have said anything.'
'Perhaps not. But he wanted me to know how unhappy you were. He was concerned you might resign. None of us want that. It would be a terrible loss for us if you left.'

Dylan and Toni were standing together on the patio in the rectory's rear garden. Shouts and whoops of excited laughter were coming from Sheldon, Khaled and Scarlett who were playing a hectic game of tag amongst the sculptures. Darkness had fallen and the sculpture park was now lit by several solar powered lamps which were stuck into the ground at various intervals. They cast an eerie, phosphorescent light upon the still and silent sculptures. Against the surrounding darkness these seemed alien, disturbing forms which contrasted strongly with the moving outlines of the chasing humans. In the centre of the lawn a small knot of people was gathered around Lucy Birkinshaw. She was regaling Zoe and several of the teenagers with her amusing account of the awards evening. Close by, the statues of Demeter and Apollo gleamed ghostly white now they'd been cleaned of all traces of mud and dirt.

After departing the awards ceremony, Lucy had called Dylan from the car park at Budeholme House and told him that Leefdale had won the gold medal in the small village category. She'd also repeated to him the many positive remarks the judges had made about the staff and students of the inclusion unit, including Lady Brearley's fulsome appreciation of the rectory's "exciting sculpture garden". Dylan's astonishment had quickly given way to delight. He'd immediately invited Lucy to the rectory to celebrate with a cup of coffee. However, it wasn't coffee that Lucy was holding in her hand now as she delivered her amusing anecdotes but red wine.

Dylan returned his attention to Toni. Seeing that her expression had softened slightly, he continued with his flattery. He told her how much she was appreciated, that she was doing a wonderful job and everyone valued her indispensable knowledge and experience. He praised her for the advances in literacy and numeracy the clients had achieved as a direct consequence of her teaching skills. 'Scarlett was telling me yesterday that she could never tell the time until you taught her. And you've even started Jake reading.'

Toni was suborned. She suspected that Dylan was laying the compliments on with a trowel to keep her at the unit. But even so, she couldn't fail to be flattered and gratified. She had a pathological need to feel wanted and approved of, which was why she strove so hard to improve the lives of others. Dylan's generous and heartfelt words almost moved her to tears.

'Thank you for saying that. I really appreciate it. These kids are a challenge but I get such a lot of satisfaction from their achievements.'

'That's why you mustn't leave us.'

She hesitated. 'Yes, but you don't know what it's like when Cynthia, that's my mum, puts the emotional pressure on. She keeps telling me how old and lonely she is and I've abandoned her just when she needs me most. It makes me feel so guilty. It always has. I'm really quite assertive when it involves my job or dealing with people professionally, but when it comes to Cynthia I'm unable to stand up for myself. I can't say what I want and express my needs. But Zoe's been incredibly helpful in that respect.'

'Zoe?'

'Oh yes. I had a long chat with her about my problems today. She's helping me find my "inner guardian".' Seeing Dylan's blank expression, she continued, 'It's the part of you that acts selfishly to protect your interests and makes sure your assertive rights are protected. It's the thing that stops you being manipulated and controlled by others.'

'That's good,' said Dylan. He was familiar with the concept but not Zoe's specific term for it. It occurred to him that it wasn't so very different to his father's metaphor of the sliver of ice that should be at the centre of every artist's soul.

'Yes, my talk with Zoe has helped me enormously,' Toni went on. 'She's made me realise that Cynthia is a very controlling person. I've always known it but Zoe's helped me confront it as a reality. She's also given me some techniques to help me be more assertive with Cynthia so when I next meet her face to face, she won't walk all over me again.'

Dylan had the sense that his own discipline was being overlooked and marginalised. 'Art therapy could help too, you know. If you wished, I'd be very willing to take you on as a client and develop a programme appropriate to your needs.'

Toni looked stricken. 'That's very kind of you and I'm sure it would be helpful. But I'd have to draw pictures, wouldn't I? The kids would know then that I was receiving help and I'd hate that.'

'No-one need know anything. It could be done very discreetly.'

'Even so, I think it's better for me to work with Zoe. She's given me some drama therapy techniques I can use when I'm alone. I've already tried them and they're really helpful. Particularly one: it involves using a cushion and an empty chair. Do you know it?'

'Yes, I think I do,' Dylan said, thoughtfully. His eyes came to rest briefly on Zoe, who was engrossed in conversation with Lucy Birkinshaw.

'I think I've misjudged Zoe,' said Toni. 'I never got on with her. Always resented her. I think that's because she represents what I've always lacked: the ability to be spontaneous and uninhibited. I suppose I've always feared Zoe would make me confront that inadequacy in myself, and it's made me rather afraid of her.'

Dylan was becoming slightly irritated by all these plaudits for Zoe. 'That's true,' he said, 'but there's more than one way to confront someone. The trick is to prevent other people from dominating and controlling your behaviour without violating their rights and driving them away.'

'Yes. Zoe's told me all about the difference between being non-assertive, assertive and aggressive. She explained it all so well. She said that empathy's an important factor too, because I must make it clear to mum, I mean Cynthia, that I respect her point of view. I tried it on Cynthia tonight. I told her it upset me that she was lonely and I understood why she wanted me to come home and live with her, but I also made it clear I had a right to pursue my own life and career independently. I told her I had an important job to do in Leefdale, so I wouldn't be coming back to London any time soon.'

'Excellent. How did she take it?'

'She didn't like it but she couldn't say anything because she knew I could see it from her point of view. At least we didn't end up rowing.'

'Good.'

'I wouldn't have been able to do that without Zoe's help. And the great thing is that this problem with Cynthia has made Zoe and I friends. Isn't it wonderful?'

Dylan said, 'It certainly is, if it keeps you here with us.'

Toni wondered what he'd say if she told him that he was the most important reason she was staying at the unit, and if it hadn't been for her obsession with him she'd have lost the battle of attrition with her mother weeks ago. It wasn't the kids or the work that kept her there, it was him. She couldn't bear the thought of never seeing him again. She was already regretting turning down his offer of art therapy. It would have given her lots of opportunities to be alone with him. But what was the point if nothing ever came of it? She was well aware that men weren't attracted to her in the same way they lusted over women like Zoe and Sharon. When she entered a room in the company of women like that, the men's eyes zoomed in on them as though she didn't exist. But you never knew: perhaps Zoe's assertion techniques might work on Dylan too. For a reckless, crazy moment she contemplated seizing the opportunity and revealing her feelings to him. She immediately told herself not to be so stupid. She said, 'Don't worry, I'm not going anywhere. I'm determined to put an end to

Cynthia's dominance over me. I'm 34 years old. I've a right to an independent life of my own. Anyway, Eric says I've already done the hardest thing by moving miles away from her.'

'He's right.' Dylan glanced towards Zoe again. 'But even though you can move hundreds of miles away from someone it's not the complete answer if they can still mess with your head.'

Loud laughter came from the crowd gathered around Lucy. Dylan said, 'Shall we join the others?'

They set off across the lawn. As they drew closer to the statues, Dylan noticed that there was something different about Apollo. He mentioned this to Toni.

'Yes,' she said, 'he's been cleaned up.'

'No. I'm talking about his lyre. He's holding it again.'

Toni looked pleased with herself. 'Yes. I did that.'

'Really? Well done. What did you use? Superglue?'

'No. Something much stronger. Cross lashing. I learnt how to do it in the Girl Guides. I knew it would come in handy one day.'

Dylan went over to the statue and inspected it. 'Amazing job. I can't see any string.'

Toni laughed. 'No, I used angler's fishing line. It's very fine. Almost invisible. But very hard to break.'

When Dylan and Toni joined the group around Lucy, she was loudly insisting that Leefdale should have been disqualified. 'Major Roberts and Maynard organised the demonstration using people from the Magnificent Britain Sub-Committee, which was clearly against the rules. And they were definitely going around forcing people to tidy up their gardens. Look what they did to Sid and Mary Arkwright.'

Zoe looked sceptical. 'But you just said Sid's wife admitted she'd asked them to come and tidy up their garden because she was sick of the sight of it and Sid wouldn't do anything about it.'

Lucy said, 'That's all rot. Mary Arkwright only said she'd gone behind Sid's back for help because she was frightened no-one in the village would talk to her if Leefdale was disqualified.' She paused, looking angrily around her. 'That lying toad Roberts was definitely behind the demo. Greg Maynard told us so and he should know. And there were definitely members of the Magnificent Britain Sub-Committee taking part in it, which is against the rules. I saw them myself.'

'It sounds as though you're really upset that Leefdale won,' said Zoe.

Lucy looked hurt. 'Certainly not. I wanted the village to win. But only if we stuck to the rules. We didn't and so it seems to me we deserve to be disqualified.'

Seeing that most of the kids were ignoring Lucy and getting fidgety, Zoe said, 'Well, the judges have looked into all the complaints and found nothing in them, so I suppose that's the end of it really.' Her expression brightened. 'Tell us what Lady Brearley said about the sculpture park.'

'I thought I'd told you.'

Zoe pointed to Sheldon, Khaled and Scarlett who'd ended their game of tag and just joined them, breathing heavily. 'These three haven't heard it.'

Lucy repeated the lavish praise that the judges and Lady Brearley had heaped upon the inclusion unit and the sculpture park. Sheldon and Khaled responded by raising their clenched fists in a triumphal gesture and shouting 'Yoah! Yoah!' The others laughed, shrieked and clapped their hands. 'It was me robot what done it,' Sheldon cried.

The laughter and excited talk continued. Dylan felt a strong and urgent need to ring Sharon and tell her that Leefdale had won. Surely she'd be delighted? He consulted his watch. Ten-thirty. It was too late. She and Louise would be exhausted after the first night of "Oliver". He was tempted to call her and find out how the show had gone, but decided it probably wasn't a good idea. She'd warned him not to be too pushy. Besides, she had his mobile number. If she really wanted to speak to him there was nothing to stop her.

Zoe finished her wine with one gulp. 'This is a great result. It gives me huge pleasure to know we've shafted Roberts and all the rest of those arseholes.'

It took only a small amount of drink for Zoe's tongue to get loose. She thought she'd addressed her last remark privately to Lucy, but several of the kids had heard it, which was why many of them laughed and jeered.

Dylan felt uncomfortable. He'd been dismayed to see Zoe very publicly produce a couple of bottles of red wine when Lucy arrived, but had been reluctant to remind everyone about the alcohol ban in case they'd thought him a killjoy. He was now regretting inviting Lucy round and hoped she'd go soon. He said, 'The Major still got what he wanted though, didn't he? His gold medal.'

Zoe said, 'Yes. But we won it for him. In particular, my sculpture park. That must really stick in his craw.'

'I always suspected you secretly embraced the spirit of competition,' said Toni, who had no head for wine.

'Why not? What's wrong with competition?'

'Nothing. Except you promote yourself as an idealistic socialist.'

Zoe laughed. 'All right. I'm a contradiction. So what? Aren't you? Isn't everybody?'

Lucy said, 'It was a great idea of yours to have everybody working in the front garden when the judges arrived. Completely wrong footed everyone.'

Zoe shook her head. 'It wasn't my idea.'

Lucy smiled patiently. 'I meant it was a great collective idea.'

'No, it was Dylan's idea. The rest of us were opposed to it. We thought it smacked of capitulation.' She grinned broadly. 'But you're right. Now we've won it was a great idea.'

'But you weren't opposed to letting the judges in, were you?' said Lucy.

Zoe looked horrified at the thought. 'Oh, no. We wanted them to come in. They had to see the sculpture park.'

'Well, that certainly worked in your favour. And Leefdale's!'

'Oh yes,' Zoe said caustically. 'Every one of us can claim we're responsible in some way for Leefdale's success. What do they say? Success has many fathers: failure is a bastard!'

Dylan regarded Lucy quizzically. 'Why do you think somebody as conservative and conventional as Lady Brearley singled us, I mean the rectory, out for praise?' He swept his arm round to indicate the sculpture park. 'She couldn't really have liked all this stuff, could she?'

Zoe was indignant. 'She didn't just like it, she loved it!' She gave Dylan a gentle, but nevertheless, belligerent prod in the chest. 'And don't call my sculptures, stuff.'

'They're the kids' sculptures, not yours,' said Toni.

'I know that!' Zoe retorted. Her look was withering until she remembered she was encouraging Toni to be more assertive.

'Methinks Lady Brearley had a score to settle,' said Lucy.

'Who with?' Dylan asked.

'Howard Roberts. She knows how much he loathes you and the unit. He's behaved appallingly but Lady Brearley couldn't disqualify Leefdale because she wanted the village to win. So she praised your work on the gardens and suggested Leefdale only won the gold medal because of the sculpture park.'

'You mean she didn't want Roberts to think it was his demonstration that swung it?' said Dylan.

'Exactly. Now everyone in Leefdale is grateful to you for getting them the gold medal. Exactly what Roberts didn't want.'

'Nonsense,' said Zoe, 'that diminishes all the good work the kids have done. Lady Brearley was genuinely impressed by their sculptures. All the judges were.'

Eric regarded Lucy doubtfully. 'Does Lady Brearley really have that much influence?'

Lucy laughed. 'Influence? She is Magnificent Britain!'

Mona, who'd been quiet up to now, suddenly spoke. 'Perhaps the people in Leefdale will like us better now we've helped them win.'

Sheldon scoffed loudly. 'Crap!'

Zoe quickly admonished him. 'Sheldon! Please!'

'I mean,' Mona went on tentatively, choosing her words with extra care, 'I think that's why Lady Brearley gave Leefdale the gold medal. She wanted to tell us we were welcome. That we could stay.'

A long, thoughtful silence followed her remarks. It was interrupted by what sounded like a perversion of Rossini's William Tell overture performed on a musical doorbell: the occluded notes signalling surreally to the night.

Dylan's heart sprang up like a startled bird. Knowing that he and everyone else would be in the garden for some time, he'd put the rectory's land line on

"Call Transfer" to his mobile phone. This was mainly to ensure he didn't miss Sharon if she called.

Dylan flipped open his mobile. 'Hello?'

The languid drawl of the caller was audible to all.

'Is that Dylan Bourne?'

'Yes.'

'Hello. It's Howard Roberts here.'

Everyone gathered more closely around the phone in Dylan's hand.

****

By leaving the awards ceremony almost immediately after the announcement that Leefdale had won the gold medal, Lucy Birkinshaw missed the magnum of Moet Chandon that was brought to Leefdale's table, courtesy of Magnificent Britain. After toasting each other, Greg and Howard, who were still in a state of incredulity, listened perfunctorily to the announcements of the other awards and agreed that, in view of the complaints which had been made, all the committee members had been treated very fairly by the judges. They attacked the champagne, and much else besides, with relish; and as the evening wore on and many more glasses were consumed, they collectively and unanimously came to the opinion that they really hadn't done anything very wrong at all. In fact, everything they'd done had been exactly right. Especially Howard. Greg toasted Howard's conduct which had been impeccable; he toasted Howard's strategy which had been flawless; he toasted Howard's achievement which had been immense.

The seemingly interminable awards ceremony continued. During it people took the opportunity to leave the Long Room and go out on to the terrace to contact friends and relatives and inform them of the results. Howard and Greg, conscious of their newly acquired status as winners and record breakers, had been reluctant to do this right away, thinking it might show discourtesy to their fellow competitors if they absented themselves while the other results were being announced. However, just before the cabaret was about to begin, they left their table and carried their champagne glasses a little unsteadily out on to the terrace to make their calls. Afterwards, with a well-known soprano's beautifully sung "O mio babbino caro" poignantly egressing the Long Room and soaring into the night, they decided it would be ill mannered and disrespectful to return to their table in the middle of the performance, so they remained on the terrace, sipping champagne, getting more and more self-congratulatory, sentimental and drunk.

'It was a damn close run thing but we pulled it off,' exclaimed Howard, slapping Greg's shoulder. 'We bloody well pulled it off!'

'We certainly did. Not bad, eh? Not bad!'

Howard looked piqued. 'The irony is that it looks like we owe our gold medal to Dylan bloody Bourne and his friends. Much as it pains me to say so.'

'You're right, you're right,' said Greg.

'Mind you,' said Howard, 'I don't think Celia seriously likes all that sculpture park rubbish. I mean the state of the rectory's rear garden, you should have seen it.'

'Why d'you think she said she liked it, then?'

'I think she said it to make me look small. She dislikes me, you know.'

'Really?'

'Oh yes. No question. A man can tell.'

'All the same,' said Greg. 'It was wrong to set up that demonstration. Some of the people it attracted were thugs. I've been feeling bloody awful about it all evening. Just think how you'd feel if one of your own children were in there. You know, in that rectory. And you were outside. In the demonstration, behaving like that. Being obnoxious. Being disgusting. Saying all those terrible things.'

'But they wouldn't be in there.'

'Who?'

'Our children. There's no way they'd be in there. They're well brought up. That rectory's for yobs. Yobs and recidivists.' He pronounced each syllable of the last word with great care so as not to slur it.

'Yes. That's true,' said Greg. He knocked back the end of his champagne.

'I wonder if they know?' said Howard.

'What?'

'I wonder if Dylan Bourne and the people in the rectory know they've won us the gold medal.'

'Probably not.'

'I've a bloody good mind to phone them up and tell them.'

'Do you think that's a good idea?' said Greg.

'Why? What's wrong?'

'Maybe they won't want to speak to us. I mean, after all that's happened.'

But Howard was not to be deterred. Reconciliation, like confrontation, is contagious; especially after too many drinks and the performance of a beautiful soprano whose soul, ascending on the wings of technique and Puccini's art, is escaping the bonds of earth and is giving her audience a tantalising ache for the furthest beyond, where only angels dwell.

'What harm can it do?' Howard persisted. 'It's all in the spirit of that peace and harmony Celia was going on about.' He smiled in a conceitedly smug manner. 'I think they'll be glad we rang and told them we've won. And they'll love to hear all the nice things Celia said about them.'

'OK. Good idea. I'll speak to them too. Congratulate them. Give them my apologies if they'll have them.'

Howard took out his mobile. 'All right. Let's do it.'

****

'Hello Howard. This is a surprise.'

Dylan couldn't conceal his astonishment. He raised his eyebrows at those standing around him and increased the phone's volume so they could all hear both sides of the conversation clearly.

'Yes. I thought you'd want to hear the good news: Leefdale has won the Gold Medal for the fifth year running.'

Everyone smiled. Zoe brought her hands up to her mouth and formed them into a megaphone, through which she whispered hoarsely to Dylan, 'He's pissed!'

Dylan nodded, and said into the phone, guardedly, 'Right. Congratulations.'

'I thought I'd call and tell you, as you probably wouldn't know, not being there and all that.'

Dylan looked at Lucy Birkinshaw and bewilderedly shrugged his shoulders. He was having difficulty interpreting Howard Roberts' motive for the call. 'Thank you, but, actually we do know. Lucy Birkinshaw was there. She gave us the good news.'

'Lucy. Ah!'

'Yeah.'

There was a pause, and then Howard said, 'Did she tell you it was thanks to your sculpture park that we won? Lady Brearley was very impressed with it. In fact, I'd say you saved the day for us.'

This was met by a raucous cheer from Sheldon and Khaled. Sheldon followed this up by shouting 'Jolly, jolly good,' in a grotesque parody of an upper middle class voice. Toni shook her blonde head vigorously at the two boys and placed a finger to her lips.

'Really? We saved the day?' said Dylan.

'Oh yes. Celia said many nice things about the rectory. Said something about you being innovators, combining the best of the traditional with the modern. That sort of thing.'

'That's amazing,' said Dylan, who didn't feel at all magnanimous. 'Considering how vilified we've been and the appalling scenes.'

'Appalling scenes?'

'The demonstrators. They were very intimidating. The children were terrified.'

'Ah yes. Well, you know, a few hot heads. What can you do?'

Zoe looked as though she was about to shout something, but Dylan raised his hand to restrain her.

The Major was speaking again. 'Look, I'm awfully sorry about what happened the other day. Tell that chap - what's his name, Sheldon - that it was all my fault. I just lost my head.'

Dylan tried to interrupt, but Major Roberts continued to apologise and abase himself, unaware of the audience around the phone who were giggling and finding it hilarious. Zoe alone was not amused. Roberts had obviously got sentimentally drunk, and floating in wine, had become emboldened to phone and patronise the inhabitants of the rectory.

'What arrogance,' Zoe said quietly to Dylan. 'Now he's won his stupid medal all he thinks he has to do is apologise for his behaviour and everything will be all right.'

Dylan nodded and placed his hand over the phone for secrecy. 'I'll get rid of him.' He removed his hand, and said, 'Look, Major, I suspect you've had a few and there's a court case coming up so I don't think we should talk about it, OK?'

'Quite right. Quite right. Very sensible.'

'OK. Goodnight.'

But Howard's objective hadn't been completely achieved.

'No. Just a minute. I've got Greg Maynard here. You don't know him but he was in the demonstration. He wants a word.'

Dylan threw a mystified look at those around him, then sighed and bowed his head in resignation.

'OK.'

A different voice came on, Northern and lower in pitch. 'Hello. Mr Bourne. Look, it's Greg Maynard. I want to say how sorry I am about the demonstration. I'm really sorry, I didn't know what I was doing.' His voice seemed slurred, thick with emotion, as though he was on the verge of tears. 'It all went wrong. I just want you to know that those people, those horrible people had nothing to do with me, they just turned up. I can't tell you how sorry I am for the distress I caused you and the kids inside the rectory. Particularly the kids. It was unforgivable, unforgivable.' The depth of his remorse was evident but so was the fact he was drunk. It was that which was making his guilt comic and giving all the teenagers the giggles.

Dylan's heart softened at Maynard's contrite tone. 'That's all right, Mr Maynard, try not to distress yourself.'

'No. I can't forget it. I did something terrible. I behaved very badly. Not like me at all. I just want you to know how disgusted I feel with myself.'

'All right, Mr Maynard. Thank you.'

'Just say you forgive me.'

But before Dylan could respond Sheldon had snatched the phone from his hand. 'Forgive you?' he screamed into it. 'Fuck you, you cunt! Fuck you!'

After a short struggle with Sheldon, Dylan was able to get the phone back off him.

'Hello, Mr Maynard, I'm sorry about that.'

But there was no reply. Maynard had switched off.

CHAPTER FIFTY THREE

'There's nowhere to park!' cried Louise.

'What do you expect? It's nearly quarter past.'

It was Saturday evening. Sharon and Louise were in the Passat driving to the village hall for the last performance of "Oliver". They were still a couple of hundred metres away from the building, yet along the grass verges on both sides of the road the vehicles belonging to those attending the show were parked bumper to bumper.

'What are we going to do?' cried Louise, panicking.

'It's all right. I'll drop you off and then find somewhere to park.'

They arrived at the village hall and Sharon double parked the car with the engine running. 'It's certainly a full house tonight,' she said.

'I know. I feel sick.'

'You felt sick last night and you were fine.'

'I know, but tonight's different.'

Sharon said, 'Quick. Jump out. You'll be late.' She quickly kissed her daughter. 'Don't worry. You'll be great. Last night you were brilliant.'

Louise opened her door and then turned back to her mother, alarmed. 'You are coming?'

Sharon looked puzzled. 'You know I am.'

'Sorry. I just want to be sure you'll be there.'

Sharon was touched by her child's insecurity. 'I won't be there unless I get this car parked. Hop out.'

Louise got out of the car clutching her small bag.

'Good luck!' called Sharon, as the door slammed. They waved to each other and then Louise was gone. She'd disappeared into the building through a rear entrance which was serving as a temporary stage door.

The village hall was in a cul de sac, so Sharon was forced to reverse a long way before she found a parking space. She fled the car and rushed back to the village hall on foot. As she went, she imagined Louise entering the building, finding her way to the changing rooms behind the stage and apologising to Mrs Henshall for her lateness. Sharon still couldn't understand why they were running so late. She'd collected Louise at 4pm from the Luffield Young People's Theatre where she spent most Saturdays. They'd arrived home in plenty of time to have a meal and get ready for the night's performance. But Louise had been in a very strange mood: she'd seemed nervous and listless and had even complained about having to go on and perform at all, which was most unlike her. She'd continued to dawdle and put off getting ready, until Sharon had warned her they were going to be late. Her response was to snap her mother's head off.

As Sharon approached the main entrance to the village hall the butterflies in her stomach seemed to have iron wings. Naturally, she was concerned on behalf of her daughter and anxious for her to do well. But there was another reason for her extreme nervousness: she expected Greg and Pam to be in the audience. She always felt sick with anxiety when she had to attend a social occasion or public function knowing that both of them would be present. On the rare occasions when she was forced to socialise with them in the company of other people, the sordid, morally questionable nature of her clandestine relationship with Greg was magnified into a mountain of guilt; and she was convinced that their treacherous adultery and years of deceit were transparent to anyone who looked at them.

It was a stiflingly hot evening and both doors of the hall had been wedged open to provide maximum ventilation. The windows had been flung open too, but despite this Sharon knew that once the black-out curtains were drawn and the stage lights came on it would become unbearably hot inside. That's why she'd chosen to wear the flimsiest off the shoulder dress. At least, that was her justification for it. She stood at the open doorway of the building, listening to the loud, expectant gabble from the audience within, fearful of social ambush and steeling herself for the plunge inside.

Taking a deep breath, she set off through the doorway and entered, acutely aware of each of her separate footsteps as she passed over the hall's parquet floor. Simultaneously, the small orchestra put together by Mr Ridley, the deputy head, began tuning up, which made her jump. Hearing her footsteps many heads swivelled round to discover the identity of the latecomer, and among the two hundred or so people gathered there, several smiled or nodded appreciatively at her. She responded appropriately, gratified by the admiration in most people's eyes, especially the men's. They were obviously very taken with the way her long brown hair sensuously licked at her bare shoulders and the shortness of her white summer dress. She noted that amongst the many parents and relatives there was a good representation from Leefdale's respectable elite: parish councillors, school governors and representatives of the village hall committee, but no sign of Major Roberts and Isobel. It was understandable that they'd wish to avoid the spotlight after the events of the past week, but when she'd phoned Dylan that morning in response to last night's voicemail, he'd mentioned seeing a huge, unmarked removal van parked in the drive of

Rooks Nest. She wondered if the adverse publicity was forcing the Major and his wife to move. She hoped not. But if they were selling up why hadn't they asked Parker and Lund to be their agents? Perhaps they intended to sell Rooks Nest at auction?

Her eye picked out Greg and Pam who were sitting with their two youngest children a couple of rows from the front. Greg turned and nodded to her. Sharon nodded back, and Pam turned to see who her husband was acknowledging. When she saw it was Sharon she smiled and gave a wave. Sharon fluttered a hand back and silently thanked Louise for making her so late. The hall was packed and only a few seats on the back row were vacant. She was spared the horror of sitting through the entire performance in the company of both Maynards.

Mrs Henshall suddenly appeared at Sharon's side carrying a small clutch of programmes.

'Do you want another or have you brought the one from last night?'

In the rush to get out of the house, Sharon had forgotten to bring the programme she'd bought the previous evening. She purchased another and apologised for Louise's lateness. Mrs Henshall told her not to worry and was very complimentary about Louise's performance, before she was called away to deal with some minor problem.

A long, searching glance around the hall told Sharon that the person she most wanted to be there, hadn't arrived. Disappointed, she glanced at her watch. The time was 7.25. Some teachers and teaching assistants were already taking up positions by the windows, standing by to close them and draw the black-out curtains. Perhaps the people from the rectory weren't coming after all.

Sharon took one of the last vacant seats. It was on the back row, next to the central aisle, and as she sat down she greeted Sid and Mary Arkwright who were sitting directly across the aisle from her. She exchanged a few pleasantries with Mary, who was soon telling her about her only son, Eddie, who was playing the Artful Dodger. Apparently his behaviour had deteriorated since getting the part. Sharon had never really liked Eddie much. She thought him rather sly. Perfect casting in fact. Nevertheless, she told Mary and Sid that she thought Eddie was a wonderful Dodger, and after this little social lie listened with only half an ear while Mary rambled on recounting the part that she and Sid had played in nearly getting Leefdale disqualified from Magnificent Britain.

Sharon's attention focussed on the stage. It was set for the opening number, "Food, Glorious Food!" Rostra had been adapted for use as tables on which the metal bowls and spoons for the workhouse children's gruel had been pre-set. She anticipated with pleasure the scenes to follow in which the rostra would be re-arranged to represent Covent Garden, Fagin's Den, The Tavern, and Mr Brownlow's House. Having seen the first night, Sharon was greatly impressed with Mrs Henshall's skilful direction. She couldn't wait for the show to begin so that she could proudly enjoy her daughter's wonderful performance all over again.

The orchestra was positioned in a cramped floor area to the left of the stage. The school boasted only seven children who could competently play an instrument and these tyros were being supplemented by several adult musicians who lived locally. They were all in evening dress and their ages ranged from a youth of eighteen to a woman in her eighties. The orchestra members were still determinedly tuning up, watched by a now mainly silent and mesmerised audience who seemed to regard the inharmonious, discordant din produced collectively by the musicians as some sort of overture to the performance. Meanwhile, the members of the school choir were already sitting in their positions on the floor in front of the stage, directly facing the audience. Like the pupils in the orchestra, they all wore school uniform and looked unnaturally scrubbed and smart. The choir was composed of pupils aged seven to eleven, and Sharon knew that its chief function was to augment the sound made by the children playing the leading roles who had rather weak voices. All except Louise, of course: a thought Sharon exulted in with a flash of pride. Only Louise had the vocal power and range to sing solo entirely unaided!

From where Sharon was seated on the back row, she still had a clear view of the Maynards. She recalled with some angst the conversation she'd had with Pam at the end of the previous night's performance. Pam had been distinctly offhand at first, obviously still piqued by Sharon's rejection of her offer to help find a childminder for Louise. When the atmosphere had thawed a little, Pam complained yet again about the unnecessary length of time Greg's civic responsibilities kept him away from home. "He should be here but he's at Budeholme House tonight. He's sure to have a terrible hangover tomorrow. He always comes back from the awards ceremony completely drunk. He can never resist a drink, particularly when he's stressed, and he's particularly stressed at the moment as a result of taking part in that stupid demonstration outside The Old Rectory. Do you know it cost him a whole day's unpaid leave? Don't you think he was stupid?"

Sharon had felt uncomfortable. She'd never been happy about listening to Pam's unguarded complaints about Greg. It made her feel so deceitful, like some kind of a spy or double agent, and she was never sure how to respond. She supposed that as far as Pam was concerned, it was only a bit of grouching about her husband's relatively unimportant shortcomings. But for Sharon it was torture: she'd no wish to discuss the faults of the man she'd been screwing for years with the wife they were still both deceiving.

Sharon's thoughts returned to the present. She watched Pam open a packet of sweets and give Gwen and Ian one each. Pam then turned and offered one to Greg. His hand went up to refuse but Pam jabbed the packet towards him again, smiling encouragement and urging him to take a sweet. He smiled back, had second thoughts and selected one. Pam said something to him and laughed.

She then took a sweet for herself and started unwrapping it. It was a simple little family scene, one that was probably being enacted by other families in different parts of the hall; but for Sharon this tiny vignette was a revelation that affected her with the force of an epiphany. It seemed to define the Maynards as a closed and tightly bonded group; it underscored her and Louise's positions as outsiders; and it forced her to reflect on the danger posed by Louise and herself to the very existence of this secure and stable little family unit. It made her feel like a murderer.

She continued to watch Greg and his family, all the while thinking of her secret connection to them, and simultaneously deriving a curious voyeuristic pleasure from it. If her secret were revealed it would mean that the Maynards would never be able to trust one another again. What an onerous burden it was keeping that secret safe. How she longed to be free of it!

Greg had told her so many details about his marriage, details so intimate she felt soiled by the knowledge, unequal to the responsibility of secretly knowing so much about another woman's life. Sometimes it seemed to her that she and Louise were so involved with Greg's family that they lived with the Maynards in every way except physically: yet extraordinarily, Pam and her children were unaware of this alternative family dimension. It was bizarre. Not only bizarre, it was demeaning. That's why, last night, when Pam had repeated yet again that the trouble between Jade and Louise was only six of one and half a dozen of the other, Sharon had wanted to scream at her, "This isn't a school spat, it's a blood feud. They're half-sisters for God's sake!"

She concentrated her gaze on the back of Greg's head. The subterfuge could continue no longer. She had to get out. Somehow she had to find the strength and the will to end it.

Some sixth sense must have alerted Greg because he suddenly turned round in his seat and stared straight at her. They allowed their gaze to hold for a moment before averting their eyes. Pam had been absolutely right about the hangover. He certainly looked rough. Sharon resisted the urge to laugh. During their phone call that morning, Dylan had told her all about Greg and Howard's drunken attempts at reconciliation.

Sharon checked her watch. It showed twenty eight minutes past seven. In the short time which had elapsed since she'd taken her seat, others had arrived but Dylan and his party hadn't been among them. Now, nearly all the seats in the hall were taken. If they came at this late stage they'd have to stand at the back.

A teacher or teaching assistant was now in position at every window, poised and ready to draw the blackout-curtains. The show was due to begin in two minutes. What could have delayed Dylan and the rest of them? He'd assured her that everyone from the unit would be at the show. She again recalled with pleasure their phone call. How wonderful it had been just to listen to his posh but genial voice. She'd told him how delighted she was to hear that Leefdale had won the gold medal and of the special praise Lady Brearley had reserved for The Old Rectory's sculpture park. He'd been keen to learn how "Oliver" had gone, and when she'd told him that Louise had been remarkable, he'd reaffirmed that everyone from the unit would be there that night. Then he'd reduced her to helpless laughter with his account of Greg and Howard's drunken apologies and Sheldon's response. The fact that he hadn't the slightest idea of her and Louise's relationship to Greg Maynard, somehow made it all the funnier.

But where was Dylan? She looked to the hall's entrance, impatiently. Were he and the others actually coming? Why hadn't they arrived?

Occasionally she was aware of the eyes of various men she knew in the village dwelling on her speculatively. Presumably they found her attractive and were wondering why she was always on her own. More likely they were wondering what she did for sex and if she could be persuaded that shagging them would be preferable to masturbation. Or perhaps they were convinced she was a lesbian? She'd heard that rumour about herself several times before. If only they knew.

She'd given up all hope of seeing Dylan that evening, when from the street outside came the approaching sound of laughter and the rapid, animated chatter of people in high spirits. It had to be them! A moment later the crowd's gaiety swept into the hall. All heads turned towards the source of the disturbance. Reduced to social awkwardness by the packed seats, the noisy, high spirited latecomers immediately froze, subsided into silence and stood around uneasily. Everyone from the rectory was there, even Sheldon, whom Dylan had earlier described as being "doubtful". In response to the scrutiny of so many eyes, many of them hostile, the body language of the kids had become tense and aggressive. It became even more so when someone at the front clearly said, 'Typical! You'd expect them to be late, wouldn't you?'

Sharon waved at the latecomers. Seeing a friendly face they all smiled back and relaxed slightly. Mrs Henshall approached them with a welcome. Dylan showed her their tickets and apologised for their lateness. Mrs Henshall then went off to see if she could organise some spare seats. Dylan came and stood behind Sharon's seat on the back row. He bent down and murmured in her ear, 'Sorry we're so late. A couple of them got cold feet.'

Gregg had turned round in his seat and was staring directly at Sharon and Dylan, his eyes radiating jealousy and resentment.

The caress of Dylan's warm, gentle breath on the back of her neck seemed to be lasering its way straight to the pit of her stomach. 'You shouldn't have forced them to come,' she said.

'It's all right,' said Toni, who was at Dylan's side. 'Some of them aren't very confident about this sort of thing. They need a bit of encouragement.'

Mrs Henshall re-appeared from a side room carrying two chairs. 'I'm afraid these are all we have left. But there are one or two spaces we can fit you into.'

Turning to Mona, she said, 'Look, you see, near the front there's a space. You could squeeze in there.'

Alarm appeared on Mona's face.

'It's OK,' Zoe said quickly. 'We don't want to disturb the people on that row. And I think we'd all like to stay together.'

'All right,' said Mrs Henshall. 'But some of you will have to stand.'

'That's fine.'

Zoe and Eric set about organising the kids. Jake and Liam were to share one chair; Rupa and Amy the other. Mona was directed to sit in the vacant seat next to Sharon. Everyone else was to stand at the back. As these arrangements were being made, several in the audience kept turning round and giving the latecomers long stares, leaving them in no doubt of their disapproval.

Dylan remained standing behind Sharon with his hands resting lightly on the back of her chair. With each breath she felt the slight pressure of the backs of his fingers against her shoulder blades.

'This is hardly the unobtrusive entrance I'd planned,' Dylan said quietly.

Sharon turned round to look up at him. Their eyes met and she was shocked by the power of her attraction for him. Surely it was obvious to everyone in the room? 'It'll certainly give them all something to talk about,' she said.

He smiled, and then lifted his head to focus on something beyond her. 'Looks like we're starting.'

Mrs Henshall was standing at the bottom of the aisle in front of the stage. The head teacher cleared her throat and the audience fell silent. 'Good evening, everyone,' she began, 'I'm delighted to welcome you to Leefdale Primary School's end of term production, which as you know is a selection of scenes from Lionel Bart's musical, "Oliver". The show will last for just over an hour. I do hope you'll enjoy it. Everyone connected with the show has worked enormously hard. Before we begin could I ask you to check that your mobile phones are switched off? Video cameras are allowed, but I must ask you to be sparing in your use of flash photography as it disturbs the performers. Thank you.'

Mrs Henshall went and took up her position by the light switches. The main doors were closed. The black-out curtains were drawn. The lights were switched off, plunging the hall into almost complete darkness except for the slits of light entering in a few places around the badly fitting black-outs. A childish giggle came from someone at the front of the audience. There was the shuffle of many bare feet, and then the dark outlines of several small figures appeared on stage, taking up their positions for the opening. Sharon felt a thrill of anticipation. She leaned back in her seat, and relished the momentary pressure of Dylan's knuckles against her shoulder blades, before he removed his hands from the back of her chair. The stage lights came up, revealing the workhouse children sitting at the long tables before their mean little bowls. The orchestra struck up the opening bars of "Food, Glorious Food." It had begun.

****

Louise's first entrance as Nancy was not until halfway through the show, so Sharon had to sit patiently through the scenes which described Oliver Twist's expulsion from the workhouse, his escape to London and his introduction to Fagin and his den of thieves.

The performances of Oliver, the Dodger and Fagin were much better than they'd been the previous night. Perhaps it was the size of the audience and the knowledge it was the last opportunity for them to do their best, that was making them strive so hard. Sharon regarded this as auspicious: if Louise raised her performance only half as much as the others she'd be extraordinary.

At last, Nancy's first entrance approached. Sharon felt sick with nerves, and yet buoyed by expectation and parental pride. She was dying to see her daughter's brilliant performance again; and desperately anxious for it to go without a hitch.

The lights went down on the scene in Fagin's den. In the blackout, the rostra could be heard being rearranged. When the lights came up for the next scene the rostra were now representing the bar and tables in a tavern. Pewter mugs were in the hands of drunken revellers. Nancy appeared, pouring beer into the jugs. Sharon knew immediately that she was going to give a miraculous performance. There was so much electricity around her she crackled. The nervous, uncertain girl she'd delivered to the village hall less than half an hour ago had been replaced by a completely different person. One who looked mature beyond her years, moved with an aura of total confidence and spoke in a perfect cockney accent. Listening to her, Sharon recalled how determined Louise had been to get the accent right. The many hours she'd spent watching East Enders and other TV programmes, until she could speak as though she'd lived in the East End of London all her life.

The dialogue ended and with unexpected brio the orchestra struck up the opening bars of "It's a Fine Life!" Louise launched into the song and her voice seemed to be too large for the confines of the hall. What an extraordinary sound it was! Despite having heard Louise sing many, many times, the power and fullness of her voice always surprised Sharon: it hadn't the tone or range you'd expect to find in a girl of eleven, and its unique quality penetrated the heart. Louise's dancing was every bit as good as her singing, and as Sharon watched her daughter with a mixture of astonishment and joy, she was glad she'd sent the girl to Mrs Foster's ballet and tap school in Luffield from the age of six. With a frisson of pride, Sharon saw that the audience was irresistibly warming to her daughter. They could see Louise had the verve of the born performer. Like all great talents her skill and energy enabled her to attack the song with exceptional gusto, whilst giving the impression that the lyrics were spontaneously occurring to her at the very moment she delivered them. She was living the part, as they say, and the audience was set alight by it. When the song finished she was deservedly rewarded with an unconstrained eruption of applause. As Sharon clapped and clapped along with the rest of them, there was no question now in her mind what Louise's career would be: the stage was her element.

All of Nancy's big numbers now came one after the other. As soon as the tavern scene was over the stage lights went to black-out, and came up again on Fagin's den. This was the scene in which Nancy is introduced to Oliver Twist and she and Fagin's gang parody the manners of toffs, before launching into "I'd Do Anything!" Again Louise performed beautifully, extracting all of the humour from the scene and the song.

'She's absolutely brilliant,' Dylan whispered in Sharon's ear.

Sharon turned to him, looked up and smiled radiantly. When she returned her attention to the stage, Louise appeared to be transfixed. She was directly facing the audience and seemed to be singing straight to those in the centre of the first two or three rows. Was she aware that that was where her dad was sitting?

Nancy's last big scene came towards the end of the show, and it was Sharon's favourite. It also took place in Fagin's den. Nancy, unwilling to help Bill Sykes kidnap Oliver from the sanctuary of Mr Brownlow's house, is struck a brutal blow by Bill Sykes and falls to the floor. Sykes leaves and, nevertheless, Nancy launches into "As Long As He Needs Me" in which she expresses her determination to stick by Bill come what may. Louise sang this song with enormous maturity and understanding. Sharon was relishing Louise's sensitive interpretation, when suddenly, behind her, she heard Zoe exclaim in a loud whisper, 'This song's a disgrace. It's so inappropriate for a school. It's condoning violence against women!'

Sharon twisted round and glared at Zoe. Others in the audience were turning in their seats and glaring at her too.

Angrily, Sharon returned her attention to the performance of the song, which was now drawing to its close. Louise was still standing centre stage and singing straight out to the audience. Sharon was sure Louise was singing the last verses of the song directly to Greg. Could it be that she was pledging him undying loyalty whatever happened? Surely not. She wondered if Greg was as deeply moved by their little girl's amazing talent as she was. And if he was, how pathetic that he could only take pleasure in her achievement secretly, and never share his parental pride for her publicly with anyone. The thought made her feel almost sorry for him.

The show ended with the death of Bill Sykes. Immediately the set went to black-out. There was a beat and then the lights came up again to full. The entire cast appeared together on stage, and with the support of the choir they reprised all of the show's songs. Afterwards, the cast bowed to a huge explosion of applause. It continued unabated as the players left the stage, and when the principals came back on to take their individual bows the applause was rapturous. Nancy took her bow after the Artful Dodger and Bill Sykes, and Sharon was thrilled because when Louise appeared the applause was unprecedented, and was greater and more prolonged than for the boy playing Fagin, or even Oliver.

When everyone in the cast had taken their bow, Mrs Henshall came up on stage. The applause was still continuing, and with the entire cast standing completely still behind her, she held up both arms to indicate that she wished to speak. 'I can tell from the strength of your applause that you've certainly enjoyed our little show,' she said. There were mutterings of agreement all around the hall. Mrs Henshall then turned to the members of the orchestra and thanked them for their beautiful playing. Mr Ridley, the deputy head, was thanked for his conducting and Mrs Woodman, the special needs teacher, was thanked for all the work she'd put in as musical director. Mr Ridley, Mrs Woodman and the orchestra members stood up and took a bow and received an enthusiastic round of applause. Mrs Henshall turned to the choir and thanked them for their magnificent singing. The choir stood up and received their applause. It was then the turn of Mrs Milton, who'd designed the scenery and costumes, to be thanked by Mrs Henshall. Mrs Lucas too was thanked for sewing and repairing the costumes on her old hand operated Singer sewing machine, and also received a round of applause. Mrs Henshall then thanked all of the staff and parents who'd worked so hard to produce the scenery and costumes.

'Finally,' said Mrs Henshall, 'I should like to thank all the children who have spent so much of their own time working on this show and have made it such a success.' This produced the loudest applause of the evening and during it, as rehearsed, Louise and John Phelps, who played Oliver Twist, left the stage and went off into the wings. A few moments later they returned carrying a huge bouquet of red roses between them.

Louise waited for the applause to die before she spoke. 'Mrs Henshall, these flowers are from everyone who's been involved in this show. They're to show you our appreciation for all the hard work you've done and your magnificent direction. Without you, this show wouldn't have been possible.'

The two children presented the flowers to Mrs Henshall who responded by looking suitably surprised and delighted. 'Thank you. Thank you so much, they're lovely,' she said, beaming.

Sharon was thrilled that Louise had been one of the two children chosen to present the bouquet. She was also impressed by the confidence and composure with which Louise had made her short speech. It had obviously been learnt by heart but she'd delivered it with touching sincerity, in a strong, clear voice that could be heard at the back of the hall. Sharon was a little staggered, however, because Louise had never mentioned that she'd been asked to do it, although it had obviously been pre-planned. Perhaps she'd intended it as a surprise.

John Phelps took a couple of steps back to re-join the rest of the cast as Mrs Henshall turned toward the audience and prepared to bring the evening to a close. But Louise remained standing alongside her.

Louise said, 'I'd just like to say something else, if I may.'

Mrs Henshall looked at the girl with the quizzical and apprehensive expression of a performer whose fellow actor has gone off script. The evening had gone so well because it had been meticulously planned: she was anxious that it shouldn't be spoiled at the last moment by some spontaneous improvisation. However, to refuse her star performer at this point might seem churlish and offend many in the audience.

'Go ahead, Louise.'

Capping a straightened hand over her eyes to shield them from the fierce lights, Louise peered directly out into the audience. 'Mum,' she said. 'I can see you're sitting right at the back. Would you stand up please?'

Sharon stared at her daughter with incredulity. What was Louise doing? Surely this hadn't been planned? Row after row in the audience was turning round, staring expectantly, willing her to stand up. She shrank at the sudden, unwanted attention.

'Go on, mum. Stand up please,' came Louise's plea.

The eyes of everyone in the room were now fixed firmly on Sharon. A terrible shrinking horror came into her. This was actually happening. She was going to have to do it. She was going to have to stand up in front of all these people. Whatever Louise was doing it could only be embarrassing for her, of that she was certain.

'Yes, Miss Makepiece. Do stand up.' This was Mrs Henshall, thinking that her encouragement was needed.

'Go on,' Dylan urged in Sharon's ear.

Slowly, self-consciously, Sharon rose to her feet. Something strange was happening. She felt in the grip of something manipulative and malign that was using her for its own purposes and which she was powerless to resist. She stood there with everyone's eyes on her, the unwilling centre of attention, exposed and vulnerable.

Louise had now transferred her gaze to the front rows. 'There's another person I'd like to stand up,' she continued. 'Mr Maynard, the chair of governors.' She smiled sweetly at Greg. 'Stand up please, Mr Maynard.'

Standing at the back, publicly exposed, naked and apprehensive, Sharon's imagination was tumbling in all directions and every scenario it produced was dangerous and threatening to her peace. Louise was up to something. Why else had she asked Greg to stand up too? No. It wasn't possible, surely? She fought back the overwhelming urge to run out of the hall and tried to compose herself.

Greg remained in his seat. He'd not had a happy evening. The heat and closeness of the hall had intensified his hangover: his head was throbbing, his mouth was dry. He longed for a glass of water and for something cool and soothing to be placed on his brow. And now Louise was doing this. Why was she drawing attention to himself and Sharon? What was she up to? Did Mrs Henshall know what was going on? Or was this a trap sprung by Louise? An animal sense told him to be afraid.

'Yes, go on Mr Maynard. Stand up.' Mrs Henshall was being helpful and jollying things along again. But what else was she to do? She had no idea where all this was leading.

Slowly, Greg got to his feet. A weak smile was on his face. He turned round to face several people he knew and grinned at them. Play this as though you're in on the act, he told himself. It's the only way to get through it.

Louise was speaking again. Her voice was strangely flat and uninflected, as though she was speaking from a deep trance. 'I've asked the two of you to stand up because you've both helped me so much.' Looking at Sharon, she went on, 'Mum, you've always looked after me, no matter how difficult things have been for you. You sent me to ballet school and singing lessons. You got me a place in the youth theatre in Luffield. I wouldn't have been able to learn my lines for "Oliver" or been able to give this performance without your help. You've had such a hard life and I wanted everyone to know how good you've been to me.'

Someone, whether from sympathy or embarrassment, began to meekly applaud and soon the whole room was joining in. Sharon blinked hard as she received the applause and her mouth twisted in spontaneous emotion, but she managed to whisper a flustered 'Thank you' to Louise, before she sat down with the tears streaming down her cheeks.

The applause stopped and all eyes were now on Greg Maynard, who remained standing. People were puzzled and curious to know what Greg had done to help the little girl.

Louise fixed Greg with a curious smile. He stared back at her, unable to raise a smile now, wide eyed and fearful. Mrs Henshall had the strongest feeling that she ought to do something to end it, but she felt powerless to intervene. Louise had everyone in some kind of thrall, as though she'd cast on them all an irresistible spell.

Louise spoke again: 'Mr Maynard. You've always been there for my mum and me. Always dropped in to visit us and cheer us up, and help me with my reading.' She suddenly took her eyes off him and lifted them towards the audience. 'I want to thank him like this because, you see, he's my dad and I never get the chance to thank him properly in front of people because no-one's supposed to know he's my dad, but he is. He's my dad. My real dad. Thanks, dad.'

CHAPTER FIFTY FOUR

Louise couldn't remember when the idea first formed in her mind. Was it the previous evening when the spontaneous bursts of applause after each of her songs and exits from the stage induced in her a rare sense of approval and belonging? Was that when she made the assumption that the crowd would be delighted with her no matter what she did, and that those clapping so enthusiastically were entitled to share in her great secret? Or was the idea planted earlier than that, when she'd drawn the picture of the girl trapped under the ice and Dylan had asked her what she thought would happen to the girl and she'd said the girl would either die or find some way of smashing through the ice? Or was it even further back than that, on one of those occasions when she'd been tormenting Jade, unable to reveal her true relation to her half-sister, and finding instead intimacy of a kind through the deviant relationship of bully and victim? Or had the intention to reveal all begun on that first day when she'd assumed the burden of the secret her parents had imposed upon her? When she was a small child and the man she'd known all her life as "Uncle Greg" had shockingly been revealed to her as her father? When he'd solemnly made her swear that she'd never reveal his true relationship to her? Or perhaps the idea had formed more recently than that: when she'd seen how publicly humiliated the MP had been in front of all those people when Clarissa's dad told him she was pregnant and the Major had punched him in the face. Was it then she'd seen the dramatic possibilities inherent in public revelation and humiliation?

She'd certainly known that evening she was going to do it. Even before the final performance of "Oliver" had started. It was the perfect opportunity with mum and dad in the audience. Heaven. That's why she'd been so nervous beforehand, hadn't wanted to come: had felt like throwing up and not going through with it. The enormity of the act intimidated her, making her reluctant even to perform. But as soon as she'd got on the stage, the knowledge that both her mum and dad were watching seemed to galvanise her. She'd acted as one possessed: every movement, every gesture, every line, every note in her voice, although predetermined and choreographed, was delivered as convincingly as if it had occurred to her that very moment. It seemed that she moved through the scenes and songs in a trance, as though she was involved in some glorious dream in which she was simultaneously both participant and spectator: deeply involved and yet curiously detached; so that she experienced intensely all the emotions her role demanded and yet through some magical third eye was able to take immense pleasure in her own performance of it. The feeling was out of this world! She was inhabiting the stage as though she wasn't subject to the laws of gravity or indeed, any corporeal laws. And then there was the added bonus of the applause; each burst becoming progressively louder and longer. On and on the applause had gone, motivating her, encouraging her, empowering her; and nourished by it, she'd craved even more: but to get it she'd had to reward them with more and more of her talent, until the climax of her final bow when her personal applause lifted the roof. Afterwards, she'd looked around the huge room filled with people, many of whom she'd known all her life, and revelled in the love that was unreservedly radiating from them directly to her. It was exhilarating to receive this pure expression of total approval. Surely there was no greater love than that which this audience had for her? But the show was over: she'd no more of her talent to give them in return. And that's when she knew it was possible. Surely, she reasoned, people who loved her so much couldn't be deceived any longer? It was wrong to keep her precious secret from them. They had to know, and if they knew what did it matter? If they knew, surely they would forgive her? People who loved her this much could forgive her anything. And wouldn't they love her all the more for telling them?

Even when she was delivering her short speech of thanks to Mrs Henshall she was deciding it had to be done. She would do it. She knew it was a cheek not re-joining the rest of the cast after the presentation of the flowers, and telling Mrs Henshall that she'd something else to say: and then seeing the surprise and anxiety in the woman's eyes. But after her brilliant performance as Nancy she was certain Mrs Henshall couldn't possibly refuse her. And she was right. Her acute sense of drama told her that mum and dad should both stand up. Even though there were hundreds of people separating them, she could feel the apprehension and anxiety filling her mother when she'd asked her to stand; and she could see that her mother suspected her of being about to perpetrate something awful. For a second she was sure her mum would refuse, and she saw that it might not be as smooth and easy to accomplish as she'd thought. But good old Mrs Henshall had stepped in to encourage mum to her feet. Then she'd heard herself asking him to stand. His face said he was terrified; that he suspected a trap. He sat frozen in his seat, but Mrs Henshall helped out again and encouraged him and he got to his feet. The sentences expressing her thanks to mum for all she'd done for her flowed naturally, without thought: they came straight from her heart and were the residue of years of agonising over mum's situation. And then there'd been that lovely applause when she'd finished, and she knew it was going to be all right. They wanted her to tell them. They could see him standing there and they wanted to know what part he'd played in all this. And then she'd thanked him for visiting and helping her with her reading, and she saw his features relax, he thought he was going to get away with it, she could tell. So she told them. You see he's really my dad. Thanks dad. And she'd stood and stared at them and waited for the enormous tidal wave of applause. But there was nothing. They were all silent. They were all staring back at her, silent.

****

'Please join the rest of the cast, Louise,' Mrs Henshall said, firmly. She was sensitive to what she imagined to be the child's painful state of mind but this was the most embarrassing finish to an end of term production she'd ever experienced, and somehow the nightmare had to be brought to a close. Gently, she took Louise by the arm, guided her upstage and placed her between Fagin and Bill Sykes. Despite their instructions to "freeze" at the end of the show, all the children in the cast kept turning their heads towards Louise. They were all aware that something momentous had happened.

Mrs Henshall, noticing that Jade Maynard's face was wet with tears, quickly turned and addressed the teachers standing in the wings and asked them to lead the cast back to the dressing rooms. The children began to leave the stage in a subdued manner and the audience started to applaud yet again; but their applause, which had previously been spontaneous and full hearted, was now sporadic and unsure, probably because the adults in the audience were still recovering from Louise's shocking exposure of her father's identity, and were uncertain what their public response should be. Thankfully, even this scant applause petered out as the last cast members left the stage and Mrs Henshall was left standing on it alone, clutching her bouquet.

Mrs Henshall now turned to face the audience. She glimpsed her husband's kind and serious face in the front row and took comfort from it. She thought of the glass or two of sherry she would share with him at home and the conversation they would have once this ordeal was over. She decided to make no reference whatsoever to Louise's revelation. She was certain that the best course was to pretend it hadn't happened and confine herself to mundane organisational matters. However, as she was about to address the audience she became aware of a fiercely whispered altercation going on between Greg Maynard and his wife. Mrs Henshall faltered, but quickly recovering her composure she reminded everyone that the village hall was available only until nine o'clock and the caretaker was anxious to have all the chairs put away by then. She therefore requested that people did not linger. She asked those parents whose children were in the choir to collect them straight from the hall, and she requested those parents whose children were in the cast to wait for them outside the rear entrance. She once again thanked everyone for coming, bade them all good night and wished everyone a happy summer holiday.

Sharon heard Mrs Henshall's words but they had little meaning for her. She was only aware of her enormous relief that the head teacher had intervened swiftly to bring an end to the painful exhibition Louise was making of herself, and had prevented her from making any more scandalous disclosures.

Her feelings of relief gave way to near panic and desperation as she looked around the hall and saw that those parents who had video cameras were still focussing them on Mrs Henshall as she delivered her closing remarks. So, her public disgrace had been recorded! Her humiliation was now complete. She felt crushed by the thought of all those parties and social gatherings where the image of Louise on stage announcing that Greg Maynard was her natural father would be played and replayed for the benefit of drunken friends and neighbours wanting a good laugh; perhaps accompanied by a salacious first-hand account from those who'd been present on the night of the village's greatest scandal.

Fortunately, there were some things the video cameras hadn't recorded: the way her self- esteem had diminished to zero, the feeling of shame which had engulfed her so that she now had no sense of herself existing as anything other than this dishonoured and disgraced creature. The conviction that she was standing in front of everyone completely naked. The video camera that could capture those images hadn't been invented.

Sharon wished she could stop re-enacting in her mind the moment Louise's true paternity was revealed. Immediately, Pam had turned round to stare at her, her pathetic features disintegrating in amazement and betrayal. Then, just as suddenly, she was turning back to her husband; "Is this true? Is this true?" You didn't need to be a lip reader. Turning back to stare at Sharon again; and then back to her husband in a grotesque attitude of horror and disbelief; exchanging words with him in vicious, harsh whispers. And even now they were still sniping at each other in their furtive, whispered fury.

Despite the wretchedness of her thoughts and feelings, Sharon was beginning to feel strangely elated. It could be just the effects of shock, but she was convinced something positive was going to emerge from all this. She knew that her reputation had been destroyed: that she was now exposed as a liar and a deceiver, but although she'd lost, in a kind of way, she'd also won. Louise's treachery (or was it honesty?) shocking as it was, had provided her with the means of her liberation. It had forced her to face up to something in herself she'd been unwilling and unable to confront for a very long time. Now, thanks to Louise, the decision had been forced upon her. Life would definitely change.

Mrs Henshall came down from the stage and went to speak to her husband. Simultaneously, there was a tumult of noise as everyone began getting up from their seats and talking loudly and excitedly at once. From the way people were stealing glances in her direction, Sharon was in no doubt what their main topic of conversation was about.

Mona suddenly turned to her. 'Was that man really Louise's dad?' Sharon was about to answer when she felt the comforting grasp of Dylan's hand on her shoulder. 'We need to talk,' he said, leaning over her.

Sharon stared back up at him and nodded numbly.

'Well? Is he her dad?" demanded Mona.

'Yes, he is,' said Sharon, rising quickly to her feet desperate to get away. All around her now there were signs of dissolution. The members of the orchestra were packing away their instruments. The blackout curtains were being removed and the light was pouring in, illuminating the hall's darkest, most hidden recesses: stripping it of glamour and restoring it to its soulless functionality; eradicating all trace of the shared and intimate atmosphere created by the performance and the scandalous revelation which had occurred. Most of the audience were already on their feet now, shuffling out of the rows of seats and filling up the crowded central aisle, impatient to be out of the hot, oppressive space. Around them, members of the village hall committee were stacking the vacated seats prior to taking them off to the side room where they would be stored until the next event. The crowd passed by her in the aisle: most people averting their eyes but some looking straight at her, darting stares of disapproval that scalded her cheeks; stony looks and moralising frowns that made her feel like a piece of shit. Yet, occasionally, here and there, in the same crowd, particularly on the faces of the few men who dared to look directly at her, was the approval of worldliness: knowing little smiles, twinkling eyes, nods of recognition. Sharon could bear it no longer. She had to get to Louise, collect her and get her to the safety and security of home, away from this confusing combination of moral hostility and lecherous insinuation. She forced her way into the exiting crowd and immediately found herself face to face with Pam Maynard.

Sharon stopped dead. So did Pam.

Pam's arms were around her two younger children whom she was solacing with the comfort of her body, clutching them to her sides like a bird shielding young beneath its wings. A look of violation was on her. Her sudden stop had brought the crowd behind her to a halt. 'You fucking slag!' she screamed into Sharon's face. All those standing around gasped. Pam gave a sob and hurried on.

The attack was so unexpected that Sharon was speechless. Then, recovering quickly, she had an overwhelming need to rush after Pam and explain. She plunged into the debouching crowd, forcing people out of her way as she ran towards the entrance in pursuit. But Dylan quickly caught her.

'Sharon, leave it. You must go to Louise.'

She ignored him and ran out of the hall. When she arrived in the street she was just in time to see Pam closing the door of her car. The children were in the back seat looking at her bleakly. Sharon stood for a moment, uncertain what to do. People were staring. She ran over to the car waving her arm to attract

Pam's attention. Pam's cheeks were glistening with tears. She shook her head despairingly at Sharon and drove off.

****

Although Dylan was shocked by Louise's astonishing public admission that Greg Maynard was her natural father, it clarified for him what Louise had been struggling to communicate through her art therapy work. He'd always suspected that she'd had problems relating to the significant others in her life. Now he understood the subtext of the art products she'd created: particularly the picture of the girl trapped beneath the ice. He saw why Louise was constantly accusing people of drawing attention to her fatherless state; and he understood the sibling rivalry between herself and her half-sister. In retrospect it all made complete sense. Her inability to reveal the identity of her father had blocked her "felt self" and had led to her revealing Greg Maynard's paternity obliquely, through codes, hints, and outrageous behaviours. However, he was sure that the minimal art therapy he and the others had provided for Louise couldn't have been responsible for tipping her over the edge into confession.

It was clear to Dylan that Louise had been a victim of severe mental and emotional abuse, and that the psychological damage done to her had to be extensive. He tried to imagine what it was like to see your father several times a week, to have him help you with reading, and yet be unable to acknowledge him in public. To go to the same school as your half siblings, even be in the same class as your half-sister, and yet be unable to relate to them as close relatives. What kind of hell was it when you were forced to deny the connection to your own flesh and blood, and yet constantly be in their presence day after day? Pure torture. No wonder Louise had bullied Jade and others and felt the overwhelming desire to act out her guilt so publicly. When she'd stood in front of that packed hall and claimed Greg Maynard as her father, she hadn't been just trying to shock people: she'd been the girl under the ice smashing her way out of the frozen pond.

Such were Dylan's initial professional reflections on Louise's astonishing disclosure. But as a man, Dylan had other responses: he had a strong, physical attraction to Louise's mother; and the revelation that Sharon had conducted an illicit relationship with Greg Maynard and kept it secret for so long revealed in her a sexual loyalty he found irresistible. There was something immensely erotic about the secrecy with which she'd conducted her long affair, and he derived a sexual frisson thinking about it. At the same time, he found himself intensely jealous and resentful of Greg Maynard. He tried to objectify these feelings and reflect on the psychological processes which were causing his unusually subjective reaction, but failed. It was impossible to be objective when powerful feelings such as love and lust were dominating you. That was why, when Sharon rushed out of the hall in pursuit of Pam he felt compelled to follow her.

He found her forlornly watching Pam's car disappearing out of sight. He went and stood by her side, but before he could speak to her seriously, Zoe and the others came out of the village hall and joined them.

'I must go and get Louise,' Sharon said, and set off down the street towards the hall's rear entrance.

'We'll come with you,' said Dylan.

'No. I think you've done enough. I should never have left Louise with you. Look what it's done to her.'

Sharon strode purposefully along. Dylan stayed doggedly at her side while Zoe and the rest followed noisily behind.

'Sharon, I'm sure that none of the work we did with Louise could have been the catalyst for what she's just done. Now I know the circumstances, it's obvious she's been threatening to do something dramatic for some time.'

But Sharon appeared not to be listening. She hurried on, grim faced, anxious to get to the rear of the hall, collect Louise and return to the sanctuary of home.

'She's going to need a lot of professional help,' Dylan continued. 'Obviously she'll be feeling upset after what's happened. Elated, but full of guilt too. The last thing anyone should do is be judgemental and reject her or punish her. She needs sympathy and understanding. She's obviously been under extreme pressure for years. She needs to work it through.'

Sharon stopped dead and turned to face him. Her expression was withering. 'Work it through? How? Draw another picture?'

Zoe, who was on the other side of her, said, 'She'll need counselling and therapy. What we saw tonight was the expression of years of suppressed emotion.'

They had arrived at the rear entrance. Sharon turned to stare at the large group of parents waiting for their children. Some of them had their younger ones held by the hand. Was it her imagination, Sharon wondered, or had their grip on their children tightened at her approach? She glanced shyly at the parents' faces, and was again frightened by their scalding looks of disapproval. Surely, they can't think I'm a threat to them, she thought, in the grip of a sudden paranoia. But how easily she could see what it looked like from their simple point of view: to them she was the wicked parent governor who'd screwed the chair of governors behind his wife's back and born his child in secret. Not at all the sort of person they'd want to invite to dinner.

Loud laughter came from Mona and Scarlett, and they started chasing each other high spiritedly round and round. The other kids were being noisy too, laughing and joshing each other, talking excitedly and making something of a din. They were boisterous rather than unruly, but Dylan and the other adults were doing nothing to stop it and this made Sharon feel uncomfortable. She thought of the awful impression it must be having on the waiting parents. No wonder they were staring so disparagingly. She turned on Dylan. 'Please, go away and leave me alone. All I want is to collect Louise and take her home quietly, without any fuss.'

'The kids want to congratulate Louise on her wonderful performance,' said Zoe. 'We all do.'

'We also want to help you, Sharon,' said Dylan. 'Louise wasn't the only one carrying this secret for so long. You were too. You must have been deeply traumatised by it. We can't just behave as though nothing's happened.'

These kind words of Dylan's seemed to absolve Sharon of all her guilt. She stared at him, not knowing what to say, aware only that he was voicing the truth: that the years of secrecy had been intolerable and had destroyed her.

'Here,' said Zoe, offering her a tissue.

Sharon took the tissue and began dabbing her eyes. All the other parents gathered around the stage door were staring, whispering and muttering to each other. She knew all of them. Several had sought her advice as a school governor at various times, or approached her when they'd had a complaint to make about the school. What the hell! She thought. How dare they look at me like that? What do they know about it?

A woman in her thirties detached herself from the group she was with and came over. Sharon knew her vaguely. Dianne was a notorious trouble maker and also no friend of Pam. She began to praise Louise's performance. Sharon responded by telling Dianne how well her son, a member of Fagin's gang, had performed. They then went on to talk about various aspects of the production. Dianne was soon complaining about Mrs Henshall's organisation of the event: she felt electric fans should have been placed around the hall; refreshments should have been available, and Mrs Henshall had spoken for far too long at the end.

Sharon was still so distracted by the trauma of Louise's public revelation she could barely focus on Dianne's complaints. In any case, she knew what this conversation was really all about. Dianne was the playground gossip, and Sharon could see she was trying to inveigle her into making some comment about Louise's astonishing disclosure.

Finally, unable to finesse the conversation into those areas which were exciting her curiosity, Dianne changed tack and made a frontal assault. 'I suppose you and Mr Maynard worked very closely together?'

Sharon said nothing. Her eyes had become slits.

'As governors, I mean,' Dianne continued, less certainly.

Sharon took a step towards Dianne and brought her face close to hers. 'It's no-one else's fucking business!' she hissed.

Dianne recoiled as though she'd been slapped. 'Oh, sorry! Sorry!' She turned round and trudged back to where her friends were standing. They said something to her and she shook her head. Louise assumed Dianne would soon be recounting what had just passed between them, prefacing it with, "And do you know what she said?"

Some of the children who'd been in the cast were now emerging from the rear of the building. They ran to their parents, talking excitedly. Sharon wondered if they were talking about Louise and the momentous thing that had happened. Or was it about their own little concerns? But, whatever they were saying, their parents silenced them and hurried them away.

Mrs Henshall appeared at the stage door holding Louise by the hand. Louise was crying, wiping away her tears with the knuckles of her tightly clenched free hand.

Seeing Sharon, Mrs Henshall brought Louise over. 'She's rather upset,' said Mrs Henshall.

'Jade and the others have been horrible to me!' Louise wailed.

Quietly but firmly, Mrs Henshall said, 'Now you know that simply isn't true.' Turning to Sharon she went on, 'It really isn't. No-one's said a word to her. I've kept her apart from the other children and personally supervised her while she changed and got ready.'

Sharon put a comforting arm around her daughter. Louise instantly buried her face in her mother's bosom.

Mrs Henshall said, 'We really need to talk about what's happened tonight. Obviously, now is not a good time. I'll be in school for a few days before I go on holiday. Perhaps you could come and see me on Monday?'

'No, I don't think so,' said Sharon, harshly.

'Why not?'

'There's no need. From today, Louise isn't at your school anymore.'

Mrs Henshall looked shocked. 'That's strictly true. But I must warn you I shall have to contact social services and inform them what Louise revealed tonight. It's in Louise's interest that we discuss the situation.'

Sharon raised herself to her full height. 'Have you any idea how devastated Louise was that you wouldn't let her come to the leaver's ceremony this afternoon?'

Mrs Henshall looked defensive. 'She was excluded. Children who are excluded aren't allowed in school.'

'But Louise has contributed so much to this school. So have I, as the parent governor.'

Mrs Henshall said nothing.

Sharon brought her face closer to Mrs Henshall's. In a low, controlled voice she said, 'You're a heartless old cow. I'm glad Louise embarrassed you tonight.'

Mrs Henshall considered this for a moment, and said, 'Oh no, Miss Makepiece. It was you who was the most embarrassed here tonight, as you very well know.'

Mrs Henshall turned and went back into the village hall.

During this short conversation, Louise had drifted away from her mother and was now standing with those from the inclusion unit. They were all milling around, some still talking about "Oliver" and Louise's performance, telling her how wonderful she'd been as Nancy. Liam and Rupa were acting out their favourite parts of the show.

Sharon went over and joined them. She took Louise's hand. 'Come on. Let's get home.'

'Why don't you and Louise come back to the rectory for some coffee?' said Eric.

'Thanks,' said Sharon, 'but I've really had enough for tonight. I'm feeling very tired and I just want to get Louise home.'

'Please mum, let's!' pleaded Louise. Sharon hesitated. Dylan and Zoe joined in the encouragement.

'We can give Louise a bit of supper,' said Dylan. 'After all that effort she must be hungry.' He gazed down at Louise. 'Are you hungry?'

'Yes.'

Under their combined assault Sharon relented. After all, what would she do if she went straight home? Just give Louise a snack. Berate her for all the humiliation and crack open a bottle. She said, 'OK. That would be nice. But just for half an hour or so.' She took Louise's hand and they walked down the road with Dylan and the others following close behind.

They'd barely gone a few yards when Sharon froze.

Greg Maynard was walking towards them.

Mona said, 'Look, Louise. There's your dad.'

****

Greg Maynard was hot and distressed. He was still in a state of shock and it was manifesting as intense surges of anger. He couldn't believe that his own child could have done such a thing. Thank God Mrs Henshall had managed to shut the little cow up. He would never forget sitting down afterwards, shaking and seeing the look on Pam's face. The hurt and reproach in her eyes. The strangeness in her voice as she'd demanded of him in an angry whisper whether it was true. The way she'd kept turning round to stare at Sharon, then at Louise and then back to him, whispering to herself in disbelief. It had been terrible to watch. And Ian and Gwen had been totally confused. What does she mean you're her dad, daddy? How can you be Louise's dad, daddy? You're our dad, aren't you? Then Pam grabbing the kids and bundling them away the moment Mrs Henshall finished speaking and everyone was starting to leave. He understood why Pam had run: his own impulse had been to get out of there as soon as possible too. But he'd left it too late. He'd been about to chase after them when Mrs Henshall had collared him. She'd seemed as shaken as he was. He recalled everyone's eyes on them as she'd drawn him aside and asked him in a quiet but emotional voice if it was true. Obviously he couldn't deny it. All he could do was nod. Then she was saying something about needing to speak to him about it later, after the weekend. That's when he'd told her he was resigning from the governors and saw the immediate relief on her face. But before she could say anything else, there was Pam at the other end of the hall screaming at Sharon that she was a fucking slag. He and Mrs Henshall had both turned in the direction of the disturbance and then ignored it, as though it was nothing to do with either of them. "This isn't the time to discuss anything," she'd said, and asked him to come and see her next week. He'd agreed. He would have agreed to anything to get out of there, away from all those people staring at him, talking about him, sniggering. Enjoying his humiliation. He wanted to find Pam and the kids. And so he'd bolted.

He'd made his way up the aisle and towards the entrance, ignoring the stares of those whom a short time earlier he'd have been pleased to stop and pass the time of day with. But he couldn't face them. His head was throbbing, his heart pounding and his mouth seemed full of sand. He longed for a big glass of mineral water or even a pint of beer to get rid of the dehydration. Then, as he neared the open doors he came face to face with Arthur Meakins. Meakins had smiled knowingly, nudged him and told him he was a dark horse. He'd wanted to deck him. How could the bastard have been so tactless as to raise it there and then? Instead, he'd let him know it was all over. Meakins had started to protest but he'd walked off and left him.

It was true, it was all over, he told himself as he'd gained the street. He'd have to resign as a councillor, of course, so no more parish council meetings. No more Magnificent Britain, no more Community Watch, and, of course, no more chairing the school governors. Those were positions of enormous responsibility, requiring the trust and confidence of the people he represented. Already they would be writing him off as a fraud and a confidence trickster, an adulterer and a liar. They'd be wondering how extensive the reservoir of his deceit was and asking themselves how he could have deceived them all so successfully for so long. How could anyone ever feel that they could trust him with public office again? He'd always prided himself on seeming above reproach, and now everyone knew he wasn't. Thanks Louise! He cursed himself for his pig-headedness. Why hadn't he encouraged Sharon to leave the village and take Louise with her, years ago?

He stood in the street looking for his car, and then realised Pam must have driven it off. He hoped she hadn't gone to her mother's. He began to panic. Jade! What about Jade? Had she collected her? He decided he'd better go and see.

He turned and began to trudge towards the stage door. And that's when he saw them.

In the moments following his public betrayal and his immediate fall from grace, Greg had thought only of the effects on himself, his wife and their children. He'd barely given Sharon a thought except as a provider of a roof should Pam refuse to allow him back into the house. As for Louise, just thinking about what she'd done overwhelmed him with a fervent hatred for her. Over the years, this hatred would attain greater and greater levels of intensity, and eventually would become moulded by events into a form of detestation so complete it would result in his total estrangement from her, as well as her mother. But all that was in the future. Now, coming face to face with Sharon, finding her strolling with Louise in the company of Dylan and those appalling yobs, he was suddenly presented with the means of absolving himself of all guilt: of transforming his despair into a rage which could be directed at those responsible for bringing about his present misery. He felt justified in taking his revenge.

He went straight up to Sharon and Louise.

'I hope you're pleased with what you've done tonight, Louise,' he shouted into the child's face. 'You little bitch!'

Sharon tightened her grip on Louise's hand. 'Come on!' she cried and started to hurry her along.

'Don't walk away from me,' bawled Greg. He grabbed Sharon by the arm. 'I've got something to say to you!'

Dylan and the others had by now caught up with them. Dylan took Maynard by the arm. 'Greg, calm down!'

Maynard rounded on him. 'Calm down! You bastards have ruined me. You put her up to this. If it wasn't for you none of this would have happened!'

Sheldon and the rest of the kids started to make a long hoot of derision which started low and rose higher and higher in pitch.

Dylan said, 'You're wrong, Greg. This has got nothing to do with us.'

Sharon was struggling to get away from Maynard, but he had her arm in a firm grip.

'No? Don't make me laugh! You're knocking her off, you scum. You're all scum!'

Dylan again moved in on Maynard and attempted to put an arm round him in a conciliatory way, but Greg shrugged him off. Suddenly, he swung a punch at Dylan. It caught Dylan on the jaw and sent him reeling.

Sharon turned. She grabbed Greg and tried to prevent him going in and landing another blow. 'Leave him. Leave him alone!' she shrieked.

Dylan had recovered and was now on his feet. He was Buddha calm and his arms were by his sides. 'This is madness. You're only making things worse. There's nothing between Sharon and me.'

'You lying bastard!' Greg shouted.

He went to swing at Dylan again. But Zoe had moved in on him from the left. With her right hand she gripped Greg's shirt, whilst simultaneously her other hand grabbed his right arm. At the same time, she straightened her left leg and jammed it under the crook of his right knee. Then, using Greg's own weight and her left leg as a pivot, she threw him backwards. He landed with a thud on his left side, gasping, all the breath knocked out of him. But Zoe was still grasping his right arm. She flung herself on him, forcing him face down on to the ground and pinioned both his arms high up his back making him scream out in agony. Afterwards, there was a moment of complete silence. Then all the kids from the rectory broke into a huge cheer.

Sharon didn't wait. She rushed off with Louise. Glancing back she saw Greg pinioned on the ground with Zoe on his back. They were surrounded by those from the rectory and a swiftly growing, stunned crowd.

CHAPTER FIFTY FIVE

Sharon flicked back the flap of the cigarette packet and examined the contents. Four left. She knew it was sometime around eleven o'clock. If she went to bed at midnight she could have one now, and then another every twenty minutes or so. Why not? She deserved it. She took out one of the cigarettes, lit it with a match, inhaled deeply and with conflicting feelings of guilt and satisfaction, exhaled and watched the smoke drift upwards towards the stars. She knew she shouldn't have started smoking again, but hadn't she been lucky to find the packet? It was the several glasses of Australian red that had brought on the craving. Strange how this time she'd known she hadn't the spirit to resist. Even as she'd implemented her usual anti-smoking strategies she'd been willing them hard not to succeed. The night's awful events had affected her so badly only a cigarette could provide the appropriate relief. But where to get one? No chance of buying fags at that time of night, and, anyway, she was too pissed to drive. Where in the house could there be a dog-end, or better still, a whole cigarette? And then she remembered. Nine months ago, when she'd given up, she'd left a packet with a few fags in it somewhere as an insurance policy. Where? Where?

The look on Louise's face as she'd watched her ransacking the house! She'd started in the bedrooms: going through bedside cabinets, looking under mattresses and rummaging through dressing table drawers; leaving a trail of disorder and minor damage behind her with the reckless indifference of a housebreaker. Finally, after ten minutes of this she'd emerged from a fitted wardrobe with a wild cry, triumphantly clutching a packet of Lambert and Butlers retrieved from the pocket of one of her winter coats. "All right!" Louise had screamed, before storming out of the room. "If you must kill yourself do it outside. I can't stand the smell!"

That's why Sharon was now moving slowly up the garden, drawing greedily on her third cigarette as she went. She felt bad about upsetting Louise. The poor little thing was terrified of losing her to cancer, she knew that. But the child was directly responsible for the dreadful state her nerves were in; and after what Louise had done to her that evening, what right had she to complain if mum succumbed to the old temptation? Not that it was doing any good. Despite the welcome cigarettes and wine, she still couldn't rid her mind of the image of Louise telling all those people she was Greg Maynard's daughter; or the mortification on Pam's face as she'd screamed, "You fucking slag!"

How intolerable for Pam to have been completely unaware of Greg's infidelity and then to have found out about it in such a publicly humiliating way. Although Louise's ambush had equally devastated Sharon, at least she'd always known that Greg was Louise's father. So, what had been shockingly divulged to that packed hall had come as no surprise to her: the knowledge was her daily reality, and therefore wasn't the thunderbolt it had been for Pam. Pam's life had been bisected by the night's events, and from now on her experience would be divided into the world as it had existed "Before Oliver" and the world as it was now, after it. "Before Oliver", Pam had been a trusting, unsuspecting wife and mother. "After Oliver", she was a betrayed woman whose husband had been leading a double life right under her nose: for over eleven years committing de facto bigamy, until it had been scandalously exposed to the whole village by his secret daughter whom he'd been hiding all the time in plain sight.

Surely, Sharon reasoned, Pam must now be thinking back to all those times "Before Oliver" when life had seemed so normal but quite clearly hadn't been. With the retrospective irony afforded by hindsight, wouldn't she be feeling the anger of a double betrayal? So many simple, treasured memories of her married life must now have become poisoned by suspicion; violated by the certainty that "Before Oliver" the constant subtext of her husband's deceit had been running like an invisible thread through her everyday normality. Without doubt, Pam would be remembering all the times Greg had said to her, "I'll just pop round to Sharon's" and she, poor fool, had innocently replied, "OK, love. See you later." And now she knew the ulterior motive for all those visits she would be reconfiguring every one of them: conjecturing what had gone on between her husband and Sharon behind the closed door of Honeysuckle Cottage; imagining the worst and knowing it had been worse than she imagined. And in this frame of mind she'd go forward into her new life, tortured by uncertainty, jealousy and loss; painfully accommodating herself to her new and utterly changed perspective on reality, which is the lot of those who come face to face with a lover's deceit and betrayal. Poor Pam, thought Sharon. What will she do now? But more importantly, what would Greg do? It was strange that he'd made no attempt to contact her. He hadn't even sent her a text. For that she was glad. If Greg thought he'd be moving into Honeysuckle Cottage to play happy families he could think again. His behaviour outside the village hall had been unforgivable.

Sharon came to the fence at the end of the garden which separated it from the field beyond. Darkness had fallen some time ago but a huge moon was creating an illusion of daylight, illuminating the fields and low hills which rose up on every side of the village, so that they glowed with unusual clarity. It was a clear night and the constellations were singular and distinct. How heavenly it was to smoke. She stood gazing up at the moon and stars, puffing vigorously, and along with the tobacco smoke inhaled something else: something invisible and eternal which seemed to hint at some unrevealed design. Her mother and father, could they be up there? In all those spaces between the stars?

She dropped the cigarette on to the grass and, swaying unsteadily, crushed it under the sole of her foot. She then turned to stare at the rear of the terrace. All the other houses were in darkness. The only light was in the upper storey of her own cottage: Louise's room. She wondered if Louise was still awake. She hoped not. Even as a toddler she'd been unable to sleep unless the light was left on. Time to perform the nightly ritual of looking in on her to check if she was asleep, and then quietly turning off the light. Anyway, the midges were biting worse than ever.

She moved up the garden towards the rear of the cottage. After silently opening the back door, she made her way through the kitchen, into the sitting room and up the open staircase to Louise's room. She still couldn't get out of her mind how upset the child had been by Greg's violent attack on Dylan. Poor thing. She'd kept turning round and staring through the car's rear window as if she expected to see Greg chasing after them. "They won't call the police will they?" she'd kept asking. "Dad won't go to prison, will he?" Sharon had managed to calm her down and reassure her, although she too was anxious about the way things might turn out for Greg. And for Dylan too. She hoped he wasn't badly hurt.

When they were safely inside the cottage, she'd presented Louise with lemonade and chocolate éclairs, the post-performance treat she'd promised her. At first, Louise couldn't be tempted. She cried and kept repeating that everything was spoilt and it was all her fault. Sharon was determined to follow Dylan's advice not to be judgemental or punitive and she'd given Louise a great deal of sympathy. This had been strangely easy because she felt profoundly grateful to her. Now that the whole of Leefdale knew their dark and sordid secret it hardly seemed to matter at all. It really was such a small thing. She couldn't understand why she'd got herself into such a state about it.

Louise was eventually persuaded to try the éclairs. Sharon listened silently as the child ate with growing relish and explained why she'd felt an overwhelming need to tell everyone the identity of her father. It seemed she'd been convinced that the audience had been willing her to tell them her secret and would reward her with even more applause when they heard it. "But they didn't," she said. "They should have clapped. Why didn't they?"

Sharon felt an overwhelming surge of compassion for Louise and took her in her arms and comforted her. Looking into the child's wounded eyes, she promised her that by Monday they'd no longer be living in Leefdale. Louise looked astounded. "By Monday! How?" "Trust me," Sharon had said. Now, gently opening the door to Louise's bedroom and observing her daughter's sleeping form, she thought of that reply again and felt the strength of her own resolve. She placed her fingers to her lips and blew Louise a kiss before turning out the light. In the darkness she whispered a promise, more to herself than her child: 'I won't let you down, Lou. Not this time.'

Sharon closed the door to Louise's room and came down the stairs wearily, holding on tightly to the banister for support. She assumed that her tiredness was an effect of all the alcohol. Or was it a deeper tiredness? In the sitting room she poured out the last glass of red, and was wondering whether to carry it outside into the garden and enjoy it with another cigarette when there was a sudden noise: a light tapping on the front door which made her jump like a startled hare. The wine in her glass sloshed around and threatened to spill. She stared at the door which had suddenly become a dangerous and unpredictable beast. Then came a second sound: thump, thump, thump. With a shock, and some relief she realised it was the sound of her heart racing. She listened for the tapping to come again, praying it was a product of her imagination. No. There it was again filling the room with foreboding. Could it be Greg? Had Pam chucked him out?

The outside cover of the letter box was raised and through the aperture came a voice, barely above a whisper. 'Sharon. Are you there? It's me. Dylan.'

She put her glass down on the coffee table and moved quickly across to the door. 'What is it? What do you want?'

'I need to see you. Please, just for a few minutes. Open the door. Please.'

'I don't know.'

'Please,' he said, low and urgently.

She heard the pleading tone in his voice and relented. Gently she eased back the bolt and carefully swung the door open. Although she was anticipating him, his actual presence gave her a tremendous start. He seemed to fill the whole doorway. He stood there staring at her like a traveller who couldn't believe he'd found refuge.

She took a step back, allowed him to go past her and then quietly closed the front door. Her first thought as she followed him into the sitting room was that the top of his head almost touched the ceiling.

He said, 'I've been up in my studio trying to paint, trying to take my mind off things. But I couldn't. I kept thinking about what happened this evening. I just had to see you.'

'You'd better sit down,' said Sharon, slipping on to the sofa. She folded her legs under her and fruitlessly attempted to cover her knees with the hem of her short dress.

'Thanks.' He eased himself into an armchair opposite her. 'Lovely room.'

'Thank you.' She picked up her glass from the coffee table in front of her. 'I'd offer you some wine but this is my last glass.' She took a long sip.

'That's OK. I probably shouldn't anyway.' He pointed to his face.

She noticed that the cheekbone below his right eye seemed puffy and raised. 'Are you all right?'

'Yes, fine. I'll probably have a black eye though. That was quite a punch Greg threw.' He gingerly touched the developing bruise on his cheek. 'Does it show?'

'A bit.'

'Much?'

It occurred to her he might be quite vain. 'Not much.'

'So, how's Louise?' he said.

'She's sleeping. We'll have to be very quiet. I don't want to wake her.' She told him how upset Louise had been about the scuffle between him and Greg. 'I'm sorry I ran off. I just had to get Louise out of there. What happened after I left? Were the police called?'

He smiled and shook his head. 'No. Eventually we managed to calm Greg down. He went as meek as a lamb. I was able to convince him that none of us had anything to do with what Louise did tonight. After that he was quite reasonable. Even apologised to me.'

'You won't be reporting him to the police for assaulting you, then?'

'No. I don't think any of us needs that.' He smiled. 'Fortunately, Jade missed seeing her dad being pinned down by Zoe.'

'Zoe was amazing,' said Sharon. 'How was she able to do that?'

Dylan gave a gentle laugh. 'She's a martial arts expert. Got a black belt in Jiu Jitsu.'

'Oh.'

'Actually, we're all taught how to restrain violent young people so they can't harm themselves or others.'

'Good thing, too.' Sharon took another sip of wine. 'So what happened to Greg?'

'His wife arrived in the car. Someone must have rung to tell her that Greg had been involved in a fight. They went and collected Jade and then drove off. Actually, I thought...'

He hesitated.

'Yes?'

'I thought he might be round here.'

'Well, as you can see, he isn't.'

'No.'

'It didn't stop you coming here, though.'

'No. I wanted to be sure, I suppose.'

Sharon stared at him surprised. What was it that he wanted to be sure of? That she and Greg were still together? Best not to go there. Not yet, anyway. She took another sip of wine and said, 'As a matter of fact when I heard the knock I did think it might be him.'

He looked at her quickly. 'You're disappointed?'

'No.'

There was a long pause. Dylan was finding it hard to raise the subject that was at the forefront of his mind.

'So, what will you do now?' he said.

'Leave Leefdale.'

'Really? Is that necessary?'

'You saw what Louise did tonight. It'll be all over the village by now. It's impossible for us to stay.'

'But where will you go?'

'I'm not sure. As far as possible.'

There was another long pause. She knew what he wanted to know but she wasn't going to help him.

He said, 'Forgive me for asking this, I know it's none of my business, but after what's happened are you hoping he'll leave his wife and move in with you?'

She shook her head. 'No. That's the last thing I want. If Pam kicks him out he might suggest we move in together, but the answer will still be no.'

He wanted to ask her why, but felt inhibited. 'I see.' He paused, and then said, 'So, it's over?'

'It's been over for long time. I just didn't have the guts to end it.'

She drained her glass and put it back on the table. 'It's getting late. You said you needed to talk to me. Why?'

'To fill in the gaps, I suppose. You see, tonight, when Louise revealed that Greg was her dad so many things fell into place. I suspected Louise had problems with the adults in her life but it never occurred to me that...' He paused, struggling to find the words to precisely express his thoughts. 'What I'm trying to say is that I have an insight now into the cause of Louise's problems but there are so many things I don't understand. Things I'd like to know.'

'Like what?'

He looked slightly embarrassed. 'Well, for example, the night we went to The Trout you told me you had a boyfriend. Was that Greg Maynard or someone else?'

'It was Greg.'

'So Greg was the only man in your life?'

'Oh yes. There's never been anyone else.'

'Never been anyone else?' He was thinking hard. 'But surely you've been out with other people?'

'No. I said there's never been anyone else. Greg's the only man I've ever been with. I've known him since I was eighteen.'

'I see. So you've been having a secret affair with Greg for years?'

'That's right. Before tonight no-one in the village knew about us.'

'Including his wife?'

'Including Pam, yes.'

'But Louise knew he was her father?'

'Yes.'

'Louise is eleven. That means...'

'That's right. We've kept it a secret for over eleven years.'

'And how long has Louise known Greg was her father?'

'Since she was eight.'

'And she's kept it to herself since then?' Dylan couldn't keep the astonishment out of his voice. 'Never told anyone?'

'Not until tonight.'

Dylan sat staring into space. He seemed to be struggling to comprehend what he'd been told.

'It's not been easy, you know. There've been times when I wanted to chuck it all up and find someone else, you know, a proper relationship.'

'So why didn't you?'

'I don't know. I had Louise to bring up and Greg was around a lot of the time. I didn't want to mess things up. I'd got used to things the way they were. So, if anyone wanted to start a relationship I always told them I already had a boyfriend.'

'You were very convincing.'

She said nothing.

'How did you get involved with Greg?'

'It was after my parents were killed.' She hesitated. 'I was in a very strange place.'

'Look, if you'd rather not...'

'No. It's OK. It'll help you understand.'

She hesitated again, but he waited.

'I knew Greg and Pam because they bought their house from Parker and Lund's. I'd just started working there as a trainee and I helped arrange their purchase. After that I used to bump into them in the village occasionally, but I really didn't have much to do with them. She was heavily pregnant and they seemed happily married. Besides, I was only eighteen. They were quite a bit older than me.'

Sharon paused here and sighed heavily. She'd never told a soul before how or why it had happened, or explained how she'd inexorably created the conditions which had effectively imprisoned her. Besides, it was late and the thought of embarking on a tale of such complexity was daunting. Even so, she willed herself to continue. It was an appropriate night for catharsis.

'Anyway, a few weeks after Greg and his wife moved here, the village hall committee organised a treasure hunt. My friend Jenny and I went along to it. We all met outside The Woldsman to receive our clues. Greg was there too. He was on his own because Pam had gone to visit her mother for a few days. I was one of the few people he knew in the village and as he didn't know the area at all, out of politeness, I invited him to come with Jenny and me in my car. I was rather hoping he'd say no but he jumped at the chance. So, off we went. Unfortunately, the treasure hunt had been planned by Mr Casey, who was the head teacher at the primary school then, and the clues were very hard to understand. They needed a really good knowledge of the history and geography of the area, which none of us had. So, we ended up following lots of red herrings and doing loads of U turns. Well, when it was nine o'clock and we'd only found half the answers we decided to call it a day. There was a bar meal booked at The Woldsman for all the treasure hunters. When we got there, we found we were the last to arrive and everyone else was at the pudding stage. We handed our answers over to Mr Casey and found a table and started into the wine quite heavily. While we were eating our meal, Mr Casey presented us with the wooden spoon for having the least number of right answers. It was very embarrassing. It wasn't that important but the three of us felt very stupid. I think that's why we drank a lot more wine than we should have. Greg was a real laugh. He was taking the piss out of the treasure hunt, doing impersonations of Mr Casey and making up unbelievably difficult, complicated descriptions of the simplest things, just like Mr Casey's clues. Around about ten o'clock people started drifting off home. But the three of us stayed on drinking. Eventually, even Jenny left but Greg and I lingered on, drinking and telling each other about ourselves. I liked him. He was very attractive. A real man. I'd only been out with boys before. I got the impression his marriage wasn't very happy. He had ambitions. Around politics. That sort of thing. But Pam wanted him to concentrate on getting promotion.'

Sharon stretched out her legs, crossed them and sat up, leaning forward.

'We stayed in The Woldsman's restaurant until closing time. I was in no state to drive so I left the car there, overnight. Greg and I both lived on the same side of the village, so we walked home in the same direction. I remember feeling that I didn't want to stop talking to him. I wanted the evening to go on. I was lonely, I suppose. I'd been pretty much on my own since my mum and dad were killed.'

'We came to my house first. We lingered outside for a minute or so, then I invited him in for a cup of coffee. But we didn't have coffee. We had more wine.' She held Dylan's eyes. 'That was the night Louise was conceived.'

Tentatively he said, 'Were you...?'

'Yes, I was. And very innocent for my age. Imagine my feelings when I discovered I was pregnant. The child's father was married. I was eighteen. Both my parents had been killed the year before and I was still badly affected by their deaths. I had no-one to talk to. It was hardly surprising that my emotions were see-sawing all over the place. One day I'd be sure that termination was the only solution. The next day I'd have a complete change of mind and be determined to keep the child at all costs. So, I'd make plans to sell the house, move to another village before my condition became obvious, and have the child in secrecy. Another day I'd feel I could go on as though nothing had happened, ignore the village gossip and refuse to discuss my situation with anyone. Then, maybe a few days later I'd be considering abortion again. That's how it went on, day after day, until I was in such a state I seriously considered killing myself.'

'You never told Greg?'

'What was the point? It would only have made trouble and he'd probably have denied it. His wife was pregnant. I didn't expect him to leave her. Anyway, it was a one night stand. Pam returned the day after we'd slept together, and after that I never saw him again for ages. No, I never told him. I calmed down and stayed in Leefdale for most of the pregnancy and somehow fronted the whole thing out. I thought what the hell! Let them all construct their own theories about whose child it is.'

'So Greg didn't know?'

'No. He found out eventually, though. One night he appeared on my doorstep completely drunk, demanding to be let in. It was six months later and my pregnancy was apparent to even the most unobservant male. Greg said there'd been much talk of it in the village and around the bar of The Woldsman. He said that he felt the finger was being pointed at him, although nothing precisely had been alleged. So I told him.'

'How did he take it?'

'Very well. Once he'd got over the shock, he accepted it was his. He said he could see no reason why I should be dishonest. You see, I'd made it perfectly clear I didn't want to break up his marriage or anything. That's when we devised our plan. We decided we'd both stay put and ignore each other. We thought if neither of us moved out of the village no-one would suspect Greg of being the father. Meanwhile, I'd let it be known quietly that the father was some guy I'd had a one night stand with while I was staying with my aunt in Norwich, and I wanted nothing more to do with him. Greg promised to support me in any way he could. He said he'd fallen in love with me, couldn't live without me, that sort of thing. He wanted us to go on meeting secretly after Louise was born.'

'Did you love him?'

'I thought I did.' She stopped, considered, and then corrected herself firmly. 'No, I did love him, then. But I was eighteen and pregnant. My hormones were all over the place. So, I agreed to stay put. It was the most sensible thing to do. We both had our houses to think of. He'd never find another as good as the one he had for the same price, and I had no wish to leave this lovely cottage. It's full of memories of my mum and dad. It's where I grew up. I couldn't bear to sell it and move into some pokey place in some strange village, or a tiny flat in town.'

'Anyway, Pam's baby was born in October. She was christened Jade. That was embarrassing. They invited me to the christening.' Sharon laughed at the recollection. 'In late February, I went to my aunt's house in Norwich and had my baby in the local hospital. In April I came back to Leefdale with Louise and things just went on from there. I was able to keep my job, although it meant leaving Louise with a childminder in the village. Later, I was able to find a place for her in a nursery. The weird thing was that Louise and Jade started school at the same time. They were in the same class and became best friends. You can imagine how that made me feel. Through birthday parties, school events and so on, I came to be thrown together quite a lot with Greg and Pam. That too was pretty difficult.'

'Were you and Greg still...?' Dylan let the question hang in the air.

'Fucking? Yes. Whenever we could find the opportunity, which wasn't easy. Greg had the solution to that though. He began to get involved in local politics. He got elected to the parish council and joined Community Watch. He encouraged me to become the secretary. It gave him a good excuse for dropping round to see me and Louise.'

'So Louise knew from the start that Greg was her father?'

'No. At the beginning she only knew he was Jade's father. We always referred to him as Uncle Greg when he came round. Ever since she was able to talk, Louise asked me where her daddy was. I used to tell her that he'd gone away. But when she was seven she became much more demanding and started to question me about it a lot. She wanted so much more information. What was he like? What did he do? And so on. I suggested to Greg that we told her the truth, but he wouldn't hear of it. He said it would confuse her and make her resentful. But I think he was really afraid that if she knew he was her dad she'd blurt it out to someone and destroy his position in the village. We had a very big row about it and he made me promise that I wouldn't tell her. But one night, when she was again asking me about her father, I decided I'd had enough of all the evasion and the secrecy. So I told her that her dad was really Uncle Greg. She didn't believe me at first, because Greg already had a family and Jade was her best friend. I managed to convince her in the end though. I said it had to be our secret, and I made her promise she wouldn't tell a soul what she knew, not even Greg.'

'How old did you say she was when you told her?'

'Eight.'

'Quite a responsibility for an eight year old.' He wanted to tell her more than that. He wanted to say that the burden of guilt she and Greg had imposed on Louise was intolerable and well within the definition of mental cruelty. But instead, all he said was, 'How did she take it?'

'Oh, really well. She was thrilled. Each time Greg came round she'd be more and more affectionate towards him. Everything was going fine until one night when she was sitting on his lap, reading to him. Suddenly, she said, "You're my dad. I know you're my dad. Mum's told me."'

'How did he react?'

'He was astonished and got very angry. Right away he made Louise solemnly swear she'd never repeat what she knew to anyone else. He told her that if she broke her promise, her mum and dad would be very hurt and she might never see us again. He also told her that Jade, Gwen and Ian were not just her friends but her brother and sisters, and if she broke her promise, terrible things would happen and she wouldn't see them again either. She got a bit confused, poor thing. She asked us if Pam was her real mummy.'

Dylan decided this had to be one of the worst cases of emotional abuse he'd come across. He said, 'So, she's been keeping this important secret since she was eight?'

'Yes.'

'No wonder she's been exhibiting disturbed behaviour. Didn't it occur to you that by doing this to Louise you could be causing her enormous emotional harm?'

Sharon shook her head. 'At first she didn't seem to mind. It thrilled her, honestly. She loved to call Greg, daddy, and it stopped her asking where her real father was. But then, as she got older she started asking me very difficult questions. She wanted to know why daddy had to have two families, why he couldn't be with us all the time. When I failed to address these issues she got very resentful. Then, at the beginning of this year the school nurse gave her class a talk on sex education. After that, she became very difficult. You see, the nurse and her teacher emphasised that sex ought to take place in a loving and caring relationship. In a family. That was the catalyst. I think it made her see herself as abnormal. Someone who has to be hidden away and not spoken of. Someone who knows her father but can't acknowledge him in a normal, natural way.'

'Poor Louise. If only I'd known this earlier.'

'Why? Do you think it would have prevented what she did tonight?'

'Probably not. Who knows? But I could have understood her conflicts more. Worked them through. Zoe would have been a great help with that too.' A sudden insight changed the tone of his voice. 'But that's exactly what you feared, wasn't it? Us finding out?'

'I nearly told you everything on Thursday night when you showed me her paintings and said you thought she was being abused.'

'Why didn't you?'

'I don't know. I suppose the habit of secrecy is very hard to shake off.'

He nodded. 'Yes, I can see that.' After some thought, he said, cautiously, 'Didn't it bother you that Greg was still producing children with Pam while you and he were having an affair?'

'While we were fucking, you mean?'

'Yes, but I'm intrigued why you keep using that harsh word for it.'

'Because that's all it comes down to end in the end, isn't it? Fucking? And death too, of course.'

Dylan's expression lightened. 'There's a bit more to life than that, isn't there?'

'Really?' She laughed bitterly, and shook her head from side to side as though it was all too much. 'It's all right, ignore me. I'm just rather low at the moment.'

'Understandably.'

'Anyway, I was quite relaxed about Greg and Pam having kids. It threw everyone off the scent. Who'd believe Greg was Louise's father when he was happily producing his own offspring?'

'But why didn't you simply move away from here?'

'I told you. I couldn't bear to leave my home. It's my life. It's where I was brought up. Where my parents lived all their lives.'

It seemed to Dylan that this was the justification of someone who was deeply frightened of maturity: terrified of growing up. You would never know it, looking at this beautiful, poised and confident woman. But we all have at least one fatal flaw, he thought, and most of us usually manage to conceal it exceptionally well.

He said, 'Are you sure that's the only reason you stayed on here?'

She didn't respond at first. She was deciding how honest she could afford to be without turning him off; and then it occurred to her that what he'd learned about her tonight should have already turned him off, so why was he there? She decided to risk it.

'Well, there was the sex, of course. It was fantastic, and as time went on I couldn't get enough of it, even though it had to be furtive and quick. I'm not going to be hypocritical about that. I really loved it. And there was the added thrill of the secrecy. Secrecy is such an incredible aphrodisiac. But all that was fine when Louise was younger and could be put to bed early. The problems started when she got older. And after eleven years the secrecy began to wear me down. I began to long for a normal existence. You know, a normal relationship. That night you took me to The Trout was one of the happiest I'd had for years because it felt so normal. Then you asked me to go out with you. You've no idea how much I wanted to say yes. I knew things had to change, that Louise and I were leading really abnormal lives. But I was frightened to make the move, so I fell back on the old excuse that I had a boyfriend.'

This was deeply upsetting for Dylan. It was hard for him to imagine what Louise's childhood must have been like. How intolerable it must have been for her to have seen her father on a regular basis, lived in such close proximity to him, and yet been forbidden from publicly acknowledging his existence. The emotional and psychological damage done to her must have been immense. Again, he thought of the girl trapped under the frozen pond, hived off from her family who were enjoying themselves on the ice. He thought of the extraordinary significance for Sharon of their night out in The Trout, and the rare, conventional happiness it had given her; in doing so he appreciated the extent of the social isolation she and Louise had experienced. The thought that Sharon had been yearning to take up his offer to go to Budeholme but had been prevented by her secret life filled him with sadness and regret. If only he'd known.

Sharon said, 'Do you think what Louise did tonight has damaged her, you know, psychologically?'

He made an inconclusive gesture. 'I don't know. Possibly. On the other hand it may have been cathartic, and in that sense beneficial. It will have released her from the tension of unbearable irreconcilable dissonances.' Sharon looked at him blankly. 'I mean, over the years she's been trying to resolve impossibly contradictory demands. Trying to keep her parents' secret whilst maintaining an elaborately constructed façade which was at complete odds with her own reality. Think of all the little lies she will have told every day about her dad in order to preserve the false presentation of self you created for her. The guilt she would have experienced worrying that one day she might make a slip and the secret would be out. I'm sure the emotional pressure of all that has been incredibly stressful for her and she's glad to be free of it, even though it creates other problems for her.'

'God. What have we done to her? I feel awful. You make me sound like a monster. I didn't realise.' Sharon buried her face in her hands.

Dylan gave her a tender, sympathetic look. 'What's important is that we help her come to terms with the consequences of what she's done tonight, and liberate her from her suppressed guilt. There's a great deal of anger in Louise and many unresolved issues to do with her identity and the way she relates to the world. She really needs the opportunity to explore these with a trained therapist.'

Dylan was standing now. Sharon took her hands from her face and looked up at him. Her cheeks were wet with tears and she was smearing them away with her fingertips. 'I'm so sorry. You see, I didn't realise.'

He said, 'You know, over the next few days and weeks Louise will probably exhibit disturbed behaviour. She may become increasingly withdrawn. Or subject to excessive mood swings, lack of concentration or unexpected outbursts of rage. Now that she's told everyone the identity of her father she'll feel she's publicly let you and Greg down, so she'll probably be full of remorse and guilt. It's very important that she's able to explore her conflicts and contradictory feelings with a therapist. I'm willing to do anything I can to help Louise, and I know that Zoe, Eric and Toni feel the same. You're very welcome to keep bringing her to the rectory over the summer holidays, Sharon.'

Dylan's offer was genuine and heartfelt, but he was very much aware of the self-interested motive behind it. If Sharon kept seeing him because of the help he was giving Louise, then hopefully, he could progress things to the point where one day she might become his. She looked so lovely sitting on the sofa with her legs curled under her, her dark hair and bare shoulders reflecting the soft highlights from the subdued light of the lamps. Everything she'd said had encouraged him to think he now stood a good chance with her. But he didn't want to rush things. It was clear that she was much more complex and vulnerable than he'd imagined. Taking her on would make him responsible for two emotionally bruised people. It would be a great responsibility, and in truth, he felt a little daunted by the prospect of it. Her personal life might be bizarre but she had excellent qualities, qualities that would obviously help her surmount her present difficulties. She was practical and business-like, a good organiser with sound common sense; and she was obviously caring, you could see that by her concern for Louise. She appeared secure and grounded, characteristics he valued and which he knew he was personally deficient in, although, he was improving all the time. He was also impressed with the loyalty she'd shown Greg, and her ability to persevere in conditions and circumstances she must have found unbearable at times. And God, she was gorgeous!

Yet a professional voice warned him that there must be something missing in her. How could she have failed to see the damage she and Greg were doing to Louise, and why hadn't she done her best to prevent it? Surely more than simple negligence and inertia had been responsible for Louise's situation persisting for so long? Hadn't Sharon exhibited an almost psychopathic level of selfishness by refusing to remove herself and Louise from their domestic situation? An innate instinct was telling him that she was inimical to him in some way and he should keep as much distance between himself and her as possible. His experience with Zoe had taught him that involving yourself in another person's hell in addition to your own always carried a huge risk. But what were you supposed to do? Become an isolate? That way too lay death. Besides, it probably hadn't been Sharon's intention to deliberately inflict such misery on Louise, just carelessness; and it occurred to him that now he was aware of the extraordinary, secret relationship she'd been in with Greg, he ought to be more assertive, speak out and offer her the mature, conventional adult relationship she obviously yearned for. But he baulked at this, because he feared he might not be able to provide her with that sort of relationship, or even want to. He suspected that he wasn't sufficiently grounded enough for her: was too intellectual, far too interested in abstract theories, too arty. They might prove totally incompatible. On the other hand, they might complement each other's deficiencies perfectly. And she was so beautiful!

She saw him looking at her and sensed that his offer was more than professional. The thought frightened her. If he became Louise's therapist he'd probably try to persuade her that it was in her and Louise's interests to remain in the village, and that was something she was determined not to do. And yet, the thought that he and she might have a future together thrilled her. Then again, she wondered if it was wise to start a relationship with someone so soon after Greg, while her life was still in turmoil. Yet if Louise continued to visit the rectory they would at least still see each other from time to time. She certainly didn't want to lose contact with him.

'Thank you for the offer,' she said, and then, because she couldn't help herself, she went on, 'But are you sure there's not more to it than that? I get the feeling you want us to become close. You know what I mean, don't you?'

For a while he said nothing and she was afraid she'd offended him. But this impression was dispelled when he smiled, and said, 'Yes. That's why I was so glad yesterday when you said you'd still like to go to the concert at Budeholme House. Ever since that night in The Trout when you told me you had a boyfriend, I've been hoping that one day you and I would get together. The feeling's just as strong now as ever.'

'Even now you've found out how deceitful I've been?'

He came towards her and took her hand. 'You've explained why you behaved as you did. It's perfectly understandable. You became involved with a much older, married man at a time when you were at your most vulnerable. You shouldn't underestimate the trauma you were feeling from the loss of your parents at such a young age.' He raised his hand and traced his forefinger gently across her wet cheek. 'For years now you've been clinging to your childhood; the only period of emotional security you've ever known.'

Her spine stiffened at the sensation of his touch. She felt the tips of his fingers caress her cheek and come into contact with her lips. She found herself rising from her chair.

A door slammed somewhere in the house. They both jumped apart like the guilty couple in a farce. Sharon pointed urgently towards the stairs. 'It's Louise!'

Dylan turned away and went quickly to the mantelpiece. Sharon shot over to the bottom of the staircase. As she got there Louise arrived on the top stair and looked down at them, puzzled.

'Mum? I could hear voices. Are you all right?'

Sharon fought to control her racing heart. 'I'm fine. Dylan's just popped in to see if you're OK.'

Dylan joined Sharon at the bottom of the stairs. 'Hello, Louise.'

'Hello. What happened to dad? Did the police take him away?'

'No. He's fine,' said Dylan. 'We didn't have to call the police.'

'Oh good.' The child's relief was obvious and quite genuine. Her face puckered as the tears came. She closed her eyes. 'I've been worrying about him so much!'

'Come down for a moment, Lou.'

Louise came down the stairs slowly. She was wearing pyjamas and slippers and was still half asleep. She came to Sharon who immediately gave her a hug.

Dylan said, 'It must be difficult to sleep after giving such an exciting performance.'

'It's not because of that.' There was a catch in her voice. 'It's just that I keep thinking about what I said, you know, after "Oliver". About dad.' She looked up at her mother. 'And about you. I had these awful dreams.'

'Sometimes dreams are our way of having a conversation with ourselves,' said Dylan. 'That's why, if we can remember them it's good to draw them. It helps us understand what we're trying to say.'

'That might be a bit above her head,' said Sharon, going to a box of tissues.

Louise looked intrigued. 'No, mum. I'd like to draw my dreams.'

'Listen, Louise,' said Dylan, as though he'd just remembered something. 'Tomorrow, Zoe is taking everybody to the beach at Filey to make some sea sculptures. Eric and Toni are going too. Would you like to go with them?'

Louise was wiping her eyes with the tissue Sharon had given her. 'What's sea sculptures?'

'Oh, just sculptures made out of stuff that you can find on the beach. Anything really, sand and seaweed, shells, bits of driftwood. I'm sure you'd find it fun.'

Sharon stroked Louise's hair, tenderly. 'Would you like to go, love?'

'Yeah. I would.' She looked Dylan directly in the eyes for the first time. 'Thank you.'

'Bring her round about ten.' He looked at Sharon. 'You can go too if you want.'

'Go on, mum,' urged Louise.

But Sharon had seen that this was a wonderful opportunity to get Louise off her hands while she took control of her life.

'Actually, I've got a lot of things to do tomorrow.'

'What things?' Louise asked.

'Just things. Things to do with a surprise I'm organising for you.'

'Oh, what?'

'I'm not telling you. It wouldn't be a surprise.'

'Are you going to the beach too, Dylan?' said Louise.

'Afraid not. I'm going to use the opportunity to get into my studio and do some serious painting.'

Sharon filed this information away with interest.

'I love your studio,' said Louise.

'Yeah, it's nice, isn't it?'

'I love the colours and all the pictures. It's a great place to hide.'

'Hide?' He smiled. 'Well, yes, I suppose it is. I'd never thought of it like that.' He turned to Sharon. 'I'd better get back. Goodnight.'

After they'd returned from seeing Dylan to the door, Louise gave her mother an insinuating look. 'You and Dylan are going out tomorrow while we're at the beach, aren't you?'

Sharon laughed. 'What gives you that idea?'

'I'll bet you are,' said Louise.

Sharon sent Louise up to bed. Later she picked up her cigarette packet and her matches and went out into the garden.

CHAPTER FIFTY SIX

When Dylan arrived back at The Old Rectory, the house was in darkness and everyone appeared to have gone to bed. Wearily, he enabled the alarm in the hall. He did this every night before turning in. It was a tedious chore but he felt it was necessary to keep the house safe from burglars; and also alert him to any clients who might have decided to abscond while everyone else was asleep. As he punched in the number code he recalled, as he invariably did, the day Sharon had brought him to Leefdale to view the rectory, and how scrupulous and concerned she'd been about disabling the alarm. It seemed an age ago now but it was actually only April.

After setting the alarm, Dylan climbed the creaking stairs to his room. He'd just started undressing when he heard a footstep on the landing. This was followed by a light knock. It was Zoe.

'Can I come in?'

'It's very late.'

'Please. I've been waiting up for you.'

'All right.' He opened the door wider. 'Come in. But we'll have to keep our voices down.'

'OK.'

He let her in and gently closed the door behind her.

She said, in a whisper, 'I just came to see if you're all right.'

'Yes. I'm fine. My face is still sore, though.'

He gestured for her to take the room's only chair and then went and sat opposite her on the bed. She was wearing just her short legged pyjamas. She crossed her long, bare legs and Dylan came a little more awake. How strange sexual attraction was. Despite actively disliking her, he still found her desirable.

Zoe said, 'I came to see if I could change my day off to Monday.'

Surely that could have waited until the morning? Really, her behaviour was becoming more and more bizarre.

'This coming Monday?'

'Yes. John's asked me to meet him in Sandleton.'

'John?'

'John Carter. The photographer.'

Her expression suggested to Dylan that she was trying to provoke him.

'Oh, that John,' he said airily. 'Bit young for you, isn't he?'

'He's nineteen. I'm twenty six. The age difference is less than that between you and me, if you want to be sexist about it. Anyway, it's nothing like that. He wants to show me his collection of wildlife photos.'

'That should be interesting.'

She ignored the sarcasm. 'So, can I change Thursday to Monday?'

'I don't see why not.'

'Thanks.' She brought her knees together and leant forward. 'There's another favour I want to ask.'

'Oh?'

'Could I borrow the Ariel? It would be great to give it a run to Sandleton, and John's very keen to see it.'

Dylan wasn't very happy with this. For some reason he found the idea of Zoe and John Carter deriving pleasure from his Ariel Red Hunter, without him, distinctly unwelcome. There was also a more practical objection: he intended selling it soon and didn't want it damaged. But he knew it would be childish, if not churlish, to refuse. 'Of course, you can.'

She gave him a big, beaming smile and thanked him.

'Anyway,' he said, 'how can I say no when you saved my life?'

'Someone had too,' she said, wryly.

'Seriously, thanks again for defending me. I always knew your martial arts skills would come in useful one day.'

'You obviously need to get some yourself.'

He ignored the implicit reproach. 'But how are you feeling now? You must be traumatised. It was an astonishing thing to do, overpowering Maynard like that.'

'Not really. I've been training for it for years.' Her look became critical, almost aggrieved. 'I still can't understand why you didn't defend yourself. Why didn't you punch him back?'

'You asked me that before.'

'I know. But why didn't you?'

Dylan shrugged his shoulders. 'Oh well. You know.'

'No. I don't know. Why didn't you stick up for yourself?'

'I was trying to reason with him.'

She tossed her head, despairingly. 'Christ, Dylan, you're thirty four years old. Haven't you learnt anything? There are some people you can never reason with.'

'I was trying to avoid violence.'

'It's not violence if you're defending yourself. What would have happened if I hadn't been there to defend you?'

He sighed heavily. 'Just let it go, Zoe.'

Zoe didn't feel like letting it go. She wanted to go on with it, but Dylan's pacific nature wasn't the reason she'd come to see him. Changing her tone, she said, 'Have you been to see Sharon and Louise?'

'Yes.'

'I thought you had. You've been out a long time.'

He sensed some sexual jealousy.

Zoe waited but Dylan said nothing. 'So, how are they?' she asked.

'Both trying to accommodate to what's obviously been a momentous event in their lives. Fortunately, Sharon's taken my advice. She's being very understanding towards Louise. Treating her most sensitively.' Pointedly, he added, 'She's not being at all judgemental.'

Zoe looked sceptical. 'Really? More likely suppressing all her anger and aggression.' Her expression became fierce. 'I tell you, if my child publicly humiliated me like that I wouldn't be taking it quietly. I'd be climbing walls.'

They discussed, yet again, Louise's extraordinary and dramatic public revelation. They both admitted that they hadn't suspected for a minute that Maynard was Louise's father; or that Jade could be Louise's half-sister.

'His poor wife,' said Zoe. 'How humiliating. Did you see her? She looked like she'd been slapped with a wet fish.' Her eyes glittered, maliciously. 'I suppose he'll be leaving her now and moving in with Sharon.'

Dylan knew that this was only said to make him feel uncomfortable and claimed ignorance.

'I must say,' said Zoe, 'you've got to admire Sharon. She could give master classes in deceit.'

Ignoring her remark, Dylan said, 'Oh, by the way, I've invited Louise to come to the beach with you tomorrow. I hope you don't mind.'

'Is Sharon coming too?'

'No.'

'Then I don't mind.'

There was a long pause. Finally, Zoe said. 'Sharon must have said something to you about what happened tonight. She must have given you some kind of explanation.'

'She did.' He gave her a short, selective account of Sharon's affair with Greg Maynard. His description of the two parents binding Louise to secrecy affected Zoe deeply. She looked horrified. 'At the age of eight? What a trauma that must have been for her. No wonder she's disturbed.'

'I agree. It's an appalling example of emotional and psychological abuse.'

'They should both be referred for counselling.'

Dylan said, 'Actually, I've offered to help Louise.'

'You? How?'

'Professionally.'

'That could be dangerous, couldn't it? Given your feelings for Sharon?'

'What feelings for Sharon?'

Zoe's look was withering. 'Oh come on. Lie to me by all means but don't lie to yourself.'

Equably, Dylan said, 'I'm not lying to anyone, least of all myself.'

'Good. I'd be really worried about you if you were still infatuated with her, now you know what she's really like.'

'Oh? What's she really like?'

'A woman who deceives everyone about her child's parentage, and subjects her daughter to psychological stress just to preserve some ludicrous and outmoded notion of bogus respectability.'

'I'm surprised you don't see her as a victim, or regard Maynard as bearing most of the responsibility.'

Zoe's eyes locked with his. 'That's a given. All men bear responsibility for women's suffering.'

He resisted the bait. 'Anyway, I'm hoping I won't be the only one working with Louise. I'm sure you'll help her, if you can. Won't you?'

Zoe looked slightly embarrassed. 'Not me, I'm afraid.'

'Ah.'

'Not because I don't want to but because I won't be here. I've resigned.'

This was a shock. His first emotion was relief, until he started wondering how he'd replace her. 'That's very sudden.'

'Well, I'm impulsive. As you're always saying.'

'Am I? How much notice will you be giving?'

'Charles said I need only give the minimum.'

This was bad news. The minimum notice was only four weeks. 'I see. I'd better start looking for a replacement right away.'

He was reluctant to ask her why she was leaving as he knew it would only re-open old wounds, but it would seem bizarre not to enquire.

'So, why are you going?'

Zoe responded with a look of huge self-satisfaction. 'Actually, I'm going to resume my acting career.'

This was another big surprise. 'I thought you'd moved on from all that. Didn't you tell me that acting and the arts in general were a waste of time because they never achieved anything?'

'I was depressed when I told you that.'

Dylan was still reeling from Zoe's news. It was entirely unexpected, almost shocking. He'd known for some time she was convinced that art contributed nothing to human existence. She'd made it clear to him on many occasions that she saw it as something spurious and self-indulgent; an irrelevancy in a world where so many awful things were happening and people were leading such dreadful lives. How many starving people had Art fed? What appalling diseases had it cured? How many wars had it stopped? This had been her reasoning. Art, she'd once told him, was nothing more than a comfort blanket for those who wanted to close their minds to the awful realities of experience. This, apparently, was why she'd originally given up acting and playwriting, and thrown herself into her drama therapy work. She'd been convinced that it would enable her to do something practically useful and effect real change in people's lives. She'd even expressed to him the hope that, in time, she'd enter politics; do something that might really transform the world for the better. That's why he was finding the reasons for her resignation so extraordinary. In fact, he wasn't altogether sure he believed her.

'But now you definitely want to return to acting?'

Her eyes gleamed with conviction. 'Yes.'

'So what happened to make you change your mind?'

'It happened gradually. As you know, I've had a very negative view of acting for some time, but I've slowly realised that art has its positive and negative aspects just like anything else. And recently I've discovered it can do something that nothing else can: it can give significance and purpose to a world that seems pointless, and guide people towards a more fulfilled life.'

This struck Dylan as somewhat specious as well as embarrassingly histrionic. As long as he'd known Zoe, he'd understood that she'd given up acting because she was afraid of following the example of her father, Seamus Fitzgerald. He'd had a chaotic lifestyle, dragging Zoe and her mother all over the world, forcing them to live out of suitcases. There was never enough money and they were often completely broke, but somehow Fitzgerald had always found sufficient funds for alcohol and gambling, his main interests apart from acting.

'But you always said your father's example turned you off it.'

'It did. But I feel differently now. Just because my father didn't have total commitment to his art, there's no reason I shouldn't.'

'But you've invested so much in your career as a drama therapist. All those qualifications and skills are going to be thrown away.'

'No. Not thrown away. I'm sure all that knowledge of human behaviour will make me a much better actor.'

'But surely your work as a drama therapist fulfils you?'

'No, it isn't nearly enough. I feel I'm only working at half power most of the time.' Catching his fleeting look of disapproval, she added, 'I'd have thought you of all people would understand that. I know you'd really like to paint full time.'

'Yes, I would. But I still find my art therapy work fulfilling. And I do need the money. I can't eat my canvasses.'

'So you sell out. You compromise?'

'Is it compromise? I prefer to call it accepting reality. I can't paint if I can't afford brushes and a studio to work in. Anyway, Life's one long compromise, isn't it?'

She said nothing but he could see from her vexed expression she didn't agree. He said, 'So this change of heart has been a gradual thing?'

'Yes. I've been considering resuming my real career for weeks now. But it was Louise who really helped me make up my mind.'

'Louise?'

'Yes, that afternoon when she sang "Where is Love?" so poignantly. She made me realise what astonishing beauty the stage can bring into people's lives. How profoundly it can affect them.'

'So that's when you knew you had to become an actor again?'

'Not quite. What sealed it was Louise's contempt.'

'Contempt?'

'Yes. Don't you remember? When I told her that acting was a very difficult career and one day she might have to give it up, she rounded on me with complete contempt. She swore that she'd never, never give up. That really affected me. Her refusal to contemplate abandoning her ambition made me so jealous. Can you imagine? Being jealous of an eleven year old? I really envied her that certainty. Her determination never to give up on her art. She made me feel ashamed of myself. I thought if this child can have so much commitment, why can't I? And then on Thursday night I went to see "The Seagull".'

Dylan stared at her blankly. 'I'm sorry, I don't follow.'

'There's a character in it called Nina. When we first meet her, she's a young, innocent girl who's determined to become an actress. She realizes her ambition but at a terrible cost. She finds the life of a provincial actress in nineteenth century Russia is coarse and full of hardships. But when she appears at the end of the play, she's learnt that if you're an artist, a real artist, you can put up with anything for your art. In fact, the art itself gives you the capacity to endure whatever life throws at you. It gives you the faith to go on. That's why when Nina thinks of her vocation she isn't afraid of life.'

A strange light was emanating from Zoe's eyes. It disturbed Dylan. 'And that's what decided you? A character in a play?'

'Yes. A character in a play written a hundred years ago gave me the courage to change my life. That's when I knew art has the capacity to give life significance and effect real change. And my faith in it was restored.'

'Well, you certainly seem to have made up your mind.'

'Yes. I phoned Charles yesterday and told him I was resigning.'

'That's funny. I was on the phone to him this afternoon and he never mentioned it.'

'He agreed to keep it quiet. I told him I wanted to tell you myself.'

'Thanks, I appreciate that.' He gestured awkwardly. 'I'm sorry to lose you.'

'You don't mean that.'

'All right. I'm not sorry to lose you.'

She laughed 'So which is it?'

'I'm sorry to lose you professionally.'

'Yes. I think you do mean that.'

'I can't pretend I'm not pleased.' Carefully, he said, 'I think the situation's become untenable, don't you?'

'It hasn't worked out as I thought it would. No.'

He saw that it gave her much pain to confess this, but it was late and pursuing it further would only pour petrol on the flames. He said, 'It's certainly a surprise, though. How did Charles take it? He must have been very disappointed. He pushed so hard for you to get this job.'

'He was very understanding. Very sympathetic. At first, he said he wasn't going to accept my resignation. When I made it clear I wasn't giving him a choice he told me he was disappointed but understood my reasons. I owed it to myself to have another go and all that. He said he was more than willing to take me on as a temporary drama therapist when I wasn't acting and couldn't find a job.'

'That's very generous of him.'

'Yes. But I had to turn it down.'

'No. Why?'

'It's too easy. I don't want to get sucked back in to full time drama therapy. It'll stop me finding acting work and writing plays. You know how difficult it is when you have to take a job home with you.'

Dylan nodded. 'I certainly do. But how will you live?'

'I'll find something. As long as it doesn't take up my precious spare time; time that has to be devoted to getting acting work. I'll work in a bar or as a waitress. Jobs that give me flexibility. Anything rather than be inveigled back into a career outside acting.'

'Yes, your old maxim: "You must have a talent for having a talent". Eric was quite taken with it. Most impressed.'

'I know he's told you all about our disastrous affair,' Zoe said, coolly.

Dylan was used to her being direct but this was another bombshell. Floundering in embarrassment, he said, 'Actually, he did mention it. It was certainly a bit of a shock. Although, as you know, I had my suspicions. Not that it's any of my business. I gather it happened long after you and I split up.'

'Not that long afterwards. I was still at my lowest point. It was a consolation shag and I regretted it immediately.'

Why was she so adroit at making him feel like a heel? He couldn't resist the opportunity to retaliate. 'Regretted it so much you went back for second helpings, according to Eric.'

'Really? What a shit he is to tell you that. Yes, another mistake. It only happened because in Charles's flat I was trying to make you jealous. I was desperate for you to want me again. That's why I asked Eric for a lift. When he took me home it seemed unfair to disappoint him.'

'But that's why, when I saw the chemistry between you and Eric that night, I assumed you'd both applied for jobs here, because you wanted to be together.'

'You were wrong. I swear to you Eric left his wife and kids and followed me here without any encouragement from me. He insisted on applying for this job, even though I begged him not to. I came here to get away from him but he stuck like a leech.'

Dylan gave her a long, probing stare. 'Why did you lie to me?'

'Lie?'

'On the first night you arrived here, I suggested that you and Eric were together and you denied it.'

'Of course I denied it. I didn't want you to know I'd slept with Eric. I thought I still loved you and I didn't want anything to jeopardise us getting back together. That's why I followed you all the way up here.'

Dylan thought about this. 'So it wasn't just for the challenge of a new job?'

She looked slightly unsure. 'Well, yes, partly.'

'You seem confused about your reasons for coming here.'

'Really?'

'Yes. First you said it was for the challenge and that Charles persuaded you to apply. Then you said it was because you wanted to be near me and hoped we could get back together. Now you're saying you applied for the job to get away from Eric. So, which is it?'

'People do things for all sorts of reasons. I don't know exactly why I came here, but those three reasons were part of it and there were probably others. I'm not some predictable, one dimensional character in a third rate novel or play. That's not what real people are like. They're spontaneous. Something seems like a good idea so they do it. Very often it goes wrong, as it has in this case. Not everyone is as calculating or as strategic as you. I don't know exactly why I came to Leefdale but I'm glad I did. It's clarified a lot of things. It's defined for me what I really am. What I really want. Maybe I had an idea it might do that all along, and that's really why I came here.'

'So you're saying fate sent you here now?'

'Perhaps.'

She came and sat down next to him on the bed. She placed a hand on his shoulder. 'Why don't you give this up and come back with me to London?'

'What?'

'I could sell my flat and move in with you. We could use the money to support ourselves while you painted and I looked for acting work.'

'That's totally unrealistic.'

'Why?'

'I can't just resign.'

'Not immediately, but you could give notice now and join me later. Just think what a wonderful life we'd have together. You'd be able to paint full time at last, and I'd be happier because I'd be doing what I really wanted. We could even ride the Ariel on the heath again. It would be a perfect life.'

'Until the money ran out.'

'But it wouldn't. Have you any idea what my flat is worth now? And it wouldn't take long before we were both successful.'

'Well, I suppose if we did run out of money you could always count on Charles' support.'

Zoe blinked furiously. 'Charles? What's he got to do with it?'

'Eric thinks the man who shared your bed before him was Charles. And it's Charles you're really carrying the torch for.'

Zoe looked affronted. 'There's never been anything thing like that between Charles and me.'

'Not for Charles's want of trying, according to Eric. He said Charles made a move on you when you went out with him behind my back.'

Zoe took her hand off Dylan's shoulder.

'Is Charles going to be your talent for having a talent?' said Dylan.

'What do you mean?'

'Only that it's very easy to accuse others of selling out when you have a rich patron behind you. And it's very easy to have a talent for having a talent when you don't have to worry about where your next meal is coming from.'

'I don't like what you're implying. I don't have a rich patron. Who are you saying is my rich patron? Charles?'

'I'm not saying it. Eric is.'

Zoe stood up and moved away from the bed. She seemed to be reflecting on something. Then, she turned decisively to Dylan. 'All right, I did go out with Charles a few times. When you were spending whole weekends stuck in your studio, painting.'

'How often?'

'I don't know. Three or four times.'

'Why didn't you mention it?'

'Because I knew you'd be suspicious.'

'What else did you and Charles do behind my back?'

'Nothing!'

'Is that why you always wanted to keep our relationship secret? So Charles wouldn't find out?'

'I swear I've never slept with Charles.'

Here Zoe was telling the truth. She'd never slept with Charles, although there'd been plenty of opportunities. Unfortunately, it's a sad fact of life that when you've been found to be untrustworthy over one thing, you'll probably be thought untrustworthy over lots of others.

Dylan said, 'Why should I believe you when you lied to me about Eric?'

'I told you why I did that. Because I was miserable and desperate and I thought it would destroy any chance of us getting back together.'

Quietly, Dylan said, 'Eric says you intend to marry Charles.'

'Rubbish! Eric's stupid.'

'You've treated him pretty shabbily though, haven't you?'

'You've got a nerve, after the shabby way you treated me!'

'No, I didn't treat you shabbily. I may have treated you insensitively, bluntly, but I never hid from you the fact that it wasn't working and we had to end it. Come on, admit it. You never followed me here because you love me. You're here because I told you some unpleasant home truths, and you were determined to come after me and make me suffer for my honesty.'

'Unpleasant truths? Oh, I remember. When you said I was too forthright. Unthinkingly forthright and gushing, that's me, isn't it? Well, you won't have that problem with Sharon, will you? The last thing she is is forthright. She's been deceiving a whole village for years!'

Dylan jumped up and put a finger to his lips. 'Shh!'

Zoe took no notice. 'You made me think I was the one with all the defects but in reality it's you. I'm offering you the opportunity to be the artist you've always wanted to be, but you're too afraid to take it. Don't you see? People who don't follow their creative instincts wither and die inside.'

Dylan scoffed. 'You don't know me at all, do you? It's a marvellous offer and if it was from anyone else I'd jump at it. But it's from you, and I know if we moved in together we'd never create anything, we'd destroy each other.'

'No. You're afraid of it. Instead of being a serious artist along with me you'd rather stay in this backwater earning a regular salary and doing the odd bit of painting when you get the time.'

'I'd rather do that than be dependent on you or anyone. Besides, people who have only art in their lives are sad sacks. Doomed to disappointment. And my life is here now. I don't have romantic notions of being an artist in an ivory tower. My work as an art therapist takes me deeper and deeper into life. I may have to work at this job until I retire, but even if I paint only one day in a hundred, I'll be painting what I want to paint. I'll never paint to please someone else. That's because I work and support myself and am dependent on nobody. That's what I call a talent for having a talent!'

She threw up her hands in despair. 'I see now that following you here was a terrible mistake. I could never be happy with a man who's so weak. You wouldn't even defend yourself when someone was punching you in the mouth. God knows what would have happened if I hadn't restrained Maynard. You've always said we're completely incompatible and I see that now. I was totally blind to it before.'

'Good! We are incompatible. You're far too intense and dramatic for me. You're well suited to the stage. I hope you're successful there.'

Zoe leant towards him pugnaciously. 'And you're certainly well suited to Sharon. She's as cold blooded as a calculator. But she'll be very good for you. She'll probably make you a well-known artist. Help you market your work so it appears on tea towels and biscuit tins. She'll make you rich and famous and in the process destroy your art.'

Dylan gave a condescending laugh. 'Bollocks! Artistic snobbery of the worst kind. What's wrong with having your work depicted on biscuit tins or tea towels? It brings it to a wider audience. Just think of all those prints of "Sunflowers" or "The Hay Wain" hanging in people's rooms. It doesn't diminish Van Gogh's original painting or Constable's, does it? And those prints have given millions enormous pleasure. What's wrong with that?'

Both their voices were raised now and they were arguing fiercely; although their differences were really quite trivial, and what united them was far greater than what divided them. Such is the tragedy of the world.

They were both so wound up, a sudden knock on the door made them jump out of their skin.

Dylan went over to the door and quietly, said, 'Yes?'

Eric's voice, low and occluded, came back from the landing. 'I heard voices. Is everything all right?'

Zoe was now standing right next to Dylan. She swept him aside and wrenched open the door to reveal Eric's astonished face staring back at both of them.

'Everything would be fine if you stopped stalking me,' Zoe hissed at Eric. She pushed past him and set off to go, but then, turning back, brought her face threateningly close to his. 'By the way, it wasn't Charles who screwed me before you. It was Dylan. We've been having a secret affair for a year. And he's much, much better in bed than you'll ever be.' She cocked her head to one side and twisted her face into a vengeful smile. 'Just to set the record straight.'

Eric watched her cross the landing and go up the stairs. Then he turned back to Dylan. He looked completely dumbfounded.

Dylan gave him a broad smile. 'Zoe's resigned.'

CHAPTER FIFTY SEVEN

Dylan was standing at his easel, evaluating his work of the previous two hours. A stick of charcoal was in his hand, and on the canvas in front of him was his drawing of a large horse-chestnut tree. He'd been considering the drawing for some time, occasionally lifting his eyes to an enlarged photograph which was pinned to the wall above the easel. The photograph was of a parkland scene: two enormous horse-chestnut trees stood side by side and in their vast shade a man, a woman and their three teenage children were picnicking.

Dylan's gaze continued to alternate between the photograph and his charcoal drawing, and if there'd been an observer in the room they would, quite naturally, have assumed he was making sure his drawing was an accurate copy of the photograph. But they would have been mistaken. He wasn't attempting a meticulous reproduction of the scene captured by his camera, but the re-creation of its essential elements. The banal snapshot of a family eating lunch in the open air was being transfigured into a work of art: a visual drama of personal conflict, self-absorption and indifference to the natural world.

Finally, after several more references to the photograph, Dylan made a small and careful adjustment to the drawing and took a step back to assess its effect. He was evidently satisfied with the modification because shortly afterwards he began work on the outline of the second tree.

He'd taken the photograph some weeks before, and on seeing the print had immediately become convinced of its potential as an appropriate subject for a work in oils. He'd been keen to start work on it at once but until now that had been impossible. Fortunately, Zoe's trip to Filey beach with the kids had emptied the rectory of people and given him the opportunity to begin. Now he was relishing the house's unnatural silence and the pleasure of his own solitude. Such wonderful quiet! Not a sound entered through the windows he'd flung open to entice in the elusive breeze. The tumult of the past few days had receded: no more baying reporters or clamouring crowds. Not even the noise of the Major's ride-on mower disturbed the tranquillity. He rejoiced in the knowledge that Zoe and the others wouldn't be returning from the beach until six. The prospect of a tranquil Sunday afternoon stretched ahead of him in which his only concern was for himself. He was glad of that. He'd had a disturbed night during which, in the distorting hinterland between sleep and wakefulness, he'd been tormented by the conviction that he was going to lose Sharon. Bizarrely, mingled with this had been another torment: that he'd no longer have the skill or the talent to paint representationally, and that the picture of the picnic under the horse-chestnut trees would be a disaster. Surreal and conflated images of Sharon and the picnicking family in the portrait prevented him from attaining the deep and dreamless sleep his mind and body craved. When he awoke the fitful dreams remained vivid, especially one in which Sharon was reminding him of his own advice to draw the things that frightened you. But all that belonged to last night. Now, as he effortlessly regained his mastery of the techniques of naturalism and addressed himself to the challenges of the new work, he began to experience the confidence and satisfaction which comes from the re-discovery of an old and neglected expertise. He worked quickly and within half an hour the second horse-chestnut tree had burgeoned into verdant being.

His father had been the first to teach him the traditional techniques of drawing and painting, and throughout his youth and early twenties he'd produced many landscapes, portraits and still lifes. But some years ago he'd abandoned the representational for the abstract. This had happened after he'd been exposed to the Neo Plasticism of Piet Mondrian, whose art had been a revelation. Mondrian believed that the appearance of the natural world concealed fundamental realities. His regular and ordered paintings of horizontal and vertical lines interacting with squares and rectangles of white, grey and pure primary colour seemed to Dylan to express the universal harmonies and fundamental creative structures behind nature's appearances. The lines in these abstracts continued right to the edge of the canvas and appeared to extend into infinity, so that the work seemed to be a tiny section of an infinite cosmos. Although they didn't contain any recognizable naturalistic form: no tree or hill or woman's face, they always evoked in Dylan an immediate emotional recognition, releasing within him great chords of pure feeling. "Broadway Boogie Woogie", for example, a work from Mondrian's New York period, painted 1942-43, was a pulsating grid composed of varying lengths of yellow, red and blue that evoked perfectly the experience that was "Old Broadway": the streets, the flashing lights, the crowds, the clamour, the music, the sexuality, the energy, the excitement; all these were present and continuing into infinity without a single building or human being in sight. That's why he loved the Abstract. Why he'd adopted it as his metier.

So why was he abandoning it? Why this sudden need to return to painting the mere surfaces of things? Why go back to reproducing the appearances of reality and not the deeper, universal structures that expressed its fundamental base? It was a question he'd long avoided, worried it might be an indication that his development as an artist hadn't been as authentic as he'd assumed. Yet now he was convinced that his return to the representational was yet another aspect of his development: a consequence of his work in art therapy. Hadn't he spent his career as an art therapist looking for the archetypes, the universals behind the appearances in his clients' art work? In that respect he wasn't abandoning the principles of abstract art but enhancing them. He would be using representational art to reveal nature's universal structures. He wished Sharon was there so he could explain this to her.

Sharon! How gorgeous she'd looked last night, sitting erect and sphynx like on her sofa, recounting to him her extraordinary, clandestine affair with Greg. He recalled the bare nakedness of her shoulders, the way her dress had clung tightly to her body, the flimsy white material emphasising every curve of her thighs. He couldn't get out of his mind the look on her face as she'd recalled the greedy pleasure of her sex with Greg. Or the tone of her voice when she'd described secrecy as an incredible aphrodisiac. She'd been so completely frank about her love of sex. Surely this had been an invitation? If only he could be sure! He obsessed yet again on the way her face had lifted, nuzzling into his finger as he'd gently caressed her cheek, and how certain he'd been that she'd wanted him to kiss her. Who knows where things might have gone on from there? What might have happened if Louise hadn't appeared?

He forced himself to concentrate much harder on his drawing but the image in his mind, a fantasy of Sharon naked and eager for him on the sofa, refused to be usurped by the image of the horse-chestnut trees he was erecting on the canvas. Really, he told himself, in many ways his life had become as abnormal as Sharon's. Working in intense proximity to other people, surrounded by them the whole time, deprived of privacy, having to snatch whatever moments he could to paint. No wonder Zoe didn't regard him as a serious artist but as an art therapist who occasionally did some painting. All his life it seemed he'd been part of some larger group. Living with his father in the commune, sharing a squat at art school, then university halls of residence, and after that living and working in several closed, self-sufficient communities like The Sandleton Trust. Hardly normal, was it? He'd never had any problems with the communal life, indeed had always thought it a most natural and supportive form of social organisation. But lately, its limitations had become more and more apparent, particularly its restraints on his freedom, and he was finding himself more and more out of sympathy with it. There were times he actually yearned for the pleasure of being alone for long periods. Lately too, he'd begun to suspect that his lifestyle was responsible for his inability to sustain lasting and satisfactory relationships with women. He'd always valued the needs and interests of the group more highly than those of individuals; he needed the stimulation he received from living and working alongside a number of people and absorbing their ideas. The group also satisfied his constant need for novelty and change. For these reasons an exclusive, hived off relationship with one person had never satisfied him. Such relationships always seemed to start off so positively, and then deteriorate into battles of wills over trivia and banality, before they ultimately ended in boredom and estrangement. Yet knowing this, why was he determined to embark on a similar exclusive relationship with Sharon? Was it, like his wish to return to representational art, a longing for the reassuring appearances of everyday reality? The security of the bourgeois existence, as Zoe had implied? Or did he see it as his last chance to prove that he wasn't a commitment phobe?

Zoe! Had he been too hasty in rejecting her generous offer? He knew that at some point in the future when he was completely bogged down in planning and admin and yearning to snatch an hour or so in which to paint, he'd curse himself for turning her down. The trouble with being pig-headed and convinced of your own rightness was that as time passed it turned to regret. He tried to imagine what his father would have said. "So, a gorgeous girl wants to sell her flat to support you so you can become a full time artist? What's not to like? Why don't gorgeous girls ever make me those kind of offers?" As long as he got the sex and the money and was able to paint, Bernard wouldn't have cared a damn about the inherent potential of such a relationship to infantilise him, make him dependent and rob him of his autonomy. But Dylan had no wish to enter such a top dog/underdog relationship with Zoe, in which the one with the money would call the tune. That's why he'd rejected Zoe's offer and was prepared to risk his chances with Sharon.

Of course he wanted to have sex with Sharon, but his interest in her wasn't only sexual. He felt that she possessed qualities that might make it possible for him to share his life with her. Or was that too an illusion? He'd long felt that he was one of those people who were far too curious about the world to seek it in only one person. Yet he was also aware that his personal relationships with women had mainly been established and conducted in a communal setting. Was that why they hadn't stood a chance? Or was he psychologically incapable of sustaining a monogamous relationship? He hoped not.

He worked on, struggling with these and other unsettling thoughts. In this way, another hour passed and the drawing was complete. He took a break and sat back in a chair, reflecting on his efforts and working out the palette he would use when he started to paint. Where to begin the brush strokes and so on. There were so many decisions to be made before his conception of the work could be transformed into reality.

Through the open studio windows came a sharp, metallic click as the latch on the front gate was raised; there was the creak of a hinge as the gate was opened; and then the noise of scraping metal and a clang as it was banged shut. This was followed by the crunch of footsteps on the gravel drive. All these sounds told him that his peace and solitude were about to be disturbed. He sighed, and frowning slightly, went over to the window. The last person he expected to see was Sharon, but there she was striding up to the front door. He watched her progress for a moment wondering why she was calling. She'd been told Louise wouldn't be returning until six.

He leaned far out of the open window and called to her, loudly.

She stopped dead and her hand flew protectively to her heart.

'Did I make you jump?'

'Yes, you did,' She was looking up and smiling.

'Sorry.'

'If I'm interrupting you tell me to go away,' she shouted.

'It's all right. I'm taking a break.'

He ran down the stairs like an excited teenager, opened the front door and ushered her into the hall. Despite the intense heat she looked ice cool in her stone coloured chinos and thin white T shirt. He was overwhelmed by the unexpected presence of her beauty, and for a moment could think of nothing to say. This morning, when she'd brought Louise to the rectory she'd barely looked at him and nothing remained of the intimacy he'd thought they'd achieved last night. His gaze dwelt briefly on her nipples which were erect and straining against her tight T shirt. He averted his eyes and saw that she was holding a carrier bag. A most attractive fragrance enveloped her. She hadn't been wearing perfume when she'd called round earlier to deliver Louise, and he speculated about the purpose of her visit.

'I'm in the studio,' he said, moving towards the stairs, 'Come on up.'

He led the way up the stairs, intensely conscious of her insinuating fragrance. She followed him into the studio and stood in the centre of the room, looking at everything around her with a genuine, childlike pleasure.

'I can see why Louise loves this room,' she said.

'Oh, of course. You've never seen my studio before.'

'No, but I feel as though I have. Louise described it to me in such great detail.'

She moved across to look at the abstract paintings hanging on one wall.

'Are all these yours?'

'Yes. All mine.'

She stared intently at each of the canvasses: at the intersecting lines and blocks of colour which Louise had so enthusiastically described. But she couldn't summon up any enthusiasm for them.

Watching her he felt a sudden surge of disappointment. She seemed to be trying so hard to extract pleasure from the paintings, which meant of course that they were giving her no pleasure at all.

'Take your time,' he said. 'It's not an exam.'

She laughed nervously, and said, 'They all seem very similar.'

'They're not really. I think you'll find they have lots of subtle differences. Look at them more closely.'

She did so, with the perfunctory obedience of one whose attention has been drawn by the guide in an art gallery to something she'd missed.

'Do you like them?' he asked, after a while.

'I think I do. It's hard to say. I think I've seen them before somewhere. Or something like them, anyway.'

'You probably have. Mondrian's influenced scores of designers. Anything else?'

'There's something very angular about them. And a bit cold too. It's hard to put into words. What are they supposed to mean?'

'Now that's very hard to say,' said Dylan. 'They probably mean whatever it is they make you feel.'

She looked perplexed. 'But they don't make me feel anything.'

She saw the drawing of the horse-chestnut trees on the easel, and immediately moved towards it with a little jig of recognition.

'Now I do like this,' she said. She stared appreciatively at it for some time. 'Who did this one?'

'I did.'

She looked confused, and gestured towards the abstracts. 'But I thought you only did those kind of pictures.'

He laughed. 'I can do all kinds of paintings. I didn't start off painting abstracts. Like most people I trained to paint what you'd call "proper" pictures.' He pointed towards a corner of the room where a pile of canvasses were leaning against the wall. 'There's a whole stack of them over there.'

Sharon was relieved to hear this: it seemed to make him so much less eccentric. He was such a good looking man, interesting in so many ways and such fun to be with. She'd been thinking about him all day, wondering what might have happened last night if Louise hadn't woken up: but now she was here and alone with him, the physical intimacy that had seemed so inevitable just a few hours ago had disappointingly receded, and he was going on and on about those peculiar paintings. She was trying so hard to like them, she really was. She just couldn't understand what the attraction was. His interest in them made him seem a bit of a nerd, an anorak. It was the only thing against him. She could see that they were quite clever patterns. But when he'd said they meant whatever it was they made you feel, he'd completely lost her. Pictures of scenery made you feel; portraits and paintings of animals. The only thing those abstracts made you feel was stupid. She didn't understand them at all; and she knew she hadn't the knowledge or the confidence to develop the conversation further and clarify exactly what he meant. The abstracts made her feel ignorant and they seemed to come between her and Dylan like a kind of curtain. Which was why she'd felt such relief when he'd said he'd done a lot of proper paintings.

Sharon's eye had been caught by the photograph of the people picnicking beneath the horse-chestnut trees. She scrutinised the photo and then turned her attention back to the drawing on the easel. 'The drawing isn't quite the same as the photograph.'

'It's not meant to be.'

'Oh. Aren't you copying the photo?'

'Not exactly copying it. Using it for reference.'

'It's great,' she said. 'Is it finished?'

He laughed gently. 'No. It's got to be painted.'

She studied the drawing intently. 'Won't that spoil it? It looks finished to me.'

'No. It's got to be painted.'

'I'd sell it as it is.'

'I'm not selling it.' Seeing her baffled expression, he added quickly. 'Well, not yet. Anyway.'

'The trees seem familiar,' she said. 'I've seen them somewhere.'

'The photo was taken in the arboretum at Budeholme House.'

'Of course! That's where it is.'

'I went there some weeks ago. You weren't able to come, so I thought I'd go anyway. Alone.' Thinking this made him sound peevish, he said, 'You were right. The gardens there are wonderful.' He moved across to the photograph. 'This little group caught my eye. They were bickering with each other all the way through their lunch, and taking no notice at all of their magnificent surroundings. I had to photograph them. When the photo was developed I felt I just had to paint them.'

'I'd like to see it when it's finished,' she said. They both caught each other's eye. 'Actually, I've come to ask you for a favour.'

'Oh?'

'Yes. I was wondering if I could borrow your van for a few hours.'

It was the last thing he'd expected. 'I should think so,' he said, slowly.

'I need it to shift some of my stuff.' She could see that he was intrigued. 'This morning I went into the office. You see, we're open till twelve on Sundays. I didn't go there to work but to find a place to live. On our books we have several properties to rent which are stuck. You know, aren't shifting. So I got out the details of those that were in Luffield, made a few calls and arranged to view them.' She'd spoken in a nervous rush and now paused to take a breath. 'I've taken one of them. It was the first one I saw. The landlord knows me so he's given me the key. It's a lovely flat. Unfurnished, with a great view of the park.' She reached into her supermarket bag and brought out a note pad. 'Here, I drew a picture of it.' She flipped back the pages and showed him her drawing. It was of an empty sitting room. Through the panes of the curtainless window, a patch of grass, a few trees and some swings could be seen.

'I felt terrified after I'd agreed to rent it. Had a sort of panic attack. Then I remembered the advice you gave me when we first met. You said if something frightened you it was helpful to draw a picture of it.' She gave an embarrassed, little laugh. 'So, here it is.'

Dylan took the notebook and studied her sketch. 'It looks a very spacious flat,' he said.

'Yes, it is. It's lovely.'

'And did drawing it help?'

'Oh, yes. A lot. It seemed strange while I was doing it but afterwards I felt a lot better. More in control somehow.' She'd been shyly averting her gaze, but now looked straight at him. 'I've helped so many people to move home but never had the courage to do it myself. Stupid, isn't it?'

She retrieved the notebook and took a quick look at her sketch, as though reassuring herself of its existence. Then she put the notebook away in her carrier bag.

'When would you like the van?' Dylan asked.

'Tomorrow morning, if that's all right. I'd like us to be in the flat by Monday night. So we'll need to get some essentials in there as soon as possible. Pots and pans, clothes, the washing machine, that kind of thing.'

'What about beds? The van's big enough to take them.'

'That's OK. We'll manage with sleeping bags until the cottage is sold.'

'You're selling up?'

'Yes. I arranged for it to be put on the market this morning. It should sell pretty quickly. There's a big demand for the smaller village properties.'

'Are you sure you're doing the right thing?'

'Absolutely. Louise and I need to get right away from here.'

Dylan nodded. There were many things he wanted to say but didn't feel entitled to.

'OK. I'll bring the van around tomorrow morning. Ten o'clock all right?'

'Fine.'

'I can help you move the stuff as well, if you like.' He looked at her expectantly. A lot depended on her reply.

She smiled warmly. 'Thanks a lot. I'd appreciate that. As a matter of fact, I was going to ask if you'd mind giving us a hand. Somehow I couldn't see Louise and me carrying the washing machine between us.'

He laughed disproportionately, because he wanted her to know she made him happy.

'I hope Louise likes the flat,' Sharon went on. 'I thought I'd take her over to see it when she gets back from the beach.'

'I'm sure she'll be delighted. After all, she always wanted to leave Leefdale.'

Sharon looked at him sharply. 'How do you know that?'

'Just something she said once.'

She nodded and gazed at him. He was wearing blue jeans and an old shirt that was covered in accidental daubs of paint. At his temple was a dark streak of charcoal. She longed to touch it and tell him it was there.

Dylan said, 'I suppose this means I'll be seeing a lot less of you.'

'Luffield's only ten miles away. You've still got your driving licence, haven't you?'

He laughed, and then immediately looked serious. 'I've been thinking a lot about what you told me last night, about you and Greg and everything. I really meant what I said about Louise benefiting from art therapy. Even though you're moving away the offer still stands.'

'Thank you. Actually, I discussed it with Louise this morning. She said she thought it might help her a lot. She's really keen to do it. She said she'd like to start next week. Is that all right?'

'Perfectly OK.'

Sharon smiled at him. Then delved into her bag and with a slight flourish produced a bottle of champagne.

Dylan looked surprised. 'What's this?'

'I've made a momentous decision today and I feel like celebrating. Will you join me?'

'Sure. I'd love too.'

'It's still reasonably chilled.'

'I'll get some glasses.'

Dylan set off for the kitchen. While he was gone Sharon went over to the pile of canvasses propped against the wall. The ones Dylan called his "proper" pictures. She started going through them and was surprised at how good they were. So normal. She couldn't understand why he wanted to mess around with those things that looked like lino patterns from the 1960s, when he could draw and paint real pictures so wonderfully. There were landscapes, pictures of fruit and portraits, one particularly good one of a very distinguished looking elderly man: his father, perhaps?

She turned to the next canvas. It was a female nude.

The profuse tangle of thick pubic hair both repulsed and riveted her. It was shocking because she hadn't expected it. She tried to pass it off. Make light of it. Dylan was a painter and lots of painters painted nudes. It didn't mean anything. Then, a terrible suspicion came into her mind, and with it a more profound shock, even more disturbing than her discovery of the nude. She carried the canvas over to the window where she stood holding it towards the light, scrutinizing it closely. There was no doubt about it. It was definitely Zoe. The long red hair, the prominent eyebrows, those amazing blue eyes, the uncompromising attitude. She was sitting on a plain wooden chair, hands on knees, breasts upraised; staring out of the painting in an attitude of insouciant defiance. The knowledge that Zoe had sat in this indecent and unselfconscious way being painted by Dylan, and the look of pure love for him radiating out of her, left Sharon in no doubt about the intensity of the relationship between artist and sitter. It was so nakedly intimate it made Sharon feel like an unwitting voyeur who'd unintentionally stumbled upon Zoe at her most physically and emotionally exposed.

But had it actually been painted by Dylan? Could it have been done by someone else? Quickly, she checked the bottom right hand corner of the canvas. There were the conclusive initials DB and the date: 2000. Only a year ago. Disturbingly recent. She remembered him telling her that there wasn't anything between him and Zoe. That they were only colleagues. But the painting suggested otherwise: that there'd been an intensely passionate relationship between them once. And then the awful thought occurred to her that it still might be ongoing.

Sharon recalled Dylan's voice, just hours ago, telling her that he hadn't given up wanting her, even when he'd understood she had a boyfriend. There was still the fugitive sensation on her cheek where his finger had touched it. What was the real reason he'd come round to see her last night? Surely it was because he'd wanted her? He'd said it was "to make sure". To make sure of what? Sure that she was his? She thought of the ephemeral pressure of the back of his fingers inadvertently coming into contact with her shoulder as she'd sat back in her chair at the beginning of "Oliver".

Suddenly she experienced a surge of emotion so unfamiliar to her that it was some moments before she recognized it as jealousy. She was unnerved by her sudden, overwhelming urge to attack the painting, destroy and obliterate Zoe's naked image, and have Dylan all to herself.

Hearing footsteps coming up the stairs, she moved quickly across the room and replaced the nude amongst the other paintings propped against the wall. She then returned to her former position by the easel.

He entered the room holding up two plastic cups.

'No champagne flutes, I'm afraid. Will these do?'

'Fine.'

A sickening thought occurred to her: who else exactly had seen the nude? Zoe presumably. But what about Eric and Toni? And what about the kids? For God's sake! Had Louise seen it? She knew she couldn't ask him directly. Instead, she said, 'You've got a lot of valuable pictures and equipment here. Aren't you worried that they'll get damaged with all the kids about the place?'

He was making a space for the cups amongst the clutter on his workbench. 'No. This room is locked the whole time. People are only allowed in here when I'm around to keep an eye on them.'

His answer went some way to reassuring her. She felt sure that Louise had probably not been left alone to explore the studio on her own.

Dylan started to untwist the wire around the neck of the champagne bottle.

She said, 'Greg phoned me, you know. From Manchester Airport. He was there with Pam and the kids. They were waiting for their flight to Spain.'

'They're still together?'

'Yes.'

'How do you feel about that?'

'Relieved.'

'Are you sure?'

'Absolutely. He was ringing to tell me it was all over between us. He and Pam have patched things up. When they get back from Spain they're going to put their house on the market and leave Leefdale. It gave me a lot of pleasure to tell him not to bother on my account. That I was moving to Luffield anyway.'

Her words sent a thrill through him. If she was telling the truth, and he had no reason to doubt it, the main obstacle to his happiness had been removed. But it also made him feel a little apprehensive: there was no excuse now for not telling her how he felt, and he was worried about her response.

Dylan turned the cork carefully until it popped and a spume of champagne gushed into the first cup. He handed it to her and poured one for himself. Raising his cup, he said, 'To you, Sharon, and your new life!'

She raised her cup too. 'Thank you.'

They both drank.

'I hope I can be part of it,' said Dylan.

'My new life?'

'Yes.'

She returned his gaze, uncertainly. Did he really mean what she understood him to mean?

She said, 'Do you remember when I brought you to view this house?'

'I certainly do.'

'You said you'd like to paint me sometime, remember?'

'Yes.'

'Well, I think I'd like that. I'd like that very much.'

He put his cup down and came towards her.

****

THE LUFFIELD ADVERTISER

AROUND THE COURTS

Charges against Leefdale man dropped.

Charges against Howard Roberts, a retired army officer, of Rooks Nest, Church Lane, Leefdale have been dropped.

Mr Roberts had been charged with causing actual bodily harm to a minor at The Old Rectory, Church Lane, Leefdale on Tuesday the 17th July 2001; also with causing actual bodily harm to the Right Hon Peter Kellingford MP at Rooks Nest, Leefdale on Wednesday the 18th July 2001.

At the hearing on Monday, 23rd July, the prosecuting solicitor informed the court that no evidence was being offered by the Crown Prosecution Service in respect of either charge. An application was made for the hearing to be discontinued under Section 23 of The Prosecution of Offences Act 1985 and Mr Roberts, who was not present in court, was acquitted of both charges.

****

THE LEEFLET
The Newsletter of The Leefdale Parish Council
August 2001
Pages 3-4
In the Garden with "The Major"

Well, we did it! Leefdale is now the only village to have won the Magnificent Britain Gold Medal (Village with Less than 500 inhabitants) for the fifth consecutive year. A staggering achievement and a record that will take some equalling. Congratulations everyone! Particularly to all those industrious souls who worked so hard to ensure that their gardens were at their very best for the judges.

Now it's hardly a secret that I doubted we would manage to pull it off for a fifth year running. You may recall that, prior to the final, several gardens in the village were not, shall I say, at their best. Fortunately, however, common sense prevailed in the long run. Those who for various reasons were unable to put the necessary time and effort into their own gardens, wisely took advantage of the excellent help that was offered by Greg Maynard and his team. They rolled their sleeves up and brought nearly all of the neglected gardens back to A1 condition. Well done Greg! Well done everybody!

Now, I feel that I must say a word about the demonstration outside The Old Rectory on judgement day.

It really wasn't necessary, you know.

Of course, it is every Englishman's right to demonstrate against a presumed injustice, and many were concerned that the state of The Old Rectory's gardens would adversely affect Leefdale's chances. But, as Lady Brearley said at the awards ceremony on Friday, although horticulturalists are by nature conservative with a small "c", nevertheless, they are always innovative and on the lookout for something new. As an example, she cited the gardens at Budeholme, which are constantly being altered year by year, yet never break faith with horticultural tradition. That's why, I presume, her Ladyship especially commended Dylan Bourne and his colleagues for converting The Old Rectory's rear garden into an organic sculpture park. She even indicated that it was a decisive factor in the judges' final decision. Paradoxically, what many of us perceived to be a negative turned out to be a positive. So there we are, there was no need for a demonstration. Taking to the streets is always the last resort, in my view.

By the way, if anyone still hasn't seen the gold medal it will be on display at the next meeting of the parish council in the village hall.

Which brings me neatly to some news of my own. Many of you will have noticed that a "For Sale" sign has appeared in the front garden of Rooks Nest. Yes, Isobel and I are moving to pastures new. For some time now it has been our dream to own and run a small garden centre and we've decided to take the plunge before it's too late. We are both tremendously excited at the prospect. Sadly, it means that I've had to relinquish my civic duties. I have resigned as chairman of the parish council with immediate effect. I have also resigned as chairman of the Magnificent Britain Sub-Committee. No bad thing, perhaps. Five years is a long time to have been chairman and it is perhaps fitting for me to give up my position at the zenith of the village's achievements. I should like to take this opportunity to thank all the members of the parish council, and everyone connected with Magnificent Britain for making my period in office so enjoyable. Isobel and I are very sorry that we weren't able to wish everyone a formal goodbye, but given the adverse publicity my family and I have received we thought that before we started our new venture we'd get away from it all, have a holiday and lie low for a bit. I do hope we haven't offended anyone by keeping our sudden departure a state secret.

Sadly, this is my last "In the Garden with the Major" column. However, hopefully it is not the last edition of The Leeflet. Councillor Meakins has volunteered to continue producing the publication from now on, and he will also be its editor. I am delighted that the tradition I established will endure. It is so important to have a monthly newspaper in a little community such as ours; not only does it give us a sense of identity but it also provides a valuable means of communication and a platform for the dissemination of advice and information.

All this leaves me very little space for gardening advice. (Thanks be for that, do I hear?)

Seriously, during this summer we have seen heat waves alternating with prolonged and heavy rainfall. This has been splendid for plants but it has also been good news for weeds too. Several of you have complained to me recently that your gardens have been choked with weeds and you've had to work 24/7 to keep them down. My advice is always to try mulching. It will halve the time you spend weeding. A mulch is a thick layer of organic material which is spread over the surface of the soil surrounding your plants. All kinds of things can be used: garden compost; pulverised bark; well-rotted manure and leaf mould. My own favourite is moist peat. Apply in May around shrubs, trees and herbaceous perennials, taking care not to bring the mulch in contact with the stems. Result? End of weeds. And it's jolly good for the plants too.

Incidentally, I was chatting to Lady Brearley about weeds at the awards ceremony. She reminded me that a weed is simply a plant in the wrong place.

And who decides whether the place is right or wrong? We do. Now that really set me thinking.

Happy gardening!
The Major
(Howard Roberts)

Post Script

I have just been told that Lady Brearley was unable to attend the All Ireland Magnificent Britain Awards as she was admitted to hospital suffering from a stroke.

I am sure that all of us send her our best wishes for a speedy recovery.

THE END

Dear Reader

Thank you for reading Leefdale. I do hope you've enjoyed it. I'm always interested to learn what readers think of my work and would be most grateful if you placed a review of the novel on the Amazon site.

If you've enjoyed Leefdale and wish to learn more about the lives of Sir Maurice and Lady Brearley you might be interested to read Magnificent Britain. This companion novel to Leefdale explores the relationship between biography and the truth, and examines the hypocrisy, class consciousness and prejudice that permeated British society during the twentieth century.

Best wishes,
Michael Murray

Acknowledgements

A huge thank you to my wonderful wife Catherine for her unswerving support during the many years in which I have been writing Leefdale and who has prepared the novel for publication despite her debilitating illness. Words alone cannot express my gratitude. Many thanks also to our family for their constant encouragement.

Printed in Great Britain
by Amazon